SHE WAS HIS PRISONER,
HIS TO DO WITH
AS HE PLEASED

Sighing her enjoyment at his touch, Maria arched her back like a small cat, unconsciously pushing her upper body against the soft, black curls that covered his chest. Her breasts suddenly felt full and tingling and she instantly became aware of a burning heat spreading languidly up through her entire body. Driven by instincts she had no control over, her hands traveled hungrily over his muscled body and she reveled in the sleekness of his skin, in the power of that lithe form so near hers.

Gabriel's mouth caught her earlobe gently between his teeth and he muttered thickly, "Be still, my little Spanish tiger. Be still so that I may pleasure us both . . ."

Avon Books are available at special quantity discounts for bulk purchases for sales promotions, premiums, fund raising or educational use. Special books, or book excerpts, can also be created to fit specific needs.

For details write or telephone the office of the Director of Special Markets, Avon Books, Dept. FP, 1790 Broadway, New York, New York 10019, 212-399-1357.

The Spanish Rose

Shirlee Busbee

AVON
PUBLISHERS OF BARD, CAMELOT, DISCUS AND FLARE BOOKS

For the "roses" in my life:

CLAUDIA RAMOS, simply because you are my sister and I love you.

MRS. GALENA TERRY, because you never fail me and you know the other special reason.

JIM and LILLIAN FISHER, our Covelo cousins, who have been so very wonderful to us and have become some of our dearest friends.

And, HOWARD, because he still believes in me and because this book is his favorite!

Foreword

ACCORDING to Spanish records, there were only two hundred men in the town of Puerto Bello when Henry Morgan and his buccaneers attacked it, and the Spanish army that hurried from Panama City consisted of just over eight hundred men. Morgan claimed that there were *nine* hundred men in Puerto Bello and that it was three *thousand* Spaniards who had traveled from Panama City to fight the buccaneers in the jungle. For my purposes, I have chosen to use Morgan's account of the battles.

The real *almirante* of the Armada de Barlovento was Don Alonzo de Campos y Espinosa, and his flagship was the large frigate the *Magdalena*. I have taken the great liberty of substituting Maria's brother, Diego Delgato, for Don Alonzo, and also of substituting Diego's ship, the *Santo Cristo*, for Don Alonzo's, the *Magdalena*. The events leading up to and culminating in the battle of Barrade Maracaibo, except for the actions of fictional characters and ships, happened much the way I describe them. All ships mentioned in the book, except for the *Dark Angel*, *Lucifer*, *Santo Cristo*, *Raven*, *Caroline Griffin*, *Vengeance* and *Jaguar*, actually existed.

Part One

Vendetta

The Caribbean, 1664

Courage is to feel
The daily daggers of relentless steel
and keep on living.

Douglas Malloch
Courage, Stanza 2

Chapter One

A SUDDEN burst of drunken laughter from the waterfront *taberna* spilled out onto the rough cobblestone streets and caused the slim figure skulking in the nearby alley to jump. Her blue eyes wide with apprehension, Maria Delgato clutched the small cloth bag that contained all of her food closer to her and sank deeper into the murky shadows.

Cielos! she scolded herself, *now* was not the time to become goose-livered! Not when she had come this far unscathed. And longingly her gaze traveled across the harbor of Seville to where the tall Spanish galleon *Santo Cristo* lay at anchor amongst the other ships. It was her half brother's ship, and with the dawn it would be sailing across the seemingly endless expanse of the cold Atlantic Ocean to the warm waters of the Caribbean, to the Spanish island of Hispaniola, to Santo Domingo ... to *home!* Maria *had* to be on that ship when it sailed with the fall fleet or face exile, possibly forever, here in Spain.

For a second a rush of tears stung her eyes as she thought of Hispaniola, of the lush, tropical inland valley several miles from Santo Domingo that had been home to her since she had been barely six months old. Bitterly Maria wondered about a fate that had brought her here, to this mean alley in Spain, the land of her birth, some sixteen and a half years later.

The events of the past eighteen months seemed incredible to her, and even now on this warm August night of 1664 she found it difficult to believe everything that had happened in that time. The death of her father, Don Pedro Delgato, had been the beginning of it all; or rather, she pondered miserably, the duel he had fought with their deadly enemy, Sir William Lancaster, had really started it. Don Pedro had been able to kill Sir William, but not before the Englishman had inflicted grievous wounds on Don Pedro. It had taken her father six long months to die, and her poor mother, Doña Ysabel, never strong, had worn herself down to a dangerous degree nursing him during that agonizing time. No one, other than Maria, had been surprised when Doña Ysabel had died within weeks of her husband.

A small sob escaped from Maria, and savagely she bit her lower lip to stem the tide of misery that swept over her. She would *not* feel sorry for herself! But, oh, how she missed her father's hearty embrace when he would return from months at sea and swing her up into his strong arms, calling her his precious pigeon. It was her mother's sweet tranquillity that she missed the most though, Maria admitted sadly. She had been very close to her mother, and the long absences of Don Pedro while he escorted the Spanish treasure fleet from the rendezvous at Havana across the ocean to Seville, on the Guadalquivir River in Spain, had increased that closeness. Don Pedro would be gone for months, but while they missed him dreadfully, Maria and her mother had been content—they had each other and the most beautiful place in the world to live. Thinking of her gracious home, of the wide terraces, of the fields of green sugar cane, the flamboyance of the tangled, tropical forest that pressed close, Maria felt a lump rise in her throat, and her gaze slid back to the *Santo Cristo*. It *must* not sail without her—even if her half brother, Don Diego, *did* kill her when he discovered she had disobeyed his commands.

It had been her father's death that had placed the then thirty-year-old Don Diego at the head of the family. As such, he became Maria's guardian, and upon her mother's death, the sole arbitrator of Maria's future. Maria and Diego had never been close. Diego, like his father, was gone for weeks, sometimes for a year or more, from Hispaniola, and so they saw little of each other. The fourteen-year gap in their ages had not helped the situation, nor had Diego's disapproval of the affectionate laxity with which Maria had been raised. But there *was* a strong bond between the siblings, and Maria admired her older brother, despite having wished in the past that Diego was not *quite* so coldly ambitious. And she had never realized just *how* ambitious he was until her parents had died and she had come into his power.

Still grieving for her father, stunned at her mother's demise, before she realized it, Maria found herself whisked away from Hispaniola, from everything she had ever known, and on the *Santo Cristo* bound for Spain. But much worse, they had barely arrived in Spain when Diego informed her that he had arranged an outstanding match for her and that he expected the betrothal to be announced within the next few months.

Her mouth twisted with distaste. If only Don Clemente de la Silva y Gonzales, the man her half brother had chosen to be her husband, had been different. Even now, thinking of the thin, narrow features of Don Clemente, Maria grimaced. It wasn't that he was particularly *un*handsome—there were many who declared that he was quite, quite good-looking—but the cruel curve to his bottom lip and the cold gleam, like a reptile's, in those black, unblinking eyes had made Maria shiver. His manner too was cold, and try though she had when she had first been introduced to him, Maria could never bring herself to feel anything but revulsion and contempt for him. And in the weeks and months that had followed, she had discovered that there really was nothing else behind that icily polite exterior of his. Don Clemente's one thought was for his own pleasure, his own gratification, and it hadn't taken her long to realize that he was simply a vain, self-centered popinjay, a puppet to be manipulated by Diego.

Diego, she had come to learn painfully, for the most part viewed the people around him as mere pawns in his quest for power and more wealth—it was an obsession with him. Maria's marriage to Don Clemente would have given him entree to the inner circles of the court of Philip IV, where titles and positions of power were dispensed.

It had soon become apparent that Diego had been courting Don Clemente and his family for months before her father had died, and she had often wondered if her father had approved of the man Diego had selected as her husband. Sometimes, when she was very depressed, she believed that it was so—after all, she had always known that her father wanted her to marry well, to increase the position and power of the Delgatos through a magnificent match. But somehow she sensed that her marriage to Don Clemente had been all Diego's idea. Just as it had been Diego's idea to take her away from home and bring her here to Spain.

Maria hated Spain. Nothing was familiar to her except the language, and she was more comfortable with the simple, untrammeled life she had lived on Hispaniola. The coldly aristocratic families she had met and the stiff, calculated deportment and ridiculous airs of the members of the gloomy Spanish court in Madrid had repulsed her. Certainly they held no appeal for warmhearted and outgoing Maria! During the past months, she and Diego had argued bitterly over her dislike of the situation, but Diego had always had the final word. Until last month . . .

In the darkness of the alley, Maria couldn't suppress the little giggle that bubbled up inside her. Oh, how angry Diego had been and how amusing the foppish and enraged Don Clemente had looked with the ornate silver honey pot upside down on top of his head. The honey pot that Maria herself had dumped on his carefully coiffed and perfumed curls only moments before. It had been outrageous, and normally Maria would have been horrified at her own antics, but she had been *driven* to take drastic action. Only the evening before she had begged Diego not to announce her betrothal the next morning to Don Clemente. Her small face determined, she had swallowed her pride and pleaded abjectly for him to reconsider. But nothing would sway Diego, and so, during the very formal breakfast that was to have ended with the announcement of her betrothal to a man she detested, Maria had done the unthinkable—she had refused to obey her guardian and had publicly humiliated the arrogant Don Clemente. There had been shocked titters of laughter at the sight of the dandified Don Clemente leaping up from the flower-bedecked table with rivulets of golden honey spreading stickily across his forehead and down his back. If the situation had not been so vital to her, Maria would have burst out in delighted laughter; but for her, at that moment it had been no laughing matter—she had been fighting for her very future.

Of course, after that, there was no possibility of a betrothal. She had never seen Diego quite so furious, and for the first time in her young life, she had learned the dangers of enraging a man who has complete control of one. After the guests left, which naturally was almost immediately, Diego ordered her to her room, and there brother and sister faced one another. Diego's handsome face was hard, the scar that twisted his left eyebrow, a result of the same duel that had caused their father's death, was livid; but Maria couldn't believe that he really meant to beat her with the slim round rod he held in his hand. In the end, he finally threw down the rod. "I do not intend to beat you—even though there are those that probably think you deserve it!" he stated coldly. The next morning Diego escorted her to a convent nearby, and there she had languished without a word from him about her fate until two nights ago.

Thank goodness, she thought fervently, that he had decided to personally inform her of his imminent departure for Hispaniola—otherwise she would have learned of it too late to do anything about his plans for her. Diego's stated intention of leaving her immured in the prison-like convent until he returned to Seville months later had, at first, left Maria dumbfounded. She had swallowed painfully and then in a husky voice asked, "And when you return? What will happen to me then?"

Unbending slightly, Diego said calmly, "By then I shall hope that Don Clemente will have recovered completely from the blow you gave his pride and will once again be in favor of the joining of our two families."

Maria's eyes flew to his. Her face a picture of astonishment, she blurted out, "You can't possibly mean to continue to pursue that course! Besides, after what I did, surely nothing would make Don Clemente reconsider!"

Diego smiled faintly. "You underestimate your own charms, little sister. In spite of those blasted Lancaster eyes, you have grown into a pleasing young creature, and Don Clemente is not unaware of it."

Those blasted Lancaster eyes! How often had she heard both the men in her family deplore them and how often had she felt wounded over it? It wasn't my fault! she brooded angrily. Could she help it if their great-grandfather Don Francisco had kidnapped their great-grandmother, Faith Lancaster, from the English court of Elizabeth I and brought her to Spain as his unwilling mistress? It was Faith Lancaster's sapphire blue eyes that had come down in succeeding generations to her great-granddaughter, Maria. It also had been Faith Lancaster who had been the cause of the long enmity between the Spanish Delgatos and the English Lancasters. The Lancasters had never forgiven the insult, even though Don Francisco had eventually married Faith. Some ten years later, when the Spanish Armada sailed against the English fleet, Faith's brother fought Don Francisco's brother and killed him on the deck of his ship . . . just as Maria's father, Don Pedro, had fought and killed Sir William Lancaster only two years ago. The vendetta that had started with Faith's abduction, Maria thought regretfully, was still going on, despite all the years and generations that had passed; and she, with her sapphire blue eyes, was a constant reminder to everyone of the reasons behind the killings and the deep enmity between the two families.

Diego's voice suddenly jerked Maria away from her thoughts, and realizing that she had not been paying attention to what he had been saying, she asked quietly, "What was it you just said? I'm afraid I didn't hear you."

Diego threw her a dark look, and carefully enunciating each word, he stated sarcastically, "I said—that it isn't just your pretty face and form that will make Don Clemente reconsider the betrothal, nor is it the gold that will pour into his coffers, but the fact that your, er, frank manners have caught the fancy of the Queen."

Her mouth an O of astonishment, Maria finally squeaked, "The Queen? She remembers *me?*"

Casually, Diego replied, *"Sí.* It came as a surprise to me—although it shouldn't have; after all, we *are* Delgatos, and our position and wealth are not to be ignored—but evidently, during your infrequent appearances at court in Madrid this spring, the Queen found your"—Diego's mouth thinned—"rustic ways refreshing. She has referred to you as her 'Spanish rose'—I presume because you gave her that rose when you were presented to her."

Maria was stunned at Diego's words. The Queen of Spain, Mariana of Austria, had actually remembered her!

Maria had not liked the two months she and Diego had spent in Madrid at the gloomy, debt-ridden court of Philip IV, but it warmed her heart to hear that she had given the poor, plain-faced young Queen a moment of pleasure. The few times that she had actually been in the Queen's company, she found herself extremely sympathetic to her. After all, it couldn't have been easy, being far away from home, married to a homely old man who was well known for his licentious behavior—it was rumored that Philip IV had fathered more than thirty-two illegitimate children; but until the birth of a son, Charles, two years ago, there had been no heir to the throne. The Queen had aroused all of Maria's protective instincts, and it had been to see her smile that she had shyly presented the Queen with an exotically scented crimson rose. And the Queen had remembered *her!*

Sharply, Diego broke into her thoughts. "Maria! *Dios!* Will you stop this daydreaming and listen to what I have to say!"

Her little features suspiciously meek, Maria answered softly, *"Sí, mi hermano.* I will listen."

Diego took a deep breath, his swarthy face full of impatience. "You have been spoiled outrageously all of your life—your *madre* letting you run wild in that vile jungle you call home. And *Padre* was not much better—he should have beaten you soundly at least a half a dozen times that I can think of—but all that is behind us. You are my ward now, and as such, you will obey me in all things."

Maria's face took on a mutinous expression, the sapphire blue eyes glinting with resentment. Seeing it, Diego commanded sternly, "Take that look off your face or I shall be forced to beat you!" But Maria's expression didn't change, and unwilling to make the situation worse between them, he said more calmly, "I know that since *Padre* died things have not been easy for you—but that is because you are so stubborn! You must learn the ways of a proper young woman. I am only trying to do what is best for you. You must forget about returning to Hispaniola. Your home is in Spain now. You will marry here and

live here for the rest of your life. You must accept that
fact."

Diego's words were like a sentence of death to Maria.
Her belligerence fading, she grasped Diego's arms and
begged, "Por favor, Diego! Do not say that!" Her blue eyes
filled with pleading, she promised miserably, "Let me go
home; I will marry anyone you say. I only ask that it be
someone from Hispaniola, so that I may live there. I hate
Spain! I will die if you make me stay here!"

Diego's face softened slightly, but he would not allow
himself to be swayed. Hardening himself against her
pleas, he snapped, "Don't be ridiculous! You were born
here; this is your home, not that provincial estate where
you grew up!" Afraid he might weaken in the face of her
unhappiness, he added harshly, "Faugh! It is useless
trying to reason with you! When I return next year I trust
that you will have come to your senses." Before Maria
could say another word, he had spun on his heels and
marched from the small cell that had been assigned to
her when she entered the convent.

Maria was numbed by his actions, but soon she roused
herself, determined to somehow be on the Santo Cristo
when it sailed. Her immediate thought was to escape at
once from the convent, but then caution held her back—
if her disappearance was discovered too soon, Diego would
know right where to look for her, and he wouldn't sail
without first tearing apart the Santo Cristo from stem to
stern until he found her. No. She had to wait until the
very last moment to make her escape. That evening she
slipped from her cell and made a small raid on the convent kitchen. Hastily, she stuffed olives, cheese, and bread
into a small cloth bag. She added a small bottle of wine
to the food and then crept back to her cell.

The next day, she waited with fevered impatience for
the hours to pass and night to fall. Finally, after the last
Te Deum had been sung and nuns and novices alike had
retired to their bare cells, Maria silently crept through
the empty stone halls, determined to reach the Santo
Cristo and be on it when it sailed at dawn.

Her journey to the Seville waterfront had been without
incident and she had been congratulating herself on her
success at arriving unscathed when the burst of laughter

had made her jump only a moment before. Of course her disguise had helped—she had managed to steal a pair of baggy breeches and a coarse cotton shirt from items donated to the convent for distribution to the poor. With her small, slim stature, her fine features half-hidden by a floppy hat worn by so many peasants, she had been easily mistaken for a young boy and had been unmolested as she made her way through the dark and often dangerous streets that led to the waterfront where the *Santo Cristo* lay at anchor.

There was another burst of laughter from the *taberna*, but this time Maria didn't jump; all her attention was on the tall galleon that was so close, yet so far away from her. Through the dimly lit darkness, she could make out two tough-looking seamen who loitered near the plank that led up to the ship, and at the railings of the *Santo Cristo* she saw the occasional movement that betrayed the presence of other men on the galleon.

Having gotten this far, how was she now to gain the ship undetected? Wistfully, her gaze lingered on the two men near the long, wide plank. If only they were Paco and Juan, two Delgato seamen who had known her since her infancy—they would help her hide in the hold until the *Santo Cristo* was well at sea. She had been so determined to escape the convent and reach the harbor that a plan for actually getting on the ship hadn't occurred to her. Disgustedly she looked down at her small bag of food. What good was it going to do if she couldn't even gain the ship!

A little subdued, but undaunted, Maria glanced around, searching for something that might help her. Almost as if in answer to a prayer, she heard the rumble of a cart moving across the cobblestones toward the *Santo Cristo*. Eagerly she looked at it, noticing the trunks and barrels that it contained. Trunks and barrels that were destined for the hold of the *Santo Cristo!*

Her heart began pounding in her chest, and she held her breath as she watched the driver of the cart step down and begin to walk over to the two men near the *Santo Cristo*. Could she make it to the cart? And once there, could she open one of the trunks and get inside?

Summoning all her courage, she bolted from her hiding

place in the alley and swiftly ran the short distance that
separated her from the cart. The sound of the three men
talking came clearly to her. Praying that they would continue to talk at the front of the cart for several more minutes, she hastily climbed over the tailgate. With trembling
fingers, she fumbled at the lock on the first chest. It
wouldn't budge, and frantically she tried the next and the
next. They were all securely locked and her heart sank.
Cielos! Surely she hadn't been offered this opportunity
only to have it disappear?

Crouching there in the dirty cart, she glared at the
leather-bound trunks. She *was* going to get one of them
open! The sound of approaching footsteps startled her, and
in her desperate attempt to escape detection, she bumped
solidly into one of the haphazardly packed objects. With
a loud crash it fell from the cart onto the cobblestones
below.

Her eyes huge in her small face, Maria froze. She heard
one of the men exclaim, *"Ay de mi!* You see what has
happened? I told you, *amigo,* that you were putting too
much on my poor cart. Now what are we to do?"

Another voice said, "The lock is broken, but no harm
is done. We will put it back on the cart, and when Don
Diego comes to inspect it, we will say that it was that
way when you picked it up from the warehouse, *sí?*"

There was a mutter from the cart driver, but after a
little more argument he agreed. Together the three men
loaded the trunk back onto the cart. Maria slunk further
back into the small hiding place she had found behind
one of the barrels.

"José," one of the men suddenly said, "you had better
inform Don Diego that the last cart of goods has arrived.
I will go tell the boatswain to alert his men that there is
more loading for them to do. As for you, *señor,* you guard
your cart until we return."

Maria heard the sounds of retreating footsteps and a
moment later the sound of the cart owner grumbling as
he walked toward the front of the vehicle. Maria waited
a tense second, then gingerly crept from her hiding place
and crawled toward the damaged trunk.

The lock was indeed broken, and with the blood pounding painfully in her temples, Maria slowly raised the lid

of the trunk. It was, to her profound delight, only partially full of silks and satins. Not giving herself time to think about it, she swiftly climbed inside and gently lowered the lid.

It was stuffy and cramped inside the trunk, and for the first time in her life, Maria was thankful that she was small and finely boned. She wiggled around trying to get comfortable, and as a further guard against discovery, she managed to cover herself with several layers of the material within the trunk.

The sound of approaching voices made her heart beat even faster, and when she heard Diego's angry voice, her mouth went dry. She almost cried aloud when the lid of the trunk was suddenly flung up. "At least you've stolen nothing!" Diego said coldly after glancing into the trunk. "But I shall dock the cost of a new lock from what is owed to you." The lid slammed shut, and Diego snapped, "Now get these things loaded. We sail at dawn."

The swaying motion as the trunk was lifted and carried onto the ship nearly made Maria sick, but manfully she forced herself to remain still and ignored her lurching stomach. The trunk was set down with a thud a few minutes later, and then there was silence.

The silence went on for a long time until finally, thinking it was safe, Maria very carefully raised the lid of the trunk. Casting her eyes over the trunks, barrels and bales that surrounded her, Maria realized she was in the hold of the *Santo Cristo*.

A little smile crossed her expressive face as she nimbly climbed out of the trunk. Finding a fairly comfortable perch on a sack of grain, she stared around her. She had done it! She was on the *Santo Cristo* and she was going home!

Chapter Two

MARIA DELGATO was not the only person boarding a ship that warm August night of 1664. Across the English Channel, up the River Thames, in the bustling port of London, England, Gabriel Lancaster had just descended from an elegant coach and was idly inspecting the *Raven*, the sturdy merchantman which rode at anchor in London's fine harbor.

In the morning the *Raven* would be taking Gabriel and his small family to the Caribbean, to the English settlement of Port Royal, Jamaica. His young bride of less than six months, Elizabeth, and his sixteen-year-old sister, Caroline, were already comfortably settled in the large cabin that would be their home for the next seven weeks. In the hold were all their possessions as well as the goods that Gabriel intended to sell once the ship reached Port Royal—glasswares, paper, utensils, arms and clothing.

He was not by nature or inclination a merchant. The Lancasters had all been fighting men, but since the ship had been a gift from the King himself, Charles II, and since there was a voracious demand for manufactured goods in the Caribbean, it had seemed only practical that he take advantage of the opportunities afforded him. Besides, until the virgin lands the King had so graciously granted him in the interior of the island of Jamaica were showing a profit, he might find himself in need of the extra monies. Especially so, considering the pleasant news Elizabeth had given him only the night before . . .

Gabriel smiled faintly in the light from the ship's lanterns. At thirty years of age, how very respectable he had become! Not only was he on his way to settle down to the placid life of a sugar-cane grower in one of the lovely inland valleys of Jamaica, but he was married and soon to be the father of a child! How extraordinarily different were the present circumstances from the uncertain, dangerous life he had known for the past eighteen years. . . .

He had been only twelve years old in 1646 when he and his father, Sir William, a minor official in the court of Charles I, had followed the then Prince of Wales to France. And in the turbulent civil war years that had followed, years that had seen the Lancaster estates in England sequestered and had seen the Roundheads, led by Oliver Cromwell, seize control of the country and order the beheading of Charles I, the Lancasters had been fighting on the side of the Royalists. They had been with the Prince when he had gone to Scotland to be crowned Charles II in 1651; and later that same year they had fought at the battle of Worcester, which had seen the humiliating defeat of their newly crowned King. Like many others, they had once again fled to France, still intensely loyal to their King and willing to share his poverty and uncertain future.

Gabriel, however, then eighteen and growing up into an adventurous young giant—he stood well over six feet tall—had soon found the enforced inactivity and wretched penury the Royalists were forced to suffer at the French court intolerable. When Prince Rupert, a prince of Bavaria and Admiral of Charles' pitiful royal navy, had embarked on a privateering mission to the West Indies in the hopes of shoring up the royal coffers, Gabriel had promptly begged leave to join it. With the blessings of both King and father, he had done so, and it had been then that he had first fallen under the spell of the Caribbean.

The clear, inviting turquoise waters of the sea; the lush, verdant growth of the palm-dotted islands; and the brilliant purple and crimson hues of the tropical sunsets had bewitched him. All during the long, dispiriting years that had followed his return, as he and his family had determinedly followed their King as Charles had moved through the various courts in Europe, always seeking money and assistance in the hopes of regaining his stolen throne, Gabriel had often thought of the Caribbean with a fierce longing. And after Cromwell's death and the glorious Restoration a few years later in 1660, when the King had spoken privately with Gabriel and Sir William about their reward for all the years they had shared his miserable exile, it had been Gabriel who had quietly suggested the possibility of land in the Caribbean.

The King had been utterly delighted. Not wishing to cause more civil strife by displacing those of Cromwell's adherents who had been given confiscated Royalists' lands, yet eager to justly compensate his own loyal followers, Charles had found himself forced to tread a delicate path between two hostile factions. Rewarding the Lancasters with a lavish grant of land in Jamaica in the far-off Caribbean gave him a painless and very practical solution.

The island of Jamaica had been wrested from the Spanish back in 1655 during Cromwell's Protectorship. A contingent of men led by General Robert Venables and Admiral Sir William Penn had landed and driven off the few Spanish settlers and soldiers who had been living there. Determined to keep the island English, with his father's approval, Cromwell's son Richard had ordered the kidnapping of Irish men and women from the streets of cities and towns in Ireland and had had them shipped to Jamaica. It had not proved successful—the men ran away to join the buccaneers who cruised the area, and of those men and women who remained, most had died of the fevers that abounded in the area. Until recently, few honest English settlers had been found to colonize the island, and Jamaica had become a haunt for all manner of lawless men. But now the King intended to change all that, and the settling of the interior of the island by men of the caliber of his loyal Lancasters was a step in that direction.

Sir William and Gabriel had sailed for Jamaica in the fall of 1661, full of hope and enthusiasm. At last they would have a permanent home and could, for the first time in far too many years, begin to think of a future. Disregarding the primitive conditions of Port Royal, the heat and the insects, joyously they had ridden inland and just as joyously laid claim to the twenty thousand acres of virgin forest and jungle that composed the generous

land grant from the King. They had named their plantation Royal Gift; a site for a home had been chosen, and
African slaves had been purchased to start the back-
breaking work of clearing the land. There was so much
to be done, and with no one except young Caroline in
England to miss them—Lady Martha, Sir William's wife,
had died years ago—the two men had been completely
absorbed in the pleasure of taming the wild, fertile land.
It had been early in the summer of 1662 when they had
finally sailed away from Port Royal for England, intent
upon bringing Caroline and the remainder of their effects
back to Jamaica. And it had been then that tragedy had
struck.

Gabriel's handsome face twisted. Despite the passage
of over two years, the memory of his father's death still
brought him unmeasurable pain. That and an unrequited
thirst for vengeance against the hated Delgatos. His only
relief from the agony that continued to bite deep was the
knowledge that ultimately Don Pedro Delgato had died of
the wounds Sir William inflicted before the Spaniard's
blade ended his father's life. That and the grim satisfaction that Don Pedro's son, Diego, would carry the scar
Gabriel had given him during that desperately savage
fight to the end of his days.

It had been an uneven fight from start to finish and
pure bad luck that the ship the Lancasters had chosen to
take them back to England had run afoul of the Spanish
treasure fleet on its annual trek to Spain. One warship
they might have been able to outmaneuver, but not the
several that guarded the treasure fleet. The *Griffin,* a
sleek English sloop, had done her best to escape, but it
had only been a matter of time until, her main mast shattered from the cannons of the huge men-of-war, she had
been manacled to the side of a Spanish ship by grappling
hooks and overrun with Spanish soldiers. The English
crew had fought valiantly, Gabriel and Sir William,
though not seamen, among them, their skillful blades
making them a welcome addition in the vicious hand-to-
hand fighting that followed the boarding. But for the Lancasters the battle had taken on an even deadlier hue when
they had caught sight of Don Pedro and Diego amongst
the boarders.

Gabriel's emerald green eyes were hard as he remembered that fight, remembered the rage he felt when he
saw his father go down under Don Pedro's blade, the blind
fury that attacked him as he fought frantically to reach
his father's side, and the wave of anguish that swept
through him when he realized sickly that his father was
dead. Something had died within him then, but he had
fought on grimly, even though it was apparent that without some miracle there was no hope for the *Griffin* and
all aboard her. Even coming face to face with Diego Delgato aroused no great emotion at the time, and he felt
only a flicker of satisfaction when his blade slashed down
across Diego's face. With a scream Diego fell backward
onto the blood-slick deck of the *Griffin.* Before Gabriel
could strike the killing blow, however, another Spaniard
engaged his blade, and in the ensuing fight he lost sight
of Diego.

How long the fight went on, Gabriel could never recall.
It seemed that he had fought for hours, his sword arm
aching from the constant thrust and parry as he slashed
his way through the Spanish attackers, searching obsti-
nately for Don Pedro. He never found him, but at some
point he became aware that there seemed to be fewer
Spaniards on board, and then suddenly it dawned on him
that the *Griffin* was slowly drifting away from the Spanish warship. Miraculously, someone had been able to chop
through the stout ropes that had linked the two vessels
together, and gradually the distance between the two
ships was widening. There was a shout of joy from the
English, and with renewed vigor they intensified their
attack on the Spanish still aboard the *Griffin.*

It seemed luck hadn't deserted the *Griffin* after all, and
more help unexpectedly appeared on the horizon—a heavily armed buccaneer frigate. The Spanish instantly had
more important game to hunt than the harmless *Griffin,*
and in the ensuing flurry of battle, the Englishmen managed to recapture their ship, taking the remaining Spaniards still aboard prisoner. The battered *Griffin* then
gratefully limped back to the safety of Port Royal, but it
had been a bitter blow for Gabriel to discover that neither
Don Pedro nor Diego was among the Spanish prisoners
captured. With a lead weight in his breast, he had buried

his father on a small knoll which overlooked the land they had so joyously claimed just months ago. His eyes on his father's grave, Gabriel had vowed fiercely that someday the Delgatos would pay dearly for this latest attack upon the Lancasters. Sir William's death would be avenged . . . with Delgato blood.

"Gabriel!" a soft voice complained from the confines of the coach, interrupting his unpleasant memories and jolting him back to the present. "I simply cannot believe that you mean to part from me this way," Thalia Davenport murmured huskily. "Surely, you could bend that ridiculously rigid honor of yours for *one* night! Elizabeth need never know—she's aware that the King keeps late hours and that it might be dawn before you return." Coaxing him, she purred, "Come home with me now . . . my bed is lonely these nights without you. For tonight let us pretend that we are lovers once again. Come with me now. . . ."

Gabriel sighed impatiently under his breath. He should have known better than to have accepted a ride from Thalia Davenport. Up until nine months ago, when he had decided it was his duty to marry and he had offered for young Elizabeth Langley, Thalia had been his mistress. She had been a very satisfactory mistress, and he had parted from her quite amicably, the elegant coach and matched quartet of bays that drew it, his parting gift to her.

Unfortunately, Thalia had never understood why he had found it necessary to break off their relationship simply because he was getting married. Lovely, amoral and totally unscrupulous, she gave short shrift to the concept of fidelity. Widowed three years ago at the age of twenty-two, Thalia had been perfectly delighted to become one of the gay butterflies who flitted about the King's then bachelor court. Gabriel had suspected that upon more than one occasion she had even entertained the King himself, but as she aroused in him none of the possessiveness for which the Lancaster men were noted, he had shrugged his shoulders and made no comment. He had even found it amusing that she had actually tried to use the King's behavior to strengthen her argument that Gabriel was being a fool for allowing his marriage to stand in the way

of their continued relationship—after all, the King had
continued to keep Barbara Villiers as his mistress after
his marriage to the Infanta Catharine of Portugal two
years ago. Surely, if the King saw no wrong in being married and having a mistress . . .

But all that had been months ago, before his marriage
to Elizabeth; and tonight, leaving Whitehall after a farewell audience with the king, Gabriel had genuinely believed that Thalia's offer of transportation to his ship had
been given out of simple friendship. A faint gleam of
mockery at his own naivete flickered in the emerald eyes.
Was *any* relationship with a woman ever simple?

Thalia's beautiful face, framed by a profusion of silky
red curls, suddenly appeared in the window of the coach
door. Her lovely, limpid brown eyes full of promise, the
lush, red mouth temptingly pursed, Thalia breathed seductively, "Oh, Gabriel, do say you will come with me!
There's never been anyone like you in my bed." Hungrily
her gaze traveled over his tall, broad form, lingering on
the straight shoulders under the short satin doublet, before traveling down to the petticoat breeches trimmed
with lace and the silk stockings that clung to his muscled
calves. A large hat festooned with a huge ostrich plume
was held under one arm and his slim dress sword hung
gracefully down one side. He was quite, quite debonair as
he stood there before her, and Thalia was certain she
would die if he didn't give in to her pleas. With a catch
in her throat, she added, "I've missed you dreadfully these
past months—what is one night to your wife—she will
have you for the rest of her life, while I, I have only tonight."

Torn between amusement at her theatrics and increasing embarrassment at the situation, Gabriel said dryly,
"Thalia, aren't you carrying this a bit to the extreme? I
have it on the best authority, yours, that Lord Rochester
has been sharing your bed of late, and as his prowess is
well known, I cannot believe that you are so desperate for
my embrace."

Thalia pouted and said with vexation, "Why are you
being so stubborn? It isn't as if you are in love with your
wife!"

Gabriel's face hardened. His voice full of steel, he said quietly, "We will leave my wife out of this conversation."

The conversation wasn't going as Thalia had planned and she was annoyed. Annoyed and just a little angry—she wasn't used to her advances being rebuffed, and she didn't like it at all that Gabriel seemed impervious to what she was offering him. Anger sparkling in her pansy-brown eyes, she spat, "Why? She's just a woman like any other! And just because the great Gabriel Lancaster married her doesn't make her a saint!" Sneering, she added, "Or perhaps I have misread the situation—perhaps you are under the cat's paw—ruled by your wife!"

Gabriel looked at her steadily for a moment; then, his tone *very* polite, he said, "Good night, Thalia. Thank you for being so kind in having your coachman bring me here."

Thalia's slim fingers tightened into a fist. He was really going to do it. Refuse her. *No* one refused Thalia Davenport! Driven by rage and hurt pride, she said furiously, "Damn you! You always were an arrogant bastard! So certain of your charm and abilities! I wonder how poor Elizabeth bears being married to you!"

Thinking of his young wife and the shy way she clung adoringly to him, Gabriel couldn't help the gleam of mockery that suddenly leaped into his eyes. Dulcetly, he replied, "Actually, she does very well, thank you."

Thalia nearly strangled on the thwarted rage that surged up through her, and completely losing her temper, she snapped, "I wonder. You've never loved any woman and I wonder how she will feel when she discovers that all of you she will ever have is merely your body—that you have no heart!"

Gabriel did not reply; he simply bowed gracefully, turned on his heel and began to walk toward the *Raven.* It was more than Thalia could bear. Her voice was uncomfortably clear in his ears as she cried out spitefully, "Someday, Gabriel, I pray you meet a woman you cannot have! And if God is good, she will break your heart!"

It was very bad of him, but he could not resist. Glancing back at her, he said lightly, "But, m'lady, you just said that I *have* no heart!"

There was a small shriek of rage from Thalia, and then

to his relief, he heard the coach drive away. Oddsfish! but Thalia was a sharp-tongued shrew! Thank God Elizabeth was a sweet-tempered young thing!

Gaining the deck of the ship, he nodded to the night watchman and slowly made his way to the stern of the ship where his cabin lay. Entering the silent, darkened room, he laid his hat aside on the small chest he knew sat near the door.

In the gray gloom of the room, he could dimly make out the bed where his sister lay asleep and across from her the small partition that had been erected to create a tiny cubicle for him and Elizabeth to sleep. He crossed to Caroline's bed, and in the shadows, he could barely make out her fine features. Her fair hair was spread out across the pillow, her eyelashes dark fans upon her cheeks. She looked so very young sleeping there that he wondered again if he was doing the right thing in taking her to Jamaica with him. But then he sighed. Caroline was only two years younger than Elizabeth and there had been no question of not taking his wife!

Caroline suddenly stirred in her sleep, and as if aware of his regard, her eyes flew open. She blinked, then recognizing her brother's tall form, she asked softly, "Are you just returned from the King?"

"Yes," he answered just as softly. "I'm sorry, I didn't mean to wake you."

"It doesn't matter," Caroline said quickly. "I'm so excited about leaving in the morning that I am surprised I was asleep at all."

A slight frown creasing his forehead, Gabriel asked seriously, "Caroline, you *are* happy about coming with Elizabeth and me? You wouldn't rather remain here with father's sister?"

"Stay with Aunt Amanda! I should say not!" Caroline replied forthrightly.

He smiled at the vehemence in his sister's voice. "Very well, then, my dear, come with us you shall!"

They talked a few minutes longer, and then bidding his sister an affectionate good night, Gabriel entered the tiny room where his wife was sound asleep in their bed. As he had done with Caroline, he stood for a second near the bed, gazing down in the darkness at his wife's face. Was he wrong in taking her with him? Perhaps he should have gone out first and seen that the house was properly constructed before he brought out the women. The conditions would be primitive for quite some time and Elizabeth was such a delicate young creature . . . and she was expecting their first child. For a moment he was lost in a dream of the future, the day he would hold his firstborn child in his arms; then smiling at his own folly, he turned aside and began to undress.

Elizabeth was sleeping so deeply she barely moved when he slid into bed. Gathering her slender form next to his, Gabriel kissed her lightly on the nape of her neck and then tried to fall asleep himself. It proved a fruitless exercise. His mind was too full of the future, and he suspected that like Caroline he was excited about the beginning of the journey. After several minutes of restless tossing, he finally gave up any pretense of sleep, and slipping into a pair of breeches and a loose white shirt, he silently left the cabin where the women were sleeping.

Standing on the deck of the ship, he gazed at the river where it slapped gently against the *Raven.* For some inexplicable reason the conversation with Thalia kept buzzing around in his mind. There had been a little too much truth in her words for him to completely dismiss them and he moved uneasily.

It was true, he didn't love his wife. He had a great deal of fondness for her and he would never treat her dishonorably, but he didn't love her; nor, he suspected idly, would he ever love her. She was a good woman though, and he would make her a good husband, even if they never shared that heady rapture of true love that his parents had known.

Until the day Don Pedro's blade had ended his life, Sir William had been in love with his dead wife, Lady Martha. And Gabriel was aware that his father had never quite recovered from her death seven years previously. Gabriel had always been conscious of the great love between his parents, and he knew as well as anybody that the Lancasters were noted for loving only once and then with an intenseness that was legendary, but so far he had scoffed at the idea when it pertained to himself. When Thalia had accused him of loving no woman, she had been correct. He *had* never loved any woman except his sister and mother. He enjoyed women though; he pampered and teased them and was fond of them, but there had never been one that had aroused any deep emotions within him. Mayhap Thalia had been right about that too—perhaps he didn't have a heart, he thought with a faint smile.

It was probably just as well, he decided slowly, he certainly wouldn't want to suffer the pain his father had when Lady Martha had died, and if that was part of loving someone deeply, then he would just as soon forgo it. Let the poets sing of love, but he wasn't going to be caught unaware. Besides, he was married to a fine young woman and he had every intention of remaining true to his vows. That too, he remembered lightly, was a Lancaster trait. He apparently possessed, he conceded thoughtfully, all of the qualities of his ancestors, except one—the ability to fall deeply in love. Gabriel shrugged cynically. It was just as well; from aught he could ever learn on the subject, love was an overprized emotion, and he could do very well without it.

A yawn suddenly escaped him, and turning aside he found his way once again to his cabin. This time when he slipped into bed, his head had barely hit the pillow before sleep overcame him.

Elizabeth woke him with a shy kiss on the cheek, just as the dawn light was filling the tiny cubicle. He turned to her, but to his surprise he discovered that she was already up and fully dressed. Sleepily he regarded her, noting with pleasure her large gray eyes and soft sweet mouth. Her hair was light brown and was caught neatly at her neck, a few curls clustering around her ears and across her forehead. She was dressed in a sensible gown of blue cloth, a pristine white apron covering almost all of her full skirt.

Gabriel grinned at her and said teasingly, "Practicing already to be a hardworking planter's wife, my dear?"

He was in the act of getting out of bed, and at the sight of his powerful naked body in the clear light of day, Elizabeth blushed delightfully. After six months of marriage she still wasn't used to the idea that this handsome, utterly charming man was her husband, the father of the babe that was growing within her. Remembering how the babe had gotten there, her blush increased to a fiery hue.

Elizabeth was not a beauty, but she was a very handsome girl, tall and slender and fine boned. Her father had been a long-time friend of Sir William's, and the possibility of a marriage between the two families had been discussed at one time or another ever since she could remember. But even so, she had never really expected that someone as exciting and wonderful as Gabriel Lancaster would ask her to marry him, and when he had, she had nearly fainted with pleasure. She adored him, and during the short time they had been married, he had done nothing to shake her belief that she was the most fortunate girl in the world. Gabriel Lancaster, able to choose just about any woman in the kingdom, had chosen to marry *her!*

Caroline's voice drifted into the small room. "Gabriel, Elizabeth! Oh, do come quickly! We are leaving! The ship is moving away from the dock! Hurry, it may be our last sight of London forever!"

Gabriel threw her a laughing reply and nimbly scrambled into his clothes, taking just a second to throw some water onto his face from the pitcher that Elizabeth handed him. He ran a hasty hand through his tousled black locks and then, grabbing Elizabeth's hand, pulled her from the room with him. Full of excitement and anticipation, they joined Caroline on the deck.

The three of them stood together watching the towers and spires of London gradually disappear as the *Raven* sailed leisurely down the Thames toward the English Channel. They were leaving home, leaving everything they had ever known for a new life, and for just a second the enormity of it all hit Gabriel.

What the devil did he know about being a planter? Was he going to be able to make a home for the women in his family? Take care of them? Would they be happy in Jamaica?

As if sensing his doubts, Caroline looked up at him. Her blue eyes, the Lancaster blue eyes, were bright and clear, and merrily she said, "Oh, Gabriel! I cannot bear it, I am so excited! I want to see Jamaica now! I don't know how

I am to survive all the weeks at sea, I am so eager to be there!"

Caroline was a true Lancaster. She had the family sapphire blue eyes and the golden hair that Sir William had possessed. Gabriel had inherited his mother's coloring, her blue-black hair and striking emerald green eyes, and yet seeing brother and sister standing side by side, their relationship was unmistakable. They were both tall; both had the same slashing black eyebrows, and their finely chiseled features were similar in many respects, Caroline's being simply a feminine version of Gabriel's. And despite the gap in their ages, there was a deep bond of affection between them, perhaps made even stronger now that their parents were dead.

For a long time, the three stood at the railings of the *Raven* staring at the receding skyline of London. Then almost as one they turned their faces in the direction of the English Channel. Out there lay their future, and each in his own way was unbearably eager for it. And none was aware that across the Bay of Biscay in the Port of Seville the *Santo Cristo* had also set sail and that all too soon the Spanish ship would bring them tragedy and death.

Chapter Three

MARIA woke with a violent start, the frightening sound of voices very close to her instantly driving away any remnant of sleep. Her heart thudding wildly in her breast, she leaped off the soft bed she had made amongst the grain sacks and hid behind some trunks.

In the days that had passed since the night she had stolen aboard the *Santo Cristo*, she had been extremely careful of where she had slept, usually choosing a place well hidden from the main cargo area. But this afternoon the hold had seemed uncomfortably hot and airless, and she had dozed off without taking any of her normal precautions against discovery. The grain sacks where she had been sleeping were piled out in clear sight of anybody entering the hold, and angry at how close she had come to being found, she crouched down behind the leather-bound trunks and warily eyed the two men who had just come down the steps into the hold.

The hold was a dark, gloomy place as Maria had soon discovered, the sunlight from above never piercing beneath the various decks down to it. But in the time that had passed, she had grown used to living in this musty world of murky shadows and little light, consoling herself with the sweet knowledge that with every hour that went by she was safer from being found and returned ignominiously to the convent in Seville. Her greatest danger lay in the fact that they would soon be stopping at the Canary Islands, and if she was found before then . . . Maria sighed unhappily. If she was found before then, it was more than probable that Diego would instantly secure passage for her on the first ship leaving for Spain. It was a discouraging thought.

Her meager supply of food, though carefully rationed, was rapidly dwindling, and she knew that she hadn't much more time before she would have to make her presence known on board the *Santo Cristo*. In this world of darkness, the murmurs of the sea pressing close against the hull of the galleon, she had used the sounds of the men moving about above her to determine time, and according to her crude calculations, the *Santo Cristo* had been at sea now for several days. The Canaries couldn't be far away, and once they were passed, she could breathe easier—even Diego wouldn't turn back then, she thought with a little smile of satisfaction.

The two men who had awakened her had apparently come down to the hold to fetch a new barrel of fresh water, and Maria watched them as they struggled to get the heavy cask up the steps. It had been fortunate for her that the water was stored here. Her small bottle of wine hadn't lasted very long, and in the time since she had finished it, she had been getting her water from one of the barrels.

It was quiet again in the hold once the men with their awkward object had disappeared from view, and thankfully Maria sank down on her haunches. *Cielos!* but they had given her a start, and if they had found her and taken her to Diego . . .

It was inevitable that she face Diego, she knew that, but she wasn't looking forward to the event. He was going to be absolutely furious—more furious than he had been the morning she had dumped the honey pot on Don Clemente's head, and a slight shiver of apprehension rippled through her as she remembered his threat to beat her. What would he do to her this time? The method of Diego's probable punishment wasn't something that Maria cared to think about a great deal, and she had deliberately refused to allow herself to brood over it, focusing instead on the joy of seeing her home again. *Any*thing Diego did to her would be worth being able to be home once more.

But as the days slowly passed, Maria found it more and more difficult to tear her mind away from the coming confrontation with her brother. Her small supply of food had run out on the morning that the *Santo Cristo* had left the

Canaries, and for the past three days Maria had eaten nothing. Sitting dejectedly on a wine cask, she surveyed her situation.

She was hungry. She had no food. She was unarmed except for the small Toledo blade she had brought with her. She was dirty, grubby and utterly bored with her own company. The Canaries were behind the *Santo Cristo* now, and she had absolutely no excuse not to seek out Diego. Certainly she couldn't remain here the entire journey—she would starve to death by the time the ship reached Hispaniola. As if in agreement with her gloomy summation, her stomach gave a hearty rumble just then and Maria grimaced.

Straightening her slim shoulders, she stood up. Her small face set with determination, she walked slowly toward the steps that led to the upper decks. Her foot on the bottom step, defiantly she jammed on her floppy-brimmed hat, stuffing her long, inky-black hair up inside it.

Now came one of the most dangerous aspects of her journey—reaching the main deck of the ship. The crews aboard most galleons were cruelly mistreated and they were notorious for their hatred of their captains. If she were to fall into the hands of one of the crew belowdecks . . . She would rather think of what Diego was going to do to her than what would be her fate if she found herself at the mercy of men who probably had good cause to hate her brother.

Luck must have been on her side, she thought gratefully several heart-stopping moments later as she crouched near the stern hatch. From the shafts of sunlight that filtered down, she knew it wasn't night, but what time of day it was, or more important, where Diego was right now, she had no idea, and for a second she hesitated there. Once she climbed through that hatch to the main deck, there would be no going back—it was highly unlikely that her presence would be undetected as soon as she stepped out into the daylight on the deck above her. And if Diego or one of his officers was not immediately at hand . . . She swallowed painfully. And in that instant her luck ran out.

A burly sailor on his way to the main deck spotted her

small figure lurking in the shadows near the hatch, and he called out harshly, *"Arriba!* What are you doing hiding there like a thief?"

Maria started so violently at his words that any opportunity of bluffing her way clear was lost. Sudden suspicion creasing his heavy brow, he started toward her, and for the first time since she had begun her adventure, Maria lost her nerve. Dark blue eyes huge in her white face, she bolted for the hatch, screaming Diego's name at the top of her lungs.

She gained the deck only seconds ahead of the now thoroughly suspicious seaman, but the bright light of the sun blinded her, and she stood there frozen, blinking uncontrollably, unable to see clearly. A pair of huge hands clamped down on her shoulders and spun her around, the force of the movement sending her hat spinning. Her long hair tumbled wildly around her shoulders, and as her vision gradually returned to normal, she saw the stupefied expression on her captor's face.

"Dios! A female!" he growled in stunned tones. Other members of the crew came racing over, and seeing their dark, menacing faces closing in on her, Maria began to fight madly. The small Toledo blade flashed silver in the sunlight as she wielded it with desperate efficiency against the man who held her prisoner. A yelp of astonishment and pain came from him as the knife cut across one of his hands. Instantly Maria found herself free.

The freedom did her little good—her back was against the railings, and there was only deep blue ocean and brilliant blue sky behind her; in front of her was a group of decidedly hostile sailors. Tensely the protagonists eyed each other, the brutish faces of the sailors reflecting a variety of emotions that made Maria clutch her knife all the more determinedly. There was no fear on her young face, only grim resolution as she met their stares boldly.

Maria made an incongruous figure there against the high railings of the *Santo Cristo,* the sea breeze that billowed the huge white sails above riffling through her tangled black locks, her rumpled and grimy boy's clothing emphasizing the fragility of her slender frame, and the knife she held so threateningly at complete variance with the elfin beauty of her features. The dark blue eyes, heav-

ily fringed with thick black lashes, were narrowed and
intent, the normally sweetly shaped lips were taut and
determined, the delicate chin was firmly held; and from
the fierce expression on her face, not one of the men in
front of her had any doubt that she would fight savagely
if any of them tried to touch her.

Several increasingly strained moments passed, neither
the men nor Maria willing to make the first move, neither
knowing what the first move should be. There was a low
unfriendly mutter from the sailors as the tense standoff
continued, and Maria sensed that it would be only seconds before they made a concerted rush at her. Her fingers tightened whitely about her small blade.

"Caramba! What is going on here?" an authoritative
voice suddenly demanded from the quarterdeck.

Maria recognized it and almost sagged with relief on
two counts—she was saved and not by Diego. The voice
belonged to Diego's cousin and second-in-command, Ramon Chavez, and Maria couldn't have chosen anyone else
that she would rather have appeared just then.

Sullenly the sailors made way for him as he approached
the knot of men gathered in front of Maria. Seeing the
object of their attention, his dark gray eyes widened.
"Dios! Maria! What in heaven's name are you doing
here?"

A hesitant smile curving her mouth, she said shakily,
"Coming to Hispaniola with you."

"Ah." Ramon sighed meaningfully and then, glancing
around, ordered mildly, "Back to work, men. It is only
our beloved captain's young sister come to pay him a surprise visit."

There was a murmur of snide amusement at this comment, and from the quick way the men obeyed him, it
was obvious that they respected him. It was also apparent
that they were enjoying the thought of Diego's displeasure when he was presented with his sister.

A slightly exasperated expression on his darkly handsome face, Ramon asked resignedly, "Would you like to
explain things to me . . . *before* we see Diego?"

Maria had known Ramon all of her life. His mother and
Diego's had been sisters, and though she was no actual
relative of his, Maria viewed him as member of her fam-

ily. The Chavez plantation was only a few miles away
from her home on Hispaniola, and Maria had spent many
a happy afternoon and evening laughing and visiting with
Ramon's large and delightful family. His sister Justina
was a particular friend of hers, and Maria had often
wished that Diego would treat her with the same teasing
affection that Ramon lavished on his younger sister.

When Maria remained silent, Ramon prodded gently,
"Pigeon, if you want me to help you, you had better tell
me what this is all about."

Maria nodded her dark head vigorously and the words
just came tumbling out. "Oh, Ramon! I *had* to do it! Otherwise, he was going to leave me in that wretched convent. I didn't have any other choice, you *must* believe me!
I hated Spain and I wanted to go home so very badly. I
begged him, Ramon! Pleaded with him, promised to do
anything, but he would not listen!" Her eyes bright with
growing indignation, she added, "He was still going to
try to make me marry Don Clemente! I had to do something! You do understand, don't you?"

Ramon smiled faintly. Knowing Maria rather well, he
understood perfectly. Actually, he would have been more
surprised if she *hadn't* done something drastic like this.
He had even argued bitterly with Diego about the other's
plans for her, and the situation between the two cousins
had been extremely cool since then. But as Diego was
Maria's guardian, and as Maria herself had never requested his aid, there had been nothing that Ramon could
do to help her ... until now. His dark gray eyes full of
affectionate sympathy, he said slowly, "*Sí.* I understand
... but will Diego?"

Ramon could have cursed his choice of words when he
saw the spasm of very real fear cross her face. His voice
kind, he muttered soothingly, "Don't look like that, pigeon! I won't let him hurt you and he's not likely to throw
you overboard to the sharks ... even though he may
threaten to do so." Taking her small hand in one of his,
he added briskly, "Come along now, let us find you some
fresh clothing and see if we can't get you a little cleaner.
As it is now, Diego will smell you coming long before he
sees you!"

Maria was exceedingly grateful to Ramon an hour later

as she stood nervously awaiting his return to his quarters. He had procured several buckets of warm water, and while she had not been able to take a *real* bath, for the first time in days she felt clean. Her hair had been washed, and though still damp it was beginning to curl in little unruly ringlets all over her head and shoulders. Ramon had even found appropriate clothing for her—a delicate chemise intended for Justina lay next to her skin; frothy petticoats lavishly trimmed with Flanders lace, meant as a gift for Juanita, his older, married sister, rustled pleasantly with every step she took; and on her feet were little silk slippers that Ramon had bought for his youngest sister, Consuelo. A gorgeous satin bodice of rose-colored silk, the sleeve slashed with green, and a full, canary yellow outer skirt of heavy silk completed her transformation. The bodice and skirt had been presents intended for Ramon's mother and another sister, and while the bodice fit rather well on Maria's small frame, the skirt had a decided tendency to drag on the floor. Before Ramon had left the cabin, Maria had stared down ruefully at the trailing material and declared, "I always knew that your sister Josefa was older than Justina and me, but I never realized that she was so much *taller!*"

A teasing glint in his gray eyes, Ramon had retorted, "I do not think, pigeon, that she is so tall as that you are . . . shall I be kind and say not fully grown?"

Maria had wrinkled her straight little nose at him and Ramon had smiled. But his smile had vanished a moment later and he had said quietly, "I don't know why we're smiling—I still have to see Diego and inform him of your presence aboard the *Santo Cristo.* But don't worry, *chica,* I'll not let him harm you."

Her eyes darkening, Maria had nodded her head, but Ramon must have sensed that she was not fully convinced, for he had walked over to her and, tipping up her chin, had promised, "Do not worry. My father and I should never have let Diego take you away from Hispaniola. We have no right to usurp his authority over you, but in the months since you have been in Spain, we have talked much about you." A slight smile had flitted across his dark face. "Justina would not let us do anything else! And we had decided that when I returned to Spain this time I would speak to Diego about you." Ramon's mouth had twisted. "I did, and I am ashamed to admit that I let him convince me that you were happy and you, *chica,* are as much to blame—did you not tell me that you were perfectly content when I asked you about it not two months ago?"

Reluctantly Maria had admitted, "I should have told you the truth, but, Ramon, I never thought that Diego would prove so, so unfeeling! I didn't want everyone to know how unhappy I was because it would seem as if I was being disloyal to my brother. Besides," she had added in a small voice, "I didn't think you would listen to me or do anything anyway."

Ramon had made a sound of disgust. "Do not let misguided loyalty betray you again! Now that we have that settled I must go and seek out my cousin and make certain that he understands the situation also. He may be your guardian, but my father is his *tío* and I think has some control over him. We will not let him make you too unhappy." He had then gone in search of Diego.

As the time passed and Ramon did not return to his cabin, Maria's fears increased. What was he saying to Diego? And more important, how was Diego taking the news of her presence aboard his ship?

Not very well, she thought a few moments later when the stout door to Ramon's cabin came bursting open and Diego stalked in, a slim rod held in his hand. His anger was obvious, the scar above his eyebrow white and throbbing. His mouth was a thin line of displeasure, and when he spoke, Maria was thankful that Ramon had not deserted her. Ramon had followed Diego, and as Diego stamped around the room he lounged carelessly in the doorway, but his gaze was intent upon his cousin.

Diego glared at Maria, making no attempt to hide his rage. *"Por Dios!* How dare you do such a thing!" Anger getting the better of him, he raised the rod to strike her, but Ramon moved swiftly to interfere. His hand tightening painfully around Diego's, he said softly, "Do not, *mi primo,* for if you beat her with it, I shall be forced to do the same to you."

The cousins were unusually tall for Spaniards, Ramon, standing above six feet, being the taller of the two; but they were evenly matched otherwise, and for one terrible moment, Maria was certain they would come to blows. Diego fought to bring his temper under control, and a second later, he wrested his hand away from Ramon and snarled, "Very well. I shall not beat her, although she deserves that and more." Turning to stare at his sister, he growled, "I am very angered at what you have done, and be aware that it is only because of Ramon's interference that I do not throw you overboard! And since," he added nastily, "my cousin has taken it upon himself to act as your protector, let *him* see to keeping you in hand— I shall have nothing to do with you until we reach Hispaniola. Pray, Maria, that by then my anger against you has cooled, and remember"—he threw a challenging look at Ramon before continuing—"that my cousin will not always be nearby!"

Spinning on his heel, he marched from the room, leaving a relieved silence behind him. Shutting the door gently, Ramon turned to smile at Maria. "It seems," he began lightly, "that I have, at least temporarily, become your guardian."

A breathless little giggle came from Maria, and running across the room, she flung her arms around his hard body. "Oh, Ramon! I was so frightened! I thought you were going to actually fight with him!"

Ramon gently ruffled her hair. *"Chica,* your brother never starts a fight he knows he will lose. Now, shall I find something for you to eat?"

Her heart lighter in her breast, Maria nodded her head. Ramon left in search of food, and alone in the cabin, Maria danced gaily around the small room. She was safe! Diego had been bearded, and whatever dreadful punishment he would eventually mete out had been delayed.

In the meantime, the *Santo Cristo* was sailing farther and farther away from Spain, closer and closer to home, and Maria's steps were light in the days that followed as she was escorted by Ramon or one of the other young officers about the ship. Ramon had turned over his cabin to her and had sought quarters elsewhere, but he took his duties as her interim guardian very seriously. When he was busy, he made certain that someone he could trust was near her side, and he had given orders that if at all possible, her every wish was to be granted. It was Ramon who introduced her to his fellow officers and those members of the crew that it was appropriate for her to know; Ramon who entertained her during the long days at sea, pointing out the porpoises that gamboled near the *Santo Cristo* and identifying the other ships which were part of the fall fleet to the Caribbean that sailed nearby.

At first Diego had refused to acknowledge her presence at all, but since she ate with him and his officers, it became ridiculous for him to pretend that she wasn't there, and by the time a week had gone by, he unbent enough to send conversation her way. As the days flowed swiftly by, he gradually began to take more of an interest in her welfare, asserting his authority over her more and more. Diplomatically, Ramon let himself be pushed back into the role of interested onlooker, and while there was a not unexpected stiffness between brother and sister, Diego and Maria were soon acting more normal with each other.

Maria didn't mind the situation. She was going home, and she was grateful for Ramon's interference, but she had never expected him to be saddled with the care of her forever. It was inevitable that eventually Diego would exert his control, and Maria was just happy that things were easier between her and her brother. She loved him dearly, but she wished again and again that he wasn't so, so *unbending!*

She might not have been quite as happy, however, if she had been privy to Diego's thoughts. His fury at Maria's blatant disregard of his orders had only faded when it had occurred to him that perhaps returning her to Hispaniola was actually a very good idea.

While his words to her in the convent had been full of confidence, if the truth be known, even Diego had doubts that he could soothe Don Clemente's wounded pride. It would take much to make the supercilious Castilian forgive Maria's outrageous actions, but Diego was determined to try. Gold, he reminded himself dryly, had a way of making a man forget the most offensive insult, and Don Clemente had as much love of gold as the next man. Diego was certain that in time he could get the other man to prove reasonable . . . especially if Maria were presented to Don Clemente in the most flattering light possible.

Even Diego would admit that Maria had not shone to her best advantage while in Spain. She had been unhappy, and her natural, outgoing charm had, for the most part, been subdued. Her attractiveness had suffered also, for much of Maria's beauty was in her warm, generous nature, and Diego was quite certain that if Don Clemente were to meet her under different circumstances, he would be enchanted. Watching her as she laughed winningly up at Ramon as they stood near the railings watching the ocean, Diego smiled grimly. Her long black hair was tousled by the sea breeze, there was a rosy bloom on her cheeks, her sapphire blue eyes were sparkling gaily, and her brother was convinced that few men would be able to resist her natural charm—particularly when that natural charm and elfin beauty were coupled with a great deal of wealth.

Actually the more he thought about it, the more pleased with the situation Diego became and his satisfaction increased when he mused over the fact, unbeknownst to either Maria or Ramon, that Don Clemente would be coming out to visit Hispaniola with the spring fleet. If Don Clemente were to see Maria as she was now, Diego had no doubt that the other man would begin to see anew the desirability of marriage to her. And once Maria and Don Clemente were married . . . Diego almost rubbed his hands together with anticipation. Once they were married, then with a highly influential brother-in-law like Don Clemente to ease his path, Diego was certain that the titles and power he lusted after would be granted to him.

Though wealthy and of the minor aristocracy, Diego was highly dissatisfied with his lot in life. He lusted for more—more wealth and more power. Especially power. He was not content to live a life of privilege and comfort on Hispaniola; instead he wrested every doubloon he could from his island plantations and used the money to increase his stature and position in Spain. Assiduously he curried favor with anyone who could help him in his quest, and Don Clemente, only heir to a grand title and member of a powerful family at court in Madrid, was in a position to help Diego along his way to glory. Maria *must* marry Don Clemente! With careful prodding, Don Clemente would see that his brother-in-law gained a title and a position of great authority. Lovingly Diego thought of his future—the Marquis Delgato, Viceroy of Panama, Spain's greatest treasure city in the New World. It had a nice ring to it, and he was willing to sacrifice everything to gain it, even his sister, and no one, not even Ramon Chavez, was going to interfere with his plans.

His eyes narrowing, he glanced again at the two by the railings. *That* could not be allowed to continue and, determined to make certain his cousin understood the situation perfectly, in the evening Diego called him aside for a private word. They were in Diego's cabin, and his face cold, Diego said bluntly, "I cannot but help notice that you have been spending an inordinate amount of time with Maria lately. I do hope that you are not entertaining any hopes in that direction. She is not for you, and I will not under any circumstances countenance a betrothal between you."

Ramon looked stunned. "Betrothal? To Maria?" he got out finally. A faintly contemptuous look crossing his handsome features, he murmured, "I do not understand you these days, *mi primo*. You are being ridiculous! I love your sister, it is true, but only as a sister. She is as dear to me as Justina and Josefa, and I spend no more time with her than I would with them. I think you dwell too much on the matter."

Diego stared at him intently. There was no guile on Ramon's face, and his words had the ring of truth to them. Relieved, he unbent slightly and muttered, "I am sorry. It is just that I did not want your attentions to her to become serious. I would not like to have to refuse you."

Ramon shrugged and turned away. Coolly, he asked, "Will that be all?"

"*Sí!*" Diego bit out tautly. For several seconds after the door closed behind his cousin's broad form, he continued to stare in that direction. He believed that Ramon had told him the truth, but what about Maria? How did she feel about Ramon? Was she falling under the spell of his far too charming cousin?

The next morning, an affable smile on his face, Diego approached his sister as she stood on the forecastle deck, staring at the churning blue water as it foamed along the side of the ship.

"Buenos días! How are you this morning?" he asked jovially.

A smile lighting her face, Maria returned brightly, "Very well, thank you. And you?"

He made a polite reply and they talked desultorily for several minutes; then, noticing Ramon crossing the deck below them, Diego said idly, "You seem to enjoy his company a great deal . . . are you in love with him?"

Maria glanced at him, astonishment written all across her lovely face. "In love with Ramon Chavez?" she repeated dumbly. Then, seeing that her brother was very serious, she burst out laughing. "Oh, Diego! Don't be silly! Of course I don't love him . . . at least not in the sense that you mean. He has always been very kind to me, but . . ."

She shrugged her shoulders helplessly and Diego finished for her, saying dryly, "But you have always thought of him as a brother."

Maria nodded her head eagerly. *"Sí!* That is true! I care for him very much, but only in the way that I care for you."

He sent her a long, considering look, but satisfied that only friendship existed between the two, he was willing to let the matter rest for the moment. With a bland remark, he changed the subject.

The subject may have been dropped by Diego but it created a feeling of concern in Maria. Was she being too friendly with Ramon? Perhaps misleading him about her affection for him?

A similar thought had occurred to Ramon, and later that day, as he escorted Maria for a walk around the ship, he said gently, "Maria, last night Diego brought up the subject of our friendship . . . it had him concerned that I might be enjoying your delightful company more than I should." His eyes on her face, trying to see the effect of his words upon her, he continued softly, "I told him that I loved you very dearly . . . as a sister." He waited, hoping he had not misread the situation and that he had not unknowingly crushed her hopes of some other type of relationship between them.

A beguiling little dimple appearing in one cheek, her blue eyes full of amusement, Maria said teasingly, "And now you're worried that you have shattered my aspirations! Don't be a donkey, Ramon! We don't either one of us think of the other in *that* way! And if Diego weren't so blind, he would have known it instantly."

Laughing softly, Ramon nodded his head, and then with a teasing glint in his own eyes, he asked, "And what do you know of *that* way?"

Maria blushed. "Very little, I am afraid, but I know how Josefa was when she fell in love with your father's overseer, and I know I don't feel that way about you!"

Ramon flicked a careless finger down her cheek and they continued on their walk for several more seconds in companionable silence. Then Maria glanced up at his hard face and asked curiously, "Have you ever been in love, Ramon? I mean deeply in love and wanting to get married?"

Ramon stiffened, his features becoming stony. Levelly, he admitted, "Yes, I was in love once. Her name was Marcela Domingo and we were very much in love. We planned to marry and I was the happiest man in the world." His voice growing husky, he continued, "She was beautiful, Maria. Beautiful and kind and young. She was everything I had ever dreamed of in a woman." He stopped, his gaze fixed on some distant spot on the horizon.

"And what happened?" Maria inquired softly. "Why didn't you marry her?"

A muscle jerked in his cheek. "Because," he said in a rough voice, "she was raped and then killed by a band of filthy English pirates! We were to have been married at the beginning of this year, and she was coming out from Spain with her parents last fall for a long visit at my home to let our families know one another better, when their ship was attacked and destroyed." His emotions held tightly under control, he ended with, "Only her father survived, along with a few crew members who had been able to escape the sinking ship, and it was he who told me her fate."

"Oh, Ramon! How terrible for you!" Maria cried sadly.

His eyes blank, an ugly twist to his fine mouth, he muttered, "Yes, it was terrible, but not as terrible as the punishment I will inflict on the English. They and their women will suffer greatly for what they did to Marcela and her family. I swear it."

"You still love her," Maria stated unhappily.

Ramon slowly shook his head. "I don't know. It is almost a year since she died, and though I grieve for her, it is hard to remember her face anymore." Sending Maria a painful little smile, he added, "Wounds do heal, *chica*, and time is the best physician, but I will always have her memory with me, always wonder of the life I might have had if those savages hadn't attacked her ship."

Lying in bed that night, staring at the beams overhead, Maria remembered the pain in Ramon's face, the anguish in his voice when he had spoken of Marcela. He had loved the other woman deeply, that much was certain, and Maria wondered if she would ever feel that strongly about someone. She had loved her parents, and after a fashion she loved her brother, but those emotions did not mirror the powerful intensity that Ramon had experienced.

In the darkness she frowned. How did one know when one was in love? And how did the mysterious feeling come about? There were many young men that she had known since childhood on the island, but none of them had aroused anything but mild affection within her breast. She had tried to like Don Clemente, but though he was considered handsome and sophisticated, she had found herself repelled by him. All during the months she had lived in Spain she had met no man who had kindled any strong emotion within her. Was there something wrong with her?

She got up and wandered over to the windows that lined the stern of the *Santo Cristo*. The moonlight silvered the crests of the waves, and staring at the endless motion of the sea, she pondered the possibility of loving someone as Ramon had. Somewhere out there, across this huge ocean, was there a man who would awaken her to love? A man that she would love all the days of her life?

Her heart beat a little faster as she thought of that mythical creature who would one day, she was suddenly very confident, come into her life like a whirlwind. He would be tall, and strong and dark, and they would love each other to distraction, she thought blissfully. A faint smile curving her lips, she crawled back into bed and promptly fell asleep, her dreams filled with a dashing figure who swept her into his arms, his mouth sweetly touching hers.

Chapter Four

THE *Santo Cristo* along with the rest of the fall fleet from Seville had been at sea nearly six weeks when disaster struck. A late-forming hurricane had roared through the fleet, sinking several ships and leaving those that survived the fierce onslaught of gigantic waves and savage winds disabled and widely scattered throughout the Atlantic Ocean.

On her first morning abovedecks since the hurricane had battered them, Maria was relieved to discover that the *Santo Cristo* had sustained only minor damage—a few torn sails and little else. But gazing at the empty blue ocean, not a sign of another ship in sight, she realized just how alone they were and felt a shiver of apprehension. Alone, they were at the mercy of the vicious buccaneers and bloodthirsty pirates who roamed this area, and remembering the fate of Ramon's Marcela, she swallowed painfully. Would that happen to her? Rape and murder? She prayed fervently that such would not be the case.

The sails were repaired immediately and the *Santo Cristo* was soon under way again, but everyone was much more alert, every eye peeled for the sight of another sail on the horizon. They were not far from Hispaniola now, but without the protection of the other ships in the fleet, the huge galleon was vulnerable to attack and there was an air of tenseness about the ship.

Shortly after sunrise the next morning, Maria awoke to the noise of much hurried movement about her, and recognizing the sound of the heavy cannons being dragged across the gun deck just below her, she leaped out of bed. Scrambling into her clothes, she threw some water from a porcelain pitcher into her face and dragged a comb hastily through her hair; then, her heart beating rapidly, she flew out of her cabin and up to the main deck.

The sight that met her eyes was not at all reassuring. Knots of heavily armed men stood about; marksmen with their muskets were in the riggings, and from the sounds coming from the gun deck Maria knew that another ship must be near. An enemy ship . . .

With alarm she glanced out at the blue expanse of ocean. In the distance, she could make out the sails of another ship, and suddenly spying the English flag that flew from the shattered mainmast, she sucked in her breath in dismay. Ramon, his face unusually somber, walked up to her. Giving her a brief smile, he said quietly, "The lookout spotted her at dawn. At first we hoped it was one of our own ships, but as you can see she flies the flag of England."

Maria swallowed tightly. "Will we fight them? Is it a pirate ship?"

Ramon's eyes squinted as he stared out across the bright cobalt sea. "Not a pirate ship, I think. From this distance, she has the look of a merchantman, but it wouldn't be the first time those devil buccaneers have disguised themselves so, in order to lull their prey." Sending her a reassuring glance, he added, "Don't worry, *chica,* the *Santo Cristo* is well armed. We shall be just fine. I do think, however, that it would be best if you went back down below to your cabin. There will be a fight at any rate, and I do not want to have to worry about you during the battle."

Reluctantly Maria nodded her head, and taking one last look at the approaching English ship, she went below. Consumed with a restless energy, she paced the small confines of her cabin, her every sense alert to what was happening around her, the sounds of preparation for the coming fight increasing as the moments passed.

When her door suddenly flew open, she jumped with startlement, but then, seeing it was only Diego standing there, she went limp with relief. A half-ashamed little smile crossing her features, she said, "You frightened me! I was certain you were an English pirate!"

"How foolish of you," Diego replied bluntly. "There has not even been a shot fired yet."

Biting back a sharp retort, Maria merely shrugged. "Is there something you wanted?" she asked politely.

Diego nodded his head. *"Sí.* I want you to stay below here until after we have sunk the Englishman. I do not want you getting in the way of my crew."

"Ramon has already told me as much," she snapped back, just a little annoyed at his manner. Unable to help herself, she added tauntingly, "Are you so certain you will sink the Englishman? Perhaps she will sink you!"

Diego gave a nasty laugh. "Hardly, my dear little sister. She is only a clumsy merchantman, not very well armed. And it is obvious from the way she is sailing and from what we can see of her condition that she is badly damaged. Like us, she must have been struck by the hurricane. But unlike us, she did not escape unscathed. It should be an easy victory."

A small frown wrinkling her brow, Maria asked, "But do we have to attack her? If she is only a merchantman and not a buccaneer ship, must we sink her?"

Diego sent her a contemptuous look. "Have you forgotten that an Englishman caused the death of *Padre?*" he demanded savagely. "Or that an Englishman gave me *this?*" His finger gently touched the white scar that twisted his eyebrow. "I haven't!" he snarled. "And I will sink every English ship that crosses my bow."

"I understand," Maria replied dully. She grieved for her father deeply, but the thought of killing other people simply because they were English disturbed her. Unlike most Spaniards, Maria was not imbued with a fanatical hatred of the English. She was aware that there was a long history of enmity between the two countries and she was dismally conscious that if positions were reversed the English would probably take much joy in sinking the *Santo Cristo.* Yet it all seemed wrong somehow. Would the killings and butchery never stop between Spaniards and Englishmen? For a second, she thought of Marcela Domingo. Would murdering women aboard this English ship bring Marcela back to Ramon? No. So why make innocent people suffer for something they had had nothing to do with? She glanced across at her brother's set face. It was futile to ask him such a question and unhappily she turned away. Her back to him, she asked, "Do you know the name of the ship?"

"The *Raven,*" he replied. "A fat English merchantman. Perhaps I won't even sink her—she may be loaded with worthwhile cargo. At any rate, we will certainly gain some slaves from the encounter."

It was indeed the *Raven* that was rapidly coming under the guns of the *Santo Cristo,* and everything that Diego had said about her was true. The hurricane that had whipped through the Spanish fleet had also caught the poor *Raven,* and while she had been lucky enough to stay afloat, she had sustained nearly fatal damage. Her bowsprit had been ripped away; the stays of all the masts were gone, the shrouds which remained were loose and useless; and she had lost both main and top mast.

From aboard the *Raven,* a sick fury churning in his breast, Gabriel Lancaster watched the *Santo Cristo* sail confidently closer to them. His wife and sister were below in their cabin; his men, those that had survived the hurricane, were armed and ready, but he was aware of how pitiful their small strength would be against the bigger and better-armed Spanish vessel.

Ordinarily, the *Raven* would have been able to avoid a confrontation and could have simply sailed away from the heavier, more cumbersome galleon, but not in her present condition. With only the mizzenmast remaining in working condition, they could make little headway. If there had been time to repair what remained of the foremast, replacing the yardarm and adding shrouds and sails, the *Raven* still might have stood a chance, but as it was, in spite of the brisk breeze that blew across the ocean, her maneuvering was clumsy at best.

The journey of the *Raven* up until the hurricane had struck had been uneventful, and after several weeks at sea, everyone had been eagerly looking forward to arriving in Port Royal. But the ship had barely survived the vicious tropical storm, and while there had been hope that she could be repaired enough to get them to Jamaica, everyone had been aware of how dangerous their position was. If an enemy ship should chance upon them . . .

Well, an enemy ship *had* found them, and there was

nothing they could do except prepare to fight and pray
that a miracle would happen. A terrible feeling of déjà vu
creeping over him, Gabriel clasped his broadsword more
firmly. Had he escaped this situation once, only to have
it occur again? And this time what would be the bitter
cost to him and his small family? Death for him? Enslavement of his wife and sister? He closed his eyes momentarily in anguish. His own death he could face, but the
thought of Elizabeth and Caroline in the captivity of the
Spanish was intolerable. He knew what their fate would
be—rape and degradation and a life of brutal mistreatment at the hands of the Spanish. It *must* not happen!
His mouth set in a grim line, he walked over to the captain of his ship.

"Have we a chance?" Gabriel asked calmly, his tone
hiding the fear he felt for Elizabeth and Caroline.

The captain, a small, grizzled man of indeterminate age,
reluctantly shook his head. "I doubt it. Our only hope will
be that she'll think we're too unimportant to bother with
and beyond sending a shot or two our way, will leave us
alone . . . and that's a frail hope at best."

The *Raven* was not heavily armed, she had two 1-pound
swivel guns and ten bronze nine-pound cannons; but beyond that, other than the swords and muskets of her crew
she had little else with which to fight. As for the *Santo
Cristo,* the galleon had as many as sixty guns and probably three times the number of fighting men. In the *Raven*'s crippled condition, she would be easy prey.

But there was hope. Usually the galleons chose not to
fight, unwilling to risk the loss of their precious cargo,
and as a rule they shunned all contact with other ships.
In most cases, upon sighting another ship, the galleon
would run rather than commence battle. Obviously, such
was not the case today, Gabriel thought sourly as the huge
galleon continued to bear down on them, her sails snowy
against the bright blue sky.

The *Santo Cristo* had the advantage of the wind; the
Raven would be forced to fight a defensive battle, lying
as she did in the lee-gauge position. Striking first as the
Santo Cristo bore down on them, the *Raven* let loose with
her cannons, the roar of the guns shattering the silence
of the sea.

The range of the *Raven*'s guns fell disastrously short, and with growing dismay and anger, Gabriel could see that the *Santo Cristo* was preparing to rake them with a broadside. When the expected attack came, even he was unprepared for the power and frightful accuracy of the Spanish guns. The air was filled with the smell of smoke and powder, the sounds of the cannons deafening, and the *Raven* trembled like a wounded animal as the missiles found their targets. The *Raven* reeled helplessly from the fierce pounding, and as the *Santo Cristo* came about with cannons blazing, Gabriel felt the ship leap beneath his feet as once again the Spanish guns found their mark.

The riggings and the mizzenmast came thundering down, the cries of wounded men carrying far too clearly over the sounds of the cannons, and though the *Raven* tried once more to bring her guns to bear, it was hopeless. The dreaded shout of *"Fire!"* rang out, and to his horror, Gabriel realized that the last barrage they had taken had started a fire belowdecks in the stern of the ship . . . the stern where Elizabeth and Caroline were . . .

His heart thudding painfully in his breast, Gabriel raced in that direction. Without thinking he plunged belowdecks, only to stagger backward as he was hit with an enveloping, acrid cloud of ugly black smoke. Gasping and blinking, he stumbled forward, crying out the names of his sister and wife. In the distance he heard a faint, answering shout, and ignoring the ominous crackle of flames nearby, he forged a path through the debris that choked the passageway. Reaching the door to their cabin, he discovered it was blocked by fallen timbers, and frantically he tore at the shattered wood that impeded his progress. Smoke was seeping out from the room, and he knew that their cabin must have taken a direct hit.

Bursting through the door at last, he was met by Caroline, who flung herself into his arms, saying huskily, "Oh, Gabriel! Thank God you came! The door was jammed and Elizabeth—" She stopped speaking, her voice suspended by emotion.

Gabriel gave her a quick reassuring hug, not quite realizing the implications of her words. He glanced around swiftly, searching for his wife, one part of him noting with shock the frightful damage done to the cabin. Smashed

beams and timbers lay willy-nilly here and there; a fire
was burning fitfully in one corner; even as he stared,
flames began licking hungrily along the walls. Seeing no
sign of Elizabeth, he shook Caroline lightly and said,
"Where is she?"

Caroline smothered a small sob, and turning her head
away from him, she pointed toward the back of the cabin.
He started forward, but she caught at his arms. Her face
poignant with grief, she murmured softly, "She's dead,
Gabriel. Don't go back there. There is nothing you can do
for her now."

Gabriel froze, his mind refusing to believe her words.
"No!" he shrieked with anguish, throwing himself violently in the direction she had indicated. He spotted the
edge of Elizabeth's blue gown peeking out from underneath one of the huge beams that had come crashing down
during the last barrage of cannon fire from the *Santo
Cristo,* and a curious numbness creeping over him, he
knelt down beside that patch of bright color. The beam
had completely crushed her slender body; only one slim
hand and a few curls of long, brown hair gave any other
sign that she lay buried beneath that massive beam.

His fingers trembling, he reached out almost timidly
and gently touched her motionless hand. It was still
warm, and he was filled with an unbearable sensation of
pain and loss. He had not loved her, but he had cared
deeply for her—she had been his wife, the mother of his
unborn child . . . she had been his future and now it was
all lost. Elizabeth was dead. A great terrible rage suddenly surged up through him. *They* had done this! Those
filthy, murdering Spaniards had killed his wife!

A look of wild fury on his face, he stood up, and gripping his sword more tightly, he hurled himself toward the
door. It was the sight of Caroline's apprehensive expression that stopped him. There was a streak of blood
streaming down the side of her cheek, and with an oddly
gentle motion, he wiped it away with his hand. Gravely,
he said, "I am sorry, Caroline, for bringing you along. I
should have left you and Elizabeth safely at home in England. Then she would still be alive and you would be
safe."

Bravely Caroline shook her head. "No," she replied

stoutly, "we wanted to come. We would not have allowed you to sail without us. You must not blame yourself—it is not your fault."

His face twisted. "I wonder," Gabriel said almost to himself, "if I will ever really believe that."

There was no time for further words, the fire was spreading rapidly and the sound of the battle had increased above them. Taking her hand in his, he guided them through the smoky passageway to the upper deck. "Stay behind," he commanded softly as they reached the hatch. "There may be boarders on now and the fighting will be bloody." He glanced back at her. Silently, he handed her a small knife. Not looking directly at her, he muttered, "I will protect you for as long as I can, but we are badly outnumbered and I fear the worst. Use the knife as you see fit, my dear . . . and remember that I love you and will die to save you."

Tears blinded Caroline's eyes but words would not come to her. She felt Gabriel's hand tenderly caress her hair, and then they were abovedecks.

As Gabriel had suspected, the *Raven* had been boarded, and as they reached the main deck, the sound of naked steel against steel rang savagely in the air. A pall of blue smoke hung over the decks, the ping and pop of musket fire sounding now and then above the cries of wounded and dying men. It was a ghastly situation. Men in Spanish uniforms seemed to be swarming everywhere, falling on the defenders of the badly listing *Raven* like ravening wolves. He had no time for further impressions; a swarthy Spaniard with a bloodied sword instantly engaged him.

His blade clanging powerfully against the Spaniard's, Gabriel met thrust for thrust, driving the soldier backward with the sheer fury of his defense. The man faltered and Gabriel's sword struck with lightning swiftness, sinking in deep. The mortally wounded man crumpled, but his body had barely hit the deck when Gabriel was confronted with another enemy, and so it seemed to go indefinitely—with each Spaniard dispatched another seemed immediately to take his place, and as the battle wore on, Gabriel could feel the muscles and tendons in his arm screaming with exhaustion. Doggedly he fought on, only dimly aware of what was going on around him, of the sounds of battle that seemed to be decreasing, of Caroline's slender form behind him.

Gradually he and Caroline were driven back, Gabriel's reflexes and reactions becoming slower and slower, his sword arm feeling like a lead weight. He knew he was wounded, he could feel the wetness of the blood dripping down his other arm, but when he had received the wound, he couldn't remember. It seemed he fought for hours, he and Caroline the only two English still resisting the Spanish horde, but finally, their backs against the railings at the stern of the ship, Gabriel knew that he could not fight much longer—this last Spaniard was too expert for him to best in the condition he was in now. But still he fought on, determined to die rather than be captured. There was a black film forming in front of his eyes, the tall Spaniard in front of him wavering.

Suddenly the other man stepped back. "Surrender, Englishman. You have fought too bravely for me to slaughter you," Ramon Chavez said quietly.

Blearily, Gabriel gazed at him. *"Never!"* he snarled, his sword poised and ready. He heard a slight sound of a movement to his left, but even though he spun to meet it, he was too late. To his horror, he caught a glimpse of Diego Delgato's face as the other man brought the hilt of his sword down hard upon Gabriel's temple and then there was nothing but utter darkness.

Wearing a smile of smug satisfaction, Diego surveyed his fallen foe. *"Gabriel Lancaster!* The saints have been inordinately kind to me this day." His gaze traveled over to where Caroline stood frozen, her slim body pressed tightly against the railings. Almost purring, Diego said, "And his sister . . . I would recognize those Lancaster eyes anywhere. What joy I shall have in despoiling you in front of your brother. How he will writhe when he hears your cries for mercy . . . and believe me, my dear, before I am through teaching you who is your master you *will* scream."

Ramon, who had remained silent until this moment, spoke up just then. His voice cool and confident, he stated bluntly, "No. She is my prisoner . . . as was the Englishman, until you took matters into your own hands."

Diego glared at Ramon, but Ramon met his stare unflinchingly. Almost gently, Ramon added, "Technically, I could claim the man also. Take your choice, the woman or the man, but not both."

Indecision written clearly across his features, Diego gazed at Caroline, the knife Gabriel had given her tightly clasped in her hand, the sunlight creating a halo of gold around her blond head. She was lovely and Diego felt lust stirring within, but then he looked down at his greatest enemy, the man who had scarred him for life. Thickly, he muttered, "The man, I claim the man." Spinning on his heel, he shouted an order to his men, and seconds later, the unconscious Gabriel was dragged away before Caroline's terrified gaze.

She stepped forward, but the tip of Ramon's blade pressing gently against her breast halted her. Her sapphire blue eyes wide with defiance and pride, she met his considering stare, her fingers clenching whitely on the knife.

Softly, Ramon commanded, "Loose it, *señorita,* or I shall be forced to hurt you."

Following her brother's lead, she cried, "Never!" and hurled herself forward, but Ramon was too quick, and in an instant, she found herself disarmed and held captive by a hated Spaniard.

Ramon looked down into her upturned rebellious face. He smiled crookedly. "The English took my bride ... I think it only fair that you pay the price." His voice deepened. "I'm certain you will find that I will make a far less cruel master than my cousin." And gently he pushed her in front of him, guiding her over to where Diego stood near the forecastle deck of the *Raven* overseeing the soldiers who were dispatching those of the English too badly wounded to save and manacling those who would become Spanish slaves. At Diego's feet lay Gabriel, his face white and still, his powerful body bound by chains. Gabriel stirred, slowly shaking his dark head as if to clear it. Diego prodded him none too gently with a booted foot and prompted, "Awake, Lancaster, and learn your new position as my slave. It will be my pleasure to instruct you in the kind of obedience I expect from my servants."

The emerald green eyes flashing with hatred and contempt, Gabriel painfully raised himself up. Oblivious of the chains that held him prisoner, he ground out, "Won't that be more like the dog teaching the gentleman?"

His face convulsed with fury, Diego struck Gabriel viciously across the cheek, the blow breaking the skin and leaving a thin trail of blood. "Insolent English swine!" Diego shrieked. "We shall see who is the gentleman here." He drew his sword, his intention clear, but Ramon's voice stopped him.

Calmly, Ramon said, "Won't that be a waste of a strong healthy slave, cousin? And won't it give you far more amusement to taunt him indefinitely than to take all of your pleasures in one moment?"

Sullenly, Diego sheathed his sword. "You're right, of course," he muttered, and turning away he called to some men who waited nearby. "Take this creature on board the *Santo Cristo!*"

"The woman also," Ramon added. Giving the four rough seamen a hard stare, he continued coolly, "Take her to my quarters—and if she is hurt or touched disrespectfully . . . then I shall rip out your entrails and feed them to the sharks. *Comprenden?*"

Nodding swiftly, the four men took Gabriel and Caroline away with them. Watching the group as they made their way across the shambles of the *Raven's* main deck, Ramon asked idly, "What do you intend to do now with the ship? Sink it? Or is the cargo valuable enough to put a prize crew upon her and take it to Santo Domingo with us?"

His eyes still on the others, Diego pulled nervously at his lower lip. "Take it with us. The hold is full of very practical items that will fetch a good price in Hispaniola. It will take some time to get the ship rigged and ready, but I think the profits to be made outweigh the risks."

Ramon shrugged. "Very well, I will order a prize crew to board her and repair immediately what they can."

Throughout the fighting, Maria had remained below as she had been ordered, but once the cannons stopped booming and the sounds of battle had faded, she was impatient to leave her room. She waited several minutes longer, and when no one came to tell her of the outcome, although she was certain the *Santo Cristo* had beaten the other ship, she decided to see for herself what had happened. On curiously leaden feet she slowly made her way to the upper decks of the galleon. The thought of having destroyed the English ship gave her no joy—it had been so senseless, so unnecessary for Diego to attack; and without even seeing them, her tender heart was full of pity for the surviving English. She took a position on the poop deck, able to oversee everything that was going on around her, and it was from there that she saw Gabriel Lancaster for the first time.

She didn't know who he was then; she only saw a tall, handsome man with an air of fierce pride about him, in spite of the chains that held him captive. He boarded the *Santo Cristo* like a conqueror, instead of a prisoner, his head held high, his features arrogant and proud. The sea breeze ruffled the thick, almost shoulder-length black hair; his white shirt of fine Holland was open nearly to his waist, exposing the strong chest with its mat of fine black curls. The shirt was torn and dirtied from the battle, one sleeve and shoulder stained with the unmistakable signs of blood; his leather doublet was barely recognizable and hung on his wide shoulders in tatters; the full knee-length breeches were ripped, and his once-elegant stockings were ruined by several rents, the bright gleam of the silver buckles of his shoes seeming oddly out of place. He was a magnificent figure with his proud carriage, and with his great height he towered above the shorter, squatter Spaniards.

Maria was so transfixed by the man that she barely noticed the tall, slender girl who followed him. It was the flash of gold as the sun touched Caroline's hair that caught Maria's attention, and seeing the girl walking so proudly between the two seamen, Maria was conscious of a feeling of great pity. How very frightened I would be, she thought unhappily, if I were in her situation, and I pray that I would be able to act with as much composure. She sensed that the other girl was hiding fear, and she felt a bond between them. So she would act, determined not to let her captors know her true feelings.

But it was the man who fascinated her, and irresistibly her gaze went back to him as he stood there in the center of the deck, just below her. He must have felt her eyes upon him, because he suddenly glanced upward and Maria was trapped by the intensity of those thickly lashed emerald green eyes. There was such suffering in their depths, such unbearable anguish, that she was aware of an almost overwhelming urge to fly across the distance that separated them and offer him comfort. And yet, despite the pain so evident, there was also fury and hatred warring with the anguish; and as his eyes wandered slowly over her, she became increasingly uncomfortable, a chill beginning to creep along her spine, displacing any yearning to offer him comfort. *Cielos,* but he hates us! And with good cause, another part of her reminded. Haven't your countrymen this day captured his ship, and killed his men? And who knew what fate awaited the young woman at his side.

Who was she? Maria wondered suddenly. Wife? Relative? Passenger?

Becoming aware of the direction of Gabriel's intent gaze, Caroline looked up, and as her eyes met Maria's they both experienced a shock, recognizing in the same instant the Lancaster eyes. Maria sucked in her breath with a great gulp. That girl was a Lancaster! *Dios!* What evil thing would Diego do to her? She noted with growing horror the similarity between the two below her—their height, the slashing eyebrows and the finely molded features—and with a sickening lurch in her heart she knew that the man must also be a Lancaster . . . *Gabriel* Lancaster!

For just a second, a feeling of justice rippled through her. This man had scarred her brother and this man's father had been the ultimate cause of her own father's death; wasn't it only just that he should be delivered into their hands for punishment? The feeling lasted only a second, and then she was ashamed of it. Was she as much of a barbarian as Diego? Unhappy with herself and full of a strange sadness at the situation, she started to turn away, but the man's mesmerizing gaze would not let her and helplessly she glanced back at him.

Gabriel had recognized those beautiful, distinctive Lancaster eyes at the same moment as the other two, and with new speculation he studied the small figure above him. She had to be Diego's sister. No other Spaniard would have those sapphire blue eyes. A yearning for vengeance suddenly flooded him. *She* should pay for what he had suffered this day. *She* should be lying dead under that huge beam, not his dear Elizabeth!

Even as one part of him thought of all the lovely ways he would take his revenge, another part of him was very aware of the elfin beauty of the delicate features, of the straight little nose, of the full, sweetly curved mouth and the womanly curves that were apparent underneath the bodice and full silken skirts. Her hair fell in long black ringlets to her slim shoulders, intensifying the smooth fairness of her skin, strengthening the impact of those almond-shaped, darkly lashed bright blue eyes. Another time, another place and Gabriel might have been more aware of her ethereal beauty, but not today . . . not with his Elizabeth lying dead beneath the decks of the *Raven*, not with his sister about to face degradation and shame. Hatred for all Spaniards nearly choked him, the feeling increasing a hundredfold when Diego came aboard and joined his sister on the poop deck.

In a sudden burst of affection, Diego put his arm around Maria, giving her a quick hug. His eyes sparkling with self-righteous satisfaction, a smug smile of anticipation upon his face, he stared down at the captured Lancasters below him.

It was more than Gabriel could bear; his teeth bared in rage, he charged forward, unmindful of the chains or the men who stood beside him. He took two steps before a powerful blow brought him to his knees. He would have fought on, forced them to kill him; only Caroline's voice stopped him.

"Gabriel!" she pleaded. "Stop! Please! Don't let them kill you!"

The decision was taken from him; he was instantly surrounded by numerous Spaniards and immediately hustled toward the main hatch. With his foot on the first step he glanced back at the two on the poop deck. Someday, he vowed fiercely, someday, I will kill you, Diego Delgato, and your sister will be *my* captive! And I will show her as much mercy and kindness as you showed my dear Elizabeth . . . as much mercy as Caroline will be given. You will suffer for your deeds this day, and the woman at your side will pay the price for all that I have lost. I swear it by all I hold dear!

Chapter Five

THE advent of the Lancasters into her life changed Maria in some inexplicable way. She felt profoundly guilty about what had happened to them and their ship, which in turn left her confused and uneasy—wasn't she a true daughter of Spain? Hadn't the Delgatos been feuding with the Lancasters for almost a century? Shouldn't she be elated at their fate? To feel otherwise was shamefully disloyal to her father's memory—or had she forgotten that Gabriel Lancaster's father had been the cause of her own father's death?

She hadn't forgotten, nor was the pain of her father's death lessened, but she failed to understand how being cruel and abusive to the remaining Lancasters would do any of them any good. She tried to explain this to both Diego and Ramon, but neither man seemed particularly moved or interested by her passionate arguments. Diego's attitude didn't surprise her, but Ramon's indifference did, and by the time they finally reached Santo Domingo, almost a week later, she was thoroughly annoyed with both men.

The arrival in Santo Domingo should have been a happy occasion for Maria—she was home at last—but because of the Lancasters and the brutal taking of the *Raven,* somehow it wasn't very happy at all for her. She was too conscious of Gabriel and Caroline lying chained in the hold, facing a life of servitude, to take any real joy in her own freedom. They obsessed her—Caroline because she was young and lovely and Maria could picture herself in the same situation, and Gabriel . . . Gabriel because she simply could not get the thought of him out of her mind. She brooded over his fate during the day, and at night he filled her dreams. She relived over and over again the moment she had first seen him step on board the *Santo Cristo,* only in her dreams it wasn't quite the same—he was unbound; his clothes were impeccable; a warm, welcoming smile was on his face; and with a cry of delight she ran to him. His arms opened and she was engulfed in a fierce embrace, his lips raining sweet kisses over her upturned face. It was such a lovely dream, but in the morning she would awake, dispirited and angry with herself for being so foolish—she had never even seen him smile, so how did she know what his smile would be like? Reluctantly she admitted that he fascinated her as no other man ever had.

And as the days, weeks and months went by, to her intense mortification, the fascination persisted unabated. The excitement and pleasure of returning home was tempered by the knowledge that somewhere on the vast lands of the Delgatos there was an emerald-eyed English slave named Gabriel Lancaster . . . and that she was helpless to alleviate his suffering, that in many ways she was as much Diego's slave as he was.

Maria tried to break the fascination, forcing herself to act unconcerned about his fate, and to some extent she was successful. She was ecstatic to be home, and during those first weeks as she was warmly reunited with the smiling servants she had known since infancy, as she wandered happily through the sprawling hacienda she had grown up in, as she rode her favorite mare across the wide savannas that lay beyond the fields of waving green sugar cane and was reacquainted with friends and neighbors, it was comparatively easy to push the Englishman and his sister to the back of her mind. But once the initial joy of homecoming had fled, she became aware of an underlying emptiness within herself, and though she did not see Gabriel, she was nagged by thoughts of him—Diego often taking delight in relating to her the tortures he inflicted upon the Englishman.

It would have both pleased and horrified her if Maria had known that she occupied a great deal of Gabriel's thoughts. Only his were not pleasant thoughts, nor were they filled with half-understood longings—his interest in Maria Delgato had only one driving motive . . . revenge.

All during the miserable days he had spent chained in the hold, one part of him grieved deeply for his lost wife and child and for the uncertain fate he had inadvertently brought upon his sister, while another part of him coldly began to plan for vengeance. Diego's death by his hand was inevitable, and he wasted little time in plotting how the Spaniard was to die. Ah, but Diego's sister was another matter—and Gabriel swore that before he killed Diego, Diego would be given just a small taste of what he was suffering now. The Delgato woman would be forced to be *his* slave, just as Caroline was going to be the slave of some Spanish family; and just as he knew that his sister would be defiled by some nameless Spaniard, so he plotted that Diego's sister would know the same fate. Only her despoiler would not be nameless, and Diego would know precisely when and where it happened . . . a feral grin flashed across Gabriel's face in the darkness of the hold. Oh, yes, the daughter of the Delgatos would one day pay dearly for all the evil deeds of her infamous family.

The parting from Caroline in Santo Domingo had been especially painful for Gabriel, and watching her being led away by the tall Spaniard who had claimed her, his thirst for revenge had increased. Someday, he thought savagely, someday they will pay for this. And as the days turned into weeks and the weeks into months; as he suffered from Diego's taunts and vicious treatment; as he labored in the sugar cane fields, his bare back crisscrossed and scarred from the whip marks of Diego and the brutal overseer; as he lay at night chained in a filthy hut, his desire for vengeance obsessed him, until it was the only emotion he was capable of feeling. The dirt, the cruel mistreatment, the insults, the heat, the insects, nothing touched him anymore—there was only one thing that he hungered for—revenge!

Perhaps if he had known of Maria's distress at his fate; if he had known that Caroline was well cared for; that she and Maria had actually met and that a strange bond was tentatively developing between the two young women, he might have had second thoughts. But Gabriel knew nothing beyond the cane fields and the disgusting hovel where he slept fitfully at night, knew nothing beyond the kicks and lashes given him by his Spanish captors. It was only the need for revenge that kept him alive.

Maria's first meetings with Caroline were not particularly notable or intimate. Visiting with the Chavez household late in January of 1665, Maria saw the English girl for the first time since the *Raven* had been captured almost four months previously. The family was sitting in the grand *sala* enjoying the fading tropical sunlight that spilled in from double doors that had been thrown wide when Maria noticed the tall, golden-haired young woman who was serving refreshments. It was Caroline, and with relief Maria noticed that in spite of an air of remoteness and the hint of sadness in the curve of her full mouth, the English girl looked well.

Maria's visit lasted only two days, and though she saw the other girl at a distance several times, they exchanged no conversation. It wasn't until the middle of February, when Maria returned for an extended visit with her dear friend Justina Chavez, that Maria had a chance to meet and get to know Gabriel's sister better. Accompanied by a prattling Justina to the rooms she usually stayed in when visiting, Maria was startled when Caroline suddenly entered the room from the connecting doors that separated Maria's rooms from Justina's. Justina noticed her start of surprise and said lightly, "It is only Caroline—she is my maid now and during your visit will serve you too." Then, grasping Maria's hand, Justina excitedly pulled her toward the other room. "Do come, Maria! I want to show you the new silk petticoat and lovely satin skirt that *mi padre* bought for me when he was in Santo Domingo! They are *so* beautiful and I have begged him to give a fiesta while you are here so that I may show them off. Caroline will unpack for you. *Come!*"

Justina Chavez was exactly one month younger than Maria; like Maria she also had masses of heavy black hair and was small in stature. The resemblance between the two friends ended there. Justina was a frivolous creature, her head full of nonsense.

The darling of her family, she was petted and pampered outrageously by everyone, but all the attention had left her curiously unspoiled; she was unfailingly generous and her heart was easily touched. Her greatest sorrow was that she had not yet attained the slender, lithe form of her dearest friend, Maria. Pleasingly plump with bright, merry dark eyes, a smile nearly always upon her soft mouth, Justina was much like a happy, roly-poly puppy that had never known a harsh or cruel word. She fairly bounced into the next room, and somewhat reluctantly, Maria followed her.

It wasn't until later that same day that Maria had a private word with Caroline. Justina had already gone to join the family in the *sala* before dinner, but Maria had purposely lingered over her own toilet, hoping for an opportunity to speak with Caroline. What she was going to say to the English girl she had no idea; there was just a compelling need to somehow express her distress about what had befallen the Lancasters.

Her strategy worked. Justina had not tripped merrily out of her room five minutes previously when Caroline entered Maria's rooms. She had some extra pillows in her arms, but she halted instantly as her gaze met Maria's.

An odd, considering stillness filled the room as the two girls stared at each other, Caroline's beautiful eyes widening as she really looked at Maria for the first time. "The Lancaster eyes," she said slowly, almost to herself.

Maria nodded her head. In simple Spanish she said, "We share the same ancestors, you and I . . . it is not good that we be enemies."

A bitter curve to her mouth, in slow Spanish Caroline retorted flatly, "What else can we be? Look what your brother did to me and my family—we can be nothing *but* enemies!" Her sapphire blue eyes suddenly full of tears, she asked huskily, "My brother? Is he still alive?"

Maria got up from the velvet bench where she had been seated, and crossing to Caroline, she grasped the other girl's hand. "Listen to me!" she implored softly. "I will be your friend if you will let me." The expression on her face grave, she added, "Yes, your brother is still alive . . . but I have not seen him, since we arrived at Casa de la Paloma, my home. I know that Diego, my brother, has him working in the cane fields, but I know nothing beyond that."

Caroline's Spanish was not extensive, but in the five months since her capture, as Spanish was the only language she heard spoken, she had learned rapidly and she followed Maria's speech easily. Speaking it was another matter, and she groped helplessly for the right words. Haltingly she got out, "If you meant what you said, would you tell my brother where I am? And that I am . . ." She hesitated, then added lamely, "That I am well."

"Oh, sí! I will!" promised Maria eagerly, so very pleased that the English girl was willing to meet her halfway. It was the beginning of a strange friendship.

But though she had promised to speak to Gabriel upon her return to Casa de la Paloma, it proved to be far more difficult than she had imagined. To her disappointment, her cautious queries about the English slave, Lancaster, were met with indifferent shrugs by the servants she questioned. Wary of asking Diego outright where Gabriel was on the far-flung lands of the estate, Maria took to taking long rides, her eyes always searching for one particular tall, broad-shouldered slave.

Finally after several days of having no success in finding Gabriel, one night in late March, as she and Diego sat at the long walnut table in the dining room, Maria asked with deceptive idleness, "I have not heard you speak of the English slave since I have returned from Justina's home . . . have you grown tired of baiting him so unmercifully?"

Diego smiled wolfishly, well aware that his sister violently disapproved of his treatment of Lancaster. Carelessly, he replied, "No. But he actually had the temerity to attempt to attack me last week—I had him beaten soundly and put in the pit for a while. *That* should break his damnable English pride!"

Maria hoped that the shudder of horror that rippled through her was not apparent to Diego. She knew of the pit's existence, but it was not something that she had ever really thought deeply about until now.

Situated near a small grove of banana and palm trees just behind the slave quarters, the pit was a small excavation in the earth, the sides lined with metal. Inside this area there was not even enough room for a man to turn around, and the hole was not deep enough for the poor creature put there to do more than half crouch. A massive cover of heavy steel had been fashioned to seal it off completely, plunging the occupant into utter darkness, and with the tropical sunlight pouring down on the metal, Maria knew that the pit must be unbearable during the day. It was an invention of Diego's—during her father's time it had not existed—Don Pedro had been a kind master.

Hiding her revulsion at the thought of anyone being put there, she inquired as indifferently as possible, "Oh? And when do you intend to release him?"

"Perhaps tomorrow—after all, I don't want to kill him." His mouth curved into a decidedly ugly grin. "It is far too enjoyable having him alive and constantly at my beck and call. It gives me great pleasure too, I must confess, to know that I can cause him much suffering." Unconsciously his fingers touched the scar that twisted his slim black eyebrow. "Far too much pleasure to let him die," he very nearly purred. Sending her a calculating glance, he murmured, "Would you like to be there when I release him? You might find it interesting."

It was on the tip of her tongue to hurl his invitation back into his handsome face, but wanting to reassure herself of Gabriel's condition, as much for her own peace of mind as Caroline's, she muttered, "*Sí.* Tell me when and I will be there."

The next morning as she stood beside Diego and the head overseer, Juan Perez, watching the two burly servants struggling to move the heavy lid, she wondered at the wisdom of what she was doing. Would she be able to conceal from Diego all the horror and pity she was certain to feel? Her heart a painful lump in her chest, she stared at the opening of the pit. How horribly had Gabriel suffered from this cruel confinement?

Gabriel's appearance as he slowly, painfully unbent from his cramped position within the pit was every bit as bad as Maria had feared, and he bore little resemblance to the man she had first seen on board the *Santo Cristo* or the man who haunted her dreams. He was filthy—ragged dirty pants hung loosely on his hips; a thick iron chain was around his neck; the black hair was matted and grew well past his shoulders; a heavy, equally black beard covered his chiseled features; the magnificent body was gaunt and scarred. Seeing him stumble weakly out of the pit, it

was all she could do not to cry out and catch him in her
arms. There was little pride in his bearing as he stood
there swaying, blinking in the bright light. But when his
eyes finally adjusted to the sunlight and he saw Diego and
Maria standing there, such an incandescent glitter of
hatred entered those emerald green eyes that Maria took
an involuntary step backward.

Diego laughed at her actions, saying, "Maria, don't be
such a goose! Do you really think this pitiful creature
could harm you?" Arrogantly he strolled across the clearing and, standing in front of Gabriel, gave him a push
with one finger. Weak and unsteady as he was, Gabriel
went tumbling down in a heap, causing Juan Perez and
his men to snicker. Ashamed and appalled at the cruelty,
Maria turned away, unable to watch this ugly scene any
longer. It was made all the more galling by the instinctive
knowledge that any outburst on her part would only make
the Englishman's lot worse. It wasn't until she and Diego
were walking back toward the hacienda that she was able
to ask the question uppermost in her mind. Staring intently at the ground in front of her, she inquired dully,
"What will you do with him now?"

Diego shrugged. "Probably nothing for a few days—he
will need time to recover somewhat before I can send him
back to the cane fields."

A bitter note in her voice, she retorted sarcastically,
"Isn't that being too kind to him?"

"Why, no," Diego answered easily. "Remember, I don't
want him to die . . . too soon."

Fortunately, before Maria lost her temper and told Diego precisely what she thought of his iniquitous actions,
they arrived at the hacienda. During the next few days
she avoided him whenever she could and was shamefully
delighted when he informed her that he would be leaving
at the end of the week for a protracted stay in Santo Domingo. The entire hacienda and plantation seemed to
breathe a collective sigh of relief the afternoon Diego and
a contingent of his men rode away. And in the time that
followed there was a happier air about the Casa de la
Paloma; laughter was heard often, and smiling faces were
frequently seen as the servants went about their chores.

Maria was very conscious of the change in atmosphere,

aware that her own spirits had soared with Diego's departure. He had enlisted the services of a nearby neighbor and his comfortable wife to stay at the Casa de la Paloma with Maria while he was away. Overseen by a benevolent pair of guardians who had known her since infancy, Maria was the person in actual control of the hacienda, and she ran it with a far gentler, more compassionate hand than it had known since the death of Don Pedro and his wife. Beyond the hacienda though, she had no authority, Juan Perez having direct orders from Diego on the running of the plantation itself, and that included everything but the servants of the household. She considered seriously the possibility of requesting that the Englishman be sent up to the hacienda for the far easier work in the luxurious gardens that surrounded the coral limestone building, but regretfully decided against the idea. There was no doubt in her mind that when Diego returned, such an action would have particularly unpleasant consequences for both her and the Englishman.

True to her word, Maria did give Gabriel Caroline's message, but his reaction to her gesture of kindness was not what Maria had hoped it would be. Not wanting her interest in the Englishman to have repercussions for him, Maria had waited for several days to pass before she sought out Gabriel in the fields. A meeting with him was very difficult and fraught with danger—whenever she rode near the fields, the weasel-eyed, ubiquitous Juan Perez would suddenly appear and insist in his oily voice that he escort her. She knew that if she attempted any conversation with the Englishman it would be reported to Diego the instant he returned. Maria didn't like to think about what his reaction would be . . . more for what he would do to Gabriel than for herself.

It finally happened one day that as she and Juan were riding through the cane fields, Maria ostensibly making sure that the work was progressing as her brother would have wanted, Juan was called aside by one of the field overseers for a brief word. Spotting Gabriel's tall form just ahead as he worked in the hot sunlight next to the road they were traveling, Maria casually urged her horse forward. Coming abreast with Gabriel, she stopped her horse, and after sending a wary glance back down the road where Juan was still deep in conversation, she bent over, apparently to check her stirrup. Instead, she muttered, "Englishman! I have news of your sister for you!"

Gabriel wasn't more than three feet away from her and he heard her words quite clearly. He stiffened, the movements of the scythe in his hands faltering for just a moment. Then taking a vicious swipe at the tropical weeds that persisted in growing between the upright stalks of green cane, he demanded coldly from the corner of his mouth, "Now, why would you say that? Has Diego enlisted your help for a different sort of torture?"

Angry that he should doubt her sincerity, she sent a harassed look in Juan's direction and hissed, "It is true! She is at the Chavez plantation some twenty leagues from here. And she is well. I have spoken with her and she asked me to tell you this."

The scythe never missing a swing, he shot her a considering look. She was very pretty as she sat there on her little black mare, a broad-brimmed hat protecting her delicate skin from the burning sun; the riding habit of dark blue fit her slender shape admirably and intensified the impact of those brilliant blue eyes. But the days were long past that Gabriel's attitude could be swayed by a lovely face and form and he replied insolently, "Very well, you've discharged your act of charity, now ride on and leave me and mine alone!" The green eyes flashing in the sun-darkened face, he snarled, "The Lancasters need no pity from you!"

Whatever Maria might have said was lost, because at that moment, Juan rode up and asked, "Is this bit of offal annoying you, *señorita?*"

Hastily, Maria answered, "Oh, no! I had just stopped to check my stirrup! Shall we continue now?"

It was the end of the incident, but she didn't like the look Juan had sent Gabriel, nor could she forget the expression in Gabriel's eyes. There was such hatred gleaming in their depths and she wondered why, in spite of everything, he continued to hold a dark fascination for her. She knew little about him; the only time he had actually spoken to her, he had been insolent, his bitter dislike obvious. He hated her and her family, and in her heart she knew she was being foolish beyond belief. She

wasn't even certain *why* he held such a strong fascination, and telling herself her interest had its roots in guilt
and pity did absolutely no good.

Maria made one or two trips more to the cane fields,
wanting to allay any suspicions Juan might have had, but
after that she avoided any sight of Gabriel Lancaster; his
effect upon her emotions was too confusing and painful.
While she avoided the cane fields, she still took frequent
rides upon her small fiery mare. Rising at dawn, just as
the streaks of pink and gold appeared on the horizon, Maria would run for the stables and—sometimes using a sad-
dle and sometimes not—she would urge the spirited mare,
Diablejo, into a swift gallop. Away from the hacienda they
would race, taking the road that passed by the slave quarters, their destination a small clearing set amongst a
mixed grove of cinnamon, satinwood, sassafras and man-
chineel trees. A huge mahogany tree towered over the
others that pressed toward the opening in the forest and
shaded during the midday heat a tear-shaped pool of clear,
cool water. Maria came here often—it was well known
amongst the servants that if the little *señorita* could be
found nowhere else, someone would have to be sent to this
tropical glade. Certainly, Gabriel soon learned of it, and
that knowledge was the beginning of a half-formed plan
of vengeance.

He took to watching for her on these dawn rides, and
though he didn't know when he would make use of this
routine of hers, he knew deep within himself that one day
his time would come. All he had to do was to wait pa-
tiently. He *would* escape . . . and he would not be denied
vengeance.

Precisely when or why Maria became the object of his
need for revenge on the Delgatos, Gabriel was never positive. He only knew that from the first time he had seen
her, in spite of his fury and his grief, she had made a
lasting impression upon his senses. And after she had spoken with him that day in the cane fields, it seemed she
began to find her way into his troubled, violent dreams
far too often for his liking. True, they were dark dreams
of death and revenge, but whenever her elfin features appeared in these night tossings, a subtle change overcame

the tenor of his dreams. It was nothing he could explain, it just happened and it bothered him.

A note from Diego, informing Maria that he would be returning by the middle of the month with guests, arrived the first day of June. In his note he gave explicit orders for the house to be scrupulously prepared for these guests and after reading his letter, Maria frowned. Why hadn't he mentioned who was coming to stay? She shrugged her slim shoulders dismissingly, and turning away, she called together the house servants and explained the situation. From then on, the Casa de la Paloma was a hive of activity—rooms being aired and beds dressed with fresh linens, silver and crystal being polished, the gardens being trimmed and scythed ... And from the kitchens at the rear of the hacienda came forth mouth-watering, spicy aromas as tasty dishes were prepared in anticipation of Diego's arrival with his important guests. It was not so much a labor of love, as the certain knowledge that if everything was not precisely as he wanted someone would suffer for it.

To Maria's surprise, she found that she was actually looking forward to the prospect of entertaining visitors. She took special care in dressing for their arrival, and as she wandered around the grand *sala* the afternoon Diego had written he would arrive, she was conscious of a happy excitement within her.

Wearing a scarlet bodice with sleeves slashed with gold, the fine lace of her chemise flowing over the low-cut neckline of the tight-fitting bodice and a skirt of yellow silk gracefully draped over petticoats of scarlet and gold, Maria was very like an exotic flower. Her black hair was piled on her head, a gold comb securing it, and a few tendrils of hair had been allowed to dangle near her cheeks and ears. She wore little jewelry—a long string of pearls fell across her small bosom and a gold brooch that had been her mother's was at her slender waist. She looked a true daughter of Spain, only the sapphire blue eyes giving any indication that other blood flowed in her veins.

Impatiently she flitted about the handsome room, and then, hearing the sounds of many horses, a welcoming smile on her sweet mouth, she flew out of the *sala* to the long portico that ran the entire length of the front of the hacienda. The front courtyard seemed filled with horses and riders, but spying her brother's tall form as he dismounted gracefully, she walked over to him.

"*Buenos días,* Diego. Welcome home," she said simply.

Diego looked at her, and from the set of his mouth and the inimical gleam in his black eyes, she knew that he was greatly displeased, furious in fact. "What is it?" she asked instantly. "Is there something wrong?"

Smiling sourly, he said, "No, why should you think that? Come, let me introduce you to our guests. Or rather *re*-introduce you." He took her hand and, turning around, said carelessly, "You remember Don Clemente, don't you? But I don't believe you met Doña Luisa while you were in Spain last year. Allow me to introduce you to her."

Maria's eyes widened with shock at the sight of the slim man standing a few paces behind her brother. Oh, she remembered Don Clemente very well . . . too well! And looking into that swarthy, supercilious face, seeing the way his small black eyes undressed her, the lascivious curve to his thin lips, her hand itched to connect with his cheek. Icily, she replied, "Of course I remember Don Clemente . . . he wore the honey pot rather nicely, I thought."

It was a deliberately provoking statement, but Maria didn't care, she was blazingly angry. Diego was apparently still scheming, still trying to force her into a marriage with Don Clemente. Why else had he failed to mention the other's impending visit?

She was so furious that even Diego's warning crush of her fingers didn't control her temper, but before she could say more, Diego interrupted smoothly, "As you see, Don Clemente, she still has not learned any manners." Politely he added, "I must apologize for her provincial upbringing, and you may take great satisfaction in the certainty that your new bride would never cause you half the embarrassment that my sister so frequently causes me!"

Diego sent her a quelling look, but Maria only smiled dazedly up at him, the full import of his words sinking in. Don Clemente was married! And if he was married . . . It was all she could do to choke back the giggle of laughter that bubbled up in her throat. She had little trouble guessing what Diego's plans must have been and what a shock he must have suffered when Don Clemente arrived in Santo Domingo with a wife! For all his clever manipulating, this time Diego had been the one to be outfoxed!

Almost kindly Maria turned to the young woman, who was being helped down from her horse by a servant. Walking up to her, she said sincerely, *"Buenos días,* I am Diego's sister, Maria. Welcome to our home. I hope your stay with us will give you much pleasure. *Mi casa es su casa."*

Maria's greeting was met by a haughty stare, Doña Luisa being every bit as unpleasant as her husband. She was only a few years older than Maria, but it was quite obvious that she held herself in high esteem and that she had no time for provincials. A bored note in her voice, Doña Luisa asked, "Are my rooms prepared? The heat on this wretched island has given me a headache—to say nothing of riding over the rutted and disgraceful roads. My father," she ended pompously, "the Duke of Zaragoza, would never have let *his* roads get in such a shocking state!"

Doña Luisa was not a pretty woman in either personality or appearance—muddy brown eyes, sallow skin, tightly pursed lips, a dumpy figure and overweening pride were her main attributes—and a more striking contrast to Maria's fresh, vibrant beauty could not have been found. That Doña Luisa herself was very aware of that fact was apparent in the hostile glance she sent Maria. It was, Maria thought resignedly as she followed in the wake of the other three a few minutes later, going to be a *very* long and uncomfortable visit.

Chapter Six

ACTUALLY, the visit went by swiftly and, to Maria's astonishment, smoothly. Diego had to take the credit for most of that—his manner toward their haughty visitors had been almost fawning, which seemed to please them. Maria avoided being around either of the de la Silvas, spending a great deal of time in her favorite forest glade. Doña Luisa she could dismiss easily, but Don Clemente's attempts to waylay her, his constant sly touching and the look in his eyes whenever they fell upon her made Maria decidedly uneasy in his company.

But the end of their visit finally came, and on the tenth of August, Diego threw a grand fiesta to mark their departure. They were leaving in the morning for Santo Domingo, where they intended to stay for several more weeks before eventually leaving for Spain in the fall.

Knowing it was the last night that she would have to put up with either of them, Maria was very polite to the de la Silvas, but then she had other more important things on her mind. To her outrage, she had discovered that Diego had ordered that the Englishman be chained at the far end of the rear courtyard so that he could display him to his guests. She hadn't learned of it until after the guests were arriving, but her blue eyes fairly spitting fury, she insisted upon a word with her brother. Alone in the small *sala*, she demanded hotly, "What is the purpose of having the Englishman humiliated so?"

Diego smiled carelessly. "He is nothing more than a trophy of war—why shouldn't I exhibit him?"

"I think it's disgusting!" Maria retorted furiously, for once forgetting to hold her tongue on the subject of the

72

Englishman. "And *you* are disgusting for treating him this way! It is cruel and barbarous!"

Diego's eyes narrowed and he asked silkily, "Why this sudden concern for Lancaster? Or is it so sudden?"

Instantly realizing that her outburst was far more likely to harm the Englishman than help him, Maria forced herself to say more calmly, "There is no sympathy—it is just that . . . that I think you could have chosen a more appropriate occasion to . . . to show off your trophy of war!"

"But then, what you think really doesn't matter, does it, little sister? Don't ever forget that *I* am master here!" Diego replied coldly. "I have decided that I want him there, and there he will remain . . . is that understood?"

It was times like these that she almost hated her brother, and she took a deep angry breath, struggling violently to keep her temper in check. *"Sí!"* she spat out in a curt tone, and spinning on her heels, silken petticoats and skirts flying, she fled the *sala*.

After that, the evening lost whatever pleasure it might have held for her. No matter what she did or where she was, as she moved about the gaily dressed throng, her thoughts were on the tall, green-eyed Englishman chained like a dog at the far end of the courtyard. She heard the sniggering comments about him, heard the jocular congratulations thrown to Diego, and her heart bled for the Englishman's humiliation. It wasn't until very late in the evening when some of the guests had departed that she could bring herself to walk in that direction. To her relief, it appeared the Englishman was no longer so callously displayed, and with a heavy sigh she sank down onto a stone bench, her sapphire skirt and cream-colored petticoats rustling about her.

The courtyard had been strung with small lanterns, and their fitful light danced upon the flagstones and over the looming flowering shrubs that were tastefully interspersed throughout the area. It was a little cooler out here and much quieter, only the faint chatter and laughter from the hacienda spilling into the tropical night air.

Maria had only been seated a second when, to her discomfiture, she saw Don Clemente coming toward her. She stood up, desperately trying to think of a polite way to avoid being alone with him. But nothing came to her, and forcing herself to smile courteously at him, she asked civilly, "Have you come out to enjoy the night air, *señor?*"

Don Clemente was slimly built with almost delicate features that gave him great pride. Large, liquid dark eyes were set above a slim nose; his lips were finely sculpted and his lustrous black hair was perfumed and curled and fell to his narrow shoulders in wavy splendor. While he moved with a dainty languidness that was deceiving and took much delight in clothing himself in costumes lavishly trimmed in lace and ribbons, he had as much masculine appreciation of a lovely woman as did the next man. As his wealthy, powerful father's only heir, a grand title to be his one day, at twenty-seven years old, Don Clemente had been denied few things. The young woman standing in front of him represented the only serious blow to his high self-esteem that he had ever suffered. But his conceit was such that he had thoroughly convinced himself that she had belatedly realized her drastic mistake in rebuffing him and was now ready to treat him as was only fitting to a man of his handsomeness and fortune.

A smirk crossing his faun-like features, he answered Maria's polite question insinuatingly. "It is not the night air that I have a mind to enjoy...." To Maria's utter astonishment, he lifted her limp hand and pressed it ardently to his lips. "You are very lovely—it is unfortunate that I did not realize *how* lovely while you were in Spain. If I had, I would have forgiven you much and wouldn't now find myself married to a harpy like Luisa. Of course," he continued pompously, "my marriage was for convenience and does not mean that you and I ..." His voice trailed off, the hot black eyes moving salaciously over her. His gaze lingered on the soft swell of flesh above her low-cut sky blue satin bodice, and he murmured, "If you are very nice to me, I am confident that I can make certain arrangements with your brother that will be advantageous to all of us."

Maria opened her eyes very wide. "Oh?" she asked innocently. "And do you think that Doña Luisa would also find it advantageous?"

The smirk was wiped instantly from his face, and he said coldly, "You are unwise to toy with me this way! You

forget who I am, how wealthy and powerful I am—there
are many women who would be honored to be under my
protection."

Gently removing her hand from his loosened grasp, Maria said sweetly, "Then I suggest, since there are so many,
that you go in search of one of them."

Throwing her a furious glance, he flounced away with
less than his usual mincing grace. Her hands shaking,
Maria sank back down to her stone bench. *Cielos!* Thank
goodness he had done nothing more than kiss her hand.
Unconsciously she began to rub that member against her
silken skirts as if trying to remove all trace of his touch.
Hearing a slight rustle to her left, she looked in that direction, her heart constricting as she recognized the Englishman coming from behind a large shrub.

A polished steel collar was around his neck, a chain
leading from it to his manacled hands and from there to
an iron stake driven securely into the ground. While the
length of chain afforded him little movement, it did allow
him to stand tall and square-shouldered; and despite the
trappings of slavehood that bound him and his nearly naked body clothed only in a clean pair of baggy white
breeches that ended at the knee, there was an air of indomitable pride about him.

Across the short distance that separated them, they
stared at each other, contemptuous green eyes clashing
with startled blue ones. For this occasion, Diego had obviously had him bathed and shaved; the thick black hair
on his head was neatly cropped. Wonderingly Maria's gaze
traveled over his gaunt features. In spite of nearly ten
months of cruel captivity, he was still a strikingly handsome man, though the shape and bones of his face were
more starkly defined. High cheekbones intensified the patrician cast to his features, emerald green eyes were deep-
set under distinctively slashed, black eyebrows; a bold
straight nose with faintly flaring nostrils and a mouth
that was at once sensuous and hard created an extraordinarily masculine face. Her heart beginning to beat with
thick, painful strokes, Maria rose from her seat and slowly
walked over to him.

Staring up into his dark face, she said softly, "I didn't

realize that you were still out here. I thought that Diego must have ordered you taken back to the slave quarters."

"And I thought that the only reason you were not more . . . accommodating to your lovesick swain was because you knew I was here," Gabriel answered bluntly.

Maria's eyes darkened. "That is an ugly thing to say!"

Gabriel gave a mirthless laugh. "I should care what I say to you?" he asked grimly. "Tell me, what could you have done to me that could be worse or more painful than what I have already suffered at the hands of the Delgatos?"

Aware that it was a futile exchange, Maria sent him a look of mingled resentment and pity; then, her slim shoulders stiff with pride, she marched away from him, leaving Gabriel to stare after her with something that might have been regret. He smiled bitterly to himself. Now, why should he have any regret? She was a Spanish slut and a Delgato! But even though he dismissed her so contemptuously from his mind, her image as she had stood before him this evening would not be banished.

Night after night, as he tossed on his sweat-damp pallet through the long, hot hours of darkness, she would appear before him, the expression in her sapphire blue eyes making his chest curiously tight, the curve of her sweetly shaped mouth arousing emotions within him that he had felt were long dead. And at dawn, when he heard the sound of her horse's hooves as she rode by, he would become aware of an odd leap in his blood.

The de la Silvas had departed as planned, and Diego had escorted them back to the city of Santo Domingo. With the master gone once more, there was a pleasant tranquillity again about the hacienda. Such was not the case in the fields; as August faded into September there was increased activity among the ripening stalks of cane. Activity and brutality, Juan Perez and his men applying the lash of their long, black bullwhips with savage frequency, demanding more and more work from men who were worn out by the heat, lack of food and the fevers so constant in the tropics.

Lying on his filthy straw pallet one morning, in the purple gray mists of predawn, listening to the hoofbeats of Maria's horse die away as she rode past and hearing the grunts and groans of the other men who shared his hovel as they were kicked and jabbed awake by Perez, Gabriel knew that he had reached the end of his endurance. He could not take another day of this brutal mistreatment; live or die, he had to strike back now or his pride would be broken forever. He had no plan; all his energies had been spent in merely staying alive and in giving no satisfaction to Diego and his bullies. Plan or not, he knew that he could bear it no more. There was only an insistent buzz in his brain—now, now, *now!* I will not suffer another day of this degradation! I will die first!

When Perez at last reached him, like a coiled tiger, Gabriel struck, rising up from the pallet in one lightning-swift move. Before Perez had time to realize what was happening, Gabriel wrested the whip from his hand and brought the handle down against his temple with a mighty blow. Perez groaned softly and crumpled to the dirt floor. Bending down, oblivious to the other poor creatures who stared dumbly at his actions, Gabriel quickly found the key from the ring that hung around Perez's leather belt and unlocked the manacles that were around his feet and wrists. He snatched up the wide blade that lay near Perez and ran from the hut.

There was no one else stirring in the slave pens yet; there would be no alarm until Perez was discovered and Gabriel had little fear that his fellow slaves would betray him; he was armed and the sword felt good in his hand, but he knew that his situation was bleak. The coast was miles away across territory unfamiliar to him; he had no money, and with the steel collar still around his neck, his status as a slave was obvious. His only chance, and it was frail at that, was to find a stray band of buccaneers, who were known still to occasionally hunt the abundant wild cattle and pigs that were to be found in the inland valleys of the north coast. But in his heart he knew it would be impossible; sooner or later, Perez's absence would be noted, and then the alarm would be out.

He spared a thought for Caroline, wondering if he dared try to find her and take her with him on his perilous journey. He had faced the near impossibility of his own escape and he realized sickly that even if he knew in which direction the Chavez plantation lay, finding his sister

amongst the unfamiliar surroundings, of discovering precisely where she was kept—if she was still there—was a
hopeless task. And dare he subject her to his own uncertain fate? Dare he make her situation possibly worse? By
his own determination not to abandon her, bring her further pain and possible death?

Common sense told him he should flee as quickly as he
could, that only by escaping Hispaniola could he ever hope
to free Caroline. But his heart, his heart ached at the idea
of leaving her behind without a word, without making
some attempt to find her. In the end, he knew it was what
he must do—only by freeing himself did he stand a chance
of one day wresting her from these hated Spaniards.

He smiled grimly. For all his accomplishments, he had
only gained himself a precious few hours of freedom—the
odds were too overwhelming that he could escape completely, and knowing that his death was a foregone conclusion, he made the instant decision that before they
killed him, there was at least one act of vengeance against
the Delgatos that he would not be denied. His face hard
and set, he took off at a fast lope in the direction Maria's
horse had taken just moments previously.

It was unfortunate, he thought acidly, as he ran through
the forest, that Diego was still away—he would have enjoyed killing him. But if he could not have the brother,
the sister would do just as well. . . . He might not ever
have another chance, and he was going to take it and
damn the risks! And as the moments passed and he heard
no outcry behind him, a faint hope rose within him—who
knew, he might have it all—revenge and freedom!

Maria heard the slight noise the passage of his body
made as he ran through the underbrush in her direction,
but thinking it was only a servant come to fetch her, she
was not frightened. Diablejo was tied to a small cinnamon
tree nearby, and Maria had been gathering a bouquet of
scarlet and orange hibiscus blooms when Gabriel suddenly plunged into the clearing.

The broadsword was clasped in one hand, his chest was
heaving from his exertions and there was a look in the
emerald green eyes that made Maria drop her flowers and
slowly start to inch toward Diablejo. Gabriel's words

halted her. "Don't," he said, almost quietly. "I can reach the horse before you can."

Maria swallowed with difficulty, sickly aware of the great danger she faced. She was wearing only a simple cotton skirt and bodice; her feet were bare and her hair hung down her back in a mass of black curls. She looked very young and small and for just the slightest second, Gabriel hesitated, but then the memory of all he had suffered came flooding back, and with determined steps he approached her.

Whether he intended to kill her or take her captive, Maria didn't know, but in neither case could she just stand here helplessly and let it happen. Throwing him off guard for a moment, she suddenly leaped toward her horse, but the mare was tied too far away for Maria to reach her before Gabriel's hand closed around her shoulder.

The force of his grasp spun her around, and truly frightened now, Maria began to fight like a wild creature, her small fists plummeting against his broad chest, her feet kicking against his shins. Dropping the sword, Gabriel caught her about the waist and threw her over his shoulder, then carried her a little distance away. With a less than gentle movement, he tossed her down on a clump of ferns, his own body following quickly afterward.

The breath was knocked out of her, and there was a moment when everything went blank, but then as her gaze cleared, she caught her breath in a sob of half anger, half fear as Gabriel's dark, bearded face loomed over her. His intention was obvious as his fingers touched the front of her bodice, and once again she began to struggle and fight, fingers clawing and body twisting desperately to escape from him.

It was no use, his big body pinned hers to the ground, and with horror she heard the bodice rip, felt his hard, callused fingers against her breasts. On a breathless little gasp, she got out, "Oh, please, please, don't!"

Gabriel too was breathless, as much from their struggle as from the sensations that were flooding his body as her slim form brushed against his in her attempts to escape. He hadn't meant to feel passion, not *real* passion; he had only meant to take her quickly, in the most brutal fashion possible, and then be on his way, but something was hap-

pening within him, something over which he seemed to
have no control. He suddenly wanted to possess her slender body for reasons that had nothing to do with revenge,
but had everything to do with her soft, warm frame twisting wildly beneath his. It startled him, this reaction to
her nearness, but, he told himself savagely, it was only
because he had not made love to any woman since his
wife had been killed.

The memory of Elizabeth's body crushed beneath the
ship's beam exploded through his brain and brutally he
brought his mouth down on Maria's. He hurt her, as he
meant to do, his lips forcing hers apart, his tongue fiercely
assaulting the inner sweetness he found within. With one
violent movement he shoved her skirts up around her
waist, intent upon finishing the act as quickly as possible,
determined to make her pay the price for all that had
been taken from him, but somehow, as his mouth moved
on hers, his hands searching her slim body, the desire for
revenge gradually blurred again and another inexplicable
emotion came over him.

Confused by the conflict within himself, he paused, and
raising his head, he looked down at Maria, as if he might
find the answer he sought in her face. Her hair was spread
out in an inky mass across the bright green of the ferns,
her incredibly lovely eyes, almond-shaped, framed with
thick black lashes stared up at him, the brilliance of their
blueness intensified by the shimmer of tears that gleamed
there. His gaze dropped to her mouth, noticing almost
with surprised remorse the swollen rosiness that increased the naturally seductive curve of her lips. Unable
to help himself, his eyes dropped even lower to the small
breasts with their coral nipples that had been exposed by
his actions. God's wounds! but she was enticing . . . and
he was a fool for letting himself be trapped by her beauty!
he reminded himself savagely, furiously holding on to his
thoughts of revenge. But they kept slipping away, and he
was left with the insane desire to taste that sweet mouth
again, only not with brutality, with tenderness and need.
He fought the battle within him, but something stronger
pulled at his senses, and with a groan of defeat, his lips
hungrily closed upon hers.

How very different this kiss was from the other, Maria

reflected dumbly with one part of her brain. The other had been full of ugliness and pain, but this one, this one was the kiss she had dreamed of, and helplessly she responded to it. She would have fought incessantly against his earlier brutal attack—it had frightened and angered her—but this time as his mouth intoxicatingly searched hers, she was aware that he was far more dangerous to her now, now that her own body was betraying her. Sensations she had only half dreamed coursed up through her; her nipples hardened under the gentle pull of his fingers as a warm, sweet ache built in the pit of her stomach. It was madness, even she knew that, but it was a madness she was unable to resist; and almost against her will her arms closed around his broad shoulders, her fingers tingling at the feel of his naked skin, her mouth opening wider to allow him to possess her completely.

Her totally unexpected response bewildered him, and dazedly Gabriel raised his head again. What was happening to her? To him? Why didn't she fight him? Why was he so very hungry for her? Wanting her with an intensity that stunned him? He didn't know the answers and none knew better than he the insanity of what he was doing, but he could not resist the irresistible attraction of those lips, that slender body. Damning himself for a fool, he let the yearning passion that clamored in his veins to sweep over him, his lips once again seeking hers, eager to taste the sweet wine he knew he would find there.

Attacked by emotions and sensations she had never before experienced, Maria was oblivious to everything but the man who kissed her, whose sure hands traveled so stimulatingly over her body. The touch of his hand as he cupped her breast was an unbearable delight, and when he bent his head, his teeth sensuously grazing the swollen nipple, his warm tongue suckling hungrily on that sensitized tip, Maria moaned with pleasure, her body arching up under his. A tightness, almost painful in its intensity, seemed to grow deep within her and she yearned for even more intimate contact with him, not even knowing what she was yearning after. But her body did, and instinctively her hips brushed up against Gabriel's bursting manhood, exciting them both. The feel of that throbbing, swollen muscle between their locked bodies drove Maria

to wilder, more evocative thrashings beneath him as she
sought to assuage the hungry ache that was growing more
and more demanding and insistent with every passing
moment. Her fingers clenched in his dark hair, urging his
mouth back to hers, and when he lifted his head from her
breast, the glazed expression of desire in his eyes pierced
her with a shaft of joy. Softly, tentatively, she began to
kiss his brow, her lips tasting his skin, reveling in this
new sensation as she slowly brought their lips closer together.

When their mouths met at last, Maria was trembling
with the force of the unleashed passion that Gabriel's
touch had freed within her, and she was eager for whatever he would do to her. Nothing else mattered; she was
aware of nothing else, not even of the crushed ferns beneath her back, nor the knowledge that they could be
discovered at any moment. There was only the Englishman in her arms, kissing her as she had dreamed he
would, and the world and everything else in it had faded
away.

Gabriel too was lost in a world of desire, a desire that
consumed him as nothing ever had before in his life. He
wanted this woman, wanted her so desperately that he
could hardly endure the sweetness of her caresses. Her
fingers in his hair, the wanton movements of her body as
she pressed herself against him, and the flick of her small
tongue as she hesitantly probed his mouth were more than
he could bear. Feverishly his hands slid between their
bodies, his fingers seeking the soft curls between her legs.
Urgently he touched her there, stroking and searching,
inflaming both of them even further by his fondlings.

Maria shivered uncontrollably as his fingers gently
probed between her thighs, her breath coming in short,
almost painful gasps. There were too many new sensations exploding through her body for her to think clearly,
to realize what was actually happening to her. It was almost as if she were dreaming this sweet assault upon her
senses, almost as if the man in her arms were a fragment
of all her half-understood longings. She was responding
to his blatantly sensuous touch with blind instinct, all the
newly awakened passions of her young body clamoring for
fulfillment. Only when Gabriel's body slid down between

her thighs, his hands reaching to free his aching manhood from his breeches, did the enormity of the situation hit her.

As if she had suddenly received a douche of icy water, Maria stiffened, shock and horror at her own lascivious conduct shooting through her. Oh, *Dios!* What had come over her? Had she been under the spell of the devil? Tearing her mouth from his, frantically she pushed against Gabriel's shoulders. Pleadingly she cried, *"Señor!* Stop! I beseech you, *stop!"*

Gabriel seemed to hear her words through a red haze, but they made no sense, and even her sudden struggles to escape didn't immediately impinge upon his consciousness. But he was faintly aware that something had changed, that the body beneath his was no longer softly yielding, that the sweet mouth was no longer burning against his lips. Still in the powerful grip of a mesmerizing passion, he shook his head, denying the increasing evidence that she was no longer a willing victim, and buried his mouth in hers, hungry to join his body with hers. It was then that he heard the sounds that plunged him savagely back into reality.

Passion gone, in one swift leap he was on his feet, the noises of the approaching men and dogs suddenly very loud. Across the clearing he sprinted, reaching the sword and scooping it up in his hand just as the first man burst into the clearing.

The Spaniard was armed, his musket primed and ready. Not a second later a second man pulled by two baying dogs arrived. Gabriel was filled with a sense of impotent rage. He had been a fool to loiter in this area, a fool to let thoughts of revenge keep him from running as far and as fast as he could, and a double-damned fool for having allowed himself to be caught up in a web of passion for a daughter of the Delgatos! But then, he shrugged mentally, he had known the risks and he had known that he had faced probable death. He readied himself to die, his hand tightening on the broadsword. He spared a moment to regret that he had not been able to kill Diego or that he had not . . . He stopped, even now his emotions too confused to understand what had happened between himself and Maria Delgato.

It was a taut tableau there in that tropical clearing. The Spaniards, determined he should not escape; the musket trained on Gabriel's chest as he stood there proudly, defiantly, holding the broadsword with menacing confidence; the dogs lunging against the rope that held them back; and just a little distance away the slim form of a beautiful young woman. Her clothes were rumpled and torn, and she sat there staring with paralyzing terror at the tragic scene that was unfolding before her.

She must have made some sound, some movement, because Gabriel turned to look at her, and in that instant, Juan Perez, a purpling bruise darkening his left temple, stumbled into the clearing beside the other Spaniards and screamed hysterically, "Don't let him escape! Shoot him, you simpleton! Kill him!"

Gabriel was already starting to swing around to meet this new danger when the musket boomed and belched black smoke. As the darkness exploded in his brain, out of the corner of his eye, the last thing he saw was Maria's face. Then there was nothing, only utter oblivion.

Maria sat there upon the bed of ferns, staring dazedly at his fallen form. It couldn't be, she thought dully, watching with numb fascination as the ground near his head slowly turned bright red. He couldn't be dead! But as he lay there, unmoving, the words became a shriek of elemental anguish in her brain. No! No! *No!* He cannot be dead! Not my Englishman!

On shaky feet she rose, unaware of the other armed servants now spilling into the glade. She was only vaguely conscious of holding her torn bodice together as she stumbled toward Gabriel's body, but before she could reach him, Juan Perez caught her arm and demanded hoarsely, *"Señorita!* Are you unharmed? This miserable English swine did not . . ."

Like a sleepwalker, Maria slowly shook her head, her eyes still on Gabriel's form, willing him to move, willing the blood that stained the ground to disappear. At Maria's negative gesture, Perez heaved a hearty sigh of relief. It was bad enough that the Englishman had escaped him, but he did not like to think what Don Diego would have done to him if his sister had been defiled by the Englishman. Gently Perez pushed her in the direction of one of the other servants. "Take her to the hacienda at once! Have the women see to her needs. *Pronto!*"

Maria protested blankly, still in the grip of a nightmare, still too dazed to realize anything but that the man who only minutes before had held her passionately in his strong arms was lying there motionless on the jungle floor. A sob suddenly broke from her as the truth seared through her body, and then weeping brokenly for shattered half-formed dreams, she was quickly hustled away to the hacienda. Only one thought remained with painful clarity in her mind—*her Englishman was dead!*

A silence seemed to fall in the glade for a moment after she was led away, and disgustedly Juan prodded Gabriel's still form with one booted foot. A shame the Englishman was dead, he thought absently, as he ordered the dogs taken away. Waving away the rest of the servants except for two of his favorite henchmen, he continued to stare down at Gabriel's unmoving body. Then he shrugged. What did it matter? After this morning's attack, the Englishman would have had to be gotten rid of anyway.

A callous bully who ruled through fear, Juan could afford no challenge to his authority, and though he knew Diego was going to be furious when he learned of the Englishman's death, it didn't really bother Juan very much. He spat on the ground near Gabriel's body. There were always other plantations who could use a man like him. He would miss the profitable little agreement he had with a certain slave dealer in Santo Domingo though. . . .

Juan Perez was a newcomer to the Casa de la Paloma—Don Pedro would never have tolerated a man of Perez's ilk on his lands—and it hadn't taken him very long to realize that Diego cared nothing for the plantation, that as long as the gold poured in from the crops, he didn't look very closely into what was happening in the fields. Hitting upon the scheme of arranging apparent "deaths" for the past year and a half, Juan had been discreetly selling the occasional slave to an acquaintance in Santo Domingo. It had proven quite profitable and he could have gotten a good price for the Englishman. . . .

Regretfully he gave Gabriel's body another glance and started to turn away when a groan wafted on the air. Spinning around, Juan saw that Gabriel's chest was still moving, and bending over, he looked at the wound more carefully, a crafty smile curving his fleshy lips when he realized that, though it had bled profusely and would probably render him unconscious for quite some time, the wound to the Englishman's head was not fatal. Rubbing his hands together in anticipation of the gold that would soon cross them, he called to his two henchmen.

And so it was that three days later, when Gabriel finally became groggily aware of his surroundings, he found himself not at the Casa de la Paloma, but in the hold of a ship. For a moment he thought he was reliving the nightmare of his capture, but as his eyes gradually became adjusted to the gloomy shadows, he saw that instead of the hold of the *Santo Cristo* he was lying chained and manacled in an entirely different ship. A slave ship!

His head aching almost unbearably, he wearily turned to the pitiful creature chained next to him and asked dully, "Where are we? Where are we going?"

"We're at sea, on our way to be sold to the mines in Peru," came the equally dull reply.

With a groan, Gabriel's head fell to his chest. The mines in Peru! Only certain death awaited him there, and for the first time since that awful day that he had spotted the white sails of the *Santo Cristo* on the horizon, his spirit cracked. There was no hope now. Nothing. Only death.

Two days of unspeakable misery went by as he lay there in his own filth, the darkness of the hold pressing in on him, the stench of the other poor wretches like himself almost choking him. But then suddenly on the dawn of the third day the tenor of the ship changed; there was much movement overhead; the sound of the cannons being rolled across the gun decks rumbled through the hold, and with a curious tingle down his spine, Gabriel realized that the ship was preparing for battle.

As the cannons roared above him, as he heard the thundering reply of the other ship, renewed hope surged up through him. Perhaps it was not to be his fate to die nameless in the bowels of some Peruvian mine, after all.

Belowdecks the sounds of the fierce battle could be heard clearly—the booming crash as the masts came tumbling down; the crack and pop as the wooden timbers gave way before the punishing bombardment of the other ship.

Suddenly the vessel shuddered as the other ship rammed her side; and the screams of dying and wounded men, the clash of metal against metal told Gabriel that hand-to-hand fighting was taking place above him. And then almost as quickly as it had begun there was a curious silence.

His ears straining, he listened with all his senses, his heart leaping as he heard the sound of English voices spreading throughout the ship, the tramp of booted feet coming down to the hold. Bright light from a lantern pierced the darkness, and a merry voice rang out, "Rise up, me boyos! We've beaten the Spanish dogs and you're safe in the hands of good, honest, English pirates!"

It wasn't until he stumbled on deck a few minutes later, his eyes blinded at first by the bright sunlight, that Gabriel got a look at his liberators. They were not an encouraging sight.

A more savage, motley collection of men he had never seen in his life, their gaudy garments stained and ill-fitting, some obviously having just been torn off of the previous owners. Most had shaggy, greasy locks that fell to their shoulders; several sported black eyepatches; all were heavily armed, with swords, knives and pistols draped all over their bodies. But it was the leader of this crew of cutthroats who caught Gabriel's attention.

The man dominated the center of the quarterdeck. He was not very tall, but there was such an air of vitality about him that one tended to endow him with more height than he actually possessed. Very dark, he could have passed for a Spaniard; a gold earring glittered through the black curls that fell to his shoulders; shrewd black eyes missed nothing as they moved over the assembled men. His clothes were cleaner than those of his followers, but he was dressed every bit as gaudily; a slashed doublet of crimson and gold topped breeches of emerald green, and his stockings were violet. Hands on his hips, he approached Gabriel and the others. Consideringly, those fine dark eyes moved over them.

"I've a mind to add me some more crew," he said in a rich, melodious voice. "Would you men be looking for a chance to win yourselves a fortune and kill some Spanish dogs in the process?"

There was a low rumble of affirmation from the wretched men just freed from the hold, but Gabriel forced himself to ask, "Who are you?"

A roar of laughter rose up from the ranks of the gathered pirates, and with a shout of amusement, black eyes gleaming merrily, the man said, "Who am I? Why, I am Harry Morgan, and I will be the greatest pirate that ever lived! If you doubt my words, join me and see for yourself!"

Part Two

The Dark Angel

Port Royal, Jamaica, 1668

Of all the causes which conspire to
    blind
Man's erring judgement and misguide
    the mind,
What the weak head with strongest
    bias rules,
Is pride, the never failing vice
    of fools.

Alexander Pope
Essay on Criticism, Part II

Chapter Seven

THE sleek, fourteen-gun frigate *Dark Angel* rode proudly at anchor in Port Royal's fine harbor, her sails neatly furled around the yards of the three tall masts which rose skyward. Sunlight, bright and hot, danced across the glass casement windows that lined the stern and intensified the gleam of the gilded, lavishly carved quarter galleries.

The harbor was crowded this warm, sun-splashed day in early March of 1668; schooners, pinnaces, brigs and English galleons were anchored nearby. In the distance, on the island of Jamaica, rose the green-covered mountains of the interior; closer at hand, on the narrow sand and limestone island of Cagua, lay Port Royal.

Port Royal's waterside fairly bristled with wharves and the bowsprits of several ships jutted comfortably across their wooden lengths. Farther along, in the town, drunken laughter and raucous shrieks of amusement spilled out from the many grog shops and brothels that lined the winding cobblestone streets.

On the *Dark Angel*, in the surprisingly elegant great cabin, Gabriel Lancaster stood looking out of the casement windows at the vivid turquoise waters of the sea below him. He wasn't alone; behind him, sprawled easily in a handsome chair of black leather and oak was Harry Morgan, his dark eyes fixed speculatively on Gabriel's back.

There was a companionable silence between the two men, and as he continued to stare at Gabriel, Morgan marveled at the great difference between this broad-shouldered, powerful man and the half-starved, filthy wretch he had first seen almost two and a half years ago.

That other pitiful creature had barely been able to stand, while this man, Morgan well knew from past experience, was swift and sure on his feet. And if the man he had freed from the bowels of the Spanish ship had been unwashed, his hair matted and soiled, this man was known for his fastidiousness. To the disapproving amazement of his crew and most of the Brethren of the Coast, as the buccaneers liked to call themselves, he bathed almost daily. His thick, shoulder-length black hair shone with cleanliness, and his clothes were always fresh and unstained, unlike those of most of the men he commanded. But if his personal habits aroused scoffing comment, his expert swordsmanship aroused nothing but pious awe and deferential respect. Above all, the Brethren valued courage, and Gabriel Lancaster had that in abundance, Morgan thought to himself. It had been his unquenchable courage which had marked his swift rise up through the ranks of the buccaneers, and today, Lancaster was one of the leading captains among the Brethren of the Coast. Morgan smiled. Indeed there really was no resemblance between the man he had met initially and the man across from him ... except for a deep, abiding hatred of the Spanish.

Gabriel moved just then, glancing back at Morgan. "Have you discussed this with any of the other captains?"

Morgan slowly shook his head. "You should know by now that it isn't Harry Morgan's way to babble his plans with everyone ... only with those I trust," he answered. He added meaningfully, "And those are damn few!"

Gabriel smiled ruefully. Henry Morgan, or Harry, as he preferred to be called, often puzzled him. At thirty-three years of age, Morgan had already risen to the highest rank among the buccaneers, and yet it had been barely ten years ago that he had first appeared in the Caribbean. He was also, Gabriel had noted upon more than one occasion, extremely reticent about his background—a not *un*common trait among the Brethren.

Morgan would freely admit to being a Welshman—he was proud of it. He was also literate, indicating that his father had probably been a gentleman; and yet in all their years together, Gabriel had never heard him mention a word about his parentage. Which was a little strange, considering that his uncle, Lieutenant Colonel Sir Edward Morgan, had been knighted by Cromwell and had been Modyford's Deputy Governor on Jamaica until Sir Edward had died during the English attack on the Dutch island of St. Eustatius in 1665.

But Morgan had seldom remarked upon his relationship to his late uncle, although he had just recently married his first cousin, Sir Edward's second daughter, Mary Elizabeth. And while Gabriel hadn't thought it particularly strange that his friend hadn't talked about a dead man, he had found it odd that Morgan *never* spoke of his life in Wales, never gave any clues to his background, not even how he had come to be in the Caribbean—not even to his most trusted companions would he speak of his past. He was just Harry Morgan, clever, crafty, more than a bit unscrupulous, a fierce fighter and for the most part damnably secretive! And considering Morgan's secretiveness, Gabriel was rather honored that he had chosen to speak so freely to him.

Walking over to a wide oaken table near Morgan, he leaned his buttocks against it and, folding his arms over his chest, studied the silver buckle on his shoe for a moment. "The men won't like it," Gabriel said finally, looking at Morgan.

Morgan snorted. "S'blood! I don't intend to tell them! At least not at first," he amended fairly.

"What about the Governor? Does Modyford know what you plan? And has he given you a commission for this raid?"

A faintly sly grin flitted across Morgan's swarthy face. "He has made me a colonel and has ordered me to gather together the English privateers and capture Spanish prisoners to find out if the Dons truly are preparing a fleet to attack Jamaica as we have been hearing for months—I believe the commission restricts me to only Spanish ships at sea. . . ." Looking very innocent, a roguish gleam in his black eyes, he added, "Unfortunately, the original document has disappeared, so I shall just have to take matters into my own hands. . . ."

A rich chuckle escaped Gabriel. "By Christ's wounds, Harry! Was there ever such a hell-fire scamp as yourself?"

With an attractive conceit, Morgan answered affably, "No, I don't believe there ever was—didn't I tell you long ago that I intend to be the greatest pirate that ever lived?" His light air vanishing, Morgan suddenly leaned forward, his dark features intent. "The Brethren have elected me their Admiral, but as you know, they're a surly, unpredictable lot. If I told them outright what I plan, they'd desert, thinking it impossible, but I know it can be done!" Warming to his theme, his black eyes full of passionate determination, he continued, "Why should we search the seas for the treasure galleons—never certain our paths will cross, or that we'll be able to cut one away from the men-of-war that guard them—when we can find several fat merchantmen fresh from Spain, in one particular place, at one particular time?" Savoring the sound of it, he rolled the name off his tongue, "Puerto Bello in the spring!" Shooting Gabriel an impatient look, he ended with, "At the proper time, will you join with me in convincing the other captains? Are you with me?"

Slowly Gabriel nodded his dark head. "Aye, I'm with you," he said quietly. " 'Tis a mad plan, Harry, but if anyone can do it, it has to be you." A grim smile suddenly flashed across his chiseled features. "Who knows," he added dryly, "luck may finally be with me and I'll find a Delgato there—ship or person, either would satisfy me."

Morgan nodded his head. Over the years he had come to know Gabriel intimately, and he was very conscious that while Gabriel had plundered several Spanish galleons, none had ever been the ship his friend hungered for the most—a Delgato vessel. But Morgan was aware that even more than waylaying a Delgato ship, Gabriel thirsted to cross blades with Diego Delgato and that though there had been many prisoners taken, Maria Delgato, the one prisoner Gabriel wanted almost as desperately as he wanted Diego dead, had eluded him. Curiously Morgan asked, "Have you ever heard anything of your sister's fate? Do you even know if she still lives?"

A spasm of pain crossed Gabriel's face, and looking away, he answered flatly, "No. I've heard nothing—of Caroline or of the Delgatos." His fist clenched. "Someday though, Harry, someday I will, and when I do . . ." With an effort, Gabriel shook off the dark, savage thoughts that crowded his brain and focused on the matter at hand. "What are you telling the Brethren in the meantime? What target have you chosen to strike first?"

Morgan leaned back in the chair. "I've sent a call out to Tortuga and many of the other places the Brethren frequent, that all those who would follow Harry Morgan for a raid against the Spanish should rendezvous at Twelve League Cays off Cuba's coast at the end of the month. We can decide then which target on Cuba the men prefer to attack." That sly smile crossed his face again. "After all, I do have to capture some Spanish prisoners for the Governor, but after Cuba . . ." The smile widened, avarice glittering in the black eyes. "After Cuba, there is Puerto Bello on the coast of the Spanish Main!"

For a long time after Harry Morgan had departed from the great room of the *Dark Angel*, Gabriel had lounged in the same position against the oak table, staring blindly at the empty chair. When he had first been freed and had joined Morgan's band of buccaneers, there hadn't been a day, an hour that he hadn't thought of Caroline; hadn't prayed that soon he would be able to lead a raid against that great stronghold of the Spanish in the Caribbean, Hispaniola; that miraculously, he would somehow find his sister and free her from her wretched captivity and, at the same time, take a prisoner of his own—Maria Delgato. But as the days had passed, as the weeks had turned into months and then years, that dream had blurred and faded; in his heart of hearts, he knew that Caroline was dead by now and that Maria Delgato . . . With a disgusted snort, he tore himself away from that particularly dangerous subject, concentrating grimly on his sister's plight. If the cruel conditions in which the English slaves were forced to live hadn't killed her, the diseases and fevers of the tropics would surely have done so by now. But though he had accepted the idea of Caroline's death, Morgan's simple questions had been like a knife slash to his vitals, tearing open an old, painful wound that never seemed to heal.

In his blackest moments, Gabriel wondered bleakly if he would ever be free of the tormented guilt he felt over Caroline's captivity and ultimate fate—whatever it had been. And it was in those dark moments that his savage unabated thirst for vengeance against the Delgatos would be fiercest, clawing its way up through his body, until it was as strong and alive as it had been in the beginning. It was an odd fact, but while he could go days without thinking of Caroline's fate, thoughts of vengeance against the Delgatos were with him always. Especially the thought of having Maria Delgato in his power, his to do with what he wished forever . . .

It was an even odder fact, and at times, it drove him to the brink of violence, that he had absolutely no difficulty in conjuring up Maria's lovely features, remembering exactly what it had been like to hold her in his arms, what her mouth had tasted like, how unutterably sweet had been those moments in that forest glade; and yet he could not recall his dead wife's face no matter how desperately he tried. He mourned Elizabeth's needless tragic death and that of his unborn child, but to his savage despair, it was memories of Maria that he recalled most vividly, most clearly, and he cursed his own folly.

With a violent motion, he shoved himself away from the oak table and restlessly prowled the elegant cabin he called home for most of the year. Blankly his gaze fell upon the smooth-planked floor, the scrubbed surface broken by a thick yarn rug, woven in shades of russet and green. Would vengeance ever be his? Would the day ever come that he could put the past behind him and look forward to a future that was not tarnished by memories of what he had suffered and what he had lost? Or was he damned to always have this gnawing pain of loss within him, this feeling of rage and frustration?

In his more rational moments, when he was not blinded by his yearnings for revenge, Gabriel knew that he had much to be grateful for these days. His ship, the *Dark Angel*, was probably the most powerful in the buccaneer fleet; his reputation as a captain and his expertness with a sword ensured that when Gabriel Lancaster went a-hunting for a Spanish vessel, there were plenty of men eager and ready to join his crew. Of course, it had not always been so—when Morgan had freed him, he had owned nothing but the filthy rags on his back and acres of fallow, almost worthless land in Jamaica. Nearly everything the Lancasters had owned had been on the

Raven, and having lost it all when the *Santo Cristo* had captured his ship, Gabriel considered it only right and fitting that he should regain his fortune by joining the buccaneers.

Driven by hatred and the hunger for vengeance, his rise up through the ranks of the cruel, barbarous buccaneers had been meteoric. Within six months, he was able to outfit his first ship, a pinnace that sported six cannon; and with a crew that was as blood-hungry as he was, Gabriel soon progressed to a second, bigger and better ship, a fine sloop with ten guns. His reputation grew among the Brethren, his fierceness against the Spanish becoming legendary, and when a crew signed on with Lancaster, they knew that though he adhered to the buccaneer motto, no prey, no pay, they had nothing to fear—Lancaster *always* found prey.

Eighteen months ago he had purchased a fourteen-gun frigate, and when he had christened her the *Dark Angel,* there had been no surprise among his companions. To the Spanish, he *was* the Dark Angel, Satan himself, and there were even those among the Brethren, a few superstitious souls, who hastily made the sign of the cross whenever he passed by them. Yet the very qualities of ruthlessness and savagery that made him feared and detested by the Spanish were the same qualities the buccaneers admired, and he was well respected among his peers, even if he was very different from most of them in his manners and dress.

Gabriel might have become a buccaneer; he might in the heat of battle be as cruel and merciless as the next man, but he had retained a certain modicum of the gentlemanly traits which had been instilled in him since birth. Once the battle had been won, there was no gratuitous brutality on his ship; there was no mercy, but neither were there wanton acts of despicable violence against the hapless prisoners.

And unlike most of the Brethren, his gold and booty did not find its way into the greedy hands of the unscrupulous tavern and brothel keepers who abounded in Port Royal. No, once he had gained his second ship, the sloop *Caroline,* his share of the plunder taken from the Spanish had been poured back into the lands he had been granted from the King. While there was much that still had to be done, this past year the plantation had yielded its first crop of that "noble juice of cane," and he had sold the sweet sugar crystals at a handsome profit. A sugar mill had been built, and a house, more a fortress than a home, had finally been completed only a few weeks ago. He had even upon occasion idly toyed with the notion of one day in the not-too-distant future settling down on the plantation as had been his original intention.

A caustic smile curved his mouth. Now *that* was folly! As long as he was eaten alive with this unbridled hatred of the Spanish, what peace could he ever hope to find? His life was empty except for the driving hunger to strike back at those who had savagely destroyed his world that fateful day three and a half years ago. There was no question of seeking a wife, of watching his sons and daughters grow up, of becoming happily domesticated—not as long as Diego Delgato walked free ... or as long as he was tortured by the haunting memories of a lovely face; of almond-shaped, sapphire blue eyes; of a soft, provocative mouth that turned to flame beneath his.

It had often puzzled him, his reaction to Maria Delgato, as well as her response to him that day in the little jungle glade, and it had taken him months of brooding speculation before he had decided upon reasons for their actions that satisfied him. His own reactions were the easiest to solve—he had been a long time without a woman, and Maria had been undeniably young and beautiful; few men, even those bent upon rape, as he had been, would have been able to remain unmoved by her delicate charms. But Maria's inexplicable yielding was not as simple to explain, and he had finally realized with a dawning fury that she must have been wooing him into letting his guard down, disarming him with the sweetness of her kisses, the erotic movements of her soft body, keeping him a willing captive until Juan Perez and the other men could pick up his trail and find him. He had cursed her a thousand times since then, cursed his own stupidity, reminding himself viciously time and time again of the cunning and cruelty of the Delgatos.

Unconsciously, his fingers went to the gold band that loosely encircled his strong neck. It had replaced the iron slave collar that he had worn before being freed by Morgan, and while the gleaming band was a thing of beauty, expertly crafted to resemble a thick, golden rope, for Gabriel it only served to remind him of the perfidies of the Delgatos. He wore it proudly as a symbol of what he had suffered, just as he wore the gold hoop in one ear to signify his association with the Brethren of the Coast. The broad, round earring hung from an emerald stud as green and hard as his eyes—the glittering jewel had been part of his share of the booty taken from his first foray against the Spanish, and for him, the emerald represented more than just a successful raid—it signified the beginning of his quest for vengeance.

There was a rap on the cabin door just then, jerking Gabriel away from his unhappy thoughts. Briskly he called out, "Come in."

The stout door opened to reveal a huge, powerfully built man the color of café au lait. His head was clean-shaven; from each ear dangled heavy golden hoops, a pair of leather baldrics crisscrossed his massive chest, a sword hanging from one, a brace of pistols from the other; he was naked save for a pair of baggy purple breeches that ended at the knee. In his hands he carried two large pewter tankards. A smile creasing his wide mouth, he said, "Ah, *mon capitaine,* I have brought you some bumbo—and we will drink to the success of this wild plan of Harry Morgan's to attack Puerto Bello, *oui?*"

Amusement glittering in the emerald green eyes, Gabriel reached for the bumbo, a concoction of rum, water, sugar and nutmeg, remarking dryly, "Listening at the door again, Zeus?"

An angelic expression crossing his face, Zeus murmured, "But, *mon capitaine,* the door was open—a very little, you understand—and, of course, I had to stand very close to it, to make certain that no one else disturbed you and the Admiral." Innocently, he added, "It is not my fault that the Admiral has such a booming voice."

Gabriel snorted, but he said nothing more on the subject of eavesdropping, knowing it was useless. Since the day two years ago when he had saved Zeus' life during a particularly bloody fight with a Spanish ship off the coast of Havana, Zeus had appointed himself as Gabriel's guardian. And there were times that Gabriel was uncertain whether it was a blessing or a curse. It was definitely a blessing in the thick of battle to know that his back was protected by the very able sword of this giant of a man; it was also comforting to know that he could leave the *Dark Angel* in Zeus' capable hands or that among the violent and savage men with whom he associated daily, he could trust his life to Zeus. However, in return for this unasked guardianship, Zeus felt that nothing that touched *le capitaine* was sacred. Gabriel could have no secrets from Zeus, Zeus assuming that it was his natural right to oversee the smooth running of the captain's life, whether the captain liked it or not—if Gabriel selected an article of clothing that did not appeal to Zeus, somehow the piece of clothing would mysteriously disappear from Gabriel's wardrobe; if Gabriel took as his mistress a woman who did not conform with Zeus' ideas on the type of beauty that was appropriate for *le capitaine*, the woman also mysteriously disappeared. After this particular form of zealousness had occurred twice, Gabriel had demanded angrily, "What in hell have you done with them? Murdered them?"

Looking as much like a brown cherub as someone of his splendid proportions and barbaric splendor could, Zeus had replied dulcetly, "But *non, mon capitaine!* Murder is only when someone will not see reason—these women were satisfied with the handfuls of doubloons that I gave them. It was very simple. Do not worry over them—they were just common whores, not worthy of you."

Fortunately for the deep bond of affection that had grown up between the two men, Zeus knew precisely when he could blithely rearrange Gabriel's life and when he could not. He also knew when it behooved him to tread warily, and seeing that Gabriel was not going to make further comment on his eavesdropping, he settled down comfortably in the chair that Morgan had vacated several minutes ago. Light brown eyes fixed keenly on Gabriel's face, he asked, "When do we set sail?"

Gabriel smiled faintly. Next to ordering Gabriel's life about, Zeus loved nothing better than to fight against the Spanish. But unlike Gabriel, Zeus bore the Spanish no definite animosity; they merely represented booty and plunder to him.

Gabriel and Zeus were nearly the same age, but their lives had been vastly different, although both had grown up into fighting men without equal. Zeus had been born on the island of St. John; his mother had been a comely octoroon who had caught the eye of a French buccaneer. When his mother had died at his birth, Zeus had been raised by his father, and he had lived most of his life in that den of depravity, haunt of every murderous rogue in the Caribbean, Tortuga. A rarity among the buccaneers, Zeus' father had been an educated Frenchman, and even rarer still, before his death in a drunken brawl some ten years ago, he had taught his son many things, among them reading and writing. There had been rumors that Zeus' father had been the younger son of a marquis and that his wildness and drunkenness forced his expulsion from French society. Whether it was true or not, one thing was very apparent—he had taught his son the rudiments of social behavior practiced among the aristocracy, and Zeus could, when it suited him, adopt the airs of a fine gentleman. He preferred the life of a buccaneer though, and he and Gabriel formed an invincible team.

Gabriel took a deep draught of the fiery mixture Zeus had brought before he answered the other man's question. Then, putting the tankard on the long oak table, he said quietly, "Within the week." Throwing a mocking smile at his friend, he added dryly, "As you probably heard, Morgan has named Twelve League Cays as the meeting place and has set it for the end of the month. You may tell the men of that particular destination, but keep your tongue between your teeth about Puerto Bello. Harry Morgan wouldn't appreciate having his plans bandied about by the likes of you!"

Zeus looked wounded. *"Mon capitaine!* You stab me deep! Would I ever betray you?"

"Only if you thought it might be best for me," Gabriel drawled, the emerald green eyes glittering with affection.

"But of course! Sometimes, little angel, you are too fierce for your own good," Zeus returned affably.

Gabriel snorted. Only someone of Zeus' magnificent size would have dared to call him "little angel," but as Zeus topped his six-foot-plus frame by almost a full head, Gabriel bore the affectionate nickname with good humor.

The end of the month found Gabriel and Zeus at the rendezvous at Twelve League Cays. Almost a dozen ships were anchored there, and as many as seven hundred buccaneers had heeded their Admiral's call. With the exception of the *Dark Angel*, most of the pirate craft were a sorry-looking group, running the gamut from a fifty-foot sloop with eight guns down to the small pinnaces that were scarcely larger than longboats. But Harry Morgan was undaunted—his election as Admiral was relatively recent, and he was aware that there were those of the Brethren who were still uncommitted to his rule and who would be watching from afar his early raids against the Spanish. If he was successful, they would then flock to him in droves, if not . . .

The meeting of the leaders of the buccaneers was brief and blunt, and it was decided not to attack Havana, but to strike instead at Puerto del Principe, the second-largest city on the island of Cuba. Next to Havana, Puerto del Principe was rumored to be the wealthiest town on the island, having grown rich in trade in hides and cattle. Besides, several of the men had been imprisoned in Havana at one time or another, and none wished to go up against its well-known defenses.

In the end, it might have been better if they *had* attacked Havana—a Spanish prisoner who could speak English overheard their plans and escaped to warn the residents at Puerto del Principe. After a brutal twenty-four-hour march through dense forests and across rolling hills, for all their efforts in the bloody four-hour skirmish that saw the town fall into their hands, they only gained fifty thousand pieces of eight and a thousand head of cattle. It was a paltry sum and caused much grief among the buccaneers. Harry Morgan's career as Admiral of the Brethren was not off to a magnificent start. But he brushed aside the grumblings and turned his crafty mind to the target he had really wanted in the first place— Puerto Bello on the coast of the Spanish Main.

Morgan did accomplish one thing though—he had learned a little more about the possible attack on Jamaica and had immediately sent notice to Governor Sir Thomas

Modyford. Considerable Spanish forces, Morgan had written Modyford, from Vera Cruz and Campeche were to rendezvous at Havana, and forces from Puerto Bello and Cartagena were to rendezvous at Santiago off Cuba for an attack against English Jamaica.

Gabriel wondered sardonically if Morgan really believed the information wrested from the poor tortured prisoners of Puerto del Principe. Certainly he did not act as if he did; instead of returning to defend Port Royal from this supposed attack, he soothed the rumblings of his buccaneers with tantalizing hints of a secret mission. Mesmerized by Morgan's dark Welsh charm, the pirate crews followed him blindly, and for the next month they spent their time among the Cuban islands, careening their ships and killing cattle and curing the meat for a long trip ahead.

One night in May, as Gabriel and Morgan finished their evening meal aboard the Admiral's ship, Morgan leaned back in his chair and, raising his wineglass, said merrily, "I would propose a toast, my friend." And at Gabriel's quizzical look, he murmured, "To our secret mission, Puerto Bello—may we both find great treasure there."

Gabriel raised his glass in acknowledgment. "Aye, to Puerto Bello"—his green eyes hardened—"and may I find the vengeance I seek there."

Chapter Eight

On a hot, sticky afternoon at the end of June, Maria Delgato found herself crossing the plaza in the center of the city of Puerto Bello. She had only arrived a few hours ago, and already she was eager to be on the ship that would take her home to Santo Domingo from a protracted visit with a great-aunt in Panama City. She had come by mule train from Panama City, and after that torturous journey, she had looked forward to finally reaching Puerto Bello, but it was proving to be a disappointment.

Puerto Bello was an extremely unhealthy place, surrounded as it was by swamps on three sides, and except for the troops that manned the two forts, San Geronimo and Triana, which protected the town itself, and the castle of San Felipe, called the Iron Fort, which stood guard at the entrance to the mile-long harbor ringed with brothels, shops and taverns that relied upon the Spanish soldiers for their sustenance, the place was usually deserted. Deserted, that is, except for about forty days out of the year, during the time of the town's annual fair, which coincided with the arrival from Spain of the merchant ships. The colonists who lived in the Pacific provinces all flocked to Puerto Bello for the fair, and the town hummed with vitality—colonists milling about, eager to see the latest merchandise from home; ship's merchants, loudly hawking their goods, avid to sell their wares and to refill their rapidly emptying holds with all the gold, silver, emeralds and pearls that had been produced in the far-flung provinces since their last visit. It was during this time that Maria had arrived, and she had discovered the usually sleepy town bustling and crowded, inns and taverns overflowing with people. Only by chance had she and her companion, Pilar Gomez, been able to secure a room for themselves at one of the better waterside taverns.

Actually, it had been Pilar who had secured the room. Having noticed a man and woman departing with their leather trunks, she had promptly approached the innkeeper, inquiring after accommodations. It had been obvious that the tavern keeper was more than willing to let the room, but at an exorbitant price—at this time of year, he had no fear of the room remaining empty for very long at any price. But Pilar wasn't about to be cheated; she took her duties as duenna very seriously, even including the prices her charge paid for necessities. A haughty look on her handsome face, the fine dark eyes flashing with disdain, she had stated regally, "My good man, what you are asking is outrageous . . . and I am certain that the *alcalde* would be very interested to know of your criminal practices! My charge is related to him, and I feel positive that he would take a *very* personal interest in how she is treated during her stay here." The innkeeper had hesitated, discretion battling with greed, and after taking a long look at Maria, standing quietly at Pilar's side, and noting her costly skirt of blue silk, the elegant cut of her satin bodice, the sapphire earrings and the lovely necklace of matched pearls that hung around her throat, he was clearly vacillating. But Pilar wasn't about to give him time to consider the matter fully, to ask why the *alcalde* wasn't providing accommodations for his relative; and smiling at him kindly, she had said smoothly, "Of course, if you are willing to be reasonable, there is no need for us to cause you any inconvenience, is there? And, you must remember, we shall only be here for a few days. . . ."

In the face of Pilar's cool confidence, reluctantly the innkeeper had relented and named a much lower figure than he had first put forth. It met with Pilar's approval, and shortly thereafter Maria and Pilar had found themselves the victorious possessors of a small, dank room on the second floor which overlooked the stables. A bed with a straw mattress and a wobbly washstand with a cracked pitcher and dirty-looking bowl completed the furnishings.

Pilar had sniffed and murmured, "If I had seen this wretched hovel, I wouldn't have paid two pesos for it, much less what that fat thief wanted!"

Remembering that scene, Maria smiled, and Pilar, who was walking by her side as they wandered about the crowded plaza, asked, "What makes you smile, my dear?"

The sapphire blue eyes full of affection, Maria responded instantly, "You do! What would you have done if the innkeeper hadn't fallen for your guileful story of my being a relative of the *alcalde*'s?"

Pilar shrugged her shoulders and answered airily, "Oh, I should have thought of something. I am most resourceful!"

And indeed she was, Maria admitted fondly to herself, recalling the day that Pilar Gomez had first come into her life over two years ago. It had been a day full of driving rain, a tropical downpour that had flooded Hispaniola, turning the roads into quagmires of foot-sucking, slippery mud. Diego had been away at sea again, and lonely and depressed, much against the wishes of the stableman and her maid, the instant the rain had lightened, she had gone for a ride on Diablejo. She had not ridden far when the rain became heavier and heavier, and feeling the water seeping through her sodden riding habit, she had just disgustedly turned Diablejo about when she heard a cry for help. Peering through the rain in the direction of the call, she could barely distinguish the outline of another horse and a cart. The cart was tipped on its side, and approaching it cautiously, Maria suddenly realized that the cry she had heard had come from within the cart. Slipping off Diablejo, she had slogged her way through the mud to the cart, and rounding the tipped side of it, she had called, "Is anyone there? Can I help you?"

An exasperated feminine voice had replied tartly, "Well, of course you can! Why else would I have cried out?"

Taken aback, Maria had stood there motionless, until the voice had demanded, "Well! Are you struck dumb or do you intend to help me?"

"Oh! *Sí!*" Maria had answered helplessly and began to pull at the heavy trunks and valises that hid the speaker from her. A few minutes later, she was rewarded by her

first sight of Pilar Gomez as the older woman had finally
scrambled out of the tumbled pile of luggage. Shaking out
her damp, heavy skirt, she had regarded Maria with surprise. *"Cielos!* It is a mere child! Whatever are you doing
out in this fiendish weather? Do your people take no better care of you than to allow you to roam about this way?"
Pilar had asked in a kinder tone.

Mutely, Maria had stared at her, bemused by the sheer
magnificence of Pilar's tall, full-bosomed figure. Dressed
all in black and standing six feet tall in her stockinged
feet, Pilar Gomez, simply by her regal size, had an overwhelming effect on most people, and Maria was no exception. It was obvious from the twinkle that suddenly sprang
to the intelligent dark eyes that Pilar was aware of her
effect on the uninitiated, and a teasing smile curving the
full mouth, she had said, "I am not an ogress, I assure
you, only cursed with my father's height."

Maria had flushed and stammered with embarrassment. "I—I—I d-d-didn't mean t-t-to stare; please forgive
me!"

In her mid-thirties, Pilar was a very handsome woman—
her creamy, mat skin was without a blemish; her jaw and
chin were masculinely firm; and with her fine, large dark
eyes and wide, full-lipped mouth she just missed being
truly lovely. But she had charm and warmth to spare,
when she chose, and looking down at Maria's small frame,
she had said with concern, "My dear child, you are soak-
ing wet!" Before Maria could open her mouth, Pilar had
spun around and, after rummaging about in one of the
leather-bound chests, had a second later flung a black velvet cloak about Maria's slim shoulders. "There," Pilar
had pronounced triumphantly, ignoring the fact that the
cloak dwarfed Maria's fragile body. "That should keep
you dry until we reach shelter! Now then, child, before
we both drown, which way is your home?"

As if under the spell of some magical creature, Maria
had pointed dazedly in the direction of the Casa de la
Paloma, and before her startled gaze, Pilar had instantly
unhooked the horse from the cart and with black skirts
a-flying had expertly straddled the animal. Looking down
again at Maria, she had said gaily, "Now, mount your

horse, child, and let us be off. I do not know about you, but I cannot wait to be dry!"

From that moment on, Pilar Gomez had become a delightful part of Maria's life. She was both friend and mentor, fierce protector and benevolent martinet. Her background was impeccable, except for the regrettable blemish of having had an English mother. Pilar had been the only child of a minor official of the Spanish court who had married the daughter of a visiting English diplomat during one of the lulls in the nearly constant hostility between England and Spain. But despite Pilar's being half-English, her father had been able to arrange an excellent marriage for his tall, outspoken daughter to a young lieutenant in the Spanish Army, and she might have spent the rest of her life being a not very dutiful Spanish wife if her husband had not died some five years after the wedding. Neither her husband's death nor the manner of it—he had died from a wound received in a duel over another woman—had surprised Pilar in the least; he had been unfaithful to her right from the beginning and his hotheadedness was well known. As Pilar had said to Maria once, "*Chica,* I was so thankful that he never beat me!" A twinkle in the fine eyes, she had added, "I would have abhorred having to break a stool over his head!"

The death of her husband had freed Pilar from an unhappy marriage, and disliking the cloistered life that awaited her as a widow in Spain—and a half-English one at that—she had promptly offered her services as duenna to the youngest daughter of a wealthy family returning to their vast estates in Panama. She had never looked back since then, although there had been times that she had blessed her unfaithful husband for having left her a tidy sum which allowed her to choose her employment as the fancy took her. She had traveled a great deal in the New World, changing employers and locations as the whim struck her, and had been fleeing from the unwanted advances of her latest charge's father when her cart had overturned. "If I were pure-blooded Spanish, they would not treat me so!" she had explained later to Maria. "I cannot tell you all of the most *im*proper suggestions that have been put to me, as soon as those arrogant *hidalgos* discover why I am able to speak such good English. I am thankful for this last one though—it brought us together! My cart turning over was most opportune, wasn't it, *chica?*"

Maria had been very nervous about Diego's opinion of Pilar, and in the beginning he had been displeased about the older woman's presence in the hacienda. "What were you thinking of?" he had demanded of Maria his first evening at Casa de la Paloma after a long absence. "She is nothing but a wayward, half-English creature with a far-too-outspoken manner! And you want her for your duenna? Are you mad?"

"Oh, Diego, please!" Maria had pleaded, her hands unconsciously clasped against her small bosom. "I know she is outspoken and that you cannot like the fact that her mother was English, but she *is* well born and respectable. After all, her father was at the court in Madrid, and she has all of the attributes that anyone would wish for in a duenna—she's older, competent, educated, responsible . . ." Diego had snorted, but he had not looked so unyielding, and Maria had ended softly, "It is very lonely for me while you are gone and Pilar is much company to me."

Diego had looked at her for a long moment and then had asked in a quieter tone, "This matters to you a great deal? You really want this woman to live with you and oversee your actions while I am gone?"

Encouraged by his words, Maria had nodded her black curly head, the blue eyes very wide and beseeching. Half severely, half teasingly, he had inquired, "And you will behave in a proper fashion? You will cause me no displeasure by acting unseemly?"

"I promise!" Maria had breathed fervently.

Grudgingly, Diego had finally said, "Very well, then—we shall try it and see what happens."

Impulsively, Maria had thrown her arms around her brother, and smiling up at him, she had said, "Thank you so much! You will see that it will be wonderful."

"I doubt that!" Diego had replied caustically but continued in a far more affectionate voice than she had ever heard, "When you smile like that, I begin to understand why your *madre* and our *padre* spoiled you so outrageously. Now run along, before I have second thoughts and change my mind." And so it was that Pilar had become a permanent member of the Delgato household, but only Maria knew how much Pilar's presence had lifted her spirits. . . .

The time between Gabriel Lancaster's death and the arrival of Pilar into her life had been most unhappy for Maria. She had grieved deeply for the Englishman, blaming herself for his death, torturing herself by having been swept away by emotions she couldn't even yet name. His death left a great void in her life—she felt as if her very heart had been ripped out of her breast—and yet she had no reason for feeling his death so intensely—she had seen him seldom, had not exchanged fifty words with him, but in some mysterious way, he had possessed her. She mourned his passing, unable to even approach that little forest glade where he had died, unable even to ride past it, avoiding it at all cost. Her dreams were tormented, and again and again as the weeks passed she would wake up with tears on her cheeks, the memory of his magnificent body lying so still in the glade searing across her brain. She mourned for she knew not what—a dream lost, a future that might have been? She didn't know, she only knew that with his death, something vital had gone out of her life, as if something within her that had been struggling to burst forth had suddenly withered and died.

Telling Caroline had been dreadful. Unable to reveal her own misery, driven by some deep emotion, she had ridden over to the Chavez plantation the next day. She had explained to Justina why she had come, and her merry face suddenly sad, for she had grown to like the English girl, Justina had seen that Caroline was told of Gabriel's death in privacy by Maria. Her own blue eyes filling with tears, her voice thick with pain and grief, Maria had haltingly informed Caroline of her brother's death. Caroline had been seated on Justina's bed and her face had paled. Her hand had closed hurtfully over Maria's as she had demanded harshly, "You are certain? You saw him dead?" Mutely, Maria had nodded her dark head. Dully, Caroline had muttered, *"Gabriel dead!* I cannot believe it! He was so, so vibrant, so full of life and now he is gone . . . now I am the only one left alive." Blue eyes so like Maria's had clouded with tears, and suddenly Maria could bear it no longer, and impetuously she had thrown her arms around the other girl, murmuring over and over again, "I'm sorry. I'm sorry. So very sorry."

How long they remained that way, neither knew, but finally, her tears lessening, Caroline had become aware of Maria's distress; and with wonder in her voice, she had gazed at the other girl. "You cared for him," Caroline had said slowly.

"I—I—I don't know," Maria had stammered. "H-h-he seemed a g-g-good man. It was not fair what happened, what my brother did to you and those aboard your ship." Her small face passionate, Maria had vowed fiercely, "If I could have undone the dreadful wrong done to all of you that day, I would have—no matter what the cost!"

Caroline had believed her, and the bond between the two young women had strengthened, the tragedy of Gabriel's death bringing them closer together. Maria had even attempted to buy Caroline from Ramon, but, his gray eyes dark and unreadable, he had asked dryly, "And could you protect her from Diego? You who can't really even protect yourself?" Maria's heart had sunk as she instantly became aware of how foolish her actions had been, but, her eyes fixed on Ramon's, she had demanded, "But who will protect her here?" His mouth had tightened and he had replied curtly, "Leave Caroline's fate to me! But have no fear, as long as she is mine, no one *else* shall harm her." It was an odd thing to have said and Maria had looked at him closely, but his dark face had revealed nothing, and she had forced herself to be content with his promise.

If telling Caroline of Gabriel's death had been dreadful for Maria, seeing Diego's rage when he had returned from Santo Domingo and had learned of the Englishman's demise had been terrifying. She had been with Diego in the small *sala* when Juan Perez was announced, but before she could leave the men to their business, Juan had bluntly and without preamble related the events, as he knew them, that had led up to the Englishman's being killed. *"What?"* Diego had fairly shrieked upon hearing Juan's words. "Dead, you say?" he had cried, his face darkening, the scar that twisted his eyebrow white and throbbing. When Juan sullenly confirmed it, Diego had struck him viciously across the cheek. "You fool!" he had yelled. "You damned, *damned* fool! *I* wanted to be the one! I could kill you for robbing me of that pleasure!" Before Maria's horrified gaze, Diego had picked up his riding whip, which had been lying on a nearby table, and in a white-hot fury he had begun to rain blow after blow upon the hapless Juan. Maria had been transfixed by the ugliness of the scene unfolding before her eyes, but shaking herself free from its horrible fascination, she had thrown herself across the room, desperately hanging on to Diego's arm as he prepared to strike Juan again. *"Don't!"* she begged. *"Por favor!* Diego, stop this madness!"

Her voice seemed to reach him, and recovering himself somewhat, he slowly lowered the rod. Harshly he ordered Juan, "Out of here! Gather up your belongings and leave here this instant!"

An oily note in his voice, Juan had whined, *"Señor,* I am sorry for what happened, but he was only an English swine . . . surely I have proven myself over these many months to be worth more than that? I know that you are angry with me, but must I leave?" Suggestively, he had added, "A man with my talents is hard to find."

Still breathing hard, his rage obviously only partially under control, Diego had stared at Juan a long moment, but then he had slowly nodded his head as if in agreement. Thickly, he had said, "It is as you say. You shall stay, but for the moment, get out of my sight!"

Life had been most unpleasant in the following months at the Casa de la Paloma, Diego's fury over the death of the Englishman touching everyone from the youngest stableboy to Maria herself. In many ways it was Maria who bore the full brunt of his thwarted rage, and she was treated constantly to his almost maniacal ravings against the Lancasters and Juan's handling of the affair. It was very hard for her to hear him speak so spitefully of the dead man and his family, and it was made even harder by the fact that she had to conceal the grief that Gabriel's death had brought her. She took a guilty relief in the fact that Diego, or anyone else for that matter, hadn't known precisely what had transpired between her and the Englishman that tragic day. If Diego had learned of her shameful actions ... She had shuddered just thinking about it.

But ranting against a fate that had robbed him of the pleasure of killing his vanquished foe wasn't the only thing that occupied Diego's dark thoughts those days—he also had a great deal to say about the marriage of Maria's erstwhile suitor, Don Clemente. Again and again she had been scolded for having upset all his careful plans for her marriage to the man of his choice. Maria had bitten her tongue and had borne his bad temper for as long as her own temper would allow, but finally one afternoon she had faced him and had said angrily, "Diego, you must cease this harping on Don Clemente! It is over and done with. He is married to another now."

But Diego could not let it rest, and leaning forward in his leather chair, he had demanded, "Do you realize what it cost me when you so foolishly threw away the honor of marriage to Don Clemente? Are you aware of how humiliated I was? How difficult it was for me to swallow my pride and pander to him, hoping he would forgive your provincial stupidity? And for what? For *nothing!*"

"Diego," Maria had said quietly, "I'm sorry that I ruined your plans, but if you would have listened to me in the first place, you would have realized that they were destined to fail. Doña Luisa will make him a far better wife than I ever would have—they are alike—and if I had married him, I would only have brought you even greater embarrassment at some time in the future when, as his wife, I know I would have done something even more outrageous than merely dumping a honey pot on his head." Thoughtfully she had added, "More than likely he would have eventually driven me to slit his gullet!"

Diego had given a reluctant laugh, and from that day forward things had been improved greatly between them. Three weeks later he had departed for Spain, leaving Maria and the other harassed residents of Casa de la Paloma to recover some semblance of tranquillity. Diego was gone for nearly a year, not returning to Hispaniola until the fall of 1666, and it had been during this long absence that Maria had met Pilar Gomez. Maria had been looking forward to his reappearance. The two letters she received from him while he was gone had been warmer and more

affectionate than she had expected; it seemed as if the
time in Spain had mellowed him somewhat. He had been
promoted to Vice-Admiral and was being considered for a
most important post with the Spanish fleet in the South
Seas. To Maria's delight, he had even eventually admitted to being pleased with Pilar's presence in the hacienda,
telling Maria one night as they had walked alone through
the gardens, "I should have thought of a duenna for you
before now—" He had frowned slightly before adding, "Of
course, I hadn't expected to have the care of you this long
either—you should have been married to Don Clemente—
but we won't dwell on *that!* Your meeting with *Señora*
Gomez was most fortuitous for me. I shall be gone much
of the time in the near future, and it is only fitting that
you have a respectable, older, wiser woman to be with you
to see that you do nothing foolish or unseemly while I am
gone. She may," he had gone on dryly, "even teach you
your duties to your brother, and the next time I propose
a match for you, you will obey me."

Maria had said nothing, only smiling faintly in the
darkness. Pilar was far more likely to incite her to rebellion against such a fate, but she kept that thought to herself! When she had repeated this conversation to Pilar,
Pilar had laughed gaily, saying with a gleam of amusement dancing in her beautiful dark eyes, "My dear child!
I pray you do not disillusion your brother about my ca-
pabilities! If he believes that I shall condemn you to the
wretched fate I suffered in the marriage my father arranged for me, then let him—so much the better for us, to
plan a way to confound him!"

To Maria's great surprise, Diego had appeared to be
totally disinterested in arranging a marriage for her—
once Don Clemente had escaped his net, he had not apparently been in any haste to snare another useful suitor.
Maria had puzzled over this frequently, but it had been
Pilar who had unerringly put her finger on the probable
reason. Smiling across at Maria one day as they rode in
a small open cart around the boundaries of the plantation, Pilar had said, "*Chica*, it is very simple, if you stop
to consider the type of man your brother is—I know you
are fond of him, but he is hungry for power and wealth,
and will, it is obvious to me, use anything he can to propel

himself up the path he has chosen. At the moment though, he is content—he has his promotion, he is by his own efforts gaining the power he wants ... and so he has no need to marry you off to a man he can manipulate to his own advantage." Cynically, she had added, "However, I am quite positive that sooner or later he will remember that he has a very useful pawn—you—and then will begin to cast about for a husband for you. But until then, do not worry about it overmuch. When the time comes, we will think of something. Trust me for *that!*"

It had seemed that Pilar had been right; Diego had not even mentioned a husband for her the few times Maria had seen him during the following years. He had seemed content that she remain unmarried, and for that Maria was fervently grateful, as much because he hadn't found a husband for her, as because he hadn't seemed to think it odd that a young woman of her age wasn't the least inclined to fall in love and want to marry. Pilar, however, was another tale, and last September when Maria had reached the grand age of twenty-one, she had commented thoughtfully, "I worry about you, pigeon. I would not want you to marry a man you didn't love, but I think it is unnatural for a lovely young creature like yourself not to have been snatched up by some ardent gentleman by now." Her intelligent dark eyes fixed intently upon Maria's suddenly averted face, she had said slowly, "I know that there are several young men about the island who would, with a little encouragement, be absolutely enchanted to woo you, but I am also aware that you very cleverly keep them at a distance." Her voice speculative, she had murmured, "If I didn't know better, I would think that you were waiting for some lost lover to return. . . ."

Maria had not answered her; instead she had become very interested in the clothes she had been selecting to be packed for their trip to Panama City in October, and Pilar had shrugged her shoulders and had allowed the subject to lapse, much to Maria's relief. But later that night, Pilar's words had come back to haunt her, and as she had lain tossing restlessly in her bed, she had wondered bleakly if there hadn't been some truth in what Pilar had said. *Was* she waiting for a lost lover to return? It was a ridiculous notion—there had never been a lover in her life, never been a man that she could have lost her heart to ... except the Englishman. And he, she had thought sorrowfully, had been killed before he could become her lover. . . . To her dismay, she had felt the prickle of tears in her eyes. After all this time, did she still mourn him? It couldn't be, it was madness, but even telling herself vehemently that it was so didn't banish the terrifying idea that it was true. That unconsciously she still searched for him, that no man of her acquaintance had ever caught her affections because none could compare with the tall, broad-shouldered, emerald-eyed Englishman's image she carried in her mind's eye. It had been a depressing thought, and all during the visit to Panama City, Maria had tried, sometimes almost with a desperate intensity, to fall in love, with any of the many eligible young men who came to call at her great-aunt's palatial home. She hadn't though, and she had been both relieved and angry with herself when their visit had finally come to an end.

Maria had been eagerly looking forward to returning once more to home, to the Casa de la Paloma, hoping that somehow she would be able to exorcise the ghost of the Englishman. She prayed that it would be so—she really didn't want to spend the remainder of her life tormented by half-formed dreams and longings, never to become a woman in the arms of a lover, never to be a beloved wife, a proud mother. . . .

She had been rather melancholy the first few days of the journey to Puerto Bello, staring blindly at the verdant jungle growth that crowded the edges of the narrow, well-worn trail that the mules plodded slowly along, brooding over her silly fixation on a man who was dead and buried. Dead and buried for almost three years, she had reminded herself fiercely only hours before their arrival in Puerto Bello.

They were not to stay long in Puerto Bello. The ship that was to take them the final leg of their long journey home was already snug in the harbor, and within a matter of a few days, she and Pilar would once again be on their way.

Neither she nor Pilar slept well that night, the noise of the patrons below and the lumpy uncomfortable straw mattress combining to keep them awake. When the dawn came, with a sigh of relief Maria left the bed. Crossing the room, she poured some water from the pitcher and began her morning ablutions.

She had just finished and had turned to greet Pilar, who was struggling from the bed, when they both heard the sounds of a great commotion in the distance. Suddenly the peaceful dawn was shattered by the church bells frantically pealing out an alarm, and then without warning, there was a thunderous, earthshaking explosion, the blinding flash of light that followed it briefly illuminating the small room where Maria and Pilar stood transfixed.

Her eyes wide and startled, still in the fine lawn chemise she had slept in, Maria darted out of the room. In the narrow hallway, she was greeted by others garbed much as she was. There was an excited babble of voices, a sensation of fear and apprehension rippling through everyone. The innkeeper's frightened face appeared at the top of the stairs, and hysterically he cried, "Run! We are being attacked by pirates! They have blown up Fort San Geronimo and are now attacking the Iron Fort that guards the harbor. Run for your lives—*the pirates are coming!*"

Chapter Nine

IT was indeed the pirates. Harry Morgan's pirates, to be exact, and they were falling on the unprepared city of Puerto Bello with a rapacious ferocity.

After the not-so-successful attack on Puerto del Príncipe in the spring, Gabriel had wondered for how long Morgan would be able to continue to exert his influence over the buccaneers. But though there had still been some dire mutterings among the men when they had finally sailed south from Jamaica in May, these had soon ceased. There had continued, however, much speculation about the twenty-three canoes Morgan had ordered to be carried aboard the many ships that followed him off on his "secret mission." Despite repeated questioning by the other ships' captains, Morgan had not revealed his reasons and had only smiled and murmured tantalizingly, "You shall see soon enough, me boyos . . . and then see if you don't think that I'm a damned clever rogue!"

Unlike any of the other buccaneer captains, Gabriel at least knew what that destination was, but try as he might, he had not been able to induce Morgan to give him some idea of how the pirate leader intended to take the reportedly invincible city. Morgan had grinned, his black eyes dancing with mockery, and he had drawled, "All in good time, my friend. Be content that I have told *you* where we are going!"

It hadn't been until they had sighted the peak of Pilon de Miguel de la Borda near the mouth of the Chagres River on the coast of the Spanish Main that Morgan had finally gathered together his buccaneer captains and had told them what he intended to do. There had been many

118

surly complaints and startled protests from the men that sat around a rough oak table in the great cabin of Morgan's sloop when they had heard their Admiral's scheme, but most of the grumblings had come from the French buccaneers.

"*Sacré bleu*, Harry! Puerto Bello! Are you mad? It is too strong!" one Frenchman had cried, the others vociferously echoing him. "There are as many as sixty cannon!" "Take the Iron Fort that guards the harbor? Bah! It cannot be done, *mon ami!*"

The babble of raised voices had continued for several moments. Morgan had said nothing from his position at the head of the table, but his black eyes had been watchful as his gaze had traveled slowly over each of the men, obviously weighing his strength in the contest of wills. Wisely, he had let the captains talk themselves out, and the tumult had gradually died. The men had begun to look to their Admiral for a decision when the French buccaneer François du Bois had spoken, summing up the main objections to the plan.

Du Bois had been a serious rival for the position of Admiral of the Brethren, and he had not been pleased when Morgan had been elected over him. He had grudgingly followed Morgan, but it had been apparent that he still harbored hopes of gaining control of the buccaneers. Tipping back his chair and hooking his thumbs in the baldrics that crisscrossed his massive chest, he had stated aggressively, " 'Tis a mad plan, Harry! A foolish one too. We have not the numbers to take Puerto Bello, no matter how many mules laden with treasure are assembled there. Have you forgotten that three forts well garrisoned with Spanish soldiers guard the town? Or that this time of year there are many armed men within the town?" Du Bois' light blue eyes had moved appraisingly over the others, trying to judge the effect of his words. There had been several nodded heads, and du Bois had continued confidently, "There is better prey to be had—we are too small a force for what you suggest."

It had been a crucial moment, but Morgan had been certain of his power, and he had leaned forward and cried passionately, "What does it matter, man! If our numbers are small, our hearts are great! And the fewer we are, the better shares we shall have in the spoils!"

Clever Harry, Gabriel had thought from his vantage point at the other end of the table, appealing to both the buccaneers' courage and cupidity. And it had been obvious from the affirmative murmurings that had arisen that Morgan had correctly gauged the mettle of the majority of the buccaneers.

But if the majority had thrown their lot in with the Admiral, the French had not, and with many woeful prophecies of doom, they had departed one by one, until only du Bois had remained of the French captains. One elbow had rested on the table, his fingers had been idly caressing his long blond mustaches, and his cold blue eyes had been fixed unwaveringly on Morgan for several increasingly tense seconds before du Bois had spoken. "I think," he had finally drawled, "that I shall come with you, Harry." A grim smile had curved his thin lips and he had added, "I would not want to miss either your success . . . or defeat."

Morgan and Gabriel had exchanged glances over du Bois' head, and later when they were alone, Gabriel had said coolly, "You know you're going to have to kill him, Harry. He means to have the Admiralty."

Morgan had snorted. "I don't fear the likes of that scoundrel! But you're probably right—he'll not rest until he is either Admiral or I've slain him," he had replied disgustedly. Then, that sly twinkle in the black eyes, he had continued, "Unless of course, *you* kill him! He loves you as the devil loves holy water!"

A cynical smile had flitted across Gabriel's handsome features. What Morgan had stated was true—du Bois held no love for Gabriel Lancaster, and the two men had clashed on several occasions, du Bois openly envious of Gabriel's expertise with the sword as well as his rapid rise up through the ranks of the buccaneers. Gabriel's close association with Morgan had only increased the French buccaneer's dislike of him, and Gabriel had suspected that it was only a matter of time until they shed blood. The green eyes hard, Gabriel had glanced across at Morgan and had said quietly, "I can kill him if you like— there was no excuse for the way he tortured that young

girl from the Dutch ship we took last fall. The treatment
of female captives is normally none of my concern, but,
God's wounds, Harry! Do you know what he did to her?"
At Morgan's negative shake of the head, Gabriel had
growled, "After he had raped her in full view of our ship's
crew, he used her to practice his skills with a knife, and
when he was through amusing himself, he had her tossed
over the side of the ship to the sharks! Bloody French
bastard!" His hand had made a fist and he had uttered
fiercely, "If for no other reason than that he deserves to
die."

Morgan had looked thoughtful. "I had heard that you
two had exchanged some nasty words and that the men
had been forced to keep you from attacking him, but I
hadn't heard the cause of the altercation." Sending Gabriel a shrewd glance, he had added, "You might have
joined the buccaneers, my friend, but I think now and
then that your conscience is a little too gentle—I've seen
worse done, and in time you learn not to let it touch you."

Gabriel's mouth had twisted. "You're right, of course.
It is just that sometimes I can't help imagining how I
would have felt if I had been forced to see my sister or
my wife suffer that fate before they died. Men, I can fight
and kill, but the others . . ."

Nodding his head slowly, Morgan had said nothing for
a moment, and then in a brisk voice had commented,
"Someday, if you remain a buccaneer long enough, such
thoughts will not occur to you. As for du Bois, I think
we'll let him run his length for the time being—I want no
disruptions within the Brethren at the moment. And now,
let us talk about the canoes. . . ."

The reasons for the canoes had soon been made apparent to everyone. Morgan had had no intention of attacking Puerto Bello's Iron Fort from the harbor side—to have
done so would have been folly and he had been well aware
of it. Instead he had planned to circle around, and striking from the rear, capture one of the other forts before
the Spaniards even realized they were in the area. Leaving their ships guarded with a small contingent of men,
Morgan and the others had taken to the canoes and had
paddled along the coast until they had reached a point
several miles from Puerto Bello. Abandoning their canoes

a few hours before dawn, they had plunged into the lush, primeval jungle that lay between them and their objective—Fort San Geronimo.

Before the startled Spaniards had known what had happened, they had been overrun and captured by the savage horde that had poured out of the jungle. Of the one hundred and thirty men who had garrisoned the fort, only fifty-five remained alive and might later have been ransomed, except that within the captured fortress, the buccaneers had found eleven Englishmen chained in the dungeons below. Their condition was wretched—far worse than Gabriel's had been when he had been set free by Morgan, and with the low growl of rage that issued from many buccaneer throats at the pitiful sight the men made, the fate of the surviving Spaniards was sealed.

Coldly Morgan had ordered the Spaniards locked in a central room of the castle. Several barrels of gunpowder had been found within the fort, and once the buccaneers had deserted the interior, at Morgan's order, the gunpowder was set afire. The entire castle, hapless Spaniards and all, had been blown up, the sounds of the colossal explosion shattering the early morning air and making the earth shake.

Broadsword held firmly in one hand, Gabriel, his face bathed in the bright golden light from the exploding castle, had stared intently at the flames shooting skyward, curiously unmoved by what had just happened. It was a savage age he lived in, and only one cruel law prevailed—atrocity *must* be met by further and greater atrocity. He took one last look at the smoking, burning hulk of the fortress, and then, rousing his own men, Gabriel had raised his sword high above his head and shouted, "To the Iron Fort! It must be taken before the Spaniards have time to rally themselves! Follow me!"

The Iron Fort fell quickly; with its many cannons pointed seaward, the defenders were helpless to repel the invaders that burst in from the opposite direction, and within a shockingly short time, the buccaneers had overrun the fortress. With the fall of the Iron Fort, only the remaining fortress of Santiago Castle, which guarded the city itself, stood between the Brethren and their total subjugation of Puerto Bello. Leaving the captured castle of San Felipe in the hands of a group of trusted men, Gabriel and Zeus began to fight their way toward the center of the city. The Spaniards they met fought fiercely, but Gabriel's sword flashed again and again, leaving death in its wake, until they had managed to slash their way into the heart of the city. They found Morgan, his swarthy face alight with satisfaction, near the plaza. Seeing them, Morgan had shouted exultantly, "It's ours, me boyos! I told you we could take her. And by Christ's wounds, we have!"

Gabriel smiled faintly at Morgan's excitement, absently pushing back a rebellious wave of heavy black hair from his forehead. Unlike the majority of the buccaneers, he did not wear his hair in flowing splendor past his shoulders. Instead the thick unruly locks were ruthlessly cut short, only the tips allowed to brush against his hard jaw and the back of his neck. But the emerald stud in his ear and the gold hoop that hung from it, as well as the collar of gold around his neck, made him appear as barbaric as any of the savage men who followed Harry Morgan. Gabriel was garbed much as the others were—white shirt with long full sleeves lay open to reveal his naked chest; loose scarlet breeches were topped by a wide leather belt that rode low on his lean hips; his hose and shoes were black; and in his belt were carelessly thrust two pistols and a long-bladed knife.

Replying to Morgan's jubilant statement, Gabriel motioned with his sword in the direction of the last fortress that lay just beyond the city and said dryly, "Puerto Bello will not be ours, Harry, until Santiago has been taken. And unless I misread the situation, some of the men are already forgetting that fact and beginning to loot."

Morgan cursed virulently under his breath. "Bloody fools! I gave orders that there was to be none of that until after we had completely secured the city, and by God, I'll kill the first man I see disobeying my command!" he thundered, the black eyes glowing angrily.

But the nearly defenseless city was proving too much of a temptation for many of the buccaneers as they swarmed through the streets of Puerto Bello, the panic-stricken population running ahead of them as deer do before a pack of ravening wolves. Even as Morgan ceased speaking, a woman, her face contorted by fear, burst out

of a nearby alley, closely followed by two corsairs. The
men caught her within a few feet, and spinning her struggling form around, with rough hands they began to strip
her, one man pulling at his breeches, his intention obvious. Morgan cursed again, and drawing one of the three
pistols that reposed in his belt, he calmly fired at the men.
A strangled gasp broke from one of the men and he fell
facedown in the littered street, a red stain spreading
across his back. The other buccaneer, the sobbing, terrified woman forgotten, crouched low, his sword poised, and
looked in the direction whence the shot had come. Seeing
Morgan standing there with a smoking pistol in his hand,
the buccaneer made a ludicrous facial expression. Morgan
glared at him and bellowed, "Whoreson! Until the town
is secure, control your lusts! Now get on with making
certain we have crushed all resistance!"

Utter chaos reigned in the city; the buccaneers, their
cutlasses gleaming with fresh blood, systematically
herded together the dazed and terror-filled inhabitants
that had fled their homes in the frail hope of escaping.
The streets were alive with movement—chickens squawk-
ing underfoot; goats bleating as they ran wildly through
the crowds; the frantic, stunned population blundering
blindly into the hands of the buccaneers; the buccaneers
darting here and there to cut off any avenue of escape.
All the exits to the city were quickly manned by the invaders, stemming the flow of those citizens lucky enough
to scramble for the questionable protection of the jungle.

The sounds of the church bells were still pealing forth
the alarm in the increasingly warm morning air; useless
cannon fire from some Spanish galleons anchored in the
harbor boomed in the distance; flames crackled and black
putrid smoke billowed out from the remains of Fort San
Geronimo, hanging over the city like a shroud; and Gabriel wondered if he would ever forget this unfolding scene
of death and destruction. But as he and Zeus plunged back
into the thick of the action again, it was the horrible
screams of men dying as they fell beneath the cutlasses
and pikes of the rampaging corsairs, the terrified shrieks
of women as they suffered unspeakable brutalities from
their captors, and the pitiful sobs of frightened, bewil-

dered children that made the most vivid and lasting impact on Gabriel.

They are my enemies, he told himself repeatedly, as he raced down the street toward the remaining fortress, Santiago. They are Spanish, their kind killed my wife and my sister, enslaved me, why should I feel pity for them? Doggedly he fought down an unexpected feeling of revulsion and distaste for what was happening, reminding himself fiercely, they *are* my enemies! But the sight of a young child dying from a ugly, gaping wound in its small chest, the body of a woman, her skirts bunched up around her waist clearly revealing the brutal fate she had suffered before dying, made the bile rise up thick and burning in his throat.

A young boy, not more than twelve, pathetically armed with a stick of wood, suddenly leaped in front of him. Staring at the frightened, determined face, Gabriel's sword arm stayed, and avoiding the desperate blow aimed at him, he swiftly disarmed the youth. Grasping the neck of the boy's shirt, he shook him and snarled, "Run, you young fool! Run and hide and pray that someone less mad than I am doesn't find you! Run!"

Gradually, the tumult within the city died as the buccaneers slowly tightened their cruel grip. Commandeering the churches, they used the cavernous buildings as prisons, crowding those poor wretches unfortunate enough to fall into their hands into what had been, only moments before, a blessed sanctuary. The inhabitants that still remained free cowered, hiding in their homes, or fearfully sought to escape from the city to the jungles. Only Santiago remained unconquered.

The massive fortress stood just to the north of the town, and it was composed of an impressive, daunting series of ramparts and bastions that rose some ten feet in the air. Santiago was constructed of impenetrable, ochre-colored stone, and above the outer defenses towered the crenellated keep and the heavily fortified roofs of the barracks and storehouses. As the buccaneers slowly approached the castle, it could be seen that the entire fortress was packed with crossbowmen and arquebusiers.

Gabriel whistled with dismay when he saw the nearly impregnable structure and the armed men who ringed the upper reaches. Standing next to Morgan as the Admiral studied the situation, Gabriel said quietly, "We cannot take it, Harry . . . not without losing far too many men. Our losses have been light so far, but half our force could be wiped out just scaling those walls."

Morgan grunted, the black eyes hard and unfathomable. Du Bois, his shirt bloodstained and dirty, approached them. Like the others, he stared at the fortress for several seconds. "Leave it!" du Bois finally growled. "The town is ours and my men are impatient to start looting. We've obeyed your orders and none of the buildings have been searched yet—there are many rich, fat merchants and spoils just waiting to be found by us . . . and women too." Du Bois smiled salaciously, licking his lips in anticipation of the rape and plunder of the city that awaited them. Sending a dismissing glance at the fortress, he added, "What do we care if some of the Spanish dogs have locked themselves up in the castle? As long as they stay there, they cannot hurt us, *mon ami. We* control the town."

The words had hardly left his mouth when the cannons of Santiago, which had been trained upon the town, suddenly roared, belching forth smoke and fire. *"Mon Dieu!"* du Bois burst out as he scrambled for cover with the others. "Those madmen are firing at their own city!"

It was true. In a desperate attempt to drive out the buccaneers, the commander of Santiago, Don José Sanchez Ximenez, had grimly ordered his men to commence firing upon Puerto Bello. The grapeshot and iron cannon balls began to fall in a deadly rain upon the city, killing ally and foe alike. As the cannons and arquebusiers continued to fire, the carnage was awful, the streets soon littered with the rubble of buildings, the bodies of townspeople and buccaneers.

Hastily withdrawing to a safe distance beyond the range of the cannons, Morgan called his captains together. It was a furious, motley group that assembled before their equally furious Admiral. Many of the brutal faces were blackened with powder burns, not a few showed signs of wounds and they were all adamant about one thing—Santiago could not be taken. Glaring at them, his long black locks waving wildly about his shoulders as he moved his

head, Morgan snarled, "But we will take it—and the cost
be damned! Are you buccaneers or milk-fed maids?"

A low dangerous mutter of anger came from the assembled men, but his black eyes glittering with a fiery spirit,
Morgan said forcefully, "Are we to give up now? Now
when everything is within our grasp? We control the city,
it is only one fortress that stands between us and complete domination. Think of the jewels that are just
waiting for us; of the women and wine, rich merchants to
be held for ransom; of the gold to be stripped from the
churches. . . ."

Greed overcame their reservations and the moment of
near rebellion was gone. "How do we take it, Harry?" one
of the men asked. "What do you plan?"

Morgan smiled oddly. "Watch, me boyos, and you shall
see! But first . . . find some carpenters from among our
prisoners." The odd smile widened. "I have some important work for them to do."

Gabriel had remained silent during this meeting, but
something in Morgan's dark face, something in that odd
smile, made him vaguely uneasy. Without terrible loss of
life among the buccaneers, Gabriel could see no way of
taking the castle, and loyal to Morgan or not, he would
not order his own men to die needlessly.

Filled with increasing disquietude, Gabriel watched silently as several prisoners began to construct the long
ladders that Morgan had ordered they build. By mid-
afternoon the ladders were completed, and Gabriel walked
over to the wine shop that Morgan had taken over as his
headquarters. Noncommittally, Gabriel said, "The ladders are made. Now what do you intend to do?"

Morgan didn't answer him at once. Instead he turned
to one of his other lieutenants and muttered, "Gather up
all the holy folk of Rome and have them brought here."
After the man had left, Morgan sent Gabriel a considering glance, then dropped his gaze, almost as if he feared
Gabriel might read what he planned. Forcing a hearty
note in his voice, he said, "You'll see soon enough, what
I plan, me boyo. Just remember before you condemn me
though that desperate situations call for desperate means.
There is only one way we can take the fortress without

having our men cut down like sheep in a slaughter yard. . . ."

It wasn't until Gabriel saw the assembled priests, monks and nuns in their long black robes, laboring under the heavy ladders as they stumbled and walked in the direction of Santiago that he realized what Morgan was planning. Whipping around to look at Morgan, his handsome face full of horror and disgust, he cried, "You're going to use them as a living shield—hiding our men behind them!"

The black eyes unreadable, Morgan slowly nodded his head. "Aye, I will! But don't concern yourself over them—the men of Santiago will not dare to fire upon their own priests."

Morgan started to stride away, but Gabriel caught his shoulder. "Harry, you can't! What if they don't hold their fire?"

Gently Morgan removed Gabriel's hand from his shoulder. Staring intently into Gabriel's eyes, he said fiercely, "I intend to take Santiago no matter what the cost, and if it must be paid in the lives of those"—he gestured at the straggling line of priests and nuns—"then, by God, I'll do it!" Looking away, he added gruffly, "Your conscience is too delicate, sometimes, Dark Angel. You forget that *all* Spaniards are our enemies—no matter what the cut of the cloth they wear." Turning away, Morgan stumped determinedly in the direction of Santiago.

Face flushed with anger and an odd resolution, Gabriel took a step forward, only to be stopped by Zeus' powerful grip on his arm.

The light brown eyes full of understanding and warning, Zeus said quietly, "Do not, *mon ami.* You cannot stop him, and if you think to challenge him, you will only die."

Furiously Gabriel glared at his friend and snarled, "Oh? Instead I am to stand idly by and watch this monstrous atrocity take place? I'd sooner meet the devil! Now, loose my arm and get the hell out of my way!"

Sadly Zeus regarded him and then reluctantly released him. Gabriel spun away, intent upon catching up with Morgan, only Zeus' deep voice stopped him. *"Mon ami!"* Zeus cried softly, and instinctively Gabriel swung around to face him. It was the last thing he remembered for a long time as Zeus' iron fist exploded under his jaw.

When he awoke a few hours later in the wine shop that Morgan had used as his headquarters, his head was aching abominably. He found that he was lying on a wooden table, and groggily he stared around him. The shop was empty, all signs of Morgan's brief stay within gone; and as he sat up, he became aware of the sounds coming in through the doorway—the splintering noises of doors being broken down, the screams and pleading of women and the shouts of coarse drunken laughter as the buccaneers raped and pillaged the town.

With a groan he sat up, gently touching his bruised chin, realizing from the sounds of the raucous carousing outside that the battle for the city was over . . . that Santiago must have fallen and that Puerto Bello was now completely in the less-than-kind hands of the buccaneers. The debauchery would no doubt be in its full, fierce glory, and with a strangely heavy spirit, he reached for his cutlass that lay nearby and swung his feet off the table.

A slight movement near the doorway caught his eye, and instinctively his hand tightened on his sword as he whirled in that direction. Zeus, his expression just a bit uncertain, loomed in the entrance and a note of coaxing in his voice, he said, "Ah, *bon!* You are awake at last and ready to forgive me my most necessary action, *oui?*"

Gabriel shot him a look that spoke volumes, but knowing that in the same situation with positions reversed, he would have duplicated Zeus' act, he nodded his aching head and growled, "Someday, my large friend, you are going to overstep yourself." At the huge smile that curved Zeus' mouth, he added caustically, "And don't think for one minute that you've heard the last of this incident!"

Zeus nodded his shaved head vigorously, replying with a blandness that didn't fool Gabriel for one moment. "Oh, *oui, mon capitaine!* It was most unworthy of me and you have every right to be angry. I don't know what overcame me. . . ." He sent Gabriel a sly look and added dulcetly, "Unless, of course, it was the desire to keep you from killing yourself."

Gabriel's mouth twisted, acknowledging the truth of Zeus' statement. Pushing away from the table, he walked toward the door. Stepping outside in the fading light of dusk, he asked, "How bad was it? Did we lose many men? And the church people . . . did many die?"

Following him outside, Zeus answered reluctantly, "It took a little longer than any of us thought it would, but we didn't lose as many men as we could have." He hesitated, shot Gabriel a quick, assessing glance and then said bluntly, "The holy folk took the main barrage. The commander of Santiago didn't spare them—he ordered his men to fire and to ignore the pleadings of the priests and nuns for protection as Morgan forced them up ladders, hiding our men behind them."

Gabriel made no reply. What could he say? Perhaps Morgan was right, perhaps his conscience *was* a little too delicate. Shoving the unwelcome thought aside, he inquired disinterestedly, "And now? With the city ours, what does Morgan plan next?"

Zeus grinned. "Except for pickets to stand guard, Morgan has turned the men loose—we do as we please. Some of the men found the dungeons where the Inquisition had been at work on more captured Englishmen, and they now are using the instruments of torture discovered there to, ah, persuade the Spaniards to tell us where they have hidden their treasures. Others, as you can tell, are busy drinking and, willing or not, enjoying the charms of the women of the city."

When Gabriel remained silent, Zeus sighed. He had never quite understood why his captain, such a fierce fighter against the Spaniards, never took part in the savage reveling that usually followed a victory. Shaking his head at his captain's odd behavior, he said quietly, "Morgan expects us to remain here for several days—he thinks it will take some time to loot and plunder the town. He has ordered that the ships be brought into the harbor, but I have secured a fine house for us to use while we are here and the booty is gathered. Would you like to see it?"

Gabriel smiled slightly and nodded his head. Zeus understood him well and he was aware that the only fault his friend would lay at his door was his curious reluctance to rape and pillage. His smile faded, the emerald green eyes hardening. There was only one woman he had ever wanted to hurt, and she had unexpectedly trapped him in a web of desire, driving revenge from his mind. It wouldn't happen again, he thought grimly, wondering if the day would ever come when he would have Maria Delgato in his power once more. If that day came it would be different, *very* different, he vowed savagely.

The two men walked slowly through the city, Gabriel ignoring with a steely determination the brutal sights and heart-wrenching sounds that abounded everywhere in the stricken city. He was a buccaneer, he reminded himself harshly, and by now he should be immune to these unwanted feelings of pity for the vanquished. But the innate decency that dwelled within him recoiled from the ugliness of the fate of the women and children, and he wondered if the time for him to give up the buccaneer life hadn't come. Perhaps the taking of Puerto Bello would be his last foray with the Brethren.

Ahead of him in the littered street, Gabriel saw du Bois swaying drunkenly toward him. The Frenchman had two women, one on each side of him, his ham-like hands cruelly holding their wrists in a firm grip as he dragged them along with him. One was a slight female, who stumbled and fought determinedly every step of the way, and the other nearly topped her captor in height and fought with equal determination. Gabriel stared with astonishment at the taller of the two women, thinking she was the tallest female he had ever seen in his life. A veritable amazon, he thought with dawning admiration.

Zeus spotted the trio about the same time, and it was obvious from the note of awe and blatant admiration in his voice that he was quite taken with the amazon. "*Sacré bleu!*" he breathed reverently. "What a woman! I have never seen such a glorious creature! It would be a sacrilege for that swine du Bois to have her—I shall have to steal her from him!"

Just then the amazon broke free, and clawing at du Bois' eyes, she screamed, "Run, Maria, run, little one!"

The slight female aimed a furious kick at du Bois and joined in the attack. Drunk and caught by surprise, du Bois toppled under their combined attack. The two women, freed from his hold, unaware of the two men approaching, bolted right into the arms of Zeus and Gabriel.

Zeus made certain he caught the taller of the two, and

his light brown eyes full of appreciation, he pulled the startled woman closer to him, his powerful arms closing around her. "Ah, *ma chérie,* the pleasures we shall have together. The magnificent sons we will make together!"

Gabriel smothered the laugh that suddenly rose up in his throat at the astonished expression on the woman's face, but then he was too busy subduing the small bundle of fury that twisted in his grasp to pay the others any head. "Be still," he grumbled in exasperation as the little creature fought incessantly to escape his grip on her slim shoulders. "I don't intend to hurt you—despite what you may think. Now cease this foolishness!"

At the sound of his voice, the woman's head jerked back instantly, and her wide blue eyes full of utter disbelief, she stared up into his dark face. *"Englishman!"* she croaked stupidly. "You are not dead!"

Gabriel stiffened, his hold tightening fiercely, the emerald green eyes searching hungrily the lovely features of his captive. "Maria," he said slowly, savoringly. "Maria Delgato."

Chapter Ten

LIKE many of the terrified inhabitants of Puerto Bello, after hastily throwing on some clothes, Maria and Pilar had raced from the dubious protection of the inn into the streets of the city. Unlike many of the others, they were not captured in the first sweep through the city by the buccaneers. Catching sight of a villainous group coming their way, they had managed to avoid being caught by instantly hiding in a deserted stable not far from their inn. All through the frightful hours that had followed, they had remained hiding, their hearts beating at a frantic pace.

The sounds of the battle that came to them were not reassuring, and in time, they knew that the city had fallen, that the dreaded buccaneers had won the day. Their only chance for survival lay in escaping to the jungle, hoping to find others like themselves and praying that someone could make it through the miles of jungles to Panama City and alert the military of the terrible calamity that had overtaken Puerto Bello.

The hours spent hiding in the stables had been some of the worst Maria had ever spent in her life. Only the time following her parents' death and the demise of the Englishman had affected her so deeply, and then she had not been filled with such a feeling of utter terror and helplessness. She and Pilar didn't need to see it with their own eyes to know the fate of other females throughout the city; the screams and sobs of the women intermingled with coarse laughter and curses of the buccaneers came to them unpleasantly clearly as they lay frozen, concealed in the hay.

The staccato sounds of the muskets and pistols being discharged in the distance had made Maria flinch, and in helpless fear she and Pilar had clung to each other all during the long, nerve-racking hours of the day. Her voice dry, she had finally managed to whisper, "What will happen to us, Pilar? What can we do?"

Pilar's arms had tightened around Maria's small frame. She had dropped a kiss on Maria's head and murmured, *"Chica,* I don't know." She had hesitated and then asked quietly, "Maria, do you know what those men are doing to their female captives?" Painfully she inquired, "Do you have any idea of what to expect if we are captured?"

Maria slowly nodded her head, deliberately not admitting her innocence to ease Pilar's distress. She wasn't totally without knowledge, but she had only the vaguest conception of what went on between a man and a woman. The Englishman had awakened her sensuality that afternoon in the glade, but it had never been touched since, and she was very certain that what had happened between her and the Englishman was far, *far* different from what would happen if she fell into the hands of the buccaneers. She had shuddered, visualizing the cruel hands of some brutish stranger touching her as the Englishman had that never-forgotten afternoon.

There was not much conversation between the two women as the afternoon passed, and it was only when dusk began to fall that, after a hurried, low-voiced discussion, they had decided to risk leaving the safety of the stables. If they were very careful and *very* lucky, they might manage to slink undetected through the increasingly shadowy streets of Puerto Bello. They had embraced each other and Pilar had gently touched Maria's cheek; then, without another word, they had cautiously slipped out of the protection of the stable.

At first, luck was with them, and they had almost made it to the outer reaches of the city when a drunken buccaneer had suddenly erupted out of nowhere. In one swift movement, he had caught Maria and tossed her effortlessly over his shoulder, roaring his delight. *"Mon Dieu!* A sweet young *poulet* for my bed tonight!"

The buccaneer had not reckoned either with Maria's almost hysterical fight to free herself or Pilar's attack.

Like an enraged tigress Pilar launched herself at the astonished man, her not inconsiderable strength catching him unprepared.

While Pilar struck him again and again in his stomach, her shoes creating painful bruises as she kicked viciously at his shins, Maria was very busy doing some kicking and striking of her own, her legs flailing wildly about, and her fists hitting him with surprising force on the back and shoulders.

Attacked on two fronts, du Bois—for it was he—had unceremoniously dropped Maria on the hard ground and with a snarl had lunged after Pilar. Pilar almost got away from him, but he had caught a handful of her long, dark hair and had jerked her backward. She had fallen and he had aimed a brutal kick at her. The blow was cruelly effective and Pilar had nearly fainted from the pain that had exploded in her chest as his heavy foot made contact. Bravely, she had struggled to her feet, crying breathlessly, "Run, Maria, *Run!* Don't worry about me!"

But Maria could not have deserted her friend no matter what the danger to herself, and resembling a small, infuriated jungle cat, she had flung herself upon the powerful buccaneer, her fingers outstretched to claw. She had scratched several bloody furrows down his cheeks before he had been able to catch both of her hands in one of his. A satisfied smirk on his coarse features, he had surveyed her gloatingly. "I like a spitfire," he had muttered.

Pilar was nearby, swaying from the waves of pain that racked her body, but before she could recover enough to fight back, he had captured her two hands in his other ham-like fist. He had glanced from one to the other, assessingly taking in Maria's slender body and Pilar's handsome curves. His smile had widened. "Ah, tonight will be *most* memorable for us all . . . I, du Bois, will see to it!" He had leered at Maria, his long, shaggy blond hair sticking out like a lion's mane around his loutish features. "I shall take enjoyment from teaching you what a real man is like, my little firebrand." Looking then at Pilar, he had murmured suggestively, "As for you, you will learn not to be quite so quick with those hands and feet!" Dragging both women along with him, he had staggered off toward the center of town.

Maria and Pilar had fought him desperately every step
of the way, both knowing that unless they escaped immediately, any chance of avoiding the terrible fate he had
planned for them would be impossible. His drunken
lurches gave them both hope, and calling on all the re-
serves of strength that she possessed, Pilar finally managed to free herself and hurled herself at him, clawing at
his eyes, screaming again for Maria to run. And like her
first attack, Pilar's assault surprised du Bois and he took
an uncertain step backward. Maria was quick to take advantage of his surprise, and she kicked him soundly, jerking her wrists from his slackened hold. Unexpectedly du
Bois toppled to the street, and wasting no time, both
women picked up their skirts and petticoats and began to
run . . . right into the waiting arms of Zeus and Gabriel.

To say which of the two, Maria or Gabriel, was the more
astounded to see the other would have been impossible.
Maria had believed him dead, and yet at the first sound
of his voice, she had known instantly whose powerful
hands held her captive. The sapphire blue eyes nearly
black with the deep emotions that roiled through her
body, after her initial, involuntary words, Maria could
say nothing; she could only stare at the dark, lean face
above hers, searching those harshly attractive features
with the same hungry intentness that shone in Gabriel's
gaze.

It was both ecstasy and terror to feel his strong hands
painfully gripping her slim shoulders, and she was torn
between a feeling of incredulous joy that he lived and
utter dread that she was now the prisoner of a man who
had good cause to despise and hate the Delgato name. A
man who had good cause to seek revenge for the tragedies
her family had created for him. She studied his face a
moment longer, seeing for the first time the fine lines that
radiated from the hard, emerald green eyes and the uncompromising slant to his chiseled mouth. His face was
very dark, deeply bronzed by the burning tropical sun,
and between the strands of the thick black hair, she
caught a glimpse of the emerald stud in his ear, the gold
hoop earring glittering brightly as it swung near his lean
cheek. His features were far more cynical than she remembered, the green eyes colder and more penetrating,

the years among the Brethren of the Coast clearly having
left their mark upon him. There was an air of reckless
indifference about him, and risking one more glance at
the granite jaw and strong, square chin, noticing for the
first time the gold slave collar around his neck and guessing accurately what it represented to him, she trembled
slightly. Gabriel Lancaster had no reason at all to treat
her kindly, and she was now completely within his
power—his to do with as he pleased, and she found that
knowledge both strangely exciting and yet equally terrifying.

Gabriel's first coherent thought, after the shock and
savage delight of actually having her in his arms again
had lessened, was that she had grown up into an aston-
ishingly striking young woman. The passage of almost
three years had matured and sculpted her delicate features into a rare and unusual beauty. Not a classical
beauty, he thought idly with one part of his mind, but a
creature possessed of such an ethereal loveliness that he
found himself oddly breathless as he continued to stare
down into her upturned face. Set under slim, arching dark
brows, cat-slanted sapphire blue eyes dominated her
heart-shaped face, a fringe of long thick black lashes only
increasing their impact. A straight little nose, almost
haughty in its form; a full, enticingly curved mouth; and
a surprisingly firm chin and jaw only seemed to empha-
size the very delicacy of her features. Waves of tousled
midnight black hair cascaded from a central part on the
top of her head and brushed gently against her cheeks,
intensifying the alabaster clarity of her skin. His eyes
dropped, dwelling for a moment on the swell of her firm
breasts where they rose above the low-cut lavender bodice
she was wearing. She was very desirable, he admitted
slowly to himself, *very* desirable and she was his. . . .

Strangely enough, there was no thought of revenge in
his mind as he stared at her. Only a confusing, irrational
sensation of relief and pleasure. He had found her, the
child-woman who had haunted his dreams all these years,
the bewitching creature who had so befuddled his brain
that it was her face he remembered most vividly and not
that of his dead wife. He stiffened as that thought occurred to him, and it was only then that he remembered

the fierce desire for revenge that was never far from him.
His mouth thinned and he swore under his breath. Already the little witch was working her wiles on him, making him forget who she was, who he was and why he could
never feel anything but hatred and contempt for her. Deliberately he tightened his hold on her shoulders, making
her wince from the pain. "Fate," he said slowly, "does
indeed work in mysterious ways. And you, sweet witch,
will soon learn precisely what sort of fate I have in mind
for you—it will be no more than the daughter of a Delgato
deserves to suffer from the hands of a Lancaster."

Zeus had been very busy subduing Pilar, who, despite
the pain that still wracked her body from the vicious kick
delivered by du Bois, had fought spiritedly. But he had
finally won the day simply by his far superior strength.
Easily avoiding her lashing fists, he had caught her gently
to him, his powerful arms imprisoning her twisting body
next to his. *"Ma chérie,* do not fight me so. It is useless,"
he crooned softly into her ear. "You will only hurt yourself and that would make me very sad. Be still, sweet
Juno, and I will see that no harm ever befalls you again."

His voice had an oddly soothing effect upon Pilar, and
realizing the futility of continued resistance, she sagged
exhaustedly against his huge chest. *"Bon!"* he murmured, and then before she could guess his intentions, he
had swept her up into his arms. Looking down into her
apprehensive, furious features, he said gaily, "See! Is this
not better? Now, there is a fine house I will take you to
and you will be bathed and rested before we share the
delights of love together."

Momentarily the fight had gone out of Pilar, and almost
resigned to her fate, she looked up into his undeniably
attractive face. She was mesmerized by his sheer magnificent bulk, and as she stared dazedly at him, noticing
with vague interest that at least he appeared to be human
in spite of the gold hoop earrings in each ear, she was
aware of a queer feeling of relief. His shaved head caught
her eye and she blurted out, "You have no hair!"

Zeus smiled widely. "Petite, if you want me to have
hair, for you I will grow it. I am a very amiable fellow,
oui?"

It was at that point that Zeus heard Gabriel say the

Delgato name, and swinging around to look at his friend, he asked with surprise, "Delgato? Is that little creature the woman you have been searching for these past years? The sister of the whoreson Pedro Delgato?"

Gabriel nodded his head, the satisfaction he felt clear to see, but before he could make some reply, du Bois' voice interrupted them. Stumbling to his feet, the Frenchman lurched in their direction, shouting jovially, *"Merci beaucoup, mes amis,* for catching those two spitfires for me. When I am done with them, you may have them."

Gabriel's arm dropped to Maria's waist, pulling her to his side as he drew his broadsword with his other hand. The sword held menacingly in front of him, he drawled, "Wrong, my friend. The women are ours. You let them go and we caught them."

Du Bois' brutish features darkened and he howled with rage, *"Non!* They are mine! Me, I, du Bois, caught them and they are mine! Give them to me!"

The emerald eyes cold with the threat of violence, Gabriel replied flatly, "No."

"We'll just see about that!" du Bois snarled, his own sword drawn and ready, but catching sight of Zeus, who had gently lowered Pilar to the ground, drawn one of the pistols from around his waist and was now standing next to Gabriel, he faltered. His light blue eyes traveled frustratedly over the quartet, and he promised sourly, "You may have won this encounter, Dark Angel, but we'll just see what the Admiral has to say. Women are common property. You must share them."

Gabriel shook his head. "No," he said again in that same flat tone that brooked no argument.

Du Bois threw them a last angry glance and then spun away, the fury he felt obvious from his stride and the set of his bull-like shoulders. Watching the French buccaneer stomp off, Zeus said slowly, *"Mon capitaine,* we have not heard the last of this. He is right, women are common property. If we wish to keep them for our own, they will cost us part of our share in the booty."

Looking at him, Gabriel asked dryly, "Do you care? Do you want to use her and then give her to du Bois?"

Zeus glanced at Pilar, who hung limply at his side. His arm tightened around her slender waist and he shook his head in vehement denial. "No, she is mine. I will pay whatever price is put upon her."

"I too," Gabriel said grimly, pulling Maria even closer to him. Looking at her down-bent head, he muttered, "She is mine and *no one* is taking her from me!"

But du Bois was not going to let the matter rest, and before Gabriel and Zeus, greatly slowed by the exhausted, lagging women, even reached the house that Zeus had secured for them, they were met with a message from Morgan. His face grim and hard, Gabriel read the scrawled handwriting on the note handed to him by one of Morgan's buccaneer aides.

Crumpling the paper slowly in his hand, he glanced at Zeus and said tautly, "The Admiral wants to see us immediately . . . and with the women. Du Bois has lodged a complaint against us and Morgan wants it settled at once."

Without further conversation, Gabriel and Zeus, Maria and Pilar trudging helplessly along with them, stepped out at a brisk pace, heading for the former *alcalde*'s residence that Morgan had commandeered as his own for their stay in Puerto Bello. The handsome house fronted on the main plaza, and when Gabriel and the others arrived, the plaza was ringed by several buccaneers; many of them Gabriel recognized as belonging to du Bois' crew. Du Bois himself lounged arrogantly against the lip of the tall stone fountain that reposed in the center of the plaza, and from the smirk on his face, it was obvious he felt confident that he had already won the day. Morgan was waiting for them on the steps of the house, and with an abrupt motion he waved Gabriel closer to him. Leaving Maria to Zeus' tender care, Gabriel slowly mounted the few steps until he stood next to Morgan.

It was apparent from the way Morgan nervously chewed on his lower lip and the faintly uncertain expression in the usually confident black eyes that he wasn't quite comfortable with the situation. But whether the uncertainty had to do with his control over the buccaneers or concern over this first meeting with his friend since they had disagreed over the use of priests and nuns in the taking of Puerto Bello, Gabriel couldn't guess. He could tell nothing more from Morgan's face, and the firm clasp with which the other greeted him gave nothing away.

There was an air of tenseness about the plaza, but seemingly oblivious to it, Morgan cried jovially, "Come inside, my friend, and we will discuss this, er, disagreement that has arisen. I am sure," and he shot a quelling look in du Bois' direction, "that it can be settled without bloodshed."

Swiftly ushering Gabriel inside the house, as he shut the twin doors behind him Morgan growled, "This is a damned nasty business—du Bois has accused me of favoring the English buccaneers. You'll have to give up the wench and find another if I am to keep him from inciting the others." With almost a note of pleading in the deep, rich voice, Morgan added, "Surely, you can find another woman who will satisfy you as well."

Gabriel shook his head and said quietly, "No. She's Maria Delgato, Harry, and I'm not giving her up!"

Morgan appeared both pleased and dismayed. "Maria Delgato! You have found her at last! This is wonderful news—I only wish that you had caught her before that devil du Bois did!"

Knowing what the capture of Maria Delgato meant to Gabriel, Morgan swiftly abandoned any further thought of attempting to convince his friend to relinquish his claim to her—it would have been folly to do so and he was well aware of it. Besides, after what had happened this afternoon, he wasn't prepared to further test the bond of friendship between them, and recalling how they had parted, he asked abruptly, "Are you still angry with me for what happened during the taking of Santiago?"

Gabriel shrugged his shoulders, saying noncommittally, "It is over with now. I can't undo it, but I must confess to disliking your methods, Harry. It is one thing to fight and kill armed men, another to sacrifice helpless innocents—Spanish or not."

"Tell me," Morgan demanded harshly, "if sacrificing those helpless innocents, as you called them, and I would hardly call those that serve the Inquisition innocent! But if sacrificing them would have saved your sister and wife . . . wouldn't you have done the same?"

Although the situations were not similar, Morgan's

question was unanswerable, and Gabriel turned away, asking bluntly, "What do you intend to do about du Bois?"

For several seconds, Morgan paced agitatedly up and down the wide entranceway where they were standing. Finally, gently fingering his chin, he looked at Gabriel and asked, "Will you give up the other one? Perhaps I can persuade du Bois to be content with just the one."

A slight smile tugged at the corners of Gabriel's mouth. "It is not for me to say—Zeus has taken quite a fancy to her—he has sworn to keep her for his own."

"By God's blood! This is a hellish predicament!" Morgan burst out angrily. "Of all the females available, why the devil did the two du Bois captured have to be the only ones that will satisfy you and Zeus?"

Gabriel smiled crookedly and said softly, "Morgan, we're both willing to pay whatever ransom is put upon them. Shouldn't that settle the matter?"

"I hope so, but knowing that du Bois is ripe for mischief, just looking to cause trouble, and since it is out of the question for you to give the Delgato wench up, I doubt that anything less than splitting your head open will mollify him now. Unless . . ." He glanced again at Gabriel before asking slowly, "Unless Zeus might be convinced . . . ?"

"Ask him," Gabriel replied unencouragingly.

But a few minutes later, when they were once again outside and Morgan did just that, Zeus proved to be implacable. "Non! She escaped from him and I caught her—she is mine and I will pay the price for her."

Morgan's announcement that Gabriel and Zeus were willing to have whatever price was put on the women deducted from their share of the plunder seemed to satisfy most of the buccaneers gathered around the plaza. It was a fair bargain, and as Maria's identity began to filter through the crowd, many of the pirates understood and supported Gabriel's stance, his quest for revenge against the Delgato family being well known. But du Bois was not to be pacified, and pushing away from the fountain in one violent motion, he drew his cutlass and snarled, "Non! I will not accept this! We will fight for the little one—Zeus can keep his amazon! But I demand the younger woman and we will fight, now!"

Morgan threw Gabriel a helpless look and muttered, "So be it . . . but only until first blood is spilled, I'll not have buccaneer slay buccaneer!"

Maria had only been dimly aware of what was going on around her, too exhausted from the terrors of the long day and the astonishment of finding that Gabriel Lancaster lived. Dazed and numb she had followed blindly where he had led, wondering bleakly about what sort of fate he planned for her. Certainly not a pleasant one, of that she was positive, but not even the knowledge that she was his prisoner could dampen the sweet joy that flowed through her body at his touch upon her arm. *He lived!* Her Englishman had not died! When he had received the note and then had dragged her willy-nilly to the plaza, she had known that something was very wrong and when he had left her in Zeus' care and had disappeared inside with Harry Morgan, she had felt a spasm of pure fright knife through her vitals. What was happening? What was wrong?

Zeus must have sensed her fright, for with an almost kind smile on his big face, he had dropped a large protective arm around her shoulders and had said gently, "Do not fret, petite, he will be all right . . . and you need not fear that he will let du Bois have you."

In spite of the horrors of the situation she found herself in, there was something extremely comforting about Zeus' huge bulk, and catching du Bois' hot, greedy eyes on her, Maria swayed closer to him, glad of his intimidating size. From the relative safety of Zeus' protection, she glanced around her, avoiding du Bois' lascivious gaze. What she saw was not at all reassuring; the hard, brutal faces of the buccaneers who crowded the plaza filled her with an almost overwhelming feeling of panic. *Dios!* All that stood between her and their cruel hands was Gabriel . . . and he hated her! A shudder went through her, and it was then that Morgan and Gabriel appeared once more.

Events happened quickly after that. Maria barely had time to assimilate that Gabriel and Zeus were determined to ransom her and Pilar when du Bois had pulled his cutlass. Her heart had leaped in her breast as Gabriel had slowly descended the steps of the *alcalde*'s residence, his own sword drawn and poised. Ah, *Dios!* She could not bear it—just to have found him again, and now he was about to risk his life . . . for her.

The plaza was an eerie place as the two men cautiously circled each other. Twilight had fallen and several torches had been lit, the firelight flickering over the cobblestones, illuminating the savage features of the men who ringed the area. They were a terrifying group, their bodies fairly bristling with armament—pistols, knives, swords and pikes. Most had long, wild-looking hair that fell in unkempt glory to their shoulders; a few were, like Zeus, completely bald; some wore fashionable hats festooned with feathers, others wore knotted gaily colored handkerchiefs about their foreheads. Their clothing ranged from simple shirts and breeches to obviously stolen finery—silken vests and hose, satin doublets and collars of exquisite lace; but in one respect they were all the same; each face was clearly stamped by the wicked, barbaric life they lived, and Maria couldn't help the shiver that went through her. If Gabriel were to lose this fight . . . She swallowed and closed her eyes in a small fervent prayer.

At the angry sound of naked steel against naked steel, her eyes flew open, and with her blood pumping frantically through her veins, she watched with frightened eyes the ugly battle taking place before her. The torchlight that danced across the plaza clearly outlined the two combatants—Gabriel's black hair nearly blue in the wavering light, du Bois' blond locks touched by gold as they fought each other, circling around and around the arena formed by the press of the other buccaneers.

Fiery sparks exploded upward in the night air as their swords met and clashed time and time again, Gabriel gradually driving du Bois before him. Du Bois fought savagely, furiously parrying each thrust of Gabriel's blade, trying desperately to find an opening that would allow him to wound his enemy. But Gabriel wasn't about to let the other's sword touch him, and with a sudden feint he broke through du Bois guard, his sword plunging deeply into the Frenchman's right shoulder. Howling with mingled rage and pain, du Bois dropped his sword to the cobblestones, and with his left hand he clutched at the wounded shoulder. Blue eyes full of hatred and rage, he glared at Gabriel and swore, "Someday, Dark Angel, someday you will pay for this!"

Gabriel smiled wolfishly and bowed with an insulting flourish. "It will be my pleasure to meet you again, whenever you choose, du Bois," he said mockingly. Then, spinning on his heels, he walked over to where Morgan stood at the top of the steps of the *alcalde*'s house. A quizzical lift to his dark brow, he looked up and asked dryly, "Am I free to leave now? Or is there someone else who challenges my right to the woman?"

There were no further challenges, and moments later, Gabriel and his small party were once more heading for the house that Zeus had procured for them. Gabriel's arm was around Maria's slim waist, supporting her slender weight for most of the walk, but when they reached their destination, he suddenly surprised her by scooping her effortlessly up in his strong arms and carrying her into the elegant house. Stopping before the door of the rooms that Zeus had indicated would be his, Gabriel looked down at Maria, an odd expression on his features. Their faces were only inches apart as they stared at each other in the darkness, and Maria's heart began to beat very fast. She swallowed painfully and finally managed to ask apprehensively, "What do you intend to do with me?"

A smile, not quite kind and yet not quite cruel, crossed his handsome face. "I have every intention," he murmured huskily as he kicked open the door and walked into the room, "of finding out if revenge is as sweet as I have been led to believe it is."

Chapter Eleven

WITH one swift movement of his shoulder, he slammed the door behind them and slowly walked into the center of the room, glancing around him. The room was of handsome proportions, and he noticed immediately that an opened door at the far side led to a smaller connecting chamber. Glancing inside he saw a second door in the little room, and he guessed that it led to the main hall. Judging from the size and quality of the furnishings of both rooms, Gabriel thought, they had obviously belonged to the master of the house.

Against ivory-colored walls were set several pieces of dark, heavily carved Spanish-style furniture; on the scrubbed wooden floors were scattered brightly colored Moorish rugs; and dwarfing everything else was a huge canopy bed set upon a dais at the far end of the main room. The bed was draped with yards and yards of wispy, creamy-white mosquito netting, and walking up to the bed, Gabriel said dryly, "A bride's bower." Lightly pushing aside one of the filmy curtains, almost contemptuously he tossed Maria onto the enormous feather-filled mattress. She landed on her back in the center of the bed, frothy petticoats and rustling purple silk skirts flying in all directions. Determined to remain calm at all costs, once she had caught her breath, she raised herself up onto her elbows and solemnly regarded Gabriel, wondering what would happen next. Would he fall upon her like a ravening savage?

He was standing next to the bed, hands on his hips, the emerald green eyes traveling appreciatively over her slim form. Maria had no idea how very enticing she looked as

she lay there, her slender ankles and calves clearly revealed by her rucked-up skirts and petticoats, her firm
little breasts rising and falling agitatedly beneath the low-
cut lavender bodice. The lacy edge of her chemise framed
her bosom and shoulders, and the long black hair tumbled
in attractive disarray about her face and down across her
breasts to her waist. Her sapphire blue eyes were fixed
warily on Gabriel, the conflicting emotions she was feeling making them almost purple; the generously curved
mouth, despite its taut line, was a rosy invitation; and
staring down at her, Gabriel felt something stir within
him. Lust? Desire? Or some other, less fleeting senti-
ment? It made him angry that he felt anything other than
the need for revenge, angry that the increasingly apprehensive expression in her beautiful eyes dulled his sense
of enjoyment of the situation.

Against another man, Gabriel was a fierce, uncompromising foe, but when it came to women and children, he
could never bring himself to treat them with unnecessary
cruelty—the memory of his wife's senseless death and the
probable fate of his sister were constant bitterly painful
reminders of the innocent lives that were shattered so
needlessly. To his helpless fury he could feel himself softening toward Maria, and he was uncomfortably conscious
of an insane desire to take her into his arms, to comfort
her, to do something, anything, that would banish that
wary, apprehensive look from her face.

Grimly he jerked his thoughts away from the path they
were following, reminding himself coldly that the situation with Maria Delgato was different—she was no innocent bystander, she was his enemy, the sister of his
deadliest adversary. He would be a double-damned fool if
he let her apparent air of vulnerability sway him from
his purpose. Had Caroline's youth and beauty swayed Diego from forcing her into slavery and certain degradation
and death? No! And by God! He would not be swayed
either!

Infuriated with his confusing reaction to her, Gabriel
reached for Maria with ungentle hands, determined to
deny any emotion except vengeance. Ruthlessly he
dragged her up against his muscled body, one hand catching the back of her head and holding her twisting face

still; his punishing mouth found hers, his lips pressing almost brutally against hers.

He meant to be cruel, meant to act as callously as possible, to treat her with the disdain and contempt he had always promised himself that he would, but instead of it bringing him the pleasure he had dreamed of, he discovered that it was oddly distasteful and extremely dissatisfying. There was no enjoyment to be gained from what he was doing, and he kissed her with an increasing desperation, as if by sheer force of will he could make himself feel the joy this moment should bring him.

Angry and frightened at the same time by Gabriel's actions, Maria struggled violently to escape from his touch. His savage embrace awoke her from the dazed state she had been in since she had first felt his arms around her, had first heard his voice; and she fought wildly to escape from him. She battled fiercely, as fiercely as she would have if he had been du Bois, her fingers recklessly clutching at the dark hair on top of his head, her body twisting frantically to free herself from his hold. Getting a firm grasp of a sizable hank of his hair, she gave it a sharp pull, and with something between a yelp and a curse, Gabriel promptly released her.

His eyes were smoldering green fires beneath the scowling black brows as he glared at her across the short distance that separated them. Maria glared back, her bosom heaving, anger having momentarily driven away her fear. A tense, awkward silence fell as they glowered at each other, each one almost daring the other to make the first move.

Any other buccaneer would have beaten Maria soundly for her actions, beaten her and then raped her as casually as quaffing a tankard of ale, and Gabriel was gallingly aware of it. He was also furiously aware that he could not, as much as he had dreamed of it, planned it and hungered for it, treat her in such a brutal fashion. Oh, he wanted to, but something deep inside of him rebelled against degrading her in that manner. Enraged with himself at this sign of weakness on his part, he snarled something virulent under his breath, and spinning on his heels, he stalked out of the room, slamming the door with a thunderous bang behind him.

In openmouthed astonishment, Maria had watched him leave, and when the fact that she had apparently won this particular contest of wills dawned on her, with a little part-giggle, part-sob, she sank back onto her haunches. Dazedly she stared around her at the empty room. What would happen now? Would he desert her? Give her, she wondered with a shudder, to du Bois?

Gabriel had no such intentions of ridding himself so easily of her, but he desperately needed some time to come to grips with the unsettling effect she had upon him ... and the sweet dreams of vengeance he had nourished for years. She was his enemy, he reminded himself savagely as he stormed down the wide hallway in search of Zeus. She was his enemy, and by Christ's wounds, he was going to take his revenge upon her! She would not deter him later tonight! No matter how defenseless or helpless she looked! She would not make *him* feel the least contrite or compassionate! By God, she would not! He was through with those soft, emasculating emotions—hadn't they died the day his wife had? Hadn't he taken an oath to make the Delgatos suffer? Hadn't he rightfully earned the name of Dark Angel for his bloodthirsty pursuit of the Spanish? Why now, when the moment he had lusted after for so long was upon him, did he waver in his sworn resolve? She would not bewitch him again, as she had that day on Santo Domingo ... weaving silken chains about him to hold him prisoner until Perez and the others could arrive. Coldly, he reminded himself that the situation was different now—she was *his* prisoner this time and he was a buccaneer—and when next he walked through that door, he would show her absolutely no mercy! None!

Having just made that grim promise, catching sight of a frightened servant scurrying down the hallway, he called to him and somewhat tersely ordered that a bath be prepared for the young lady in the master's rooms and that some food and drink be taken to her. Sardonically he convinced himself that he was only seeing after her comforts to confuse her, to prolong the agony of suspense she must be feeling. But as he continued on his way, there was a black frown marring his handsome face as the disturbing thought occurred to him that it wasn't *just* the desire to confound her that had prompted his actions.

He was in a vile temper when he flung open the door to the large *sala* at the front of the house. Finding Zeus comfortably seated in a leather chair, slowly sipping a glass of fine Spanish sherry, did not soothe his exacerbated temper. Sending an unfriendly glance at his friend, he halted just inside the doorway and demanded nastily, "What! Not busy enjoying the charms of your amazon? Or has she proved to be a disappointment already?"

Zeus sent him a considering look, and seeing the baffled rage that flickered in the emerald green eyes, he gestured gently toward the heavy glass decanter of sherry that sat upon a long walnut sideboard. "Pour yourself something to drink and sit down, *mon capitaine,* and let us enjoy some of the lesser delights of our labors."

His bad temper vanishing instantly in the face of Zeus' calm words, Gabriel grimaced and did exactly as directed. A glass of sherry in his hand, he threw himself down onto a small sofa of embroidered leather and muttered, "Forgive my earlier greeting—I am in a foul mood."

Wisely, Zeus refrained from comment or question, and for several moments the two men sat quietly sipping their sherry, sherry that until this morning had belonged to the rich merchant whose house Zeus had commandeered for his captain. A tranquil silence spun out, and feeling himself relaxing for the first time since they had left the ships to embark upon this mad mission, Gabriel asked idly, "What *is* your amazon doing?"

A beatific smile crossed Zeus' face. "When last I left her, she was busy throwing anything she could lay her hands on in my direction. Not unnaturally, I decided to give her time to become more accustomed to her fate. Such a temper! And yours? What is your elfin beauty doing?"

Gabriel chuckled at Zeus' words and murmured, "My elfin beauty, as you call her, only tried to make my head as bald as yours—like you, I left her to consider her situation." Dryly, he added, "It is perhaps as well that Puerto Bello was not guarded by women, at least not by the likes of the two spitfires that have taken our fancy."

"And has she?" Zeus asked shrewdly. "Has the little Delgato taken your fancy? Or is it just the desire for revenge that makes her your prisoner . . . that brings her to your bed?"

Gabriel stiffened, Zeus' question coming too close to the mark. But there were no secrets between the two men, and his smile fading, he answered levelly, "I don't know. If I were face to face with her brother, there is no question of what I would be feeling, but she is a woman. . . ." His voice trailed off and an expression of bewildered anger crossed his face.

His reply seemed to answer some question of Zeus', for the other man gave a grunt of satisfaction and said jovially, "Enough of this talk of revenge—I long for nothing more than a good meal, a hot bath and a warm woman in my arms . . . and in that order!"

With his commandeering of the house, Zeus had also laid claim to several servants, and within a short time, he and Gabriel had been served a rather pleasant repast in the spacious dining room across the hall from the *sala.* Tossing aside the chicken leg he had been eating and glancing around again at the elegant appointments of the room, Gabriel remarked thoughtfully, "Your merchant must have been extremely wealthy. The house, servants and furnishings are worthy of a lord."

Zeus nodded his head. *"Oui,"* he said slyly. "I wanted something that would please you—especially since I had just given you that gentle tap on the chin."

Gabriel grinned at him and raised his wineglass in a toast. "I owe you one of those, my large friend. Be warned."

Zeus raised his own glass in salute and drank heartily, apparently not a bit concerned by Gabriel's threat. They sat there discussing the day's events for quite some time and then fell into a friendly wrangle over who *really* wanted to bathe first in the former owner's rare and prized copper tub. Gabriel finally convinced Zeus that he did indeed wish to enjoy more of the merchant's fine wine before retiring for the evening. With a smile of anticipation on his large face, Zeus ambled out in search of the tub and servants to heat and bring him water.

Finishing his second glass of wine in pleasant solitude, Gabriel wondered at the stroke of luck that had brought Maria Delgato into his power. To think that he had searched the entire Caribbean, always hoping to find her, and yet when he least expected it, she ran right into his arms! Not even to himself would he admit that he *had* been searching for her and that his reasons for wanting her to be his captive had very little to do with wanting to take revenge. Refusing to speculate about the state of his own emotions, he preferred to savor this moment of triumph, and he smiled faintly as he recalled the look of astonishment on her face when she had realized who held her prisoner. He stood up from the table, suddenly eager to see her again, eager to assure himself that she was truly his captive, that she waited for him just down the hall and that she had not been some fevered image from a dream.

But first, like Zeus, he too went in search of the copper tub, the idea of his first real bath in weeks very appealing. To his pleasure he discovered that Zeus had finished his own bath several moments previously and had ordered that the tub be placed in the small room that adjoined Gabriel's chambers. More water had also been heated in anticipation of his needs, and so in a matter of minutes, Gabriel was comfortably submerged in soapy water to his chest, a large bar of sweetly scented soap in his hand. He had wrinkled his nose at the spicy scent, but then had shrugged his shoulders. At least there was soap available, and if he smelled like a fop mincing through the corridors of Whitehall, so be it.

Clean clothing had proved to be no problem; several trunks of confiscated garments had been brought to the house earlier, and Gabriel had selected a rich robe of fine russet silk to put on after his bath. He had just wrapped the garment about him and was absently rubbing his freshly washed hair dry when there was a tap at the door that opened onto the main hallway. At his command to enter, he was somewhat surprised to see Zeus, a sheepish expression on his face, walk into the room.

At Gabriel's quizzical lift of an eyebrow, Zeus muttered, "I have no intention of spending the entire night subduing her—she has promised that she will be loving and docile if I allow her to talk to you first. She has sworn that she will not try to escape or kill me during the night, if I will just grant her this one request."

A gleam of laughter in his eyes, Gabriel said mockingly, "Then by all means, I must talk with this fierce creature of yours. It would sadden me to find your dead body in the morning."

Zeus grinned at him, both of them knowing the ridiculousness of that statement, but it was also obvious to the meanest intellect that Zeus was deeply enamoured of his amazon and was prepared to indulge her outrageously. Another woman would have discovered by now precisely how ruthless he could be and how very much he disliked not getting his own way; but somehow Pilar had managed, in a matter of hours, to slip beneath his guard and he was clearly putty in her hands.

With a great deal of curiosity, Gabriel watched as Zeus ushered Pilar into the room. She was, he noticed again, a magnificently endowed woman, and with her tall, queenly stature, fine dark eyes and handsome features, it was apparent why Zeus was under her spell. She was also, Gabriel decided admiringly, very brave as she marched right up to him and demanded fiercely, "You must not hurt her! She is very young and innocent and she does not fully understand the ways of a man with a woman."

For Zeus' sake, Gabriel was prepared to humor her, but there were some areas in which he would tolerate no interference, and his relationship with Maria was one of them. The emerald green eyes shuttered, he replied dryly, "I think that you forget your position in this household. I also think that you forget that Maria Delgato is *mine* and I will treat her as I wish!"

Aware of the dangerousness of her situation, aware that she and Maria were being treated with far more respect and kindness than they could have ever dreamed, considering the circumstances, Pilar bit back the sharp retort that automatically sprang to her lips. This tall, arrogant man wasn't about to be swayed from his plans for Maria, and Pilar swiftly abandoned her militant stance. The dark eyes full of pleading, she said simply, "She is a virgin, *señor*—be kind to her, that is all I beg of you. Be gentle."

An almost imperceptible nod of his dark head was her only answer, and with that she had to be content. To her amazement Zeus had honored the desperate bargain she had struck with him, and now there was nothing else she could do to help Maria. But Pilar's spirit was a little lighter as she allowed Zeus to escort her from the room.

This Gabriel Lancaster was obviously a man of good birth and breeding; he was also extremely handsome, handsome enough, she thought slowly, to steal any woman's heart. If he was the tiniest bit kind to Maria, she had no doubt that Maria would not find the night that was to come the ordeal it so easily could have been. As for herself, she smiled faintly. Zeus was clean, he had already shown that he was not entirely without finer feelings and he was certainly not *un*attractive. Who knew what pleasures she might find in the strong arms of this half-gentle, half-savage giant. . . .

If Pilar had known of the leap Gabriel's pulse had given at her words, she would have laughed at her worries over Maria's fate. Gabriel might tell himself that it was revenge that was driving him to Maria's bed, that the reason he was so pleased by what Pilar had revealed was because it made his revenge that much sweeter, but there was a part of him that knew he was only deluding himself. Unwilling to think any deeper on the subject, with an odd eagerness, a bridegroom's eagerness, he opened the door that led to the bedchamber.

The room was in darkness except for one small candle that flickered on a table near the bed. Quickly crossing the room, he stopped when he reached the bed, one hand slowly lifting the drape of netting. The candlelight danced across Maria's sleeping form, and Gabriel was conscious of a queer jolt in the region of his heart as he looked down at her.

She was very lovely as she slept, a faint rosy flush staining her cheeks, the long black hair curling near her temples, increasing the alabaster whiteness of her skin. The tropical night was warm, and she had tossed aside the sheets and coverlet, the slender shape of her body clearly revealed beneath the thin, silken chemise that had been provided by one of the servants from the trunks of clothing. As Gabriel stood staring down at her, he was aware that she aroused emotions that he had never before experienced, that not even on his wedding night had he come so eagerly to the bridal bed. That thought confused him and angered him too, as much because he wanted to feel nothing but the satisfaction of at last extracting a measure of revenge against the Delgatos, as because the

knowledge that had the vendetta between their families
not existed, he would have still wanted her, would have
still fought du Bois for the right to claim her as his captive. It was unsettling knowledge, and there was a faint
frown on his forehead as he continued to stare down at
her sleeping features. What was there about her that
twisted his emotions, that made him forget thoughts of
revenge when he looked at her and left him only with the
desire to taste again the sweetness he had known that
afternoon on Santo Domingo? He could find no answers,
and with a snort of exasperation at his own muddled
thinking, he shrugged aside his robe and slipped swiftly
into the bed.

Maria stirred a little in her sleep as he moved closer to
her, and almost as if sensing that she was no longer alone,
she slowly opened her eyes. Catching sight of his lean face
only inches from hers, she smiled sleepily and muttered,
"Englishman! You were gone such a long time—I thought
that you had deserted me!"

Involuntarily Gabriel smiled back at her, and pulling
his arms around her, he pulled her next to him. "Desert
you? Never! Not when I have yearned to have you right
here for so long!" That he was speaking a deeper truth
than he knew never occurred to him; he only knew that
she felt warm and sweet in his arms and that he very
much wanted to kiss that soft mouth so close to his. Gently
his lips found hers and he kissed her with an unexpected
tenderness that surprised both of them.

Still half-asleep, not even aware of what she had said,
Maria responded instinctively to the tenderness of his
kiss. She *had* feared at first that he had deserted her, but
the arrival of the tub and food had lessened her fears if
not her confusion. When the hours had passed and he had
not returned to her, she had grown apprehensive once
again, but worn-out from the terrors of the day, she had
fallen asleep only minutes before he had joined her in the
bed. That he was with her now, filled her with an odd
contentment, as if she could face anything as long as he
was near; and the startling warmth of his kiss seemed to
banish all her fears of the future. She was his prisoner,
his to do with as he pleased, and while that knowledge
should have filled her with fright and despair, as he con-

tinued to kiss her so sweetly she decided hazily that perhaps being his captive wasn't such a terrible fate after all.

Unlike Gabriel, Maria suffered from no illusions about what she was feeling: this man had always fascinated her; from the moment she had first seen him aboard the *Santo Cristo,* he had awakened some deep emotion within her, and she knew that what she felt for him was unique, that no other man had ever, or would ever, make her feel like this again. She didn't call it love, she only knew that when she was in his arms nothing else mattered—not the fierce enmity between their two families, not the wrongs that had been done through the years; nothing mattered but here and now, and with all the warmth and generosity of her loving nature, she returned his kisses, eager to become a woman in his arms—and *damn* the reasons that brought them together this night.

As it had that afternoon on Santo Domingo, Maria's uninhibited response surprised Gabriel, surprised and delighted him, his blood leaping in his veins as she warmly returned his kiss, her soft body molding itself to his. He could feel the heat of her skin through the thin chemise that separated them, and with impatient hands, he quickly stripped it from her body, groaning with satisfaction when he pulled her back against him and her naked flesh touched his. Her skin was like silk, and pleasurably he gently kneaded her shoulders, his fingers moving with a slow, rhythmic pressure.

Sighing her enjoyment at his touch, Maria arched her back like a small cat, unconsciously pushing her upper body against the soft, black curls that covered his chest. Her breasts suddenly felt full, the nipples hardening and tingling as she moved against him, and she instantly became aware of a burning heat spreading languidly up through her entire body. His long legs were pressed next to hers, and between their locked forms, she was extremely conscious of his warm, rigid manhood pressing intimately against her belly. Driven by instincts she had no control over, her hands traveled hungrily over his muscled body, and she reveled in the sleekness of his skin, of the power of that lithe form so near hers.

Those soft, gentle hands, moving so lightly up and down

his spine, were a sensual delight to Gabriel, and unable to control the passion that was building so powerfully within him, he sought a deeper intimacy, his lips parting hers, his tongue seeking and finding the moist, exciting warmth within. He kissed her with a growing intensity, his exploring tongue filling her mouth, enflaming both of them as his hands reluctantly left her shoulders and slid to her breasts. Gently, he cupped the firm flesh, his thumb deliberately caressing one nipple as he stroked and fondled her, but he was hungry for the taste of those sweet buds, and leaving her mouth, his lips scorched a path to her breasts.

His mouth was warm and insistent as it moved across her nipples, tasting one and then the other, his teeth arousing Maria even more as he teased and suckled the swollen tips. Her breathing was uneven, her heart hammering in her chest, her body feeling as if it were being consumed by fire as his tongue lightly flicked across the sensitive nipples, and helplessly her fingers tangled in his dark head, pulling him closer, wanting him to kiss her, wanting him to continue what he was doing, wanting, wanting. . . .

Feverishly she twisted up against him, and when he threw one leg over her to still her restless movements and his bulging shaft rubbed erotically between her thighs, she moaned with pleasure and frustration. This was a sweet madness that had possessed her and she wanted it to go on, but there was an increasingly demanding ache in her loins that overpowered all other sensations, and helplessly she moved against Gabriel.

Gabriel was deliberately prolonging the moment until he possessed her, deliberately arousing her until she was wild with desire, determined that when he at last joined their bodies together they would both find pleasure in the moment. But he was so hungry for her, so full of an urgent need to drown in the sea of ecstasy he knew awaited them, that every time Maria's twisting body touched him, he nearly lost control. His mouth leaving her breasts, he caught her earlobe gently between his teeth and muttered thickly, "Be still, my little Spanish tiger. Be still so that I may pleasure us both." He gave a breathless laugh and added, "After tonight, you have no fear of tardy behavior on my part! But until you are fully a woman, I do not want to move too quickly."

Maria stilled instantly at his words, and her eyes big with astonishment, she asked shyly, "You know?"

An almost-tender smile curved his chiseled mouth as he looked down at her flushed features. Gently he kissed the corner of her lips and murmured, "I know. And later, I'll tell how . . . *much* later."

Not giving her time to question him further, his mouth found hers again, and he kissed her with a passionate intensity that plunged them both back into a warm, sensual world inhabited only by lovers. But there was a fevered urgency about his movements, his hands skimming hungrily over her flesh, teasing and fondling as they traveled from her breasts, down across her flat stomach to the junction of her thighs.

When he touched her there, Maria's breath caught in her throat, and she knew a moment of apprehension, but Gabriel muttered softly against her mouth, "Don't be frightened. I'll be as gentle as I can—and if I do hurt you, it will only be this one time." He kissed her deeply, his tongue probing against hers, and then lifting his mouth from hers, he added huskily, "After tonight, it will never hurt again, sweetling—it will only become more pleasurable."

With a slow, sensuous movement, Gabriel's hand moved through the tight little curls, gently stroking and caressing her, arousing her virgin passion unbearably, causing her to push up against the invading fingers, eager to know his full possession. His kisses became more and more demanding, and with the same hungry urgency that drove him, Maria kissed him back, her tongue flicking excitedly against his.

Gabriel could bear it no longer and he shifted slightly until his body slipped between her legs. Gently he pushed her thighs further apart, one hand sliding beneath her to lift her hips slightly, the other parting the soft flesh, gently probing and preparing the way for his possession.

Maria was lost in a maelstrom of sensations. The headiness of his kisses, the warm masculine scent of his body, the voluptuous movements of his hand made her entire body ache with the need for fulfillment, and helplessly she surged up against his probing fingers, her hands pulling him even closer to her. She felt him move slightly, and then to her intense pleasure she was breathlessly aware of the shaft of warm, male power slowly entering her. Her body trembled from the very sweetness of that invasion, and eager to have all of him, she arched up, desperately wanting more than his teasing thrusts within her.

Maria's movements were nearly his undoing, and the silken heat of her body as she so ardently accepted him was the most intensely sensual feeling he had ever experienced in his life. Groaning his pleasure, he cupped her buttocks, and with a control he had not known he possessed, he slowly slid his full length within her.

His taking of her had been so gentle, so sweet that Maria felt only one tiny jab of pain as his body completely possessed hers. She was stunned by the pleasure that flooded her being at knowing that she was now a woman, that her Englishman had been the man to take her virginity, and erotically she arched up to press herself even nearer to his hard, warm body.

At her actions, Gabriel's hands tightened on her buttocks, and almost lazily he began to move on her, his movements making Maria stimulatingly conscious of how totally he filled her, how powerfully built a man he was and how much more pleasure there was to experience. The demanding ache that had been voraciously growing within her loins seemed to intensify with every stroke he made, and she found herself instinctively rising to meet his every thrust. She was on fire, helplessly assaulted by a wonderfully fierce emotion that had her writhing wildly beneath him, sobbing out loud her pleasure every time their bodies met. Suddenly, when she thought she would go mad with the pleasure that was shooting through her, the wildness within her seemed to explode in a glorious feeling of rapture, and Maria's small frame trembled from the force of her ecstasy.

Her soft cries of gratification sent a shudder of delight through Gabriel, and groaning his own satisfaction, he let the frantic urgings of his body control him. Passionately he drove himself faster and deeper into her fiery sheath, his body stiffening with indescribable pleasure when at last he too knew fulfillment and spilled his seed.

Maria was only vaguely aware of his movements, she was still dazed from her own reactions, and it was only when he slowly slid from her body that reality came flooding back. But it was, at least for the moment, an exceedingly agreeable reality, she thought dreamily as Gabriel pulled her into his arms and lightly brushed a kiss across her forehead. As if it were the most natural thing in the world for her to do, she nestled next to him, her head resting comfortably on his broad shoulder. She might be his captive, she mused sleepily, but at present it was such a sweet captivity that she wondered how she could ever have dreaded it.

Chapter Twelve

GABRIEL was awake a long time after Maria had fallen asleep, and his thoughts were not pleasant as he lay there frowning up at the canopy overhead. By rights, tonight should have been very different: instead of sleeping so confidingly next to him, Maria should have been treating him with revulsion and repulsion, and he should be feeling great satisfaction at having shamed and degraded the daughter of the Delgatos. But such was not the case. . . .

How had it happened? he wondered frustratedly. When had his desire for vengeance changed? When Zeus' amazon had told him that Maria was a virgin? Or had it been earlier, when Maria had run into his arms, and he had been stunned by the feeling of savage delight that had coursed through him at knowing she was his captive?

He shifted his body slightly and scowled down at Maria's sleeping features. What was there about her that affected him as no other woman ever had? She had tormented his thoughts ever since that afternoon on Santo Domingo, and tonight her body had given him pleasure such as he had never before experienced.

He had made love to many women during the thirty-four years of his life, but none had ever made him feel the way this small creature at his side had . . . not even his wife. His lips thinned and he was aware of a deep sensation of guilt, as if it were not right that a Delgato woman could have aroused him more, pleasured him more, satisfied him more than his dead wife. Anger at himself and Maria gusted through him.

She is a witch, he decided with a baffled sort of rage. A witch whose touch makes me forget everything but the sweetness of her kisses, the pleasures to be found within the soft beguiling flesh. Even now, angry and frustrated, he could feel desire stirring in his veins, and silently he cursed his own folly.

There were all manner of excuses he could put forth to explain his conduct this evening, but none of them pleased him. Yes, she was young. Yes, she had been a virgin. He would even concede that she personally had never done anything to harm him—her only sin being born a Delgato. He could even argue that his kindness had come from the ridiculous hope that Caroline had known the same sort of gentle induction into womanhood that he had shown Maria this night, but he was cynically aware that those reasons had nothing to do with his inexplicable actions. Nor did it explain why Maria herself had responded so ardently to his embrace. . . .

She should have fought him, done everything within her power to keep him from taking her, but she had not done so . . . if anything she had encouraged his advances. His scowl increased and he knew an irrational desire to shake Maria from her sleep and demand to know why she had not defended herself against him. If he hadn't known for himself that she was a virgin, and he *had* known the moment he had vanquished the delicate membrane that was proof of her virgin state, he could have convinced himself that she was simply a wanton creature, easily aroused by any man. But that particular argument appeared ludicrous in the face of her untouched condition . . . unless, Gabriel thought stubbornly, she would have reacted to *any* man the same way she had him, virgin or not. He didn't like that idea, finding it distasteful, and furiously he pushed it away.

There seemed to be no answers to explain either his own illogical actions or Maria's sweet yielding, and a sense of great frustration boiled up within him. *Nothing* seemed to be going as his dreams of vengeance had led him to believe it would.

And yet, if Maria had somehow bewitched him, she could not banish his deep-seated need to avenge what Diego had done to Elizabeth and Caroline. His wife was dead because of *her* brother, his father had died at the hands of *her* father and his sister had been sold into slavery and

certain death by *her* brother—it seemed an ugly travesty
of justice that she should lie so trustingly next to him,
that he should allow her to do so and that he should have
taken such care in bedding her. Twenty-four hours ago,
he would have sworn in blood that he would as soon sleep
with a viper as have Maria Delgato share his bed and yet,
here they were side-by-side like husband and wife. . . .

Angrily, he turned away from her and the puzzles she
represented. His back coldly presented to her, he lay there
confused and enraged by the events of the evening, feeling vaguely cheated and, with masculine irrationality,
blaming Maria for his condition. It didn't help his state
of mind either when she moved closer to him, her slim
body gently aligning itself to his. To his annoyance, he
discovered he liked her there, and with a sigh of exasperation at his own vacillating thoughts, he gradually drifted
off to sleep.

When Maria awoke in the morning, she found to her
mixed emotions that she was alone in the huge bed, the
spot where Gabriel had lain during the night now cold
and unwelcoming. She was conscious of a faint disappointment and blushed when she realized that she would
have liked to have had him make love to her again. But
she was also glad of these moments alone to come to grips
with all that had happened to her in such a short space
of time. Yesterday, she had awoken to the horrifying
knowledge that the dreaded buccaneers were attacking
the town; she had spent the remainder of the day in terrified hiding; for some time she had been the prisoner of a
savage brute and she had feared that she would be ravished
by that same monster, but today. . . . Today, she met the
morning with the sweet awareness that she had become a
woman in the strong arms of the fascinatingly attractive
man she had thought dead these past years.

With a sleepy smile of contentment on her face, she
stretched and instantly became conscious of the slight
tenderness between her thighs, and she blushed again,
remembering explicitly what it had felt like to have her
body locked with Gabriel's. She didn't honestly regret last
night; if anything she was pleased to be a virgin no longer,
to know fully now what went on between a man and a
woman. She felt so much older this morning, so much

wiser, as if she had just discovered a brand-new world, a world of sensual delights, and she rather thought she was going to enjoy sharing it with Gabriel Lancaster. . . .

A little frown marred her forehead. She hadn't expected such kindness from him, and it suddenly occurred to her to question his motives for acting as he had. And to wonder how he had known she was a virgin—only Pilar could have known and told him. . . .

Pilar! With a little gasp of dismay, full of contrition that she had not given her friend's fate one thought until this moment, she sat bolt upright in the bed. What a wretched creature she was! Who knew what terrible things Pilar had suffered at the hands of that huge brute Zeus?

Realizing that she was stark naked, she quickly rummaged around the bed until she found the silk chemise that Gabriel had tossed aside last night. Hastily dragging it on, she had just scrambled to the edge of the bed when the door that led to the main hallway opened and the object of her concern strode confidently into the room.

Maria noticed instantly that Pilar certainly did not look as if she had suffered any great harm; there was a sort of soft glow about her and she was dressed in fine garments, her scarlet and black satin skirt rustling as she crossed the room. A hint of worry in her large dark eyes as they rested on Maria's lovely face, Pilar asked anxiously, "Are you all right? Did he hurt you? Was it very bad, pigeon?"

Maria flushed and looked away, saying shyly, "It wasn't very bad at all. He, he was very kind to me."

Pilar heaved a sigh of relief, but her eyes narrowed at Maria's reaction and words. Thoughtfully, she inquired, "Do you want to talk about it?"

Maria gave a vehement shake of her head, and Pilar, after a long, searching appraisal, said slowly, "I see." Unwilling to force confidences, but extremely curious about several things, she sat down next to Maria and remarked, "You knew him, didn't you? He wasn't a complete stranger to you, was he?"

An odd little smile curved Maria's mouth and she gently shook her head. "No, he wasn't a stranger to me . . . he was once a slave at Casa de la Paloma."

Pilar wasn't going to let the conversation stop there,

and in a very few minutes, she had the entire tale of the Delgato–Lancaster vendetta and the events of the past several years. But knowing the situation made the previous night's events all the more confusing and didn't explain Gabriel's consideration of Maria, or Maria's reaction this morning, and Pilar looked slightly confused as she stared at her young friend. "I just don't understand it," she finally muttered.

"I don't either," Maria confessed readily, "but I'm grateful that it was Gabriel Lancaster who captured me . . . and not the monster du Bois!"

Pilar made some vague reply, her thoughts very busy on the contrary actions of certain people.

A small silence fell and tentatively Maria asked, "And your night—was it simply horrid?"

A strange expression flitted across Pilar's handsome features, and Maria could have sworn that there was a hint of a blush on her friend's face as the older woman replied airily, "Oh, it was nothing *un*pleasant! *Señor* Zeus is not quite the savage he would lead one to believe, nor," she added darkly, "the malleable simpleton I first thought."

Maria would have liked to have known what was meant by that remark, but Pilar would say nothing more and instead began to consider their situation. A slim finger tapping her mouth, she admitted glumly, "I doubt that we have much chance of escaping from either of our captors—and realistically assessing the conditions in Puerto Bello at this time, I think we would be foolish beyond belief to attempt to escape their protection."

As leaving Gabriel was the last thing that Maria wanted to do, she wholeheartedly agreed with Pilar's assessment of their predicament, but that their situation was perilous at best couldn't be denied. And precisely what their future would be was something that Maria preferred not to contemplate at present. But it had to be faced, neither one of them could simply let events drift, and hesitantly, Maria asked, "Did Zeus give you any hint of how long they intend to be here? Or what his plans for you are?"

To Maria's astonishment, Pilar's face was suffused with a bright red blush, and the older woman muttered in a somewhat flustered tone of voice, "That dolt! He spent a large part of the night telling me of the sons we would have and talking utter nonsense about settling down on some miserable tract of land in Jamaica! He is mad! Completely mad!"

Maria sighed. How she wished that Gabriel had said something of that nature to her last night, and she suddenly realized with a start that their lovemaking could have created a child. Almost wonderingly she looked down at her flat stomach. Was his child even now growing within her? It was a disturbing and tantalizing thought. If she were to have his child, no matter what the future might bring, she would always have a part of him with her. But then her mouth twisted dejectedly. What a silly rabbit she was, letting her romantic nature carry her away with such *foolish* ideas. And they *were* foolish in the extreme—she was Gabriel Lancaster's *prisoner!*

Giving herself a firm mental shake, she asked abruptly, "What are we to do? What *can* we do?"

"At the moment," Pilar answered dryly, "we can do nothing but what our captors allow us to do." A brisk note in her voice, she added, "Zeus did tell me that we are safe as long as we remain in the house and its grounds. Apparently Lancaster has ordered several of his most trusted men to guard this area, so I believe that we can take him at his word. And provided we do not attempt to concoct any rebellious schemes amongst the servants, your young man has informed me that we may treat them and the house as our own." Sending Maria a sly look, she murmured, "Your Gabriel is very handsome and seems to have retained his gentlemanly qualities—despite his unfortunate profession!"

But Maria would not rise to the bait, and not meeting Pilar's interested gaze, she muttered, "What am I to wear? My clothes were all taken away last night, and I cannot go about wearing nothing but this!" And she gestured to the silk chemise that clung enticingly to her slender body.

Finding some proper clothing proved to be no problem; several things were selected from a few of the trunks of booty that were scattered throughout the house, and in a reasonably short period of time, Maria had washed and was appropriately attired in a soft rose-colored bodice with slashes of cream silk in the sleeves and a full, sweeping skirt of deep burgundy. Lace-edge petticoats rustled whenever she moved, and she deliberately tried not to think of the fate of the unknown woman whose clothes lay against her skin. But as the day progressed it became increasingly difficult for her to tamp her growing feelings of dismay and repugnance for the entire situation in which she found herself.

It wasn't that the powerful pull of attraction she felt for Gabriel was any less, or that she had experienced any great feeling of revulsion for him, it was simply that she was now becoming more aware of events outside of the personal ones that had so deeply affected her. As the hours sped by, the full horror of what had transpired in just less than twenty-four hours began to distort and cloud her judgment, and as her outrage grew at the bloody attack on Puerto Bello, it was only understandable that some of her indignation and abhorrence would spill over onto Gabriel.

In the beginning, with all the traumatic events she had experienced, it had been relatively easy to let herself be carried unresistingly along with the current; the savage buccaneer attack had been a terrifying occurrence, and then to discover so dramatically that Gabriel Lancaster was not dead had left her stunned, unable to comprehend truly what was happening all around her. That had been yesterday, and last night was only one small segment of the unreal sequence of incidents that she had been part of; but this was today, and the full enormity of what had happened to not only her, but to Puerto Bello itself, was finally, painfully seeping into her consciousness.

The house Zeus had commandeered sat on a slight rise above the city, and standing on the front portico, looking down at the blackened, smoking ruins of several buildings, the streets still littered with corpses and various smashed and broken articles, Maria was appalled at what she saw. The two heavily armed, burly buccaneers who stood guard at the bottom of the steps sent her hurriedly back inside, but even there she could not escape signs of what had transpired—the cowering servants who scuttled up and down the hallways of the house; the furtive, apprehensive glances they sent her way made her even more

aware that this was real . . . that her life and Pilar's, as
well as countless others, depended solely upon the cruel
whims of a band of cutthroat pirates! And *she* had lain
with one of them last night . . . eagerly given her virgin
body to him, had longed for his touch, yearned for him to
possess her. . . . Maria's face paled and she was filled with
remorse and guilt. How could she have acted that way?
While her countrymen were being ravaged, murdered and
tortured, she had blatantly given herself to one of the
very creatures who had caused their suffering. Even
worse—she was a Delgato and he was a Lancaster!

Her features twisted with distaste and contempt for
herself. She must have been insane! And remembering
how she had even fleetingly dreamed of his child this very
morning, inwardly she writhed with shame and anger. No
Delgato woman, she thought fiercely, would ever *willingly* bear a Lancaster bastard! Ever willingly allow herself to become the plaything of a Lancaster!

She was a disgrace to her family, a disgrace to the proud
name and heritage of the Delgatos! But not ever again,
Maria vowed passionately, her blue eyes dark with the
violent emotions that roiled through her, never again
would she lay eager and yielding in Gabriel Lancaster's
arms! When next they met, he would see a true daughter
of the Delgatos, not that weak, mewling creature he had
known last night!

Deep within her breast there was a part of her that
cried out violently against this harsh rejection of something that had been wonderful and sweet, but caught up
in the savage grip of outraged Spanish pride and the
equally savage sensation of having betrayed her family,
of having shamed the proud name she bore, Maria was
deaf to more rational thought. At the moment, she was
only aware of the carnage caused by the ruthless buccaneers, of the suddenly bitter knowledge that last night
she had given herself to the son of the very man who had
caused her own beloved father's death! Tears of rage and
shame flooded her eyes, and angrily she dashed those tell-
tale signs of despair away. She was a Delgato, not some
whimpering timorous creature!

As the day wore on Pilar noticed that Maria seemed
unusually quiet and withdrawn, and she was puzzled by

it. If Maria had greeted her with this attitude earlier, she would have assumed that it was caused by what had happened during the night, but Maria hadn't been so subdued, nor had there been that slightly grim cast to her fine mouth when they had met this morning. . . . No, then there had been an air of sweet satisfaction about her, and she had seemed oddly content with her situation. But not any longer . . .

Frowning, Pilar asked, "Maria, little pigeon, what is wrong? You have been standing there scowling at that unoffending rose for the past half hour."

They were at the rear of the house, on a pleasant patio, enjoying some late-afternoon sunlight. Like the house, the patio revealed its previous occupant's pride in his home. Glorious damask roses had been placed attractively around the edge of the flagstoned patio, and comfortable pine chairs were scattered about; an arbor covered with white jasmine blossoms was at one end, and not too far distant, the lush green foliage of the tropical forest pressed close.

It was undoubtedly a lovely place, but Maria found no pleasure in it; even from here, the raucous sounds of the carousing buccaneers could be heard. The faint smell of smoke still hung in the air and the sight of armed guards standing discreetly beyond the fringes of the patio did nothing to lessen her anger at the situation. Tearing her gaze away from a particularly beautiful crimson rose, Maria glanced over her shoulder at Pilar, who was sitting nearby, idly plying her needle on some half-finished bit of embroidery that she had found earlier. With almost an accusing note in her voice, Maria demanded, "Doesn't it bother you? The fact that we are prisoners, that our fellow Spaniards are being mistreated by these, these *savages?*"

Consideringly, Pilar regarded her young charge, the needle flashing in the sunlight as she calmly continued to sew. "What would you have me do?" she asked quietly. "Attack those hulking brutes over there?" And she nodded her head in the direction of the armed guards. "Or would you prefer," she went on reasonably, "that I do away with myself? Of course, I could try to kill Zeus when he is asleep tonight and escape into the streets where more dangers await . . . but do you really think that will help our situation?"

Frustration written all across her lovely features, Maria glared at her friend. Her hands forming two tight fists, she replied hotly, "We *should* do something! Not just stand idly by this way!" She gestured toward the ruined town and added, "They are suffering—why aren't we? It is wrong for us to be here safe, well fed and clothed in these garments." She looked down with revulsion at the rich burgundy skirt she wore. "The woman who wore this yesterday is more than likely dead . . . or down there enduring who knows what fate, while I, *I* wear her clothes and grace the bed of probably the very man who killed her!"

Pilar was not unmoved by Maria's words, but she was a survivor and a realist, and gently she said, "Maria, I don't believe that Gabriel goes about killing defenseless women, nor do I think that you are doing yourself any good torturing yourself this way. Don't you think that I don't grieve for our people? That I don't wish yesterday's attack had ended differently?" The dark eyes full of compassion, she continued, "But I cannot undo the past. I cannot change the present. At this moment I can only hope and look for the opportunity to help others less fortunate than we are."

Pilar's placid reading of their situation didn't resolve the conflict within Maria's breast, but it did have a calming effect. Some of the tenseness disappearing out of her small figure, Maria stated gloomily, "At least we don't have to *enjoy* our captivity!"

Raising a slim, dark eyebrow, Pilar asked, "Is *that* what is troubling you? The fact that you find our predicament not as *un*pleasant as it could have been?"

An attractive blush staining her cheeks, Maria turned her back to Pilar and stared out into the distance. In a low voice she muttered helplessly, "I don't know . . . probably."

Conversation lapsed after that, but Pilar's gaze was unhappy whenever it strayed to Maria. Life was never simple, and the choices one was occasionally forced to make were not always easy. She could understand Maria's feelings, and while she was far more cynical about the world, even she would admit to wondering if perhaps they hadn't surrendered to their captors too easily. She sighed and then shrugged her shoulders. If Maria were realistic she would realize that there really hadn't been any choice to make, and Pilar strongly suspected that the real root of Maria's angry frustration with the situation was because she was being pulled in two opposite directions—the dictates of pride and family honor ordering her one way and the promptings of her heart another. Only time and Gabriel Lancaster himself could furnish a solution. . . .

It was well after dark before Zeus and Gabriel returned to the house. It had been a long, grueling day for them, almost as dangerous as the previous day as they had lent themselves to the arduous task of consolidating and strengthening Morgan's already powerful grip on the city. While Puerto Bello had fallen to the buccaneers yesterday, there had still been pockets of resistance, and Zeus and Gabriel, along with others, had managed to finally annihilate the last of the stalwart defenders. It had been an ugly business, and both men were tired, grimy and bloodstained when they finally reached the house.

Pilar had smoothly taken over the running of the household, and to the two exhausted, hungry men, it was especially gratifying to find that water had been heated in anticipation of their arrival and that once they had bathed a hot meal would be instantly served. Gabriel said nothing, but he noticed immediately that Maria was notably absent. She had not been there to greet them when they came home, nor did she later join them for a meal in the dining room.

The green eyes hard and unfathomable, he looked down the long table at Pilar and asked in a disturbingly calm voice, "Where is Maria? Why isn't she here with us?"

For such a usually unruffled individual, Pilar suddenly seemed very uneasy and almost nervously she replied, "She said she wasn't feeling very well. She is lying down and resting."

Gabriel gave her a long, considering look. Dryly he murmured, "One hopes that it is nothing that will entirely incapacitate her for very long."

Pilar remained silent a moment, and then as if having come to some decision, she said forthrightly, "Señor, I know that we are your prisoners and that you have treated us very kindly under the circumstances, but I would beg that you make further allowances for Maria's youth and inexperience." The dark eyes asking for understanding, she added, "Maria is very proud ... and sometimes she lets the Delgato pride and temper overrule her normally gentle nature." It was as much as Pilar could say—she could hardly relate the heated argument that had suddenly sprung up between the two women when they had left the patio and Pilar had begun seeing that things were made ready for the men when they returned. While Maria might be willing to admit that they could do nothing to change their situation, she had been adamant about not doing one jot more than was commanded of her. The blue eyes flashing with fire, she had spat, "I may be his captive, but I will not make things comfortable for that English barbarian! And you, you should be ashamed at yourself for so tamely pandering to the needs of the enemies of Spain!" Appalled and distressed by Maria's reaction, she had watched unhappily as the younger woman had stormed off. And seeing the grim slant that now curved Gabriel's mouth, her heart sank. There was bound to be trouble.

A bite to his voice, Gabriel remarked, "You don't have to remind me of the Delgato pride—I am well aware of their arrogance!"

Pilar swallowed uncomfortably, damning her unfortunate choice of words, but Zeus, quick to stem a disagreement between his woman and his friend, finished his wine and, carefully putting down the goblet, murmured teasingly, *"Oui,* he knows a great deal about the Delgato pride—especially since it is only exceeded by the arrogance and pride of the Lancasters!"

A twinkle suddenly leaped to Gabriel's eyes, and a mocking smile on his lips, he said to Pilar, "I must warn you about that abominable creature who has claimed you—he always speaks the truth as he sees it, but he often neglects to tell the *entire* truth—in this case, while he jeers at my pride, he is silent on the fact that *his* arrogance far outstrips mine!"

The tense moment passed, and in spite of herself and the circumstances, Pilar found herself responding to the considerable charms of both men. They were both excellent raconteurs, and since the stories they told were carefully expurgated and none involved conflicts against the Spanish, on more than one occasion, Pilar found herself laughing delightedly. When the time came for her to retire she was amazed at how enjoyable the evening had been. It was only when she walked down the hallway to the rooms she shared with Zeus that she began to worry about Maria. If only the little donkey didn't allow her pride to force her to do something foolish . . .

Unfortunately that damnable Delgato pride wasn't allowing Maria to think very clearly, and while she had considered and discarded several wild schemes, she had finally had to content herself with stealing a small-bladed knife from the kitchens. Refusing to dine with the men was also another act of defiance, and munching unenthusiastically on some stale bread and sour cheese (it was all her pride would now allow her to accept from a Lancaster) in the darkened bedroom, she wondered about her course of action. One thing was certain—Gabriel Lancaster was not going to find the same willing creature he had last night, and she concluded rather gloomily that probably the most she could hope for was that he didn't kill her out of hand.

The rose-colored bodice and burgundy skirt had been, in another gesture of defiance, returned to the trunks from which they had been taken, and Maria had made a little vow that if she had to wear rags, she would accept nothing that had been pillaged from one of her countrywomen. She had traded the pair of sapphire earrings she had been wearing when captured to one of the servants for a clean shift and a few other articles of clothing.

On one level she was very much aware that her acts would be mere pinpricks to Gabriel, but she took a certain amount of satisfaction from them, and they seemed to soothe her troubled conscience. Even when her stomach growled protestingly at the meager fare she presented it with, she told herself grimly that there were others in the looted city of Puerto Bello who would have given much for her stale bread and sour cheese.

The dissension that existed between her and Pilar troubled Maria deeply. In all their years together, there had

only been the mildest of disagreements, and she was saddened and feeling a little forlorn about the rift that had
so suddenly developed between them. And as the hours
passed, as her stomach made her increasingly aware that
it needed more sustenance and the coarse cotton of the
servant's shift scratched her delicate skin unbearably, she
became a bit disgruntled with the entire situation. She
was hungry, she wanted a bath and she was lonely too.
The fact that it was also entirely her own fault was cold
comfort, but by reminding herself sternly of what others
were going through at this very moment she was able to
bolster her sagging resolve.

The sudden opening of the door had her sitting bolt
upright in the big bed and reaching determinedly for the
small-bladed knife. The moment of ultimate defiance was
upon her! Stiffened with an overabundance of Delgato
pride, she waited tensely for the hated Lancaster to touch
her.

The darkened room gave Gabriel pause, as did the
added advantage of Pilar's words. It hadn't taken him
long to discover the trade of the sapphire earrings and
the fact that Maria had so contemptuously returned the
clothing, and so he was already prepared for battle. The
problem was that he was in no mood for more fighting—
he had spent the day doing just that, and for the moment
he longed for nothing more than ten hours of uninter-
rupted sleep. The warm bath, delicious meal and several
goblets of wine had left him in a drowsily amiable state
and certainly not in a mind to fight—not even the tantalizing Delgato wench!

Stifling a huge yawn, he slowly walked across the room,
and reaching the table near the bed, he fumbled for a
second before he was able to light the candle that reposed
there. The flickering yellow light danced across the bed,
and somewhat gingerly pushing aside the voluminous
mosquito netting, he glanced inside.

Sitting on her haunches, garbed in a rough chemise
many times too large for her small frame, a knife held
menacingly in her hand and the brilliant blue eyes dark
with purpose, Maria awaited him. Gabriel thought he had
never seen anything more adorable . . . even if she was a
Delgato.

Tonight he was too tired even to wonder at his reactions to her, and keeping a cautious eye on the knife, he put one knee on the bed.

Maria, her heart jumping in her breast at the sight of him and not quite certain what her next move should be, promptly scooted to the far side of the mattress. If he touched her . . .

At her actions, a faint smile flitted across his face, and keeping a wary eye on her still form, he discarded his clothing and carefully climbed into bed. He lay there for a long moment, wondering what she would do, and when there was no further movement from the other occupant, he raised up and calmly blew out the candle. As the darkness descended, Gabriel murmured, "Good night, sweet tiger—we can fight in the morning." To Maria's frustrated astonishment he proceeded to fall asleep immediately.

Chapter Thirteen

LONG after Gabriel's even breathing told her that he was asleep, Maria sat there glaring in his direction. Her fingers grew cramped from holding the knife so tightly, and though she toyed lovingly with the notion of driving it deep into his arm, eventually she regretfully discarded the idea. Despite everything, she could not bring herself to harm him, and Pilar's words came back to haunt her— "I could try to kill Zeus when he is asleep . . . but do you really think that would help our situation?"

Even if she could have brought herself to strike out against Gabriel and could in some miraculous way escape from him, she suspected dolefully that her position would be even more perilous than it was now. Better the devil she knew . . . Confused, depressed and feeling just a bit silly, she finally lay down a short distance from Gabriel. Inexplicably exhausted, the knife unconsciously clutched to her bosom, after a very few minutes she fell into an uneasy slumber.

Her sleep was extremely restless the entire night, the raging conflict within her breast invading even her dreams. Images of her father and brother floated through her brain, their expressions harsh and condemning; the next instant it would be Gabriel's face that she saw, his mouth curved in a singularly endearing smile that lifted her spirits. She was constantly being torn in two—loyalty and affection for her family ferociously urging her in one direction, the powerful stirrings within her heart in the other. There were horrifying nightmares during the long night in which she vividly relived the brutal taking of the *Raven*, savage, ugly fights between her brother and Ga-

briel dominating the action: one time it would be Diego's
sword seeming to strike Gabriel a fatal blow and even in
her sleep she would moan softly in anguished denial; the
dream would change and then it would be Gabriel's sword
that mortally wounded her brother, a shaft of pain and
regret knifing through her as she slept.

Du Bois' leering face also danced through her unpleasant dreams, and though asleep she trembled with fear
and revulsion at the idea of his hands upon her. But it
was the ugly, violent duels between her brother and Gabriel that disturbed her the most, the torment she experienced then at its strongest, and she woke at daybreak
with tears upon her face.

As had happened the previous morning, she was alone
in the bed, but there was no feeling of contentment, no
joy in her waking. Listlessly she stared around the room,
longing for the turmoil within her to cease; almost longing to hate Gabriel Lancaster and all he stood for with
every fiber in her being . . . or for the feelings he aroused
in her heart to be so powerful, so strong that nothing else
would matter—not the past, not their warring families,
not even the long enmity between their two countries.

As she slowly slid from the bed, there was a sad little
smile on her lips. What she wanted was an immediate
solution to her dilemma, and she was very much aware
that it was highly unlikely to happen. Only time would
resolve the situation, and facing that fact squarely, she
straightened her shoulders and prepared to face the day.

After splashing some water in her face from the china
pitcher and bowl that had been placed on a marble-topped
washstand, she hurriedly dragged an ivory-inlaid comb
through her tangled locks, restoring some semblance of
order to them. Looking with disfavor at the unappealing
shift she had bought from the servant yesterday, for just
a moment she let herself think of the costly silks and
laces she could be wearing if she wished. But then reminding herself how those same articles of clothing came
to be in this house, her resolve stiffened, and with good
grace she slipped on the coarse garment. She was a prisoner and she would dress as one.

Pilar, of course, was angry and scandalized at Maria's
actions. Fruitlessly, she argued with her not to be such a

stubborn little fool, but Maria remained adamant—she was a captive, a slave, and she would act as one. Seeing the determined slant to Maria's full mouth, Pilar's heart sank, and with every passing hour of the day, Pilar's dismay grew. Not only did Maria refuse to eat at the dining table with her, she insisted upon sharing the rather meager and unappetizing fare of the servants in the kitchens. But even worse, grimly resolved to take nothing from the Englishman, Maria proceeded to spend the day doing various subservient tasks. She lugged several heavy buckets of water from the well at the side of the house; she helped sweep the halls with a rush broom; she carried in armloads of wood for the cook fires and graciously obeyed the meek orders of the thoroughly confused and greatly disconcerted *mayordomo*.

Maria worked with a sincere diligence the entire day, driving herself mercilessly, as if by doing these menial chores she could somehow erase the terrible sin of having given herself so shamelessly to the Englishman. Unused to hard physical labor, as the day drew near its close every muscle and sinew in her slender body ached unbearably and once again she thought yearningly of the pleasures of a hot bath. For a blissful moment she shut her eyes and visualized the scene; she could almost feel the warm water touching her skin, almost smell the sweetly scented soap. . . . With a regretful sigh she brought herself back to reality and clumsily struggled with one of the large buckets of hot water that had been heated in anticipation of the return of the masters of the house this evening.

It had been a long, exhausting day for her, the tropical heat, poor fare and the unceasing labor taking their toll of her slim resources. Limp wisps of hair clung to her forehead and cheeks, perspiration trickled uncomfortably down her back and there was a weary slump to her shoulders when at last she joined the other servants at the long, scrubbed pine table for their evening meal.

The servants themselves still weren't quite certain how to treat her, and while some of them had watched with admiration and some with scorn her activities during the day, most were unhappy and uncomfortable with the situation. Consequently, she sat in solitary splendor at one end of the table, the others carefully keeping their eyes averted from her and talking in soft tones to themselves.

A spicy paella bubbled in a pot hung over a corner of an open fire. Chickens were roasting over the main part of the blaze, freshly baked loaves of bread reposed on a nearby table and the kitchen was filled with delightful, appetite-tempting odors; but looking at the thin gruel that filled the wooden bowl before her, Maria felt her stomach lurch. Sour wine and stale bread were the only other accompaniments to the meal, and she was conscious of a great rage building up through her. *Her* servants had never been treated to such fare, and she counted it as another black mark against Gabriel.

There was a sudden commotion as the *mayordomo* bustled into the room and commanded, "José and Juan, bring those buckets of hot water—the masters are home and *Señor* Lancaster is in need of his bath. *La cena* is to be served within the hour."

Maria's throat was instantly inexplicably dry, and she swallowed with difficulty. *He was home!* And what was he going to think of her actions . . . more important, how was he going to react?

Even Gabriel himself couldn't answer that question—at least not immediately. Despite last night's rather tame outcome, he was fairly certain that Maria would not simply abandon her aggressive stance, and he had to admit that all during the day as he had helped to oversee the collection of booty and had visited with Morgan and the other buccaneer leaders, he had wondered with a sort of indulgent amusement what form her next act of rebellion would take. She was never far from his thoughts, and though he told himself it was because he was merely curious and that it was only normal that he savor the sensation of having one of the hated Delgatos in his power, there was a strangely eager lift to his steps as he and Zeus had made their way home that evening.

When Maria was again not there to greet him, he wasn't surprised, but he was aware of a feeling of growing annoyance. She was his prisoner and she should dance to the tune of *his* piping! Not take matters into her own hands! But he was in an extremely tolerant mood this evening—the day had been most pleasant, and as he had watched the magnetic Morgan charm the high-born Spanish ladies who sought the Welshman's protection, Gabriel had been struck by the sharp contrast between yesterday and the present. Yesterday he had been risking life and limb, while today he drank fine Spanish wine, had wandered at will through the fine house that Morgan had decided to occupy during their stay in Puerto Bello and had made idle conversation with the other buccaneer captains who had thronged Morgan's residence.

There was no longer any doubt that Puerto Bello was firmly in the power of the Brethren; guards had been posted at strategic positions and pickets patrolled the perimeters of the city. In the dungeons beneath one of the fallen castles, the instruments of the Inquisition were being used with great glee by the buccaneers to extort the hiding places of family jewels and gold from wealthy aristocrats and merchants, and the piles of booty grew with every passing moment. With the taking of Puerto Bello, Henry Morgan was undisputed Admiral of the Brethren, and while there could have been a few more galleons to loot, the plunder wrenched from the pillaged city was going to be more than satisfactory.

Being a captain, Gabriel's own share of the spoils, even with the ransom Maria would have brought deducted from it, would be quite high, and he was feeling very pleased with the whole situation. He had helped strike a humiliating blow against the Spanish, he had as his captive the daughter of the Delgatos and he had even begun to think that he had finally been recompensed enough for all the material things he had lost on the *Raven*. But only material things—*nothing,* he thought with a darkening brow as he slid into the heated bathwater, could ever repay him for Elizabeth's death, Caroline's unhappy fate, whatever it had been, or his own time of brutal enslavement on Hispaniola. Some of his tolerant disposition vanished, and he was suddenly conscious of a strong sense of savage frustration.

Vengeance still seemed to elude him—even Maria's capture had not given him the satisfaction he had been so certain it would, and he was only now becoming dimly aware that his desire to have Maria Delgato in his power had little to do with his thirst for revenge against Diego.

But he was unwilling to pursue that avenue of thought, and instead he focused on the real reason he had joined the Brethren in the first place—he had wanted Diego Delgato! He had wanted to meet the man who had killed his wife, sold his sister into slavery and certain death, with sword drawn. He wanted desperately to strike the crippling, killing blows for Elizabeth and Caroline that had been denied him that day the *Santo Cristo* had attacked the *Raven.* Only when Diego lay dying at his feet would the poisonous bitterness within him begin to dissipate. . . . And only then would he be able clearly to examine the emotions that Maria Delgato aroused within him—until that time, for his own sanity and pride, he *must* remember that she was Diego's sister, a Delgato, and that the Delgatos were the sworn deadly enemies of the Lancasters.

The bathwater had grown cold, and rising in one swift movement, he hurriedly dried himself and put on the clean clothing that had been laid out on the bed by one of the servants. Maria's absence from the bedroom didn't disturb him, but he had been quite positive that she would be waiting with the others in the dining salon. When she was not, his mouth tightened, and he ate the expertly prepared meal set before him in growing anger. He said nothing until the meal was finished, and then taking a long drink of his wine, he carefully set down his goblet and looking at Pilar, asked neutrally, "Where is Maria, tonight?"

It was the question Pilar had been dreading he would ask ever since he had arrived home. She had considered explaining the situation to Zeus, but she had been uncertain what good that would have done, and at any rate, she was so used to handling Maria's and her own affairs that it never occurred to her that Zeus might have been able to avert a clash between Maria and Gabriel. Putting down her knife, she glanced at Gabriel and said quietly, "I believe she is in the kitchen."

"Oh?" Gabriel remarked, his eyebrow lifting questioningly. "And what is she doing in the kitchen that is of such importance that it keeps her from dining?"

Pilar took a deep breath and murmured, "I really couldn't say . . . I haven't seen her all day. I would suggest, however," she added cautiously, "that if you wish to know what she has been doing you go ask her yourself."

Gabriel's eyes narrowed, and rising from his chair in one swift movement, he began to stride from the room. As he reached the door, he said over his shoulder, "And that, madam, is precisely what I intend to do!" He glanced at Zeus and said, half-serious, half-mocking, "If I were you I'd beat her—her tongue is far too ready for a suitably abject captive!"

There was a little silence after Gabriel disappeared, and it was Zeus who spoke first. "I wonder," he rumbled consideringly, "if he isn't right. But more importantly, *chérie*, you should have told me about this first. *Mon capitaine* does not always have the sweetest temper . . . especially when he is being thwarted, and in a contest of wills, the petite pigeon will surely be the loser."

Pilar's chin went up, and a rebellious sparkle in her eyes, she demanded spiritedly, "Would you care to wager on it?"

Zeus smiled slowly, a sensuous curve to his mouth. *"Oui!* You shall let me do all the wicked things that I wanted to do to you last night . . . and if I lose, then you shall decide how we spend the evening."

It wasn't perhaps the wager Pilar would have preferred, but she really didn't think it mattered whether she won or lost—she was becoming *very* aware that Zeus had a way of arranging things exactly to his liking. . . .

It took Gabriel a few minutes to find the kitchen, and during that time, his temper became thoroughly aroused. Pushing open the door to the kitchen, his expression was grim and his unexpected appearance in this area of the house caused a collective gasp of surprise and dismay from the servants assembled there. Fearfully they glanced at him, wondering what terrible things this English buccaneer would do to them, but Gabriel never even spared them a glance; he had eyes only for one small woman still wearily seated at the long table, her back stubbornly presented to him.

A tingling along the back of her neck as well as the servants' reaction had warned Maria who it was who stood in the doorway behind her, and she was conscious of an almost overpowering urge to flee, an urge that was in direct conflict with the wild exhilaration that was pumping through her veins. It took a great deal of steely determination to remain where she was, to pretend that she didn't notice the utter silence that had fallen over the room. As the seconds spun out, the confusion and fear of the servants became nearly tangible, and for their sake alone, Maria wondered how long she could sit staring at the unappetizing remains of her unappetizing meal.

Staring hard at her slim little back, Gabriel was startled at the great gust of rage that swept up through him. It wasn't that she was making her opinion of him so insultingly clear, so much as it was that he found her *here!* Here in the kitchens, obviously acting the part of a servant, and *that* enraged him . . . it also vastly amused him, and as the moments passed he was torn between a strong desire to beat her soundly and a equally strong desire to laugh out loud. Amusement won out, but determined not to let *her* know it, he walked with nerve-racking slowness across the distance that separated them. Resolved to make the most of the situation that Maria had created, he stood directly in back of her for several long, deathly silent minutes, deliberately letting the tension within the room build.

Maria could *feel* him standing so still behind her, and she felt so breathless it seemed almost as if her heart had stopped beating. Her mouth went dry and she was suddenly very conscious of the folly of her actions. She was, after all, a captive, a captive of a buccaneer, a man who hated her family, and she had dared to insultingly deny his unexpected, if not kindness, at least consideration. She swallowed with difficulty, wondering with increasing trepidation what he was going to do with her.

Gabriel could see her increasing nervousness, the slight stiffening of her body and the involuntary fidgeting of her fingers on the table. He glanced around the room, and the expression of complete terror on the faces of the servants had him hard-pressed not to burst out laughing—it was apparent that they expected him to murder her right before their very eyes. Stifling a chuckle at the ridiculousness of the entire affair, he put one booted foot upon the bench where Maria sat, and resting his forearm across his bent leg, he murmured conversationally, "The fare served in the dining room not to your taste, princess?"

Maria bit her lip, not quite certain how to deal with him. He didn't sound angry ... and her eyes flitted quickly to his face and back again to the table before her, a little frown beginning to pucker her forehead. He didn't look angry either; there had been, she was positive, a gleam of amusement in his green eyes, and it perplexed her. Surely he didn't find this situation *amusing?* A small flicker of annoyance shot up through her, and she looked at him again, noting indignantly the faint amused curve of his mouth, and this time the green eyes were fairly dancing with laughter. He was *laughing* at her, she thought with resentment, and she grew very angry. Insufferable beast! Finally she sent him a haughty look, and her voice dripping with disdain, she said, "It wasn't the fare, so much as it was the *company!*"

Innocently, Gabriel replied, "My friend Zeus doesn't meet with your approval? Or has your *duenna* somehow offended you?" He smiled intimately. "She certainly didn't discharge her duties very adequately the other night ... but then," he added with a thread of laughter in his voice, "I doubt I would have paid her much heed, if she had tried to stop me from bedding you."

Maria's bosom swelled with wrath, and a becomingly rosy flush stained her cheeks. Her lowered voice shaking with embarrassment and rage, she hissed, "How dare you speak so publicly of your disgusting depravity!"

One of Gabriel's thick black eyebrows arched. "Disgusting depravity?" he retorted, not bothering to keep his voice low. "I seem to recall that my *disgusting depravity* didn't bother you in the least ... as a matter of fact, you seemed to enjoy it!"

Maria was certain her entire body was scarlet with shame, and in an agony of embarrassment and fury, she tore her gaze from his mocking face and stared stonily at her congealing bowl of gruel. A hint of angry tears in her voice, she said huskily, "Go away! You've had what you wanted from me—now leave me in peace with the other servants."

"Not," Gabriel said slowly, some of his amusement having fled at the change in her voice, "until you tell me

why I find you here ... surely, it isn't ..." His words
trailed off as his eyes rested upon the remains of Maria's
meal. "God's wounds!" he burst out in astonishment.
"What in the name of all that's holy is *that!*"

Inordinately pleased that something had disconcerted
him, Maria said smugly, "That, *señor,* is the fare that
your poor servants are forced to eat while you gorge yourself on rich meats and viands."

All signs of amusement had vanished from his manner,
and standing up, he sent a dark look over to the *mayordomo.* His voice hard, he demanded, "What is the meaning of this? There are provisions enough here to feed many
mouths—why are the servants eating this"—he glanced
at the gruel again and continued—"pig swill, instead of
proper food?"

Nearly wringing his fat hands in distress, his pudgy
face the picture of terror and dismay, the *mayordomo*
stammered, "T-t-the o-old master ordered it so ... and I
just assumed ..."

"I am *not* the old master!" Gabriel said through his
teeth. "I am your master only as long as we remain in
Puerto Bello, and during that time, you will see that these
people are fed properly or I'll have your hide to hang upon
the walls in my home on Jamaica!"

Quaking with fear, the *mayordomo* nodded his head
vigorously, and his face whitened when Gabriel added
ominously, "They are to eat well, and I would suggest
that you not try to fatten your own pockets at the expense
of the others. ..."

Swinging around to look at Maria, who was watching
him with openmouthed startlement, he smiled grimly and
said, "I am not very much like your brother, am I? Starving those who serve me is not one of my pleasures." He
reached out and bodily plucked her up from her seat.
"However, those that serve me, serve at *my* pleasure, and
I decide what their duties are ... and you, sweet witch,
serve me best in bed!"

Ignoring the gasp of outrage and shame that came from
Maria, he flashed an intimidating glance across to the
others and said coldly, "She is not to be found here again.
She is my personal servant and she serves *only* me!" His
eyes on Maria's mortified and indignant face, he added

silkily, "And if she chooses to disobey me and any of you help her . . . I'll see to it that the guilty one is flayed to within an inch of his life. Obey me and you will find that I am not an *un*generous master; defy me and you will suffer greatly for it." Seeing that his message was clearly understood by the frightened servants, Gabriel lightened his tone. "And now I would like some water heated." He glanced at Maria's soiled clothes and wrinkled his handsome nose. "You, sweetling, are in sad need of a bath!" When the servants remained uneasily standing about, Gabriel said softly, "I want that water, *now.*"

Instantly, there was a flurry of activity, and feeling extremely satisfied with the situation, Gabriel tightened his hold upon Maria's arm and effortlessly dragged her out of the kitchen with him. Maria objected strenuously to his hold on her arm, but she could not escape his grasp as he calmly strode down the hallways of the house, his destination the rooms they shared together.

Breathless, annoyed and confused, Maria fought him every step of the way, and when he was not one bit deterred, she finally decided angrily that fighting against him was like trying to halt a hurricane. *Nothing* seemed to sway him from his path, not her fingers scratching and clawing at the hand that kept her prisoner, nor her feet kicking viciously at his long legs. He appeared impervious to her tactics and Maria's frustration and rage grew.

Reaching the doors to their rooms, he pushed one open, and jerking Maria in behind him, he shut the door and then released her. Coolly, the green eyes shuttered, he looked her up and down. Thoughtfully, he observed, "You surprise me—one night I am met with warmth and eagerness, the next a knife and tonight . . ." He frowned. "What precisely was the object of tonight, sweet tiger? What was it you were trying to accomplish by those antics? Am I to feel pity for you? Remorse that you are my captive? Or was it merely to arouse pity amongst the servants? Or simply sheer perversity?"

It was a reasonable question, but one she couldn't answer. How could she say that it was a form of penance for herself, that by demeaning herself, she could somehow atone for the terrible sin of having so blatantly given herself to the enemy of her family and on a larger scale, the enemy of Spain? How to explain the need to throw as many barriers as possible between them, to deny the fascination he held for her? How to explain to this dark-faced stranger that her conscience writhed at the thought that others were suffering in the ravaged town of Puerto Bello and that it seemed obscene and cowardly to consort with the enemy, to have all the comforts and ease that were denied the rest of her people. And because she didn't know how to answer and because she was once again in danger of succumbing to his undeniable charm, she averted her face and said stiltedly, "I am your captive, and considering the enmity between our families, it seemed only natural that you would want me to take my place along with your other servants . . it is what Diego demanded of you. How, as his sister, could I expect to be treated any differently?"

"Oh?" Gabriel replied interestedly, his brow arching. "And because your brother is a cruel, sadistic bastard, I am to be one too?"

Angered at his slur against her brother, Maria's eyes flashed brilliantly blue, and she burst out passionately, "How dare you say such things of my brother! And are you any better? Haven't you slaughtered my people these past few days? Attacked and pillaged this innocent city?" Her eyes sliding from his, she said lowly, "Didn't you force yourself upon me and take my virginity?"

"Take, my dear?" Gabriel inquired dryly. "I seem to remember that you were willing . . . *very* willing, if my memory serves me right!"

Driven by the devils of pride and family honor, Maria could not bear for him to say the words aloud and she cried out, "No! *Never!* A Delgato would never willingly lie in the bed of a foul Lancaster!" And pain as well as pride goading her, she struck him with the flat of her palm across the cheek.

He closed his eyes against the blow, but he made no move to retaliate. Thumbs hooked in the broad leather belt around his waist, Gabriel slowly opened his eyes, and Maria was frightened at the cold rage she saw flickering there. "Don't ever," he said with soft menace, "strike me again . . . you won't, I can assure you, like the method I would choose to teach you better manners."

Maria drew herself up proudly. Sneeringly she replied,
"There is *nothing* I like about you now, so there is nothing that you could do to me that would surprise me."

She resembled a small, bedraggled and angry kitten as
she stood so defiantly before him, and Gabriel was aware
that he didn't really want to fight with her ... at least
not tonight. Another time and he might have welcomed
this confrontation, might have welcomed the excuse to
vent all of his bottled rage and frustration over his own
conflicting emotions. It would be a pleasure to join lustily
in the battle she seemed so intent upon provoking, but
not tonight. Tonight, despite her antagonistic attitude,
she looked too weary and dispirited to be a worthy oppo-
nent, and Gabriel had never cared overmuch for clubbing
kits in the den. Besides, he discovered uneasily, he would
far rather make love to her than fight or brood over the
past atrocities committed by their families on each other.

Confused, tired and unhappy, Maria stared at him,
wishing he weren't quite so attractive with his dark hair
and rakish air and that she wasn't so unbearably conscious of a desire to throw herself against his strong chest
and damn the future. But no, she thought forlornly, she
had allowed herself to do that once, and she could never
allow it to happen again; it would be a final betrayal of
her family and country. He was an enemy and it would
be the greatest dishonor imaginable for her to treat him
with anything less than hatred and contempt.

Despairingly she sent him another look from under her
lashes. Nothing had worked out as she had thought it
would. Instead of reacting with anger or indifference to
her actions, he had appeared to find them amusing, and
even when she had been driven to strike him, even that
hadn't provoked the reaction she had been expecting.
Confused, she almost hated Gabriel for his restraint, for
the very kindness he was showing her—he was an enemy
and she wished fiercely that he would *act* like one! She
was certainly doing her very best to behave like a true
Delgato!

There could never be anything but enmity between
them, and it was unfair of him to continue this pretense
of consideration. Unfair too, she admitted dejectedly, for
her heart to feel such delight in merely looking at him—

unfair of him to be so charmingly attractive. But sternly, Maria steeled her wayward heart. She *must* not think such thoughts! She must remember at all times that he was a Lancaster and that she was a Delgato! And that it was her duty to uphold the family honor and pride—at *all* costs.

Chapter Fourteen

HEARING the sounds of the servants moving about in the room next door and guessing what they were doing, Gabriel suddenly grinned at her and murmured, "Ah, m'lady's bath must be ready . . . and it will be my privilege, nay, *pleasure* to act as your maidservant this night."

Grimly hanging on to her pride and stony resolve, Maria glared at him and gritted, "Don't be ridiculous! You certainly will not! I need no help, and definitely, I don't need yours!"

He grinned sardonically and said mockingly, "Have you forgotten that as your captor, I am the one who makes the decisions? I have decided that I'm going to give you a bath . . . and there is nothing you can do to stop me!"

As if to prove his words, before she had a chance to react, he scooped her up into his arms, and swinging around, he walked through the other doorway to the small dressing room where the huge copper tub had been set up. A goodly amount of water had already been poured into the tub, and several more buckets of steaming water stood nearby. A large bar of soap floated gently in the water, and weakly Maria decided that it wouldn't really be *too* sinful to allow herself to be clean. But she didn't dare let *him* bathe her. She might have made all sorts of righteous resolutions, but she was also aware of how easily they could be destroyed by this man. And remembering her dreams, remembering her father's face, stiff with contempt for her actions, she began to struggle in Gabriel's arms.

"Put me down!" she commanded breathlessly, not liking the way her body was beginning to respond to the nearness of his.

"Whatever m'lady desires," Gabriel replied lightly and gently lowered her feet to the floor. A warm glint in his eyes, his fingers began to search for the fastenings of the shift.

Hastily Maria slapped his hands away and said sharply, "Cease that! I can bathe myself! Leave me now!"

Gabriel only grinned and murmured, "And deny myself the joys of touching that delectable little body of yours? Hardly, sweet tiger."

His fingers found the fastenings, and despite Maria's struggles to stop him, in seconds he had her stripped naked in front of him. Her face was flushed with embarrassment and she was positive that she would die of shame as his gaze slowly traveled over her.

A reverent note in his voice, Gabriel breathed softly, "By all that's holy, you're a lovely sight." And slowly, gently, his hands wandered over her breasts and waist. Cupping one breast, he bent his head and kissed it, murmuring, "So small, so sweet . . . and *mine.*"

To her increased shame, she could feel her nipples stiffening, feel a warm languorous sensation stealing over her. Horrified, she jerked away from him and pleaded, *"Señor!* Please, I beg of you, stop this! No man has ever seen me naked before, never touched me as you do . . . please, stop."

His eyes, dark with passion, met hers, and huskily he said, "Don't you think I know that? But you belong to me now, my body has claimed you, made you a woman . . . *my* woman, and I alone have the right to touch you, to caress you and to look at you whenever I desire. . . ."

Maria swallowed, fighting against the seductiveness of his words. Her eyes downcast, she stammered, "I—it—it m-m-makes me feel ashamed to have you stare at me this way."

"Ashamed to have me see your loveliness?" Gabriel muttered thickly. "Oh, Maria, you should never be ashamed of your sweet charms—you are beautiful and everything that a man could ever wish for in his woman." His eyes moved over her, lingering on the high, firm bosom, the coral-tipped nipples before dropping to the narrow waist and gently flaring hips. Though small, Maria was perfectly formed, her shoulders proud and straight, her stomach flat, almost concave, the thighs slimly muscled and ankles finely fashioned. She was exceedingly lovely and Gabriel's gaze strayed to the vee between her thighs, to the soft, silky black hair that grew there. Regretfully he tore his eyes away and said gruffly, "In the bath with you, m'lady, or I'm very much afraid my plans for later will take place here on the floor!"

Once again he caught her up in his arms, only this time he lowered her into the waiting tub of water. If Maria had been embarrassed before, it was nothing to what she suffered now. It wasn't very bad when he contented himself with washing her hair; as a matter of fact she rather liked the feel of his strong fingers moving over her scalp, but when he knelt at the side of the tub and began, despite her vehement protests to the contrary, to bathe her body, she was certain that nothing could ever be so shameful, so sinful and yet so beguiling. . . .

For a big man, his hands could be seductively gentle, and when he lingered over her breasts, lightly rubbing the bar of soap across them, his fingers sensuously pulling on her nipples, Maria was aware that her resolutions were in desperate disarray, that all she wanted was to give in to the sensual mood he was deliberately creating. His hands seemed everywhere, touching and sliding over her flesh with provocative movements, the soapy lather making them silky and slick against her skin. It was all she could do not to reach up and touch the dark, intent face as he bent above her, his eyes seeming fascinated by the soft flesh beneath his hands. She longed to caress that chiseled male mouth that brought her such pleasure, to wind her fingers in the thick, unruly black hair, to pull his face down next to hers, to have their mouths meet . . .

She swallowed with difficulty, helplessly attempting to tear her thoughts from the path they hungered to follow, and with something between a sigh and a moan, she pulled his hands closer to her, trying to stop their distracting wanderings, and almost frantically, she cried, *Señor!* You must cease this! I'll, I'll . . ." She hesitated as his green eyes, the desire he felt very evident in the emerald depths, met hers. For a moment, she let herself be wooed by the promise of ecstasy she saw there, but then with a little gasp she said wildly, "If you don't stop, I'll get you all wet!"

Gabriel smiled sleepily, thinking that he had never seen such an enticing sight as Maria in her bath. The freshly washed hair hung in damp tendrils that displayed a tendency to curl as they gradually dried; her shoulders were like pearlized silk, the dampness shining in the light of the candles that lit the room; and her breasts with their rosy nipples were just visible above the foamy lather of the soap. He let his gaze slide downward, and through the haziness of the soapy water, he could just barely discern the shape of her slender legs, and he sighed deeply. His voice husky, he murmured, "If this tub were large enough, I would join you . . . but don't worry about getting me wet—I don't intend to remain in these clothes much longer—the way I feel right now, I'm about to burst my breeches!"

Maria blushed right up to the roots of her hair, and Gabriel laughed merrily at the sight of it. Gently tweaking her nose, he said lightly, "Such sweet blushes—a shame that living with me will soon drive them from your cheeks. Although," he added with an intimate smile, "I suspect I shall see them often . . . at least until I've taught you all there is to know about a man and woman making love."

Her mouth dry, Maria regarded him with something between delight and terror. It was obvious that he was going to make love to her soon, and unless she was prepared to sink her pride and allow the honor of the Delgatos to be dragged in the mire, she *must* do something to stop him. If he continued in this gentle, teasing manner, she wouldn't be able to resist him, and calling up all the haughtiness she possessed, she raised her chin in the air and said darkly, "Do not think it will be an easy task, señor. I will tell you here and now that I intend to fight you every step of the way. I may be your captive, but you do not control what I feel inside, what is in my mind and heart. I am a Delgato—you are a Lancaster . . . there is much enmity between us, and you would do well to remember it."

His indulgent mood vanished instantly, and a hard edge

to his voice, Gabriel returned harshly, "I seldom forget it, m'lady, but you would do well to remember *this*—it is not wise for one in your position to provoke one's master!" The emerald eyes suddenly cold, he added, "I have been kind to you ... I can be cruel, never doubt it! Continue in the manner you have chosen tonight and you will soon discover just how cruel. Do not push me too far, m'lady, or you will have cause to regret it—*that* I can promise you!"

Of course, after a challenge like that, it would have been impossible for Maria not to have met it head-on. A decidedly belligerent sparkle in the sapphire blue eyes, she retorted angrily, "Do you think to frighten me? Bah! You can do nothing worse to me than you did the night when you took my virginity." With great daring she snapped her fingers under his nose and to reassure herself, as much as to let him know that she wasn't so easily cowed, she said hotly, "I'm not afraid of you—you're a mere Lancaster and we Delgatos know how to deal with your like!"

It wasn't the wisest thing she could have said, and whatever remnants of indulgence he might have felt disappeared the second the words left her mouth. Full of rage that she dared to speak to him so, infuriated that the willing little creature he had held in his arms not two nights previously had vanished to leave in her place this sharp-tongued virago, Gabriel's temper exploded. Rising to his feet, his eyes narrowed, and almost silkily he drawled, "So I can do nothing worse to you?" A nasty smile played across his fine mouth. "I think I'll just have to show you how very lucky you were the other night!"

Alarmed now that she had aroused the beast, Maria tried frantically to avoid his hands when they came down and settled heavily on her shoulders. With one swift movement, he jerked her out of the water, and oblivious to her attempts to escape him, he roughly wrapped her in a soft cotton blanket that had been left for just such a purpose. Sweeping her struggling form up into his arms, his face grim and set, he carried her back into the bedroom, slamming the door to the smaller room behind him. Walking to the bed, he pushed aside the mosquito netting, and as he had done the first time, he tossed her lightly on the mattress.

But unlike that first time, he didn't then leave her; instead, with short angry movements, he began to strip off his clothes and before Maria could fight her way clear of the tangled blanket, he had joined her on the bed. His naked body fell heavily on hers, and she struggled wildly to escape from him. Twisting frantically, she managed to slip from beneath him and had half-scrambled away when his hand came out and caught her firmly around one ankle. He gave a violent jerk and began to pull her squirming, thrashing body down next to his. Hauling her up against his muscled chest, his mouth found hers, claiming her lips almost cruelly.

It was a nightmare for Maria, and she could take little comfort from the fact that what was happening was of her own making. That he intended to take her just as brutally as he was kissing her was very evident and she was more fearful than she had ever been in her life. Like a wild creature, she thrashed and twisted, desperately trying to free herself from his increasingly paralyzing hold.

Sobbing with anger and terror, she finally managed to tear her mouth away from his and to jam her elbow between their bodies, momentarily keeping him at bay. They were both panting, their chests heaving from their exertions, his lower body pressing warmly, intimately against hers, and despite the circumstances, to her utter horror, Maria felt a treacherous weakness invading her lower limbs. Her eyes met his and she was surprised to find that they were no longer hard and cold; instead the emerald green eyes were bright with desire ... and some other emotion that made Maria's heart beat very fast.

Gabriel dropped his head and lightly kissed her shoulder. Softly he murmured, "It doesn't have to be this way, sweet tiger. . . . I would far rather have you willing than fighting me."

Maria stiffened, fighting down a traitorous urge to give in to the coaxing note in his voice. She could feel the heat of his hard body against her own, could feel the shape and texture of his long, powerful legs pressing against her and between their bodies, his manhood hot and swollen thrust against her stomach. It would be so sweet, so wonderful to relax, to let her body cling to his, to have those strong hands that were holding her prisoner move caressingly across her body, to have that mobile mouth take hers with gentle passion, and for one moment her resolve wavered. But then, almost as if they stood condemningly at the edge of the bed, she heard her father's voice and Diego's crying out contemptuously, *"Puta! Slut!* Where is your pride? You are a Delgato! He is a Lancaster! Do you dare think to bring more dishonor on the proud name you bear?"

An anguished sob rose out of her throat, and violently she pushed Gabriel away. With a feverish intensity, she cried out, "No! *Never!"* And catching them both by surprise, in her struggles to reject him, her knee caught him hard in the groin, and with a smothered curse Gabriel rolled away from her, doubled over from pain. Uncertain what had happened, Maria hesitated; but then seizing this unexpected chance, she scooted swiftly across the bed, intent upon putting as much distance as possible between herself and this man who fascinated her so, but who was, by the enmity of their ancestors, beyond her reach.

Maria had just made it to the edge of the bed, one slim foot actually groping for the floor, when Gabriel recovered himself enough to, in one lithe movement, hurl himself across the distance that separated them and catch hold of her upper arm. Dragging her roughly back against him, he growled, "Oh, no, you don't! I'm afraid that you've finally made me lose my temper, and the devil with treating you gently!"

He threw her down on the bed, his mouth taking hers bruisingly, his hands sliding down to her thighs, parting them forcefully. His big body held hers pinioned, but Maria fought him strongly, pride as well as fear driving her. But nothing seemed to stop him and with a start of apprehension, she could feel his hard manhood probing between her legs ... and it was then that she remembered the knife.

Using all the strength contained in her slender body, she reared up, nearly tossing him aside. Stretching and straining, she fumbled for the knife beneath the pillow, and with a gasp of satisfaction, finally felt her fingers curl over it. Not thinking, reacting with blind instinct, she

struck at him and with something between pain and relief, she heard him cry out. Rising up on one elbow, she
discovered that the knife had caught him in the face, the
blade leaving a neat slice across his cheekbone near his
eye.

For a long, tension-filled moment they regarded each
other, the cut on Gabriel's cheek bleeding freely, the blood
sliding unheeded down his hard face. Filled with remorse,
a tight ball of pain coiling in her chest, Maria threw the
knife away, looking at it with revulsion. The blue eyes
nearly black with contrition, she got out shakily, "Englishman . . . I—I—I never intended to . . ." The words of
apology died on her lips as she caught the expression in
his eyes.

Never in her life had anyone ever quite looked at her
that way. Contempt, fury, disbelief . . . desire and regret
were all revealed for one split second before his lids
dropped, hiding what was in his eyes. Something dark
and dangerous slowly entered the room, Maria could feel
it, building up all around her, and her mouth went dry.
Sickly she was aware that she had crossed some invisible
boundary, that she had changed, possibly forever, the situation between them, and she was suddenly very frightened of this tall, powerful buccaneer. Gabriel Lancaster
had fascinated her . . . but she had the curious feeling
that the Gabriel she had known had gone a long way from
her, and that now, through her own pride and folly, she
had brought herself face to face with the Dark Angel so
dreaded by her Spanish compatriots. She swallowed
tightly, mourning the passionately gentle lover who had
awakened her to womanhood, yet unable to stop herself
from following the path dictated by the past.

The green eyes hooded, Gabriel looked at her a second
longer, and then almost indifferently, he reached up to
touch the ugly gash, his fingertips coming away crimson
with his own blood. In a chillingly remote voice, he ground
out, "I made a vow the day Harry Morgan freed me from
the bowels of that wretched slave ship—Never again
would a Delgato best me, never again would a Delgato
spill Lancasterian blood . . . promised myself that I would
seize every chance to make certain that the Delgatos lived
no more, that they could no longer foul the earth with

their hateful presence." He smiled, a savage sort of smile that held no amusement, and Maria shivered, courage making her lift her chin proudly, her body tensing as she prepared to fight for her life.

"It would appear, however," Gabriel went on in that same chilling voice, "that I'm going to have to break that vow. . . ." His voice hardened and he spat, "I won't kill you, sweet tiger, but by the time I'm through with you, you may very well wish that I had!" He gave a bitter laugh. "It was good of you to remind me so forcibly of the treachery of your family . . . and it behooves me, if I am to uphold the Lancasterian family honor, to treat you with the same brutality and violence that your brother visited upon me and mine!"

Numbly Maria stared at him, still deeply shocked that she had struck him so viciously, still stunned at how very much it hurt to look upon the bleeding wound that *she* had given him. And yet she could not entirely regret it . . . the battle lines between them were now clearly and irrevocably drawn; there would be no turning back for either of them. There would also, she realized with a mingled sense of satisfaction and sorrow, be no more heart-searchings on her part—by the blood spilt by their ancestors, by the acts committed this night, Gabriel Lancaster would be her enemy.

When Gabriel reached for her this time, she was half-prepared for his actions, but nothing had quite prepared her for the unleashed strength of that powerful body. His hands were like iron talons as they caught her shoulders, and though she struggled wildly, her efforts to escape him were useless. Frantically she sought to avoid his descending mouth, but one steel-muscled arm slid around her waist, jerking her next to him, as his other hand caught her twisting head and held her still as his mouth angrily trapped hers. Ruthlessly his firm lips parted hers, his probing tongue filling her mouth, demanding and insistent as it hungrily explored the exciting warmth bound there.

It was a frenzied battle between them, Gabriel effortlessly destroying her fragile defenses as swiftly as she erected them. Their locked bodies rolled and thrashed across the big bed, Maria's hands and arms flailing vio-

lently about as she furiously tried to strike a disabling
blow. Her clenched fists struck him again and again on
the back, shoulders and head but seemed to make no impact, and a sob of half fright, half fury broke from her.
Her breath was coming in rapid gasps and her heart was
beating painfully fast as the uneven fight continued. Gabriel's hands and arms felt as if they were everywhere,
first touching her breasts and hips, then holding her
strongly against him, his legs tangling with hers, his
mouth on hers one second, the next sliding hotly down
her throat before returning to capture her lips once more
in a pillaging kiss that was gradually draining her resistance. Maria fought him with every fiber of her being,
her slim body constantly twisting and arching, never allowing herself a respite from the intense struggle they
waged against each other.

A terrifying violence filled the room, the very air feeling heavy and oppressive; Maria could taste blood on her
tongue, and whether it was his from the wound she had
given him, or hers from the fierce pressure of his lips on
her tender mouth, she didn't know, but it seemed sym-
bolic somehow that it should come to this between them.
Generations of Delgatos and Lancasters had inflicted
grievous hurts on each other, so why should it be any
different between them? she wondered sickly. A terrible
sense of defeat began to destroy her urge to continue this
wretched, one-sided fight, and while she still made every
attempt to escape from Gabriel's powerful grasp, she
found herself weakening, not really caring anymore what
he did to her this night.

As the minutes passed, Maria suddenly became aware
of new emotions swirling up through her body, emotions
that shocked and appalled her, and to her utter shame,
she discovered the dark side of passion. A wild, hungry
heat was spreading up from her loins, the half-bruising,
half-seductive touch of Gabriel's hands and muscled body
against hers instantly became perversely exciting as they
tumbled and struggled on the bed. His hard, callused
hands on her breasts, the fierce urgency of his mouth on
hers was no longer hurtful; instead there was a willful,
savage pleasure to be gained from his ungentle embrace.
When his mouth sought hers again, this time she didn't

avoid his kiss, her lips parting helplessly under his, her tongue darting like a flick of fire into his mouth.

A primitive, primeval passion had been unleashed between them, explosively sweeping all other thoughts and emotions away. Revenge and pride had no place in what was happening between them—they were only uncivilized, barbaric man and untamed feral woman fighting a battle as old as Adam and Eve, a battle that had only one ending. . . .

At the touch of Maria's tongue against his, Gabriel groaned deeply, his fingers tightening in the tangled black hair as he forced her head backward, hungrily taking the kiss she so shamelessly offered him. He was consumed with desire, ablaze to drive himself into the sweet flesh that so infuriated and yet aroused him beyond thought. He ached with desire, a primitive desire that he had no control over, the thrashing of that slim body so near his was a fiery torment; her resistance, a carnal goad that ripped aside the thin veneer of civilization and awakened the elemental urge to conquer his woman, to claim her so completely, so fully that his taking of her would forever mark her as his and his alone.

Maria was drowning in a mindless well of earthy passions as Gabriel hungrily returned her kiss, his long legs wrapping around hers, holding her next to him, making her achingly conscious of his swollen, upthrusting manhood. He hadn't released his hold on her head, and when his lips left hers to travel scorchingly along her exposed throat, she struggled to change her position, wanting to kiss him, to taste him, but he would have none of it. His head dipped lower as he sought the stiff coral nipples just below him. With a low growl of satisfaction, his mouth closed over first one and then the other, his teeth grazing the tender tips, almost hurting her. But it was an oddly pleasurable hurt, one that made her moan aloud with frustration and desire, the heat in her loins becoming stronger as primitive passion shot up through her. She was trembling from the force of the emotions blazing in her blood, unable to think of anything but the craving need to have Gabriel take her, to have his body join with hers. His mouth caught hers again, his hold on her hair lessening as he pushed her back against the soft mattress, his other hand seeking and finding the tight black curls at the junction of her slender thighs.

Unable to help herself, she arched up against his invading hand, nearly crying out with shamed pleasure when he parted the tender flesh and caressed her deeply, stoking the fires that burned within her to a white-hot heat. Helplessly she writhed beneath his arousing touches, not even caring that his caresses were not the gentle ones he had shown her that first night . . . she was completely ensnared by the dark passions that surrounded them and only later would shame and horror attack her. . . .

Despite the base feelings that overpowered his finer sensibilities, there was a sensuous savagery to Gabriel's actions—he was not tender with her, nor was he cruel; but he was in the grip of such a basic, barbaric passion that nothing Maria could have said or done would have deterred him from possessing her. That she too seemed consumed by the same relentless wildfire that raged through him aroused a fierce satisfaction within him, and he was mercilessly compelled to take full advantage of it. But while there was a twisted, bitter delight in driving her beyond herself, in forcing her surrender to him, in making her feel emotions she didn't want to feel, his own hungry needs would be denied no longer; and pulling her beneath him, his hands slid to her hips, raising her up to meet the powerful thrust of his hard body. An almost animal growl of intense pleasure came from his throat as his rigid, swollen member sank deeply within her hot, yielding flesh.

It was an ungentle mating, both of them trapped and driven by the past and the present, both of them mindless with the dark desires that swirled about them. With a ruthless eroticism Gabriel crushed her slender body against his, his hands on her hips controlling her movements as again and again his big body met hers, each thrust driving them both closer and closer to a carnal ecstasy. Voluptuously Maria writhed beneath him, lost in the red haze of wild desire, eager to reach that exquisite peak of pleasure she knew awaited them. Unconsciously her fingers dug into his back, her legs locking around his lean driving hips, her own body now meeting and joining the rhythmic movements of his. He filled her fully, completely, and she ached from his sheer size, but it was such a potently sweet ache that there was great pleasure to be gained from it, and when at last the first tiny tremors that heralded fulfillment rippled through her, she gasped with astonished delight. Suddenly she was assaulted by such an intense explosion of physical rapture that uncontrollably she arched up wildly against Gabriel, her eyes opening in stunned pleasure.

Gabriel felt her response, and his mouth lifted from hers, the green eyes ablaze with passion meeting hers for just a second before his features stiffened and his body jerked as elemental pleasure surged through him. His lashes dropped, and urgently he captured Maria's mouth, kissing her hungrily, his movements wild and almost desperate until the fierce sensations that had consumed him gradually ebbed.

But if the feral passions that had dominated them both had been momentarily appeased, the violent emotions Maria had so unwisely loosed this night had not. Gabriel had been right when he had stated that when he was done with her she would wish she were dead—she did. The moment he rolled away from her, a chill swept over her body. Shame and revulsion clawed their way up through her as she realized painfully precisely what had taken place between them, how different tonight was from the first time he had made love to her. Her mouth trembled. He had not made *love* to her this night—he had conquered her, possessed her, made her do things she hadn't wanted to, had made her respond wildly, savagely to him, and she despised her own weakness and hated him for the power he seemed to wield over her. There had been no gentleness in his taking of her, no sweet coaxing; his possession had been insultingly blunt, and a cold lump of angry despair settled in her chest, her only consolation—and it was bitter at that—the fact that at least she had made him fight in the beginning for what he wanted. A furious resentment surged in her blood and with a disdainful movement of her body, she put some distance between them.

Gabriel was lying on his back, his eyes fixed on the canopy overhead, his muscled chest rising and falling slowly as the candlelight flickered over the gold rope-shaped chain around his strong neck. His face and upper body were smeared with blood from the deep gash just above his cheekbone, and almost against her will, Maria reached out a hand but then let it drop limply on the bed. At her action, he glanced over at her, the green eyes empty and blank, almost as if he didn't recognize her, and that seemed to be the most painful insult of all.

Rage nearly choking her, she spat, "I hate you! You are a beast!"

With an effort, Gabriel brought himself back from the dark place he had gone to, but reality was no better, and there was an acrid taste in his mouth, a sick depression permeating his very being. He had promised himself revenge, and tonight he had taken it, but while his body had known an intensely primitive pleasure, he was repelled by what had happened between them. And yet, like Maria, he too was driven by devils, and at her words, his expression hardened, the emerald eyes turning to green ice. Rising up on one elbow, he looked across at her, the blood on his face and chest giving him a savage appearance, and his mouth formed a tiger's smile. "I expected little else from a Delgato . . . nor wanted anything else. As long as your body gives me the pleasure it has, I shall be content, and whether you hate me or not matters not at all to me." The tiger's smile widened. "As for being a beast . . ." Something flickered for just a moment behind the green eyes. "Be glad I didn't show you *real* bestiality! But enrage me again and I can promise you that tonight will become a most pleasant memory for you!"

Chapter Fifteen

HAVING uttered those infuriating words, Gabriel sprang up from the bed and, indifferent to his nakedness, stalked across the room to where his russet silk robe had been laid out on the chair. After shrugging into the garment, he carelessly knotted the sash about his waist and without another word disappeared through the main doors of the room.

For a long time after the doors had slammed shut behind him, Maria had continued to stare in that direction, unwilling to face the unpleasant fact that she had deliberately brought tonight's events upon herself. That with her own two slim hands she had destroyed the fragile, tenuous thread that had miraculously existed between them. Her head bowed and a great painful sob of utter misery rose up in her chest. Tears streamed unheeded down her cheeks, and weeping piteously, she flung herself facedown on the pillows of the bed. She cried for what seemed endless hours, and whether she wept for herself or Gabriel, she never knew. She was only aware that pride and arrogance had relentlessly compelled her to the ugly position in which she now found herself, and as the darkness slowly gave way to the dawn, she could see no way out of the trap into which she had fallen.

That damnable Delgato pride would not allow her to retreat and she quailed at the thought of what Gabriel's probable reaction would be if she were mad enough to attempt to rectify matters between them. He had made it very clear how he viewed the Delgatos, and she shivered as she remembered the expression on his face when he had spoken of his vow never to allow a Delgato to get the

better of him . . . and that he would kill to keep that vow.
That he had treated her as he had this night should not
have surprised her, what *should* have surprised her was
that he had shown her such gentleness and restraint the
first time he had made love to her. A shudder of revulsion
swept through her when she viewed the difference between tonight and her sweet initiation at his hands into
womanhood. How, she wondered dully, could he have
acted so differently? How could the two acts that she had
experienced with him both be called lovemaking? Sickly
she realized that they couldn't, that tonight's events had
nothing to do with love. . . . But neither had the first time
. . . Or had it?

Was she in love with Gabriel Lancaster? Or had she
been merely fascinated by him . . . had her untaught body
simply responded to the caresses of an experienced man?
That last thought was extremely distasteful and angrily
she pushed it away. But the idea that she might conceiv-
ably be in love with him was equally distasteful—especially after tonight and after she had gone to such great
pains to put him at a distance, to remind both of them of
the vendetta between their families. Yet if she was not in
love with him—and she assured herself fiercely that she
was not!—then why was she mourning the loss of the
tender lover who had shown her ecstasy for the first time?

With an angry hiccoughing sob, Maria sat up, furiously
wiping away the tears that still continued to fall. She
didn't mourn him! she told herself savagely. *She hated
him!* She hated him for what he had done to her this night
and for being a detestable Lancaster. She was *glad,* she
thought vehemently, that he had shown her his true side
this night—now she was under no illusions about him,
now she knew the *true* beastly creature who occasionally
hid behind a smiling mouth and laughing green eyes. She
would not be tricked by him again!

She might not have been so confident of her feelings, if
she had known what was going through Gabriel's mind
at the same time. What had taken place tonight had
shocked and horrified him almost as deeply as it had Maria, and he was conscious of a powerful desire to call back
the moments that had led up to that violent mating. He
was aware of a strong feeling of shame, of disgust for his

acts, and yet he could not deny that there had been a mad
excitement and pleasure in what had happened. His fine
lips thinned. Was he, like du Bois, simply a lustful, rut-
ting creature, intent upon his own pleasure? Uncaring
that he hurt or degraded his woman?

Aimlessly, he prowled through the darkened house, his
thoughts as dark and shadowed as the area around him.
God knew that despite the vendetta that had long existed,
he had never intended to treat Maria as he had this night.
At least, he amended fairly, not once he'd held her in his
arms and tasted the sweetness of her lips. He would freely
admit that he had dreamed of vengeance and that the
vengeance he had planned had been founded on rape and
degradation; but that, he almost cried aloud with pain,
had been only dreams—not reality! He could take little
consolation that in the end, it hadn't really been rape—
but his *intent* had been rape and that shook him to the
very core of his being.

A black frown marring his forehead, he slowly wandered out onto the patio at the rear of the house. Above
him the stars winked like diamonds on sable velvet, and
the scent of thousands of tropical flowers floated on the
night air, but he was oblivious to anything but his own
dark thoughts.

What was there about her that made him frustrate his
own desires? He hadn't *wanted* tonight to end as it had!
Nor, he discovered perplexingly, did he want to continue
to force Maria to accept him in her bed night after night.
What he desperately wanted, he admitted fiercely, was to
have the beguiling, sweet little creature he had known
that first night back in his arms! It was a damning ad-
mission, all the more so since it concerned the one woman
he should view with contempt and disdain! And she had
made it very plain how she felt about him! he thought
angrily.

Gingerly he reached up to touch the wound on his cheek.
It still bled slightly, and he swore under his breath at the
faint throb of pain the light pressure of his fingers caused.
Vixen! She had marked him well, and he grimaced ruefully at the knowledge that tomorrow he was going to
receive many ribald and bawdy remarks from his fellow
buccaneers. But while he could accept with equanimity

the teasing of his comrades, the situation with Maria was intolerable. And yet, wasn't it the way it *should* be? Wasn't it far more acceptable to be at drawn daggers with Maria Delgato than to be tormented by half-formed yearnings? Wasn't it better for his own peace of mind, for the years that he had thirsted for revenge against the Delgatos, to have it this way? To have her hating him? To know that each time he possessed her, that she was fighting him, that he was forcing her to submit to his embrace, just as his young innocent sister had probably been forced to accept the body of her captor?

Thinking of Caroline, his face hardened. By God's wounds! He was a fool to wish tonight had ended differently! The Delgatos had taken more from him than just a wife and sister that fateful day the *Raven* had been attacked—he had lost his future, the entire fabric of his life had been ruthlessly ripped apart, and now he should feel remorse for having subdued the daughter of the Delgatos? Unconsciously his hands formed two rock-hard fists and the green eyes glittered with a savage light. Zounds! Was he mad? He should feel no regret! If any event was to be regretted it was his gentle taking of Maria the first time!

Stubbornly he held on to those ugly thoughts, unwilling to allow his finer instincts to overcome his deep pride and vengeful emotions. Glaring furiously up at the diamond-studded black sky above, he vowed that never again would he allow the Delgato viper to confuse him, to cloud his judgment, to sway him from extracting a fitting revenge!

He could not, however, bring himself to return to the bedchamber that he shared with that ill-tempered hellcat, and being too wide awake to sleep anyway, he spent the remainder of the night hours pacing the confines of the patio. Broodingly he dwelt on all the wrongs inflicted upon the Lancasters by the Delgatos, and by the time dawn came, he was in a foul, bitter mood and ripe for trouble.

Returning to his bedchamber just as daylight was spreading across the tropical sky, he approached the bed with determined strides. The sight of Maria's tear-stained face caused his step to falter ever so slightly, and he was angrily aware of a sharp pang in the region of his heart. But steeling himself, he ignored those soft, emasculating emotions, and reaching out a hard hand, he roughly shook Maria awake.

Maria had not slept for very long, or very deeply, her painful thoughts having kept her awake until only minutes before Gabriel's arrival. And to wake and find his dark, hostile features only inches from hers was unnerving. She gave a start of half surprise, half fear, her eyes widening as she took in the full extent of the wound she had given him last night.

The blade had sliced a long groove just along the top of his cheekbone and in the morning light she could see from the swelling and green-and-purple bruises that surrounded it that she must have cut him deeply. Stupidly Maria stared at him, her heart banging hurtfully in her chest, aware of a painful longing to touch him, to soothe the wound that she had so violently inflicted upon him. But then, remembering what he had done to her, she stiffened and a resentful sparkle lit the sapphire blue eyes. Her chin lifted belligerently and nastily she demanded, "Yes, master? Is there something that your humble servant can do for you?"

Gabriel's jaw tightened and the green eyes narrowed. With an ungentle movement, he dragged her from the bed and snarled, "Aye! Your *master* wants some warmed water—go see to it!"

Tamping down a strong desire to smack his arrogant face, Maria contented herself with a mocking bow, saying sweetly, "Oh, master! It gives me much pleasure to serve you . . . but did you wish me to leave the room naked? After all, *you* took my clothes last night . . . or have you forgotten?"

For a moment, Maria feared she had overplayed her role, the expression on Gabriel's face thunderous as he glared at her. Then, spinning on his heels, he stalked furiously to the adjoining room; and scooping up the tattered shift from the floor where he had discarded it the previous night, he marched back to where she stood and with a violent motion threw the garment at her feet. Hands on his hips, he ground out, "I believe that should satisfy modesty's demands! Now get out of my sight!"

Deciding that it would be wisest to retreat in swift order, Maria hastily donned the rumpled shift and left the room quickly. Reaching the kitchens, she wasn't surprised to find that the fat *mayordomo* and the cook were already bustling about; and suppressing a mighty yawn, for it was only minutes after daylight, she walked over to one of the buckets filled with cold water that sat near the outside door. After splashing some water in her face, she attempted to make some semblance of order out of her tangled locks with her fingers, but it was a fruitless task. Giving up on it, she looked at the two servants who were warily regarding her. Recalling Gabriel's threats to them last night, she muttered. *"He* sent me here! He would also like some warmed water."

"Si!" the cook replied instantly. "I shall see to it immediately!" And then he busily set about pouring some water into a black iron kettle which reposed on the hearth. A small fire flickered there, and laying some more wood on it, the cook said briskly, "It shall only take a moment or two."

Maria nodded, and discovering that she was hungry, she helped herself to a hunk of warm bread that had just come from the brick oven. Slathering it with butter from the crock that sat on the table, she waited impatiently for the water to heat, wondering what the day would bring. Probably something utterly dreadful, she decided glumly as the cook motioned that the water was warm enough.

A thick rag was wrapped about the handle of the kettle, and as she lugged it through the hallways of the house, Maria toyed with the idea of simply dropping the kettle and walking out of the house. But then remembering the dangers of the streets and the burly buccaneers who guarded the perimeter of the house, she regretfully discarded that idea. She didn't, however, forget about escaping, a vigorous yearning to put as much distance between herself and Gabriel Lancaster taking possession of her. After last night, whatever fascination he may have held for her, whatever half-understood dreams she may have fashioned about him were shattered, and the thought of having to endure another night like the previous one was intolerable. She must escape! And somehow, some way, she would find a way!

Pushing open the door to the bedchamber, she said ungraciously, *"Señor!* Here is the water you wanted."

Gabriel had partially dressed while she had been gone, and despite all her protestations to the contrary, the sight of him, his powerful upper body naked above the full black breeches, left her curiously breathless. Despising herself for her reaction, she kept her eyes away from his magnificent body and stomped angrily toward the adjoining room, spilling several small puddles of water as she did so.

His eyebrow lifted sardonically and he murmured hatefully, "Such a sloppy little servant . . . I wonder if I should beat you?"

Maria shot him a look full of daggers, but held her tongue, suddenly guessing that he would like to provoke an unwise response from her. When she remained silent, he shrugged his broad shoulders, and pointing to a marble-topped table with a china bowl on it, he commanded, "Put it there—and then go and find yourself something else to wear other than that disreputable garment."

"Why?" she inquired tartly. "I find it perfectly suitable for the role that I must play."

His voice full of a dangerous silkiness, he said softly, "And I find that it offends me. Change it, or I shall change it myself! Need I say more?"

Her sweet mouth set in a tight line, she shook her head and retorted in choked tones, "I am free then, to leave your presence, master?"

"Only to go find something else to wear, and when you've done that, I expect you to join me in the dining *sala*—with," he added mockingly, "your hair combed!"

Maria pivoted sharply, eager to get away from him before she did something completely foolish, but his voice halted her just as she reached the doorway.

An almost purring quality to his words, he said, "And Maria—make certain that you *are* wearing something appropriate! Come to me in anything but proper clothing, and I shall strip you naked and parade you through the streets of Puerto Bello!"

His infuriating words ringing in her ears, she slammed out of the room, and whether she was more furious at his unerring perspicacity or his cold-blooded threats, she wasn't positive. Her small face marred by a ferocious scowl, resentfully she went in search of *proper* clothes.

Rifling through one of the trunks of booty she found in a small room near the rear of the house, she finally settled on a black damask skirt, a bodice of black-and-gold satin, several petticoats trimmed with frothy lace and a charming chemise of delicate gold silk. Shoes and stockings as well as other underclothing would have to be found elsewhere. The other items she ferreted out a second later, and plunder in hand, she returned to the bedchamber. Opening the door cautiously, she breathed a sigh of relief when she discovered the room empty.

There had been enough of the warm water left over from Gabriel's morning ablutions for her to manage a most satisfactory scrub. She rubbed herself unmercifully, almost as if she were trying to remove all traces of his touch upon her skin. Feeling refreshed, she dressed hurriedly in her finery and quickly combed her hair before fashioning the unruly locks into a long braid which she artfully curled around her head.

Taking a quick glance in a cheval glass, she left the room, entering the dining *sala* a few minutes later. Maria had hoped that despite the early hour Zeus or Pilar would also be up and stirring about, but her heart sank as she realized that Gabriel was the only other occupant in the long room.

There was an awkward silence, and then Gabriel rose from his chair and said coolly, "Thank you for obeying my orders and not giving me reason to mistreat you further. Now, if you will be seated, I shall ring for the servants to bring our meal."

They ate in that same awkward silence, Maria nearly gagging on the expertly prepared sweet cakes and hot chocolate; Gabriel overwhelmingly relieved that she had chosen to follow his orders and that he would not be forced to carry out his threats. He could have wished too that she didn't look quite so young and vulnerable in the black-and-gold apparel, the severe hairstyle enhancing the delicate beauty of her features. But then the faint throb from his wound reminded him that though she might look like a sweet angel, in reality, she was a deadly viper, at least as far as he was concerned.

The appearance of Zeus and Pilar just as the two hostile occupants were finishing their uncomfortable meal put an

end to the silence. Pilar, after a quick, encompassing
glance to see how Maria had fared the night before, had
then noticed the ugly gash upon Gabriel's cheek and unthinkingly cried out, *"Señor!* What has happened to you?"
As soon as the words left her mouth, she realized precisely what must have happened, and her lips shut with
a snap as she sent a worried look in Maria's direction.

It was left to Zeus to cover the embarrassed pause that
followed, and seating himself at the table, he murmured
unperturbedly, *"Ma chérie,* you really must do something
about this distressing habit you have of blurting out such
tactless questions." Helping himself from a large plateful
of cold meats that had been untouched by Gabriel or Maria and apparently oblivious to Pilar's gasp of outrage, he
continued, "It is obvious that the petite pigeon was driven
to teach our surly Dark Angel some manners. And since
they are both here together this morning, we can assume
that all has ended just as it should." He cocked a quizzical
eyebrow at Gabriel and inquired softly, *"Oui?"*

Gabriel snorted, but pushing aside his plate with its
half-eaten contents, he said calmly enough, "Let us
merely say that it ended, shall we? And without further
bloodshed." He shot Maria an odd look before adding quietly, "But I suspect that we both bear scars that the eye
cannot see."

Startled, Maria glanced at him, but unwilling to read
anything into his words, except idle conversation, her gaze
dropped instantly to the plate in front of her. There had
been a queer expression in those emerald green eyes
though, one almost of regret? Apology? Grimly, she banished such thoughts, her mouth taking on a mulish slant
that Pilar at least recognized immediately. Stubborn, pig-
headed, Delgato pride!

The remainder of the meal passed pleasantly enough,
and it was only when the men rose to leave that a strained
note entered the conversation. Stopping by Maria's chair,
Gabriel stared at her stubbornly down-bent head and said
harshly, "When I return this evening, I expect you to be
here to greet me *properly.* I don't want to find you in the
kitchens, nor do I want to find you garbed as you were
last night. If I do . . ." He didn't need to say any more,
the threat in his voice was explicit.

The door had barely closed behind the two men before Maria jumped up angrily from her chair, and her blue eyes blazing with fury, she spat, "Foul English dog! I cannot wait until they leave this place and we are left in peace!"

"Are you so certain he intends to leave you behind?" Pilar asked dryly.

Maria stared at Pilar with astonishment; the idea that Gabriel might *not* leave her behind obviously hadn't occurred to her. She swallowed painfully, suddenly assailed by a whole host of new sensations. Her face pale, she sank slowly back down in her seat, the bitter knowledge that she didn't really want to see the last of the Englishman striking her with the force of a blow.

Blankly, she stared across at Pilar, her thoughts and emotions in a frenzied turmoil. Pride and honor demanded that she take the stance she had, that she act the way she had and that she continue to do so, but her heart ... Her heart ached at the situation in which she found herself, a part of her longing for last night never to have occurred, yearning pitifully to forget that she was Maria Delgato and that he was Gabriel Lancaster, an English buccaneer, a lifelong foe of her family. A blind expression in the bright blue eyes, she asked dully, "What am I to do?"

"I don't think that you will have much say in the matter," Pilar returned matter-of-factly. "If *Señor* Lancaster decides that he is taking you back to Jamaica with him, you won't have any choice."

Maria was vaguely aware that under different circumstances the thought of leaving behind everything she had ever known and traveling with Gabriel Lancaster to Jamaica, of becoming a part of his world, would have been irresistibly appealing and exciting, but as things were ... She shivered, the dangers and pitfalls of her defenseless position crushing down on her. She glanced across at Pilar. With almost a note of wonder in her voice, she asked, "It doesn't frighten you?"

"No," Pilar answered calmly. "But then," she added sternly, "I wasn't quite mad enough to take a knife to him!" It was difficult to speak to Maria this way, very difficult not to fold the slender little body into her arms and offer comfort, but she could not. Maria *must* be made to understand that their very lives depended upon the two men who had captured them, and that Maria must, for the time being, control her unruly temper and willful Delgato pride. At the flash of pain that appeared in the dark blue eyes, Pilar almost relented, but steeling herself, she said grimly, "Maria, I warned him of your youth and innocence . . . I didn't think I would have to warn him of your lack of intellect! Are you insane? If you had fought and stabbed him that first night, I could have understood it, but now? For mercy's sake, why now?"

Hurt by Pilar's apparent desertion, confused and uncertain, Maria said forlornly, "I should never have allowed . . ." She swallowed with difficulty, tears stinging her eyes. "That first night should never have happened . . . for a little while, I forgot who he was and who I was . . . but then I remembered . . . and it all seemed horribly wrong somehow." Anguish in her voice, she cried out, "His father murdered mine! How could I lie with him? How can I forget what my own brother did to him? Or that it wasn't love that brought him here, but hate and the need for vengeance?" Almost shrilly, she added, "Do you think it was *me* that he wanted—it wasn't, it was merely that I was Maria Delgato—the sister of his sworn enemy!" The tears would be held back no longer, and as they spilled uncontrollably down her cheeks, she rose from her chair so abruptly that it tipped over onto the floor. Unmindful of the loud crash of the falling chair, she raced for the door and disappeared down the hallway.

Distressed and concerned, Pilar ran after her, catching her just as Maria prepared to dart into the bedchamber. Throwing her stern resolve to the winds, Pilar wrapped her arms about the sob-shaken young body and muttered, "Ah, pigeon. Don't cry so! And don't condemn yourself so! Why shouldn't you be attracted to him? He is handsome and utterly charming. What does it matter that you are a Delgato and he is a Lancaster?"

"Because," Maria got out woodenly, "his pride will not let him forget it—nor, I fear, will mine!" Shrugging out of Pilar's embrace, she said tiredly, "Leave it be, my good friend. There is nothing that you can do or say that will change anything." Bitterly she added, "My fate and Gabriel Lancaster's were decided long ago . . . in blood."

Maria spent a most unhappy day, her tangled emotions and thoughts giving her no respite. She was downhearted and miserable, one part of her aware that there was much to be said for Pilar's attitude, another part of her recoiling from the idea of betraying all those Delgatos who had gone before her and letting herself respond to the fascination she knew Gabriel Lancaster could hold for her. It was small and cold comfort to know that her actions last night had ensured that he would come no more to her with beguiling smiles and sweet, coaxing manners. It was equally small and cold comfort to know that his despicable actions last night had shown her a side to herself that she had never known existed. Just thinking of how she had been caught up in that mindless, elemental passion appalled her and gave her more reason not to listen to the softer prompting of her nature.

Pride might drive her to extreme lengths, but common sense dictated that she dare not disobey his commands, and consequently, though her very spirit rebelled, she forced herself to greet Gabriel and Zeus politely when they returned at dusk. And while Maria may have endured an unpleasant time of it, Gabriel's day had been no better.

Every ribald comment thrown his way from his highly amused friends and acquaintances only served to remind him of a night he would have preferred to forget. Only served to remind him of the tantalizing little witch who had somehow managed to infuriate him beyond reason. Gabriel was a man who prided himself on always being in control of his emotions, and Maria Delgato was wreaking havoc with his deepest feelings. She had thwarted his original intent to take a justly deserved revenge on one of the hated Delgatos, and then she had driven him against his will to treat her abominably. His actions of the previous night shamed him, and as the day passed, he was conscious of a building resentment against Maria inside of him. It wasn't that she had necessarily provoked the beast within him, so much as it was that, in spite of all the reasons against it, he found himself drawn irresistibly to her. He wanted her, and the wanting, he was dimly aware, had little to do with vengeance. Except for last night, she evoked the gentler side of him—the teasing, affectionate side his mother, sister and, briefly, his wife had known, and he resented it greatly. She made him recall another life, the life that had been his before Diego had brought it crashing down around his ears, and he found it somehow repugnant that Maria Delgato, of all women, should be the one to make him suddenly yearn for those half-forgotten dreams. It also enraged him unspeakably to discover that she alone aroused one of the Lancasterian traits he had always presumed had passed him by—that deep-seated possessiveness of the men of the Lancaster family. And it was brought home to him just how *very* possessive he felt about her when du Bois had remarked idly, "Ah, *mon ami,* you should have let me have her—she wouldn't have marked *me* that way—I would have taught her better manners!" Du Bois had laughed coarsely, rolling his eyes expressively, and Gabriel had been consumed by a blind, primitive rage at the merest idea of Maria in another man's embrace. Before anyone knew what happened he had been across the room, his hand crushing the startled du Bois' neck. His face inches from the other's, Gabriel had snarled, "Touch her just once, du Bois, and I'll gut you from throat to groin!"

Almost contemptuously, he had tossed du Bois away, and in the astonished silence that had fallen in the tavern where a group of the buccaneers had gathered, he had stalked majestically from the room. Glances of mingled dumbfoundment and amusement were exchanged between Zeus and Harry Morgan. Staring perplexedly at the door where Gabriel had disappeared, Morgan said thoughtfully, "My good Zeus, I really do think it behooves me to have further conversation with the little Delgato. It appears that she has a most remarkable effect upon our usually so amiable Dark Angel."

Zeus slowly shook his head. "It would not be such a good idea, I think. At the moment, there is, I fear, much trouble between them. Later, when they have both discovered the truth would be better."

"The truth?" Morgan asked curiously.

Zeus smiled mysteriously. "They are such blind fools, the pair of them. And when you see them together, you will understand exactly what I am saying."

It was fortunate that Gabriel didn't hear that particular conversation or he might have had a dangerous falling out with his friends. But while he hadn't heard Zeus' comments, his temper was still unsettled when they returned home that evening, and Maria's apparently docile acceptance of his orders didn't help matters any. Paradoxically, he was enraged to find her waiting so meekly for him, becomingly gowned in shades of russet and green, her hair neatly parted in the middle and caught in a pearl-studded chignon in the back. Eyeing the pearls of the chignon, he said sharply, "I see you managed to find the jewels."

There was disdain in his voice, as if she had done something wrong, and the blue eyes darkening with rising temper, she glared at him a second before snapping, "You said to be properly dressed!"

Zeus interfered before a full-blown argument could erupt by saying dulcetly, "And so lovely you look, petite pigeon . . . I wonder that I was so blind to choose Pilar."

Gabriel's jaw clenched, and with fire in his eyes, he turned on his friend, but Zeus was already laughing as he pulled a highly affronted Pilar into his arms. "Ma chérie," Zeus rumbled easily, "I but jest. There is no one for me but you. Now come along and I shall show you how very much I have missed you this day."

The evening meal was somewhat more enjoyable than the morning one had been; once again Zeus and Pilar covered any lapses of conversation on the part of the other two. As the hours passed, Maria felt some of the heavy ball of tension that had been forming in her chest gradually dissipate—beyond that first biting comment, Gabriel had been, if not conciliatory, at least polite. But as the time grew near for them to retire, a feeling of dread and revulsion began to spread through her. Was she to be forced to endure another night like the last?

Another night like the previous one was the last thing on Gabriel's mind when they were finally alone in the bedchamber. Full of a sick rage at his own loss of control, he couldn't have brought himself to touch her that way if a sword had been held to his heart, and when she stood stiffly in the center of the room, the faint flicker of fear undisguised in her lovely eyes, he felt compassion stir.

He started to reach for her, to take her into his arms and offer what comfort he could, but Maria, not unnaturally, recoiled violently from his touch. His outstretched hands fell, and wearily he muttered, "I won't hurt you—I won't even touch you, if that's what you want."

Her heart twisted at the faint hint of defeat in his voice, but steeling herself to resist his perfidious charms, she asked stonily, "Since when, *señor,* have you taken into account the wishes of your lowly servant?"

Stung, all thought of comfort vanished, and throwing her a look almost of contempt, he snarled, "Thank you for reminding me . . . *again,* of our differences!" Turning his back on her, he strode angrily to the bed, and wrenching off one of the pillows and a blanket, he threw them at her. "Since you *are* my servant—sleep on the floor at my feet and the devil with you!"

Chapter Sixteen

MARIA almost threw the bed things back at him, but deciding that it would be most unwise, she angrily picked up the blanket and pillow and moved to the far side of the big room. She might sleep on the floor, but not like a dog at its master's feet!

Sleep didn't come very easily to either one of them, Gabriel missing the feel of her small shape next to him, regretting all that had passed between them, yet unable to retreat from the position that pride and the past injustices between their families had placed him in. For Maria it was no better—worse, perhaps, in that the floor made an extremely *un*comfortable bed, and every time she squirmed around trying to find a more agreeable position, the reasons that she found herself here came flooding back to haunt her and at the same time stiffen her resolve. During the days that followed, the resentment and hostility between the two protagonists did not abate one jot. The animosity continued to simmer dangerously just below the surface; each one refused to be the first to alter the pattern that had come about through the unyielding, obstinate pride of the other. During the day, Gabriel made certain that Maria was kept busy with menial chores that related to his personal well-being—icily she was ordered to mend his clothes, clean his shoes, wash his clothing and keep their room in an impeccable state—no easy task, since he deliberately went out of his way to leave things haphazardly scattered about, making Maria's work that much harder. Every time she glared at him, he smiled grimly, his eyes gleaming with challenge, daring her to defy him. Gritting her teeth, muttering under her breath

language that would have shocked her only a fortnight
ago, she would angrily turn away. The nights were the
easiest to endure, Maria continuing to sleep on the floor,
each night wrapping the blanket about her slender body
with a majestic disdain for the other occupant of the room.

Fortunately, Gabriel was not about often; he and Zeus
were gone from daybreak to dusk, busy with the overseeing of the gathering of booty. The buccaneer ships had
been brought about from the coast, and they filled the
harbor; every day more and more plunder was stowed in
the increasingly bulging holds. When he was at the house,
Gabriel treated Maria with a cool contempt, making it
painfully clear to her who was master and who was captive.

That the buccaneers would one day leave Puerto Bello
could not be ignored. It was obvious from the haste with
which the loot from the stricken city was being gathered
and loaded on the ships that Morgan did not wish to remain longer than necessary. But it was not always easy
to keep command of the rough, boisterous crew he led,
and the town frequently rang with the bawdy, raucous
sounds of the corsairs as they continued to pillage, rape
and plunder the Spanish city they had conquered. As the
days passed though, and the signs of departure became
clearer and clearer, Maria became aware of an oppressive
feeling of despair and confusion.

Undoubtedly, she would be overjoyed the day Harry
Morgan and his crew of cutthroat buccaneers sailed away,
but the thought of never seeing Gabriel Lancaster again,
despite all the reasons that she should be delighted at
that prospect, filled Maria with despondency. Yet the half-
exciting, half-terrifying idea of being compelled to go with
him to Jamaica filled her with an odd feeling of relief and
fear. What sort of life would she face as the Englishman's
slave? She would be in a foreign world, among people
whose ways were strange to her, whose very language she
could only partially understand and that only because of
her association with Caroline Lancaster and Pilar. She
spared a thought for Caroline, her sympathy deepening
for the other girl as she realized how frightening Hispaniola and its inhabitants must have been to the English
girl. And now she might be faced with the same fate that

had befallen Gabriel's sister—captive of an enigmatic man who had no reason to treat her kindly. . . .

And yet, except for that one savage night and his infuriating manner with her, Gabriel had not been unkind. And hearing the frightened whispers of the servants as they discussed the brutalities and sordid conditions of the city of Puerto Bello, Maria discovered, despite the hostility and open antagonism that flowed between them, that she was profoundly grateful that it had been Gabriel Lancaster who had captured her. Just remembering du Bois' leering features sent a spasm of sheer terror rocketing through her slender body, and listening to the appalling tales told by the servants, belatedly she began to realize how *very* kind the fates had been to her and how very sheltered she and Pilar were from the realities of what was befalling the plundered city. They lived in a cocoon of luxury and splendor, their two captors treating them with unheard-of benevolence and patience. Immured in the house, except for their treatment at the hands of their buccaneer captors, they were untouched by the events that had shaken the city. Not for them the horror of rapine and murder, not for them the degradation of being forced to barter their bodies to one brutal buccaneer after another simply to stay alive; nor did they face the pain and cruelty of the instruments of the Inquisition that were employed gleefully by the buccaneers against their Spanish captives, torturing out of pain-racked bodies the locations of hidden treasures. They were not forced to see their homes invaded and laid waste by the rampaging corsairs, nor compelled to beg for the lives of their loved ones; all that was spared them, but hearing the ugly stories only made Maria feel more guilt-stricken at the near-normalcy of their days. Every time she put on one of the fine silken petticoats and skirts or touched the rich brocaded bodices or even ate the succulent dishes prepared by the cook, she was filled with repugnance and conscious of a growing great rage against Harry Morgan's buccaneers and most of all against Gabriel Lancaster.

As the days passed, her resentment and fury increased, the tension between her and Gabriel becoming an almost tangible thing, the very air crackling with electricity whenever they were in each other's company, so much so that Pilar and Zeus began to avoid being present whenever the other two were in the same vicinity. More and more Gabriel's eyes rested on Maria's lovely features with a sort of baffled fury, and there were moments when the threat of violence hung heavy in the air and his green eyes would flash with anger at some provoking act of Maria's. And while she knew she had been most fortunate to fall into his hands, Maria could not prevent herself from deliberately enraging him, pushing him to the very limits of his endurance, constantly testing his patience, almost daring him to strike her, to treat her with all the cruelty that had been visited upon the other inhabitants of the city. She didn't understand her own actions, and she was so very weary of the battle that was waged continually within herself. Occasionally the guard she kept rigidly on herself would slip, and her eyes would follow Gabriel wistfully about the house, but then she would remember, reminding herself viciously, that he was a buccaneer, an enemy of Spain, a deadly foe of her family, and for the time being the traitorous feelings he aroused within her would be vanquished. . . .

The idea of escape occurred to her time and time again, but knowing that no help lay within the city, that her only chance of safety lay in reaching Panama City and that between Puerto Bello and Panama City lay miles and miles of savage untracked jungle, jungle filled with hostile Indians, poisonous snakes, swamps and feral beasts of prey . . . Sighing, she pushed the thoughts away, but persistently they returned night after night as she lay on her makeshift bed on the floor, hating Gabriel for the conflict within herself and hating herself for the weak-willed yearning for events to have been different between them, but most of all for the painful stab that knifed through her whenever she contemplated life without him.

For Gabriel the time was no easier, his emotions so tangled and lacerated that it was a wonder he didn't come to blows with the amiable Zeus. Full of rage and frustration at his own inability to destroy the sweet longings Maria had awakened within him, he watched her with a brooding bitterness. She was his prisoner, his slave, and yet he could not bring himself to mete out the degradations he had once promised himself. Oh, he could order

her about, treat her with an icy disdain, provoke her,
make the sapphire eyes sparkle with temper; but as for
the spirit-destroying punishments he had dreamed of, that
was beyond him. Instead of breaking her pride, clothing
her in rags and manacles, forcing her to grovel before
him, humbling that Delgato arrogance by the same mis-
treatments that had been heaped upon him, what did he
do? Like a besotted fool, Gabriel thought one night, as he
lay sleepless in the big bed, he clothed her in plundered
riches, saw to it that she was protected and cared for and,
most galling of all, denied himself the pleasures of her
body! Scowling, he glanced over to where she lay huddled
on the floor, the faint stream of moonlight that lanced the
darkness of the room outlining her slender form. God's
blood! he thought wrathfully. He must be bewitched to lie
here night after night aching to have her in his arms and
yet unwilling to repeat the violence of the last time he
had possessed her.

It was a situation that could not last. Sooner or later
the smoldering rage that built within him or the seething
resentment that rose in her would have to be released.
Finally, one morning when the buccaneers had been in
control of Puerto Bello for about ten days, events came to
a head and in a manner that surprised both of them.

Waking that morning just as the tropical sun bathed
the horizon in gold and pink hues, Gabriel looked across
at Maria's sleeping form. During the night, her light covering had come off, and the skimpy shift she slept in had
slipped off one of her shoulders, giving an enticing glimpse
of one small, coral-tipped breast. Mesmerized, he stared
at that gentle rounded globe of creamy flesh, desire sweet
like honey and warm like wine surging up wildly through
his body. Her face was turned toward him, a shaft of sunlight gilding the fine features with gold dust, making the
long, dark lashes appear even darker, the sultry shape of
her mouth more kissable; and without thought, he slid
from his bed, filled with an inexpressible yearning to
know again the intoxicating ecstasy they had shared that
first night together. But he took only two steps before the
memory of that other, no less pleasurable, but distinctly
shameful mating came back to haunt him. He could not
bear for it to be repeated, and his expression bleak, he

returned to his bed. Grimly he regarded her, an irrational rage replacing the desire that had flooded him only a moment ago. He must be quite mad, he decided angrily, staring at her small shape, against his will his eyes lingering on the rise and fall of her breasts. Was she not his prisoner? As captor wasn't it his right to possess her body as he pleased? And hadn't he promised himself that if she ever fell into his hands he would extract some measure of revenge for what had been done to him by her family? If the answers to those questions were yes, he asked himself sarcastically, why then did he sleep alone? Furious at his own confusing actions, he glared at her and vowed relentlessly that his lunacy was at an end! Tonight, willing or not, hating him or not, she would be in his bed and in his arms. . . .

Still in the grip of his own brooding bad mood, he picked up one of his silver-buckled shoes lying nearby on the floor and with unerring aim, tossed it at her. The shoe landed with a clattering thud not two inches from Maria's sleeping body, and at the sound she jerked upright, her eyes opening wide with fright.

Perhaps she wouldn't have reacted so if she hadn't been once again caught up in another of those heart-dividing, terror-filling dreams of fatal conflict between her brother and Gabriel. But as it was, she had been. In her nightmare the cannons had been booming thunderously, even as Gabriel and Diego faced each other across a blood-slick deck, their swords flashing and feinting as each sought to strike the killing blow against the other. The sound of the shoe hitting the floor so near her head had echoed the roars of the cannon in her dreams, and it was no wonder that she woke with such a look of utter horror on her face, her heart banging painfully in her chest.

Seeing her expression, never guessing the cause of it, Gabriel coldly quelled the treacherous urge to gather her to him and to soothe away with tender kisses her obvious discomfort. And determined to show her no more kindness, swearing from this moment on to treat her as he had always promised himself he would do, he said icily, "A well-trained slave does not lie abed longer than the master. And if you don't want me to mar that pretty hide of yours with a whip, get yourself up off that floor this instant and go to the kitchens at once and bring back the water for my morning ablutions!"

It took Maria a second to orientate herself, to realize that the horrid dream was just that, a dream; but then as his tone and the import of his words sunk in, she was consumed by temper. *Dios!* And to think that only moments before she had been, in her dream, terrified for his life! Biting back the hot words that crowded her throat, she jumped to her feet and struggled into a simple skirt and bodice. Throwing him a look full of anger, she took a certain satisfaction from the thin scar upon his cheekbone that now marred his handsome face. It was, she thought viciously as she stormed from the room, a pity that she had not cut out his black heart!

Still not fully awake, but more furious than she had been in a long time, upon reaching the kitchens and spying the buckets of cold water that had just been brought into the house that morning, she was struck by a wicked inspiration. Giving herself no time to consider the consequences of what she planned, she swiftly grasped the handle of one of the buckets and started to stalk from the room, but the cook's voice slowed her step.

"Oh, *señorita!* Not that one! It is very cold. I have already heated some water for the master and will get it for you this very moment."

Maria smiled at him sweetly. *"Very* cold, you said?"

"Sí! It has just been drawn from the deepest well."

Her smile widened mischievously. "Then it shall do just fine!" she replied demurely and swung out of the kitchen.

Thinking that she would be gone longer, Gabriel had dozed off into a light sleep. Vaguely he heard the opening of the door and the soft sounds of her footsteps approaching the bed. Always on the alert for danger, the fact that she was not going on through to the small dressing room impinged upon his consciousness, and his eyelids flew open. But it was too late.

Her voice fairly purring with satisfaction, she murmured dulcetly, "Your water, master." And proceeded to dump the entire bucket of cold water over his head.

The shock of the icy water so unexpectedly dousing his upper body took Gabriel's breath away. When he could breathe again, a gasp of painful astonishment came from him, and he sat bolt upright in the bed, shaking his head like a dog, sending droplets of water spraying in all directions.

The enormity of what she had done swept over Maria, but no matter what he did to her, she knew she couldn't wish it undone; and torn between amusement and horror she clasped a hand to her mouth, holding back the hysterical gurgle of laughter that threatened to bubble forth. It was as well that she did not laugh for Gabriel was *not* amused.

Naked as the day he was born, the emerald-and-gold earring gleaming through the wet strands of black hair, the gold slave collar beaded with water, he sprang from the bed. "Why, you little vixen!" he snarled. "When I get my hands on you, you'll have cause to curse the day we ever met!" The green eyes were as hard as the emerald that pierced his ear, and to her complete mortification, Maria discovered that she had never found him more irresistible.

He was a magnificent creature as he stood there unadorned before her, his chest lightly heaving, crystal rivulets of water slowly, almost sensuously sliding down his tall, muscled form. She could not tear her eyes away from him, her gaze moving over his superb, sun-darkened body with a hungriness that would have shamed her if she had known it. Wide shoulders tapered down to a hard waist and lean hips, his chest covered with an attractive sprinkling of black curls that narrowed just below his waist before flaring out again thicker and more abundantly across the groin.

Maria had never really seen a naked man before, and helplessly she continued to stare at him, a slow heat building in her loins, her breath seeming trapped in her throat as the minutes passed and a new element entered the room. His legs were long and elegantly muscular, but Maria found her eyes compulsively drawn to where the hair grew thickest between his thighs, and under her wondering gaze, she watched as his manhood suddenly swelled, bulging and rising upright, his desire obvious.

Reluctantly, she ripped her eyes off of his imposing organ and met his stare, somehow not surprised to find the anger gone, his eyes dark now with an urgent desire that was reflected in her own gaze. Her hand left her mouth and dazedly she swayed toward him. In one stride he had her in his strong arms, his mouth coming down hungrily on hers. Feeling his hard body pressed ardently next to hers, reveling in the fierce sweetness of his kiss, Maria blindly gave herself up to the ecstasy she knew they would find, so very weary of fighting herself, so desperately weary of trying single-handedly to uphold the pride and honor of countless generations of Delgatos.

Neither one of them heard the sudden opening of the door, but they both jumped as if shot at the sound of the door hitting the wall from the force of the shove Zeus had given it. Gabriel's eyes full of murder, he swung around in that direction, but seeing his friend standing there in the doorway, obviously full of vital news, he dropped his hands from Maria's shoulders and demanded, "Yes? What is it? What is wrong? The Spanish?"

Zeus nodded his no-longer-bald head, now covered by a faint fuzz of dark hair. Not one whit flustered by the intimate scene he had just interrupted, he replied, *"Oui!* I've just come from Morgan's house—an Indian messenger arrived while I was there—the Viceroy and Captain General of Panama is fast approaching the city with a military force of nearly three thousand men . . . and speculate, if you will, who marches by his side."

Gabriel's eyes narrowed, studying Zeus' satisfied smile intently. Incredulously, he finally said, "Not Delgato?"

Zeus nodded smugly. *"Oui!* The new Vice-Admiral himself! It seems from what the Indians discovered that Delgato sailed into the capital city only hours before de Bracamonte, the President, departed and immediately offered his services." He cocked an eye in Maria's direction. "Do you think he knows she is here?"

Hastily pulling on breeches and shirt, Gabriel glanced at Maria. His voice noncommittal, he asked her, *"Does* he know you are here?"

Her thoughts in a whirl, elated and frightened at the same time, Maria stared at him dumbly for a moment. What should she say? Try to trick him? Or tell him the truth? And what did it matter what she told him? Finally she answered honestly, "I don't know . . . he might guess I *was* here—but he won't know whether I was able to sail away before your attack. . . ." A bitter note entered her voice, "Or if I was unfortunate enough to be captured."

His mouth grim, the emerald eyes hard and cold, he spat out bitingly, "Then before I kill him I'll have to make certain that he learns of your *unfortunate* capture, won't I?"

A second later, he and Zeus were gone, nearly running from the house in their haste to reach Morgan's and learn how the Admiral of the Brethren planned to counter this new threat. They reached Morgan's headquarters moments later, and upon going inside, they were not surprised to find several buccaneer captains assembled there, their various states of undress clearly revealing that they had just tumbled from bed, but all were heavily armed.

Morgan, however, was fully dressed and lounging near the rear of the long room; watching as his friend coolly answered the questions hurled at him, Gabriel decided that Morgan was also fully in command. The black eyes flashing, Morgan eventually put a stop to the hubbub. "By Satan's tail! Are you men or frightened babes? Do you think that having come this far, we'll let those Spanish dogs snatch our booty from our very hands! Bah!" As the silence fell, he leaned forward confidently, a look of supreme conviction on his swarthy face. "I've a plan . . . the Spaniards don't know that they have been spotted nor that the Indians have apprised us of their approach. . . ." He glanced around to see how the men were taking his words, and emboldened by their intent gazes, he added craftily, "A short march from here, there is a narrow pass . . . the perfect place for, say, a hundred men or more to ambush the vile popish swine. What say you?" There was not an immediate response, but not giving them time to consider it further, Morgan said slyly, "And for every man who volunteers, there will be an extra share of plunder!"

That settled any indecision, and in a relatively short time, a group of about a hundred buccaneers were making rapid preparations to plunge into the jungle and reach that narrow pass. Alone with Morgan a moment, Gabriel asked him, "Is it true that Diego Delgato is with the Spanish?"

"Aye! The Indians know him well—and hate him equally well for his brutality and cruelty to them—one

still bore the scars from the lashing that Delgato gave
him two years ago when last he was in the vicinity."
Casting Gabriel a considering look, he added mockingly,
"This venture is proving quite profitable to you, is it not?"

A tigerish smile curved Gabriel's chiseled mouth. "Aye,
it is, Harry! And as for the extra share of plunder—keep
mine!" Almost lovingly, his hand tightened on the handle
of the broadsword at his waist. "Gutting Delgato is all
the reward I ask!"

It was only as he and Zeus were racing back to the
house to issue brief orders before they left the city that
Gabriel thought to ask the other man what he had been
doing at Morgan's place that early in the morning. Zeus
hesitated a moment, then said bluntly, "I wanted him to
release a priest so that I might marry Pilar."

Gabriel stiffened. Something that could have been hurt
in his tone, he inquired quietly, "Why did you say nothing to me?"

Gently Zeus answered, "Because, *mon ami*, in the mood
you are in these days, you would have tried to prevent
me."

"I see," Gabriel said slowly. But unable to help himself,
he demanded dryly, "And nothing will sway you from this
mad folly?"

Smiling hugely, Zeus replied jovially, "Nothing, *mon
ami!* I love her and last night she agreed to marry me—if
I would find a priest to say the vows. I have long searched
for a woman like my Pilar, and having found her, I shall
not let her go."

Recognizing that at present further argument on the
subject would gain him naught, reluctantly Gabriel held
his tongue. His only hope to stop this folly, this marriage
he was certain would only bring grief and pain to his
friend, was after they had routed the Spanish. Perhaps
then he could somehow make Zeus see reason. But watching the way Zeus enfolded Pilar in a powerful embrace
and tenderly kissed her when they reached the house, his
heart sank. Zeus was truly ensnared.

Taking his eyes off the other couple, he looked at Maria
as she stood before him, her eyes wide and full of apprehension. Angry on several counts and not certain why, he
cupped her chin and asked sardonically, "Will you miss

me, sweet, while I am gone? Or will you pray that your
brother's sword carves out my liver?"

Maria swallowed with difficulty, pain slashing through
her at the picture his words conjured up. Racked by the
conflicting emotions that tore through her, she could only
stare up at his handsome dark face, one part of her longing to cast herself into his arms, to rain kisses over that
hard mouth, to beg that he stay with her, that he not risk
his life, but another part, a part of her that she was beginning to hate, rejected those softer emotions and longed
to be free of him. The news that her brother was coming,
that rescue was within reach had done nothing to still the
turmoil that ate at her; and the knowledge that rescue
might mean Gabriel's death or at least that she would
never see him again took away whatever joy news of Diego's approach might have given her. Realization that
whatever the outcome of the confrontation with Diego,
this might be the last time she would ever see him alive
chilled her. To both their astonishment, unable to help
herself, her eyes brimming with unshed tears, she
brushed feather-light fingers across the scar on his
cheekbone and choked out, "I shall pray for both of you!"
then spun on her heel and, ignoring Gabriel's cry of her
name, raced from the room.

He took a step after her, but Zeus placed a restraining
hand on his arm. "We must go, *mon ami*. There will be
time enough for that later."

Full of frustration, Gabriel glared at his friend, but
then, knowing Zeus was right, resolutely he put Maria's
contrary actions out of his mind. There was only one thing
that he could think of now—somewhere out there in the
jungles that lay between Puerto Bello and Panama City,
Diego Delgato was approaching. Diego Delgato, who had
killed his young wife, enslaved his sister and nearly broken his own spirit. Diego Delgato, his greatest enemy, the
one man, above all others, he wanted dead. All thoughts
of Maria vanished from his mind, and there was only one
thing in his brain as he followed Zeus into the jungle—
find Diego and kill him!

Chapter Seventeen

THE house seemed unnaturally silent once the men had departed, and alone on the big bed that she had shared so few times with Gabriel, Maria lay sobbing as if her heart would break. He was gone. And she might never see him again—in a matter of hours, he might be dead. Her slender body trembled with horror at the idea, and for one anguished moment she relived that terrible day on Hispaniola when she had stared down at his still, unmoving form and had thought him dead.

A low moan of denial escaped her. It might be wrong, it might be against everything she had been taught, but she could not wish him dead. She could, she realized bleakly, face anything but his death. She might hate him, and at this moment, she wasn't so very certain that what she felt for him was *hate*, he might be insolent, provoking, infuriating and the enemy of her family, but she could *not* wish for his death! Even if she never saw him again, never saw that hard, implacable face again, never heard that deep-timbred voice again, she wanted him *alive!* And he was going to fight her brother—her brother, who would free her from this dark captivity, who would spirit her away to Casa de la Paloma—Casa de la Paloma where she would live out her days, always remembering the laughing green eyes of the Englishman. . . .

A choked cry came from her, and sitting up, she buried her face in her hands. What was she to do? Never, she decided wretchedly, had there been such a vacillating captive as herself. Her brother was on his way to rescue her, and did she find that gratifying? No! All she could

231

think of was the danger to the very man who had captured her!

Guilt swept over her. Vile, wicked creature that you
are, she cursed herself silently, your brother's life is at
stake and you shed tears for the man who may kill him!

Straightening her slim shoulders, she roughly scrubbed
her tears away, angry with herself for giving way like
that, angry that she was caught once again on the same
treadmill of pride and family honor battling with the feeling that Gabriel Lancaster aroused within her. A small
hiccoughing sob came out as she stared dumbly about the
room, her brain frantically seeking some way to escape
from the powerful emotions that clashed within her. But
there was no escape, the tension mounting inside of her
as scenes from her nightmares came back to haunt her.

Her nightmares, she realized sickly, were about to come
true. Soon, in some jungle clearing, the two most important men in her life would come face to face . . . and try
to kill each other. She closed her eyes in pain, guilt once
more sweeping through her. She didn't want her brother
dead, but she could not admit to any deep affection for
him either, and that, perhaps more than anything, increased her feelings of guilt. Especially since buried in
the most hidden recesses of her mind was the knowledge
that her choice of who would live and who would die had
already been made. A trail of tears trickled pitifully down
her cheeks. She was, she was quite certain, the most
treacherous, despicable, base creature alive! If only, she
thought despairingly, there were some way to avert that
coming confrontation. If only she could be there to somehow avert the needless tragedy.

Suddenly, she stilled, a wild, desperate idea bursting
across her brain. If she was there . . . If miraculously, she
could be in the midst of the battle . . . If she was present
the instant Gabriel and Diego laid eyes on each other,
couldn't she prevent one from killing the other? Throw
herself between them? Deflect the killing blow?

In a saner, less emotional state, she would have dismissed the idea as ludicrous, but as it was, the reckless
thought took violent hold of her mind. She *must* be there!
She must not let them kill each other!

Tears gone, her forehead furrowed in concentration, she

jumped up from the bed, restlessly pacing the confines of the room. How? How was she to accomplish this miracle of hers?

Pilar's entrance into the room momentarily distracted her, and though knowing there could be no news yet, she glanced fearfully across at her and asked, dry-mouthed, "Is there word? Have you heard something?"

Sending her a sympathetic smile, Pilar shook her head. "No, pigeon. They have only been gone but a short time. We will not hear anything for hours." Her smile faded, anxiety peeping into the fine dark eyes. "And then," she added heavily, "the news we hear may not be what we want."

In all their years together, Maria had never seen Pilar so obviously distressed, and gently she asked, "What do you want to hear?"

"That Zeus is alive and well and is coming back to me," she answered without hesitation, the love she felt for him suddenly blindingly apparent from the expression on her handsome face.

"You're in love with him!" Maria burst out almost accusingly, not quite able to believe that this sophisticated, worldly woman could have fallen in love so quickly—or with a man she should view as her enemy.

Pilar smiled ruefully. "*Sí!* I am very much! And do not ask me how it came about, for I do not understand it yet myself! It is absolutely impossible that at my age and position, I should find myself as giddily in love as a child of sixteen and, worse, with a buccaneer!" Her voice had a soft, wondering lilt to it as she added, "But so it is! From the first moment he held me in his arms and I looked up into his face, I knew that something vitally important had happened in my life, but it has only been these past few days that I have known precisely what it was that happened to me! I love him madly, Maria!" Her face glowing, she continued with an odd shyness, "Last night he asked that I marry him and . . . " She hesitated, ending in a rush, "I said yes!"

Maria was aware of a pang of envy at Pilar's words, but she pushed it away, unwilling to speculate on her own emotions at this time. Smiling warmly at her friend, she said affectionately, "I am so very happy for you! But, but when will you marry and where will you live? In Jamaica? Will he continue to, to . . ." Her voice trailed off, not wishing to mention Zeus' way of life.

An understanding smile on her face, Pilar walked over to where Maria was standing, and putting a fond arm around the slender shoulders, she said merrily, "Oh, he has promised to be a lawful man—he says that he has many acres of land in Jamaica and that he will do as Gabriel has been suggesting for some time and become a respectable planter." A twinkle danced in the dark eyes. "He says that if he is to become a married man and the father of a growing family, it is indeed time for him to give up his wild ways."

Again, Maria was conscious of another pang of envy, this one stronger and more insistent, but stubbornly she refused to examine its cause and asked blankly, "A family? Are you? But you wouldn't know for certain this soon! Would you?"

Glad to talk of something that would keep her mind off of Zeus and the danger he was facing, Pilar answered lightly, "According to Zeus it is only a matter of time until I am big with his child. He, as he has informed me frequently these past few weeks, has certainly been doing *his* share to ensure that I am!" She hugged Maria to her and admitted huskily, "Oh, Maria! I am happier than I have ever been in my entire life!" Her voice faltered, "And so very frightened! I could not bear it if something happened to him now. Now when I have just discovered the only man I could ever love!"

The fear that was in both women couldn't be ignored, and her face buried against Pilar's shoulder, Maria said in a muffled tone, "Nothing must happen to either of them! They must be safe! They *must!*" For a moment she considered telling Pilar of her reckless scheme, but then she discarded the idea, knowing that Pilar would do everything to stop her from carrying out her desperate plan.

There had been an estrangement between the two women of late, but the common bond of worry and fear for the two men who ruled their lives banished it, and for the first time in a long time the closeness they had once known was in full effect. With a great deal of discipline, they both avoided speculating on what Zeus and Gabriel were doing at this moment; by unspoken tacit agreement, they also avoided any conversation that dealt with Maria's situation, but Pilar found much to talk about, and not so surprisingly her favorite subject was Zeus. Listening to her sing his praises, Maria smiled to herself, wondering if Zeus would recognize himself from Pilar's descriptions. But she was only paying attention to Pilar's comments with half her mind; the other half was busily scheming to find a way, without hurting Pilar's feelings, of bringing this tête-à-tête to an end so that she could set about putting her admittedly farfetched plan into action. Fortunately, after several minutes, Pilar inquired quietly, "Would you mind being alone for a while, *chica?* I—I—I think that I have babbled on long enough, and if I stay here, sooner or later, I will not be able to hold back my fears for his safety. If I keep myself busy about the house, I shall be better able to control my thoughts; so if you have no objections, I shall leave you now."

If Pilar's mind hadn't been so full of images of Zeus, she might have noticed that Maria's agreement was quickly given, too quickly, and she might have paid more attention to the younger girl's actions. But as it was, giving Maria an affectionate kiss on the cheek, she wafted from the room.

Knowing that time was passing swiftly, that in order to avert the fatal clash between Gabriel and Diego she must act immediately, Maria was in motion almost before Pilar had shut the door behind her. Racing across the room to a chest containing, among other things, several pieces of masculine attire, she knelt before it and frantically rummaged through the contents.

There were many obstacles in her path, not the least of these her very sex, but Maria had already thought of a way to circumvent that problem—she would disguise herself as a boy! A boy buccaneer! If she had had time for more rational thought, the sheer lunacy of her thinking would have no doubt occurred to her, but she was driven by the twin devils of fear and guilt, and impulsive as always, she gave herself no time to consider her actions, no time to question the wisdom of what she was doing.

Moments later, clothed in an ill-fitting shirt and baggy black breeches with a length of knotted yellow silk acting

as a belt around her waist, she surveyed herself critically
in a cheval glass. Thankfully, her small breasts proved to
be a decided asset under these circumstances, she thought
with a nervous giggle, and flattened as they were by the
cloth she had bound around them, no one would guess of
their existence. The clothes though were obviously far too
large for her, but she consoled herself with the knowledge
that from what she'd seen of some of the other buccaneers, sartorial elegance meant little to them! Her slender calves were covered by a pair of cotton stockings that
fit no better than the rest of her raiment, but undeterred,
grimly she secured her long black hair with an ivory comb
on top of her head. She would need shoes and a hat of
some sort to cover her hair, as well as disguise her features, and once she had obtained those items, she decided
with an unpleasant thrill of fright, she had *only* to escape
the house, find Gabriel and miraculously stop him from
killing her brother, or Diego from killing him!

In the end, everything worked out much better than
she could ever have dreamed it would. Sidling into the
kitchens, she happened upon one of those rare moments
when it was deserted, and she took instant advantage of
it. Grabbing a floppy-brimmed straw hat that hung on a
hook by the door, she slapped it on her head, rubbed some
soot from the hearth across her face to further her disguise and found, to her great delight, in the pantry, a
well-worn pair of shoes that must have belonged to one of
the younger servants, judging by the small size of them.
They didn't fit much better than the rest of her clothing,
but all in all, she was satisfied. Grabbing an empty bucket
that sat on the scrubbed wooden table, she darted out the
door that led outside before she could change her mind.
Next, she thought determinedly, she must escape from
the buccaneer guards Gabriel had placed around the
house. But that too proved to be relatively simple—Gabriel had given them orders to watch the *women* of the
household, not a grubby little servant boy on his way to
get water from the well.

Her heart thumping madly in her breast, her breath
coming in half-excited, half-fearful gasps, Maria scurried
down the brown-cobblestoned streets of the city, almost
unable to believe the ease with which she had crossed her

first hurdles. Well away from the house, she dashed into
an alley, tossed her bucket away, and then after sending
up a fervent prayer for help and guidance, she set out
upon her mad journey.

Finding the trail the buccaneers had taken into the jungle was not hard, the recent passage of a hundred men or
more could not be easily obliterated in the scant time that
had passed since Gabriel and Zeus had left the house.
Pleased with herself, buoyed up with a sudden burst of
confidence, Maria followed the signs they had left as
swiftly as possible. She would not think of what she was
going to do once she caught up with the buccaneers. *When*
she found them, then *some*thing, she was certain, would
occur to her!

They had over an hour's head start on her, and grimly,
Maria forced herself to move through the encroaching
gloom of the jungle at a rapid pace. She had to catch up
with them; she had to be there *before* the battle began—
and most important of all, in that dangerous motley collection of corsairs, she *had* to find Gabriel!

The deeper she went into the jungle, the closer the verdant growth seemed to press. In the treetops monkeys
chattered and screamed, hundreds of blue-and-green par-
akeets darted through the tangled growth and parrots and
toucans squawked. Stopping to catch her breath near a
huge cinta tree, Maria glanced uncertainly around her.
The jungle was full of dangers, pythons and jaguars and
the deadly *tabobas* and *coralis* snakes lurked here too. As
if to prove it, what she had assumed was merely a hanging vine near her head unexpectedly slithered off, and she
smothered a shriek of terror as she jumped away. Shaken
but undaunted, she plunged on into the orchid-splashed
greenness.

How long she ran, she never knew—it seemed like
hours—but then just as frantic despair nearly overtook
her, she became aware of a subtle difference in the sounds
around her. There *was* no sound; the jungle was suddenly
deathly silent and that meant only one thing—man was
nearby. Carefully now, she moved through the dimly lit
forest, her eyes trying to pierce the gloom that surrounded her, searching for what had caused the jungle
inhabitants to still their usually noisy chatter.

So intent was she on catching her first sight of the buccaneers that she wasn't watching where she put her feet, and stumbling over a half-rotted log, she plunged headfirst into the brush and right on top of the brawny corsair who had lain there concealed in the green darkness. There was a muffled curse and rough hands shoved her down onto the moist leaf-covered floor of the forest.

"For God's sake, boy! Keep down! You want to alert the popish dogs that we are here?" the buccaneer growled.

Her heart somewhere in her throat, Maria shook her head, inordinately grateful that her hat had not sailed off when she had fallen. *Cielos!* She had wanted to find the buccaneers, but this wasn't quite what she had planned! When the man beside her remained silent, she cast him a cautious look and was dismayed to see him looking at her with a suspicious frown. He was not a particularly encouraging sight—a dirty green-and-gold handkerchief was wrapped turban-like about his head, hanks of grimy black hair escaping here and there from the confinement; there was a black patch where his left eye should have been; a gold earring glittered in one ear, and he had the longest pair of black mustaches she had ever seen. But apparently he had not plumbed her disguise because after a tension-filled second, he turned away, muttering, "Godamercy! You're a bit young for this, boy! But stay close and old Jenkins will try to see that you come to no harm." As if struck by something, he looked back at her and demanded, "Your weapons? Where are they?"

Maria's tongue was stuck to the roof of her mouth, her eyes widening with dismay, utter horror roiling through her at the knowledge of her own stupidity. But Jenkins obviously misread her expression, for cursing softly, he reached into the wide leather belt about his waist and, to her astonishment, thrust a huge dagger into her hand. Turning away again, he grumbled something about, "Bloodthirsty little jackanapes with more guts than brains!"

It took several moments before Maria's heartbeat gradually resumed some semblance of normalcy, and she wasn't at all surprised to notice that the hand that clenched Jenkins' dagger shook slightly. She took a deep steadying breath and then carefully glanced around her.

At first she could see nothing but jungle, but then as her eyes examined the foliage more closely, she could discern the shapes of several buccaneers cleverly hidden in the shadows of the rampant growth. Casting her gaze upward, she was astonished to see even more men in the trees above her, the barrels of their long arquebuses aimed at something just beyond her sight. Warily she scooted forward and parted the bushes that obscured her view.

She sucked in a frightened breath at the sight that met her eyes. A narrow pass lay below her, the ground plunging steeply down on both sides of the jungle gorge . . . a perfect place, even to her untrained eye, for an ambush; and looking across the width of the pass, she wasn't at all surprised to pick out more buccaneers lying in wait for the unwary line of men who were even now marching through the pass below her.

The hot tropical sunlight glinted brightly off the steel morions worn by the men beneath her as they slowly worked their way through the underbrush, their yellow-and-black uniforms and high leather boots clearly identifying them as the Spanish troops led by de Bracamonte from Panama City. Desperately Maria searched the straggling line of men, straining to pick out her brother's face amongst them. But she could not and a little groan of helplessness escaped her.

The sound made Jenkins send a sharp scowl in her direction, and Maria ducked her head, biting her lip in angry despair at bringing attention to herself. She kept her face carefully averted, willing Jenkins to turn away again, but as the seconds passed, he didn't, and Maria would have been terrified if she had seen the narrowing of his good eye as he studied her more carefully. The scowl increased as he took in the small frame, the slender calves and dainty hands. Suspicion in his voice, he rumbled, "Whose crew ye belong to?"

Maria swallowed with difficulty, then hoping her Spanish accent would not give her away, she replied gruffly, "Lancaster's . . . Dark Angel."

"Ah," he said softly as if that explained everything. "That be so—passing strange I didn't recognize you—considering I be part of Dark Angel's crew too!"

"New member," Maria choked out, cursing a fate that had landed her right next to one of Gabriel's men.

Jenkins sent her another long look, then turned away, his eye trying to pick out where his captain lay in wait for the Spanish. The captain's wench was a dainty piece, if he recalled right, just about the size of this little morsel beside him. . . . Not able to find Gabriel and unwilling to lose track of the *boy* beside him, Jenkins settled himself more firmly in position for the coming battle. Who'd've guessed, he thought sourly, that outnumbered nearly thirty to one, he'd spend his time playing guardian angel to the captain's green goose!

In an agony of indecision, Maria watched the scene unfolding beneath her. Every nerve within her slender body was screaming out for her to warn the men below her, to warn her brother of the deadly trap that was about to be sprung, and yet . . . and yet . . . to do so would be a betrayal of that enigmatic man who so carelessly commanded her wayward heart. An angry, smothered little sob of denial broke from her. No! He did not command her heart! She did *not* love him! She *hated* him! But still she lay frozen, gripped by a terrible paralysis, heart fighting against head, unable to make the decision to betray either her brother or the Englishman. More than once she opened her mouth to shriek the warning to the Spanish troops slowly winding their way deeper into the pass beneath her, but she could not, the image of Gabriel lying dead on the ground in Hispaniola shimmering before her eyes. Writhing with shame at herself, furious that there was even a question of choice, she finally gathered her scattered emotions and prepared to make one last effort to do the *right* thing.

Whether she would have been able to call out that warning to the Spanish suddenly became moot, as Jenkins came to a decision on his own. Not one to take chances and decidedly uneasy with the situation, he handled it in his own way. Removing a fine French pistol from the leather baldrics that crisscrossed his chest, he somewhat matter-of-factly gave Maria a smart tap on the head. Watching her instantly collapse into unconsciousness, he grunted with satisfaction. Better to face the captain's wrath at treating the wench this way, than for all of them to be put in jeopardy by this little Spanish viper in their midst.

For Maria, the moment Jenkins' pistol connected with the back of her head, there was nothing but a burst of pain and then blessed darkness. Darkness that she embraced with an odd gratitude . . . now there was no decision to make, no betrayal to face. . . .

Almost as if Jenkins' actions had been a signal, the battle commenced, the buccaneer arquebusiers, from their excellent position in the treetops that lined the narrow jungle pass, letting loose with a volley of shots that tore through the ranks of the marching Spaniards with disastrous results. Men fell screaming where they stood, others thrashed around in terror and pain, most immediately scrambled for cover, of which there was precious little, their commanders frantically trying to bring order to the sudden chaos.

Watching intently from the concealment of a huge palmetto, just a short distance up from the floor of the gorge, Gabriel was searching the faces of the Spaniards below him, eager for the sight of just one man. . . . As the minutes sped by and the firing of the arquebusiers continued, he grew impatient for the hand-to-hand fighting to begin—for *his* part in this foray to start. The knowledge that Diego Delgato was somewhere in the midst of the carnage just below him only intensified his feelings about joining the battle, and he was, ironically, terrified that a shot from one of the buccaneers' weapons would take Diego's life. A grim smile curved his mouth. He was, he admitted cynically, praying that Diego remained unharmed, unharmed until at last they were face to face. . . .

Finally the moment Gabriel had been waiting for arrived, and with blood-chilling shouts he and the other buccaneers came leaping and running from their hiding places, falling upon the Spaniards with a stunning ferocity. Cutlasses and knives flashing in the sunlight, they fought their way through wavering ranks of the Spanish, the sheer violence of the attack destroying whatever defenses the Spaniards might have been able to muster against the savage buccaneers.

This was fighting as Gabriel liked it—man against man, no innocents to worry over, no reason to question the fate of the men he killed—and the fact that the buccaneers were vastly outnumbered only added to the thrill of the fight. In the midst of the battle he *was* the Dark Angel the Spaniards had named him—he seemed everywhere, his cutlass delivering death wherever it struck as he plunged deeper and deeper into the struggling mass of men. With each thrust, with each parry, with each man that fell before his striking blade his only thoughts were— This for Elizabeth! This for Caroline! This for my dead child! *This* for my innocent family!—it was a vengeful refrain that knew no end, a refrain that drove him like a madman.

As he fought, his white shirt had opened to his lean waist, revealing the powerful muscles underneath, sunlight glinting on the gold rope around his neck and intensifying the bronze hue of his skin. With every movement he made, the wavy, blue-black hair swung wildly near his hard jaw, giving an occasional glimpse of the emerald stud and hoop of gold that hung from his ear. The green eyes glittering fiercely, the white, even teeth flashing in a tiger's smile, Gabriel was without question a most magnificent sight as Spaniard after Spaniard fell beneath the relentlessness of his attack.

The Spaniards had begun to withdraw haphazardly, unable to withstand the merciless onslaught of the buccaneers, when Gabriel finally caught sight of Diego. Diego was near one side of the gorge, his Toledo steel blade covered with blood, his thin lips curled back disdainfully as he drove his sword into the belly of a buccaneer. Seeing Diego scant yards away from him, a savagely exultant cry rose up from deep within Gabriel, and heedless of anything but his hated enemy, he leaped across the distance that separated them.

"*Delgato!* Whoreson! Come and taste death!" Gabriel thundered when at last he was within sword range of his quarry.

Even beneath the narrow brim of the steel morion, Gabriel could see Diego's eyes widen with angry disbelief. Almost with pleasure he watched the expression of stunned outrage spread across the other man's swarthy features.

"Lancaster!" Diego breathed furiously, his blade instantly rising to meet Gabriel's.

Expertly parrying Diego's sword, Gabriel smiled, not a nice smile, the green eyes hard and cold. "Aye! Lancaster himself—although it is by the name Dark Angel that you may have heard of me most recently."

From the way Diego stiffened, it was obvious that he had indeed heard of the Dark Angel. Rage shook him and unthinkingly he lashed out wildly with his sword. "English swine! I was told that you were dead! But this time I shall make certain myself that you are truly dead—despite the enjoyment it would give me to take you prisoner again and mete out a slow and lingering death."

Gabriel nimbly avoided Diego's blade, his own sliding swiftly under the other's guard, and almost gently he nicked Diego across the throat. For Gabriel this was a moment of supreme satisfaction—he had dreamed of it, had hungered for it and had lived for it since that fateful day the *Santo Cristo* had so brutally destroyed his life, and he wanted to savor it. Memories of Elizabeth and Caroline danced through his brain, and for them, he was determined to make Diego suffer dreadfully before dying.

Yet each time their blades met, it was apparent that the two men were almost evenly matched; but it was the coolness of purpose that gave Gabriel the edge and repeatedly his cutlass slipped under Diego's maddened, furious lunges. Gabriel did not give the fatal thrust, however, each time drawing back, toying with his victim, each time letting Diego know how close to death he had come.

Neither man was aware that the Spaniards were now in full retreat. They only saw each other, the hatred they felt a tangible thing as their blades continued to meet and clash in the hot jungle sunlight.

Just above the two men, on the rim of the pass, Maria stirred and raised her aching head. Blankly she stared around, at first not remembering anything, but then as the sounds of the battle drifted to her; as the smell of smoke and blood assailed her nostrils, memory exploded in her brain and she jerked upright with a gasp. Stars danced in her head, but doggedly she forced herself to concentrate, her gaze instantly focusing on the scene below her.

At first everything appeared to be a jumbled mass of bodies, but gradually, despite the painful throbbing of her head, she began to see more clearly, and with growing fear and distress she searched desperately for Gabriel or Diego. Panic rose up within her as the minutes passed, and she could see no sign of either man; then just when she was about to give way to hysteria, she spotted them locked together in battle almost directly below her.

Sliding and stumbling, falling and slipping, she came down the side of the narrow pass, her eyes fastened fearfully on the two men below her, oblivious to everything but those two figures. Her hat went flying, the thick black hair tumbling down and around her slender shoulders, her hands cut by branches and roots as she fought her way toward those two struggling men. She never saw the ever-watchful Jenkins when, about three-quarters of the way down the side of the gorge, he erupted out of the brush and grabbed her.

Feeling those brutal hands on her, she screamed and spiritedly struck out, using every ounce of strength she possessed. Sobbing and fighting she twisted in Jenkins' increasingly cruel hold.

Caught up in his own dream of revenge, closing in for the kill, Gabriel was unconscious of Maria's screams; it was only when he saw the look on Diego's face that he realized that something momentous was happening. Risking a glance over his shoulder, he was thunderstruck to see Maria struggling wildly in the arms of his boatswain.

Diego recovered himself first and taking advantage of the other's distraction, he struck swiftly, cutting open a long slice the entire length of Gabriel's upper arm.

Moving with lightning speed, Gabriel jerked himself around and deftly parried the next blow, but the wound was a telling one, and he could feel the blood gushing down his arm. Aware that he must now end the fight quickly, Gabriel put all his strength into driving Diego backward, determined to kill him before he became too weak. He coldly pushed Maria's presence to the back of his mind.

An almost maniacal gleam in his eyes, Diego demanded, "How is it that she is here?"

In spite of the pain, Gabriel smiled. "She is my captive—my slave, my *thing* to use as I wish! Does that thought strike you with fear and loathing? I trust it does, I trust that it will haunt and torment you for an eternity, that when I kill you, you will die knowing that your sister is *mine!*"

Diego's breath hissed through his teeth and he redoubled his efforts to bring a quick end to this conflict. But, even badly wounded and loosing blood rapidly, Gabriel was an indomitable fighter, his blade striking strongly and fiercely against Diego's.

In their fighting they had gradually moved away from the edge of the gorge and into the mainstream of the battle, and a fresh wave of men suddenly swept between them, separating them. Despite frenzied attempts to reach each other, more and more men came between them, and in helpless fury, Gabriel soon found himself surrounded by struggling Spaniards and buccaneers and was unable to clear a path to Diego. In much the same situation, Diego was filled with frustration and rage as he was carried along with the tide of retreating soldiers, pushed further and further and further backward until Gabriel was lost to his gaze.

With a valiant stubbornness Gabriel continued to fight, unwilling to admit that his thirst for revenge would remain unslaked this day, unwilling to admit that Diego had once again eluded death at his hands and *most* unwilling to consider Maria's part in what had happened. But his vigor was fading swiftly; he had lost dangerous amounts of blood and his spirit was sick within him. A sharp rap on the temple from the pike of a frantic Spaniard sent Gabriel spinning around, his ears ringing from the force of the blow, and hazily he stumbled away from the fighting, collapsing not far from where Jenkins and Maria were still struggling.

Both combatants saw Gabriel go down, and with a ferocious shake of her arm, Jenkins snarled, "Spanish bitch! You may have cost the captain his life!"

A small groan of denial came from Maria and oblivious to everything but Gabriel's limp form not six feet away,

with a burst of strength that surprised them both, she
tore out of Jenkins' grasp. The terrible memory of that
afternoon in Hispaniola leaping in her brain, tears of
fright and despair trickling down her pale cheeks, she ran
to where Gabriel lay so still. Dropping to her knees beside
him, hesitantly, she touched him, her fingers trembling.

And in that fateful moment, she realized so many
things—why he had always fascinated her, why his touch
turned her body to liquid fire and why his mere presence,
despite all the reasons against it, filled her with joy. . . .
She loved him! Adored him and had since that first moment she had laid eyes on him as he had stood so proudly
defiant, even in defeat, on the deck of the *Santo Cristo*.
She loved him . . . and now he might die.

The slow rise and fall of his chest and the warmth of
his skin beneath her questing fingers told her that he was
still alive, but he looked dreadful—his face pale, the skin
near his temple where the pike had struck already beginning to turn an ugly purple, and the blood . . . Dear Lord!
The blood seemed to be everywhere. Unaware of what she
was doing, she cradled his head to her breast, her lips
caressing his brow, one hand frantically trying to stop the
flow of blood that seeped at an alarming rate from the
wound Diego had given him. Dear *Dios!* she thought
pleadingly, don't let him die! Not now! Not when I have
just discovered that I love him—let him live so that I may
win his heart. He must not die! He *must* not!

Part Three

Royal Gift

Jamaica, Summer, 1668

There is light in shadow and shadow
     in light,
And black in the blue of the sky.

Lucy Larcom
Black in the Blue Sky

Chapter Eighteen

ON August 17, 1668, Harry Morgan returned triumphantly to the city of Port Royal, Jamaica, the holds of
his ships fair to bursting with all the booty from the
plundered city of Puerto Bello. All in all, he and his buccaneers had held Puerto Bello from the Spanish for
thirty-one days, and the treasure the buccaneers had so
methodically wrested from the stricken city was esti-
mated to be nearly three hundred thousand pieces of
eight—in addition to an untold amount of silks, laces and
other costly goods.

Port Royal went wild with delirious excitement at Morgan's arrival; the twin pleasures of having the tail of
mighty Spain and the seemingly unlimited supply of gold
spilling freely from the hands of the returning buccaneers
unleashed a raucous celebration among the populace that
seemed to have no end. Brothels and grog shops rang with
the shouts of laughter and bawdy songs; along the cobblestoned streets near the water's edge, drunken buccaneers
lurched and staggered, tawdry harlots hanging from their
brawny arms. Drunkenness, womanizing and an unpar-
alleled orgy of spending was the order of the day, with
some inebriated buccaneers buying entire casks of rum
and offering liberal swigs to anyone passing by on the
street . . . and inclined to take great offense if the drink
was refused, knives flashing in the hot sunlight before the
thing was settled. There were fights and brawls almost
every hour, but despite the rowdy behavior, even the most
staid merchants in the more respectable parts of town
were exceedingly pleased by all the plunder being thrown
about so lavishly—buccaneer spoils were still Port Royal's

lifeblood, and sooner or later, *every*one profited from the arrival of pirate ships full of booty.

The audacious raid on Puerto Bello established Harry Morgan as undisputed prince of the pirates, and now there was no one to gainsay his power and authority. He was second only to Governor Modyford on the island; and the rich planters, of which there were beginning to be a few, and other men of power all flocked to him, eager to claim friendship with the conqueror of Puerto Bello.

But if the successful raid on Puerto Bello brought great delight to Port Royal and its residents, there was at least one person who viewed the town and surrounding area with decided trepidation. From the glass casement windows that lined the stern of the *Dark Angel,* Maria Delgato stared out apprehensively across the expanse of the blue water that separated her from the dubious charms of the buccaneer stronghold.

The *Dark Angel,* most of its crew in town adding their noise to the boisterous festivities, was currently riding at anchor in the sheltered lagoon on the landward side of the island of Cagua, where the town of Port Royal had been built; the far larger island of Jamaica rose green and majestic nearby. The water was very deep here, and Cagua protected the harbor and any ships anchored there from the violent storms and hurricanes that swept so fiercely through the area. But on this bright humid sunny day there were no storms to fear . . . except the storm that raged in Maria's heart as she continued to gaze around her, wondering bleakly about the future these islands might bring her.

From this distance, Port Royal looked relatively innocuous—wharves, cobblestoned streets and stoutly constructed brick buildings, several of them three stories high, were strung out tidily along the limestone and sand spit that formed Cagua. On a point overlooking the harbor stood a sturdy fort; several cannons gleamed dully in the hot sunlight, and the small figures of soldiers could be seen as they moved about the upper ramparts of the fort.

The town appeared to bustle with life and color; black slaves carrying huge bunches of yellow plantains upon their shoulders walked the streets; buccaneers in scarlet

and green swaggered about; women in gowns of purple
and rose strolled along the wharves; and Maria even
glimpsed the occasional carriage and horseman as some
of the respectable and wealthier members of the town rode
through the winding streets. But Maria had no interest
in them, she was too intent upon watching for one particular person, the man who owned her body and soul . . .
and heart too, she admitted unhappily. Gabriel Lancaster.

Even now it still astonished her to realize that despite
everything that had happened in the past, she was
blindly, madly in love with her captor, the son of the man
who had brought about her own beloved father's death.
And thinking back over the weeks that had just passed,
it was only a little less astonishing to her that she was
still alive and relatively unharmed. A slight shudder went
through her slender frame as she remembered with chilling clarity that terrible journey back to Puerto Bello,
Gabriel's bloodied, unconscious body carried so effortlessly and gently by Zeus.

Just the memory of the way Zeus had glanced at her
after he had so carefully picked up Gabriel's body was
enough to make her shiver uncontrollably in the sun-
warmed great room of the *Dark Angel.* Unemotionally
Zeus had murmured, "Pray, petite, that he lives. For if
he dies . . . I shall kill you with my bare hands."

She had believed him implicitly, and though the words
of explanation had trembled on her lips, she had kept
silent. How could she possibly explain her own tangled
emotions? Explain her motives and actions when she
didn't even understand them herself? And what did Zeus'
threat mean to her anyway—if Gabriel died, life would
have no meaning for her, and she would welcome the dark
oblivion Zeus had promised.

For the moment her own uncertain fate had been the
last thing she had worried about; all her thoughts had
been on Gabriel. Filled with anxiety and fear for him, she
had stumbled numbly along in Zeus' wake as he had
turned and begun the long walk back to Puerto Bello. It
was as well, she could admit now, that she had been in
such a haze of misery, that the black looks and muttered
threats that had followed her progress hadn't actually im-

pinged upon her consciousness at that time. All she had been able to cling to was the idea that Gabriel *must* live.

It hadn't been until much later that evening that anyone had spoken to her again, and it was then that Zeus had made her aware of the contempt with which she was regarded. When they had reached the house, he had ordered that she be put under guard in one of the smaller rooms at the rear of the house. Maria had cried out, had begged to stay with Gabriel; but Zeus had merely looked coldly at her, and his usually warm voice full of ice, he had said, "Haven't you done enough today? Be assured, *mam'zell,* that I can see to the safety of my friend. Certainly he will receive far more tender care at my hands than yours!"

Gulping back the sobs that had torn at her throat, her head held high, she had been marched past the white-faced Pilar and placed in solitary confinement in the small, bare room. She had been tired, dirty and hungry, but still her only concerns had been for Gabriel. What was happening with him? Had the physician arrived? Was Gabriel in imminent danger of dying?

There had been little for her to do but nervously pace the confines of the small room, her ears constantly cocked for the sounds of approaching footsteps as she wondered fearfully what news would be brought to her.

When what had seemed like hours later she had heard the noise of people approaching, her heart had stood still. Had Gabriel died? Were they now coming to kill her?

A little quiver of hope had gone through her when she had seen Pilar entering the room closely followed by Zeus. Pilar had held a tray in her hands and there had been food and drink upon it. Zeus had tossed the feminine clothing he had been carrying over his arm onto the narrow bed that graced the room, and looking sternly at Maria, he had said quietly, "He will live. The physician has dressed his wounds and the bleeding has been stopped. He is very weak but he will live . . . provided there is no infection and the wound does not fester."

Maria had felt tears of gratitude and joy sting her eyes and huskily she had murmured, "I know you will not believe me, but I never meant him harm. My brother was

among those he was going to fight—and the men he led
were my countrymen."

Zeus had sent her a long, unsmiling glance. "You care
so much for your brother? That is not the impression I
have gained from Pilar."

Maria had swallowed uncomfortably. How could she explain the complicated love-hate relationship that she
shared with Diego? How to make Zeus understand that
while Diego enraged and disgusted her frequently, he *was*
her brother, her only close relative, and that when he did
not let ambition blind him, he could be kind and caring?
Mutely, she had stared at Zeus' skeptical features, words
failing her.

After a tense moment, Zeus had shrugged and had said,
"It doesn't matter now what your thoughts were at the
time—*mon capitaine* nearly died because of your interference, and neither he, nor myself, nor the men who follow
him will ever forget it. For that reason you will remain
here in this room. It is for your own good—until Gabriel
is well and able to decide what to do with you, you would
not be safe from reprisal from one of the buccaneers, even
in this house. I have placed armed guards at the door to
this room—men who I can trust not to take justice into
their own hands. Except for Pilar or myself you will see
no one else." He had given her a sharp look. "You do
realize what I am saying? That if you were foolish enough
to try to escape your life would be instantly forfeit? Even
Morgan himself had raged that you should die for today's
deed. Your only protection lies in doing *precisely* what I
say . . . until Gabriel is recovered."

Unable to offer more in her defense, Maria had nodded
slowly, her expression clearly miserable. But for once Zeus
seemed unmoved by her bedraggled condition and obvious
unhappiness. Without another word to her, he had turned
on his heel and stalked from the room.

A heavy silence had fallen when he had left the room,
and uncertainly, Maria had stared across at Pilar. "Do
you despise me too? Do you think that what I did was
wrong?" she had asked in a tiny voice.

Pilar had put down the tray on a rough wooden table
nearby, and holding out her arms, she had muttered, "Ah,

chica, where has that foolish Delgato pride led you this time?"

Wordlessly, Maria had flown into Pilar's welcoming embrace, and muffling her sobs against the other woman's bosom, she had let the tears she had held in check for hours flow freely. Pilar's arms had been warm and comforting, and as the minutes had passed and Maria's slender body had finally ceased shaking from the force of the emotions that had ripped through her, Pilar had said gently, "This is very bad, little one. I can do nothing to help you very much. And everything that Zeus has said is true—you are only safe here in this room. Under no circumstances leave it without me." She had then pushed Maria a little away from her and had fumbled under her bodice for some object. A second later she had slid a small knife into Maria's nerveless hand. "I should not do this, and if it is found out, I may join you here. But while Zeus feels that he can trust the men guarding you, I do not feel the same and want you to have at least *some* protection against them, if his trust is ill-founded."

Having gently wiped the last traces of tears that had fallen down Maria's cheeks, Pilar had murmured, "I will do what I can to help you—you know that! But"—and she had sent Maria a pleading glance—"please, *chica,* no more foolishness! We are prisoners of these men—and though I love that brute Zeus shamelessly, I am under no illusions about what kind of man he is—he will give you no further protection than what you have right now. Your only hope lies in the swift recovery of the Englishman." Her mouth had turned down. "And who knows," Pilar had added pessimistically, "what manner of punishment he will order meted out to you for your actions this day?"

It had been on that depressing note that Pilar had left Maria. And it had been then, as she had stood in that barren little room, the wooden table and narrow bed its only furnishings, that reaction had set in and the full impact of her precarious position had hit her. Looking around at the bleak confines of what was her prison, a shudder had shaken Maria's body. She might be murdered here! Any second the door might burst open and brutal men with vengeance on their minds might fall upon her! Zeus, Harry Morgan, the buccaneers, all were against her; and the only man who could save her—if he was even willing to!—lay gravely wounded somewhere in this house.

With a heavy heart she had trudged to the small bed, and seated upon it, her body braced as if for a blow, fearful images of her own death had danced through her brain. But unwilling to dwell on her own fate, she had shoved those thoughts aside, and only concern for Gabriel's wellbeing had filled her mind. He *must* recover, she had vowed fiercely and had clung pathetically to Zeus' statement that Gabriel would indeed live. She had longed desperately to see him herself, to assure herself that what Zeus had said was really true, but there had been nothing that she could do but sit and wait . . . and pray.

But Gabriel was not the only man that Maria had prayed for that night. Kneeling before that mean little bed, she had uttered fervent prayers for Diego's safety too, had wondered helplessly of his condition and had prayed most pleadingly that if these two men who meant so much to her survived, never again would she have to choose between them.

Eventually, exhaustion had claimed her and she had slept soundly until the sound of the door opening had brought her springing upright to her feet, her fingers clenched whitely around the knife. It had been Pilar and Maria had felt the terror that had swept over her slowly drain away. She had guessed that it was morning and had hastily rubbed the sleep from her eyes and had demanded anxiously, "Gabriel! How is he?"

There had been a worried expression on Pilar's face, and she had seemed to hesitate before she had admitted reluctantly, "He has a fever, *chica.* It rose about midnight and we have spent the night trying to keep him cool and comfortable."

"Oh, let me go to him!" Maria had cried out pitifully. "Let me help him!"

Pilar had shaken her head and had said dully, "*Chica,* it is best that you remain here—in the temper Zeus is in now, I fear he would slay you out of hand, were he to lay eyes upon you."

Defeated, Maria had turned away. "Pilar . . . do not worry for me. If . . . if . . ." Her voice had faltered but then had gained strength. "If he dies, then I would *want* to die!

Zeus would merely be ending my own hell. Do not fear
for me if the worst should happen."

Pilar had asked gravely, "You love your Englishman
very much, don't you?"

Maria had smiled sadly. "*Sí!* But I did not know it until
yesterday. I wish . . ." Wistfully, she had continued, "If I
had known, how very different I would have acted in the
past."

"Would you have still tried to warn Diego?"

A stricken expression had flashed across Maria's elfin
features. In a voice laced with pain she had whispered, "I
think not—but it is a terrible thing to contemplate."

"Well, we will not brood over what did not happen,"
Pilar had said, suddenly brisk. "The Englishman *is* going
to get better. And once he is better you shall have a second chance to win his heart. I know it! I am certain that
he feels very deeply for you—only you are both too stubborn and proud to let the other one know!" Severely, she
had ended with, "And you both spend far too much time
thinking of this ridiculous vendetta between your families. What happened in the past is over and done with—
you both have your lives in front of you—will you let the
wrongs done years ago—wrongs done, in most cases, to
people that are now dead—ruin your future? One hopes
not!" Pilar had turned away and had opened the door. "I
am going to get you some fresh food—I see that you did
not eat last night—and when you have filled your stomach, I shall bring you some warm water and you may
bathe." Ever practical, she had added calmly, "When you
are clean and fed, you will find that things look much
brighter."

Maria had felt somewhat better after she had followed
Pilar's advice, but in the long, lonely days that had followed, her spirits had remained low. Finally, however,
one morning a week later, Pilar had entered the room
with a huge smile upon her handsome face and Maria's
heart had instantly lifted. Blissfully, Pilar had announced, "He is *much* better, *chica!* He actually threw his
bowl of broth at me and had a ferocious argument with
Zeus! He is driving us all to distraction and he is refusing
even to stay in bed!"

Arms around Pilar's waist, Maria had dragged her

about the room in a joyful little dance. When they had stopped for a breath, her eyes shining with pleasure, Maria had asked eagerly, "When may I see him?"

Pilar's smile had faded and she had said quietly, "That, I'm afraid, is up to him."

It had been three endless days later before Zeus had come to her and had said curtly, "He wants to see you."

Suddenly fearful of what this interview might herald, Maria's eyes had gone wide, and apprehension had flickered in their sapphire depths. She wasn't afraid that Gabriel would order her killed—*that* he could have done any time in the past few days. No, it was the knowledge that he was far more likely to banish her from him, to leave her here in Puerto Bello when the buccaneers sailed away that swamped her with an icy terror. Never to see him again would be a living death, and her face had whitened at the thought of his disappearing forever from her life.

Perhaps now that Gabriel was no longer in danger of dying, Zeus had felt compassion stir at the sight of her pale and strained features. At any rate, he had murmured gruffly, "He doesn't intend to throw you to the others, petite! Now come along!"

In many respects, Maria admitted heavily, as she continued to stare out at the rippling blue water that gently lapped the hull of the *Dark Angel,* throwing her to the others might have been a kinder punishment. Certainly it would have been easier for her to bear than the cold indifference with which Gabriel had treated her these past weeks.

Caught up in the wonderment of her newly discovered love for him, worn down by the constant fear for his health, she had never given his reactions to that fateful day any thought. Consequently, she had been completely unprepared for the glacial-eyed, granite-jawed man who had confronted her that morning weeks ago in Puerto Bello.

Gabriel had chosen not to meet with her in the bedroom they had shared; instead the painful interview that had followed had been held in a room in which Maria had never been, a little antechamber a short distance from where she had been cloistered. The room had been cheerlessly empty except for Gabriel's tall figure when Maria

had entered, but her heart had leaped with joy at the
sight of him. His back had been to her, and apparently
he had been engrossed in staring out a tiny window at
the far end of the alcove.

A moment had passed, and with new eyes she had surveyed his broad-shouldered form as he had stood there,
taking pleasure in the proud tilt of his head, the hint of
muscles beneath the white shirt he had been wearing, the
lean waist and hips that had been covered by a pair of
loose-fitting black breeches and the elegantly shaped
calves that had been displayed in a pair of white silk
stockings. As the minutes had passed and he had still
made no acknowledgment of her presence she had asked
uncertainly, "*Señor?* You sent for me?"

Gabriel had stiffened and then had very slowly pivoted
to face her. The sun had been streaming in behind him
and had shadowed his features, but for one fleeting second
she had thought she had seen a flash of delight in his
green eyes. *If* he had been pleased to see her, he had immediately hidden that fact, and in a voice full of icy disdain, he had said, "Good morrow, *Señorita* Delgato. I am
overwhelmed that you have deigned to meet with me—
particularly since you must have been praying most fervently these past days that your brother's expertise with
the blade might have relieved you of the unpleasant ne-
cessity of ever laying eyes on me again!"

Both his words and his appearance had shocked her.
He had been very pale, the toll his illness had extracted
from him clearly evident in his coloring and also in the
gauntness of his features. But the obvious signs of his
ordeal had not detracted from his attractiveness: the pal-
lor of his skin had only intensified the raven hues of the
thick black hair that had waved near his temple and chin,
and the chiseled features had only appeared more so; his
nose had become almost aquiline, the hollows under his
high cheekbones calling attention to the aristocratic cast
of his face. The emerald eyes had been a glacial green
beneath his heavy black brows as he had regarded her
across the short distance that separated them, and as the
full import of his words had sunk into her consciousness,
Maria had been aware of a feeling of bitter despair.

There had been no doubt that he believed she had

wanted his death, that he thought she had deliberately tried to warn Diego so that her brother could kill him. Remembering the anxious time she had just spent desperately worried about him, praying, yes, most fervently, but *for* his life not death, a bubble of half-angry, half-hysterical laughter had nearly burst from her throat. A hard gleam in her sapphire blue eyes, she had glared up at him and snapped, "You are a fool, Englishman! And after the way you have treated me and the things you think that I am capable of, you *should* be overwhelmed that I deigned to meet with you!"

Gabriel had appeared taken aback for just a second, but then, his own eyes shining with temper, he had growled, "I'll not mince words with you, you viper of the Delgatos! You forget yourself, and in the future you had better learn to control that wicked tongue of yours or I'll beat you so soundly that you will think death a welcome reprieve!"

It would have been unwise, even Maria could see that, to have provoked him further, and so biting back the hot words that had surged up within her, she had looked away and had remained silent. But there had been a mutinous slant to her full bottom lip that had made her thoughts transparent, and a sardonic smile on his mouth, Gabriel had murmured, "Damn me in your mind all you want, but never, *never* forget that I am your master! You are *my* slave now, and be grateful that you will find me a far kinder master than your brother ever was to me!"

Maria had haughtily averted her head as he had spoken, and with a less than gentle motion, Gabriel had captured her chin and jerked her face in his direction. Those cold green eyes had traveled slowly over her features, taking in the sweet curve of her mouth, the deep blue of her eyes and the tousled black hair, and he had said with a note of furious wonderment in his voice, "You don't deserve any kindness from me—you forswore that the day you sought my death, but I find that I am not villain enough, though I long to be, to extract a suitable revenge from you. I should, by all that is holy, give you to du Bois or let the others have you to do with as they will, but the memory of my sister and wife will not let me."

Maria's eyes had widened fearfully at mention of du Bois' name, and Gabriel had smiled cruelly and had said coolly, "Aye, little viper, du Bois. Every time you think to disobey me—just remember that even I can only be pushed so far and that if you are too troublesome I may be able to overcome my own scruples, few that they are, and give you to him anyway."

In a voice barely above a whisper, Maria had asked, "What do you intend to do with me?"

"Such docility!" Gabriel had drawled, a mocking gleam in the green eyes. "Do, little viper?" For just a second the iciness had left him, and his lip had had a decidedly sensual curve as he had murmured softly, "There are many things that I can think of that I would enjoy *do*ing with you." His thumb had lazily brushed across her mouth and he had seemed to be fascinated by its shape. But then, as if remembering something unpleasant, he had instantly dropped his hand, and his entire demeanor had changed from gentle teasing to sardonic aloofness. "For the present, however, I intend to take you back to Jamaica with me. Harry has given the order that we sail by week's end and you will be coming with me." A hard glint in his eyes, he had finished coldly, "You will be my slave for the rest of your life, and believe me, little viper, I have vowed to take my own revenge in my own fashion."

Maria had swallowed with an effort, the love she felt for him warring with despair and rebellion. Stiffly she had demanded, "Why don't you simply hold me for ransom? My brother will certainly pay you richly for my return." And determined not to lose face, grimly resolved not to let him have any inkling of her true emotions, she had spat, "Surely, having to suffer your touch has been punishment enough for me—and you can salve your twisted pride by making Diego pay an exorbitant sum for my release."

His eyes had narrowed and thickly he had snarled, "Never! You are *mine!* And only Diego's death will *salve my twisted pride!*"

There had been no further exchange between them, and uncertain whether to be joyful or terrified, some days later from the deck of the *Dark Angel* Maria had watched Puerto Bello disappear on the horizon. She had glanced across the huge expanse of blue ocean that separated her from her destination in Jamaica, and her spirits had been heavy. Who knew what the future would hold for her? she had thought unhappily.

To her astonishment the trip had proven not to be unpleasant. Good weather had held, and since Pilar had naturally been accompanying Zeus to their new home, she had not been without female companionship. Maria and Pilar had spent the majority of the time immured in the great room of the ship, though Zeus and occasionally Gabriel had escorted them for short walks about the ship in the mornings and evenings. The fact that no one had forgotten her part in Gabriel's brush with death had been made abundantly clear by the attitude and manner of the buccaneers she had happened to pass during these walks. Several had turned and spat contemptuously on the decks, others had murmured ugly threats that had made her ears burn and had caused a flush to stain her cheeks; but there had been no overt acts of violence—Gabriel and Zeus had seen to that—a stern look from either of them, and the offender had immediately become engrossed in the deck.

Throughout the long days and nights at sea, Gabriel had treated her with a maddening sort of cool indifference. He had ordered that it was her duty to keep the great room in impeccable order, and angrily determined to give him no cause for complaint, she had done so; even the brass fittings at the windows had gleamed from her zealous polishings. She had also been forced to act as maidservant to Gabriel, Pilar and his various officers who ate with their captain in the great room. Gabriel had seemed to take a perverse delight in the sight of Maria scurrying about the long oak table as she had diligently served food and poured wine, and not even Pilar's distressed expression as she had sat next to her husband and had had her one-time ward perform such a menial task for her had deterred him. He had been intent upon making it clear that Maria was his possession, his slave to order about as he wished; and she had been equally intent upon showing him that no Lancaster could ever humble a Delgato.

The one thing that Maria had feared the most had not happened—he had not taken her to his bed. During the journey to Jamaica she had slept in chaste isolation in

what had been a large storage cupboard just off the great
room. It had made a *very* small bedchamber and her bed
had been a hammock strung between the walls. But she
had managed, and by the time they had been at sea a few
days she had decided that she actually enjoyed the swaying motion of the hammock.

Gabriel's health had improved dramatically once they
had sailed from Puerto Bello, and by the time the buccaneers had reached Jamaica there were no outward signs
of his illness. He was darkly bronzed from the blazing
Caribbean sun, his movements once again lithe and full
of energy, and it was obvious to everyone that he was
fairly bursting with vitality.

Since their arrival three days ago Maria had not seen
very much of him—he had gone with Morgan to report
their success to Governor Modyford, and Gabriel had been
spending much of his time in town. Beset by worries of
her future life, Maria had been uncertain whether to be
glad or distressed at his absence. But thinking of the way
his eyes had traveled with increasing frequency over her
slender form as she had moved about the great room the
past week, she had decided that what she felt most was
relief.

While Gabriel treated her in the manner he had been,
it was relatively simple to keep her mind filled with angry, rebellious thoughts. Stubbornly ignoring Pilar's very
sensible advice, she had kept her mind filled with memories of the age-old vendetta that existed between the
Lancasters and Delgatos, telling herself, at least for the
time being, that he didn't deserve her love, that she was
mad to have ever even thought that what she felt for him
was love. He was a buccaneer, an enemy of Spain, a hated
Lancaster, the man who had taken her innocence, a man
to be despised at all cost. And yet she knew deep in her
heart that he had only to reach out and touch her for all
the barriers she had erected between them to be shattered. She was only safe from his unfairly abundant
charm as long as he ignored her. But if he were to change,
if he were to smile at her with the warmth he had once
so surprisingly displayed, she was sickly aware that she
would be lost. And if the expression in those green eyes
was any indication, it would appear that his desire for

her body had not abated, that sooner or later, he would reach out for her. . . .

Her heart beating painfully in her chest, Maria fixed her eyes on the wharves of Port Royal. She would not think of *that!* Instead she would focus her mind on what lay in front of her. She was a slave and before her lay the islands that would be her home for the rest of her life. Who knew what awaited her here?

Chapter Nineteen

LOUNGING comfortably in the Governor's salon, his long legs stretched out indolently in front of him, Gabriel too was thinking of the future, more particularly about Royal Gift, his sugar plantation, and Maria's reaction to it. Would she, he wondered with far more interest than he would have cared to admit, find it too uncivilized and primitive? How indeed was she going to view this home that he had carved from the verdant wilderness . . . and did it really matter to him? *Should* it matter—after all, she was *only* a slave!

A little angry with himself for considering, even for a moment, what her reaction might be, he frowned blackly at the silver buckle on his shoe. He was icily determined not to retreat from the stance he had taken—she was a Spanish bitch, a Delgato. She had very nearly been the death of him—at the very least her interference had destroyed his chance for taking revenge once and for all on Diego Delgato—and he wasn't about to let himself forget it. He would *not* allow himself to be blinded by a breathtaking smile and a pair of bright blue eyes this time!

The trouble, he admitted moodily to himself, was that he was finding it difficult to remember precisely what a little viper she could be, finding it hard to remember that she was a Delgato. Almost unconsciously his hand rose to the small silver scar that marred his cheekbone. Let *that,* you fool, he thought furiously, be a constant reminder that she is no different from all the other Delgatos—certainly that she is no different from her double-cursed brother, Diego!

Gabriel didn't like to think of those last days in Puerto

Bello. Particularly he didn't like to think of the terrible pain of betrayal and disbelief he had experienced when he had finally realized that Maria had been going to warn her brother. That she had, in fact, been racing down that hillside to join her brother when Jenkins had caught her. It was an ugly thought, and it, as much as the pain from his wounds, had tormented him madly during those days he had lain so ill. He didn't really know what the future would have held for them, but he had been on the verge of being willing to admit that she touched something deep within him, that she had awakened an emotion that he had never felt for any other woman. . . .

His frown increased, the scowl on his handsome face making the Governor exclaim, "My dear Lancaster, if the wine is that bad, I beg you say it! Do not simply sit there glaring so!"

The frown vanished in a moment, and a singularly charming smile flashing across his sun-bronzed features, Gabriel murmured, "Forgive me, sir! I am ashamed to confess that my thoughts were far away from here." He took a swallow of the wine and added, "As always, your taste in all things is exquisite."

Seated across from Gabriel in a large gilt-and-tapestry chair, Sir Thomas Modyford sent him a tart look and snorted. "And you, young scoundrel," he retorted dryly, "have far too glib a tongue!" A sly grin curved the Governor's pink mouth. "Although, in this case, you are absolutely correct!"

Sir Thomas Modyford was a pleasant-faced man, some twenty years older than Gabriel. He had been a former Governor on the island of Barbados, a successful planter and quite satisfied with his lot in life, when Charles II had offered him the post of Governor of Jamaica. Like the dutiful royal servant he was, he had promptly packed up his family and retainers and without a backward glance had sailed to the buccaneer harbor of Port Royal, intent upon turning that den of vice into an Eden of respectability. That had been four years ago in 1664, and his attitude had changed greatly since then.

He had arrived at Jamaica full of purpose, the proposals he had laid before the King for the proper settlement and growing prosperity of the island firm in his mind.

Piracy was to be stamped out; there would be no more safe harbor for the buccaneers at Port Royal; privateer commissions would no longer be issued. A House of Assembly would be established, the voting members elected from the free men of the population.

With him, Modyford had brought nine hundred and eighty-seven hardworking, honest settlers. These people were to be the nucleus of the respectable community he had envisioned. They had been provided free passage to Jamaica and had been promised thirty acres of free land when they arrived; and it said much for Modyford's charm and position that so many had followed him from Barbados to the notorious environs of Port Royal.

In the time that had followed, the Governor had worked hard to create the economic stability and decorous atmosphere that was so vital for the survival and prosperity of his settlers. The island would thrive, he was confident, if decently planted; and to this end he had introduced a far superior strain of sugar cane to the area. A twenty-one-year period in which there would be no duty on trade had been established. Overall, he had done more for the island of Jamaica than all the other Governors in the past, but in one area, he had failed as lamentably as they—the buccaneers could not be ousted. . . .

Oh, he had attempted quite diligently in the beginning to banish them, but it had been to no avail. He had confiscated ships and had hung a few pirates in chains on a point overlooking the harbor, leaving the wretched men to die from thirst and hunger as a warning to returning buccaneers.

Modyford might have succeeded if he had held firm to his purpose, but the declaration of war between England and the Dutch in 1665 had forced him to reconsider his position. With huge, well-armed Dutch warships roaming the waters of the Caribbean, preying upon English settlements, the idea of a harbor full of heavily weaponed buccaneer ships manned with experienced fighting men suddenly became very attractive. So attractive in fact that he organized, using many buccaneers, an attack against the Dutch islands in the West Indies.

From that point onward, Modyford never made any further serious attempt to dissuade the buccaneers from gathering at Port Royal. Simply by their very presence the Brethren of the Coast provided Jamaica with ample protection against not only the Dutch, but the French and Spanish as well. And not to be dismissed, their cargos contributed overwhelmingly to the island's growing prosperity. So mindful of the rewards for continued association with the buccaneers was Modyford that he had even upon occasion written long letters to the King, defending the acts of the Brethren.

But it was a precarious tightrope that Modyford walked. London might demand that the buccaneers be expelled from the vicinity of Jamaica, but London was far away—and certainly in no position to protect the fledgling colony that could face harassment at any time from the Dutch, Spanish or French! Worse, in the early days when Mody-ford had first attempted to drive out the buccaneers, he had discovered to his dismay that several merchants and traders were preparing to leave; their reasons were simple—without the goods the buccaneers brought in there was no business for them, so why should they stay? Reluctantly, Modyford had seen the wisdom of continuing to offer the buccaneers the safe harbor and commissions that they wanted.

Determined to appease the King, who wanted the lawless pirates exiled from his islands, Modyford in 1666 had his Council prepare a resolution stating why it was so important that the colony actively encourage the buccaneers. The buccaneers' raids, the resolution had stated, would replenish the island with coin, bullion, logwood, hides, tallow, indigo and many other things which would encourage traders from New England to come to Jamaica, and many merchants would then settle on the island. The slave trade would be increased. If the port prospered, more planters would arrive to take up residence. And perhaps, most vital of all, remaining friendly with the buccaneers ensured that they would not become hostile to the English and attack the plantations on Jamaica. Equally important, their presence helped deter the Spanish, who were still demanding that Jamaica be returned to them; the buccaneers also provided excellent intelligence on Spanish activities in the Caribbean; and last, the booty the buccaneers brought to Port Royal helped to enrich the King and his brother, the Duke of York.

And so it was that while the powers in London publicly deplored and condemned the Brethren of the Coast, privately they had made no *real* attempt to oust them from Port Royal. That cynical attitude also helped to explain why Harry Morgan always received a warm welcome from Sir Thomas Modyford and why the buccaneer known to his enemies as the Dark Angel was so comfortably sprawled in the King's House which served as the Governor's residence.

But it wasn't only his connection with the buccaneers that made Gabriel such a frequent and eagerly sought visitor to Modyford's home—there was the added cachet of his earlier intimacy with the King and the fact that he was rapidly turning Royal Gift into one of the premier plantations on the island. Lancaster was a man with each foot firmly planted in the two conflicting factions which ruled Jamaica, and the Governor had found that situation extremely useful.

So useful was Gabriel to the Governor within the society of the Brethren that the news that Gabriel was going to give up his buccaneer ways almost made Modyford regretful. Almost. The Governor might have had to accept and even embrace the presence of the buccaneers in Jamaica, but that didn't mean that he had discarded his original plan of making the island a respectable, viable community of honest planters. Lancaster was the type of man the Governor had always yearned to have settle on Jamaica—well born, educated and willing to fashion the wild, lush jungles into productive fields of bright green sugar cane. Modyford had buccaneers aplenty—*too* plenty, he sometimes admitted caustically—but what he didn't have was an excess of men of Gabriel Lancaster's background and caliber. And so while he might feel a little regret in losing a man he could trust within the buccaneer camp, he was more than delighted to add a valuable member to the growing ranks of successful planters on Jamaica.

But there was one tiny speck of disquietude on the happy horizon that the Governor foresaw in Gabriel's future, and he remarked thoughtfully, "There may be trouble over the wench, you know."

"Why?" Gabriel asked bluntly, the green eyes suddenly very watchful.

Modyford sighed and moved his slightly plump frame uncomfortably in his chair. "Because she is Spanish and because her brother is a man of power and position. If she were some mere little nonentity, there would be nothing to concern us. And then there is this vexatious situation with Spain. . . ."

Gabriel didn't need to have the "vexatious situation" explained to him; he was well aware of it. England and Spain had been at war with one another intermittently for almost a hundred years, and with the treacherously shifting winds at the Spanish and English courts, one never knew from moment to moment whether peace prevailed between the two countries or if war, undeclared or not, had erupted again. The situation in the Caribbean was even more complex—it took months for news of the constantly changing policies between the two hostile nations to reach the area, and so the Governor never knew when he was acting properly in authorizing attacks on Spanish shipping or if he was in fact, because of recent developments in Europe, going directly against the wishes of the King.

But Gabriel cared little for the political battles that waged an ocean away from him, and certainly, he saw no reason why the enslavement of Maria Delgato should cause any disastrous repercussions—he had been enslaved by the Spanish and it had engendered no dramatic outburst—and *he* could call the King of England friend!

The handsome face set and grim, Gabriel replied, "Who she is or what she is doesn't matter—she is mine by right of capture and I doubt even the King himself would demand that I release her. She is *mine!*"

Hastily Modyford soothed, "Quite right, my dear fellow! I only meant that if her ransom could be arranged it might not be such a bad thing."

"Have you forgotten precisely who it is we're talking about?" Gabriel demanded sharply.

Modyford looked unhappy. "No, I haven't forgotten," he returned a little testily. "It is just that the situation between Spain and England is so delicate that I want nothing done in my province to upset the balance between the two countries." Speculatively he eyed the tall man across from him. Harry Morgan had been quick to share the jest of the usually coolly contained and unruffled Lancaster's inexplicable behavior in the tavern in Puerto Bello, and that coupled with his so obvious disinclination to free Maria Delgato under any conditions gave Modyford pause and a great deal to consider. Almost idly the Governor murmured, "I suppose you could marry the wench if the situation became too volatile. After all, no one could *demand* the separation of man and wife!"

Gabriel sat up like a man who had just been doused with icy water. The green eyes glittering fiercely, he spat, "Have you gone mad, man! Marry Maria Delgato—I would sooner spend the rest of my days in a pit full of vipers!"

Having said that, Gabriel rose in one fluid motion and bowed low to the slightly startled Governor. "Good day, sir," he said levelly. "It has been a *most* instructive visit! I shall call again when next I am in Port Royal. For the present, should you have some serious need of me, I can be found at Royal Gift."

Without another word, he stalked from the room, his broad shoulders stiffly held under the perfectly cut coat of mulberry-colored cloth. Divided between exasperation and amusement, the Governor stood up and walked over to a pair of double doors that opened onto a balcony festooned with clinging vines of English morning glory. Standing half-hidden under the overhanging eaves of the house, he looked down below to the courtyard and watched interestedly as Gabriel appeared and strode purposefully across the flagstones to his horse. From his movements, it was apparent that Lancaster was still very angry, and the Governor sighed. Who would have thought that the calm, congenial and normally even-tempered gentleman he had known in the past would take such violent umbrage so quickly and over a mere idle comment? It would appear, the Governor decided with a small smile creasing his face, that where Maria Delgato was concerned, one must tread *very* carefully with her suddenly volatile captor. Frank amusement gleaming in his hazel eyes, he watched as Gabriel galloped away on a rakish bay stal-

lion. Turning back toward the house, the Governor shook
his head slowly, thinking lightly that he really must share
this interesting little scene with Morgan. Harry would
find it, he was certain, as diverting as he did. One thing
was very apparent though—whatever Lancaster might
claim, revenge was not the *only* emotion he felt for his
captive.

Unfortunately for his own peace of mind, Gabriel was
bitterly aware of the fact that he was acting contrarily
and that the root of all his unpredictable actions of late
could be traced to the moment he had realized precisely
who it was he held in his arms that evening in Puerto
Bello. A black scowl marring the handsomeness of his
features, despite the heat of the day, he spurred his horse
on to greater speed, his thoughts giving him little joy.

Nothing had gone as it should have from that very moment, he admitted furiously to himself. Instead of treating her with the cruel disdain and brutal savagery he had
promised himself he would, he had acted more in the
manner of a lovesick calf! And he had continued to do so
even after he had faced the unpalatable reality that she
had nearly been the cause of his death, that only Jenkins'
quick thinking had saved his life. I should have, he decided sourly, either ordered her slain or given to du Bois
the instant I regained consciousness. But no, he continued
to berate himself angrily, I didn't do that! No, I proceeded
to bring the treacherous little viper home with me! It's
not the Governor who is mad, you fool, it is yourself! She
has so addled my wits, he thought with ever-increasing
rage, that all I seem to want to remember is the sweetness of her beguiling body. With mingled despair and fury
he faced the unpleasant truth—that despising her for who
and what she was still didn't stop him from aching to lose
himself in her poisonously seductive flesh!

He had told himself, time and time again, that the *sole*
reason for bringing her to Jamaica with him had been to
extract the revenge he had been unable to take in Puerto
Bello, that she was a hated Delgato and that having her
as his slave would lessen some of his pain and shame at
the loss of his wife and sister. But as the days had passed
and as the buccaneer fleet had neared Port Royal, he had
realized unhappily that the need for vengeance had only

been part of why he had brought her here. The idea of leaving her behind in Puerto Bello had not even been considered by him; the prospect of giving her to one of the other buccaneers had been flatly rejected before his brain had even completed the thought, unaccustomed possessiveness filling him with rage at even the hint of the possibility of another man's touching her.

In a vain attempt to ease some of the guilty fury that consumed him at his own inability to act as he was positive he should, he had had to content himself with treating her in a cool, contemptuous manner, demanding that she act as his servant, giving her trifling and insulting tasks to perform to make it obvious that she *was* a slave! But even that had had its disconcerting effects, the sight of her on her knees vigorously scrubbing the floor of the great room had flooded him with anger and the violent urge to kick aside the wooden bucket of water and jerk her upright into his arms. Watching her slender body as she had walked gracefully around the long table, meekly acting as a maidservant to his officers and Pilar had not helped his temper any either. He had been conscious of a sensation of shame, of a wild impulse to order her instantly to cease these menial duties, but perverse pride would not let him.

But worse yet were the nights when his body burned to possess her and the days when just the sight of her moving about the great room had sent a jolt of urgent desire coursing madly through his veins. And it was then that he had painfully, angrily admitted that vengeance had been only one of his reasons for bringing Maria Delgato to Jamaica with him—she had bewitched him, inflamed him with an insatiable need to have her near, to know that he could touch her whenever he pleased, that he had only to reach out, to take her into his arms, to kiss her, to caress that smooth, pale skin, and that if he chose, he could at any time once again taste the sweet ecstasy of her slender body. . . .

Furiously he felt himself suddenly harden with raw, hot desire at the mere thought of possessing her again, and with a smothered curse, he pulled his horse to a stop in front of a small shop. He sat still a moment, forcing his unruly body to return to normal, deliberately emptying his mind of the unwanted desire that had so unexpectedly flooded him. When he was at last under control, he dismounted and quickly tied his horse to the lower limb of a nearby tree.

It was a dressmaker's shop that he had stopped at before, and with a grim little smile on his face, he walked up and opened the wooden door. A tiny middle-aged woman with snapping black eyes, her equally black hair pulled back into a unbecoming bun, greeted him, her heavy French accent betraying her country of origin. *"Monsieur!"* she cried playfully. "You've arrived just when I had begun to despair that you had forgotten your Suzette."

Gabriel smiled more easily, and putting his hands about her slender waist he swung her up and around, bestowing a lusty kiss upon her as he did so. "Ah, sweet Suzette, you are insatiable! Was I not here, not two days past? And did I not then let you know that you are the only woman who has my heart?"

Removing herself from his teasing embrace, she sent him a droll look. *"Monsieur,* I may be an old woman, but I am not without my wits! Your heart is too well guarded for any ordinary woman to capture it." Shaking a finger at him, she added, half-serious, half-mocking, "But someday, someday, when you are least prepared . . ." She flashed a most superior smile at him. "When you are least prepared that wary heart of yours will be hopelessly enslaved by a pair of lovely eyes. Me, Suzette Teissier, I promise you this!"

Some of Gabriel's light air disappeared and carelessly he replied, "I have been told that I have no heart, and certainly I am in no danger of losing it any time in the near future." Avoiding any further conversation on that particularly sensitive subject, he asked abruptly, "The garments I ordered from you—they are ready?"

Suzette glanced at him, her puzzlement obvious. *"Oui, monsieur,* they are! But why such dowdy clothing? Your women have always been a pleasure to gown, but these garments! *Mon Dieu!* They are only fit for a servant!"

His face suddenly hard, Gabriel returned flatly, "Exactly. Now if we can settle accounts . . ."

Giving a very Gallic shrug, Suzette turned away, call-

ing to someone in another room. A few moments later,
Gabriel left the dressmaker's shop, a parcel under his arm.
Mounting his horse, he guided the spirited animal toward
the waterfront.

Shortly thereafter, leaving the horse at the stables he
maintained when in Port Royal, he swiftly returned to
the *Dark Angel*. Seeing one of his men loitering near the
railings, he called out, "Goodwin! I have made arrangements for my carriage to pick me up at dockside. When
it arrives, let me know, please. I'll be in the great room."

Goodwin nodded and Gabriel headed in the direction of
his quarters, the package from the dressmaker's still
firmly held under his arm. As he neared his destination,
he was conscious of a queer mixture of reluctance and
anticipation, wondering how Maria was going to take to
the "gifts" he had bought especially for her.

She had been staring out the casement windows at the
blue waters of the lagoon when he entered, and her
thoughts must have been far away, because when he shut
the door, she jumped and swung around to face him, her
startlement obvious. For a long moment they regarded
each other across the distance that separated them, tension slowly building within the confines of the room as
the silence spun out.

Gabriel deliberately did nothing to break the mood, and
with measured steps he approached the oak table in the
middle of the room. Carelessly he tossed the parcel he had
brought from the dressmaker's onto the table.

A sardonic expression on his face, he said, "Your new
wardrobe, m'lady. I have decided not to force you to sully
your high principles by making you wear stolen finery
any longer." His voice dripping with sarcasm, he added,
"I trust these garments please you—and lay your delicate
conscience to rest—they were purchased with good English coin."

To still the leap her heart had given at the sight of him,
Maria looked fixedly at the innocuous package lying on
the table, and then rising to meet the challenge of his
sarcastic manner, she raised her eyes to his and retorted
sweetly, "Good English coin, no doubt earned by the suffering of untold innocent Spaniards!"

His face dark and anger glittering in his green eyes, he

he was across the room in a trice, his hand curling brutally around Maria's upper arm. *"Innocent Spaniards!"* he fairly spat the words. "Shall I tell you about your innocent Spaniards? We don't need to mention what your brother did to me and mine, but shall I tell you about Jenkins? Jenkins, who watched his brother and father die in the flames of an *auto-da-fé* in Madrid, simply because they were English Protestants who had the misfortune to be on a merchant ship stopped by your countrymen." His grip on her arm tightening with every word he spoke, he went on grimly, "Shall I show you the scars that Jenkins bears, constant reminders of the tender treatment he received from the Inquisition? And then there is my second mate, Thomas Cleaver, who saw his entire family slaughtered by a group of murdering Spaniards who attacked the settlement where he was living on Saint Kitts—his wife was gutted in front of his very eyes—his infant daughter roasted on a spit. I could go on further, but be aware of this, half the men who belong to the Brethren of the Coast are there because of the cruel and inhuman treatment they have received at the hands of *your* countrymen. They were good, honest, Englishmen trying to live good, English lives until it was their merciless misfortune to cross paths with the Spanish." He tossed her arm aside contemptuously. "Don't *ever,"* he grated out, "speak to me again about *innocent* Spaniards!"

Maria was horrified and repelled by his angry words, but there was nothing she could say to refute them. While she had no personal knowledge other than what had happened to the *Raven* and its occupants of the atrocities that he had spoken of, she had no doubt that every word he had hurled at her was true, and she was aware of a feeling of despair and shame. The brutality and ugliness of the acts committed by *both* of their countrymen created a black, jagged-spiked chasm that would always lie between them.

A sharp rap on the door broke the menacing silence that had fallen, and his cold green eyes still on her, Gabriel called out impatiently, "Yes! What is it?"

"Your carriage is here, captain, and I've ordered the dinghy readied for you."

quietly. His tone hardening, he said to Maria, "I'm afraid that you'll have to wait to try on your new garments." A derisive smile curved his mouth. "Another few hours of wearing pilfered silks and laces shouldn't do much damage to your far-too-nice scruples."

As he finished speaking he reached across the table and scooped up the package he had thrown there only a few minutes ago. His other hand once more around her upper arm, he said mockingly to Maria, "Come along, m'lady, our carriage awaits us!"

Willy-nilly, she was dragged toward the door. When he stopped to open the door, she got out breathlessly, "Where are we going?"

He looked down at her, that infuriatingly derisive smile again curving his chiseled mouth. "I can see that I shall have to teach you the proper manner of a slave. And your first lesson shall be—never question . . . and certainly never complain!"

Maria's blue eyes flashed angrily and she gritted out, "You'll forgive me, kind master—I have not been a slave for very long!"

"True, and I shall forgive you this time and even deign to give you our destination. We go to Royal Gift, my plantation and your new, if not home, then definitely slave quarters!"

Chapter Twenty

THE several-hour journey to Royal Gift was one of the most uncomfortable, unpleasant and tension-filled times Maria had ever spent in her life. It almost rivaled the nerve-wracking hours she and Pilar had remained hiding in the stables in Puerto Bello, the sound of the buccaneer attack coming with dreadful clarity to their ears.

One of his men driving the pair of spanking bay horses, Gabriel rode with her in the well-sprung carriage, and so she did not have any private time to recover her composure, no time at all to contemplate her future quietly. During the entire trip Gabriel lounged carelessly across from her, his long body swaying easily with the bumps and jolts of the carriage, his eyes half-closed, his very silence and apparent indifference to her presence almost as unnerving as openly aggressive behavior would have been.

While the carriage was well constructed and expensively outfitted, gray velvet interior and black, gilt and scarlet exterior, the road, if it could be called that, was not. It appeared to be a mere dirt track that wandered aimlessly through the tropical lushness that threatened to engulf the road at any time. The cabbage-like leaves of the banana and plantain trees created welcomed patches of dappled shade where they overhung the track; the spiky fronds of tall, slender coconut trees could be occasionally glimpsed through the rampant wilderness; and here and there grew clumps of vivid green ferns and wild orange trees, their sweet scent filling the air. The palm-like leaves and globe-shaped yellow-orange fruit of the papaya trees could be seen too as well as the profusion of liana vines that grew everywhere. Clouds of jewel-hued birds would rise screaming to the brilliant blue sky above as the passage of the carriage startled them, and monkeys would chatter angrily at the disturbance—to Maria it reminded her vividly, painfully, of Hispaniola, and in some small way it also comforted her.

But the condition of the road did not allow for any great appreciation of the tropical beauty that was everywhere the eye could see, the constant bouncing and shaking of the carriage jerking Maria about so, that she was certain every bone in her body had become dislocated. The heat inside the carriage was oppressive, and as the hours passed, she could feel an uncomfortable trickle of perspiration sliding between her breasts and running down the middle of her back.

Gabriel's brooding presence did not help matters, and he, rather than the rutted track and the humid warmth, caused her the most discomfort. If only, she thought half angrily, half apprehensively, he would say *something!* At this very moment she would have even welcomed an infuriating, scathing comment or two from him—anything would have been better than his silent, almost menacing form, tension and strain building within the carriage with every mile that they traveled. And it was, she decided waspishly, sending him a dark glance from underneath her long lashes, all *his* fault! One would have thought, she mused acidly, that he would have had the decency to let her have some peace. But no! He must ride with her, forcing her to endure his despicable company!

It was an effort to keep her eyes averted from his tall form, to studiously avoid even looking in his direction. It was even more of an effort as the hours passed to keep her own expression serene and unruffled, to give not one hint of the wild turbulence that was beating in her breast and to pretend that this journey was nothing more than a pleasant ride through the untrammeled jungle. But the most unpleasant effort of all was to remind herself that she was on her way to a place of servitude, that when they arrived she would be among strangers, people who would regard her as little more than a trophy of war, a slave brought home by the master of the house.

A tiny sigh escaped her and she wished not for the first

time that Pilar was still with her. Somehow events hadn't seemed so very bad when her friend had been with her. But now she was all alone with Gabriel Lancaster, and she found that knowledge daunting indeed.

Of course, Pilar wasn't gone from her life forever; she would be, as they had discussed yesterday, only ten miles down the road from Royal Gift at Zeus' plantation, Havre du Mer. Maria gave a little grimace. But that wasn't quite the same as living together in the same house, as she and Pilar had been doing for the past few years.

Remembering their parting yesterday on the *Dark Angel,* Maria felt tears sting her eyes. Fiercely she glared at the unoffending countryside, willing the tears to recede, ashamed and alarmed at the idea of letting Gabriel see her distress. It had given Maria a terrible wrench to say farewell to her friend, and both she and Pilar had been near tears as the time had approached for Pilar to leave.

"Pigeon," Pilar had said miserably, "I do not like abandoning you this way, but I have no choice. I must follow my husband to his home, and we can only be thankful that it is situated such a short distance from where you will be living." Her fine dark eyes full of worry, she had added, "You will try not to enrage *Señor* Lancaster? I know it is not easy, your situation, but it is far better than either one of us could have guessed it would be the day the buccaneers attacked Puerto Bello."

Maria had sent her a brave smile, trying very hard to act cool and unconcerned about being left totally at Gabriel's mercy, without even the solace of a friendly ear. "Don't worry about me," she had muttered staunchly, "I will survive—but it is *you* who make me anxious—are you positive that you are well and able to travel to Havre du Mer? You are still too pale for my liking . . . and you lost your breakfast again this morning," she had finished uneasily.

Pilar had smiled wanly. "I am fine, *chica.* I think it just must have been the strange food we have eaten these weeks at sea. I am certain that once I am settled at Mer I shall soon regain my appetite and leave off this distressful sickliness that has overtaken me these past few weeks."

Zeus and Gabriel had entered the room just then, and

there had been no further chance for private conversation. Moments later the four of them had walked out onto the deck of the *Dark Angel* and Zeus and Pilar had prepared to disembark. The two women had embraced and Pilar had whispered urgently into Maria's ear, "Control that Delgato temper, little one! And if he harms you . . . I mean *really* harms you, dangerous or not, come to me at once! I do not know what I can do to help you, but we will think of *something!*"

Maria had hugged her that much tighter, warmed by the affection and anxiety of the other woman. Through tear-misted eyes she had watched them be rowed ashore in the gig, but once they had reached the docks and Zeus had solicitously helped Pilar from the boat, they had disappeared in the crowds that thronged the wharves, and Maria had been left bereft and aware of a stab of fright. She was alone now. At the mercy of a man who hated the very sound of the Delgato name.

Still glaring at the sun-splashed forest, she felt a lump rise up in her throat, and only by exercising the greatest self-will was she able to hold back an overpowering urge to cry. Biting her bottom lip hard, she vowed forlornly that she would not cry in front of that beastly creature across from her. She would *not!*

Fortunately, the fight within herself not to cry kept her mind from wandering onto even less pleasant subjects and for a while even managed to make her forget how uncomfortable the muggy heat and bone-jarring ride was making her. And by the time she had come to terms with her misery at saying good-bye to Pilar, she suddenly noticed that the countryside was changing.

They had been riding steadily inland, the altitude gradually rising as they traveled toward the spine of green mountains that rose in the distance, and she became conscious that it was less humid, the warmth more bearable. Papaya and banana trees were no longer so prevalent, hardwoods and lianas now dominating the terrain; waterfalls and fern bordered blue pools of water appearing unexpectedly in these mountains of the rain forest. It was, she reflected with a lighter heart, utterly beautiful.

Royal Gift was in the mountains, and when they crested a hill and the land suddenly fell away from them, reveal-

ing a verdant valley filled with acres of tall, waving green
sugar cane, Maria caught her breath in pleasure. How
much it reminded her of home. Despite her wishes to the
contrary, a wave of anticipation flooded her. To her complete astonishment, she was eager to reach their destination.

Forgetful of the events that brought her here, she instantly turned to look at Gabriel, and with eyes sparkling
with excitement, she dumbfounded him by demanding,
"Is all of this lovely land yours? This is where we will
live? Where is the house? Can it be seen from here?"

There was a startled silence, and then straightening
up, a hint of pleasure flickering through his green eyes,
he said warmly, "Yes, these acres you see all belong to
me. The entire valley from ridgetop to ridgetop is Lancasterian land. And yes, you can see the house." Leaning
toward the window, he pointed and murmured, "See? Up
there on that hill overlooking the valley, there is Royal
Gift."

His pride was evident, and from the way he gazed at
the lush valley and green, forested hills, it was obvious
that he held great love of the land too. How very different
from Diego, the thought occurred to her. Diego saw the
land as only a means to earn gold, while Gabriel . . . Even
not wanting to find one acceptable thing about him, she
had to admit that Royal Gift appeared to mean more to
him than merely a source of gold.

Vexed with herself for endowing him with a virtue he
probably didn't possess, somewhat crossly she reminded
herself that he didn't *need* gold—not when there were rich
Spanish galleons to plunder and helpless towns like Puerto Bello to sack. Her initial pleasure vanished and belligerently she asked, "And how many good Spanish ships
did you have to loot to gain such a plantation? How many
Spaniards had to die to make you wealthy?"

Gabriel's face froze, the green eyes becoming icy. In a
voice of barely controlled anger, he growled, "The land
was a gift, a royal grant from the King of England. As
for wealth—I had enough, more than enough, until your
brother stripped me of not only wealth, but wife, sister
and freedom! And if I regained my stolen fortune by preying on those who robbed me, I see little wrong or little to

be ashamed of—certainly, no amount of Spanish gold can ever repay me for the loss of my family!"

Thoroughly routed and unable to find any form of effective retaliation, Maria held her tongue, and in stony, angry silence they turned off the main trail they had been following onto a smaller but far better maintained road. It wound through the dense upright stalks of sugar cane until gradually once again the road began to rise toward the mountains. In spite of herself, ignoring the conflicting emotions that were warring within her breast, she watched impatiently for her first sight of Royal Gift.

The carriage rounded a curve, and there unexpectedly stood the house. It was situated on the highest ground and overlooked the plantation below; there were no other buildings near it, and as was the custom, the grounds had all been cleared for the distance of a musket shot. For Maria, more familiar with the sprawling gracious haciendas on Hispaniola, the first glimpse of Royal Gift was disappointing. The house more resembled a medieval fortress than the home of a wealthy aristocratic gentleman.

Built entirely of stone, its towering majesty was very intimidating to Maria; and yet the more she considered the thick stone walls, the crenellated rooftop and the "bullet wood" shutters which adorned the windows, windows that were little more than slits in the stout walls, the more it appealed to something deep within her. It looked, she decided with wonder, like a castle. A castle set down unexpectedly in the virgin wilderness of the tropical jungle.

A circular driveway curved in front of the building, and as they came nearer, there were signs that someone had tried to soften the harsh exterior: several rosebushes grew near one corner of the house and a ruby red bougainvillea rioted charmingly around the stone pillars of the wide portico which jutted out from the center of the imposing structure. There was, Maria thought pleasurably, as the carriage came at last to stop near the broad steps of the portico, an air of timelessness and grace about the house, despite its fortress-like appearance.

Stiltedly, almost defensively, Gabriel muttered, "It may not have the sprawling beauty of Casa de la Paloma, but then it was built without a woman's softening touch and it had to be built strong enough to withstand an attack—either from the Spanish or rebellious slaves. Royal Gift is on the furthermost frontier on Jamaica, and except for Zeus and Pilar we have no near neighbors for miles around."

Turning shining eyes to him, Maria said softly, "Oh, but, Englishman! It is lovely!" Then she remembered the situation between them, and unwilling to utter another compliment to her wretched captor, she shut her mouth with a decided snap.

Just as her earlier artless comment on the loveliness of the land had dumbfounded him, so now did her compliment, and he found himself inordinately pleased by her reaction. *Not*, he reminded himself grimly, that it mattered what she thought! After all, he hadn't brought her here to be happy!

But there was a curious sense of harmony between them as they mounted the steps and prepared to enter the house. Gabriel's manner was almost solicitous to her, his hand warmly cupping her elbow, his dark head bent in her direction as he casually mentioned that someday when Jamaica was more settled trees and shrubs would be planted nearer the house to soften its stark solitariness. Maria was left with the curious impression that, against his will, he cared about her reaction to his home, that for some inexplicable reason he actually wanted her to like it here, and to her dismay she found herself responding to his suddenly gracious conduct.

A pair of huge double doors were flung open the instant they approached them, and a little man, correctly attired in black-and-white livery, was standing there, his merry blue eyes full of delight and pleasure. "Sir," he cried happily, "it is wonderful to have you home once again! Mrs. Satterleigh is busy in the kitchen just this very minute cooking you a hearty meal—curried mutton with saffron rice, and she has also baked a gooseberry tart, knowing it is your favorite dessert."

Gabriel smiled warmly. "It is good to see you also, Satterleigh. When I am at sea I long for nothing more than to be here and think often, you can be sure, of your wife's tasty cooking. I trust that since I have now given up my sea-roving days the two of you will not grow bored with my constant presence!"

Maria sent him a sharp glance, a question hovering on her lips, but Satterleigh's indignant comment allowed her no chance to speak.

"Bored!" the little man exclaimed. "It is boring *without*, sir!"

Gabriel chuckled and murmured, " 'Tis indeed my good fortune that you, Mrs. Satterleigh and Richard were content to settle at Royal Gift with me."

Drawing himself up proudly, Satterleigh replied, "The Satterleighs have always served the Lancasters."

Nodding his head, Gabriel said easily, "So it has always been." Glancing around he asked, "But where is Richard? I thought he would be here at the house to greet me."

"And so he should be, sir! But one of the mares is foaling and she seems to be having trouble—he'll come to the house just as soon as everything is done."

Throughout the conversation, Satterleigh had been flashing quick little speculative glances in Maria's direction, and finally unable to control his curiosity any longer, he asked, "And is this the young lady you wrote about in your note to us?"

Some of Gabriel's relaxed manner fled and quietly he admitted, "Yes, this is Maria Delgato. She is here as, my, ah, slave."

Satterleigh was of middle age; he and his family had endured the privations of the Lancasterian family as they had followed the court of young Charles II throughout Europe during the King's exile, and the Satterleighs had come with Gabriel and his father on their first trip to Jamaica. While Sir William and Gabriel had left on that fateful journey to England that had seen Sir William die at Don Pedro Delgato's hand, Satterleigh, his wife Martha and their son Richard had remained on Jamaica seeing to the interests of the Lancasters. They were loyal retainers—generations of Satterleighs had served generations of Lancasters and there was little each family didn't know about the other, but at Gabriel's words, Satterleigh looked astonished. "Your *slave!*" he burst out in scandalized startlement; even his shock of thick, shoulder-length white hair seemed to quiver with outrage at such a notion. "This lovely young lady is your slave?"

Dryly, Gabriel answered, "This lovely young lady, in case you don't remember, is a Delgato. The daughter of Don Pedro." He touched his fingers to the faint silver scar that marred his high cheekbone. "And don't be deceived by her fragile appearance—she is quite capable of defending herself, as this scar attests."

"Well!" Satterleigh exclaimed forthrightly. "What you say may be true, sir, but I hardly think that you can blame this young lady for something that her father did! And as for the other"—a twinkle entered the blue eyes—"you'll forgive me, sir, for saying so, but you probably deserved it!"

Enchanted by this unexpected protector, Maria smiled shyly at him, her gratitude shining in the sapphire eyes. Satterleigh returned her smile with interest, saying firmly, "She must be exhausted from the journey from Port Royal. I shall show her to the rose chamber and then see immediately to your needs, sir."

A black frown creased Gabriel's forehead, and not liking the reaction of his most trusted servant to Maria's arrival, he said sharply, "She is no guest! She is to be treated no better than one of the field women—take her to Nell—she can assist that kind lady in preparing my meal."

Attacked by a sudden bout of deafness, Satterleigh smiled once more at Maria and murmured, "Come along, young lady. You'll feel much better after you have rested and refreshed yourself."

Impotently, Gabriel watched as Satterleigh considerately led Maria away, uncertain whether to take great enjoyment in the situation or to be angry at the calm way his authority had been usurped. There was also the unpleasant knowledge that he was going to find it extremely difficult to treat and have Maria treated in the manner of a slave. A wry smile curved his handsome mouth. Maria, he admitted with chagrin and amusement, was more than likely about to become the most pampered slave ever seen on the island of Jamaica—particularly if Satterleigh's actions were any indication of how others in his household were going to behave around her. Shaking his head at the

dilemma she presented to him, he reluctantly followed in
their wake.

Buoyed up by Satterleigh's kind conduct, with a far
lighter heart, Maria adjusted her steps to the older man's
more sedate stride as they slowly walked down the great
hall and unhurriedly made their way through the house.
Curiously she looked around her, eager and excited to see
what manner of house Gabriel had created in the middle
of Jamaica's tropical forests.

There were few rooms in the house from what she could
see, but all were impressive in size and all had wonderfully high ceilings, the massive beams of sweet cedar extremely pleasing to the eye. Partitions of mahogany
divided the house into some of the various rooms, their
eight-foot height leaving large air spaces between them
and the wooden beams of the ceilings. Jewel-toned tapes-
tries had been fastened to the walls and added to the feeling of warmth and color; elegant, intricately patterned
Oriental carpets broke the wide expanses of rich mahogany flooring; and here and there had been hung iron
sconces, all of which held thick, ivory-colored candles.
Through an arched doorway she glimpsed a room furnished with a dark, heavily carved table and chairs covered with fine tawny Spanish leather, lavishly decorated
with brass studs. A magnificent silver candelabrum
graced the highly polished surface of the long table.

As they passed through the commodious main room of
the house, Maria noted admiringly the comfortable chairs
and settees upholstered in rich fabrics—emerald brocades
and crimson velvets, sapphire silks, all trimmed with gal-
loon and fringe and garnished with brass-headed nails. A
delicate marquetry cabinet had been placed near one of
the narrow window slits, and above the massive stone
fireplace that dominated the far end of the room had been
hung a large gilt-framed painting of a man and woman.
Maria would have liked to have taken a closer look at the
room and painting, but Satterleigh ushered her through
a doorway and up a wide staircase made of sandalwood to
the upper floor.

The stairs ended, and she found herself at one end of a
spacious hall, several doors opening onto it, the latches
and hinges made of silver. Smiling gently, Satterleigh

stopped before a door, midway down the hall, and throwing wide the door, said gently, "I'm sure you will find everything to your liking, miss. I shall leave you now and see if Mrs. Satterleigh will prepare a tray of refreshments for you . . . some fruit and perhaps some lemonade?"

Maria smiled back at him sunnily and replied, "Oh, *si!* I would like that very much—you have been very kind to me, *Señor* Satterleigh."

Satterleigh drew his small, wiry frame up proudly and bowed low over her hand. "It has been my utmost pleasure, miss! I hope that your stay here at Royal Gift is most enjoyable."

Hearing that part of their conversation as he approached, Gabriel grimaced, thinking sourly that Satterleigh was really being far too charming and thoughtful under the circumstances. But then remembering how he himself seemed unable to place Maria firmly in the menial, despised position of captured enemy, a sigh escaped him. Why in the abstract did revenge appear so sweet, so satisfying, while reality was proving to be so *dis*satisfying? Or better yet—why did he find it so damnably hard to mete out the same kind of punishments and degradations that had been *his* fate under Diego?

A scowl darkened his brow and an arrow of guilt pierced his vitals. His wife had died at Maria's brother's hand, and there was little doubt in his mind that his sister had been defiled and had died at the hands of some brutal Spaniard—one of *her* innocent Spaniards. Ugly hatred surging up through him, he brushed past Satterleigh and growled, "She won't be needing anything. I'll send her down to the kitchens in a few moments."

Satterleigh looked as if he were going to be conveniently deaf again, but one glance at Gabriel's face convinced him that in this matter he had best remember who was master and who was servant. A bit crestfallen and disturbed, Satterleigh walked down the sandalwood staircase. I wonder, he thought heavily, what Mrs. Satterleigh is going to make of this?

Unaware that Gabriel was only a few steps behind her, Maria went into the room that Satterleigh had indicated, and with an appreciative glance she looked around her, immediately enchanted with what she saw. The room

was very large and airy, the high ceilings and open beams
ensuring that even on the hottest days it would be cool
and pleasant up here. And again, like the rest of the
house, here too were further signs of elegance and comfort; a truly lovely carpet of rose and ivory wool lay upon
the mahogany floor, an armoire of sandalwood stood between the two narrow window slits that let the warm sunlight stream into the room and a settee with plump
cushions and upholstered in a deep rose velvet had been
placed nearby. Against the far wall was a delightfully
feminine dressing table with an olive-wood framed mirror
and a stool covered in ivory satin, and just to her left, on
a dais, was a beautifully fashioned bed: tall, delicately
carved spires at the four corners held up the pale rose silk
canopy, and the remainder of the bed was entirely
swathed in gauzy folds of mosquito netting. Through the
netting, she could discern the gleam of the rose satin coverlet upon the mattress, and with longing she wondered
if Gabriel would ever allow her to sleep there—Satterleigh might have momentarily deflected Gabriel's plans
for her, but she never doubted for a moment that he would
be swayed from the course he had determined to follow.
And somehow she was very certain that treating her like
an honored guest in his home was *not* what he had in
mind.

Sighing unhappily, she glanced around briefly again.
She would have enjoyed using this room. It was so wonderfully feminine, so very appealing, and she knew instinctively that its furnishings had been planned
expressly for a special person. She would have wagered
her very life that it hadn't been for her that such care
had been lavished! Almost reverently she touched the arm
of the settee, liking the smooth feel of the velvet beneath
her fingers, oblivious to Gabriel's presence behind her.

From his position, lounging negligently in the doorway,
Gabriel watched her a second before asking in a curiously
remote tone, "Do you find the room attractive?"

Maria jumped at the sound of his voice so near and she
whirled about, her heart thumping wildly at the unexpected sight of his long frame filling the doorway, the
package he had first brought to the *Dark Angel* dangling
loosely from one hand. Trying to sound casual despite the

frisson of tension that suddenly splintered uncomfortably down her spine, she remarked truthfully, "It is a beautiful room. Far grander than I would have thought would be found here."

Gabriel's upper lip curled in a sneer. "Why? Is it only the Spanish who can appreciate fine things?"

A little gust of anger swept up through her, but determined not to rise to the bait, she said levelly, "You yourself have told me that Royal Gift is on the frontier—I am sure that few places in this wilderness have such lovely things—or that few, if any, buccaneers live in such an impressive home."

"Perhaps, but that is only because they spend it on rum and women and never think to the future," he drawled indifferently.

"But you *did* think of the future?"

For a moment he looked as if he would not answer her, but then shrugging his shoulders, he pushed away from the doorjamb and replied reluctantly, "No, I didn't think of the future—building Royal Gift, furnishing the house and settling the land was more to keep my father's dream for this place alive. I felt I owed it to his memory, that it was his legacy to me . . . and Caroline."

Maria frowned and asked hesitantly, "But what of your own dreams, your own future?"

Gabriel gave a mirthless laugh, the green eyes hard. "My dreams? My dreams died the day the *Santo Cristo* destroyed the *Raven!*" A spasm of pain crossed his handsome face, and harshly he demanded, "Did you know that my wife was to have borne me a child? That with her died my heirs, my hope for the future?"

Shocked, Maria stared at him, conscious deep within herself of a shaft of pain at knowing that once he had loved another woman, that some other woman had been going to have his child. But her greatest emotion was one of pity for him, for having lost so much that day . . . and so needlessly at that. She tried to speak, to convey the warm sympathy she felt for him, to try to explain some of her own feelings of guilt at her brother's often senseless acts of cruelty, especially Diego's behavior that terrible day; but she could not find the words that would adequately express what she was feeling. The blue eyes dark with pain and understanding, she looked at him, longing to touch him, to soothe the unabated anguish she was certain drove him remorselessly at times.

Gabriel instantly recognized the pity in her gaze, if not the other emotions, and stiffened with fury. His voice a silky menace, he growled fiercely, "There are many things I might want or desire in this life, but one of them is *not* the pity of the likes of you!"

Grasping her upper arm, he propelled her from the room, saying harshly, "And I'll not have you sullying the room that was prepared for my sister, should I ever be so fortunate to find her! By God's wounds, you are a slave and you'll damn well be treated as one!"

Chapter Twenty-one

MARIA'S feet barely touched the floor as Gabriel strode angrily down the hallway. Two doors down from the Rose Room he stopped abruptly before a set of double doors, and throwing them wide, he pushed her inside the room ahead of him.

She had a glimpse of a very masculine room, of massive mahogany furniture and colors of russet and emerald and guessed that this must be his bedchamber. There was no time for more impressions because, grasping her upper arm once more, he dragged her ungently across the length of the huge room to a small door set in one wall. With a violent movement he opened that door and with an equally violent motion he pushed her through the doorway.

Utter darkness met her gaze, only the light from the room behind her piercing the blackness. A sensation of smothering overcame her as she realized that there were no windows, no light of any kind in this small, black airless chamber before her. It was far worse than the hold of the *Santo Cristo;* it would be, she thought with rising fear, like being immured in a grave! Realizing that he intended to lock her in this tiny room with no light and little air was more than Maria's nerves could stand, and irrational terror rose up through her and she recoiled uncontrollably.

Gabriel's chest stopped her retreat, his hands clamping tightly around her slender shoulders. "Don't you like your new quarters, sweet viper? I'm sure you'll find them far more comfortable than the devil's pit your charming brother left me in for so long—and at least I don't intend

for you to go without food and water, nor that you stay
there indefinitely—just long enough to make your position clear within my household."

He began to push her further into that yawning darkness, but Maria resisted furiously, her heels sliding across
the flooring, her body twisting in his grasp. She fought
like a cornered tigress, and catching him by surprise with
her frantic movements, she broke his hold on her shoulders. Spinning around, she faced him, the terror she was
experiencing evident in the wide blue eyes. Breath coming in great gulps, for the first time since they had known
each other, she pleaded with him. "Englishman," she
begged, "do not do this to me! Beat me if you wish, but
do not lock me in that coffin, *por favor!* I could not bear
it!"

Moved by her obvious fright and angry because he was
sympathetic, Gabriel stared down at her, his heavy eyebrows creasing in a frown. He was furiously aware of a
need to reach out and take her into his arms, to soothe
away her terror, to tell her that she had nothing to fear,
but stubbornly he pushed the feeling away. He would not
be beguiled by a pair of speaking blue eyes! But yet, it
was not in him to act so cruelly in the face of her great
terror, and disgusted with himself, he pulled her from the
small room and snarled something vicious under his
breath about the possibility of insanity having overtaken
him. To vent some of the bottled frustration that was
churning within him he slammed the door with far more
force than necessary, and looking at Maria, the emerald
eyes decidedly unfriendly, hands on his lean hips, he
asked acidly, "Since that doesn't meet with your approval, madam, where do you suggest I put you? In the
Rose Room, I suppose?"

Relieved that he wasn't going through with his plan,
some of Maria's fright lessened, and prodded by an impulse of mischief, she nodded her head slightly and said
with feigned meekness, *"Sí señor,* I would like that much
better."

Sternly repressing a sudden urge to laugh at her brazen
change of face, he glared at her, his upper lip curling
scornfully. "I'm sure you would!" he finally snapped when

he was certain he would not laugh. "But I think you forget yourself—you are a slave, *not* here for a polite visit!"

Despite Gabriel's intimidating stance and expression, Maria had seen a tiny twitch in his cheek and rightly guessed that he was not as angry as he would have her believe, and emboldened by this instinctive knowledge, she said more brashly, "But why not, *señor*? Surely, it is time for us to put the past behind us . . . and for Delgato and Lancaster to show the world that we can rise above the wrong done by our ancestors."

To Gabriel's complete horror and wild fury, he found that proposition vastly appealing, and it was only by the greatest willpower that he was able to throttle the words of agreement that threatened to spill from his lips. With a grim effort he clamped his mouth shut and reminded himself unpleasantly of that day on Hispaniola when she had used her lovely body to hold him enthralled until Perez had arrived. She was a witch! While he should feel nothing but contempt and hatred for her, she evoked feelings within him that he had never felt for any woman. He desired her when he should despise her, he was, if not kind to her, at least not *un*kind to her when he should be cruel, and now when he should be enjoying his position of power over her, his ability to treat her in any manner he wanted, he discovered that all she had to do was look at him with those lovely sapphire eyes and he became incapable of rational thought, that all he could think of was how soft and warm she would feel in his arms, of how sweet and yielding that gently curved mouth would feel beneath his. He swallowed with difficulty, desire, sweet and strong, surging through his loins, driving all thought of revenge from his mind.

Maria sensed his mood change, if not the manner of it, and uncertainly she looked at him. There was suddenly a sensual cast to his mouth, a warm glitter in the green eyes, and she found herself instantly breathless. Hesitantly, she asked, "*Señor*? What is it that you want?"

Almost like a man mesmerized, his eyes locked on her soft, red mouth, Gabriel slowly shrugged out of his mulberry jacket, his fingers lazily working at the throat of his white shirt. "Want?" he questioned thickly. "Why, it is you, little viper, that I want . . . and now."

Discarding his shirt a second later, bare-chested, he reached for her, and Maria was powerless to resist him, just as she had known she would be. With a small moan of part-pleasure, part-denial her mouth met his, mindless, intoxicating desire exploding through her as his tongue hungrily slid between her teeth, seeking the warmth and honey beyond. Never breaking the sweet contact of his lips upon hers, Gabriel lifted her slim body in his arms and carried her blindly to his bed, gently laying her on the silken coverlet.

The remainder of his clothing joined the shirt and jacket haphazardly on the floor, his hands immediately seeking to divest Maria of the satin and laces that hid her smooth flesh from him. His movements were no longer slow; there was a feverish urgency about him, as if he had waited too long for this moment, as if he could not bear for one more second to pass until she lay naked and willing beneath him.

The same driving passion that gripped Gabriel had Maria in its sweet toils too, and eagerly she returned his hot, fierce kisses, her hands roaming pleasurably over his long, lean body, exploring him as shamelessly as he was exploring her. For these passion-filled moments she could forget the difficulties that awaited them when reality returned and could lose herself in the wonder of his possession. He had awakened her to desire, had taught her the pleasure their bodies could give each other, and she was wild to know that ecstasy again, the love she tried to hide and ignore flooding through her as his mouth clung hungrily to hers.

Gabriel was as a man possessed; he seemed unable to have enough of her, his mouth and hands moving erotically over her soft flesh, tasting, teasing and greatly arousing them both with his actions. Maria was hardly less bold in her own ministrations, her warm hand closing around his swollen manhood, stroking him so tenderly that he thought he would die of the pleasure she stirred within him. Compulsively his fingers slid through the soft curls between her thighs, finding the yielding spot he sought and gently, insistently he brought her to the peak of ecstasy before allowing their bodies to merge.

It was a sweetly urgent mating, the weeks of denial

making them both wild with desire, Maria's hips rising erotically to meet the hard thrust of his body, Gabriel unable to control or stop the almost frenzied need to lose himself within her hot, silken depths. And when the release came, it brought exquisite pleasure to them both, Maria's entire body awash with blissful sensation, Gabriel groaning aloud his intense gratification.

There was silence in the room, neither one of them seeming able or willing to break the sensual rapport that had so suddenly erupted. Their bodies still locked together, Gabriel slowly shifted until they lay side by side, their faces only inches apart.

Wonderingly he looked at her, the expression in the green eyes hard to define. Heavily, he asked, "Why is it that you seem to so easily twist my thoughts about? Your father killed mine; your brother wantonly destroyed my life; the Delgatos and Lancasters have been bitter, uncompromising enemies for generations; and yet with you, I . . ." His voice trailed off, his gaze dropping to the small breasts that almost touched his muscled chest, the coral nipples still slightly swollen from the passion they had just shared. His eyes seemed transfixed by those coral tips, and huskily he got out, "You unman me. Instead of taking revenge, I am only conscious of the pleasure your body gives mine . . . I am ashamed of what you make me feel—my lust for you is a betrayal of all I hold dear. It makes a mockery of my vow for vengeance and leaves me less of a man." He stopped abruptly, as if suddenly becoming aware of how damning his words were, of the weapon he was unwittingly giving her.

With a rough, angry movement, he rolled away from her, Maria nearly crying in despair at his change of mood. His words had filled her with joy and pain—joy that he would admit to some inexplicable emotion between them, pain that he found it shameful, pain that he could reduce what was between them to mere lust. And yet, she wondered dully, perhaps that's all it was . . . to him. But not to her, never to her, she thought fiercely.

Gabriel dressed hastily, leaving the fine mulberry-colored jacket lying where he had discarded it only moments before. He glanced back at Maria, who had sat up on the bed, having pulled the russet silk coverlet to her chest to hide her nakedness. He glanced at her, his mouth twisting. Wryly, he admitted, "I should keep you that way—naked and in my bed, but I am afraid that the devils that dwell within me would not allow it."

Again his careless words gave her both pleasure and pain, but holding her head proudly, she asked coolly, "What do you intend to do with me, señor?"

He sighed, rubbing a hand across the back of his neck, his eyes never leaving her face, thinking against his will that he had never seen her look quite so appealing, the russet coverlet intensifying the creaminess of her delicate skin, the long inky-black hair spilling wildly around her naked shoulders. Even now, with passion just slaked, the knowledge that she was completely naked beneath that clinging silk coverlet aroused him. Disgusted with himself he turned away from her. His voice as cool as hers, he replied, "Why, nothing . . . for the moment. When all is said and done, you are *still* my slave and I will not allow that to change."

Concealing the further pain his words gave her, she sat up more stiffly on the bed, and determined to give no ground, to give him no satisfaction, she said in a voice that only shook slightly, "Being your slave is far more acceptable to me, señor, than being your whore!"

He swung around at that, an inimical gleam lighting the green eyes. "Then perhaps," he snarled, "you shouldn't practice the arts of whoredom so expertly!"

An ugly silence fell, and then as if unwilling to continue this fruitless exchange, he bent down and picked up the package that had fallen from his hands when he had caught her shoulders earlier. Tossing it carelessly on the bed, he said levelly, "Your servant clothes, madam. You'll not have need of silks and laces any longer."

Her chin held firmly, she reached for the package and viciously tore it open. Two chemises of coarse cotton, three black bodices and skirts of inexpensive material were the contents.

His face carefully bland, Gabriel said, "I believe that Mrs. Satterleigh will be able to provide you with some aprons, but I think what you have there should keep you decently clothed for the time being."

In a voice dripping with scorn, she choked out, "What, no petticoats or corsets, *señor?*"

A sardonic smile flashed across his dark face. "You have no need of stays and corsets—as for petticoats, I'm afraid the only ones I can offer you are those, ah, *stolen* from the high-born ladies of Puerto Bello . . . and of course, we both know that your too-delicate conscience could not bear to accept such pilfered finery—never mind that the petticoats might have originally belonged to some gently bred Englishwoman who had the misfortune to fall into Spanish hands!"

"Like your sister!" she hurled back at him, letting anger make her reckless.

His jaw hardened and the green eyes were fairly glacial as icily he retorted, "Very like my sister! Just remember *her* fate and that of my wife whenever you think me too cruel a master. Now get clothed and out of my sight before I forget that I was born a gentleman!"

A decidedly unwise reply trembled on her lips, but a strong instinct for survival suddenly asserted itself, and casting him an uncertain glance, she muttered, "May I have some privacy to dress, *señor?*"

He smiled nastily, and propping himself up against the door frame, he said baldly, "No."

The blue eyes burned with anger, the fact that she would have enjoyed doing him an injury very obvious from the set expression on her delicate features. With a sound something like an infuriated kitten might have made, she presented her back to him. Eventually, using the coverlet as a shield and keeping her slender back to him, she was able to struggle into the chemise and a bodice and skirt. Her cheeks flushed from her exertions as well as the humiliation, she finally slid off the bed and looked at him, rebellion and dislike radiating from her almost tangibly.

Grimly she started across the room toward the doorway where he stood. When she was within a few feet of him and he had made no effort to move, she sent him a disdainful glance and said haughtily, "Señor, you have told me to get out of your sight—and I shall do so, the instant you remove yourself from my path!"

Gabriel made no effort to move, but lounged there, surveying her, a slight frown upon his face. She was dressed appropriately enough, the simple white chemise spilling artlessly out over the top and from the sides of the sleeveless black bodice as was the fashion of the day, the plain black full skirt falling virtuously to the floor. She was sensibly garbed, but with her lustrous black hair tumbling in wavy splendor down her back and shoulders, her mouth still red and slightly swollen from their lovemaking, there was something very earthy and alluring about her. She looked, he decided with angry exasperation, like some damned little Puritan in her black and white garments—a *wanton* Puritan at that! He had brought the plain, dowdy clothes to punish her, to humiliate her, she who had so proudly scorned the silks and laces he had first offered her, but now he found that he did not like her in these simple garments—that *he* felt humiliated and uncomfortable to see her dressed so and his frown increased. Now, why should he care that she was forced to wear clothing fit only for a lowly servant? Wasn't that the whole purpose behind his actions? Wasn't he determined to show her that she was nothing more than a servant here? That he was her master, that the clothes she wore, the food she ate, her very life, all depended upon his whims?

An intense feeling of baffled rage surged up through him as he continued to stare at her, his irrational dislike of the garments growing with every second that passed. This was another of those moments that should have given him great delight, he should be filled with a strong sense of justice and pleasure about what he was doing, but he wasn't. To make matters worse, he didn't even think that he could endure seeing her moving about Royal Gift in the role of his servant—those days on board the *Dark Angel* when he had forced her to serve his table had been bad enough, and he was fairly certain that he wasn't going to find it any easier in his home. Revenge, he thought for the hundredth time and with increasing bitterness, was not bringing him the joy his vows and dreams had promised him. Instead, to his utter confusion and dismay, whenever he tried to act as he had sworn he would, he discovered that something deep inside of him rebelled and that he found his actions distasteful and repugnant—certainly, they brought him no joy.

Even dwelling upon her family's wrongs against his couldn't still his growing revulsion for the situation, and like a nagging toothache, one particular thought had begun to occur to him again and again—*she* had done the Lancasters no wrong. Her father had committed a great evil in slaying Sir William and her brother had done an even greater evil by attacking the *Raven* . . . but no blame could be laid at Maria's little feet. She was as much a victim as Elizabeth and Caroline. Yet whenever that unsettling and discomforting train of thought filtered through his brain, the ugly image of the beam crushing Elizabeth's slender body beneath it and the terrified expression on Caroline's young face when she had been led away by that tall, gray-eyed Spaniard on Hispaniola would leap to his mind, and he would be filled once more with an unquenchable thirst for vengeance against the Delgatos. And no matter what Maria might make him feel, no matter how sweetly her body joined with his, no matter how much she stirred other emotions inside of him, she was still a Delgato and he was bound by blood to avenge the deaths of those dear to him.

But Gabriel was finding it increasingly difficult to remember that fact, especially when the daunting thought emerged that there was little difference between his actions and Diego's. They were both preying upon innocents—the women of each other's families, dragging defenseless females into a fight that was not of their making. If he had raped Maria as cruelly and brutally as he had sworn he would—what difference would there have been between his actions and Caroline's probable fate at the hands of that unknown Spaniard? If he had slain Maria that first night, how would that have differed from what had happened to his wife? Was he, despite his righteous beliefs, really no better than the very men he hated and condemned?

Confused, bedeviled and frustrated, Gabriel glared at Maria, wishing she didn't look quite so appealing and vulnerable, that instead of feeling fiercely protective toward her, he could hate her as savagely as he did her brother. Seeing the hint of apprehension that sprang to her lovely eyes as he continued to scowl blackly in her direction, he sighed. Even now, he couldn't bear for her to be dis-

tressed, and he sent her a wry look. Moving aside, he said
gruffly, "If you'll come with me, I shall show you the way
to the kitchens and introduce you to Mrs. Satterleigh."
Cryptically he added, "Perhaps she will succeed where I
have failed and see that your hands are kept busy."

Slightly reassured that he had apparently thrown off
his black mood, Maria ventured carefully, "And my quarters, *señor?* Will she tell me where I am to sleep?" Unable
to help herself, she glanced fearfully back at the small
airless room that he had tried to imprison her in such a
short time ago. "You will not, I beg you, put me in there."

Gabriel shook his head. "No, sweet viper, you shall not
sleep there." And despite hoping that Mrs. Satterleigh
would take an extremely dim view of Maria, but more or
less resigned to the exact opposite happening, he took the
coward's way out and said dryly, "We shall let Mrs. Satterleigh find you what she thinks are appropriate quarters."

They found Mrs. Satterleigh a few minutes later, bustling about her immaculate kitchen. As round as her husband was slim, her diminutive height and laughing hazel
eyes gave her the look of a jolly, plump elf. A pristine
white cap sat primly upon her gray head, fluffy wisps of
escaping hair framed her apple-cheeked face, but there
was nothing prim about her smiling mouth. She was, like
her husband, neatly and soberly dressed; a crisp apron as
pristine as the cap on her head covered the majority of
her gray clothing and meeting the warm, welcoming smile
that Mrs. Satterleigh flashed her when Gabriel introduced them, Maria was encouraged to believe that Mrs.
Satterleigh was every bit as nice as her husband.

Sardonically, Gabriel had watched Mrs. Satterleigh's
thorough but kind appraisal of Maria, and he wasn't in
the least surprised when she imperiously brushed him
aside and said forthrightly, "You, I'll talk to later! Now
let me see our guest!" Wise hazel eyes once again traveled
slowly over a shyly smiling Maria for a few seconds, and
then Mrs. Satterleigh pronounced her judgment. "My,
aren't you a lovely little thing! Just what I would have
wished for, and if you are as sweet as your smile, it is no
wonder that Mr. Satterleigh was all in a twitter when he
told me about you." She frowned. "But my dear, those

clothes—they will never do!" An expression of sympathetic concern crossing her plump features, she asked, "Did you lose all of your things?"

Mutely Maria nodded, her eyes very big, not quite certain what to say. She could not imagine any servant of Diego's treating the master of the house so casually, nor could she ever imagine Diego merely smiling and settling himself comfortably on the corner of a well-scrubbed trestle table and beginning to munch happily on an apple at such unheard-of treatment. Gabriel's relations with his servants were a revelation, and she wished passionately, not for the first time, that her "visit" were something very different.

A mocking gleam in the green eyes, Gabriel answered Mrs. Satterleigh's question. Innocently he said, "I gave her several costly gowns and petticoats and other fripperies, but she would not take them from me. She doesn't," he added dryly, "care for me overmuch."

A militant sparkle in her eyes, hands on her ample hips, Mrs. Satterleigh rounded on him. "And I am not the least surprised, young man! What is this nonsense that she is to be a servant? Anyone can see that she is a lady, born and bred!"

With feigned meekness, Gabriel murmured, "But, Nellie, I thought you said at the beginning of the year that you needed an extra pair of hands about the house."

Mrs. Satterleigh snorted. "I think, jackanapes, that you are being deliberately simple—when I mentioned those 'extra pair of hands' we were talking, if you will recall, about it being high time that Royal Gift had a proper mistress!"

Laughter brimming in the green eyes, a satyr's smile on his lips, he replied outrageously, "Oh, if it's a mistress you want me to have, I have no objections at all about making Maria my mistress." He glanced over at Maria standing in the center of the big kitchen and drawled huskily, "In fact, I'm certain I should enjoy her in that role far more than any other!"

Despite her best attempts to hide it, Mrs. Satterleigh's mouth twitched with amusement at his provoking words, but she said primly enough, "And that will be enough of *that* sort of talk in *my* kitchen! I think this last trip to sea

has addled your brains!" And as Gabriel reached for another ripe red apple from the bowl that sat in the center
of the table, she scolded fondly, "And leave those apples
alone! I have spent all day preparing a tasty meal for you
and I'll not have you spoiling it by eating the makings of
the sweet I have planned for tomorrow." Somewhat tartly,
she added, "Shouldn't you be at the stables with Richard?
After all, it is a fine Cleveland Bay mare that is birthing."

Keeping the apple that had elicited her comment, he
pushed away from the table and sauntered from the
kitchen, saying over his shoulder, "Ah, Nellie, 'tis a sharp
tongue you have for the returning prodigal, but I'll forgive all, if you will not teach Maria your shrewish ways—
she has a vixen's temper as it is!"

There was a little silence when his tall form disappeared out of the wide doorway, and each woman regarded the other a bit shyly. Mrs. Satterleigh recovered
herself first, and smiling encouragingly at Maria, she said,
"After that long ride from Port Royal, you must be fam-
ished, my dear. Do sit down over there and I shall fix you
a small bite to eat."

Thinking of the hasty, unfilling meal of bread and tea
she had eaten early this morning on board the *Dark Angel*, Maria's stomach suddenly grumbled loudly, making
any polite protest to the contrary impossible. But remembering Gabriel's scolding about the apples, she said hesitantly, "If it is not too much trouble . . . and will not spoil
your plans for supper."

Mrs. Satterleigh understood perfectly what Maria was
alluding to, and a twinkle in the hazel eyes, she replied,
"Pay no heed to what I say to Master Gabriel—I wanted
him to leave us women to ourselves for a while—things
are so much cozier if the menfolk are not underfoot, don't
you think?"

Cozy wasn't precisely the word she would have chosen,
but Maria instantly comprehended what Mrs. Satterleigh
meant. With Gabriel's disturbing and disruptive presence
gone, she was able to relax and was much more at ease
within herself, and his departure did give her and Mrs.
Satterleigh a chance to observe and learn about each other
without the distraction of a third party. A *very* distracting

third party, Maria thought unkindly. Her gaze meeting Mrs. Satterleigh's questioning one, she nodded her head slowly, and within a remarkably short time, she was seated at the oak trestle table in the center of the room, eating a delicious little meal of pease porridge; warm, crusty bread just taken from the brick oven; and thick slices of creamy, yellow cheese. After days of the rough fare on the *Dark Angel*, the food tasted like ambrosia to her. As she ate, she glanced interestedly around her, noting the herbs and spices hanging from the open beams overhead, their pungent aromas blending pleasingly with the cooking odor of the bubbling pot of curry that was planned for supper and the freshly baked gooseberry tart which rested on the sill of an open window. The kitchen, Maria decided as she slowly drank the glass of crisp cider that Mrs. Satterleigh had handed to her, was a wonderful place. There was a feeling of warmth and, well, she admitted with a small smile, coziness. Everything was neat and tidy, from the various iron and pewter pots, kettles and utensils that hung from their appointed hooks on the walls to the scrubbed cleanliness of the stone floor. Next to the brick oven was a raised open hearth; the black iron pot which held the curry hung there over a small fire that crackled and popped cheerfully. Several windows across the rear of the room allowed the hot, yellow sunshine to pour inside and dance across the furnishings, the stout oaken chairs, the well-built cupboards, the small russet-and-gold oaken settle near the hearth and the huge sideboard that sat against the far wall.

Her meal finished, Maria sighed happily, and flashing Mrs. Satterleigh an enchanting smile, she said, *"Gracias, Señora* Satterleigh, I greatly appreciate your kindness to me."

A faint, pleased blush stained Mrs. Satterleigh's cheeks, and she replied gruffly, "And why shouldn't I be kind to such a lovely little thing as yourself? But now that you are well fed, perhaps you would like to rest for a few more hours until suppertime. I'm sure that you must be tired and longing to refresh yourself."

Uncertainly Maria regarded her. Mrs. Satterleigh was not treating her as a servant but more in the manner of a welcome guest and Maria knew without a doubt that this was not what Gabriel had planned. Not wishing to cause Mrs. Satterleigh any trouble, she finally said slowly, "*Señor* Lancaster intends for me to be his servant—not his guest. I believe that I am to help you—that you are to see that I am kept busy and that you also are to tell me where I am to sleep at night."

Mrs. Satterleigh's small form bristled, and a militant light lit the hazel eyes. "We'll just see about that! I am not so far in my dotage that I cannot run Master Gabriel's household with the indentured servants I have at my disposal now. As for your being his servant, a more ridiculous notion I have never heard—anyone can see that he is bewitched by you!"

Chapter Twenty-two

STUNNED by Mrs. Satterleigh's pronouncement, dazedly Maria could only stare at the older woman. Taking a deep breath, she finally got out, "You must be wrong, *señora*. H-he-he hates me and my family!"

Mrs. Satterleigh raised an eyebrow and snorted. "It would appear," she said tartly, "that Master Gabriel is not the only fool in this household!" When Maria opened her mouth to protest, Mrs. Satterleigh put up one hand to forestall her comment and said bluntly, "There is nothing to be gained discussing it further. Now come along and I shall show you through the house and take you to your room."

Relieved and disappointed at the same time, Maria followed Mrs. Satterleigh as she bustled from the kitchen. Walking into the main living area of the house, Mrs. Satterleigh said proudly, "My dear child, if you could only have seen what first greeted our eyes when we arrived from England with Master Gabriel and Sir William! A veritable *jungle* there was here at this very spot—no sign of habitation and now look!" Her satisfied smile fading, she nodded in the direction of the gilt-framed portrait that hung over the stone fireplace. "That is Sir William and Lady Martha." She sighed. "Such a devoted pair you would never have met. I thought Sir William would die himself when Lady Martha succumbed so suddenly to an inflammation of the chest that winter in France. It was difficult for all of us, but Sir William was like a madman, just inconsolable. I don't believe that he ever stopped grieving for her."

Wonderingly Maria crossed the cavernous room to stand

in front of the painting. Sir William's Lancasterian blue
eyes, blue eyes so very like her own, stared coolly down
at her, the mocking expression in their depths one that
she had seen often enough in Gabriel's gaze. The face that
looked out of the painting was kinder, less hard and cynical than Gabriel's, but the features were strikingly similar, the only real difference between father and son being
the profusion of long golden curls that framed Sir William's lean face and his blue eyes. It gave Maria a pecul-
iar feeling to stand there staring up at the man her father
had killed, this elegant gentleman in silks and laces who
had sired her buccaneer captor. Sir William's long-fin-
gered hand was resting possessively on the creamy shoulder of a seated woman, her hair piled high upon her head,
a shiny black ringlet hanging careless at the side of her
smooth white neck. The Lady Martha had been quite
beautiful, Maria admitted freely, the patrician features
serene and unruffled as she sat at her tall husband's side,
but the full red lips appeared as if a smile would curve
their shape at any second and the emerald green eyes
twinkled with a hint of laughter. Softly Maria uttered,
"He is very like both of them, isn't he?"

There was no reason for her to identify the "he" of her
question, and Mrs. Satterleigh answered easily, "Aye, so
he is. He's Sir William all over with Lady Martha's eyes
and hair . . . and temper too!"

From there the two women walked into the spacious
dining hall, Mrs. Satterleigh commenting briefly, "This
room isn't used as much as I would like—most of the time
Master Gabriel prefers to eat in the kitchen with us, and
he has seldom, in the past, had very many guests to entertain."

With great interest Maria stared around the large room
they had just entered. As with the main hall, a massive
stone fireplace dominated one end of the room—despite
Jamaica's humid, tropical weather, there were times
when it was definitely chilly in the mountains of the island and a crackling fire was most welcome. The furnishings were as luxurious and fine as those in the other room,
but noticing the intricate Spanish design of the heavy,
dark table and chairs, Maria knew instinctively that they
had come from a plundered Spanish galleon, and she was

conscious of a spurt of indignation and rage. Unwilling, however, to pursue such a fruitless line of thought, she sighed and stared instead at a brilliant gold-and-emerald tapestry that graced one long wall. Despite the size of the room, it was sparsely furnished; in addition to the table and chairs, there was only a tall mahogany cabinet that stood near one of the narrow window slits and a few wainscot chairs of stout English oak lining the wall. The stone floor had been left bare, and except for the silver candelabrum that sat upon the polished table and a pair of iron sconces on either side of the doorway, there was little ornamentation. Remembering the warmth and comfort of the kitchen, Maria could well understand why Gabriel chose to eat with the Satterleighs.

There were only a few other rooms on the first floor, and glancing into them, Maria was startled to see that though they were handsomely proportioned, they were empty. She cast a surprised look at Mrs. Satterleigh, and the older woman said, "The master is often gone and most of the family's belongings were lost on the *Raven.* It has taken him a long time to regain the wealth that was lost. Fortunately, there were some items that had came out with us in the very beginning, such as the portrait of Sir William and Lady Martha, and so everything did not fall into the hands of those murdering Spaniards." Suddenly remembering whom she was talking to, Mrs. Satterleigh blushed. "Forgive me, my dear! I meant *you* no harm!"

Maria smiled faintly and murmured, "Pray do not distress yourself—I am afraid that I shall have to grow used to such comments. There will be, I am sure, many people who will look upon me with contempt."

There was no use denying that statement and Mrs. Satterleigh said staunchly, "That may be, but you can be confident that the Satterleighs will stand your friend."

Her blue eyes full of gratitude, Maria said quietly, "And for that I thank you—but are you not speaking unwisely? You do not know me."

"Aye, that is true, but I have lived a long time and I have seen many things, some of them unpleasant; and I have learned to be a shrewd judge of people—there were times our lives have depended upon it—and no one will convince me easily that you are not honest and true . . .

no matter *who* your father was!" Having said those words in a forthright manner, Mrs. Satterleigh continued briskly, "And now we shall put that subject behind us and see the rest of the house."

Leading Maria up the graceful sandalwood staircase at the rear of the house, Mrs. Satterleigh said, "You will discover that beyond the master's bedchamber and the room prepared for Miss Caroline none of the other rooms on this floor have been furnished." Shaking her head, Mrs. Satterleigh added, "I have told him time and time again that it was folly to plan for Miss Caroline's return." Her eyes grew misty and, a little quiver in her voice, she went on, "I have given her up for dead, and I know that we shall never see her again, poor child, but the master will not hear such talk. Her name is seldom mentioned these days, and I hope that at last he has finally accepted the fact that she is lost to us. But I fear that if he heard one word of her whereabouts, if he had any idea that she was still alive, that no matter how dangerous, no matter how unlikely the possibility of success, he would instantly attempt to find her and free her . . . even if it cost him his life."

Unhappily Maria stared down at the floor of the long hallway. Caroline's name had never been spoken between her and Gabriel, and now Mrs. Satterleigh's words filled her with dread and guilt. If she were to tell Gabriel that his sister was indeed alive, that Caroline was still in the power of Ramon Chavez, then she would be sending him to certain death. Caroline was too well guarded, too far removed from any port that was friendly to the English to make a rescue attempt even remotely possible. If Gabriel did go after his sister, he was certain to fail . . . and die in the attempt. A shudder went through Maria at that thought. She had faced his death once, she could not do it again; but fatalistically, she knew that someday he would learn that Caroline was alive and that when he did . . . She swallowed convulsively, desperately trying to pay attention to what Mrs. Satterleigh had been saying.

". . . why you shouldn't have the Rose Room. It is really the only suitable bedchamber for you."

Glancing inside at the graciously appointed room, Maria said hesitantly, "I do not think that *Señor* Lancaster will be happy with this. He means for me to be a servant and no servant would sleep in such a place. You must find somewhere else for me to sleep."

Mrs. Satterleigh drew herself up. "Until the day the master marries, I am mistress of this house—he has frequently said that this is so—and *I* have decided that you will stay here! If he has any objections, I shall give him a tongue-lashing that he won't forget for a long time! As for you, young lady, I'll have no more fussing! I want you to get into that bed and rest until it is time for supper. I will send a servant to you when all is ready."

Meekly Maria did as she had been ordered, wondering what the outcome of this extraordinary situation would be. Lying there on the soft feather-filled mattress, she stared at the canopy overhead contemplating the confusing events that had passed since her arrival at Royal Gift. She didn't know what she had been expecting to happen, but the Satterleighs' manner toward her had been a pleasant, if distinct, shock. She had been prepared to be treated with scorn and contempt, even hostility, on the part of Gabriel's retainers; she had considered the possibility that she would be forced to live in despicable conditions, to suffer degradation and shame; and instead, she had been greeted almost with delight. Even Gabriel's actions had left her bewildered; one moment he was grim and foreboding, the next, if not kind, at least not cruel. But how, she mused uneasily, was he going to take the information that his "slave" was not industriously working her fingers to the bone and was instead whiling away the heat of the afternoon by resting in the very room he had dragged her from just a mere hour or so ago. Her lids slowly dropped, and as sleep crept over her, she thought fuzzily that she might as well enjoy the comforts the Rose Room offered—it was highly unlikely that she would be allowed to remain here for very long—especially once the master of the house discovered where Mrs. Satterleigh had placed her!

But as the days passed, beyond the random mocking comment, Gabriel made no effort to oust her from the Rose Room. When somewhat shyly she mentioned this fact to Mrs. Satterleigh, Mrs. Satterleigh had only smiled smugly and muttered, "I am still mistress of the house and well

Master Gabriel knows it!" If her continued possession of the Rose Room was mystifying, her position within the household of Royal Gift was even more so. It would appear that she was neither guest nor servant, neither slave nor mistress of her own fate. The Satterleighs, including their strapping son, Richard, and the various maids who worked in the house, all treated her as if she were a welcome, if not precisely guest, then at least an addition to their ranks. And yet that was not exactly accurate either; she was part of the household and yet not part of the household. The maids occasionally sent her speculative looks, and she heard whispers now and then when she passed them in the halls of the house; but no one had been rude or insolent to her, no one had reminded her that she was a Spanish captive in the home of an English gentleman turned buccaneer. Among the underservants, it was very clear that no one knew how to treat her.

As for the Satterleighs, their attitude had Maria thoroughly confused. They greeted her each day with a warm friendliness and behaved toward her much as if she were *almost* the wife or daughter of the house. She was allowed to do no heavy or arduous chores; instead Mrs. Satterleigh would assign her tasks very similar to those she had performed at home. She helped with the cooking; she carefully plied her needle; she oversaw the dipping and making of candles; she helped to polish the pieces of silver and just generally was useful about the house. She had no idle time on her hands, but she was also hardly overworked.

Picking some marigolds one afternoon a week later from the luxuriant kitchen gardens behind the house that Mrs. Satterleigh needed for a quelquechose, Maria pondered her perplexing situation. She wore the clothes of a servant and yet she slept in a bed and room as fine as any in the Casa de la Paloma. She was a piece of booty, a captive, a member of a race that the English had good cause to despise, and yet she was treated kindly—in the case of the older Satterleighs, even affectionately. Her captor, a man her family had grievously wronged, seemed to find no quarrel with the way his own servants behaved around her; if anything, she thought with a frown, he seemed to find the situation amusing—almost as if he knew how very confused she was by what was happening.

Was this all some sort of diabolical torture? she wondered apprehensively. Did he plan, that once her guard was relaxed, once she felt safe and secure, to spring some wicked punishment upon her? Were the Satterleighs only acting on his orders, charming her and disarming her, so that when he struck it would be all the more painful?

Those were daunting thoughts, and yet she could find no logical explanation for his conduct since she had come to Royal Gift. He had not touched her again, nor spoken alone with her. In fact, she admitted slowly, he had hardly spoken to her at all, apparently content to let the Satterleighs handle her fate. He didn't *exactly* ignore her presence, but except for a derisive smile or a look full of mockery or the carelessly tossed-off sardonic statement, he seemed content with the situation.

Of course, Maria reminded herself as she walked toward the kitchen, he *had* been very busy since his return, and he *was* seldom at the house itself. Several mornings when she had stumbled down the stairs to the kitchen just as the sun was rising on the horizon, she would find that he had already been up, eaten and had gone to the fields, or barns, or the sugar mill to oversee the grinding of the cane or to check that the huge vats used to boil and thicken the juice to syrup were being properly maintained. Unlike Diego, she conceded reluctantly, the master of Royal Gift took a personal interest and pride in his plantation, and it showed in not only the appearance, but the atmosphere, neatness and industry being the manner of the day.

Returning to the kitchens with her basket full of bright yellow blossoms, she said to Mrs. Satterleigh, "If you have no objections and if there are no chores for a while, I would like to go to the stables and see Pandora's new foal."

Pandora was the Cleveland Bay mare that had given birth on the day Maria had arrived at Royal Gift, and Maria had been eager to see the colt. Mrs. Satterleigh nodded absently, her thoughts busy on the potage she was making to accompany supper.

Free for the moment, with light steps, Maria wandered toward the buildings that had been constructed on another slight rise some distance from the main house. Here were the hen houses, the pigpens and barns and stables that sheltered the various livestock on the plantation. Maria had only been to this area once when Mrs. Satterleigh had sent her after some urgently needed eggs for a special tansy she had been planning for dinner one night. It had been then that Maria had gotten her first glimpse of the newborn colt and had promised herself that just as soon as the opportunity arose she would come back again to make the acquaintance of the beautiful spindle-legged little creature.

Except for one or two indentured servants busy about the stables, there was no one else in sight, and with a happy smile of anticipation, she walked over to a long paddock where Pandora and Pandora's Pride, as the colt had been named, had been placed. Pride had been the main subject at the oak trestle table in the kitchen for several nights now, and with assessing eyes Maria surveyed the young horse, deciding finally that he looked absolutely handsome—despite the criticism leveled at his sire. He did look, Maria admitted, very small next to his sleekly powerful dam—but then, she excused, he *was* only a baby! A little smile curved her lips as the colt, curious about the human on the other side of the fence, slowly minced closer to where Maria stood.

Slowly reaching out her hand, she was delighted when the velvety soft little muzzle was thrust into her palm, and gently she stroked the colt, thinking that the dish-shape of his finely fashioned head was exactly right and not ugly, as Richard had claimed. But then, Richard thought the colt was a mongrel, belittling the newborn's size and even finding fault with the glossy dark brown coat. Only last night he had muttered, "Brown! Who ever heard of a *brown* Cleveland Bay!" Shaking an admonishing finger at Gabriel, he had continued, "I told you not to breed her to that—that skinny little Arab stallion you found on that deserted and sinking felucca."

Gabriel had smiled and, biting off a piece of bread, had answered, "And what would you have had me do, Richard, leave the poor creature to drown in the sea? It was obvious that the felucca had been blown far off course and that she had been abandoned, leaving only the horse on board. Despite his small size, the stallion has a spirited temperament and is far more fleet than any of our larger, heavier horses. I think that you condemn my experiment too soon. Let Pride grow up before you dismiss him so contemptuously."

Richard had continued to argue about the lack of merit in the young horse, but Gabriel had been unmoved, and Maria had been left with a strong desire to judge for herself the faults that Pride supposedly possessed. As if conscious that her thoughts had wandered, Pride nudged her limp hand more insistently, and obediently Maria began to scratch between his ears. "Oh, but you are lovely," she crooned softly to him, silently agreeing with Gabriel that the youngster should be given time to prove himself.

"Lovely!" Richard suddenly growled from her side. "If it's a lovely animal you want to see, come and look at the little filly that was born last night. She's Cleveland Bay through and through and a better horse you'll not find in all of Jamaica."

Maria turned to glance at the strongly built young man at her side, a slightly nervous smile on her mouth. Of all the people she had met so far at Royal Gift, Richard Satterleigh made her the most wary. Not because he was openly hostile, nor because he had made any overt attacks on her, but because Maria sensed that he was very disapproving of her presence in the house and also because of his abrupt manner.

He bore little resemblance to his parents in temperament or size. In the days she had been at Royal Gift, Maria had never seen him really smile; and while he possessed his mother's hazel eyes, they had never, at least so it appeared to Maria, held the same warmth and amusement. He stood a good foot taller than either of his parents, and while he seemed very fond of them, his manner to everyone was abrupt and blunt, painfully blunt. "Richard," Mrs. Satterleigh had confided to Maria, "does not mince words! He speaks his mind without hesitation . . . or wisdom!"

It was Mrs. Satterleigh's great disappointment that Richard was unmarried, and Maria had listened with amusement as the older woman had complained bitterly about this unsatisfactory state of affairs. "As bad as the master, that one, when it comes to finding himself a help-meet. Heaven knows that I have done my best—on one pretext or another, I've paraded all the eligible girls on the island through my kitchen, but he's never even lifted an eyebrow."

Richard was about Gabriel's age, with curly light brown hair and pleasant features, and Maria admitted that he was very attractive—except for his slightly intimidating behavior. If only, she thought as she accompanied him to the foaling shed, he would smile more often and wouldn't always wear such a gloomy expression.

The foaling "shed" was actually only an extension of the main stable, and walking down the wide aisle that separated the four large, roomy stalls that had been specially constructed for the pregnant mares and their offspring, Maria breathed in pleasurably the warm, earthy scent of horses, hay and leather. If she closed her eyes, she could imagine that she was at home in the stables, getting ready to have Diablejo saddled up for a morning ride, and for just a moment, she was struck by a sharp, painful stab of homesickness. Richard's voice booming nearby brought her instantly back to the present.

"Now, *that*," he stated aggressively, "is a lovely animal. Pure Cleveland Bay she is and will grow up to be just as sound and handsome as her dam and sire—unlike that mongrel Pride." Glaring at Maria as if expecting an argument, he spat, *"Pride!* Ha! What sort of name is that for a horse with no breeding?"

Looking into the box stall, she had to concede that Richard did have a point. The little filly was indeed lovely and clearly an exact, if long-legged, replica of her mother right down to the beautiful bay coat, but Maria was conscious of a soft spot for the far smaller, dark brown Pride; and she said quietly, "You should follow Gabriel's advice and wait until Pride is fully grown before you judge him—he may not have the color, nor be as large or strong as the others, but he may possess other traits that will make him a better horse."

Richard looked as if he would explode at such an idea and Maria took a nervous step backward. Colliding with a warm, hard body, she spun around, her eyes widening as she looked up into Gabriel's mocking features.

"Do my ears deceive me," he drawled sardonically, "or did I just hear you *agree* with me?"

She would have liked to be able to disabuse him of that notion, but to do so would be to turn traitor to little Pride, and she would not do it. Lifting her chin, she muttered, "*Sí!* But because I think that the little colt should be given a chance does not mean that I have changed my mind about you!"

He seemed in an extremely amiable mood this morning, and somewhat warily Maria regarded him, wishing he didn't look quite so handsome as he stood there before her. He was casually garbed: a white, full-sleeved shirt was open almost to his lean waist; his dark-green petticoat breeches were simple and unadorned; the stockings that covered his muscled calves, a pale yellow cotton; and his shoes of russet leather were plain, without the usual silver buckles. But even in such unremarkable clothing, he was a striking figure of a man with his height and broad shoulders. The thick black hair curved near his jaw line, the emerald stud gleaming between the strands, the gold hoop, swinging gently whenever he moved his head; and staring at those half-beloved, half-hated features, Maria was conscious of a warm melting feeling in her chest. When he looked at her as he did now, his manner teasing and relaxed, she found it extremely difficult to remember that they were supposed to be enemies.

Unaware that some of the conflict she felt was clearly reflected on her expressive face, she was further confused when he suddenly grinned at her and said, "Would you like to see poor Pride's much-maligned father?"

"*Just*ly maligned!" Richard muttered, reminding Maria that he still stood nearby.

Gabriel laughed, saying easily, "Only time will prove which of us is right . . . but for the present, shall we see which one of us Maria agrees with?" Sending Maria another mocking look, he added, "Dare I dream that you will agree with me *twice?*"

Richard gave her no time to answer, stating gloomily, "Time will prove me correct, and as for Frolic, that is all he is good for! What can one do with a creature like that— he is too small to pull a coach and no good Englishman would dare ride such a delicate-boned animal." Having

given his opinion of the situation, Richard turned his back
on the others and busied himself offering a handful of
brown sugar crystals to the big Cleveland Bay in the foaling stall.

A small silence fell as Gabriel escorted Maria from the
stables and ushered her in the direction of a lone paddock
quite some distance away. They walked in silence in the
hot, tropical sunlight for several minutes before Gabriel
said idly, "If you plan to be outside often, you should get
Nellie to provide you with a hat of some sort."

Glad of a topic of conversation that didn't seem very
volatile, Maria answered quietly, "It isn't necessary; I am
inside most of the day. This morning is the first time that
I have been allowed very far from the house."

There was no complaint in her voice, but Gabriel
frowned and demanded, "She is not working you too hard?
You are not overtired?"

Maria laughed naturally. "Oh, *señor!* She is very kind
to me—everyone is and sometimes . . ." She stopped abruptly, realizing that she had very nearly admitted to *enjoying* her servitude. She bit her lip and muttered gruffly,
"Señora Satterleigh sees that I am kept busy. She says
that idle hands are the devil's delight and that she'll not
have me sitting around with nothing to do, but she does
not overwork me."

They had finally reached a narrow paddock, and effortlessly lifting Maria up onto the top bar of the fence, he
said, "Well, there he is, Frolic, Pride's father. What do
you think of him?"

As if aware that he was being closely studied, the small,
delicately fashioned stallion cavorted and pranced just a
few yards away from where Maria and Gabriel were po-
sitioned. The sunlight gleamed on the horse's chocolate
brown coat, the long wavy mane and jet black tail—and
staring at the long, slender legs; the finely shaped muzzle;
the large, intelligent dark eyes that watched her closely,
Maria thought she had never seen such a graceful, spirited animal. His neck curved in a proud arch, tail held
elegantly high, he pirouetted light-footedly before them,
obviously putting on a show for his audience. But then,
startling Maria, he gave a high-pitched whistle-like neigh

and in an astonishing burst of speed raced away to the far end of the paddock.

"And *that*," Gabriel said dryly, "is why I was willing to have him mate with Pandora. If Pride has inherited his sire's wondrous speed and grace and yet still has Pandora's size, I shall be most pleased." He shot Maria a look, asking curiously, "And what do you think of him?"

"He is *beautiful, señor!* So much power and speed!" Maria breathed pleasurably, her eyes shining with the enjoyment she felt.

His gaze once more on the horse, Gabriel asked with deceptive casualness, "And would you like to ride him?— he is far too small for most of the men and far too spirited for Nellie."

Maria nearly fell off her perch at his words; as a matter of fact, she had swung around to look at him with such violence that only Gabriel's quick action prevented that from happening, his hands snaking out to catch her around the waist. Her eyes locked on his, she blurted out, "You would allow this? You would let me ride him?"

An odd expression on his face, an even odder note in his voice, Gabriel said slowly, "I find that there are many things that I am willing to let you do."

Maria swallowed convulsively, her heart hammering in her chest, her thoughts jostling wildly in her brain. She was suddenly very conscious of his strong hands about her waist, very aware of how close he was to her, of how easy it would be to bend her head and bring their mouths together. Jerking her eyes away from his, she tried frantically to think of something to say, to think of something else other than the way his lips would feel beneath hers.

That Gabriel was thinking much the same thoughts was apparent from the way his hands tightened around her waist as he pulled her in his direction. Unable to help herself she looked back at him, not at all surprised when his gaze dropped to her mouth and he said thickly, "Maria . . ."

She swayed toward him, her lips within mere inches of his when Richard's voice pierced the air.

"Gabriel!" he shouted from the stables. "A message has arrived from Zeus!"

Sighing, Gabriel loosened his hold on Maria's waist,

and a rueful smile on his mouth, he murmured, "Someday I really must speak to Richard about his decided lack of tact."

Uncertain whether or not she was relieved by this timely interruption, keeping her face averted from him, Maria hastily scrambled out of his slackened grip and jumped down lightly from the fence. Nervously straightening the folds of her black skirts, she said primly, "He is only doing as he should. Besides, the message might be important—something may have happened at Havre du Mer."

"I doubt it," Gabriel replied indifferently. "Zeus has probably only written to tell me that he has accepted my invitation to visit on Tuesday."

Her face alight with excitement, Maria glanced up at him. "And Pilar?" she asked hopefully. "Will she be with him?"

"Hmmm, I suspect so, since I have invited *both* of them to stay a few nights at Royal Gift," he answered easily, a satisfied grin tugging at the corners of his mouth. He looked down at her, and seeing the expression of pure delight that crossed her vivid features, he wondered how long it would be before the ramifications of Pilar's visit dawned on her, and he wondered again at the deviousness of his own plans. But more than that he marveled at the ease with which Maria had become a part of his household, of how very right it seemed to have her in his home, how quickly and simply she had become so important to him . . . and how contented he was, knowing that she was nearby, that at any time he could call her to him. Gabriel couldn't have explained what he felt for her, nor could he have explained why he allowed Maria the license that he did, why he could not have borne to have had her treated in a despicable manner by anyone. Precisely when he had surrendered his schemes for vengeance, had admitted to himself that he could not harm her, he didn't know, didn't even want to admit fully that he had. But somewhere during the past weeks Maria had become part of his life; his plans for her had changed drastically, and he was both troubled and confused by his own apparent vacillation and inability to hold fast to his vows. Yet he was pleased and satisfied with the way the Satterleighs had accepted her so readily, amused at the way his loyal retainers behaved toward his "slave." He was unwilling to concede total defeat where she was concerned, but he was also very aware that it was a great jest to even begin to pretend to himself that Maria was a disdained and hated enemy, suffering great hardship and degradation at his hands. An enemy, he thought sardonically, who wears the garb of a puritan and sleeps in a bed of silk and satin. Thinking of that bed a wicked grin slashed his cheeks. Ah, yes, but he was looking forward to the coming visit of Pilar and Zeus.

Maria was so thrilled about the prospective arrival of her friend that it was several minutes before a disturbing thought occurred to her. But when it did, her step faltered and her smile vanished. With suspicion darkening her eyes, she stared hard at Gabriel. To find that he was watching her closely, an unholy gleam in his eyes, didn't help banish the sudden idea that had just crossed her mind. Bluntly she demanded, "And where do you intend for them to sleep? There are only two bedrooms suitable—yours and mine."

Gabriel smiled angelically and murmured, "Hmm, I think that some sort of satisfactory arrangement can be made . . . after all, my bed is very large . . . and you are quite small. . . ."

Chapter Twenty-three

GABRIEL'S expression was so satisfied, so pleased with the situation, that despite the turmoil in her breast, Maria had to choke back an unexpected gurgle of laughter. Frowning fiercely to hide her amusement, amusement that warred with outrage, she glared at the lush foliage in the distance.

It would be silly to pretend that this captivity was cruel; ridiculous to claim or even think that she was being mistreated; folly to deny to herself that she was head over heels in love with her captor and that sharing his bed was repugnant to her. But even if she admitted all of those things, it still didn't change the basic problem—she was a Delgato and he was a Lancaster. She sighed unhappily, wishing again that he were not so attractive, not so charming and not, she thought with a little spurt of temper, so very kind.

If Gabriel had been different, if he had been the pitiless monster she wanted him to be, if he had treated her with the same calculated cruelty and brutality Diego had meted out to the Lancaster family, it would have been so easy to hate him, to feel nothing but contempt and loathing for him. But he had never truly harmed her, and a flush stained her cheeks when she remembered the night she had scarred him, the night he had made such savage love to her. Even then, he had not hurt her; even then, she had reveled in his angry embrace; and she writhed with shame and despair at her own inability to despise him, to view him with the same driving hatred her brother did. It was impossible, she admitted forlornly, the past

320

week having shown her another side of this disturbing
man who held her captive.

It was obvious that Gabriel Lancaster was a good master. The affection the Satterleighs showed him was proof
of that; the smiles and unconcerned faces of the other people on the plantation, further proof that he was no feared
taskmaster. Unaware that Gabriel's smile had faded and
that he was watching the varying unhappy emotions as
they flashed across her face, Maria admitted to herself
that, even from what little she had seen, Royal Gift was
a tranquil place, that any signs of discord and lack of
harmony were few. Remembering the wretched conditions of the people at Casa de la Paloma, the looks of
sheer relief when Diego would leave, the expression of
utter terror and loathing that would greet the news of his
return, Maria sighed again, miserably conscious that
comparing Diego with Gabriel was not the wisest thing
for her to do, that it only increased her feeling of guilt
and shame at being unable to find any point in Diego's
favor. . . .

That arrogant Delgato pride and blind loyalty still
clashed against the emotions Gabriel aroused within her
and that more than any one thing kept her from being, if
not resigned, then temporarily at ease with the present
situation. She *should* feel wretched; should hate every
moment of every day at Royal Gift; should constantly seek
ways to escape from what should be a degrading captivity; and certainly she should view the possibility of Gabriel's lovemaking with loathing and fear—and yet she did
not, *could* not, and she felt conscience-stricken and dis-
graced because of it.

"Maria," Gabriel asked softly from beside her, his voice
troubled and full of concern, "what is it? What makes you
look so? Are my embraces really so repugnant to you?"

His question cut her to the quick, slashing into her very
vitals. No! His embraces did not fill her with repugnance;
in spite of everything, she longed for his strong arms
about her, and suddenly guiltily furious with herself for
being unable to control her foolish heart, irrationally angry with him for being so attractive and appealing, for
being so bewilderingly *un*cruel under the circumstances,
she glared at him. Her eyes were shimmering with unshed

tears of anger and humiliation, and driven by the ugly conflict within herself, she spat, "I think you forget my position! As your slave it is not my right to feel anything but hatred and contempt for you!" Almost despairingly, she cried, "Why are you so, so amiable!" Her voice rising hysterically, she shouted, "I am a Delgato! Doesn't that mean anything to you!"

Gabriel's face changed, a cold expression gradually settling over his handsome features, the emerald eyes becoming bleak. "I see," he said slowly. His mouth lifted in a sardonic smile. "It is good of you to remind me . . . *again*, of what lies between us." He gave her an insulting bow and said harshly, "Have no fear that I shall force you into my bed—there are other women who are far more willing to share it. As for being amiable, if you would prefer, I can have you beaten every night and sent to work in the fields." Sarcastically, he added, "Would *that* please you, madam princess?"

They stood there glaring at each other for several moments, pride, hurt and anger billowing through both of them. It was Gabriel who spoke first, growling angrily, "I have tried very hard to put the past behind me, as far as you are concerned. It is true that you are my captive, but I would think that it has not been an arduous captivity—I have tried to treat you fairly, to treat you as I would have had Caroline treated—despite the fact that you *are* a Delgato." His voice softened for just a minute. "At times I find it difficult to remember that you are Diego's sister. . . ." He sent her a searching glance, trying to read what lay behind those beautiful sapphire blue eyes. Slowly, he said, "The vendetta between our families was not of our making . . . we could change the future . . . if we are willing to let what happened in the past not lie between us like a drawn sword." It was as close as he could come to expressing what he felt inside, as close as he could come to admitting that he found it increasingly difficult to even pretend that it mattered to him that she was the sister of his most hated enemy.

Some of her anger and despair fading, Maria stared at him wonderingly. His words left her breathless, uncertain, confused; and helplessly she asked, "What do you mean? That you will set me free? That you no longer seek vengeance upon Diego for what he did to those on board the *Raven?*"

"Don't be silly!" Gabriel snapped, the notion of ever letting her free from him sending a gust of furious denial rushing along his veins. Grasping her upper arm, he shook her gently and muttered, "You are mine and I will not let you go! As for your whoreson brother ..." His expression darkened and he said brutally, "His life was forfeit the day my wife died, the day he destroyed the *Raven,* and *nothing* will ever change that ... until he is dead, I will not be free of the vow I took that day." An inimical gleam in his green eyes, he added, "A vow you cause me to dishonor every day I am ..." He paused, a tiger's smile crossing his face. "Every day that I am *amiable* to you!"

"How dare you!" Maria burst out with angry disappointment. "You speak of letting the past go and yet you swear to kill my brother!" Glad of an excuse to vent her confusion and guilt, she said wildly, "It is no wonder that I hate you! That I cannot bear for you to touch me!"

"Then you'll just have to suffer, won't you!" Gabriel snarled, just as furious and bewildered as Maria. And jerking her closer to him, he kissed her angrily, his mouth punishing and yet oddly yearning.

For one insane moment Maria nearly yielded to the half-savage, half-seductive power of his kiss, but then with a great effort she tore her lips from his and hissed, "I despise you!" Her eyes fastened on the scar she had given him, and not even aware of what she was saying, desperate to shore up her wavering defense, she cried distractedly, "Instead of your cheek, I wish it had been your heart I struck that night!"

Something flickered in the depths of the emerald eyes and Gabriel went very still. His hold on her arm loosened and he looked at her strangely. A queer note in his voice, he murmured, "Perhaps you did." A crooked smile curved his mouth, and he muttered cryptically, "And I'm sure that wherever she is Thalia would find it vastly amusing."

Maria looked at him uncomprehendingly, and his smile fading, Gabriel said wearily, "Go back to the house Maria. Tell Mrs. Satterleigh that I shall read Zeus' message

later. I find that the prospect of his visit isn't quite as
pleasant as it once was to me."

He turned away from her, and with confusion and dismay, Maria watched him walk toward the stables. When
he had disappeared inside, miserably she began to make
her way to the house, tears clogging her throat. She had
managed once again to put him at a distance, but this
time it hurt, even more painfully than it had that night
in Puerto Bello; and listlessly she admitted to herself that
she could not continue with this battle between family
pride and the love she felt for him, that she must decide
between the two or the conflict would tear her asunder
. . . and ruin any chance she might have for happiness. If
she stood any chance at all, she thought dispiritedly as
she approached the house.

In a subdued voice she relayed Gabriel's words, and as
there were no pressing tasks to be done, she gratefully
escaped to the privacy of her bedroom. Throwing herself
down on the yielding feather mattress, lying on her stomach, hands locked beneath her chin, she stared sightlessly
at the lovely cream-and-rose carpet on the floor near the
bed.

The time had come, she comprehended painfully, for
her to make a final choice. She must decide within herself, once and for all, the path she would follow. She could
not continue as she was, constantly buffeted by the conflicting emotions within herself, continually torn between
the demands of her wayward heart and the need not to
betray the Delgato name. She *must* choose between her
unexpected love for Gabriel Lancaster and the dictates of
family honor.

There was no real choice in the matter, she admitted
mournfully to herself. Foolish or not, disloyal or not, she
loved Gabriel Lancaster, and she had finally come to realize that clinging to family honor above all else would
be folly.

She sighed and rolled over onto her back. But choosing
to love Gabriel did not make things precisely simple, did
not immediately ease the pain within her. If she were
willing to forget the past, willing to put aside her pride,
it did not mean that he would too, did not mean that she
would ever be anything more than a piece of booty to him.

Her mouth twisted. A piece of booty he was more than willing to take to his bed when it suited him! Yet she could not deny that there had been moments when his actions had surprised her, moments when he had not acted like an enemy at all, and a dreamy smile slowly crossed her face as she remembered the first time he had made love to her. He had been kind to her many times, many times, she admitted uncomfortably. *She* had been the one to bring up the hatred that existed between their families. Not Gabriel.

But what did *that* prove, she asked herself sarcastically—that he was a benevolent master? That she should be happy to be his slave? His mistress? Content to share him, content to know that it was only lust for her body that brought him to her? *Never,* she thought fiercely, suddenly sitting up on the bed. She loved him, but she would not share him, would never be satisfied being merely his mistress.

A frown marring her forehead, she recalled his comment of other women being more than willing to share his bed. Thalia? A gust of jealous fury swept through her. No! He might be the most infuriating, confusing, arrogant man she had ever met, but she loved him and she would make him love her!

Startled at that idea, her frown vanished. Could she make him love her? she wondered with growing excitement. He wanted her—that had never been any secret—but from desire could she coax love? Might one day he long for her love as she did his? A soft glow in her blue eyes, Maria lay back down. If she had not created an insurmountable wedge between them by her guilt and pride-dictated actions ...

Grimacing at her own foolishness, she vowed determinedly to try to undo the damage she had done. She wasn't certain how she was going to do it, but she was going to woo Gabriel, going to make him love her ... somehow! And to begin with, she decided grimly, she would make sure that no other woman was found in his bed ... even if she had to sleep there every night. An impish smile crossed her face and she sighed theatrically. What terrible punishments she was prepared to suffer for love!

That evening when Gabriel returned to the house, to his utter astonishment, he was met by a smiling, sparkling-eyed Maria. A Maria whose demure glances made him suddenly breathless and yet not a little wary. What, he wondered as he lay in bed that night, was she playing at? And why did it matter so much to him?

Gabriel knew that answer and he found it extremely unpleasant. All afternoon he had done nothing but think about Maria, think about the effect she had on him and the easy way that she had completely turned his emotions upside down and inside out!

He had also thought a great deal about Thalia Davenport, more particularly those words she had hurled at him the night before the *Raven* sailed. "Someday, Gabriel, I pray you meet a woman you cannot have! And if God is good, she will break your heart!"

Well, he admitted dryly, part of Thalia's curse had definitely come true—he wanted Maria, wanted her passionately, and yet because the idea of forcing her to accept his caresses was revolting, he could not have her. He smiled mirthlessly in the darkness. How Thalia would crow if she knew. As for the remainder of Thalia's angry words, he wasn't ready to admit yet that Maria was breaking his heart.

But he knew that he could never despise Maria, could never think of her with the same cold hatred that possessed him whenever he thought of Diego. Even her aborted attempt to warn the Spaniards that day in the jungle near Puerto Bello he had come to terms with and could even admire. Wouldn't he have done the same thing if positions had been reversed? And could one truly condemn loyalty to one's own family and people? He didn't believe so, even if he wished that there were some way of surmounting the differences that lay between them.

If only, he thought exasperatedly, she were not so proud, so prickly about the Delgato blood that flowed in her veins! So determined to throw the past enmity between their families in his face! If it were not for stubborn family pride, he was confident that he could woo her, could make her forget the past, could make her love him, as he . . .

In the darkness of the room, Gabriel frowned, suddenly

aware of many emotions that he had been trying to ignore
and suppress from the moment Maria Delgato had run
into his arms in Puerto Bello. And again he thought of
that last night in England and of Thalia's words.

He had scorned love then, had rejected the notion that
there would ever be a woman who could touch his heart,
could hold him enthralled; but now he was not quite so
arrogant.

Right from the very beginning Maria had twisted his
emotions, had always clouded his judgment—hadn't he
risked death and capture on Hispaniola simply to spend
precious dangerous moments in her sweet embrace? And
hadn't he thrown aside his plans for a wicked revenge in
Puerto Bello? Instead of raping her brutally, he had tenderly brought her to womanhood—and could not even now
regret it. And more damning still, didn't he yearn to have
her in his arms this very moment, to know again the dazzling ecstasy she had given him that night?

Restlessly, Gabriel tossed on his big bed, his body suddenly stiff and full of desire for her. But it was not just
desire, he realized bleakly, it was desire mingled with
some emotion he had never felt before, had never thought
to feel.

Angry with himself, he swung out of the bed and in
naked splendor stalked to one of the tall, narrow slits that
served as a window. Blindly he stared out at the black,
tropical night, wondering at the jest that fate had played
on him.

He had sworn that he did not possess the legendary
traits of the Lancasters—that he would never be possessive of a woman, that love was something he could very
well do without; and yet he now discovered to his great
chagrin that he had, perhaps, deluded himself. Certainly
he was possessive of Maria; he could not deny it, especially when he remembered his rage at du Bois for even
teasing about giving her up. Or the instant rejection that
surged through him any time the idea of releasing her
was broached. He had been furious at Modyford for even
hinting that there was a possibility that she would have
to be returned, and today, when Maria had asked if he
meant to free her, he had been consumed with anger at
the very idea.

Yet how often these past months had he cursed her? Had called her in his mind a Spanish bitch and had vowed that he would show her no mercy, only to have a glance from those blue eyes shatter his plans for vengeance? Hadn't he sworn the very morning they had left to come to Royal Gift, never to forget that she had nearly cost him his life? That she was not to be trusted? And yet, he had meekly allowed the Satterleighs to turn aside his plans for vengeance, had abandoned all thought of revenge that moment in his room when Maria had looked so frightened and terrified of that dark, little chamber where he had been determined to lock her. Instead, he reminded himself without amusement, he had made love to her. . . .

Had made love to her and taken pleasure from it, and dimly he realized that it had been then that, subconsciously at least, he had given up any notion of making Maria suffer for the sins of her father and brother. It had pleased him that the Satterleighs had accepted her so easily, that they had put her in a position of being a welcome member of the household, and for the most part he was content and satisfied with the present state of affairs, willing to forget plans of vengeance where Maria was concerned.

No, that wasn't true, he thought with a frown. He wasn't satisfied! He hated seeing Maria garbed in those dowdy black skirts; hated the fact that her servitude, gentle though it might be, galled her and that she wanted only to be free of him.

He grimaced ruefully. He had no objections to freeing her, provided she stayed at Royal Gift and shared his bed. . . .

Delightful images of Maria's lovely face, flushed with passion, darted through his mind; and for several long seconds, Gabriel was lost in a *very* erotic daydream, but then with an effort he tore himself away from such addictive musings and considered the present situation. What was he to do? How was he to cross the chasm of blood and pride that lay between them?

For quite some time, he stood there staring out at the blackness, wondering about the past and the future. Maria's question about Diego came back to bedevil him, and Gabriel admitted fatalistically that no one, not even Ma-

ria, could stop him from one day slaying the man who
had ruthlessly killed his wife and condemned his sister to
slavery and death. Knowing that sooner or later his sword
would end Diego's vile life, how could he possibly expect
Diego's sister to view him with anything but disgust and
hatred?

His jaw hardened. She would just have to learn to live
with it, he told himself grimly. There were many areas
in which he was willing, more than willing, to indulge
her, but not about Diego and the vengeance he had promised himself so long ago. Diego would die by his hand! He
must kill him or he would never be able to find any happiness, never be able to put behind him the nagging guilt
of Elizabeth's death and Caroline's uncertain fate.

Elizabeth's sweet young face suddenly swam before his
gaze, and Gabriel was conscious of a great sadness. She
had not deserved to die . . . and he had been unfair in
marrying her. He had been fond of her, but he had not
loved her, had not believed that he was capable of that
emotion, and he felt all the more guilty because of it. He
wouldn't admit even now that he loved Maria, but he was
aware that the feelings he had held for Elizabeth had
been weak and tepid when compared to the raging emotions Maria aroused in his breast.

Once Diego is dead, Gabriel thought stubbornly, once
Diego Delgato is no longer able to strike at others the
way he did me and mine, *then* I shall be content, be able
to think of the future, to discover exactly what it is I feel
for Maria. But in the meantime, in the meantime, I must
woo my own prickly rose, must make her find me . . . A
grin suddenly flashed across his face. Find me *more* than
amiable!

Precisely how he intended to do this wasn't clear to
him, but with a new determination he walked back to his
bed. Distastefully he eyed it, thinking how much more
appealing he would find it if it contained a particular infuriating, baffling and utterly adorable little Spanish spitfire! He smiled at himself, and strangely at ease, eager to
fight for his future, he slipped between the sheets. Tomorrow was a new beginning, a new day, and he intended
to make the most of it!

To his uneasy astonishment, Gabriel found the object

of his desires more than willing to meet his sly overtures of amiability. When he suggested that she might enjoy a ride around some of the more picturesque borders of the property, Maria smiled sunnily at him and demurely agreed. She seemed to enjoy his company, seemed to take delight in the beauties of the lands of Royal Gift: the glorious tumbling waterfalls; the fern-swathed, clear pools; the brilliant plumage of the exotic birds that swayed and screamed in the lush treetops of the jungle as well as the bright green expanse of tall sugar cane. It was a day that brought great contentment to Gabriel, and with growing bemusement, he fell deeper and deeper under the spell that Maria was artlessly weaving about them, wondering how he could have been so lost to reason even remotely to view her as an enemy. Watching the way she deftly controlled the spirited antics of Frolic as the small stallion cavorted and pranced under her slight weight, he was reminded of that day on Hispaniola when she had tried to give him word of Caroline, and his heart swelled with tenderness within his breast—she had tried then to help him and he had brutally thrown her aid back in her face! But thinking of that day brought a frown to his features, and as they rode slowly back toward the stables, he asked carefully, "Maria, what do you know of Caroline? Is she . . ." He hesitated, suddenly afraid of what she might tell him. It was one thing to convince himself that his sister was dead, another to hear confirmation of it. But he *had* to know, and bluntly he demanded, "Is she still alive?"

Maria stiffened; for one wild moment, she considered lying, but she could not, not about something as vital as this. Yet remembering Mrs. Satterleigh's words and picturing Gabriel's dead body, she prevaricated. "I don't know. I have not seen or heard of her for many months."

"When was the last time you saw her?" he asked eagerly, a look of dawning hope in his eyes.

Reluctantly, Maria admitted, "Over a year ago."

"Where?" The question was like a pistol shot, the eagerness he felt obvious from the expression on his handsome face.

Maria took a deep breath. Stubbornly she said, "I will not tell you!" The blue eyes full of tears and distress, she muttered, "I will not send you to your death!" And kicking Frolic on the sides, she raced away, ignoring Gabriel's cry to stop.

Reaching the stables, she flung the reins in the hand of a startled Richard and ran as fast as she could to the house. She had to get away from Gabriel! He must not be allowed to force her to divulge Caroline's whereabouts—she would *not* be responsible for sending him to his death! Oblivious to the astonished looks of the elder Satterleighs, she darted across the kitchen, intent upon reaching the relative safety of her room, but Gabriel, as she had expected, was right behind her, and catching her arm, he swung her around to face him. Fiercely he said, "Do not play childish games with me!" Shaking her roughly, he growled, "Now, where *is* she?"

Maria lifted her chin proudly, meeting his eyes defiantly. "I will not tell you!" she said from between gritted teeth. "She is well, though, and not mistreated."

His green eyes dark with temper, Gabriel snarled, "And you expect me to be satisfied with *that!* God's wounds, woman, don't be any more of a fool than you can help! Before I throttle you, tell me where she is!"

Despairingly Maria glanced at Mrs. Satterleigh. Moved by the pain in Maria's gaze, Mrs. Satterleigh abandoned the apples she had been peeling and said briskly, "Now, that's enough of that! Leave her be, Master Gabriel—she'll tell you soon enough and in her own time." Bustling over to where Maria and Gabriel stood, Mrs. Satterleigh ignored the look of outrage Gabriel sent her and gently pried his hand from Maria's arm. Giving Maria a little pat on the bottom, she said softly, "Run along, my dear. We'll talk about this later."

Not waiting to see Gabriel's reaction to Mrs. Satterleigh's unexpected intervention, Maria did as she was told, disappearing into the main room, fearful with every step she took that Gabriel would explode out of the kitchen behind her. As her foot touched the bottom of the stairs, she heard him shout, frustration evident in his tones, "Are you mad! She knows where Caroline is!"

Mrs. Satterleigh's soothing reply was lost to her and thankfully she finally reached the sanctuary of her bedroom. But for how long? she wondered as she leaned her trembling body back against the stout door. How long before Gabriel came pounding up those stairs and barging into her room?

As the minutes passed and nothing happened, Maria gradually relaxed, musing bleakly at how dreadfully such a wonderful day had ended. But I could not tell him where Caroline is, she thought guiltily.

A sudden tap on the door had her straightening with alarm, but the sound of Mrs. Satterleigh's voice calmed her. With shaking hands she opened the door.

Mrs. Satterleigh sailed into the room, and turning to look at Maria, she said sternly, "I wish you had talked to me first before you blurted out the fact that Caroline is alive."

Dumbfounded, Maria stared at her. Finally she managed to say, "What should I have done, lied to him?"

"Yes, of course! It was one thing for him to wonder about her fate, but now that he knows she is alive, he will be like a dog with a bone until you tell him where she is. It would have been," Mrs. Satterleigh ended frankly, "much better if you had said simply that you didn't know *any*thing about her."

Dazedly, Maria shook her head. "Doesn't it matter to you that she is alive? Don't you want her returned to Royal Gift?"

Mrs. Satterleigh's eyes filled with tears and her face softened. "My child, it would be my dearest wish . . . but not at the cost of Master Gabriel's life! He is safe for the present, but if he dares to go after Caroline, I fear that I will lose them *both!* Don't you understand?" Heavily, she added, "If I thought for one moment that there was a chance of the master being able to free her, I would not hesitate to implore you to tell him all you know, but if, as I fear, his life will be in danger by going after her and there is little hope for success, then I do not want him to sail away on some mad chase that will only end in tragedy for us all." The hazel eyes searched Maria's features anxiously. Softly, reluctantly, Mrs. Satterleigh asked, "I suppose there *is* no chance that he could free her?"

Slowly Maria shook her head. Dully she answered, "No chance at all."

Mrs. Satterleigh seemed to gather herself together and said in a more vigorous tone, "Well then! We shall just have to convince Master Gabriel of that fact! Now, don't you worry, I have put him off for a while, telling him that he must not snarl and snap at you so, that you will be made to see reason . . . eventually."

Doubtfully Maria regarded the older woman. "And then? What happens when *eventually* comes around?"

Mrs. Satterleigh fixed her with a severe look. "Then you will have to lie and tell him she is in a place that is safe for him to go."

"*Señora* Satterleigh!" Maria breathed, shocked.

Mrs. Satterleigh had the grace to appear embarrassed, but she said bluntly, "I will not have him dying needlessly—not even to free Caroline!"

It wasn't to be expected that after denying Gabriel the information that he so desperately wanted things would be easy between them and they weren't, but the situation wasn't nearly as dreadful as Maria thought it would be. Gabriel treated her to a cold, inimical stare whenever she was in his presence; and though he mentioned not one word about Caroline, she had the uneasy sensation that he would have enjoyed pouncing upon her and beating the knowledge out of her.

The arrival of Zeus and Pilar on Tuesday lightened the atmosphere a little, but at the first opportunity, when she had escorted Pilar up to the Rose Room, Pilar demanded, "*Chica*, what has happened? I know that you must be unhappy about your invidious position, but why is *Señor* Gabriel so obviously incensed with you? Did I not warn you to curb that temper of yours? To do nothing foolish?"

Maria smiled wanly at the affectionate scolding, wishing that it *had* been an act of temper that had caused the widening rift between her and Gabriel. "It was not because of anything I did," Maria confessed as she sank down comfortably on the velvet settee, "but because of something I will *not* do!"

Pilar cocked an eyebrow. "And that is . . ."

Maria grimaced ruefully. "Tell him where his sister is."

Looking thoroughly confused, Pilar demanded, "And who is his sister and why should you know where she is and her brother not?"

Maria glanced at her friend. Amazement in her voice,

she asked, "You mean you don't know? That you didn't recognize her—the English girl at Justina's."

"Ramon's—!" Pilar exclaimed with astonishment, the identity of the tall blond English girl suddenly taking on enormous significance and halting any further comment on her part.

"*Sí!*" Maria replied gloomily. "And now you know why I won't tell Gabriel where she is—he would be determined to wrest her from Ramon, and I doubt even Gabriel could accomplish such a thing."

Pilar slowly nodded her dark head. "*Sí.* But it is an impossible situation!" And echoing Mrs. Satterleigh's sentiments, she added prosaically, "Well, pigeon, you will just have to tell him she is somewhere else and let him find her gone. Surely we can think of someplace where it would be safe for him to go."

Maria looked at her uncomfortably. "Doesn't it bother you to lie?" she finally asked.

Pilar cocked that eyebrow again. "You would rather he died?"

The question was unanswerable, and halfheartedly Maria allowed Pilar to lead the conversation to other subjects. Glancing around the room, Pilar murmured lightly, "*Chica,* you cannot imagine how wonderful it will be to be staying in a *real* house—instead of that, that . . ."

"Hovel!" Zeus finished for her amiably. A twinkle in his eyes, he entered the room, saying innocently, "That was what you called it, *mon amour,* was it not?"

Pilar laughed and sent him a droll look. "*Sí!* But you agreed with me!"

Zeus smiled at her besottedly and admitted, "*Oui,* this is true! And is it not also true that I am building you a new home, a magnificent place that you can shape and furnish as you please?"

Walking across the room to where Maria sat, he glanced down at her and said fondly, "And, petite pigeon, how have you been?" His smile fading just a little, he continued, "And what have you done to put the Dark Angel in such a fury? Since we arrived this afternoon he has done nothing but speak to me about the contrariness of a certain infuriatingly stubborn wench."

Resignedly Maria explained, and somehow she wasn't

at all surprised that Zeus should repeat advice very similar to that which she had already received . . . twice! Bafflement obvious on her features, she demanded, "Don't any of you want Caroline rescued? Why are you all so willing to lie to him about something this important?"

Thoughtfully Zeus fingered his chin. "Petite, Caroline has become an obsession with him—he feels guilty that he is free and she is not! To rescue her, he would sail right into Havana harbor and die for his foolishness. It is not that we enjoy lying to him; rather it is to save his life."

But it was Pilar who squelched any further argument. Gently patting Maria's hands, she asked softly, "Are you so certain that Caroline *wants* to be rescued? Do you?"

Dumbly, Maria stared first at Pilar and then Zeus, and then finally, shamefully she said, "I cannot speak for Caroline, but as for myself, no."

"You see!" Zeus cried joyfully, and then startling her, he swooped down and, big hands about her waist, swung her up from the settee. "And now," he boomed, "for our news! Congratulate me, petite! My virago-tongued wife is *enceinte* and in the spring will give me the first of our many fine sons!"

Chapter Twenty-four

WITH the news that Pilar was expecting a baby, it wasn't surprising that, for the time being at least, Maria forgot about her estrangement from Gabriel, and with wide blue eyes, she looked at her friend. "Is this true?" she breathed, half-excitedly, half-enviously.

There was a blush on Pilar's face and she said sharply to Zeus, "I told you that I wanted to tell her! You promised you wouldn't say a word!"

Zeus only laughed, and loosening his hold on Maria, he bent down and dropped a kiss on his wife's dark head, saying outrageously, "But it is no secret, my heart . . . and in just a few months, everyone will know—your belly will proclaim clearly how much I love you."

Pilar snorted, obviously torn between amusement and vexation. Pointing a finger at the door, she commanded, "Go, you big lout! Go find *Señor* Gabriel and brag to him of your prowess, but leave us alone for a little while."

Not the least bit perturbed by his wife's actions, Zeus winked at Maria and ambled from the room. Once they were alone, Maria threw her arms about Pilar's neck and breathed happily, "Oh, Pilar how wonderful for you! Are you not thrilled and pleased?"

"Astonished would be more like it," Pilar replied dryly, the teasing glint in her dark eyes belying the dryness of her tone. "I thought that I was barren . . . I was married before, you know, and never conceived."

Maria smiled impishly. "But your first husband was not Zeus, was he?"

Pilar flushed like a girl, but there was a sensuous cast to her mouth as she murmured, "No, he was not!"

The remainder of the afternoon passed swiftly, and it was only as the time for the evening meal approached that Maria was reminded of her odd position in the household of Royal Gift. Ever since Pilar and Zeus had arrived, she had acted more in the manner of the lady of the house, introducing Pilar to the elder Satterleighs, taking her through the various rooms and just generallly acting the part of the hostess. No one seemed to think this strange, the Satterleighs acting as if it were perfectly normal, for the master's "slave" to spend the afternoon entertaining guests, even Gabriel raising no demur when he and Zeus returned from the stables and found the two women sitting in the main room, enjoying a glass of lemonade. It was only when the others left to go upstairs to change that Maria was aware that while she may have played the role of hostess these past hours, she was anything but! Disconsolately she wandered into the kitchen and asked quietly, "Is there anything that I can do to help you, Señora Satterleigh? I'm afraid that this afternoon I forgot my place."

Mrs. Satterleigh snorted and muttered, "Methinks that for the first time since you arrived here, you were in your proper place! But now stop this nonsense! We have guests to entertain, and I don't need you cluttering up my kitchen. Since supper won't be for a while yet, why don't you go lie down in the spare room Master Gabriel had me prepare for you yesterday."

Her surprise was evident in the gasp that came from her, and stammering, Maria asked, "A-a-a r-r-room. He had y-y-you prepare a room for me?"

Busy with plans for supper, her mind on other things, Mrs. Satterleigh said exasperatedly, "Child, isn't that what I just said? Run along now, I've got a cheese tart to make yet as well the sauce for the olives of veal."

Feeling chastened and rebuffed, Maria asked quietly, "Where is my room?"

"Your room?" Mrs. Satterleigh glanced up from the dough that had her attention. "Oh, yes, your room—it is the one across the hall from the master's." She smiled warmly at Maria. "We took several items from the storeroom and I made it as pleasant as possible for you. Now away with you!"

Walking along the long hallway upstairs, Maria heard the low murmur of voices coming from the Rose Room and she smiled faintly. How lucky Pilar was to have a husband who loved her! And to think that hardly three months ago in Panama, Pilar had sworn that she would never marry again!

Pushing open the door to the room that Mrs. Satterleigh had indicated, Maria stopped on the threshold, an expression of pleasure flitting across her face. It was true that the huge room was sparsely furnished for its size, the odd bits and pieces taken from the storeroom only filling up the far half of the area, but the effect was charming. A Turkey rug in brilliant shades of wine and gold lay upon the floor; a small, delicate armoire of rosewood stood at the rug's fringed edge; and a peacock-blue satin-covered bed had been placed in the middle of the rug. At the end of the bed was a little trunk bound in green Spanish leather, the brass studs gleaming in the fading rays of sunlight that spilled in from the one tall, narrow window. Against the wall near the bed had been set a long table, a china bowl and pitcher, a hand-held mirror, combs and brushes; and a wide, low-spreading candelabrum rested upon the table's green marble surface.

Despite the emptiness of the other half of the room, Maria was delighted with her new quarters, and sitting on the feather mattress, not so surprisingly, she felt more at home here than she had in the polished elegance of the Rose Room. This was *her* room, furnished *for* her, and she was quite certain that even after Pilar and Zeus departed she would continue to sleep here.

She had just lain down and had been on the point of dozing off when there was a sharp rap on the door. Jerking upright, she called out nervously, "Yes? Who is it?"

It was Gabriel, and without answering her question, he opened the door and, shutting it firmly behind him, strode in her direction. Her heart beginning to pound in her breast, Maria watched his approach warily, wondering if he had sought her out in private to continue to demand she tell him Caroline's whereabouts.

When he stopped only a few feet from the bed, hands

on his lean hips, and raked her with a hard look, she asked bluntly, "What is it? What do you want?"

Gabriel's mouth twisted wryly and he murmured, "There is much that I want, but I doubt you are willing to give me the two things I want most!" His gaze rested for a long moment on her mouth and from the suddenly sensual curve of his bottom lip, she was very certain of at least *one* of the things he wanted.

Shifting uncomfortably under his scrutiny, she asked helplessly, "Why are you here?"

"To see if you liked your new quarters for one thing and for another to see if you had discovered the contents of the armoire and the trunk," Gabriel replied carelessly, and walking over to the armoire, he flung the door wide to reveal several pieces of feminine clothing reposing there.

That they were not servant's apparel was clear from the abundance of lace that trimmed some of the garments, and even from where she sat, Maria could tell that the clothing was made of silks and velvets and other costly goods.

Turning away from the armoire, Gabriel walked the short distance to the trunk at the end of the bed, and flipping open the lid, he said, "I think you will find an assortment of corsets, stays and what-have-you in here— Richard," he continued with a mocking gleam, "is not as familiar with your, ah, size as I am, and so he was somewhat at a loss in this matter."

"Richard?" Maria croaked foolishly. "Richard brought these things for me?"

"Hmmm," Gabriel answered lazily. "At my request, of course. If you are to greet my guests properly, you must be clothed appropriately."

Frowning, Maria looked at him closely, wondering if he had indulged in too much ale when he and Zeus had been at the stables this afternoon. Cautiously, she said, "This is very kind, but haven't you forgotten my position here? These things are hardly the garments of a . . . a . . . slave."

"And you, my beguiling, infuriating little witch, have never been a slave in your life—certainly it is ludicrous to pretend that you have been *my* slave; we both know the folly of *that!*" Gabriel drawled, the jeering note in his voice very apparent. He glanced at her drab garb and muttered fiercely, "You wear those garments no longer, and from this night on we dispense with the less than amusing facade that you are my slave! You have not been treated as one, and I find that I have grown tired of this *game* we have been playing."

"Game!" Maria repeated, her eyes sparkling resentfully. "It has been no *game* for me, *señor!*"

"Pretense, then," he snarled, coming to stand directly in front of her. Grasping her arm, he jerked her closer to him. "I may have captured you and made you my prisoner, but there never was any question of you being a slave! *You* were the one who first called me master, and you were the one who threw the silks and laces back in my face! It has been *you* all along who has insisted we play these roles, and I for one will have no more of it!"

Her eyes meeting his, her mouth suddenly dry, she got out carefully, "Are you telling me that I am *not* your slave?"

"Aye!" he growled, his breath coming faster, his eyes dropping to the soft mouth only inches from his. "You are my hostage, that I will not deny, but you are not servant, nor slave, nor will I have you pretend that you are any longer . . . if you wish to pretend, sweet viper, pretend that you are my captive guest!"

Maria was only half listening to his words, too aware of those hard, beautiful lips so near her own, too conscious of the warmth radiating from his lean body to concentrate. The dark handsome face was so close she could feel his breath upon her cheek, and a curious weakness invaded her body, making her want to bend forward, to touch that smooth bronzed skin with her mouth. Ah, *Dios!* she thought despairingly. She loved him so much! And she longed to lose herself in the ecstasy of his powerful embrace, to let his passionate, mind-drugging kisses and intoxicating possession drive reality away for those brief moments when he claimed her body. To her horror she could feel her breasts swelling, just remembering what it felt like to have his tall, muscled form joined with hers, and with an effort she forced herself to pay attention to what he had been saying.

But if Maria had not been immune to the proximity of

his body, neither had Gabriel been unaffected by the nearness of her slender shape, and with difficulty he tried to
hold on to his train of thought. It was impossible; all he
could think of was how much he wanted to kiss that soft
mouth, how much he wanted to rip aside those offending
garments and lose himself in the silken warmth he knew
lay underneath. Throwing all his hard-won restraint and
promises to himself to the winds, he suddenly muttered
thickly, "Nay, not guest . . . never a guest . . . mistress,
more like." And compulsively his mouth dropped to hers,
his hands sliding up her shoulders to hold her prisoner as
hungrily, yearningly he plundered her lips with his.

Maria had no thought to deny him, her lips opening
sweetly beneath his, her tongue eagerly sliding along his,
exploring his mouth as thoroughly, and if she had known,
as devastatingly as he did hers. Groaning low in his
throat, Gabriel pulled her closer, his strong arms embrac-
ing her tightly, making her satisfactorily aware of how
aroused he was, the thick bulging muscle between his
thighs riding hard against her lower body.

Her arms went around his neck, her fingers tangling in
the thick black hair, and mindlessly, they sank down together on her bed, Gabriel's hand immediately going to
the front of her bodice. In a trice her breasts were laid
bare to his touch, and he was not tardy in dropping his
warm mouth to the coral nipples, his tongue gently laving
the burgeoning tips. He raised his head and gave her a
long sensual look. "You taste," he said huskily, "like
strawberries and wine . . . and I am a starving man where
you are concerned." He dropped his head again, sliding
his lips along her shoulders before returning to her
creamy breasts.

Uncaring of anything but the moment they shared, Maria's own hands had not been idle, and Gabriel's white
shirt had been pushed down around his waist as she delightedly explored his hard-muscled chest. Like a contented cat, she dug her fingers lightly into the dark, curly
hair she found there, reveling in her power when he shivered beneath her caresses. As deftly as he, she teased his
flat male breast, thrilled when his nipples filled and hardened just as hers.

His fingers were at her waist struggling with the fas-

tenings at the back of her full skirts when they both heard
Zeus' voice ring out loudly from the hallway.

"Gabriel, *mon ami,* where are you? Come, did you not
promise to show me before supper that pair of fine French
pistols that you have?"

Gabriel stilled, and then cursing virulently under his
breath, he slid away from Maria and stood up. With stiff
angry movements he straightened his shirt, and frustration and thwarted desire making his voice harsh, he
growled at Maria, "Do not come downstairs in anything
but something you find in the armoire. If you dare to show
your face in that damned puritian garb I shall take great
pleasure in beating you soundly . . . and then stripping
you and dressing you myself!"

Turning away, he walked to the door, and opening it,
he said smoothly to Zeus, "Here I am, my friend. You did
not need to bellow like a wounded bull to find me." Without a backward glance he shut the door behind him.

Dazedly Maria stared at that shut door, wondering if
she had imagined the passionate scene between them only
seconds before. Her gaze dropped to her bared bosom, her
nipples still stiff with desire, and she flushed. No, she had
not imagined a thing!

Elated, confused and perplexed by his words, she slowly
washed her body with the water she had found in the
china bowl. He had made it very clear that he wanted her
physically, and she could not pretend that she had not
wanted him just as desperately. But it was cold comfort
to know that while her desire had been motivated by love
. . . it had been mere lust that had brought him to her. It
was also, she thought a few minutes later as she looked
blankly at the clothes in the armoire, somewhat unnerving to realize that he had torn aside the last fragile defense she had against him—as long as she was able to
convince herself, albeit with growing difficulty, that she
was his slave, it had been relatively easy to keep alive a
certain resentment about the situation, but now . . .

But now what am I to do? she wondered, bewildered. It
was one thing to harbor feelings of indignation and bitterness at being reduced to a common piece of property
with no will of her own and another to be a forced guest
in someone's home. It was a slight alteration in her sta-

tus, but a telling one, and she had the lowering feeling that now she was going to find it even more and more onerous to hide the love she felt for him.

It was obvious he wanted her as a mistress, apparent, even she would concede, that a strong physical bond existed between them, but could she accept his caresses knowing that it was only lust that brought him to her? That another woman, perhaps *any* other woman, could have satisfied him? Only last week, she had admitted that she loved him, forced herself to choose between family honor and pride and the deep emotion she felt for him . . . but could she sustain that emotion, knowing she was desired for her body alone, that she, as a person, meant nothing to him?

The question was unanswerable. Dimly Maria suspected that for a while, she would be able to convince herself that his body was enough, that his intoxicating lovemaking would satisfy her and enable her to forget that she was only being *used* by him to slake an elemental hunger . . . a hunger that had nothing to do with love. Eventually, she guessed that she would come to hate him, hate him for the shameful passions he aroused within her and hate him for making her feel ashamed and disgusted that she could not resist him.

It was a bleak thought, and blindly Maria began to dress, not even aware of the garments she put on. Instinct must have guided her hands, she decided ruefully as she crossed the room and prepared to go downstairs to join the others. A black-and-gold satin petticoat trimmed with yards and yards of fine lace was revealed by the draping of the heavy silk skirt of emerald green. The short-waisted bodice with elbow-length sleeves was made of a pale green brocade, rows of ribbons and lace decorating the sleeves, the delicate lace of her chemise spilling out over the top of the bodice. There had even been several pairs of shoes, and the pair she had indifferently selected were black with a square toe and a ribbon bow. She looked lovely, her long black hair caught at the nape of her neck by a wide gold ribbon she had found in the trunk, and the gleam that suddenly lit Gabriel's eyes when she walked into the main room made her glad that she would no

longer wear those black dowdy clothes that seemed to of-
fend him so much.

The evening was a pleasant one, and Maria had no
trouble at all in forgetting for a while the uncertain, provoking situation between her and Gabriel. Zeus was an
entertaining fellow and Gabriel was no laggard either,
and it was only when she would glance up and find Gabriel's eyes upon her, an odd flicker in their jeweled depths,
that she would remember that things were not settled
between them.

She both dreaded and looked forward to the end of the
evening. Would he come to her bed? Would she spend this
night in his arms, the hunger he alone aroused finally,
momentarily, appeased?

It was late when the two women eventually climbed the
stairs to their beds, leaving the two gentlemen talking
and making large inroads into the bottle of potent French
brandy Zeus had brought with him. Too restless and bewildered to sleep, Maria lay awake for a long time, her
heart suddenly leaping in her breast when she heard footsteps coming along the hallway. With relief and disappointment she listened as the door to Gabriel's room
opened and then shut. She sat up in bed, her ears straining for any sound. Would he still come to her? Perhaps
he was merely taking off his clothes, and she blushed in
the darkness at the mental picture that flashed through
her brain of Gabriel's naked body. But as the minutes
passed and the house became still, she realized that he
had no intention of taking up where he had left off earlier.
And it would have astonished her to discover that the
same reasons that troubled her were the very ones that
kept him from her bed.

Gabriel *had* hesitated outside her door, the memory of
how sweetly she had responded to him earlier in the evening almost making him willing to forget his scruples.
Almost. In the past, he had never thought very much
about what the woman who shared his lovemaking was
thinking. Oh, he had never been thoughtless or cruel, nor
indifferent, he had always made certain that the earthy
interlude brought pleasure to the woman as well as himself, and perhaps with Elizabeth he had taken greater
care, had even fleetingly wondered if she enjoyed his ca-

resses. But with Maria it was different. Very different, he thought caustically as he flung himself into bed. With Maria he wanted more than just physical gratification . . . he wanted, he realized nervously, for her to care for him, for their joining not to be just casual animal passion.

So much lay between them, he mused restlessly, the family vendetta, the taking of the *Raven*, his slavehood, her capture by him, so many things. . . . In the darkness Gabriel sighed heavily, realizing that he was really asking too much of fate, to have Maria feel anything but hatred and contempt for him. Yet he sensed, or told himself that he sensed, that she was not completely impervious to him, and he could console himself with the fact that he knew that he could arouse her . . . whether she wanted to be or not. It was not much consolation. To his chagrin and dismay he discovered that while he desired her greatly, he did not want her in his bed, simply because for the moment, he could make her forget herself, could make her want him so desperately that her own principles were destroyed. And what, he wondered bleakly, would be the final outcome? Her hatred of him growing until she couldn't bear to have him touch her? And himself, what would it do to him eventually? Knowing the woman in his arms was hating every second of his embrace? How long would it be before he began to hate her himself, hate her because of the power she wielded over him? Hate her because he could not stop himself from forcing her to accept his lovemaking . . . hate her because she would not love him?

Cursing, Gabriel sat up in bed. Sweet Jesu! Why did his rambling thoughts always come back to that one idea, the idea of love existing between a Lancaster and a Delgato? For a second he considered his parents' marriage, the strong love that Sir William had felt for his equally adoring wife. Was he in danger of falling in love with Maria Delgato that way? In grave danger of giving his heart to a woman who would only scorn his love for her?

Gabriel's mouth set stubbornly. No. He was not so far gone with desire for her that he would allow her to touch that deepest part of him. But it was inconceivable that he couldn't, as he had promised himself only days ago, *make* her love him. And once she loved him . . . He smiled wryly.

Well, once he had forced her to admit that she loved him, he would just have to examine precisely what it was he felt for her. But he had the unpleasant feeling that he already knew *exactly* what he felt for Maria Delgato! He would have to, he admitted grimly, be extremely circumspect in his pursuit of her—if she guessed what he was about, he feared, and with good reason, that his plans would come to nought and that his hope for a happy future would be destroyed for a second time.

He frowned. And what about Caroline? Why wouldn't Maria tell him where she was? His frown fading just a little, with an increased heartbeat, he recalled Maria's words. "I will not send you to your death!" Surely that meant something! Perhaps she already cared deeply for him? A blissful smile curving his mouth, he lay back down. Silly little twit! he thought fondly, as if I would let anything hurt me, knowing you were waiting for me here at Royal Gift. And sooner or later, sweet tiger, you *will* tell me where my sister is!

The fact that Zeus and Pilar ended up extending their visit indefinitely while major construction was being done at Harve du Mer helped the situation between Gabriel and Maria. The days were busy with entertaining their guests, and they had a chance to learn more of each other in the company of *very* interested and accommodating friends. Zeus and Pilar did much to promote the match they had both long felt was inevitable, and they were ably assisted in their efforts by the Satterleighs, Mrs. Satterleigh saying one afternoon to Pilar, "My dear, it is high time that Master Gabriel took a wife! And I cannot tell you how pleased Mr. Satterleigh and I were when we laid eyes upon Miss Maria. She is perfect for him! As for that Delgato business—it is sheer nonsense! She may have been born a Delgato but she was *meant* to be a Lancaster!"

Privately Pilar thought the same thing, and one night about eight days after their arrival at Royal Gift as she and Zeus lay in bed together, Pilar asked abruptly, "Do you honestly believe that Gabriel is in love with her?"

Zeus chuckled and pulled her to lie against his massive chest. *"Mais oui, ma coeur!* But he is very stubborn, that one, and I think just a little afraid."

"Afraid!" Pilar burst out, sitting bolt upright beside her large husband. "Why should he be afraid?"

"Because your little pigeon is very apt at hiding her feelings. And I think because she is just a little confused and uncertain about the lures he has thrown her way. She is very proud, as proud as he, and I think she fears to make a fool of herself, and so while she smiles so delightfully at him and does not reject his advances, neither, you will have noticed, does she precisely encourage them."

"But, Zeus, that is not fair!" Pilar argued. "He has been very cautious in his approach too! If you were not so positive yourself that he loves her, I would not have guessed it from his actions. He is very polite to her, but I notice he is very careful not to make any overt move around her."

Dryly Zeus asked, "Assembling all the servants and announcing, with her at his side, that she was his guest? That she was to be treated with honor and respect, was not overt?"

"Well, yes, I suppose so," Pilar admitted slowly.

"And have you watched his eyes?" Zeus inquired. "The way they follow her around the room? The way they light up when she is near him? Or the way one has the impression he is only half listening to the conversation when she is gone from his side? That his thoughts are on her and what she is doing?"

There was a thoughtful pause. Reluctantly Pilar said, "It is the same with her." She sighed and said with exasperation, "They are such fools, the pair of them! I wish he would just *do* something to change the situation."

Zeus chuckled again. "And ruin my enjoyment? *Non, chérie.* It is much too amusing watching the great confident Dark Angel fumble through his rocky and prickly courtship! It serves him right for all the women who threw themselves at him and he would coolly ignore them. I suspect, though, that something will have to happen soon—he has become just a bit testy and short-tempered these last few days to be entirely restful to be around."

Something did happen, but it was not what anyone would have expected . . . or wanted. The very next afternoon, as Gabriel, Zeus, Pilar and Maria returned home from a pleasant picnic near a breathtaking waterfall in a clearing high in the mountains above Royal Gift, they were greeted by a slightly worried Mr. Satterleigh. The quartet had just entered the house when Mr. Satterleigh approached, a soiled and crumpled piece of paper in hand.

"Master Gabriel," he said anxiously, "this arrived not an hour after you had departed this morning." He handed the paper to Gabriel and added, "I think it might be important—I have never seen the man who delivered it before and he was gone as soon as he gave it to me, but he did say that you would find it interesting. He also said that he would wait at the White Horse in Port Royal for your reply."

Maria glanced at the folded paper and stiffened as she recognized the firm, bold handwriting on the outside of the note. Diego! What had he written to Gabriel?

She didn't have long to wait to have her curiosity satisfied. Gabriel read the contents of the note swiftly, his features hardening. Finished, he raised his gaze and bleakly looked across at Maria.

"What is it?" she cried, coming to stand next to him.

He looked at her a long time, some unidentifiable emotion flickering in his eyes before he hid them with his dark lashes. Coolly, he said, "What is it? Why, merely a note from your dear brother, offering me an exchange."

Her mouth dry, Maria demanded, "An exchange, what sort of exchange?"

Gabriel smiled grimly, his eyes cold and hard. "You, sweet viper. He will give me Caroline for you."

Chapter Twenty-five

FROM the deck of the *Dark Angel*, Maria strained her eyes to see the shape of the barren atoll that Diego had demanded be used for the exchange of the women. Even now, some three weeks after that terrible day Gabriel had received Diego's note, she couldn't believe she was here. That Gabriel was actually going to coolly and calmly return her to her brother. Yet, what else could she have expected? she thought dully. Gabriel cared nothing for her, despite the hopes that had risen in her breast those wonderful days before Diego's missive had shattered everything. He had used her, perhaps enjoyed her body, but it had obviously meant nothing to him. And if she had harbored any faint hopes at all that he had come to care for her, his actions these past weeks had completely destroyed them. He had been so cold, so aloof from her, avoiding her, all his thoughts on Caroline and the moment he would have his sister in his arms once again.

Maria tried very hard not to feel bitter, not to hate her brother for intruding into her life so disastrously, not to hate Caroline for simply meaning so much to Gabriel. But it was Gabriel himself who aroused her greatest acrimony, and she wondered furiously how she could have ever imagined she loved him! He was a cold, calculating monster! But it did her little good to rail mentally against him—he had never offered her anything but his body, and now she wasn't even certain that his seeming kindness to her at various times hadn't been all part of another, more devilish form of revenge—a plan to disarm her and have her fall in love with him. Well, if that had been his plan, she thought miserably, it had worked admirably, except

349

that she would rather die than ever let him know just how effective his charms had worked to enslave her heart.

The entire household at Royal Gift had been in an uproar once the contents of Diego's note had been learned, and the days that had followed had been turbulent, debilitating ones. Zeus and Gabriel had disappeared almost immediately, leaving the women without a word. Maria assumed, and Pilar later confirmed it, that they had ridden pell-mell for Port Royal and a meeting at the White Horse. But beyond that, Maria could learn nothing. The Satterleighs went about their chores with tight-lipped, worried expressions while Pilar and Maria had tried to console themselves, Maria urgently telling herself that he would *not* just give her back to Diego, but she had been wrong. When Gabriel and Zeus had finally returned to Royal Gift, Gabriel had said flatly, "We sail in less than a fortnight—the rendezvous is set for the twenty-fourth day of September." Maria had been numb, chilled to the very bone by his apparent eagerness to be rid of her. Yet, realistically, she admitted unhappily, what else could she have expected? Caroline was his sister and she was only a Delgato. His announcement had occasioned a cry of outrage from Pilar, and it had been all Zeus could do to keep his wife from attacking Gabriel. Pilar had calmed down eventually, but the looks she had sent to her host had been full of venom, although she said often enough to Maria, "I can't believe that he will do this to you. He *must* feel something for you; why else has he treated you so kindly these past months?"

Dispiritedly Maria had replied, "You forget, Caroline is his sister and he wants to free her from captivity. Can you really blame him for giving in to Diego's demands?"

Pilar had appeared nonplussed, but right up until the morning the *Dark Angel* had sailed from Port Royal, Pilar had maintained stoutly, "Something is afoot! I just know it, he will not meekly hand you over to your brother. He must have some plan that he is not telling us about—Zeus, that great lout, will tell me nothing, but we both know that he will be with you on the ship, and it gives me some comfort."

Pilar had been furious and angry that she was to be left behind when the ship sailed, and Maria's last sight of her

had been standing on the wharf at Port Royal, tears
streaming from those fine dark eyes. Maria's own eyes
had been dry; she was still too numb to feel anything but
an exhausting despair. It had been Zeus who had dropped
a warmly comforting arm about her slender shoulders,
and he who had murmured, "Come along, petite pigeon,
let me show you to your quarters."

The week that they had been at sea had been uneventful, and time had weighed heavily on Maria's spirits.
Their destination, she had learned from Zeus, was a deserted and rocky atoll set in the vast expanse of the Caribbean, and several days' sailing in any direction from any
inhabited island.

They were currently anchored five leagues away from
the atoll where the rendezvous and exchange would take
place at dawn tomorrow. Bleakly Maria realized that this
would be her last night on board the *Dark Angel*. By this
time tomorrow evening, she would be with Diego, probably on her way to Hispaniola, the events of the past
months seeming like a dream ... or a nightmare, she
mused cynically.

Tiredly, she started to turn away from the railings,
wondering where her vigor and spirit had gone, when she
bumped into Zeus' solid bulk. In the darkness he smiled
at her and said softly, "Do not despair little one, all is not
lost."

Her heart seemed to jerk slightly in her breast, and her
eyes fixed painfully on his, she asked huskily, "What do
you mean? He is *not* going to give me to my brother for
Caroline?"

Zeus ran a finger along the side of his nose, then glancing around and seeing no one standing nearby, he said in
a lowered tone, "He would have me keelhauled if he knew
I was talking to you, but Pilar would not like it, if I let
you look so sad."

They both smiled at each other, then Zeus continued in
that same low tone, "I cannot tell you what is planned,
but trust that our moody Dark Angel would never give
you up."

Maria swallowed with difficulty, hope surging so
strongly through her that she was speechless for a moment. "Why?" she finally got out. "Why has he told me

nothing? Why has he acted as if he cannot bear the sight of me these past weeks?"

Zeus sighed and answered bluntly, "Because, I think, at the moment, that he hates you just a little—you have greatly complicated what should have been a simple situation."

Downcast, Maria muttered in a mortified voice, "I see— he *will* be glad to be rid of me."

Softly, Zeus said, "Don't be a fool! There was never any question of your being returned to your brother—only the question of how we could get Caroline back! Now I will tell you nothing more, but take that melancholy expression off your pretty face—all will be well; remember, Pilar will beat me if she finds out that I have let you be unhappy."

A tremulous little smile curving her mouth, Maria threw her arms around Zeus' massive form and hugged him tightly. "Oh, *Señor* Zeus! Pilar is very lucky to have found you."

Zeus hugged her back. *"Oui,* this is true! But now, you go to sleep and dream of the future we shall all share together on Jamaica."

With a lighter heart Maria walked across the deck toward her quarters in a small room near the stern of the ship, not far from the captain's great room. But before she went belowdecks, the sound of much movement caught her ear and she glanced back.

The deck suddenly seemed alive with action, as several members of the buccaneer crew were busily preparing to hoist two long canoes over the side of the ship. She recognized Gabriel's tall form supervising the operation, and a second later she watched as Zeus joined him.

Fascinated, Maria stared as the canoes were lowered; then to her astonishment, Zeus enveloped Gabriel in a hearty embrace and she had the curious impression that he was offering his captain words of encouragement, just as he had offered her only moments before. A second later Zeus and several heavily armed men disappeared over the railings. Overcome with curiosity, she left her position and ran to the side of the ship, peering down into the darkness below, watching with growing excitement as Zeus and the others scrambled into the canoes and then silently began to row in the direction of the atoll. Was this part of the plan? she wondered with an accelerated heartbeat.

"Maria!" Gabriel's voice rang out behind her. "What are you doing here? I thought you were already in your quarters for the night."

He didn't sound precisely friendly, but remembering Zeus' half-reassuring, half-depressing words, she turned to face him. He didn't look very friendly either, she decided ruefully, noticing the taut line of his mouth, the coolness in the emerald green gaze. She also noticed, with a little pang in her heart, the obvious lines of tiredness and strain that creased his forehead and radiated out from the corners of his eyes. A gentle sea breeze ruffled through the thick black hair, causing the gold hoop earring to swing slightly, and Maria thought that he had never looked quite so handsome as he stood there before her in the ghostly light of the waning moon, his shirt a pale blur, his hands on his hips as he regarded her intently. Softly she said, "I was just on my way to bed." And driven to make him reveal something of what he was feeling, desperately needing some sign from *him* that he wasn't just going to calmly give her back to Diego, she asked rashly, "Will you be happy tomorrow evening when I am no longer with you?"

Even in the faint light of the moon, she saw his eyes darken and was filled with a wild exultation when he jerked her roughly up against him and snarled, "You will be with *me* tomorrow evening! I will not let you go—and that is my damnation!" Hungrily his mouth crushed down on hers and Maria reveled in the very ruthlessness of his kiss, joy like quicksilver pumping madly through her veins. He cared! It could not be just a need for revenge that made him want to keep her with him, and helplessly she gave herself up to the ecstasy of his embrace.

A long time later, a long time after his kiss had gentled and become warmly searching, he had finally, with obvious reluctance, lifted his mouth from hers. Thickly he said, "Go below to your bed or I swear by all that's holy I'll ravage you here on the deck!"

For just a second Maria hesitated, still too bemused by his kiss to think clearly, but then seeing that a few crew

members were still about and had been observing their
embrace with interest, she nodded her head and quickly
disappeared down below. She had dreaded this night, certain she would spend it in dry-eyed misery, staring
blankly into the darkness, but comforted by Zeus' words
and Gabriel's urgent kiss, she fell deeply asleep the instant her head hit her pillow.

She was awakened an hour before dawn by Gabriel's
impatient hand on her shoulder. "Dress yourself," he said
curtly, "we are approaching the place for the rendezvous."

Suddenly aware of the movement of the ship beneath
her and frightened of what this morning might hold, with
trembling fingers she hurriedly dressed. Deftly she plaited
her hair into a long thick braid and quickly secured it
around her head. Then taking a deep steadying breath,
trying to still the nervous tumult that raged inside of her,
she left the room and made her way to the deck above.

The first pale streaks of dawn were painting the horizon a soft pink and gold, but Maria had no thought to
appreciate the beauty of the tropical dawn, her eyes going
immediately to Gabriel's tall figure standing on the quarterdeck, staring off to the east. She followed his gaze, her
breath catching in her throat as she spotted the large
Spanish galleon, its huge sails furled as it lay at anchor
just off the small, barren dot of land that had been chosen
for the exchange. It was her brother's ship, the *Santo
Cristo,* and Maria wondered what sort of awful memories
were going through Gabriel's head as he stared at that
ship. As terrible as she had feared, she thought a second
later as she approached him. His face was grim, and there
was a dangerous stillness about his body, the stillness of
a hungry jungle panther that has just sighted prey.

He was completely unaware of her presence, and hesitantly, she murmured, "Gabriel? I am ready."

With a great effort he seemed to jerk himself from
wherever his thoughts had taken him, and he glanced at
Maria blankly for a moment before she saw comprehen-
sion slowly fill his eyes, driving out the ugly icy hatred
she had seen there. Wordlessly, he cupped her elbow and
escorted her to the side of the ship.

While she had been crossing to Gabriel's side, the *Dark*

Angel had been anchored, and the ship now lay several hundred yards away from the *Santo Cristo* on the east and the rocky atoll to the north, the gentle swells of the sea rhythmically rocking the ship. As the moments passed and nothing seemed to happen, Maria became aware of a tenseness stealing through the crew; Gabriel was rigid at her side, his eyes locked on the *Santo Cristo* as if willing Diego and Caroline to appear.

Then suddenly, there was a flurry of action on the *Santo Cristo,* and Maria watched as a small gig was lowered to the water; a second later, she recognized her brother's sleek form as he lithely climbed down the rope ladder to the gig. Then it was Caroline's turn and though the distance was too great to be certain, the sunlight glinting on the mass of golden curls as the tall, slender woman came down the ladder made Maria positive that it was she.

At the sight of the golden-haired woman, something seemed to snap inside of Gabriel and with a strangely harsh voice, he ordered, "Lower the gig."

It was quickly done and in a trice Maria found herself in the small boat, being rowed by Gabriel toward the rock-strewn beach of the atoll. Gabriel was heavily armed and Maria was conscious of anxiety and uneasiness building within her. What was going to happen?

She glanced across at the small gig from the *Santo Cristo* as it kept pace with Gabriel's strong steady rowing, Diego and Caroline its only occupants. Everything had obviously been prearranged, but Maria knew her brother, and somehow she doubted that he intended to make a straightforward exchange . . . just as Zeus had clearly revealed that Gabriel had other plans than those agreed upon. Mouth dry, she looked around her, the two ships appearing to lie so peacefully at anchor, the squat shape of the atoll coming nearer and nearer and the empty expanse of brilliant blue ocean and sky all around them. But then her heart lurched slightly as she caught a glimpse of something on the far horizon. A ship's sail? Or merely the faint outline of a cloud?

The scrunch of the gig hitting the shore distracted her and then she had no time for further speculation. Gabriel's hand was like iron around her upper arm as he silently helped her from the gig and they made their way inland a short distance.

Diego and Caroline did the same, and Maria wondered what Gabriel was thinking as he stared at his sister for the first time in nearly five years. That she had changed? Indeed she had; she was a woman now and it showed in the swell of her breast beneath the blue bodice she was wearing, and the passage of years was there in the fine bones of her face.

The quartet stopped as they reached an area where the rocky spine of the atoll seemed to spread out like two long arms on either side of them, and with several yards between them, they stood and stared at each other.

It was Diego who spoke first. A contemptuous curve to his thin lips, he said, "I see that you have done as I instructed you."

Gabriel nodded curtly, his eyes on Caroline, and stealing a quick glance at him, Maria wasn't at all surprised to see the love he felt for his sister revealed in his eyes. His voice thick with emotion, he got out, "Caro . . . is it really you?"

Caroline's beautiful eyes filled up with tears and she cried, "Oh, Gabriel! You are really alive! I didn't believe him when he told me!"

"Aye, I'm alive," he ground out, and his gaze turned to Diego, "but no thanks to that whoreson!"

Diego stiffened and snarled, "You always were a disobedient swine! How I wish I had killed you the day we took the *Raven.*"

Gabriel smiled wolfishly. "I'm sure you do—and you'll have even more cause to wish it were so before this day is through."

"Do you think so?" Diego drawled condescendingly. "Somehow I rather doubt it—especially since you will not be alive to see the sun set."

Maria had the strange impression that Diego's words didn't surprise Gabriel, that he had been waiting for them. His voice cool and undisturbed, Gabriel asked idly, "Oh? And why do you say that?"

"Because, you stupid English swine, I am not so gullible as you! And you are a fool to have so blindly obeyed my instructions." Almost purring, Diego went on, "Did it never occur to you that I might make other arrangements."

A sort of grim amusement dancing in his eyes, Gabriel murmured, "But, *señor,* you gave your word of honor that you would hold to the bargain. That we would exchange our sisters and that there would be no bloodshed between us."

"And you believed me?" Diego gave an ugly laugh. "Let me disabuse you! Pedro! Miguel! Show yourselves!"

Suddenly from behind the rocks and boulders that encompassed them on three sides there appeared several armed Spanish soldiers, their arquebuses aimed at Gabriel. Maria's heart went to her toes. Was this how it would all end? Gabriel shot to death before her very eyes? Dying on this bleak and nameless bit of earth in the middle of the Caribbean?

She looked at him again, and to her astonishment, he appeared to be enjoying himself, his thumbs hooked negligently in the wide belt around his waist. It was then that she remembered Zeus and the men in the canoes. Where were they?

It wasn't long before she found out. Unperturbed by the knowledge that several muskets were aimed at his chest, Gabriel called out cheerfully, "Zeus! My friend, are you and the others there?"

And higher up in the black rocky outcroppings, Zeus' voice rang out jovially, "But of course, *mon ami!* Where else would we be but up here and ready to kill ourselves some Spanish dogs?"

Diego's face whitened with fury as he took in the rising forms of the buccaneers as they popped up from their places of concealment behind his men. His fists clenched at his sides, his black eyes were livid with rage as he realized how simply he had been outfoxed.

There was no question of continuing this farce further. It was obvious the buccaneers could cut his men to pieces before they could turn and fire at the well-armed enemy above them; and through tight lips, he growled, "Well then, since I won't have the pleasure of . . . this time . . . of killing you, let us get on with what we came here for— the exchange of the women."

Gabriel eyed him for a tense minute and then he

drawled, "Nay, I have a better solution. You and I shall fight, and the winner shall leave unmolested . . . with *both* the women."

Diego's breath drew in sharply, a savage light flickering in his eyes. He hesitated only a second; then, his hand going to the long sword that hung by his side, he hissed, "Why not, English swine? Why not!"

And seeking to strike the first blow, he lunged at Gabriel. But Gabriel would not be caught out by such tactics, and with lightning-swift movements, he had instantly shoved Maria behind him and had swung his cutlass free to parry Diego's maddened lunge.

Pushed back against the protection of the rocks, with a sick fascination, Maria watched the duel unfolding before her—it was her worst nightmare come true, but she was dully aware of no feeling of being torn in two any longer: all her concerns were for Gabriel. Ah, *Dios,* she prayed fervently, do not let the Englishman die!

The sandy, rock-dotted floor of the atoll was not the best surface for the vicious fight that was raging across it, but neither of the combatants paid the uneven footing any heed—each man concentrating on only one thing—the death of a most hated enemy. Gabriel and Diego were fairly evenly matched—Gabriel's reach was perhaps longer, Diego's lighter build gave him a sinuous agility—but Gabriel had much to avenge this day, he had waited too long for this moment, and there was a cold-blooded ferocity about the flashing thrusts of his blade.

Every eye of every person on the atoll was riveted on the two men as they fought, and from the sudden sound of excited commotion that carried across the water, it was apparent that the crews on the two ships had become aware of the grim duel that was taking place in front of them. Despite the distance that separated the ships from the atoll it was easy to distinguish the two combatants— Gabriel's white, full-sleeved shirt, buff breeches and russet hose were in clear contrast to the leather doublet and black breeches that Diego was wearing. When Diego unexpectedly broke through Gabriel's guard and sliced a wicked gash along the Englishman's lower arm, there was a howl of rage from the crew of the *Dark Angel* and a shout of triumph from the Spaniards on board the *Santo*

Cristo, the sounds reversing a second later when Gabriel's cutlass slid smoothly down Diego's blade and Gabriel deliberately nicked him across the cheek, leaving a long crimson stripe on the Spaniard's swarthy face.

It was an ugly fight, neither man willing to give an inch, and as the minutes passed, both men bloodied and sweating hard, their swords continued to meet and clash in the bright morning sunlight. There was a tiger's smile on Gabriel's mouth as he fought, and Maria had the distinct sensation that time had receded for him, that the passage of years had never gone by, that he was fighting the duel he had wanted to fight that long-ago day on the *Raven.* The savage thrusts of his sword seemed to ignite the very air as he lunged again and again at Diego, gradually driving the Spaniard before him toward the open beach where the foam-crested blue waves lapped against the sandy shore. Diego seemed unable to halt Gabriel's charge, and the Englishman's blade was making telling contact, Diego's leather doublet hanging in shreds, as Gabriel almost toyed with him, striking here, there, everywhere, but never delivering the killing thrust.

The explosive, stupefying boom of cannon fire from the *Dark Angel* suddenly rent the air, and as one, those on the atoll turned to look out to sea. Maria's eyes widened and she felt a thrill of horror as she realized that there were no longer only the silhouettes of two ships on the horizon, but *three!* The new arrival, a thirty-gun Spanish galleon, her huge white sails spread to catch every breath of air, was fast bearing down on the atoll, although she was still some distance away and out of firing range of the buccaneer ship.

Having fired that first warning shot to alert those on shore, the buccaneer crew were now frantically pulling up anchor, unfurling sails as they hurried to bring the *Dark Angel* about to meet this new and deadly threat. On board the *Santo Cristo* there was excited activity too, despite the fact that the newcomer should pose no danger to them.

There was a moment of stunned, disbelieving silence on the atoll; then, green eyes blazing with fury, Gabriel snarled, "You bastard! You were taking no chances, were you? By God's wounds, you'll not win *this* time!" And in one graceful blur of movement, he lunged toward Diego.

But Diego, his face a curious mixture of apprehension and rage, blocked the force of Gabriel's sword, their blades crashing together as steel met steel. A strange glitter in his black eyes, his face inches from Gabriel's, Diego ground out breathlessly, "It seems we are destined to fight another day, English swine! I'm afraid that the arrival of Ramon's ship has put an end, for the time being, to my plans to rid the earth of your foul presence."

Once the initial shock had vanished, the duel between the two principals was forgotten and pandemonium broke out amongst those on land, Zeus and the other buccaneers firing at will at the Spaniards crouching down among the rocks. There was one thought in the buccaneers' minds, they must fight their way clear to the beach, to the place where the canoes were hidden, and rejoin the ship as soon as possible; every second was vital.

The Spanish soldiers fought back viciously, just as intent upon escape, and determined to slaughter as many buccaneers in the process as possible.

The two women were ignored for the moment and they clung to each other, seeking shelter behind a large boulder from the whizzing iron shot that filled the air.

On the water, the *Dark Angel*, her cannons belching smoke and fire, tried to hold her position, unwilling to run and desert the men on shore. But the newcomer seemed in no mood to fight; despite having the buccaneer ship in range, her cannons were still and silent as she sailed closer to the atoll.

Diego's words were mystifying and Gabriel's eyes narrowed. "Another day? Why? Isn't this what you planned?"

Their swords still locked together, Diego smiled twistedly. "To kill you? *Sí!* To have Ramon arrive in swift pursuit of the English bitch? No!" And surprising Gabriel with a burst of sudden strength, Diego broke the contact of their blades, sending Gabriel sprawling backward in the sand.

Like a cat, Gabriel was on his feet in an instant, poised to meet Diego's attack; but to his utter astonishment, Diego was running away, calling loudly as he did so, *"Retirada!* Hurry to the *Santo Cristo!"*

The Spaniards spilled willy-nilly from their positions among the rocks and began racing pell-mell toward the beach, the buccaneers right behind them, hand-to-hand fighting having replaced the fire of the arquebuses and muskets. Bedlam reigned on shore; blue smoke hung overhead; the sound of sword grating against sword rang in the air; the screams of dying men and the boom of the *Dark Angel*'s cannon in the distance created a cacophony of destruction. Gabriel, momentarily dumbstruck by Diego's cowardly and irrational retreat, risked a harassed glance at sea and was instantly galvanized into movement when he saw that the newcomer, still oddly refusing to fire upon the *Dark Angel*, was lowering a longboat filled with soldiers into the water. *Reinforcements!* he thought furiously as he plunged back up the beach, running for the place he had last seen the women.

He spared one frustrated and angry look in Diego's direction, the bloodlust within him reluctant to let Diego slip from his grasp again, but to his complete incomprehension, instead of returning to attack anew now that more Spaniards were on their way to the beach, Diego and some of his men were in the *Santo Cristo*'s gig and rowing frenziedly toward the mother ship. By the devil's tail! Here was confusion! Why was Diego abandoning everything so swiftly when help was fast arriving?

But there was no time to speculate, no time to wonder what the hell was going on—he had to get Maria and Caroline out of here! And he had to join his men and reach the ship—his crew would not willingly desert him, and every second he was on land put them all in greater danger—the strange galleon would not continue, he was grimly confident, to hold her fire much longer, and once Diego was aboard the *Santo Cristo* . . . His face a picture of rage and hatred, Gabriel increased his already swift pace—he would not lose another ship to Delgato!

Zeus materialized out of the confusion by his side, just as Gabriel arrived at the spot where Maria and Caroline had last been seen. Blankly Gabriel stared at the barren landscape. "Did you see what happened to them? I know they are not with Diego!" he said tautly, horror roiling through his veins at the sudden frightening notion that the two women might have been murdered and thrown behind one of the tumbled boulders. His voice filled with fear and longing, he called out, "Maria! Caro! It is Gabriel! Come to me! Hurry, there is not a moment to lose!"

To his joyous relief, Maria, with Caroline just a step behind her, came stumbling through the sand from their place of concealment. His sword dropping to the ground, with strong arms he crushed them to his chest, such a sweet jubilation surging through his heart that for one fleeting second he forgot their peril and could only revel in the knowledge that they were all alive and together. Fervently he dropped a kiss on Caroline's brow, one hand tenderly caressing her hair, as if convincing himself that she was really here with him. Then, remembering their position, he dropped a brief, hard kiss on Maria's mouth and snatched up his sword.

Before he turned away, Maria was astonished to see the sheen of tears in his eyes. He glanced down at her and muttered huskily, "Now that Caroline is returned to me, perhaps we can find a happy future. But come! We are not out of danger yet!"

And indeed they were not! In those short minutes much had changed. Diego had reached the *Santo Cristo* and the galleon was beginning to swing about, her guns pointed landward; the men from the longboat from the unknown galleon were leaping into the surf as their boat neared the shore of the atoll; further down the beach, the buccaneers had secured their canoes and the *Dark Angel*'s gig; and hovering as near as she dared was the *Dark Angel* herself, cannons aimed at the newcomer, but now following the lead of the other ship, holding her fire, waiting tensely to see what would happen.

Gabriel took in the situation in a flash and his hand gripping Maria's upper arm tightly, he said softly to Zeus, "I will trust you, my good friend, to make certain that Caro does not lag behind."

Zeus smiled and rumbled, "As if I would, after we have gone to such trouble to have her with us!" He glanced down at Caroline, sending her a commiserating grin. "Your brother is a charming man most times, but I think the excitement has driven his manners from him! But come along, young Caro, I have heard much of you and look forward to comparing all of your brother's many vices, once we are all safely at Royal Gift."

There were no more words, and together the quartet raced frantically toward the shore. The two canoes from the *Dark Angel* were already being rowed quickly toward the buccaneer ship, and at the water's edge the gig was being tossed violently about by the incoming waves, two staunch buccaneers fighting to hold the small boat's position at the water's edge, waiting loyally for their captain. Three hundred yards down the beach, the longboat from the strange ship had finally landed, and armed Spaniards were leaping through the surging waves, scrambling toward shore.

In seconds, breathless and panting, the foursome had arrived at the gig, Maria feeling as if her heart would burst from her breast, so hard was it pounding. Gasping, she tried to catch her breath as Gabriel and Zeus, along with the other two men, hastily shoved the small boat out into the churning water. The two buccaneers, who had stayed behind, slithered aboard the gig, reaching instantly for the oars. Zeus was just about to clamber over the sides when a huge wave suddenly swept the boat a short distance away. Cursing and sweating, the two men rowed the boat nearer the shore, and in water nearly to his waist, with a mighty lunge, Zeus heaved himself on board. Turning to Gabriel, who with the two women now stood in thigh-deep water, he shouted, "Give me Maria first!"

Gabriel's hands had just closed around her waist, when there was a thunderous explosion, cannon fire suddenly striking the beach as the *Santo Cristo* raked the shoreline. In stunned alarm Gabriel stared at the big galleon as she prepared to fire another round, unable to believe that Diego was crazed enough to fire upon his own men! But it appeared that he was, and from the shout of horror that rose up from the other galleon, it was obvious that those on board were as afflicted by that base act as was Gabriel himself.

From the shrieks that came from further down the beach, it was apparent too that not only had Diego fired upon the new arrivals, but that he had also managed to make his shots telling ones. Frantic now to get Maria and

Caroline safe from this madman, roughly Gabriel grabbed Maria, and with a swift, violent motion, tossed her into Zeus' outstretched, waiting hands. Another wave swept the gig askew, but grabbing Caroline's hand, Gabriel lurched deeper into the water, pulling his sister behind him, intent on getting her safely on board. To his utter consternation, Caroline resisted, her slim hand twisting frantically in his as she cried out in a voice laden with deep emotion, "Oh, wait, Gabriel! Wait! It is Ramon! He has come for me!"

Staggered, as much by her actions as her words, Gabriel's hold loosened, and he flashed an anxious glance down the beach in the direction Caroline was staring so eagerly. A tall, black-haired man was racing swiftly through the waves, his sword held in readiness for battle, and in that moment, Gabriel recognized him. The gray-eyed Spaniard who had led Caroline away from the *Santo Cristo* when she had docked in Santo Domingo all those years ago! Dazed, Gabriel looked at his sister; and Caroline, tearing her gaze away from the fast-approaching figure, half-sobbed, half-laughed, "I am sorry, but I must go to him! He does not understand all that has happened. He doesn't know that I did not leave him willingly!" The blatant expression of overpowering love and longing on her beautiful face took Gabriel aback. Oblivious to the waves swelling around them, confused thoughts darting wildly through his brain, he croaked, "You want to go *back?* With *him?*"

Already moving through the water toward the nearing man, Caroline sent him a misty smile, her brilliant Lancasterian blue eyes shining. "Oh, yes! I love him! And though he has never told me so, his actions this day prove that he cares deeply for me. Do not worry over me, dear brother, I *shall* be happy with Ramon—go quickly! Now that I know you are alive, I shall find some way to write to you and explain everything. But go! We cannot linger here with Diego trying to kill us all!"

Gabriel might have argued with her, might have tried to restrain her, but another wave swept her even farther from him. The man she had called Ramon was now scant yards away and the expression on that dark face suddenly eased the despair that was in Gabriel's heart. He didn't know how it had come about, or what had transpired between his sister and this man, but there was such naked yearning and torment, such blazing love revealed on the proud features of the Spaniard that Gabriel knew without a doubt that his sister was cherished and greatly loved by Ramon. But still he waited, torn inside to let her go to a man he clearly felt was an enemy.

The gig surged nearer, Zeus calling out desperately, *"Mon ami!* Let her go! There will be another day—but not if that madman Diego decides to fire on us again! Hurry! We must reach the *Dark Angel* at once!"

Gabriel sent another harassed look seaward, relieved and furious to see that the *Santo Cristo* appeared to be heading toward the open water, apparently intent upon putting as much distance as possible between herself and the other two ships. When his gaze swung back it was to see the Spaniard sweep Caroline up next to him in a powerful embrace.

One arm around Caroline, the other holding his sword poised for action, Ramon said across the distance that separated them from Gabriel, "Englishman! It is good that you are alive! But I will kill you if you think to take my wife from me!"

Gabriel's eyes widened and he breathed incredulously, "Your *wife!*"

"Sí!" Ramon replied fiercely. "And now if you will excuse me, I intend to split Diego Delgato from groin to neck!"

"Nay!" Gabriel snarled, coming closer, his sword held menacingly. "It is my sword that will end his wretched life! It is *my* wife who died at his hands."

Ramon hesitated, then glanced down into Caroline's upturned face. Some wordless emotion passed between them, her hands tightening on the opening of his leather doublet. He looked back at Gabriel. Grimly he admitted, "So it was. Then let us part for now, brother of my wife, and when next our two paths cross let there be no enmity between us." Exasperation lacing his voice, he added, "And tell your blasted crew that my ship, the *Jaguar,* has no quarrel with them this day!"

Gabriel laughed, his even teeth white in his sun-bronzed face. "So be it!" He looked hard at Caroline, but seeing her tranquil features flushed with the love she obviously felt for the Spaniard, he shrugged and said quietly, "Goodbye little sister—may you find happiness on the road you have chosen."

Caroline sent him a blindingly radiant smile and too full of emotion to speak, she only nodded her golden head. The sudden sound of renewed cannon fire had them all looking out to sea again and Gabriel was appalled to see that the *Santo Cristo* had changed direction again and was now bearing down fast on the *Dark Angel,* her guns belching smoke and fire.

The gig was bobbing up and down only three yards away, Zeus frantically motioning the men to row closer to their errant captain, Maria's small, white face appearing just behind his massive shoulder. At the sight of Maria, Gabriel hesitated no longer; he gave a quick salute of his blade to Ramon and Caroline, and then he dived beneath the waves, his black head breaking the water when he finally surfaced and swam strongly toward his destiny.

Part Four

Of Love and Revenge

Jamaica, Autumn, 1668

> The sea has its perils
> The heaven its stars,
> But my heart, my heart
> My heart has its love.
>
> Heinrich Heine
> *Das Meer hat seine Perlen*

Chapter Twenty-six

BUT it was not Gabriel's destiny that day to meet the *Santo Cristo* in battle, and by the time the gig had gained the *Dark Angel*, Diego had ordered his ship away, content apparently this time to run from the fight that was inevitable. In a mixture of frustration, rage and regret, Gabriel stared as the huge white sails of his enemy's ship grew smaller on the horizon.

With Gabriel and the others at last aboard, the *Dark Angel* wasted no time in loitering in the vicinity of the *Jaguar,* even if the Spaniard who commanded her *was* the captain's brother-in-law! The enmity between Spaniard and buccaneer was too well established to be easily allayed, and with a concerted sigh of thankfulness, the crew of the *Dark Angel* set to putting as much distance as possible, as swiftly as the strong sea breeze would allow, between themselves and the massive, cannon-bristling *Jaguar.* Only when the atoll and the *Jaguar* were faint dots on the horizon did the air of wary tenseness evaporate from the crew.

The journey back to Port Royal was a relaxing one— clear blue skies, miles of white-crested turquoise seas— and a steady breeze kept the sails filled and sent the *Dark Angel* skimming lightly across the ocean toward home. There had been no prey this time out, but the hand-picked crew was undismayed—the captain had made that clear at the onset and had promised each man a tidy number of gold doubloons for his efforts. And there was the feeling of having been successful—the captain's Spanish wench had been kept from her whoreson brother and the captain's sister was apparently no longer a slave and a captive, but the beloved wife of a rich Spaniard. Aye, there was much to be pleased about on this journey home.

Pilar was waiting anxiously on the quay when the *Dark Angel* dropped anchor in the bay at Port Royal very late in the afternoon a week later, and the instant she saw her muscular husband and Maria's small shape flanked by Gabriel, a joyous smile broke across her attractive features. They were safe! Her smile faded just a little when she suddenly realized that there was no sign of Gabriel's golden-haired sister. Had they failed utterly? Had Caroline been killed?

The small gig that ferried Maria, Gabriel and Zeus to the wharf had barely docked before Pilar was there, questions tumbling from her mouth. What had happened? Had Diego failed to keep the rendezvous? Or had it all simply been a trap? Or worse, had something dreadful happened to Caroline?

Laughing, Zeus swung her up effortlessly in his powerful arms, and after pressing a lusty kiss on her mouth, said gaily, *"Ma cœur!* Are you not pleased to see me? And, yes, *chérie,* I will tell you everything in just a moment, but let us first retire to *mon ami*'s fine town house and speak in private." He shot a speculative look at Maria's wan face and added noncommittally, "The petite pigeon was not well on the journey home—she lost her breakfast at least twice and has been pale and listless since we sailed away from that cursed atoll."

Maria glanced at him in alarm, shocked that he had known about something that she had taken such great pains to hide and frightened that he had discovered something she wasn't even positive about yet herself. But Zeus was already walking away, a protesting Pilar being dragged along in his wide wake.

Gabriel's touch on her arm made her jump and the frown that creased his forehead when he looked at her did nothing for her agitated state. "You never mentioned anything about being ill," he said slowly, his eyes searching her features with concern.

Maria took a deep breath, pasted a determined smile on her mouth and said brightly, *"Señor* Zeus exaggerates too much! I think it was simply that my stomach was not prepared for the fare it received on board the *Dark Angel.*"

Still not quite convinced, Gabriel stared at her an unnerving minute longer, but then as if finally satisfied, he put his hand under her arm and began to escort her along the long wharf. "You will be able to rest a few days at my house in town before we return to Royal Gift. Perhaps by then you will have recovered your spirits somewhat."

Maria bit her lip, not certain how to take his comment. This was the most conversation they had exchanged since the night before they had landed on the atoll, and she didn't quite know how to respond. But then, she thought despairingly, she had never known how to respond to Gabriel Lancaster. She loved him, but she didn't understand him, didn't even begin to guess *precisely* how he felt about her, didn't know what role she was now to play. Mistress? Guest? Hostage?

She flashed him a look from beneath her long lashes as they walked through the brown cobblestone streets of the sprawling town of Port Royal, wishing he wasn't so handsome, wishing the very sight of his lean, dark face didn't make the blood pound so wildly in her veins, wishing . . . She sighed heavily. What she wished for was for him to take her into his arms and tell her that he loved her passionately! That it didn't matter that she was the sister of his enemy! That he wanted to share the future with her as man and wife . . . that he was delighted about the child she strongly suspected grew in her womb!

She had tried to ignore the signs, tried desperately to tell herself those mornings of late that she had been violently sick, that it *had* just been the food; but she knew she had been only deluding herself. Especially when she began to count on her fingers, when it had finally dawned on her that there had been one body function that had not appeared since she had arrived at Port Royal, then the truth had stared her in the face. She could not continue to hide from it—she was going to have Gabriel's child! The child that had been conceived that very first day at Royal Gift.

The knowledge filled her with both joy and terror. The invidiousness of her position, the confusion and unsureness about what fate Gabriel planned for her, did nothing to ease the turmoil in her breast. It was true, there had been many encouraging moments since he had first exploded into her life that evening in Puerto Bello, moments that, from time to time, had given her hope that he viewed her as something other than simply an object to be used for lust and revenge. The fact that he had been so adamantly opposed to giving her back to Diego had added to that hope and those intriguing words he had uttered on the atoll—"Perhaps now we can find a happy future"—had only increased the sweet anticipation that had tantalized her since the very beginning.

Once the awful horror and numbing fright of that time on the atoll had faded, once the *Dark Angel* had been well on the way to Port Royal, Maria had thought that Gabriel would come to her and at least explain some of his feelings about her position in his life and future. But he had not, although he had been kind and infuriatingly casual to her; and as the days had passed and he had said nothing more about her fate, her spirits, not unnaturally, had begun to sink.

The baby, she realized miserably, was a decided complication and she wasn't so innocent, or so far gone in love with him, to think that once he learned of her state he would suddenly ask for her hand in marriage. Nor, she thought painfully, did she want to marry him under those circumstances—if their child was the only thing that brought them together, they were doomed to never find happiness with each other. She loved him, but she could think of few things worse than being trapped into marriage with a man who cared nothing for her, except that she had borne him a child. But the nagging thought that he might offer marriage because of the child haunted her.

The prospect of the child made Maria more vulnerable and made her view the immediate future with fear and despair. If, she thought dully, as Gabriel guided her along another winding street, it had been only the desire to thwart Diego that had kept Gabriel from giving her back to her brother, only lust that bound him to her . . . when her body grew heavy and swollen with his child, would he abandon her? Or nearly as horrible to contemplate—

keep the child and toss her like a piece of refuse on the vice-ridden streets of Port Royal?

It was a frightening idea and Maria glanced up at him again as they walked together, wondering what went on behind those emerald eyes. What was he thinking? Regretting that he had not let Diego have her? A little shudder went through her as she envisioned Diego's reaction to her pregnant state. He would be, she admitted wretchedly, absolutely livid, and she doubted anything she could say to him would lessen his fury and contempt.

Gabriel felt the shudder and looking down at her, he asked quietly, "Are you chilled? The weather is warm, but perhaps the breeze is too cold for you?"

Maria shook her head, unaware that some of the turmoil inside her was clearly revealed in the shadowed sapphire blue eyes and that the unhappiness that churned in her breast had added a discouraged droop to her sweet mouth. But Gabriel saw it, and he was disturbed and depressed by the signs of her apparent dislike and disappointment with the present situation. Maria would have laughed out loud, if she didn't scream with vexation first, to have discovered that Gabriel was interpreting her unhappiness as a sure indication that she was miserably resigned to being with him and that she had wanted overwhelmingly to be returned to her brother and to have seen the last of Gabriel Lancaster!

Gabriel was finding himself in an odd dilemma, and he was reminded once again of Thalia Davenport's words to him that last night in England, words that he had begun to believe were actually a curse. "I pray you meet a woman you cannot have! And if God is good, she will break your heart!" He wasn't certain what a broken heart felt like, but he was fairly confident it would hurt little more than the exquisite pain that seemed to have permanently settled in the middle of his chest.

For a precious few moments on the atoll, when he had held both Maria and Caroline in his arms, he *had* believed that he could overcome the difficulties that lay between him and Maria, that once they were all safe on board the *Dark Angel* and sailing for Jamaica he could begin to woo his proud Spanish rose, that he could make her love him. He had, for those brief seconds, envisioned

a delightful future for them all—a dazzling future in which
Maria loved him wildly, and the children they were sure
to have would grow strong and proud around them; a
happy future in which Caroline would marry some upright young planter and someday have a loving family of
her own.

Caroline's defection to Ramon Chavez had troubled him
greatly, despite the apparent ease with which he had accepted her decision. It had been a wrench for him to let
her go to a man he could never forget was a Spaniard,
one of the men who had been on the *Santo Cristo* that
fateful day; and yet he knew instinctively that Ramon
was an honorable man and that Caroline would be safe
and loved. It was all that he could have asked for her, but
still he grieved a little that she was gone from him forever, that she would have children that he might never
see, grieved because no matter how much he and Ramon
might wish to forge a bond of friendship, that their very
nationalities might prevent it and because of that he
might never see his sister again.

It had been those melancholy thoughts that had bedeviled him those first few days at sea as the *Dark Angel* had
sailed gracefully toward Port Royal. And by the time he
had come to grips with the loss of Caroline in his future,
accepted without regret the stunning knowledge that miraculously his sister had found love in her captivity, he
had found the one woman who had come to mean everything to him listless and preoccupied. What conclusion
could he draw but that she had wanted to be with her
brother, that unlike Caroline, she had *not* found her captivity a loving one, nor had she fallen in love with her
captor, as had his sister? That assumption had stilled the
powerful temptation to sweep her into his arms and demand that she marry him, that she love him, as much as
he had, albeit unwillingly, come to love her.

Stubbornly, he told himself that he would make her
change her mind, reassuring himself repeatedly that she
could not be totally indifferent to him, that no woman
would have responded so intoxicatingly to his kisses, have
given so generously of her body, if there were not some
spark of feeling for him within her. But he was not as
confident as he pretended, not as sure of his ground as he

would have liked to be—especially, he was afraid to declare himself for fear of facing a final rebuff, for having
the frail hope that she would one day come to love him
completely and irrevocably destroyed. He did not like to
see her so obviously unhappy either, and there was the
heart-wrenching knowledge that he might, in spite of his
very spirit crying out against it, in the end have to let
her go. . . .

His mouth tightened, the emerald eyes darkening. By
God's wounds, he would not surrender so tamely! If he
could woo other women, when it had meant little more
than a moment's gratification, could he not win the most
important one of all? Could he not bring all the charm
which he was reputed to have into full play against this
mule-headed little darling who walked by his side?

Stopping before a pleasant two-story brick building,
some distance from the main part of Port Royal, Gabriel
murmured, "This is my town house. You will find it comfortable, if less maintained than Royal Gift—I keep two
mulattoes in residence to serve my needs in town, and it
is here that I have usually stayed when returning from a
voyage." He smiled rufully. "It is a bachelor's residence,
and I trust that its amenities will be sufficient for our stay
here." He hesitated and then added casually, "Of course,
if there are any changes you would like to make—addi-
tional servants, or household goods and such, tell me and
I shall see what can be done." At the expression on her
face, one of delighted astonishment, he said more softly,
"Whenever Royal Gift becomes too boring for you, we can
come into town and stay here for a few days and enjoy
the, er, gentility of the more respectable parts of Port
Royal."

Maria gave him a sunny smile, suddenly all her worries
about the future seeming not quite so insurmountable. He
obviously was planning to keep her in his life and appeared to be willing to indulge her outrageously. But her
smile slipped just a trifle when the lowering thought occurred to her that he was probably only treating her no
differently than he would a new mistress and that, in ac-
tuality, mistress was her role. It wasn't what she wanted,
but for the moment, she was not going to quibble—she
loved him and she was going to try very hard to make

him love her! Before her pregnancy became too noticeable! She needed desperately to know that it was she that mattered to him and that the coming child would be a cherished addition to the feelings they shared, not the motivating factor!

Entering the house, Maria was pleased to see that, despite Gabriel's comments, it had much to offer. At the rear of the large central hall where they stood, a graceful spiral staircase led upstairs, the hall narrowing as it passed by the staircase and disappeared into the back of the house. On either side of the main hall were two beautifully fashioned sets of carved double doors, and she guessed that they opened into the dining hall and the main *sala.* From behind the doors on the left came the sounds of several voices, and Gabriel glanced inquiringly at the small mulatto woman who came hurrying along the narrow hall beside the staircase, her hands holding an enormous silver tray on which were piled various foodstuffs—cheeses, breads and cold meats and mustard.

"Oh, master!" the young woman exclaimed, her large liquid dark eyes sparkling with good humor. "I am so happy that you have arrived—you have guests and I did not know what to do with them!"

Gabriel laughed, saying easily, "It appears that you are doing just fine, Phoebe. I would only suggest that if you have not done so already, you find some ale and wine and bring it along too."

Phoebe giggled. *"That* I did immediately upon the appearance of Harry Morgan and Jasper le Clair!" She looked quizzically at Maria, standing silently by Gabriel's side.

Reminded of his duties, Gabriel said lightly, "This is Maria Delgato—she will be your mistress from now on. Maria, this is Phoebe, one of the servants I told you about. Her mother, Delicia, is the cook and despotic ruler, I might add, of the nether regions of the house, but I think that you will find Phoebe very helpful."

Apparently not the least concerned over the stunning impact of his words upon Maria, he took her by the arm and murmured, "And now to face Harry and Jasper—two greater rogues in the Caribbean you will not find!"

Her mind reeling from the cool way he had só casually

explained her position in the household to Phoebe, Maria held back, and grasping the only thing that made any sense, she asked breathlessly, "Jasper le Clair? Who is he? Why was he not with you at Puerto Bello?"

Gabriel's smile widened. "Next to Zeus, he is my dearest friend. His mother was English, his father a Frenchman, one of the aristocracy, but he will not talk of him—and the reason that he was not with us at Puerto Bello is because he usually prefers to sail with the buccaneers out of Tortuga. You will, I think, find him most charming and amusing." Something flickered in the green eyes. "But not," he said on a more serious note, *"too* charming and amusing, I hope!"

Maria lowered her long lashes and with great daring she murmured, "And if I did?"

Oblivious to Phoebe, still standing nearby with the tray, Gabriel swept Maria into his arms, his mouth coming down warmly on hers. He kissed her soundly, and slowly releasing her, he muttered thickly, "Then I should just have to kill him!"

Maria's eyes widened. "Your dearest friend," she blurted out, still dizzy from his kiss, "you would kill him?"

The green eyes meeting hers mockingly, he retorted, "He *wouldn't* be my dearest friend if he tried to take you from me!"

A little glow around her heart, Maria said demurely, "Then I shall make certain, Englishman, that I do not find him *too* attractive—after all, I would not want his blood on my conscience."

Both her words and her manner elated Gabriel, and for the first time in a very long time, he was certain that there *would* be a happy future for them together. With far more pleasure and confidence than he had felt only moments before, Gabriel turned away and flung open the double doors. "If you will, sweetling, our guests await us." And with a great flourish he ushered her through the doors, Phoebe following behind them.

Maria's first impression was that the long room was filled with strangers, but then as she saw Pilar seated on a plump-cushioned settee, Zeus standing behind her, one hand resting possessively on her shoulder, she realized that she was mistaken. She also, with an uncomfortable

feeling of uneasiness, recognized du Bois, as the French
buccaneer lolled about in a large chair near the far wall,
his feet propped up negligently on a handsome table of
polished satinwood, apparently indifferent that he marred
the lovely surface. Quickly Maria averted her eyes from
him, and her gaze went to Harry Morgan, resplendent in
green and gold, who stood in the center of the room, gesturing flamboyantly as he made some particular point to
his captivated audience. An exquisitely lovely woman
with flame red hair and gowned in rich silks and satins
in shades of lavender and pale pink sat on a small chair
watching Morgan with undisguised cynicism. It was, however, the tall man who lounged with careless elegance
against the marble mantel of a seldom-used fireplace who
caught Maria's attention. Dark curly hair fell to his broad
shoulders, the bronzed skin clearly marking him as a man
who was seldom inside, but it was the startling blueness
of his eyes in that dark, incredibly handsome face that
made Maria stare. He was undoubtedly the handsomest
man she had ever seen in her life; his features very nearly
perfect, from the sculpted nose and mouth to the perfectly
symmetrical arrangement of the high cheekbones and
firm, masculine chin. His eyebrows were dark, black aristocratic arches over the cerulean blue of his eyes, the
length and thickness of the lashes that surrounded those
slightly slanted blue eyes making Maria just a trifle envious. A woman, she thought idly, as she stared at him,
would give much for those eyes and lashes.

Gabriel noticed her absorption and gave a low laugh.
"You see why I warned you! And unfortunately, he has
the charm to go with his handsome face."

Maria tore her eyes off the gentleman, and looking at
Gabriel, she said softly, "But, *señor*, you are every bit as
handsome—and I much prefer green eyes to blue!"

His voice husky, Gabriel replied, "Sweetheart, I could
wish you would have chosen a better time to make your
preference known—if you continue to look at me that way,
I'm afraid I shall startle our guests by my actions! Now
come and let me introduce you to everyone."

The introductions went smoothly, the lovely lady in
pink and lavender turning out to be Gwendolyn Denning,
and Maria was not certain which of the two gentlemen,

Harry Morgan or Jasper le Clair, had accompanied her to Gabriel's house. Gwendolyn seemed *very* familiar with all the men in the room, and Maria was left with a distinct impression that Gabriel and Zeus were not very pleased by her presence. But then she found her hand in Harry Morgan's and she promptly forgot about the other woman.

"So this is the little wench who has so greatly changed our Dark Angel! I saw you but once, my dear, in Puerto Bello, and I do not think that either of us were at our best. Allow me to make amends for my surly behavior before you condemn me out of hand," Harry said with a gleam of amusement dancing in the dark eyes as he bowed over her hand and lightly kissed it. He sent Gabriel a teasing glance, and then looking back at Maria, he added audaciously, "If you find his protection too wearing, do not forget that Harry Morgan is a generous man!"

Maria felt Gabriel stiffen beside her, and when Harry burst out in uproarious laughter at the expression on Gabriel's face, she realized that the buccaneer Admiral had been teasing him. Gabriel realized it too, a rueful smile at his own quick jealousy curving his mouth.

Harry clapped him jovially on the back and murmured, "Ah, Gabriel, my friend, when have I ever stolen one of your women? Come now, you know that is not Harry Morgan's way."

"But the same could not be said of me," drawled Jasper le Clair as he strolled across the room to where Maria stood. Taking her slim hand in his, the striking blue eyes glittering with amusement, he added in his deep voice, "Lancaster and I have been stealing each other's women for some time now . . . it is a shame that I decided to stay in Tortuga this time instead of joining with Morgan in the attack on Puerto Bello—who knows, it might have been my arms that you ran into."

"Jasper," Gabriel said warningly, "I will not have you plying her with your perfidious charms. She is not *just* one of my women—she is to be—" He stopped suddenly and ended lamely, "She is mine, and not to be trifled with."

Jasper looked surprised, but seeing that Gabriel was deadly serious, an expression of dismay flitted over his perfect features. *"Mon ami,* you know that I would never betray you—*especially* not over a woman!"

There was a ripple of laughter from the others, although the sour cast of du Bois' face seemed to change little, and it was he who said bluntly, "If we could now get back to the Admiral's plans for the next raid . . ."

Phoebe had put down the laden tray and had disappeared during these exchanges, and after Harry had slapped a hunk of cold meat between two thick slices of bread and bitten off a hefty bite, he said, "Aye! It is for that reason that I am here to see you today, Gabriel—I did not know until I arrived here today that you had been away." There was a question in the dark eyes, but when Gabriel offered no explanation, Morgan shrugged and went on smoothly, "The men want to go on another raid. Their money is all gone and they have begun to clamor for us to be at sea again."

"God's wounds, Harry!" Gabriel exclaimed, half-angry, half-amused. "We've been home for less than two months—it is only the first week of October! How could they have spent all the booty from Puerto Bello so soon?"

Harry shrugged again. "You know the men—they throw their money away on women and drink. Your own Jenkins paid five hundred pieces of eight merely to see a strumpet naked! As for the others, some spend as much as two or three thousand pieces of eight in one night gaming and drinking—gold does not last long in the hands of our buccaneers!"

Ruefully, Gabriel admitted the truth of what Morgan said. The buccaneers *did* spend wildly as long as they had the money and the tavern keepers were not loath to put out their best brandy and Madeira for them, the bawdy houses were equally eager to supply them with new whores just arrived from London, the shopkeepers did not hesitate to gain their share of the gold either, happily they would display their best and most costly wares, the gold that flowed from the lavishly careless hands of the buccaneers seldom disappointing any of the various recipients. As for the buccaneers, why should they worry when their money was all gone—there were always more rich Spanish cities and ships to plunder!

Du Bois commented sarcastically, "We are not all like

you, Lancaster—the King of England did not give us a fine plantation! Nor do we sup with the Governor in his fine house! We are poor men, who live by our wits and swords, unlike you with your grand friends and rich lands!"

Du Bois' entire manner was insulting, and it was apparent to the meanest intelligence that he was looking for a fight. Gabriel's face hardened, the hand that had rested beneath Maria's elbow tightening as he fought to keep his temper in check.

Jasper's eyes met Gabriel's, a warning flashing in the blue depths, and not giving Gabriel time to speak, Jasper drawled languidly, "Oh, go away, du Bois! How stupid of you to make remarks like that in a man's own home! Sometimes you do indeed make me regret that we are both of French blood."

With all the indolent grace of a sleek cat, Jasper sauntered across the room to du Bois and dropping his foppish air, he said softly, "Didn't you hear me? I said for you to go away . . . or would you prefer we settle this outside with our swords?"

Du Bois hesitated. If Lancaster had made such an offer, he would have immediately accepted, but his argument was not with Jasper le Clair, and so with a snarled oath, he lurched out of his chair and stalked angrily to the double doors. Over his shoulder he growled, "I will meet you at the rendezvous at the end of the year, Harry." He shot a baleful look at Gabriel, his cold blue eyes resting for a moment on Maria's lovely face, and then he was gone.

In the silence that followed his departure, Jasper said thoughtfully, "I do believe you are going to have to kill him, Gabriel. He holds Maria against you, and I think will not rest until he has settled the situation to his satisfaction." Jasper pulled a face, adding, "While we awaited your arrival, he did nothing but complain about your treatment of him in Puerto Bello—he did not like losing either the women or the fight!"

A smile on his mouth, Gabriel murmured, "And you are so certain I am unable to take care of myself that you coddle me like a babe? Is that why you so quickly leaped into the fray?"

Adopting, as he so often did to hide his true emotions,

the air of a dandy, Jasper replied in mock horror, "But, *mon ami,* we could not have a brawl in front of the ladies; besides, he bores me—he has no tact!"

The strained moment behind them, the atmosphere lightened once again, and after several minutes of desultory conversation, Morgan said, "Gabriel, I would like to speak privately with you and Zeus about this latest venture. Could you both come to my town house this evening?"

Gabriel hesitated, having already formulated other plans for this evening's entertainment that had nothing to do with hearing Harry Morgan's plans for a new attack on the Spanish! Reluctantly he inquired, "Must it be tonight? Could we not meet on the morrow . . . in the afternoon?"

Not well pleased by this decided lack of enthusiasm on the part of one of his most trusted lieutenants, Morgan snapped, "If you think you can spare me, your Admiral, the time!"

Gabriel grimaced. "Harry," he began placatingly, but Morgan had recovered instantly from his fit of temper, and smiling warmly at Gabriel, he said more in his usual manner, "It is no matter, my friend, forgive me my quick words." The dark eyes traveled over Maria's slender body, and a knowing smile on his wide mouth, Morgan said gaily, "I am sure you have other commitments for this evening—and I would rather have your full attention when we talk than to have you thinking of, er, *other* things."

"And speaking of 'other' things, Harry," Gwendolyn broke in with sweet sarcasm, "did you not promise a new silk gown this afternoon?" Her bored gaze swept the room and she added, "Shouldn't we be on our way? After all, Gabriel and Zeus have just returned from some days at sea, and I am sure they are longing to do"—she waved an airy hand—"whatever it is that men do when they return from sea."

An uncomfortable pause occurred, the notion that Gwendolyn Denning was *not* a respectable lady suddenly crossing Maria's mind. It also clarified which of the men had brought the woman with him, and she rather thought that she was glad when, after a few more polite exchanges, it was Morgan who escorted Gwendolyn from the house and not le Clair. Le Clair, she had decided, deserved much better than the likes of Gwendolyn Denning! Especially after he had so gallantly deflected du Bois' barbs against Gabriel!

Jasper departed shortly, and overhearing Gabriel's "Tell Harry not to bring that strumpet here again while Maria and Pilar are in residence!" when the two men said their good-byes at the door, Maria's suspicion that *Señorita* Denning was not very respectable was confirmed. It was only later, when Pilar slipped into the room Phoebe had shown Maria at Gabriel's command, that she learned exactly who Gwendolyn Denning was. Or had been.

Zeus and Gabriel were still downstairs and Maria was dozing lightly on the feather-filled mattress of a massive, heavily draped bed while her bath was being prepared when Pilar came in. The two women exchanged embraces and talked for several minutes, Maria giving Pilar her version of what had happened on the atoll. Eventually though, their conversation came around to this afternoon, and with more curiosity than she would have liked Maria asked, "Who was that woman? Everyone seemed to know her, but I had the feeling that Zeus and Gabriel did not precisely approve of her."

Pilar snorted. "They are fine ones to be giving approval." Her beautiful eyes snapping with remembered temper, she went on, "I knew something was strange by Zeus' manner with her, and as soon as we were alone I taxed him with it—she is a well-known whore! Apparently too, she has been mistress, at least in the past, to both Jasper and Gabriel! Zeus says that Morgan is now keeping her and that Jasper and Gabriel have—" She stopped suddenly and amended uneasily, *"Had* a wager to see which one of them could steal her away from Morgan!"

Chapter Twenty-seven

It was not auspicious news with which to start her return to Port Royal, especially since she strongly suspected that Pilar had taken it upon herself to put the wager in the past tense. But once Pilar had departed to her room, unwilling to contemplate that after all Gabriel had done to keep her he would still be interested in seeking out the charms of Gwendolyn Denning, resolutely Maria turned her thoughts in other directions ... such as the far more pleasant one of remembering the way he had looked at her when he had sent her up the stairs with Phoebe such a short while ago. And the huskiness in his voice when he had murmured for her ears alone, "I shall not be long with Zeus ... and then we shall have the entire night to ourselves. ..."

Maria hugged those words to her, as well as the ones that he had spoken when they had arrived at the house and then later his introduction to Phoebe. It was obvious, even to someone as filled with doubts and fears as Maria, that he wanted her and that he was willing to treat her with more than just kindness. In some respects, that knowledge delighted her, but she didn't think that she could ever be completely resigned to being merely his mistress. It was not a state that someone reared as she had been could ever easily accept. Besides, a mistress was only a temporary creature, and she very much wanted to remain in Gabriel's world for the rest of her life. But if all he offered to her at present was the position of mistress, then she would take it with greedy hands, hoping that in time she could make him love her as she loved him.

Consequently, when Phoebe knocked on the door just a minute later and came in with a small trunk which turned out to be filled with all manner of beautiful intimate apparel and various scented soaps, perfumed oils and spicy-smelling powder, Maria did not disdain them as she once would have. After all, she told herself with a nervous little giggle, if she was to make him mad for her, she needed every weapon at her disposal . . . and if the man was willing to *give* her these weapons, then she would be a fool not to use them!

She and Phoebe spent several minutes exclaiming over the many lovely things which the trunk contained, Phoebe saying, "The master has had these things here for several weeks; I believe he ordered them for you when he was last in Port Royal, just before this latest journey. There is another, larger trunk downstairs too, which, I believe, contains many clothes." She gave Maria an assessing glance. "He has always been a generous man with his women, but he has never been *this* generous, or ever given one command over the household." A speculative look in the brown eyes, she added slowly, "Nor has he ever kept her in this house. You must mean more to him than all the others." Struck by a sudden thought, Phoebe looked again at Maria and added slyly, "Maybe he intends to wed you!"

Maria did not like the reference to other women, but she was comforted by the intelligence that Gabriel was definitely treating her very differently from his usual mistresses, and that information added a further lift to her spirits and a sparkle to the sapphire blue eyes. Sternly repressing the urge to discuss this extremely interesting topic at length with Phoebe, she said firmly, "You should not talk of such things. He might not like it."

Accepting the slight rebuke good-naturedly, Phoebe shrugged and began to carry some of the soaps and oils into the room which adjoined the bed chamber. Over her shoulder she said, "The master has his bath in here. If the water is hot, I shall haul the first buckets up to you."

Maria nodded, thinking that after the time at sea it would be heaven to have a real bath and not just a hasty wash in a bowl. Finding herself still a little worn out by the fits and starts of the past weeks, she lay back down, intending to rest for just a few minutes before exploring her new quarters further. Actually, she thought drowsily, there wasn't much to explore, the room in which she lay was very large, but its contents were few; a thick rug upon the floor, this massive bed and a large armoire were its only contents, and she began to realize what Gabriel had meant when he had said that it was a bachelor's establishment—only the barest necessities were present. A little smile flitted across her lips. She hoped that Pilar and Zeus at least had a bed in their room! As for the bathing room, she would see it in a moment, certain that it would hold very little beyond the tub itself, and she quite rightly guessed that most of the other rooms of the house were empty. Sleepily, she decided that if they were to spend some time in Port Royal it might be very pleasant to see about furnishing the house—*if* Gabriel had been serious in all that he had said to her today.

She must have fallen into a deep sleep because the next thing she heard was the sound of rapping on the door. Struggling awake, she called out, "Come in!" and was just a little disappointed when it was only Phoebe.

Entering the room, Phoebe said, "The water is hot and it is ready to be brought up. Would you like your bath now?"

"Oh, *sí!*" Maria replied, scrambling from the bed, pushing her tumbled hair back away from her face.

Together they walked to the room Phoebe had indicated earlier. Stepping through the doorway, Maria stopped in astonishment at the sight that met her eyes.

Far from holding only a tub, the room and its furnishings were the most decadent she had ever seen in her life! A large reclining sofa covered in crimson-and-gold velvet was set against a wall which was covered in mirrors. There were no windows; tall candles placed throughout the room spilled soft light everywhere; mirrors lined the ceiling; thick rugs of fur lay upon the floor; two wide, softly cushioned chairs in black satin sat on either side of a large painting of a naked man and woman in a blatantly amorous embrace. Tearing her shocked gaze from the naked forms in the painting, Maria let out a gasp of sheer surprise when she at last discovered the tub.

It wasn't until she had taken a few more wondering

steps into this sumptuous and frankly sensuous room that she realized that the object which crowned the dais just beyond the rugs was a tub. But a tub like none she had ever seen before, or probably ever would. Constructed of gleaming gold-shot black marble, it was large enough to hold three or even four people, the sides sloping gently downward; and gingerly looking into it, she saw that it was well over three feet deep. Suddenly remembering the night in Puerto Bello when Gabriel had so tenderly bathed her, she was aware of a trembling weakness stealing through her body. If he wished to join her in her bath as he had said that night ... She swallowed and tearing away her fascinated gaze, she asked helplessly, "What is this place?"

Phoebe giggled. "It was a fancy brothel until the master won it gambling. He had all the furnishings removed, except for this room." She giggled again. "He said that he rather liked it and that he was certain that he would spend many pleasurable hours here."

Flushed with embarrassment at the pictures that flashed through her mind, yet driven to know and hating herself for it, Maria got out bleakly, "Has he ever shared ... ? I mean, did he ever bring ... ?" She stopped, unable to complete her question.

The dark eyes full of amused understanding, Phoebe shook her black head. "No, miss. You are the only woman who has ever seen this room, other than me and my mama." Then, afraid her words might be misinterpreted, she added hastily, "When we clean it! The master has never, would never, lay a hand on one of his servants—he is not *that* sort of man!"

Uncertain whether to laugh or be outraged at the idea that Gabriel's town house had been a former brothel, Maria said weakly, "Oh. I suppose that explains it."

"Yes, miss. And now I'll show you what to do when you want more hot water." Walking across the room, Phoebe stopped before a small cupboard door set in the wall just behind the tub; opening it, she revealed a bucket of steaming water. "Whenever you want more water, you just pull this bell-rope right here, and from down in the kitchen I put on another bucket and pull it up to you. When you want it to go down, you just give two pulls and

I lower it." Looking back at Maria she asked, "If you like I'll start filling the tub right now. It'll take several buckets, so unless you want me to select your night things, I'll get busy."

Still a little flustered about this room and the intimate knowledge in Phoebe's eyes, Maria stammered, "Oh! T-t-that's a-all r-r-right. I am used to being my own maid."

Maria made to leave the room, but she lingered, fascinated in spite of herself. After all, she told herself reassuringly, how many women like her ever saw the inside of a brothel! Taking a second look at the picture of the man and the woman, she suddenly realized shockingly that what she had assumed was merely decorative trim around the large frame were actually human figures in various positions of lovemaking. Her cheeks flaming scarlet, she hastily glanced away, only to have her eyes be drawn back to that scandalous frame. Embarrassed at her own curiosity, uncomfortably conscious of Phoebe in the background, she moved away from the painting, noticing for the first time the tall black-and-red cabinet in the corner. She approached it cautiously, and touching the smooth surfaces, she jumped when Phoebe said carelessly, "Oh, I forgot to tell you about that—it holds some of the master's liquors and wines and such. I put your bath oils and powders in the lower drawer and there are also some towels and the like." Phoebe gave a little laugh. "The master says that sometimes he wonders why he ever leaves this room. He says that someday he might even construct such a room at Royal Gift."

Having no reply to make, Maria smiled blankly and left the room. She was aware of a warmth in the pit of her stomach, and wantonly earthy images engendered by the erotic atmosphere of that room trailed through her mind. Going through the intimate apparel once more, her hands lingered with pleasure on the silks and satins, and she wondered with longing if Gabriel would indeed join her in her bath. The idea was overpoweringly appealing, and her breath quickening slightly, she finally selected a luxurious robe of delicately spun silk, the deep rose color as vivid as the bloom on her cheeks.

Entering the bathing room once again, she saw Phoebe pouring some oils into the water, the scent of roses suddenly floating in the air. Politely dismissing Phoebe, Maria approached the tub with anticipation and a strong feeling of being very wicked. Surely, it was scandalous to bathe in such splendor and luxury, yet the pull of the warm scented depths was too strong, and tossing aside further speculation, she quickly set about undoing her outer clothes.

To her pleasure she saw that Phoebe had laid out a thick towel and some combs and brushes, and standing in her chemise, with fingers that seemed to have become all thumbs, she brushed her long black hair and secured it with a pearl comb on the top of her head, thoughts of Gabriel filling her mind. Her cheeks were flushed and hot when she finally slipped out of the chemise, and flustered by the naked images of her own body that were reflected back from the mirrored wall, with a sigh of relief and delight, she slowly lowered herself into the rose-scented water.

It was every wicked pleasure Maria had speculated it would be, the warm, silky water rising up to her shoulders: and like a child, she playfully kicked her feet, laughing at the sheer enjoyment of the water's caress along her legs and feet. Grasping a large bar of finely milled soap that Phoebe had conveniently left on the edge of the tub, she made a bubbling lather over her arms and shoulders, the smell of roses intensifying as the soap released its own fragrance.

The sound of the door opening didn't alarm her, but even so, her heart began to pound heavily in her breast and she was certain she would die of disappointment if the person entering the room was only Phoebe. She put off looking in that direction as long as she could, but finally driven to know if she had read the message right in Gabriel's green eyes earlier, she glanced over her shoulder, a little quiver of confusion and anticipation tingling through her when she saw that it was indeed Gabriel.

He was wearing a robe of black silk, and there was something almost intimidating about him as he stood there, just a few feet inside the doorway, watching her, the expression in the green eyes hard to define. The dark, lean face gave no clue to his thoughts, and Maria was aware of a feeling of uneasiness until she saw that chiseled mouth curve in a lazy smile. Huskily, he asked, "Do you know that I have been bedeviled for weeks now with dreams of you just as you are at this moment?" Walking swiftly toward her, he stopped just a step away from the tub. The green eyes traveling over her with all the warmth of a caress, he murmured, "But you are far lovelier than any dream, and my dreams did not prepare me for the reality of actually having you here."

Thrilled and nervous at the same time, Maria shyly looked up at him, her entire body suffused with a blush at the frankly carnal promise in his eyes. With a sudden shock, Maria realized that while she loved this enigmatic man with all her being and had come to be a woman in his arms, she had only known the explosive possession of his body three times. Despite all that they had shared, he was still virtually a stranger to her, a beguiling, mesmerizing, magnetic stranger who had both tenderly and savagely taught her body to respond to his, a stranger who was the father of the child that grew even now in her womb.

She swallowed with difficulty, overcome with an agonizing embarrassment that was far worse than the first night he had come to her. Now she knew what to expect, and there was not even the shadow of darkness to conceal the emotions he evoked within her, the candlelight flickering brightly in the room, and she was frightened that he might discover what was in her heart.

Her turmoil was clear to see, and mistaking it for fear of him, Gabriel dropped to his knees by the tub, his hands closing warmly about her naked shoulders. "Nay, nay," he breathed softly against her mouth. "Do not fear me, I mean you no harm . . . I mean only to love you as that sweet body of yours was meant to be loved."

Unmindful of the damage her wet soapy body did to his silken robe, Gabriel pulled her to his chest, and his mouth covered hers in a long searching kiss, a kiss that melted whatever qualms Maria had, if not all of her inhibitions. Nearly giddy with pleasure when at last he lifted his lips from hers, her sapphire blue eyes dark with awakening passion, she muttered stupidly, "Englishman, your clothes, they are all wet."

He smiled, that sensually explicit little smile of his that

made her heart beat even faster in her breast. "Aye, and did you not say much the same thing to me that night in Puerto Bello?" His voice thickened. "And did I not promise that I would have joined you if the tub had been large enough?" He looked at the watery expanse behind her and, his tongue exploring her ear lightly, added, "I believe that this tub is more than adequate to hold us both."

He stood up in one fluid motion, and completely shameless of his own nudity, carelessly he shrugged out of the robe, his state of arousal blatantly revealed. He glanced down at himself and admitted ruefully, "You see, sweet tiger, the effect you have upon me? I am very much afraid that the male of the species is unable to hide his desire." Sinking into the tub and pulling Maria's unresisting body up across his, he whispered huskily, "And, oh, sweetheart, I *do* desire you!"

The setting, the words and the man sent Maria's senses spinning, the warmth she had felt earlier in the pit of her stomach increasing as her body slid along his, the tips of her nipples brushing against his hair-roughened chest, their legs tangling beneath the water. It was all incredibly erotic, the candlelight dancing on the water, the scent of roses filling the air, the mirrored ceiling reflecting back their two bodies in the warm silken water, and helplessly Maria gave herself up to the moment, eager to share with Gabriel all the earthy pleasures she knew they would find in each other's body.

She felt both shy and bold at the same time as she lay there, her cheek resting against his shoulder, her body half on his, the water covering them both like a soft perfumed cloak. Dropping her gaze slightly, through the water she could see their entwined bodies, the whiteness of hers a startling contrast to the sun-darkened bronze of his long length. Fascinated, she stared at him, at the whorls of black curly hair that led from his muscled chest downward until they disappeared between their bodies. His head was laid comfortably against the rim of the tub; one arm was wrapped gently about her waist, keeping her close to him, while his other hand lightly and seductively played with the few tendrils of hair that had escaped from the pearl comb and dangled near her ear.

It was a tantalizing moment; they were here together,

each certain of what the outcome would be, and yet each savoring these precious seconds before passion would overtake them. With wondering eyes Maria continued to stare at his naked body, intrigued by the flat, honey-colored male nipples; and not even aware that she did it, with curious fingers she reached out and brushed them, gratified and startled when Gabriel groaned and the small fleshy nubs beneath her fingers stiffened.

His mouth near her ear, he muttered, "You see, your slightest touch enflames me."

She glanced up, her eyes widening at the green fire in his, at the unguarded expression that was momentarily revealed before his lids dropped and the thick black lashes hid what he was feeling. Breathlessly Maria watched as his mouth unhurriedly descended to hers, his lips warm and compelling as their mouths met, his arms tightening around her. Her eyes closed and with a little sigh of pleasure, her slim arms closed around his strong neck, her body lying fully on his as fervently and passionately she returned his kiss.

A slow sweet fire seemed to ignite within Maria's body, and she almost cried out with disappointment when he lifted his mouth from hers, but then those knowing lips of his slid leisurely down her throat, lingering at the base, his tongue caressing that spot where her pulse beat madly. It seemed to afford him satisfaction, because Gabriel chuckled softly and murmured, "I see that I am not the only one who is easily inflamed tonight." Maria could feel a blush of mortification rising in her cheeks, but then, his hands slipping to her waist, in one quick motion, he lifted her higher from the water, his lips finding her exposed breasts. Unconsciously she straddled his prone form and she gasped out loud at the sudden fierce stab of delight that assailed her as his tongue gently circled her sensitive nipples, his teeth teasingly rolling the swollen tips about in his mouth, stoking the fire that already burned in her body.

The touch of his mouth at her breast was so sweet, so pleasurable that Maria unconsciously arched up closer, her head thrown back, her eyes half-closed in delight as his hands moved up to her rib cage, holding her a willing prisoner to his tongue and lips. Her hands were resting on his broad shoulders; his flat, hard stomach was held between her slender thighs and his manhood, warm and rigid, rose up impudently between her buttocks. Maria trembled in his hands, her blood singing with sensual excitement, and helplessly she pulled his head closer to her throbbing nipples, a soft sound of pleasure escaping from her when he began to suck harder, increasing her arousal.

The sight of them together caught her gaze in the mirrored ceiling overhead, Gabriel's dark head moving slowly across her coral-tipped breasts, his tanned hands splayed out against her back and rib cage. Her face was flushed with desire, her mouth soft and red from his kiss, the sapphire blue eyes dark with passion; and Maria thought she had never experienced anything so deeply erotic in her life.

But she wanted more, and yearningly, her hands cupped his face, bringing his mouth to hers as she kissed him, wanting to give him as much pleasure as he was giving her, and slowly, following his lead, her head slipped lower until it was his nipples that were being so tenderly assaulted, his groan of delight that hung in the air. She suckled him as he had done her, her tongue flicking the honey-colored nipples into stiff little peaks that revealed his growing desire as plainly as his swollen staff.

"Sweet, sweet tiger," he said thickly, "I think that we shall never leave this room, but stay here forever, locked in each other's arms."

He jerked her head up, his mouth finding hers in an increasingly urgent kiss, his hand caressing her flanks and sliding again and again between her thighs, deliberately touching her there, his fingers seeking entrance to her very core. Like warmed wine, desire hot and intoxicating surged through her, and restlessly she moved about, brushing her throbbing breasts across his chest, her fingers wildly clutching at the thick black hair of his head as he caressed her more deeply, his tongue filling her yielding mouth, mimicking the thrusting motions of his fingers. Her body was trembling from the powerful sensations he was creating within her, and consumed with an age-old need to know the possession of the loved one, wanting him with a desperate intensity, Maria felt her emotions spinning helplessly out of control. She wasn't even aware of what she was saying or doing, the sweet passion Gabriel had evoked destroying her inhibitions so completely that all she was aware of was the demanding ache in her loins, an ache that grew with every passing moment. She could not bear the heady ministrations of his tongue and hands any longer, and made bold by the untamed desire that flowed through her, she moaned heedlessly, "Ah, *mi amado!* Take me, please, fill me with you!"

Gabriel's lips lifted from hers and through slitted eyes he regarded her lovely, passion-flushed features. Something that could have been satisfaction flickered across his face, and then his mouth against hers, he said huskily, "Aye, that I will, sweetling; only you shall be the one to guide us tonight." And then before she knew what he was about, he shifted slightly, and with a shock of tingling excitement, she could feel him sliding up into her, her body eagerly accepting the thick hard length of his bulging manhood.

Impaled upon him, full of him, she sat there absorbing this new sensation, her eyes full of wonder and delight at what was happening to her. Gabriel did not seem so much in control of himself anymore, his handsome face tautly held, his breath coming now as rapidly as hers, his hands tightening on her slender hips. Gratified by these signs that he was as gripped by passion as she was, Maria grew more daring, and experimentally she moved up and down upon him, delighted when he groaned out loud his pleasure, the emerald green eyes feverishly bright as he stared at her. "Kiss me," he commanded thickly, "give me your mouth, your sweetness." And blindly, Maria bent forward, her lips pressing ardently against his chiseled mouth.

The kiss he gave her then was hungrily explicit; it was as if until this moment, he had been able to hold himself rigidly in check but could do so no longer, his tongue ravening her mouth, plunging deeply between her lips, fiercely seeking the drugging warmth to be found beyond. Deliriously Maria returned his kiss, loving him, needing him, wanting him, unbearably aware of the potent shaft of male flesh lodged so breathtakingly solid within her.

Gabriel had meant to make love to her slowly, gently,

but he found that he could not. He had been too long
without her, there had been too many nights, and days
for that matter, that his yearning body had burned to lose
itself within the silken heat of hers, and now that they
were at last joined together, all his plans went flying out
of his head. Everything about Maria inflamed his senses,
the intoxicating fervency of her kisses, the delectable taste
and feel of her firm breasts in his hungry mouth, the sat-
iny smoothness of the white skin, the small sounds of
pleasure that came from her when he caressed her, and
he knew that no other woman had ever affected him so
strongly, so intensely . . . and that no other woman ever
would. . . .

The velvety heat of her body around him was almost
more than he could stand, and yet he wished acutely to
prolong this exquisite pleasure, wished to savor the sharp
sensations that were rippling through his big body, wished
to continue to kiss her, to sustain this fever peak in his
blood, to drive her as mad with desire as she was so effortlessly driving him. But he did not think that he could
bear this sweet torment much longer, every little movement Maria made, the slight brush of her nipples on his
chest, the fiery thrusts of her tongue as she returned his
increasingly frantic kisses were all far too stimulating
and his hands dug into her hips, to still the unconscious
movements she had begun to make.

But it was too late for both of them, Maria as aroused
and frantic for release as Gabriel, her body demanding
that she seek out the fulfillment she knew awaited them
both. When Gabriel's hands tightened on her, she moaned
in protest, "Ah, no, *mi amado!* Do not stop me! I cannot
bear this sweetness any longer!"

Her words electrified him, shattering whatever control
he had managed to hold upon himself, and with wildly
urgent motions he began to thrust himself further up
within her, hungrily meeting the downward plunge of her
hips. It was ecstasy for them both, the warm water of the
tub sloshing wildly from their movements, Gabriel's
strong hands holding Maria to him, his mouth hotly possessing hers.

Trapped in a web of frankly carnal sensations, Maria
moved helplessly upon him, her blood thudding in her

veins, the ache in her loins quickening until she thought that there could be no greater ecstasy. But then breathlessly she felt her body convulse, and she cried out in stunned pleasure as wave after wave of exquisite rapture shuddered through her slim body.

Feeling her quiver in his hands, groaning his own intense excitement, Gabriel too swiftly found the pinnacle of pleasure. His loins pumping madly up against her, his lips hungrily locked on hers, he emptied himself into her, the pleasure so sharp and powerful that he shook with it.

And afterward, afterward, there was the sweet bliss of holding Maria close to him, of feeling her damp cheek on his chest, of scattering soft kisses over the top of her small head, of knowing that he had brought her satisfaction. He had no desire to move away from her, no urge to change their positions, his hands gently running up and down her spine as if to reassure himself that she was really in his arms, that this repleteness was not just a figment of his dreams.

A little shy now that passion had spent itself, Maria kept her cheek against his warm chest, listening to the strong beat of his heart, wondering what he was thinking, wondering apprehensively if she had betrayed how much she loved him in the throes of her desire. She was aware of his hands gliding smoothly over her flesh, of the powerful body that lay locked between her thighs, and she longed for this moment to last, for the tranquillity she felt now to stay with her.

It was the chill of the cooling water that finally made them move, Gabriel saying huskily, "Phoebe had better have some more water heated, or I'm afraid we'll soon both be covered in gooseflesh." And reluctantly sliding Maria off his body, he rose and gave a yank to the bell-rope Phoebe had shown Maria earlier. There was a grinding noise in the wall and then a thump. Opening the door, Gabriel hauled out a bucket of boiling-hot water. Dumping it into the tub, he sent down for another one and said laughingly, "And now, sweet tiger, for our bath!"

Startled, Maria could only stare at him as he stood there before her in all his naked splendor, the green eyes glinting with amusement at her expression, the mobile mouth wearing a lazy, contented smile. Stooping, he firmly grasped the forgotten bar of soap, and sinking into the tub once more, he said, "You. shall scrub my back and then I shall do the same for you. . . . I particularly look forward to washing the front of you—especially those cherry-ripe nipples of yours!"

The bath that followed was an exquisite blend of torment and pleasure, Gabriel's hands and fingers boldly exploring her body as he ostensibly washed her, her own uncertain hands traveling less surely over his hard, muscled form. It was a revelation to her: she knew his slightest touch aroused her, but she hadn't known until now that she could do the same to him and she watched with delighted astonishment as his manhood stiffened and grew rigid under her unknowingly provocative soapy ministrations.

With a mixture of reluctance and anticipation, she allowed him to take her from the tub, the manner in which he dried her tingling body making it clear that he found her slender shape utterly enticing. When she reached for the towel to dry him, he shook his head, and scooping her up in his arms, he muttered against her mouth, "Nay, there will be time enough for that another night. . . ."

As he carried her determinedly toward the crimson-and-gold couch, Maria caught a glimpse of the pair of them in the mirrored wall. The candlelight danced on the damp blue-black of his hair, the emerald stud and gold hoop earring clearly seen, the golden rope around his neck gleaming dully. He carried her high against his chest, his sun-bronzed arms dark in contrast to the alabaster fairness of her skin, the coral tip of one of her breasts peeking over his arm, her own wet hair an inky-black stream across her shoulder. Her gaze slipped lower, shyly admiring his rampant state of arousal, before dropping to the elegant length of his long, powerful legs.

He laid her on the couch, his own body swiftly following, his mouth catching hers in a devastatingly carnal kiss. It seemed that he could not get enough of her, his hands roaming possessively, urgently over her body, seeking once again to drive her wild with hungry passion. Maria could deny him nothing and mindlessly she offered herself up to him, a willing partner to the ecstasy they would share.

Not content with what they had experienced earlier, like a man with a urgent craving to assuage, his lips traveled over her, his tongue and teeth gently nipping and tasting, his hands cupping her burgeoning breasts, bringing them to his questing lips. Maria sighed helplessly as his hot mouth tenderly ravaged her nipples, desire languidly curling and swirling in her belly. Overhead, in the mirrored ceiling, the erotic picture they made on the crimson velvet played in front of her eyes—Gabriel's black head on her breast, the muscles of his back rippling beneath his skin, the tight curls at the junction of her white thighs, the rounded firmness of his buttocks and the possessive way the knee of one leg forced itself between hers. Unable to tear her eyes away, she watched mesmerized as her own hands caressed the dark head at her breast, her breath catching in her throat, when Gabriel shifted his body to lay between her thighs and his mouth began a tantalizing trail to her navel. A terrified sort of excitement shot up through her as his lips slipped insistently lower and lower, his tongue sensually laving her flat belly, his one hand moving caressingly through the curls between her thighs, parting her, touching her, sending little tremors of pleasure spinning through her.

Frantically, she reached for him, a frightened yearning leaping in her blood as, with an incredible aching slowness, his mouth slid to the top of one thigh, his teeth lightly biting her, before he suddenly buried his lips in the softness of her womanhood. Maria jerked with a horrified delight, stunned at the wicked pleasure his mouth and tongue lavished on her, alarmed at the new, intensely erotic sensations that he was wreaking upon her body. Dry-mouthed, her breath coming in short little gasps, she stared helplessly overhead, looking on dazedly as he parted her thighs further, his hands sliding around to grip her buttocks, to lift her even nearer to his searching lips and tongue.

Her body seemed not her own; writhing and arching up to meet the fiery thrusts of his tongue, soft moans of animal delight coming from deep in her throat, Maria was totally oblivious to anything but the increasingly urgent demands of her flesh. Shaking with an elemental emotion, she was blind to everything but the sweet fierceness of Gabriel's caress, her very body feeling as if it were splintering apart with pleasure. Restlessly, her hands moved through his hair, her fingers brushing his shoulders, wanting, *needing* to touch him, to somehow impart some of the pleasure he was giving her. Suddenly, she stiffened, ecstasy such as she had never known exploding through her, a shrill whimper of rapture rising from deep within her.

Shocked and perhaps a little frightened by the power of her release, Maria jerked away from Gabriel, curling into a small ball. His hands warm on her shoulders, he pulled her next to him, nuzzling her neck, murmuring, "Nay, nay, love, do not hide from me! Let me see your pleasure so that I may gain pleasure from yours."

His body aching with desire, compelled to lose himself once more in the intoxicating heat of Maria's bewitching flesh, Gabriel kissed her, muttering, "You are mine, all mine and I will never let you go!"

Willingly Maria gave herself up to him, her arms clinging to him, her body eagerly welcoming the hard invasion of his. And then the magic began again as compulsively Gabriel drove himself into her, catapulting them both into sensual oblivion.

Chapter Twenty-eight

THE afternoon was well advanced before Gabriel appeared downstairs, and then despite the lateness of the hour and the look of satisfaction, if not smugness, upon his handsome face, it was obvious that he had not been spending his time sleeping. There were attractive blue shadows beneath the emerald eyes and a certain pleasing haggardness about the lean face that bespoke of time whiled away in pursuits other than slumber!

It had been with great reluctance that he had finally left Maria sleeping exhaustedly in the bed that had been the site of further sweetly frantic lovemaking. He had been insatiable, unable to tear himself away from the beguiling rapture to be found in her heady embrace. Again and again through the night and the morning, he had lost himself within her welcoming flesh, revealing with his big warm body what he could not yet say aloud. But if he had not spoken of his love, he had admitted it fully within his heart, and Maria's intoxicating and ardent willingness in his arms had lessened some of the fears and doubts that had been in his mind. After last night, after the ecstasy they had shared, he could not believe that she did not feel deeply about him—and he was suddenly positive that whatever had given her that unhappy melancholy air, it was *not* because she had not been returned to Diego! For just a second he relived that moment she had cried out, "Ah, *mi amado!*" She had called him her love! And he did not, *would* not believe that it had only been the wildness of the moment that had brought the words from her. She must love him! he thought fiercely. His face softened. Soon, he would force her to tell him again, and this

time, it would not be in the throes of passion. A tender
little smile crossed his hard face. And then, he would tell
her of *his* love, tell her and show her!

Finding Zeus and Pilar just sitting down to enjoy the
main meal of the day, he joined them in the long dining
salon, saying lightly, "Maria is still asleep. I've requested
Phoebe to take her up a tray around five o'clock, if she
has not arisen by then."

Pilar raised an eyebrow but, for once, made no comment. It was Zeus who spoke up. A teasing glint in the
tawny eyes, he murmured. "If your appearance is any
indication of how the night was spent, I am surprised that
you are still not abed!"

Gabriel merely grinned, and helping himself to a suc-
culently browned thigh from the roasted chicken Delicia
had prepared for dinner, he admitted ruefully, "If I had
not promised Harry that I would meet with him this
afternoon, I can assure you, my friend, that I would *not*
be down here putting up with the likes of you!"

Zeus chuckled. "And that I know to be the truth, *mon
ami!*" A serious look replacing his amusement, he asked.
"Do you mean to sail with him this time?"

Gabriel shook his head decisively. "Nay. Both Harry
and Modyford are aware that I mean to give up buccaneering. . . ." An odd expression flickered across his face,
a mixture of wonder, tenderness, bewilderment and uncertainty. "Having found Maria, I . . ." He stopped as if
conscious that he was thinking out loud, and to Pilar's
utter astonishment, a slight flush stained his dark cheek.
Somewhat gruffly, he said, "Before we left for Puerto Bello, I had told both Morgan and the Governor that I was
fairly certain that it would be my last outing with the
Brethren." He grimaced. "I don't think that either one of
them believed me at the time—or is particularly happy
with my decision. Modyford, of course, is more inclined to
view it philosophically, but Morgan . . ." He frowned.
"Harry is not going to like it!"

Gabriel was right. Harry didn't like it, and he made his
displeasure abundantly clear barely an hour later as Zeus
and Gabriel sat comfortably in Morgan's house located
just a few streets away. Jasper le Clair was also present,
his cerulean blue eyes watching appreciatively as Harry

Morgan strode violently up and down the large, richly furnished room in which the four men had met.

Morgan was magnificent in his rage; his shoulder-length curly black hair nearly bristled with indignation, the dark eyes flashing wrathfully and the fine nostrils of the handsome Greek nose flaring with anger. Even that melodious voice betrayed his great vexation, the tones less rounded, less mesmerizing as he growled, "I do not believe what I am hearing—one of the bravest, most renowned of the buccaneer captains is *not* interested in raiding Cartagena!"

Mildly, Gabriel said, "Harry, the captains have not voted on the matter yet—it may not be Cartagena that will be your goal. You won't know until the rendezvous where the Brethren mean to strike."

"Bah! So you think that worries me—*I* want to go to Cartagena, and I'll wager a year's worth of wine that the men will follow my lead!" His voice dropping persuasively, Morgan went on almost pleadingly, "Think of it, Lancaster! Cartagena, the richest city on the Spanish Main! Who knows what marvelous treasure we will find there! Say you will sail with me this one last time!"

Regretfully Gabriel shook his dark head. "Nay, Harry, I will not—there are things that I must be about."

The black eyes narrowed dangerously. "It is that Spanish wench, is it not? It is she who has turned you into the mewling, weak-spirited creature I see before me now! By God's wounds! If I had known, I would have slain the slut that very first night!"

Gabriel stiffened, the green eyes suddenly hard and cold. His voice icy with rage, Gabriel snarled softly, "I take those words from no man, not even you Harry . . . and lay your tongue on Maria again and I'll fry it before your lying eyes!"

Zeus and Jasper exchanged worried glances, Jasper leaping into the fray instantly. *"Mes amis!"* he cried lightly. "Come now, what is this? Fighting over a woman? How can it be? Surely, there is a bond between us all that will not let this small misunderstanding ruin our friendships." Slapping Morgan on the back, he urged, "Harry, you must not let your disappointment take such an ugly turn." Sending Gabriel a limpid glance, he murmured,

"And Dark Angel, you must not be so quick to take umbrage over something as trivial as a mistress."

Only a little appeased by Jasper's intervention, Gabriel snapped, "She is no mere mistress—I mean to marry her!"

There were exclamations of startlement from Jasper and Morgan, but Zeus laughed, saying delightedly, "Did I not tell you 'Arry! Did I not tell you at Puerto Bello?"

Morgan suddenly smiled, his bad temper vanishing as quickly as it had surfaced. "Forgive me, Lancaster! I meant your lady no slur." Wryly, he admitted, "It is as le Clair stated, I am gravely disappointed to lose you, and I let my damnable temper force me to say things of which I am now ashamed."

Relaxing, relieved that he was not going to be at dagger's drawing with Harry, Gabriel conceded generously, "And I am far too quick to take offense where Maria is concerned. But now to prove that I am not totally *uninterested* in your plans, tell me what has been decided upon so far."

The tense moment gone, the men talked for several minutes longer, Morgan imparting the information that he had set the rendezvous with the buccaneers for *Ile-a-Vache*—Cow Island, off the south coast of Hispaniola, and for sometime near the first of the year. His regret obvious that Gabriel and Zeus both would not be part of this newest undertaking against the Spanish, Morgan asked hopefully, "Are you positive that you will not reconsider?" Adding slyly, "After all, there is still Diego Delgato to contend with."

"Bring me word," Gabriel replied harshly, his green eyes savage, "of his whereabouts and I shall be there, have no doubt of that!"

Morgan grunted, satisfied that he had not entirely lost one of his favorite and best captains. There was some more desultory conversation, and then escorting the three men to his door, Morgan bid them all good evening.

Walking through the swiftly falling twilight of the tropics, Gabriel, Zeus and le Clair slowly made their way to one of the waterfront taverns that had known their patronage in the past. *"Mes amis,"* Jasper said thoughtfully as they seated themselves in one of the murky, smoke-hung corners of the tavern, "I find it difficult to believe all that has happened since last we met." A twinkle in his blue eyes, he looked at Zeus and marveled, "The great Zeus has grown a fine crop of curly black hair upon his bald pate, has got himself a wife and gotten her with child and *you* . . . *!*" He glanced teasingly at Gabriel, "You, the man I had thought viewed the unholy state of matrimony with as much aversion as I, are about to be married—and to the one woman I would have sworn you would hold in contempt above all others!" His beautiful mouth curved in a reminiscent smile. "Ah, the times we have shared, *mes amis!* The wine we have drunk, the women we have shared, the ships we have plundered and the riches we have spent! I find it hard to accept that those times will never come again." He cocked an eyebrow at Gabriel. "Or do I misread the situation—will you perhaps be a husband like Morgan? A wife in the country and a mistress or two in town—or anywhere else you please?"

Distaste on his handsome face, Gabriel said quietly, "Nay. I want no other than my own prickly Spanish rose." Smiling, he added, "Which reminds me—you will win our wager by default—I leave the seduction of the fair Gwendolyn to you!"

Jasper's beautiful features danced with mockery. *"Non! Non!* Instead I will bestow upon your firstborn that sum! Now tell me, when are you to wed?"

Gabriel looked sheepish. "I do not know, I have not yet asked Maria."

As the evening passed and tankard after tankard of ale was quaffed, Zeus and Jasper took great delight in putting forth increasingly ribald and outrageous situations in which Gabriel could declare himself. A lazy smile on his long mouth he took their comments in good part, thinking that he was lucky in his friends and wishing that some of the lighthearted schemes suggested for winning his lady could actually be of use to him in gaining his desire.

It had been so simple to propose marriage to Elizabeth, and perhaps what had made it so easy had been the lack of deep feeling on his part. He had been fond of her, but if she had spurned him, nothing but his pride would have been touched. With Maria, however, the situation was entirely different, the powerful emotions that she aroused in his breast could not be lightly dismissed, nor was there the comfort of having known her since childhood, of knowing that his offer of marriage would be happily, joyously accepted. And then there was the unpleasant fact that she was a Delgato. . . .

For a moment a frown creased his forehead. Was he deluding himself? Because he no longer really associated her with that hated name, did it mean that she had forgotten that he was a Lancaster? Would she be willing to bear that name? Did the feud their families had started generations ago matter to her? Her body had responded to him, but did her heart?

Maria was asking herself much the same thing. Having eaten ravenously everything that had been on the tray that Phoebe had brought as Gabriel had ordered, then bathing and dressing, she had enjoyed a pleasant coze with Pilar. She had been disappointed that Gabriel had not been downstairs when she had finally entered the main salon, but as the hours had passed and night fell, she was conscious of a sharp sensation of dismay. Having satiated his body with hers, was he now indifferent to her? Had last night meant *nothing* to him? She could not believe that it was so, but as she prepared for bed, her heart was heavy in her breast. She could not conceive that he could have made love so sweetly to her, could have lavished those many shocking intimacies that he had upon her and yet not feel *some*thing for her. But, she wondered miserably as the hour struck midnight and she still lay alone in her bed, had it been lust . . . or love that brought him to her?

The questions in both of their minds remained unanswered, but later that night when Gabriel slipped into her bed and pulled her fiercely into his embrace, their bodies knew the answers, *all* the answers. . . .

Because it had been decided previously that Zeus and Pilar would be leaving for Havre du Mer the next morning, everyone was up early and eating breakfast in the dining salon at seven o'clock. Maria was inordinately thankful that Pilar was still with her for this first meeting with Gabriel outside of the intimacy of their bedroom. It made things much easier for her, and she even managed to act as if she had not just spent the past two nights making wild, passionate love to the imperturbable stranger who sat at the head of the table. But she could not hide all of the signs, and every time Gabriel's warm green gaze rested on her face, to her mortification, Maria could feel a hot flush staining her cheeks. Gabriel thought he had never seen anything quite so adorable and a silly little smile curved his mouth.

Suddenly shyer than she had ever been with him, Maria viewed the eventual departure of Zeus and Pilar with a delicious apprehension. There would be no guests to demand Gabriel's attention; no reason for him to leave the sweet sanctuary of her bed. . . . Certain everyone could read the lascivious thoughts that were chasing through her head, Maria suddenly hugged Pilar tighter and muttered, "I will write and let you know when we are at Royal Gift. There is something I must talk about with you."

Pilar looked at her, but Maria was already turning away to be engulfed in Zeus' hearty embrace. A few more exchanges of conversation and then Pilar and Zeus were gone.

The house seemed very quiet without them, and wandering restlessly about the large salon, *very* aware of Gabriel's eyes upon her, Maria stammered breathlessly, "W-what d-d-did you p-p-plan to do n-n-now?"

A slow sensual smile lifted the corner of his mouth. "Hmmm, I can think of several things that I would like to do, but I do believe that when we arrived I promised you a free hand to refurbish the house. Would you like to go shopping? There is a fine cabinetmaker's shop on Honey Street, and right next to it is an upholstery shop that I am told has many rich fabrics and such. Shall I escort you there?"

It was an offer no woman alive could have resisted, and with a gratifying harmony, they spent the next several hours pleasurably mulling through the wares offered by the cabinetmaker and his neighbor, the upholsterer. There was a gaiety about both Gabriel and Maria, both falling deeper and deeper in love with the other, both cherishing this delightful and unexpected interlude. They argued amiably over the merits of a gilded wood-framed sofa upholstered with a Beauvais tapestry as opposed to a far darker and heavier-styled one in leather, Maria saying with an enchanting gurgle of laughter, "Señor! Did you not promise *me* the choice?"

Smiling besottedly, Gabriel replied generously, "Aye, so I did! And if I must live with a Beauvais tapestry to keep that fetching look on your face, that I shall and be glad of it!" It was all very silly and they enjoyed themselves immensely; it was only when Maria lingered over a delicately wrought cradle of fine English oak that her light air vanished. Dare she ask him for it? How would he react? With pleasure? Or rage? Her courage deserting her, she quickly walked away from the cradle, but Gabriel had noticed her absorption, and a small frown marred his forehead. As they walked unhurriedly toward the town house, he shot her a keen glance, instantly connecting Zeus' statements upon their return to Port Royal and Maria's marked interest in the cradle.

Pilar had been quite sick in the beginning of her pregnancy and Maria had been sick some mornings aboard the *Dark Angel*, and now she was looking at cradles! He swallowed as a sensation of delight snaked down his spine. Was she pregnant? Did his child even now grow beneath her breast? Conscious of a rising elation, his arm suddenly tightened possessively around her waist as they walked, his heart welling with tenderness. A child! The child that would bind her to him! But then the exceedingly painful thought occurred to him that she might not be happy about bearing *his* child, that she might very well resent her situation and that it would be one more barrier between them.

Keeping his suspicions to himself, when they made love that night, Gabriel was incredibly gentle with her, his caresses dallying leisurely in the region of her stomach, his hands tenderly cupping her breasts, as if he tried to judge for himself her pregnant state. He could tell nothing—her stomach was flat and smooth, her breasts small and firm—but by some simple arithmetic of his own, if she was indeed with child, from her condition, he knew that there was only one possible time that she could have conceived—that first day at Royal Gift!

He was conscious of a feeling of regret—he had not been overly kind to her then, and he would have wished that their child had been conceived under different circumstances. Pulling her to him, he dropped a kiss upon her dark head. *If* she was already pregnant, their second child, he swore softly, would come to her with love and joy, he would make sure of it!

A long time after Maria had fallen asleep at his side, Gabriel lay there, thinking. He yearned to have matters settled between them; wanted her as his wife, wanted urgently to know if he had read the signs right and that she was carrying his child. But he hesitated, not knowing what was in Maria's heart and yet, not so oddly enough, not quite ready to put his hopes to the test. The present was far too sweet, Maria's soft, warm body pressing trustingly against his long length as she slept—he wanted nothing to disturb the pleasant tenor of their lives. There was time, he told himself sleepily. Time in which to win her heart, time in which to persuade her gently to tell him of the child. . . . He had forced her in so many things that now, loving her as he did, he wanted her to tell him of her own accord, *not* to have him badgering the truth out of her!

Breakfast that next morning was interrupted by a surprise visit from Jasper le Clair. The blue eyes startlingly vivid in his dark face, he promptly took the seat Gabriel offered and carelessly helping himself to a hot biscuit just from the brick oven, he said easily, "Morgan sails today! We go with the evening tide and I wanted to say *adieu* before we left." He looked at Gabriel. "I shall sorely miss you; it is always good to have a friend at your side when you go into battle."

Jasper did not stay long, his mocking blue eyes lazily gauging the state of affairs between Maria and Gabriel. Standing alone in the doorway as he prepared to leave, Jasper asked quizzically, "Have you not yet settled things between you? She does not look to me like a woman who has just received a proposal of marriage."

Gabriel grimaced ruefully. "Someday, my friend, you will be faced with the same situation, and then I wonder if you will be so bold! It is not easy laying one's heart before a female—especially a female such as Maria!"

Jasper shuddered. "My dear fellow! Do not wish marriage on me! The Gwendolyn Dennings of the world suit me very well." A negligent wave of his hand and Jasper was gone. Watching that tall, elegant figure disappear down the street, Gabriel was conscious of a little stab of regret that he was not also putting out to sea with the evening tide. But then hearing Maria's voice as she spoke to Phoebe in the hallway behind him, he firmly shut the door. His buccaneering days were over—especially if he was about to gain a wife and child!

But somehow in the days that followed, there never seemed to be the right opportunity for him to broach the sensitive subject. At night, Maria welcomed him to her bed eagerly, and it was in those warmly intimate moments that he nearly blurted out his offer of marriage, but with passion blurring his brain, the right words would not come and afterward . . . well, afterward he was too replete and satiated to think of very much but how sweet she was in his arms. At least three different days he had attempted to bring himself to the sticking point, and each time Phoebe had entered the main salon, announcing that another tradesman had arrived with more wares to display to the lady of the house—word had traveled swiftly that Lancaster was setting up his town establishment. Cursing under his breath, he had stalked from the room, leaving Maria to stare openmouthed with astonishment after him. Darkly, he wondered if he was going to have to abduct her merely to propose marriage!

Four days after Morgan sailed, an event occurred which for the moment pushed the vexing question of marriage to the back of his mind. The thirty-four-gun frigate *Oxford* arrived in Port Royal, the first royal ship to be assigned to Jamaica since 1660. She had been sent out by the King's brother, the Duke of York, to help defend the island against Spanish attack and, ostensibly, to help put down piracy. The arrival of the ship itself did not disturb Gabriel, but it was the letter she carried that disrupted all his neatly made plans for the future. The *Oxford* had not dropped anchor two hours before a messenger from the Governor was at Gabriel's door informing him that the Governor wished to see him—immediately.

A frown on his handsome features, Gabriel ordered his horse brought round and a short while later found himself seated in the large room that Modyford used as his office.

The Governor sat behind a handsome desk of oak and it was apparent from his expression that he was a trifle uneasy about the letter he gravely handed to Gabriel after the initial greetings were over. Clearing his voice nervously, Modyford said, "The, um, captain of the *Oxford* brought this with him."

His curiosity sharpening, Gabriel glanced at the seal, recognizing instantly whose it was. He looked back at Modyford. "Do you know what is in this letter?"

Modyford moved his well-fleshed frame uncomfortably in his chair. Reluctantly, he admitted, "Perhaps."

Frowning, Gabriel put an end to the suspense, tearing open the packet and quickly scanning the contents of the letter within. His frown did not abate; if anything, it increased. His voice deceptively mild, he asked, "And what precisely did you write to your noble cousin the Duke of Albemarle that finds me now the recipient of a personal letter from the King of England . . . a letter that begs me in the name of our long friendship *not* to forsake my position among the buccaneers, but to stay near them so that he can rest easy, knowing that I will not let these unruly pirates cause him any embarrassment."

Modyford looked decidedly embarrassed. "I wrote to Albemarle *before* you left for Puerto Bello with Morgan—you had disclosed then that you had considered making it your last association with the Brethren, and I merely *mentioned* in my letter to him that I viewed it with some reservations." Hastily, he added, "I never conceived that he would talk to the King about it, or that the King himself would request that you continue to sail with them!" A little hesitantly, he continued, "There is much merit though in this plan—I can rely on your reports—Morgan does not always tell the truth; sometimes he is given to a great deal of, um, *em*bellishment! From you I get accurate reports about the Spaniards *and* the buccaneers." His face regretful, Modyford said earnestly, "If I had known that my cousin would go this far, I swear that I would never have broached the subject." Not liking the set expression on Gabriel's face, he inquired carefully, "And, um, what do you intend to do now that this letter has arrived?"

Gabriel sent him a derisive glance. "My dear sir, when

the King of England requests a favor of you, you do *not* refuse!"

Unhappy and yet pleased at the same time, Modyford sank back a little easier in his chair. "Will you sail immediately?"

Shaking his head, Gabriel said thoughtfully, "Nay. There are things that I must settle before I leave, and the meeting of the buccaneers is not until the first of the year. I will sail at the end of the month or the beginning of November; it all depends on . . ." He stopped, the fact that he would be forced to leave Maria suddenly striking him with the force of a blow. Slowly, he said, "It has been my intention these past days to marry Maria Delgato—this letter only makes it more imperative. When I sail, I want her position secure, I do not want her to be at anyone's mercy should I fall in battle. As my wife, as acknowledged mistress of Royal Gift, even if I die, she will be well cared for and will not be thrown willy-nilly onto the streets of Port Royal to suffer an ugly fate."

Modyford's slightly plump features split into a beaming smile. "Did I not," he fairly crowed, "suggest just such a thing some weeks ago? This is wonderful news—a marvelous solution to a highly irregular situation, considering who she is! I cannot tell you how pleased I am with your decision! As the wife of a loyal Englishman, any inquiries for her release I can safely turn aside, making it clear that it is unthinkable to separate a man and wife."

Gabriel was not certain whether the Governor was genuinely happy because he was getting married or because his marriage solved a sticky little problem for him. But then Gabriel grinned. What did it matter? Modyford was always the cynic and always quick to make certain that no wind of blame ever blew *his* way!

Leaving the King's House a few minutes later, Gabriel's step was not as light as it could have been. He could not disobey the request of his sovereign, and yet for the first time in his life he resented the royal interference. The plain and simple fact of it was that he did not wish to leave Maria, that he was eager to settle down to the tranquil life of a planter, the only dark cloud on his horizon the knowledge that Diego Delgato still lived. His heart was no longer with the Brethren of the Coast, and he viewed the prospect of falling in with Morgan's plans for Cartagena with great displeasure. But then he shrugged. There was nothing for it; with the King's letter burning a hole in his coat pocket, his course was clear and he must follow it.

There was much to be done if he was to sail within the next few weeks, not the least of it, gathering up a crew— most of the buccaneers had sailed with Morgan, including some of the men that he considered his own, and re-signedly he threw himself into the task of preparing the *Dark Angel* for sea once more. But as the days followed only half of his mind was on what he was doing; the other half was filled with thoughts of Maria and the vexing problem of marriage.

Maria had been obviously disappointed when he had broken the news that he must sail at the end of the month, her beautiful blue eyes darkening with dismay, the soft mouth having a decided droop to it. She had been openly distressed that after having stated that he was giving up the buccaneering life, a scant time later, he was prepar-ing to sail again. Unwisely, perhaps, Gabriel had held back the information that it was not of his own choice, that it was because of royal command that he was taking to the sea once more. Used to making his own decisions independent of outside interference, Gabriel never saw any reason to explain *why* he was leaving and not so *un*-expectedly Maria thought the worst—she had bored him already and he could not wait to be away from her.

The bubble of joy that had been rising within her burst, and unable to help herself, she began to withdraw from Gabriel, feeling that she must mean little or nothing to him that he could so easily abandon her in Port Royal, her only friend, Pilar, far inland at Havre du Mer. When he sailed, with him sailed her protection, and she would be left a penniless stranger in a foreign land, at the mercy of brutal men like du Bois. But even more frightening was the prospect of never seeing Gabriel again—men died on expeditions such as this, and the terrifying thought of his possible death wracked her slender body. Not only would she face the unbearable pain of a world without the laughing, green-eyed Englishman in it, but what of her eventual fate and that of her unborn child? Not even the warmth of his big, hard body during the night could drive out the chill that was insidiously spreading through her as the next few days passed.

The *Oxford* intruded upon their lives once more—the captain, unfortunately, killed the ship's master and was forced to flee for his life, leaving the *Oxford*, the most powerful English ship in the Caribbean, without a captain. Modyford requested Gabriel's presence once more at the King's House; and between them, they decided that since Gabriel could not take command, Edward Collier, a privateer well-known to them both and one of Morgan's captains during the raid on Puerto Bello, should be given command of the ship. And as the *Oxford* had been sent out with express orders to help stamp out piracy and as the best use of her would be as a privateer she promptly sailed away in search of prey—prey other than the buccaneers of course.

Having seen the *Oxford* away, Gabriel redoubled his efforts to have the *Dark Angel* provisioned and primed and ready to set sail herself as soon as possible. Deliberately Gabriel did not inform Zeus of his plans. He needed Zeus here in Jamaica to see after Maria once he had sailed, and he felt strongly that at least *one* of them should be able to enjoy the delights of marriage. To his pleasure he discovered that the one-eyed Jenkins and some others of his usual crew had chosen not to sail with Morgan and that they were more than agreeable to sign on with him. In less than a week after receiving the letter from the King, Gabriel had the *Dark Angel* nearly ready to sail; and it was then that he finally was able to turn his complete attention to the problem uppermost in his mind, Maria and their marriage. . . .

Helplessly he had watched her grow increasingly pale and strained, but there had been nothing that he could do, not even his devastatingly urgent lovemaking had seemed able to pierce the protective shell she had erected about her. A thousand times, he cursed the interference of Modyford. A thousand times, he cursed the powerful emotions that seemed to have turned him into a weak-willed, spineless creature who continued to make excuses for postponing the moment he must reveal what was in his heart.

Finally he could bear it no longer, and returning determinedly to the town house one morning during the third week of October, he discovered Maria being violently sick upstairs in their bedroom. His face curiously devoid of expression, dispassionately he helped her recover her composure, handing her a bowl of warmed water to cleanse herself and even gently sponging her flushed face.

Maria was in an agony of embarrassment. So far she had been able to hide from him this distressing morning occurrence, and to be found in this condition was not what any woman would have been comfortable with—especially not considering the uncertainty between them. When Phoebe had come and taken away all signs of her loss of breakfast and Maria had sipped a soothing cup of mint tea, Gabriel asked quietly, "Is there something that you would like to tell me? Something that I should know?"

Utterly miserable that he found her in such a distressing situation and that now he would know of the child, to give herself time to think, Maria took a deep fortifying gulp of the hot tea and, of course, promptly burned her tongue. Putting down the china cup with a clatter on the small tray nearby, she fiddled with the folds of her silken skirts, wishing that she did not have to tell him under these circumstances, wishing that she could have more time, that she had some other choice. . . .

Gabriel forced the issue. She was seated on their bed, looking, he thought unhappily, heart-rendingly forlorn, the silky black hair tumbling in curly disorder about her still-flushed cheeks, the sweet mouth that gave him such pleasure, drawn and pale. Easing himself onto the bed beside her, he captured one of her restlessly moving hands, and dropping a warm kiss on the palm, he asked softly, "Are you with child?"

Maria swallowed nervously, overwhelmingly aware of his vital presence so close to her. Refusing to look at him, she admitted baldly, *"Sí."*

There was such a rush of joy through his veins that Gabriel was nearly dizzy from it. Pulling her into his strong arms, he kissed her hungrily, murmuring, "Sweetheart! Why have you not told me? Are you not pleased?"

Dazedly Maria stared at his dark face, noticing with wonder the blazing delight in his green eyes, the satisfied curve of his mobile mouth. "You are not displeased?" she croaked.

He smiled tenderly. "Nay, I am most happy . . . the only thing that would make me happier would be if you would marry me. Would you?"

Maria's heart seemed to stop beating, a wild rush of mingled elation and despair surging through her body. She had yearned for this moment, had wanted it with every fiber in her being, but now that he had offered her his name, she wondered at his reasons. Was it *just* because of the child? What of his heart? she cried silently. What of love?

Gabriel mistook her hesitation, and his face hardening, he said coolly, "I am sorry that my proposal gives you such pause, but you really have no choice in the matter— I will not leave you here in Port Royal without the protection of my name, and my child will not be born a bastard! You *will*," he finished grimly, "marry me!"

Chapter Twenty-nine

IT was not the wisest thing that he could have said, and he swore violently to himself the split second the words left his mouth. After all his dithering, after all his plans *not* to force her, what did he do but snarl out an ultimatum. Somehow he wasn't at all surprised when her unhappy air disappeared in an instant and the lovely blue eyes suddenly sparkled with rising temper.

In spite of its being one of her dearest wishes, it couldn't be expected that Maria would meekly accept his words as final. That damnable Delgato temper surging up through her slender body, she gritted out furiously, "You cannot force me to wed you!"

Exasperation at his own folly mingled with a sort of angry despair. He loved her! He wanted nothing more in this world than to have the right to cherish her, to claim her as wife, but her not-so-startling reaction did nothing for his own temper. Torn between the desire to shake her until her teeth rattled and the equally strong desire to kiss her mindless, Gabriel glared at her. "Would it be," he finally snapped, "such a terrible fate being my wife?" And completely forgetting the one thing that he should have said, he went on harshly, "You would have everything that I possess at your command—Royal Gift, this house, money, whatever. You are not indifferent to me, so do not try to tell me that you have taken me in aversion—the time for *that* was in Puerto Bello!"

Miserably Maria looked away from him, ashamed and disgusted with herself for letting her unruly temper create another unpleasant scene between them. She did not, she admitted bleakly, want to argue with him, she wanted passionately only to fling her arms around his neck and tell him, "Yes! Yes! I will marry you!" But even more importantly, she wanted, *needed* desperately to hear him say at least *one* word of love. At least give her some sign that this was not merely a marriage of convenience, that the coming child had little to do with his proposal. Wearily, she realized that she was acting foolishly, that he would never love her, even if he did enjoy her body, and that half a loaf would be far better than none. She blinked back a sudden rush of tears and in a low, saddened voice, she muttered, "You are right, Englishman, it would not be such a terrible fate to be your wife . . . and . . . and I am not indifferent to you."

Not the most gracious acceptance, Gabriel viewed it with extreme distaste. He did not want, had never wanted her to marry him simply because she had to, and it was obvious to the meanest intelligence that she was not overjoyed by the situation. Hurt, bewildered and still very angry, he drawled sarcastically, "Well! I am glad that you acknowledge it!" The green eyes hard and unfriendly, he demanded, "But tell me, sweet viper, if it would not be *such* a terrible thing and you are not indifferent to me, why do you hesitate?"

Maria could not meet his eyes, did not want him to see what was in her heart, frightened of betraying her love for him. Her eyes locked on her lap, she admitted forlornly, "I had hoped to marry for love. . . ." A little waver in her voice, she continued, "It is not very pleasant to know that you merely use my body and that the child is the only reason that you are even suggesting marriage now."

An arrested expression on his handsome features, Gabriel stared at her downbent head, the wildest surmises flashing through his brain. His heart beginning to beat with thick heavy strokes, he reached for her chin with fingers that only shook slightly. Cupping her chin, he turned her face to his, and a curious flicker in the emerald eyes, he asked warmly, "And if I told you that the child had *nothing* to do with my proposal? That it has been my most greatly desired wish these past days to make you my wife? What would you say to that?"

Maria's mouth went dry, the pulse at the base of her

throat beginning to beat madly, a look of dawning wonder in her lovely eyes. "What?" she finally got out breathlessly. "What did you say?"

An incredibly tender smile flitted across his mouth, and his confidence increasing enormously with every passing second, his lips very near hers, he murmured huskily, "I said that it has been my most greatly desired wish to make you my wife. I think of little else but keeping you with me always, of always knowing that you are near."

"Oh!" Maria exclaimed nervously, almost unable to believe the evidence of her eyes and ears. But it was there for all to see, the deep love he felt glittering in the depths of the green eyes, the powerful emotions that moved him, obvious in the vibrant tones of his voice. Hardly daring to believe what was before her, a little frisson of delight shooting through her veins, she stared at him, her own love and uncertainty clearly revealed by the agitated flush on her cheeks, the brightness of the gaze that met his.

His lips brushed hers teasingly, his arms slowly closed around her, pulling her closer to him. "Could you not guess?" he whispered against her mouth. "Could you not tell every time that I made love to you that I was burning with love for you?" He kissed her unresisting lips lightly, savoring their warmth and sweetness. "Why else," he asked softly, "did I give you silks and satins; lay everything I own at your feet? Why else did I take such care with you that first night in Puerto Bello?"

Maria jerked slightly from the blissful, unbelievable dream in which she was drowning. Astonishment apparent, she cried, "Even then?"

"Even then," he answered deeply. "I do not know *when* I first began to love you, I only know that I could never bring myself to hurt you, that you have twisted my emotions from the very first." Almost accusingly, he went on, "Why else did I linger on Hispaniola and nearly lose my life in the process, if it was not because your sweetness drove every sane thought from my mind? Why else would I refuse to give you back to Diego?" He shook her gently. "You sweet little simpleton! I adore you!"

Tears of joy filling her eyes, Maria flung her arms around his neck, and hugging him as though she would never let him go, she muttered gruffly, "Oh, Englishman!

I never thought that you would say it! I was so afraid! Afraid that you would always view me as an enemy, that I had let my stupid pride drive you away and that you cared nothing for me!"

Nearly dizzy from the sheer exhilaration that was pumping madly through his veins, Gabriel brought his mouth down urgently on hers, all the love he felt, all the emotions he had kept carefully hidden blazingly revealed in that yearning kiss. They were both breathless when he finally lifted his head, and his expression tender, he murmured, "I tried very hard to remember that you were a Delgato, but it was useless! And now," he added softly, "it does not matter, does it? For soon you will be a Lancaster, will you not?"

"Oh, yes! Please! I would like that above all things!" Maria replied eagerly, the sapphire eyes brilliant with joy.

He kissed her again and with complete abandon Maria returned it, her body pressing ardently against his. "Oh, Englishman," she said when she could talk again, "I will be such a good wife to you, I promise!"

Gabriel smiled sensually. "I'm sure you will be, sweetheart. But have you not something else to tell me?" A teasing glint in the green eyes, he said slyly, "Having confessed my love, should I not hear something from you in return?"

Maria looked demure, loving him very much in this playful mood, still not quite convinced that she was not dreaming. Her fingers lightly traveling over his chiseled mouth, she asked impishly, "Why, Englishman, what do you mean? Have I not agreed to marry you? What more could you wish from me?"

Gabriel's eyes darkened and he kissed her roughly. "Your love," he said thickly. "I want your love!"

Her mischievous mood vanishing, she met his demanding gaze and averred solemnly, "Oh Gabriel! Never, *never* doubt that you have it! You are my life and I would die without you!"

After a statement like that, it was not surprising that Gabriel bore her swiftly back onto the bed, his mouth hungrily searching hers, his hands urgently and passionately moving over her slender body. In those moments that followed, they exchanged all the sweet promises that lovers have always exchanged, their mouths meeting and clinging with increasing desire, until, clothes scattered in wild disorder about the bed, they sealed their love in the age-old manner, their bodies merging and joining in a physically ecstatic proclamation of their love. And afterward, afterward as they lay entwined, Gabriel's head upon her shoulder, his hands gently fondling her still passion-swollen breasts, they talked lowly of the things that only lovers do, the sweetness of this moment to stay with them always.

But all too soon the real world intruded itself upon them, Gabriel recalling reluctantly that he had promised to meet with Jenkins within the hour, and regretfully he began to move away from Maria. Sitting up, he glanced down at her, thinking she had never looked so lovely to him, her dark hair spread out across the crimson coverlet of the bed, her naked body very white against the deep color of the fabric. Possession in his gaze, his eyes traveled warmly over her, and consigning Jenkins to the devil for a few minutes longer, he bent his head and tenderly kissed the smooth, warm stomach. "Do you mind," he asked huskily, "about the babe?"

Maria smiled mistily back at him, lightly running her fingers through his tousled black hair. "Would it matter, señor?"

"Aye!" he replied harshly. "I do not want you to be unhappy!"

Pulling his mouth nearer to hers, she breathed passionately against his lips, "Only one thing would make me unhappy—if you stopped loving me. . . ."

Gabriel groaned, kissing her with all the love that was within him, and Jenkins was completely forgotten for quite some time.

The wedding was set for the end of the last week of October, Gabriel unpleasantly aware that he would only have a few days with his new bride before he sailed. He also was faced with a new and ticklish dilemma—Zeus and Pilar were naturally coming to the wedding, and it wouldn't take Zeus very long to discover that he was planning on sailing without him.

Fortunately, the days that followed were very busy, the Satterleighs arriving from Royal Gift to help organize the hasty wedding; Gabriel tending to all the last-minute preparations for having the *Dark Angel* ready for sea by no later than the first week of November and giving Richard all the directions for running Royal Gift during his absence. But it was a bittersweet time too, Gabriel and Maria clinging to each other, each aware that time was both precious and an enemy, that all too soon, Gabriel would be sailing away from Port Royal, leaving Maria behind.

There was much that still lay between them, their love too newly acknowledged to be the unbreakable bond it would be in time; they were still uncertain with each other, still learning about the beloved one; and there were still too many areas that lay dark and dangerous between them. But there was such joy within them, such pleasure in knowing that they would be married and that it would be a marriage made of love, such quiet delight in the prospect of the coming child, that for the time being, all the difficult pitfalls that lay between them were forgotten, and there was only the dizzying ecstasy of knowing that against all odds, incredibly, love had come to them and they greedily embraced it.

The arrival of Zeus and Pilar swelled the numbers of those gathered for the wedding, and showing Pilar into the newly refurbished bedroom at the rear of the house, Maria was thankful that it had been finished in time. The house had been a beehive of activity of late: upholsterers and cabinetmakers delivered finished goods; the draper, swathed in various hangings, had finally made order out of the chaos of beautiful fabrics; and the entire house was taking on the appearance of a wealthy gentleman's residence.

Glancing around the handsome room, Pilar smiled and said, "Now, this, pigeon, is very nice! So much nicer than that moldy mattress we had to sleep on last time! You have done marvels with the house since then. These men!" she said exasperatedly. "If it were not for us, I believe they would still be hunched over open fires, wrapped in raw skins." She shuddered, and complacently patting her greatly rounding belly, she added, "At least by the time the babe arrives, Mer will be presentable!"

They spoke for a few minutes longer, Maria shyly admitting that she too would be having a baby in the spring. Pilar was delighted, and they spent quite a pleasant time discussing their impending motherhood and the trick of fate that had completely changed the course of their lives. The fine eyes pensive, Pilar said quietly, "Do you know, if we had not been at Puerto Bello when we were that I would probably have become a grumpy old widow woman and that Diego would have eventually married you off to some positively vile grandee in Spain. Thank God we had the good fortune to fall into the hands of Zeus and Gabriel!"

Maria could only agree with this statement wholeheartedly, and later meeting Gabriel downstairs in the comfortable room they had set aside for a study, Gabriel was startled at the warmth of the kiss she gave him. "What is it, sweetheart?" he asked softly, aware that something was different.

Maria smiled dazzlingly up at him. "Nothing," she admitted huskily. "I . . . oh, I just love you so much!" Of course this sparked an ardent response from Gabriel, and the room was very quiet for several moments, only the low whispers and murmurs between lovers breaking the silence.

Zeus found them there, and his face decidedly fierce, he wasted no time in niceties. "Tell me," he demanded angrily, "that my ears have deceived me, that Jenkins is mistaken when he informs me that you intend to sail within four days after the wedding."

Ruefully Gabriel put Maria from him, saying, "Leave us, sweetheart. There is much that I must discuss with him."

Alone, his heavily handsome face revealing his anger and hurt, Zeus growled, "Jenkins is not mistaken, I take it."

"No, I do mean to sail within the week."

"And you never thought to let me know?" The tawny eyes darkening with suspicion, Zeus said accusingly, "If it had not been for the wedding, you would have sailed away without a word."

"Aye, that I would have," Gabriel answered flatly. "You have a wife and a coming child to think of—and you are not bound by a request from the King of England." Coax-ingly Gabriel went on, "My friend, I need you here—I cannot leave Port Royal without knowing that there is someone to care for my own wife and expected child. I have no choice about going, you *do!* And though I know you mislike it, it is best that you stay here."

But Zeus would have none of it. "And what is wrong with the Satterleighs?" he inquired acidly. "Richard is perfectly capable of watching over both women, and his parents will ably assist him, I am sure, in seeing that Maria and Pilar are not distressed in any way." Throwing Gabriel a glance of mingled disgust and pain, he burst out furiously, *"Mon Dieu!* I could not believe my ears! It is unthinkable that you sail without me!" A glimmer of amusement suddenly lighting his eyes, he murmured, "Who will see to your back without me? Left to your own devices you will fall into danger and I will not have it, *mon ami.* I sail with you!"

Meekly Gabriel agreed. "Very well, then. I would prefer that you stay here, but if your mind is firm. . . ."

"It is!"

If there had not been so much excitement with the rapidly approaching nuptials and if he had not been so astonished and bewildered by Gabriel's apparent willingness to leave him behind, Zeus might have questioned his captain's serene acceptance of his words. But as it was, thinking the matter firmly settled, Zeus gave it no other thought and threw himself into the preparations.

Because of the hasty arrangements, the wedding of Gabriel and Maria was necessarily small. But married they were on a fine, warm day in late October, the Governor and his lady attending, as well as several other notables on the island, including Morgan's placid wife, Mary Elizabeth. Gabriel wished that Morgan himself and Jasper could have been present, but he spared them little thought, the wonder of Maria's love left him no inclination to think of anything but the joyous future that stretched out in front of him.

There were, however, some ominous clouds on his horizon, not the least of them, his imminent departure from Port Royal, and the frustrating stubbornness on the part of Zeus. And then, perhaps the most ominous of all, his

vow of revenge against Maria's brother, Diego. They did
not discuss it, but it lay there unspoken between them,
and Gabriel was certain that Maria believed that he was
leaving Port Royal to go in search of Diego, to kill him.

On their wedding night as they lay satiated in each
other's arms, Maria's head resting gently on Gabriel's
chest, she asked softly, "Must you leave on Friday?"

In the darkness he nodded, then realizing that she could
not see his answer, he murmured, "Aye, sweet tiger, I
must."

Maria swallowed, despair billowing through her. Since
it was not because she bored him, and as he still had not
mentioned his reasons for rejoining the buccaneers, what
else could she think but that revenge so ate at him that
he must go hunting Diego. Her voice tight, she demanded,
"Could you not let it be? Forget the past?"

Gabriel stiffened. There would be little that he could
ever deny her, but where her brother was concerned, he
was adamant. Diego must die by his hand. He could never
truly be at ease, never stop being just a bit guilty at his
own glorious future, knowing that the man who had so
senselessly slain Elizabeth still lived. It wasn't something
that he could have explained to anyone; it was just there,
a part of him, one of the inherent qualities that made him
Gabriel Lancaster. It didn't matter that Caroline had miraculously found happiness in her captivity; it didn't matter so much that he had endured the pain and degradation
that he had; but other men had died because of the brutal
taking of the *Raven*, men who had trusted him, who had
followed him and had looked to him for leadership, and
he had failed them and his own gentle Elizabeth. Young,
trusting, loving Elizabeth had died because of Diego Delgato. . . .

Wearily, he said, "Nay, I cannot forget your brother's
dastardly actions, and I would be less a man, less than
honorable, if I cowardly forsook my vows."

Frightened and furious at the same time, Maria sat bolt
upright in the bed, and her small fist clenched whitely,
she struck him on the chest. "Ah, *Dios!*" she cried fiercely.
"Must you die to defend your honor? Must my babe be
born never knowing his father, simply because you must
hunt my own brother down like a dog?"

His face hard, he caught her shoulders, and shaking her roughly, he growled, "Even loving you, I will not allow you to abuse me! I do not," he said dangerously, "go hunting your brother—I go because my own sovereign has requested it of me!" His anger abating slightly, the expression in the green eyes softened and he said thickly, "For no other reason would I leave you! And if I cannot forget the past, I will give you my promise, that I will not deliberately go searching for Diego. If our paths cross, however. . . ."

That Gabriel would kill Diego was explicit in what he didn't say, but Maria had to be content with the small comfort that he was *not* sailing from her simply because of revenge and that he would not purposely seek out her brother. It was very small comfort indeed. And she dreamed again that night, the terrifying nightmare of the blood-slick deck of a ship; the sails, sheets of fire as two men, her husband and her brother, fought a deadly duel, their swords gleaming redly. She woke at dawn, tears on her cheeks, foreboding and despair in her heart.

Maria was not the only one feeling despair and anxiety as the date set for the departure of the *Dark Angel* loomed frighteningly near. Pilar could not hide her anger and distress that Zeus was apparently willing simply to abandon her and follow blindly wherever Gabriel led. "He is determined, no matter what I say, to go with him!" she cried distractedly the afternoon before the men would leave in the morning. "They are *both* fools, and I *almost* wish I had never laid eyes on that stubborn, arrogant, misguided, ass-eared monster, Zeus!"

Coming into the room and hearing these kind words from the lips of his beloved wife, Zeus merely grinned and, kissing her soundly, said teasingly, "Such attributes! I am overwhelmed, my love!"

Not able to remain angry at him for very long, Pilar melted, saying in an entirely different tone of voice, "You great lout! Why I love you I am sure I don't know!"

Grinning wickedly, Zeus solemnly patted her protruding stomach and said brazenly, "I think the reason is clearly revealed, *ma cœur!*"

"Oh, go away!" she said crossly, and smiling faintly he ambled from the room.

Looking away, Maria bit her lip unhappily, wishing that things were as easy between her and Gabriel. They loved each other, but there were still constraints between them, and she was increasingly uneasy about this trip. Uneasy and miserable, knowing that by this time tommorow Gabriel would be far out at sea and that it would be months before she saw him again . . . *if* some disaster did not befall him.

Gabriel stuck his head inside the room and inquired, "Has either of you seen Zeus? I need a word with him."

"He was here just a moment ago," Maria replied, her heart jumping in her breast at the very sight of him. The strain of these past few days was telling on him too, she realized with a little stab, seeing for the first time the lines of sleeplessness about his eyes, the taut way in which he held his mouth. He did not like leaving her any more than she liked being left behind!

Waspishly, Pilar added, "I would hope that he will pay more attention to *your* words than he does mine! After all, I am only his wife and you are his captain! What does it matter that he is deserting *me!*"

Compassion and amusement glimmered in the green eyes. Tantalizingly, Gabriel murmured, "Pilar, cease your frettings—I have no intention of taking Zeus with me. Keep your mouth shut about it, but be assured that when I sail tomorrow, your husband will be on the wharf."

Leaving Maria and Pilar to stare after him, questions jostling madly in their minds, Gabriel too disappeared from the room.

Evening came all too soon and when Gabriel at last came to bed that night and reached for her, Maria flew to his arms, knowing that tonight would be their last together. They made love with a frantic urgency, both painfully, miserably aware of the uncertainty of life and fate. . . .

Dawn came and with reluctance Gabriel and Maria dressed and made their way downstairs. There was a subdued air about the entire house, everyone trying to act normal and casual about the impending departure of the *Dark Angel* in just a few hours. Breakfast was strained, not even the usually vocal Pilar finding very much to say. Her eyes went to Gabriel's unrevealing face many times, a hopeful, beseeching look in their dark depths. It was only when he passed her just before they all left for the docks that he gave any sign that he had noticed her expression. His hand dropped warmly on her shoulder and he gave it a quick, reassuring squeeze.

The docks were bustling when they arrived there, and as the elder Satterleighs and Richard as well as the Governor had come to see Gabriel and Zeus off, there was quite a little crowd pressing near Maria and Pilar as they kissed their husbands good-bye and tried to hide their tears.

His arms wrapped tightly around her, Gabriel's mouth clung to Maria's as if he could not bear to part from her. This was not what he planned for them, and silently he consigned Modyford and his King to the devil, vowing that this was his last trip and royal requests be damned! But eventually, his mouth left hers and he muttered, "When I return there will be time for us. I shall never leave you again!"

Her throat clogged with unshed tears, loving him so much, as the sea breeze ruffled the heavy black hair, Maria thought her heart would burst with pain. Pasting a brave smile on her trembling lips, she whispered, "Come back to me, that is all that I ask. Come back to me!"

A troubled expression in the green eyes, he murmured, "Maria, I cannot promise you . . . things happen that no one has any control over . . . but if it is humanly possible, you know that I shall and that no matter where I am or what happens to me, *I love you!*" He hesitated; then, his voice raw, he added, "But if something should happen to me . . . if I do not return, know that my last thoughts were of you and our child."

Unable to speak, the tears she had tried to hide sliding unheeded down her cheeks, Maria nodded, her fingers whitely clutching his leather doublet. He kissed her again roughly and then grimly pushing her into Richard's waiting arms, he said harshly, "Take care of her. I leave her in your care."

He swung away and walked determinedly to the dinghy that would carry him to the *Dark Angel* and away from the most precious thing in the world to him, Maria. At the edge of the wharf, he hesitated, Zeus walking in front of him. Gabriel turned and frowned, looking back in the direction of the women. "What is wrong with Pilar?" he asked.

Startled, Zeus' head swiveled in that direction and right into Gabriel's iron-hard fist. Zeus crumbled without a sound and as Pilar came running up, outrage on her handsome face, Gabriel grinned at her, saying mildly, "Believe me, madame, there was no other way—he is as stubborn as an ox and, like the ox, respects only force."

Uncertain whether to be angry or relieved at his actions, Pilar sank down beside her unconscious husband cradling his great head in her lap. Seeing that he had suffered no lasting harm, she looked up ruefully at Gabriel. "I suspect that you are right, *señor*, but I do not think that he is going to like this."

Gabriel shrugged. "Most likely not, but when he awakens I will be far at sea and there will be nothing he can do about it . . . until I return." A sudden spark of laughter lit his eyes. "And by then perhaps he will have forgiven me; but if he has not, remind him, if you will, of a day in Puerto Bello. The day Santiago fell. Tell him that I was merely repaying my debts. He'll understand."

And taking one last, long look at Maria, standing so small and forlorn in front of Richard Satterleigh, he bowed slightly and then leaped down lightly into the dinghy.

He was gone! Feeling as if her heart would break, Maria stood like a slender statue, staring at the horizon, watching as the *Dark Angel* spread her sails, caught the wind and disappeared on the horizon, taking Gabriel away from her and into danger, mercifully unaware that when they next met it would be on the bloodstained decks of the *Santo Cristo*.

Chapter Thirty

As the *Dark Angel* sailed gracefully toward the place set for rendezvous by Morgan, *Ile-a-Vache,* off the coast of Hispaniola, she did not travel alone; with her were the *Oxford* and the newly renamed *Satisfaction.* It had happened that the *Oxford* had returned to Port Royal just two days before the wedding, and with her had been her first prize—a fourteen-gun French ship out of La Rochelle called *Le Cerf Volant.* The captain and his crew had been thrown into irons and with the Governor's brother, Sir James Modyford, sitting on the Court of Admiralty, the Frenchmen had promptly been found guilty of plundering an English merchant ship from Virginia. The *Le Cerf Volant* had been declared a legal prize by the court, and Collier had instantly retitled her *Satisfaction* and had decided to join with Gabriel when he sailed for *Ile-a-Vache.*

The three ships reached their destination in late December, and they discovered anchored off *Ile-a-Vache* nearly all of the Jamaican privateers and buccaneers, as well as several Frenchmen from Tortuga. In all there were ten ships and some eight hundred men waiting there, all impatient and eager to sail with the captor of Puerto Bello, to whatever target the great Harry Morgan would name.

As the *Oxford* was by far the most powerful ship in the group, Morgan immediately named her his flagship and hoisted his flag from the mast. Meeting Morgan and Jasper later that same day in the spacious comfort of the *Oxford,* Gabriel bore their many jesting comments and sly teasings his unexpected appearance engendered with good will. He did not, however, give any indication of *what* had changed his mind, letting the others think that it had been for the reasons he had stated upon arrival—as a newly married man and intent upon setting up his nursery, it behooved him to make one last journey with the privateers to shore up as much gold as possible for the future. A mocking grin on his dark face, he had murmured, "I have discovered that a wife and a coming child can make gold disappear faster than a wild-spending buccaneer!"

Morgan and Jasper had laughed, and Jasper had added warmly, "So you did marry her, *mon ami!*" Cocking an eyebrow, he had drawled teasingly, "And left her with child after less than a week of marriage? So prolific of you!"

Gabriel had flushed slightly. Pulling on his ear, he had admitted uncomfortably, "The babe will be born some months early."

Morgan and Jasper had thought that very funny, and they had laughed and laughed until, reluctantly, Gabriel too had smiled faintly, more at their mirth than the cause of it. But he was not smiling that night as he lay in his bed aboard the *Dark Angel.* He missed Maria intolerably, his heart heavy in his breast as he viewed the weeks and months that he would be away from her. His child could even be born before he returned home! In desperation, trying to think of something other than Maria's sweet features, he turned his mind to the meeting Morgan had called for the second of January to decide upon their target. There was no doubt that it would be Cartagena— Cartagena was where Morgan wanted to strike, and so it would be . . . even if the French proved contrary and voted against it as they had with the attack on Puerto Bello.

It wasn't very likely that they would—Morgan had proved himself at Puerto Bello—but du Bois was still a thorn to be endured, and the French buccaneers in general had not been pleased about the taking of *Le Cerf Volant.* There had been rumbles throughout the buccaneer fleet as the story spread and the *Satisfaction's* presence was fast becoming a sore point with the French. In the darkness of his cabin, Gabriel frowned. A sore point that was ably kept raw by du Bois. He was uneasy about the situation, but as 1668 closed and 1669 began, his worries seemed less—hopefully, the incident was now behind them.

At the council of war held aboard the *Oxford* on the second day of January of 1669, it was unanimously decided that Cartagena would be the target of the privateer fleet, and across the table from Morgan, Gabriel wasn't at all surprised to see Morgan send him a smug glance, the black eyes full of satisfaction. It was a bold decision; Cartagena was the richest and best defended of all the cities on the Spanish Main. Even Morgan conceded that it would be much harder to take than Puerto Bello, but it was too rich, too wealthy, not to make the eyes of the assembled captains glisten with greed. The fact that it was also Spanish only whetted their appetites—the buccaneers were notorious for preferring to sack Spanish possessions rather than any of the other nationalities to be found in the Caribbean. And with nearly a thousand seasoned fighting men and the powerful *Oxford* to lead the way in blasting away the city's defenses, the privateers began to think of the city as already in their hands.

To celebrate this momentous decision, Morgan gave a wild and boisterous dinner in the *Oxford*'s cabin for his captains, while the members of the crew celebrated with increasingly disorderly drunkenness in the forecastle. During the course of the evening, it happened that Morgan, Jasper and Gabriel were all seated side by side, on one side of the long table, the three of them pleasantly, if not totally, inebriated as were the rest of the buccaneer captains. But Gabriel was still sober enough to see that du Bois was leaving, and touching Morgan's shoulder, he asked, "Why do you suppose he is departing so soon? I seem to recall that he is usually the last to leave—and then it is only when he is dragged dead-drunk from the room!"

Morgan stared owlishly at du Bois' broad back as the Frenchman walked from the crowded cabin. "Full of sour grapes, I suppose," he returned, enunciating each word carefully, a sure sign of the large amounts of wine he had enjoyed throughout the evening.

Jasper added his mite, the only indication of his wine-filled state being the bright intensity of the cerulean blue eyes. "I think, *mon ami,*" he drawled, "we really should kill him. He is *such* a disgrace to the French!"

Jasper's displeasure with this aspect of du Bois was so sincere, so serious, that Morgan and Gabriel looked at each other and grinned. Jasper promptly was affronted by their amusement, and they spent the next several moments teasing their friend into a better humor. Gabriel was just on the point of suggesting that perhaps they go out onto the deck for some fresh air, when suddenly, catastrophically, the *Oxford* was ripped from bow to stern by a thunderous explosion.

Whether it had been some careless spark from the drunken buccaneers that had lit the ship's magazine or, as an appallingly sober Gabriel and Jasper later speculated, spiteful revenge on the part of du Bois over the taking of the *Satisfaction,* was never decided. But certainly, it was a frightful moment, as in a blinding flash the ship was destroyed; shattered planks and spars and bloody bits of what had been living men were violently shot up into the night air only to fall in a grisly rain into the phosphorescent sea. The loss of life was terrible: of a crew of over two hundred buccaneers only six men and four boys were rescued from the blood-washed seas off *Ile-a-Vache.* Miraculously, Morgan and all of those buccaneer captains who had been on one side of the table in the cabin survived, while those on the other side were all killed; and Gabriel blessed his stars that he had changed his position during the evening. . . .

The loss of the *Oxford* and nearly a fifth of his men made an attack on Cartagena out of the question, and in a grimly solemn mood Morgan was forced to name the fourteen-gun frigate *Lilly* as his new flagship. His mood was not improved when Collier decided to sail off in search of his own game with the *Satisfaction.* It was not one of the Admiral's better moments. Once Collier had departed, Morgan led his somber and shaken fleet east along the coast of Hispaniola, intent upon seeking out some less heavily guarded target.

The days that followed were not ones that Gabriel cared to contemplate. Since the demise of the *Oxford,* nothing seemed to be going right as the buccaneer fleet crept along the coast, the ships beating straight into a strong east wind, which played havoc with most of the small craft that composed Morgan's fleet. Many of these ships were completely undecked, and the wind and unremitting hard world soon began to tell on the men. Raids upon the Spanish lands to replenish their dwindling supplies with wild pigs and cattle were not any more pleasant, the Spanish

seeming to be unusually alert, and several times the buccaneers made it back to their ships with the militia of
Santo Domingo hard on their heels.

It wasn't surprising then that after a few weeks, toward
the end of January, some of the men began to complain, du
Bois leading the pack. Listening to the heated argument in
the small cabin of the *Lilly* between du Bois and Morgan,
Gabriel and Jasper exchanged glances. They had discussed
with *no one* their suspicions about du Bois in connection
with the explosion aboard the *Oxford,* but both of them
would have preferred to keep du Bois with the buccaneer
fleet—at least that way they could keep an eye on him. But
though Morgan argued strenuously against it, the next day
du Bois, and three of the best ships, sailed away in search
of other game. With a mixture of regret and concern, Gabriel watched them go, uneasy about du Bois' departure, but
helpless to do anything about it but to continue with the
main part of the buccaneer fleet as they continued to beat
windward around the coast of Hispaniola.

Morgan's fleet was now reduced to a mere eight ships
and only five hundred men, barely half his original fighting force, and the Admiral of the Brethren was *not* happy
with the current situation. They had planned, after the
debacle with the *Oxford,* to sail to Trinidad and then to
sail leeward along the Spanish Main, raiding and robbing
the unprotected ports of eastern Venezuela and the
wealthy pearl island of Margarita, but that idea too had
to be abandoned in the face of the weather and the deser-
tions among the crew. It was in early February, when
they reached the island of Saona, a favorite place of the
buccaneers, at the east end of Hispaniola, that Jasper
came up with a suggestion.

Jasper, Gabriel and Morgan were in the cabin of the
Lilly discussing possible sites that would prove profitable,
Gabriel making sure that none which could prove to be
an embarrassment to the English government were selected, when Jasper said thoughtfully, "There is one place
we have not considered . . . the towns that lie within the
Laguna de Maracaibo."

Morgan looked interested and Jasper went on slowly,
"Two years ago when I sailed with L'Ollanais, we raided
there and found it very satisfactory—the defenses were

not strong and the plunder was more than adequate. After this period of time, they should have recovered enough wealth to make it worth our while."

There were several men within the crew who were familiar with Maracaibo, and there was a ripple of excitement through the crews when the possibility of attacking in that area was discussed. The fact that Maracaibo was an easy sail from Saona, just west of south from the island, added to its appeal and the site was voted upon unanimously. Their spirits lifting, the buccaneer ships stood away for the Main, visions of plunder dancing before the eyes of the crews.

Gabriel viewed the decision with indifference; a gnawing sense of disquietude was eating at his vitals, had been since du Bois had sailed away. He didn't like the thought of Maria back in Port Royal and du Bois possibly being in the same vicinity. He told himself that he was being stupid—Zeus and Richard both would keep her safe—but it didn't stop his concern, and as the days passed, for no apparent reason, his uneasiness grew.

As February passed into March, Gabriel had good reason to be uneasy—du Bois was indeed heading directly toward Port Royal, as fast as his pinnace would sail, his one purpose to capture Maria Lancaster and return her to her brother. It was not, however, revenge which drove him, rather self-preservation and greed.

When du Bois had left the privateers off the coast of Hispaniola in January there had been no definite target in his mind—he simply could not stomach watching Morgan in the exalted position that he himself lusted after so hungrily. Eaten up with jealousy and envy, he had simply sailed away, intent upon soothing his vanity. Unfortunately, he had sailed right into Diego's hands. . . .

The news that the buccaneers were on the prowl, that they had been seen gathering at *Ile-a-Vache* and that they had chosen Cartagena as their place of plunder had, through several different sources, eventually reached the Spanish authorities in Santo Domingo. The news did not travel swiftly, but by early February it had finally reached Havana and the one man who might be able to stop Harry Morgan, Diego Delgato.

Diego had risen meteorically through the ranks and

now, not yet thirty-five years old, he had been named *almirante* of the Armada de Barlovento, the Spanish fleet stationed in the Caribbean to wipe out piracy and to act as a mobile garrison. Originally it had consisted of five warships, but at present Diego had under his command only three ships. Still, these were true warships and together they amounted to a formidable force, far more formidable than the combined force of Morgan's buccaneers, even though the *Dark Angel* and Jasper's ten-gun *Lucifer* sailed with the Brethren of the Coast. In battle the buccaneers would be outgunned and outweighed, and with a gleam of satisfaction in his dark eyes, Diego had immediately set out to run down this motley crew of men who had been wreaking such havoc in Spanish possessions, his heart full of the hope that once again he would find himself face to face with Gabriel Lancaster, and this time, Diego thought viciously as his ships had sailed from Havana, this time he would find Lancaster and kill him!

Thinking to head off the privateers and to have the advantage of the wind, he set off first for the windward bastion of the Spanish in the Indies, the port of San Juan, Puerto Rico. Arriving there in very early March, some days after Morgan and his privateers had actually reached Laguna de Maracaibo, he sent a boat ashore for news, but nothing had been heard of Morgan's privateer fleet. Diego frowned, finally deciding that he had come too far windward, and leaving Puerto Rico he sailed back along the north coast of Puerto Rico, through the Mona Passage, and it was there that he found du Bois.

Having had no destination in mind when he had sailed away from Morgan, du Bois had spent the intervening weeks raiding and sailing indifferently along the coast of Hispaniola, trying to hit upon some scheme that would add glory to his name and that would make the other buccaneers look to him with admiration ... but the scheme must also make the blasted Morgan look foolish. Of course, it was impossible, and his bitterness and envy grew with every hour, his temper short and his manner increasingly surly to his crew. Things were not helped one morning when he was roughly awakened with the news that there were sails on the horizon—Spanish sails.

The battle that followed was brief and brutal, Diego

having the advantage of the wind; and his three warships bristling with blazing cannons made appallingly short work of the frail pinnaces and small sloops that composed du Bois' little fleet. Du Bois' life might have ended then, but he was one of the survivors, and as Diego was after information as much as destruction of the buccaneers, he ordered his men to haul on board the *Santo Cristo* many of the surviving buccaneers from among the scattered wreckage of their ships.

The buccaneers expected no kindness from their Spanish captors, and in sullen misery they waited for the blows to fall as they stood sodden and dispirited on the decks of the *Santo Cristo*. Eyeing them with contempt, Diego paraded in front of them, the small whip he was seldom without carried in his hands. Tapping a man on the shoulder with it, he demanded in simple English, "The others, where are they?"

A baleful glare was his answer, the buccaneer spitting unerringly on the deck just next to Diego's finely shod feet. Livid, Diego struck the man again and again, screaming, "Insolent dog! *Dios!* Would that I could kill all of you myself!" The dark eyes feverish with rage, he added wildly, "Especially, the swine Lancaster!"

Du Bois' ears perked up from his position two men down from where Diego was taking great delight in beating the other poor buccaneer to death. As the man fell to the deck, his face and chest a swathe of blood and torn flesh, du Bois, hoping to capitalize on that one phrase, called out, "We have no knowledge of the other buccaneers, or of Lancaster; we left him with the others in January . . . but I do know where Lancaster's Spanish woman is. . . ."

Diego froze as if his body had suddenly been swept by an arctic wind, and pivoting slowly, he looked at du Bois. Imperiously, he beckoned him forward and his voice silky with menace, his black eyes full of the madness that drove him, he asked, "Lancaster's woman? And who might that be?"

Unaware of who it was that spoke, du Bois said bluntly, "A Spanish wench captured at Puerto Bello. He married the slut not five months ago in Port Royal."

Diego's face convulsed with unbridled rage, the nostrils flaring whitely, the scar above his eyebrow throbbing

madly. "Her name?" he choked out, barely able to say the
words, so great the fury within.

"Maria. Maria Delgato."

Stunned, Diego could only stare at du Bois' grimy features, his every instinct crying out a denial. It could not
be! That Maria had consented to marry the Englishman
was incomprehensible, and he rejected it instantly. Striking du Bois savagely on the side of the face, he shrieked,
"You lie! She would never marry *him!*"

But it was true, he realized with a combination of despair and wild fury as he looked at du Bois' face, and
whether his reaction was because she had married his
greatest enemy or because it completely shattered his own
plans for her future and his further advancement was not
certain. His body trembling with rage, the swarthy face
nearly white with temper, Diego spun away, growling to
his lieutenant who stood nearby, "Take them below and
chain them!"

Alone in the sumptuous great cabin of the *Santo Cristo,*
Diego paced the floor in quick, violent movements, his
brain racing, his temper held barely in check. He wanted
to strike out at someone for this devastating blow to his
family pride. Maria had married Lancaster! He could not
believe it! She would not! The filthy buccaneer had lied!
But even as he told himself these things, he knew that
he was deluding himself. The buccaneer had no reason to
lie—every reason, in fact, to tell the truth.

Swallowing some of the blind rage that burned within
him, hands behind his back, he stared furiously out the
windows that lined the stern of the *Santo Cristo,* trying
frantically to bring his disjointed thoughts to order. Maria
had married Lancaster; she was in Port Royal and Lancaster was out at sea, somewhere with the other buccaneers.

That he would find Lancaster was, no doubt, in Diego's
mind, but what of Maria? What of his recently renewed
plans to marry her once again to Don Clemente de la Silva
y Gonzales, the newly *widowed* Don Clemente, the powerful
Don Clemente who had within the past three months just
inherited his father's huge estates and titles. . . . *The* Don
Clemente who could see to it that his brother-in-law was
given a much finer command than this paltry little squad-
ron in the Caribbean. . . .

It had been the news of Don Clemente's widowed state that had brought Diego hotfooted to Panama City in June last year, hoping to catch his sister before she had departed for Santo Domingo, the letter from Don Clemente that had broached the subject of marriage with Maria once again resting under his doublet, the letter in which the great man had written, "I married for wealth and more power the first time, but this time, I wish to please myself . . . and my memory of your sister pleases me very much. . . ." Diego could hardly contain his elation, but his plans had suffered a bitter setback because of Maria's capture at Puerto Bello, and in wild desperation Diego had hit upon the scheme of exchanging sister for sister to get Maria back into his hands. . . .

Thinking of that debacle, Diego's face contorted with anger and frustration. To have come so close . . . to have had everything within his grasp. Damn Ramon Chavez! Double damn him for the uncomfortable time he caused me in Santo Domingo last November, Diego thought fiercely, when he laid charges against me before the Admiralty, claiming I fired upon him. For just a second, Diego's features were smug. But it came to nothing, he recalled coolly, Ramon being unable to *prove* that I had been firing at his men and not at the buccaneers as I claimed.

Determined not to lose Don Clemente's powerful favor again, Diego had thought of little else these past months but of ways to free his sister. He had sent several letters to Spain, soothing Don Clemente's rising ire that his bride was not on her way to his side, manufacturing excuse after excuse to explain away Maria's absence. Not one hint of her whereabouts did he drop, knowing that to do so would put the possibility of marriage out of the question—what Spaniard wanted the leavings of an English swine? But as months had passed Diego had become increasingly harassed. Don Clemente's last letter, the one that had informed Diego of the other man's assumption of his father's estates, had made it clear that something must be settled soon, or he would look for his bride somewhere else . . . after all, the Delgatos were not *that* prominent, and that he was certain he could find some other beautiful young woman to be his wife. . . . Diego had received that letter at Havana, not two weeks prior to hear-

ing of the gathering of the Brethren of the Coast, and his
bafflement and rage had been growing since then. To kill
Lancaster would give him much pleasure, but to get
Maria back ... Now, that, he mused slowly, would be a
plum indeed. He would see to it that she was a widow
before he sent her on her way to Spain as Don Clemente's
affianced bride. All he needed at this point was some way
of getting Maria in his hands. . . .

Absently he stroked his chin. This buccaneer, du Bois
... Not giving himself time to think, he threw open the
door to his cabin and barked to a sentry outside the door,
"Have that man du Bois brought to me immediately!"

And so it was that du Bois found himself in Diego's
presence and was listening with startlement and savage
cunning to the plan being laid before him.

"If," Diego said arrogantly, "you can bring me my sister, Lancaster's woman, I shall give you fifty thousand
pieces of eight ... and the life of the remaining buccaneers that I will hold until your return. I will provide you
with a small ship, which will be yours when you give me
Maria in Santo Domingo."

Du Bois stared at the other man consideringly, hiding
his surprise of the relationship between Lancaster's wife
and his captor. Pulling nervously on his blond mustache,
he growled, "I cannot do it alone. And what guarantee do
I have that you will keep your word?"

Diego smiled nastily. "You have none, but if you refuse,
you will not leave this room alive. Is it not worth your
life to accept this proposal?"

Feeling a trifle braver, du Bois countered swiftly, "And
how do you know that once I sail away that I will keep
my bargain, that I will not simply go on my way?"

Almost pleasantly Diego replied, "Two things, my filthy
friend—one, the gold that I offered you; and two, the reputation that would follow you when it is learned that you
deserted your own men, that you left them to my mercy
and sailed blithely away." His face cruelly amused, Diego
drawled, "What men would want to follow a leader who
is so callous?"

Du Bois nodded his head reluctantly. The buccaneers were
a loose-knit organization of brutal men, but if du Bois simply abandoned the survivors of this unfortunate expedition,

his days as a captain were over—no one would follow him
and any dreams he had of wresting the leadership from
Morgan were finished. He was trapped, and even if he
hadn't been coming to think that this arrogant Spaniard's
plan was an excellent way to get his own revenge against
Lancaster, he would still have consented. He had no choice.
And so it was on the morrow that du Bois and twenty buccaneers sailed away in a hastily requisitioned pinnace for
Port Royal, their one purpose to stealthily capture and bring
Maria back to Diego unharmed and unmolested. Diego had
made that point *very* clear, his eyes full of dark promise,
and with thirty more surviving buccaneers miserably
chained in the hold of the *Santo Cristo,* he was quite confident that du Bois would keep his word, dishonorable wretch
that he was.

But unlike Diego, du Bois did have a sort of honor. He
would keep his word, and as soon as Maria was in his possession, he would keep her from the ugly clutches of his
remaining men and would sail with all haste to Santo Domingo to retrieve his other men and the gold. . . .

Of course, Diego never gave his promise a second thought,
and the moment the small pinnace was out of sight, he said
to his lieutenant, "Get those foul creatures out of my hold.
Kill them and throw the bodies into the sea—we have no
more use for them." He and his lieutenant exchanged
knowing glances. What a foolish swine the Frenchman had
been, death too would be his reward once Maria was safely
on board the *Santo Cristo.*

Unaware of the events set in motion by her brother, Maria waited anxiously in Port Royal, her every waking
thought on Gabriel and their coming child, her dreams full
of him too and the wonderful days that would be theirs once
he returned. After Gabriel's departure she had spent some
months at Royal Gift, but restless and not truly happy, she
had finally convinced Richard and Zeus that she would be
much more content at the house in town at Port Royal. At
least there she would hear instant news of Gabriel's return
and would not have to wait for him to come to her at Royal
Gift. Reluctantly, just after the first of the year, Richard
had escorted her to Port Royal, and she had set up her
household there, determined to be there until Gabriel came
home and her child was born.

The unborn child was a great comfort to her, and she marveled delightedly as the weeks and months had gone by and her stomach had swollen with the growing infant. Of course her stomach was not nearly as large as Pilar's, and Maria was conscious of a slight pang. Did her lack of blossoming mean all was not well with her child? Pilar had laughingly said, "You little goose, I am nearly two months ahead of you; just wait, you will be this enormous too."

Pilar and Zeus had temporarily moved in with Maria in Port Royal, Zeus saying resignedly, once he had gotten over his rage at being left behind, *"Mon capitaine* set me in charge of you, and how else can I keep watch over you, unless I am right at hand?" He had grinned sheepishly, adding, "Besides, I want to be here when he arrives too!"

Maria was inordinately grateful to have them here with her; it made the days a little less lonely, the waiting a little less unbearable. But seeing the devoted pair together made her heart ache with longing. If only Gabriel would come, if only he would sail into the harbor tomorrow, she thought yearningly as February had faded into March. He had been gone *such* a long time, and she pulled a face thinking of the months yet before he would return. Feeling the babe move within her, she gently touched her stretched stomach. "Are you lonely for him too?" she asked whimsically. And experiencing a particularly strong kick from her unborn child, she smiled foolishly and murmured, "I know, I want him home too!"

At night as she lay alone in her big bed, her hands softly exploring the roundness of her stomach, laughing when she felt the child move within her, she talked lowly to it, singing gay little songs to it and longing for the day she would hold her newborn child in her arms. May seemed such a long time away from March, she thought wistfully. In mid-March while Gabriel raided with Morgan in the Laguna de Maracaibo area and Diego was anchored off Santo Domingo seeking word of the buccaneers' whereabouts, Maria grew increasingly restless, and one night, having trouble sleeping, she tossed about uncomfortably on her bed, wishing the baby was born, wishing Gabriel was home. Suddenly she stiffened, hearing a stealthy movement outside her door. Thinking it was Zeus, she called out, "Zeus, is that you? Is something wrong with Pilar?"

There was no reply, and puzzled and curious, she scrambled from her bed, never believing that danger lurked in her own hallway. Struggling into a pretty robe of pale pink silk and lace, she had just gotten halfway across the room when the door flew open, and hard, brutal hands closed around her. She had barely time for one startled, choked-off scream before a powerful hand was crushing against her mouth and du Bois' voice hissed in her ear, "Scream again, my lovely, and you'll not live for another moment!"

Terror beat through her in icy waves, and numbly she obeyed, frightened of making any move, frightened for herself and her unborn child. In the heavy darkness of the room, du Bois grunted his satisfaction when she made no other attempt to escape and turning his head away from Maria, he whispered to someone behind him, "Strike a light and find some other clothes for her." Adding sarcastically, "The Admiral will not thank us for bringing him his sister in her night attire!"

Maria trembled at his words, questions humming in her brain, and she made some move to speak, but du Bois' hand tightened painfully, leaving her with the taste of blood in her mouth where his brutal pressure had forced her lips against her teeth.

A candle was lit, and in the wavering, dancing light, she gazed into du Bois' leering features, his cold blue eyes skimming hotly over her. His gaze widened when he noticed her obviously pregnant state, and an unkind smile played across his vulpine mouth. "I do not think that your brother counted on *this!* But then, my bargain was only to give you to him, and he did not specify in what condition . . . except that you are to be unharmed and unmolested by me and my men." He gave a low, ugly laugh. "I cannot wait to see his face when he discovers that Lancaster has been before us!"

The second man made quick work of dragging a haphazard assortment of clothing from the armoire, and in less than a minute the room was again plunged into darkness. Maria, a hastily made gag from her pillow-covering stuffed in her mouth, was thrown over du Bois' brawny shoulder, and they were out of her room and heading down the hallway toward the stairs. But though du Bois and his companion had been quiet, they had not been quiet enough, and Zeus, with long years of being constantly on the alert for trouble behind him had suddenly awakened with the vague sense that something was not right, that he had heard some sound that was not normal. Slipping silently from Pilar's side, he swiftly dragged on a pair of breeches, and reaching for the long-bladed knife that was never far from his side, with a panther-like tread he quickly crossed the room to the doorway. He hesitated, straining to hear some sound, and then, slowly, he opened the door.

Utter darkness met his gaze, but his keen ears had already heard the small movements Maria had made as she twisted helplessly about on du Bois' shoulder, and suddenly hearing the muffled whimper she was able to make through the gag, concern washed through him. Never thinking that there were others in the hallway, assuming that Maria had fallen and somehow hurt herself, he plunged forward, crying out, "Maria! Petite! Where are you? Have you fallen?"

Several things happened at once: Pilar awoke, the nagging pain in her lower back increasing; Zeus' voice had further disturbed her uneasy slumber and automatically she reached for candle and flint; in the hall, du Bois gave a smothered curse, and wasting no time, Maria slung like a bag of potatoes over his shoulder, he barged down the stairs. Zeus, recognizing a man's voice, surged forward, knife in hand, determined to make short work of the brazen intruder; du Bois' accomplice slunk down against the wall near the top of the stairs, waiting to strike; and further down the hall, Richard too had awakened and was swiftly grabbing for his own candle.

Unaware of the danger, Zeus reached the staircase, and as he stood there at the top, the second man struck him from behind, hitting Zeus solidly with a powerful blow that sent him hurtling down the stairs like a huge cannonball. The light from Pilar's candle as she awkwardly and painfully made her way toward the source of the disturbance was just beginning to pierce the darkness when Zeus' attacker nimbly leaped over the fallen Zeus. Groaning and in great pain, certain that one of his legs was broken, Zeus was able to make out du Bois, with Maria across his shoulder, in the wavering light from Pilar's candle. To his relief, from down the hall, he heard Richard calling out irritably, "What the hell is going on?"

The two intruders wasted little time racing to the door, but Zeus heard du Bois snarl quite clearly, "Now all we have to do is get the slut to her brother in Santo Domingo!" before they disappeared into the night.

At the top of the stairs, Pilar glanced down and seeing Zeus' crumpled body at the base, filled with terror, she stumbled down the stairs. *"Mi amor!* What has happened?"

Dragging himself to the wall with Pilar's help, Zeus had just managed to prop himself up, when Richard, candle in one hand, pistol in the other, appeared. For the next few minutes there was incoherent bedlam until, finally, Zeus was able to make himself heard above the questions of the others, Phoebe and Delicia having also been disturbed and coming to investigate.

His eyes, dark with pain, meeting Richard's, Zeus growled out, "It was that bastard, du Bois! He has kidnapped Maria and is taking her to Diego in Santo Domingo!" The agony in his leg made him wince and he muttered, "You're going to have to go after her—I obviously cannot."

Richard nodded grimly, saying, "I am not a sailor like you, but I shall do my best. The first thing must be for me to get a ship."

Zeus nodded. "That should be no problem—Gabriel still has his sloop the *Caroline* here in Port Royal. She's captained by a friend of ours, Will Blackwell—and more to the point, the *Caroline* just docked last week. The greatest difficulty may be in finding Will at this time of night. You'll have to try the various brothels and grog shops—I would suggest that you start with the Yellow Girl."

Richard nodded curtly, but hesitated. "What of you?" he finally asked. "Shall I get a physician first—your leg needs attention."

Her voice almost apologetic, Pilar said, "I think that a physician would be a very good idea—I know that it is too soon yet and most inconsiderate, but I am very much afraid that I am going to have the baby now."

All eyes turned to Pilar and the spreading stain that marred her nightclothes. Again there were several minutes of utter confusion, Zeus finally bellowing for Richard to get the physician, *immediately!*

It was a chaotic, tense night. The physician was summoned by Phoebe, while Richard set off to find the elusive Will Blackwell, and Delicia, proving extremely efficient, despite her great bulk, got Pilar settled upstairs and provided Zeus with some pillows and a large, *very* large tankard of brandy.

When Richard returned around ten o'clock in the morning, exhausted and bleary-eyed from searching through the many dens of vice to be found in Port Royal, he found the house oddly quiet. It was only as he started up the stairs that he became aware of the lusty crying of a newborn infant. From the multitude of sounds that wafted down the stairs, he judged that the child had an unusually good pair of lungs, and some of his fear lightening, Richard hurried up the stairs.

He halted at the sight which met his eyes when he reached the upper hallway. Zeus, his leg now set in a splint and resting on a large stool, sat in one of the chairs from the main *sala.* In his hand was an empty tankard, and on his face was the most idiotically pleased smile Richard had ever seen. From the open doorway leading into the bedroom came the murmurs of Pilar, Phoebe and Delicia, the lower sounds of the physician's voice intermingling with those of the women; and above it all, was the loud screaming of the baby.

At Richard's approach, Zeus glanced up and his eyes narrowed; the smile vanished. "Did you find him?"

Wearily Richard nodded. "We leave within the hour." His gaze strayed to the doorway. "Is all well?"

That incredibly silly smile crossed Zeus' face and blissfully he stated, *"Twins!* My Pilar has given me twin sons!"

Chapter Thirty-one

THE happy state engendered by Pilar's safe birthing of two fine sons did not last, fear and grave concern for Maria overshadowing the joyous occasion. Zeus cursed du Bois, his broken leg and the wicked fate that had overseen this night's events. Yet there was nothing that he could do but glumly bid Richard farewell and charge him not to return to Port Royal without Maria ... or some definite word as to her fate.

Richard had his reservations about his own abilities to complete the task set before him successfully, but with his usual pragmatic attitude, he sailed away on the *Caroline*, trusting that Zeus' faith in the less than prepossessing Will Blackwell was well founded. It was. There was little that Blackwell would not do for Lancaster, and as he was an able seaman, familiar with the ways of the buccaneers and privateers and more than capable of finding his way around the Caribbean, Richard was in good hands. With just a little luck, they might be able to overtake du Bois before he reached Santo Domingo and then wrest Maria from his dastardly clutches. Precisely how this was to be accomplished, Richard preferred not to think, but even less did Richard like to think of facing Lancaster with the unpleasant news that his beloved wife had been stolen right out from beneath the noses of the two men he had trusted to guard her. All Richard could console himself with was the knowledge that at least they were in fast pursuit, and that du Bois did not have an insurmountable lead.

The *Caroline* was sleek and swift, and with all her canvas spread, she was sure to cut down on the distance between the two ships. . . . And then, Richard thought uncomfortably, then the real danger for Maria would begin! He spared a thought for her, wondering if she was unharmed, wishing that there were some miraculous way that he could undo last night's terrible events. All he could do was hope that she knew that *someone* was coming to her rescue.

Maria did know it—she was positive that Zeus had heard what du Bois had said about taking her to Diego in Santo Domingo, and she was certain that help was on the way. But it was small comfort at most, and as she lay on the dirty pallet that du Bois had thrown her in the tiny, cramped cabin of the pinnace, to bolster her own failing courage, she patted her protruding stomach and muttered, "Things are not good for us right now, *chico*, but we must be very brave and not let that swine du Bois know how very afraid we are." As if in reply, the babe gave a strong kick, and despite her fears, Maria smiled. "I know we shall think of something." But Maria was not too sure that she could find a way out of this trap, and the information that she was being taken to her brother was not exactly the most reassuring that she could have heard. Of course, it *was* much better to know that Diego was behind this ghastly set of circumstances than to think that she was completely at the mercy of du Bois and his merciless crew. But Maria didn't like to contemplate her brother's reaction when she was dumped, great with Gabriel's child, at his feet. A little shudder went through her. He was going to be furious!

Bravely she told herself that she would be able to calm him, that he was her brother and that he loved her and that, after his first shock, she would be able to convince him to have her returned to Port Royal. Deliberately, she repelled the unworthy thought that she was only deluding herself, reminding herself, again and again, of the times that Diego had been kind to her, telling herself that he would not harm her. But somehow she wasn't very comforted by those staunch ideas.

Being the prisoner of a man she hated and feared did not help matters, and du Bois' ugly comments when they had finally reached the pinnace and he had locked her in

the cabin had made it clear that he was within a hairs-
breadth of breaking his unwilling bargain with Diego.
The blue eyes had roamed over her disheveled state, and
he had even dared to touch her breast as he had growled,
"Do not cause me any trouble, wench, or promise or not,
even with your swelling belly, I shall lay you on the deck
and have you as I should have in Puerto Bello." As Maria
had shrunk away from his touch, her blue eyes spitting
defiance and hate, he had smiled cruelly and added
harshly, "And when I am through with you, each of my
men shall take his turn and then we will throw you to
the sharks . . . so stay here and be *very* quiet."

Maria had not argued. There was a time to be bold and
a time to be prudent, and she had a strong suspicion that
now was definitely the time for prudence. Perhaps if she
had not been made ungainly by her pregnancy, if fear for
her unborn child had not tamped down the instinct to
strike out against du Bois, she might not have so meekly
obeyed his commands, but obey them she did, unwilling
to bring his attention to her and the child that grew in
her womb.

The journey that followed was grim. She lived in constant fear that at any moment the door might open and
that du Bois would have changed his mind and decided
that it would please him more to rape her and give her to
his men than to keep his bitterly given promise to Diego.
As the time passed and they sailed nearer to Santo Domingo, he made it appallingly clear that the bargain made
under duress grated abominably on him and his men and
that they had discussed among themselves the possibility
of simply having their way with her and then, after dis-
posing of her, going about their business, abandoning the
men held hostage on the *Santo Cristo.* Du Bois seemed to
like taunting her that way, watching with cruel amusement the revulsion and anger that she could not hide flit
across her expressive face, like the way she flinched at
his slightest touch—and he took several sly liberties, his
hand lingering on her shoulder when he brought her what
he fondly imagined was an evening meal, his foul breath
blowing hot against her cheeks as he bent too near her to
pick up her empty bowl. It was intolerable, and within
just a few days, Maria's features began to show the effects

of the strain she was under, lavender circles under her eyes proclaiming sleepless nights, gaunt hollows appearing in the gentle curve of her cheeks. It was obvious that the lack of fresh air and proper food were taking their toll. Du Bois even mocked her about it, saying coldly, "You must remember the child, little slut—I am looking forward to seeing the expression on your brother's face when he sees you with your swollen belly." Maria would have enjoyed putting a dagger through him for his taunts, but she merely dropped her gaze, unwilling to let him see the hatred and fury that gleamed in their dark blue depths.

Though Diego had named Santo Domingo for the place of transfer, du Bois was no fool, and not even to rescue his men would he blithely sail into the well-armed harbor of the Spanish. Anchoring in a small cove off the coast of Hispaniola, du Bois sent one of his men ashore for news. The news was not good. The *almirante* had sailed the previous day, on March twentieth, in search of Morgan's fleet, sailing upon word from a newly captured buccaneer toward Trinidad.

Du Bois hesitated. Should he wait? Or should he follow after Diego? There really was no decision to make. He did not want to linger in this vicinity, and he would much prefer to make the exchange on the open sea. The small pinnace was not up to fighting three Spanish warships, but one thing the past days had taught du Bois—she was fast—fast enough, he was willing to wager, to leave behind the bulky galleons with no trouble, once he had gotten his men back on board. That Diego would not keep his bargain never crossed du Bois' mind—he might be a savage buccaneer, but he had an honor of sorts and a bargain was a bargain. Without further speculation, he ordered his crew to set sail for Trinidad.

Ironically, not six hours after the pinnace had sailed, the *Caroline* slipped into the same cove and Blackwell sent one of his men on shore for news too. Like du Bois, Blackwell and Richard learned of the sailing of the Spanish fleet after the privateers, but they also learned of the pinnace that had so recently lain at anchor in this very spot. Excitement glittering in Richard's hazel eyes, he had quizzed the returning buccaneer closely, and it had soon become apparent that du Bois was following after the Armada de Barlovento. After buying some fresh supplies from the obliging herdsman who had given them their information, the *Caroline* spread her sails once more and followed swiftly in the wake of du Bois' pinnace.

The next two and a half weeks were not ones that Maria could ever look back on with anything other than revulsion and loathing, as du Bois doggedly sailed after the *Santo Cristo.* A permanent lump of ice seemed to be lodged where her heart should be, and the increasingly volatile situation that had begun to develop on board the pinnace only added to Maria's peril. The men had begun to argue and fight among themselves, and at night as she lay taut and nervous on her pallet, she could hear the angry sounds of their voices, and she shivered, curling into a protective ball around her distended womb. "Do not be frightened, *chico,"* she would say as much to comfort herself as anything else, "we will not be harmed. Your *tíos,* Zeus and Richard, will soon find us."

But so far, du Bois was keeping his promise to Diego, and she was unmolested in the suffocating confines of the tiny cabin. There were many moments of bleak despair, moments when she wondered if she would die here in this filthy little room, never seeing Gabriel again, never hearing him call her sweetheart again.

Despite the graveness of her situation, in the beginning she had been consoled by the knowledge that Zeus or Richard would be coming after her; she had even indulged in fantastic daydreams in which Gabriel miraculously appeared and swept her away from this wretched captivity. But when du Bois had given the order to sail for Trinidad, her hopes and confidence had plummeted. Her rescuers could now have no idea in which direction to look for her, and who knew what ugly fancy might overtake the brutal men who held her captive before they finally reached her brother . . . if they ever reached Diego?

She thought often of Gabriel, wondering with longing if she would ever see his beloved face again, trying very hard not to give way to hopelessness. But as the days dragged by interminably, it became nearly impossible for her to keep her courage high, and as March slid into April and the pinnace continued to zigzag its way through the

blue-green waters of the Caribbean in search of Diego's
fleet, she grew listless and dull-eyed, convinced that she
and her unborn child would suffer a grim fate.

It was far easier for her would-be rescuers to keep their
own spirits up; they knew they were closing fast and that
they were on the right track, that another day, another
hour might bring them the sight of the sails of du Bois'
pinnace. It had not always been so.

As the days had passed the *Caroline* persistently
skimmed swiftly across the Caribbean in pursuit of du
Bois, but never gained sight of the quarry, and Richard
had become frantic. Surely, he had argued with Blackwell, they should have seen some sign of the pinnace by
now. Had they been mistaken? Were they following the
wrong ship? Could she have changed course? Blackwell
had no answers, they could do nothing but continue in
the fading hope that they had not been mistaken and that
du Bois was just beyond the horizon.

Finally, though, to their great delight, they had received
some encouraging word. Hailing a passing French merchant
ship, they had learned many interesting things from its bluff,
congenial captain. The Armada de Barlovento had changed
course, no longer sailing for Trinidad—a pearl fisherman had
passed on to the fleet the intelligence that the pirates were
looting and raiding at Maracaibo, and the Spanish fleet had
immediately stood away for the Main. To Richard's impatient questions about du Bois, the French captain had replied carelessly, *"Oui!* I know the ship you mean." His brown
eyes narrowing, he had added slowly, "They too asked after
the Armada and seemed displeased by the news that I gave
them."

His voice ringing out like a pistol shot, Richard had
demanded, "When? When did you speak with them?"

The captain had shrugged. "Just a few hours ago."

It was all the men aboard the *Caroline* needed to hear,
and with a new will and energy, they set their sails, and
like the Spanish fleet ahead of them, and du Bois following in its wake, they stood away for the Main, their sails
stretched taut and full by the ocean breeze. The gloom
that had been with them evaporated, and with eager eyes
they had scanned the horizon in the following days, cer-

tain that their luck had changed and that their quarry would be sighted at any moment.

Diego had been thinking of *his* quarry as the *Santo Cristo,* leading the frigate *San Luis* and the smaller *Neustra Señora de La Soledad,* a converted French merchant ship, had sped across the waves toward the Gulf of Venezuela and a rendezvous with fate. Soon, he had told himself as he had stood on the deck of the *Santo Cristo,* his eyes fixed on the far horizon, soon he would have those insolent buccaneer dogs within his grasp and when he did . . . He smiled cruelly. When he did, he would pray that the Englishman Lancaster was among them.

Diego would get his wish. Without a doubt Gabriel was among the men busily and methodically raiding in the huge inland freshwater sea of the Laguna de Maracaibo. But Gabriel's heart was not in it; his heart was in Port Royal, his thoughts nearly always on Maria and their coming child. Yet despite having no way of knowing it, Gabriel was uneasily aware that something was not right. Never given to premonition and the like, he pushed aside his increasingly ominous feelings, telling himself sternly that his unsettling emotions were simply because he was lonely and missed Maria intolerably. But that didn't still his uneasiness, didn't dispell his longing for this particular venture to be finished and for them to be sailing home. Home to Port Royal. Home to his bewitching, beguiling Spanish rose, Maria.

In spite of his reluctance to be here, Gabriel had been forced to admit that things had gone rather well—especially considering the disastrous start at *Ile-a-Vache* and the unpleasant weeks that had followed. But once Maracaibo had been selected as their target, problems had seemed to unravel themselves and events had gone smoothly.

After departing from Saona for the Spanish Main, the buccaneer fleet had reached the Dutch island of Aruba, where they had stocked up with fresh supplies, buying sheep and goats from the native herdsmen. They did not linger, stealing away under the cover of darkness to disguise their destination. The next morning they had entered the Gulf of Venezuela. The vast gulf, a wide cavity in the Spanish Main coast, was also shallow and well known for its treacherous winds and currents, but the experienced sailors who sailed with Morgan had no trouble crossing the gulf, again by darkness. Without incident the buccaneer fleet finally arrived at the Barra de Maracaibo.

The Barra de Maracaibo consisted of three small islands, Isla de San Carlos, Isla Zapara and Isla Barbozo. The low-lying islands were surrounded by shoals and sandbanks, and they effectively blocked the entrance to the narrow stretch of water which connected the Gulf of Venezuela to the Bay of Tablazo and which opened onto the Laguna de Maracaibo and the cities within that the buccaneers had come to plunder.

The buccaneers had not found it as easy to breach those islands as they had the gulf. The dangerous twisting of the extremely shallow channel across the bar between the middle island of Zapara and the western island of San Carlos was daunting enough, but in the time that had passed since Jasper had been here raiding, the Spaniards had not been idle. A fort, the Fuerte de la Barra, had been constructed on the eastern tip of San Carlos, and it dominated the narrow channel, the shining bronze cannons making it obvious that the fort was well armed and primed to fight off all intruders.

But the Spaniards had not been prepared for the ferocity of Morgan's men. After a day of fitful firing at the attacking buccaneers, when night fell, the Spanish soldiers abandoned the fort to the intruders. The fort was dismantled by the buccaneers as swiftly as possible, the guns torn from the walls of the fort and spiked and then covered with sand. Everything else of value was divided and given to the men.

Guided by canoes manned by sharp-eyed lookouts, the privateer fleet sailed across the bar, and so the first of March had found Morgan and the others nearing their destination. But some of the ships had gone aground while crossing the Bay of Tablazo, which was not very deep and full of shoals and quicksand. The ships that *did* successfully navigate the bay's treacherous waters, the *Dark Angel* and the *Lucifer* among them, had taken on the crews of the grounded vessels. It was then easy sailing to Maracaibo.

Once Gabriel would have enjoyed this sort of foray against the despised Spanish, but now he no longer hated the entire Spanish race; there was only *one* Spaniard whose blood he yearned to spill and consequently, he did not join in with his usual grim satisfaction when the attack began. Oh, he fought well, he could do nothing else, but that craving to strike at *all* things Spanish no longer drove him, and he was conscious time and time again of his lack of enthusiasm for what he was doing.

Perhaps if the Spaniards had been better armed, if the odds had been stacked more unfavorably against the buccaneers, he might have been able to whip up some of his old hatred and contempt, but Maracaibo had already been warned of their approach and they found the city empty and deserted. Some of the residents had not fled far enough or fast enough, however, and a raiding party had scoured the nearby countryside and had returned with thirty prisoners and a mule train ladened with booty. The usual practices of looting and drunken carousing then began. Gabriel found it boring and swore that when he returned home, the first ship to England would have a letter for the King—a letter beseeching his sovereign lord to relieve him of this most unwelcome chore. Gabriel smiled. He'd put if far more tactfully than *that!*

After a week spent in Maracaibo, the buccaneers had taken over a hundred prisoners and had cleared the countryside for thirty miles inland of cattle and other valuables and moved on to their next goal—the settlement of Gibraltar at the far end of the lagoon. The events of Maracaibo were repeated and while the others drank and whored, Gabriel spent his nights alone, the only woman he wanted, he thought, an ocean away from him.

Finally, however, to his great joy, came the day in early April when Morgan ordered his crews to return to Maracaibo, where they would prepare themselves for sea. And unaware that the object of all his thoughts and longing was much closer than he realized, Gabriel was full of delight at the prospect of sailing soon for Jamaica. But if he had known of Maria's plight that April morn, if he had known that she was in Diego's power, his step would not have been so light, his heart not so joyous.

When du Bois' pinnace had at last sighted the sails of

Diego's fleet anchored off the Barra de Maracaibo, and his not unhandsome face showing his satisfaction, du Bois had told her of it, Maria had known a huge surge of relief. Surely she would be safe now! There was still Diego's rage to confront when he discovered her pregnant state, but with an outwardly calm expression, Maria allowed du Bois to ferry her across to the massive *Santo Cristo*.

Diego was startled when he saw her—he had been certain that she was waiting for him safely and comfortably in Santo Domingo. The flowing cloak she was wearing hid her swelling stomach, but seeing how worn she was, how frail she looked, he turned angrily to du Bois. "I believe," Diego said in a dangerous voice, "that I told you to take her to Santo Domingo."

Thumbs hooked in the leather belt around his waist, du Bois replied tautly, *"Oui!* You did . . . but then you were not there and it seemed . . . safer to come after you." Du Bois had not thought things out very clearly and he was not comfortable with the situation, that sixth sense developed over years of getting himself out of dangerous corners warning him that he may have made a mistake, a fatal mistake. He realized that he should have taken more precautions, that it had been stupid on his part to have so blindly assumed that the black-eyed devil before him was going to keep their bargain. Consideringly, he glanced around, eyeing the distance to the railings. If things turned nasty, as he suddenly very much suspected they would, could he get over the sides of the galleon fast enough and could he make it to the pinnace before either the *Santo Cristo*'s marksmen shot him or the larger ship turned her many cannon on his small craft? It didn't look good, and he cursed himself for boldly approaching the galleon. He should have used his possession of Maria to better advantage and should never have left himself so vulnerable. Edging nearer the rail, hiding his inward disquiet, he asked with apparent confidence, "My men? Will you now keep your part of the bargain?"

Diego looked down his nose at him. "I do not," he said slowly, "bargain with the likes of you!" And then he flicked his fingers.

Before du Bois could move, a shot rang out. He staggered and almost resignedly touched the sudden splash of bright red blood that appeared on his breast. His voice thick, he got out, "I knew I should never have trusted a whoreson Spaniard!" and fell facedown onto the deck of the *Santo Cristo,* dead.

Another signal from Diego and the *Santo Cristo*'s cannons roared, bombarding the pinnace with deadly accuracy. In a matter of minutes the pinnace had been sunk and with satisfaction Diego turned away.

In stunned horror, Maria had watched it all, and she looked at her brother with something akin to loathing. She had hated and feared du Bois, but he had kept his word, had kept the infamous bargain Diego had forced upon him, and his reward had been death. Condemnation in her glance, she breathed angrily, "He trusted you! He *believed* you! And you betrayed him. What manner of man are you?"

Diego stared at her coldly, thinking that her captivity had not improved her appearance very much. Her eyes were sunken, her color pallid, her usually shiny black hair hung about her shoulders limply, and Diego's mouth twisted with distaste. He could only hope that by the time Don Clemente saw her again she would have recovered the roses in her cheeks and that her eyes would have lost their lackluster look. Not even replying to her, he said to his lieutenant, "Take her to my cabin and see that some arrangements are made for her to bathe—I can smell her from here!"

It was not a very warm reunion between the siblings, and Maria flushed, her blue eyes darkening with anger. But she remained silent, uneasily aware that time had not improved her brother's arrogance. Still she couldn't help asking tartly, "And clothes? Could *that* also be arranged? After weeks in these garments, a bath will not improve matters much if I am forced to don them again."

Diego made a face and sent an inquiring look to his lieutenant. That young man looked uncomfortable, but he cleared his throat and mumbled, "There are some things that I was taking to my, er, mistress . . . I would be honored, if your sister could find something suitable among them."

An hour later, washed and gowned in an odd assortment of ill-fitting orange and scarlet silks that did nothing to obscure the rounded protrusion of her stomach, Maria nervously awaited Diego in his elegant cabin. Knowing that she was clean helped her confidence just a little, but only a little. Her pregnancy was too far advanced to hide, and even with the full skirts and petticoats, her state was unmistakable. It was fortunate that she did not know then of Diego's plans for her.

But his plans were very much on his mind as Diego walked toward his cabin. He had Maria safely within his power once more; tomorrow his fleet would find a way to cross into the Bay of Tablazo, and then ... Almost rubbing his hands with glee, he thought as he opened the door to his cabin, and then I shall have those hellish buccaneers trapped!

Entering the room, the very first thing he noticed was Maria's no-longer-slim form. He blanched as he realized her condition, and his eyes dilated with a nearly insane fury as once again he saw his glorious plans vanishing right in front of him. Before Maria was even aware of his presence, he was at her side and with all the force with which he was capable, he struck her, his hand catching her cruelly on the side of the face, the force of the blow sending her crashing heavily to the floor. "Slut!" he snarled. "How could you? How dare you bring this sort of dishonor upon me!"

Dazed by the unexpectedness of his actions, as well as the power behind the blow, Maria stared up at his rage-contorted face, wondering sickly if she had ever known him, wondering how she could have ever thought that she loved him ... or that he loved her. Dismayed and angered by his actions, she sought some way to calm this explosive situation. Awkwardly she struggled to her feet, and hiding her trepidation, she faced him proudly, her head held high. Quietly she said, "I really didn't have much to say about it, but lest you think that I was unwilling—I was not! I love Gabriel Lancaster! He is my husband and I am pleased to be carrying his child!"

Too furious to speak, Diego glared at her, his hands clenching and unclenching at his sides, as if he could hardly restrain himself from fastening them around her slender neck and choking the life out of her. Warily, Maria eyed him, but unwilling to be cowed, she said with more confidence than she felt, "I appreciate all that you have gone through to free me from what you must have believed was a shameful captivity, but it was unnecessary. I wish to be returned to Jamaica."

When Diego remained silent, his face hard and set as he stared at her, she took comfort from the fact that his hands were no longer moving so convulsively at his sides and she approached him. Her eyes full of pleading, she looked up into his swarthy face, telling herself that affection did exist between them, that he would not really hurt her, that in the end he would not let his fury at this situation drive him to rash action. Tentatively she touched his hand, saying softly, "Diego, let me go back to Port Royal. I am happy there . . . happier than I have ever been in my life. There is nothing for me at Santo Domingo, and if you force me to go back to Casa de la Paloma, I will only run away and try to find my husband."

Like a statue Diego stood there, his eyes black with the thwarted rage that boiled within him. Hoping that he was getting his temper under control, Maria implored gently, "Let me go. I can be nothing but an embarrassment to you now. And even if you think to pretend that these past months did not happen, and find a way to keep me prisoner, my child will always be a living reminder. . . ."

Diego's eyes flickered to her stomach. Icily he said, "Newborn infants die. I'm sure that such a fate can be arranged for the bastard that grows within your womb!"

Repelled, Maria shrank back from him, whatever affection she had ever felt for him utterly destroyed. Her hands protectively covering her stomach, she spat, "You would *dare?* Harm my child, Diego, and I will find a way to kill you!"

His eyes narrowed, a thought suddenly occurring to him. A mirthless smile twisted his mouth and he retorted, "Very well, then, the brat shall live . . . as long as you do *precisely* what I want." He grasped her wrist and dragged her up next to him. "Forget about ever seeing the Englishman again—tomorrow, if he is with the buccaneer dogs within the Laguna de Maracaibo, he will die. You will be, dear sister, a widow." He grinned nastily. "But we won't tell Don Clemente about *that,* will we? Nor will we mention the bastard I will keep at my side to ensure

that you obey me and go to your new husband a willing
and obedient bride, will we?"

Maria looked at him with horror and contempt. "You're
mad!" she cried. "I will never marry Don Clemente!" A
frown crossed her forehead, and slowly, she asked, "He is
married, have you forgotten?"

"Ah," he said lightly, "I'm afraid you are mistaken—
his wife is dead—I believe that she fell down a flight of
stairs. . . . He wrote to me last year, proposing the match
which you so unwisely refused years ago." His face darkened and his voice became menacing. "A match that *will*
take place this time! You will not destroy my chance for
advancement again. Marry him and be a docile wife and
I shall oee to it that no harm comes to your brat . . . defy
me and I will strangle the bastard with my own two
hands! Now do we understand each other?"

Maria looked at him as if she had never seen him before, numbed that he could act this way, and yet not so
completely surprised. She had always known of his dark
side, had always known of his ruthless ambition and lust
for power, but that he would so wantonly destroy her
life, would murder an innocent babe to further his way,
she had never dreamed. She swallowed painfully, realizing finally, that Diego loved *no one* but himself, that
the flashes of kindness he had shown her in the past
had been empty and meaningless, that he cared no more
for her than he would a useful dog to serve him. A hysterical little giggle of laughter rose up from within her.
To think that she had tried to warn him, to save his
life! To think of the nightmares she had suffered, the
pain she had endured torn between honor and family
pride, torn between her affection for the man she had
thought him to be and her growing love for Gabriel. It
was ludicrous! Diego was not worthy of it, not worthy
of one moment's concern, and she turned away from
him, damning herself for being a fool. But there was no
time to dwell on her past foolishness, there was her child
to think of, her future to fight for; and playing for time,
determined to find a way out of this trap, she said coolly,
"Yes, we do understand each other . . . *completely!* Now
will you leave me alone? I am very tired and wish to
rest—the past weeks have not been pleasant."

Diego bowed and left her. Alone, she walked over to the casement windows staring blindly out at the gulf. What would become of her? And even of more urgent concern, where was Gabriel? Was he with these buccaneers? Would he indeed die tomorrow? Her composure cracked a bit, her lower lip trembling. I will *not* cry, she vowed fiercely, pushing away the tears that threatened to fall. I will find a way out of this! I will find Gabriel!

A slight movement caught her eye, and with a sudden leap in her breast she stared hard in the direction of the Isla de San Carlos, just off the stern of the *Santo Cristo.* Had she seen a sail? Had that brief flash of white that had disappeared so quickly been another ship? A ship that might be coming to the rescue? Ah, *Dios,* she prayed, let it be!

It was indeed a rescue ship, but as Richard and Blackwell had discussed earlier as the *Caroline* gamely hugged the swampy, hostile coast of Isla de San Carlos and tried to keep the Spanish fleet in sight without revealing herself, it was doubtful at best and impossible at worst for them to effect Maria's rescue. Their gallant little sloop would be no match for the three large and heavily armed warships, and certainly the Spaniards drastically outnumbered their small crew and made a confrontation unthinkable.

With a grim determination, Richard and Blackwell, along with two others, had paddled the *Caroline*'s gig to the unwelcoming shore of the Isla de San Carlos, Blackwell warning that the island was inhabited by cannibal Indians, the Caribs. Leaving the gig, doggedly Richard and Blackwell had crept through the swampy shore, hoping to get a better view of what was taking place on board the *Santo Cristo* before returning to the gig and the *Caroline.* Hidden among the tangled roots of the mangroves, they had watched helplessly as Maria had been ferried to her brother's ship by du Bois, bitter frustration rising up through them. To have come so close . . .

The sound of the shot that had ended du Bois' life had alarmed them, and then when the pinnace had been blown up, a sensation of deep gloom had fallen over the two men.

It had only been the previous evening that a lookout on

the *Caroline* had spotted the sails of the pinnace disappearing on the horizon. Immediately every bit of canvas on board the sloop had been pressed into action, and the crew had been confident that by dawn they would have overtaken their quarry. But this morning, spying the huge, towering sails of the *Santo Cristo* and realizing that du Bois had reached his destination, they had sought concealment, guiding the *Caroline* as near to the shore as they dared and anchoring her out of sight of the other ships. It had been then that Richard and Blackwell had departed in the gig to observe what was happening between the pinnace and the Spanish warships. After the pinnace had been destroyed, Richard had turned to Blackwell and muttered, "We must do something! But what?" Dispiritedly he had added, "I am a landoman, not a sailor! I am no buccaneer! I only know how to plant and sow, it is the master who should be here—he would know what to do!"

Blackwell, his weather-beaten face thoughtful, had rubbed a hand across his stubble-covered chin. "Aye. If there were some way of reaching Lancaster . . ."

Richard's eyes suddenly brightened. "But of course! It will be dangerous, to be sure, but on foot, we could march for Maracaibo." Blackwell did not seem overly enthusiastic about the idea, but Richard continued dauntlessly, "We cannot sail into the lagoon—not with the Spanish fleet guarding its entrance, but if we could make it through the swamps . . ."

Blackwell glanced uneasily about at the forbidding jungle, thinking of the Carib Indians and the tales he had heard. He also thought of Gabriel's face when informed of his unwillingness to continue further, and slowly he had nodded his grizzled head. *Much* better to face the possibility of meeting up with savage, man-eating Caribs than to bear the wrath of the Dark Angel!

Returning to the *Caroline* and fearful that she might be discovered this close, Blackwell had ordered her to heel about to remove to a safer distance from the Spanish. Fortunately, only Maria had seen that brief glimpse of white sails as the sloop had changed position.

After a hasty meeting, Richard's plan was endorsed and leaving a skeleton crew on board the sloop, the others stealthily and a little fearfully plunged into the tangled, murky swamps that reached out into the very gulf itself. It was unsettling and unpleasant going, but even as night fell, they slowly and torturously fought their way toward Maracaibo. Eventually they left the deep swamps but found their way blocked by a nearly impenetrable jungle. Finally, however, they neared the outskirts of their destination. As luck would have it, Morgan and his victorious privateers had only just arrived back at Maracaibo late the previous evening.

Word of the sudden appearance of the men from the *Caroline* spread like wildfire through the buccaneer ranks, and in a scant space of time, Richard and Blackwell were standing in front of Morgan, Gabriel and Jasper in the saddler's shop that Morgan had claimed as his headquarters. Sparing himself nothing, Richard bluntly recited the events of the past weeks, his gaze steadily meeting the dawning horror in Gabriel's eyes. The news of the Spanish warships blocking the only way out from the huge inland sea that composed the Laguna de Maracaibo had not disturbed Gabriel, but the incredibly appalling information that Maria had been kidnapped by du Bois and was with her brother on the *Santo Cristo* was devastating. . . .

Richard's mere presence, here in the wilds of the Spanish Main, had caused Gabriel to stiffen, his features held tightly. He had known that he would hear terrible news, but when he had learned the worst, when he had learned that his sweet wife may have suffered vile, unspeakable degradations at the hands of du Bois, his naked anguish was painful to see. Some of the strain left his face when Richard spoke of seeing Maria ferried to the *Santo Cristo*—he could take comfort from the fact that she was at least still alive—but she was still in great danger. She was on board an enemy ship, a ship the buccaneers *must* destroy if they were to escape with their vessels out into the open waters of the Gulf of Venezuela.

Chapter Thirty-two

IT was Jasper's hand roughly clasping his shoulder that finally brought Gabriel back from the black hell into which he had fallen. With difficulty he focused his gaze, trying desperately to gather his wits about him. There was not a moment to be wasted, plans must be made, and later, much later, when he had Maria safely in his arms again, then perhaps he could come to grips with the terror and fury that coiled in his vitals. His emotions rigidly under control, his face curiously devoid of any expression, he said flatly, "I will find a way to free her ... I will need a diversion of some sort to cover my boarding of the *Santo Cristo.*"

"*Mon Dieu!* Don't be a fool! You cannot rescue her alone!" Jasper burst out angrily, the blue eyes glittering with both anger and compassion.

Somewhat thoughtfully, Morgan regarded Gabriel in the gloom of the saddler's shop. "I think," he began slowly, "that we must work out a scheme that will give us all what we want. ... We must get past those Spanish ships and at the same time ensure that your lady is freed." The black eyes glowing with supreme confidence, he growled, "No Spanish dog is going to defeat *me!* I am Harry Morgan!"

It was a long day. Jasper, Richard, Blackwell and the others made certain that Gabriel was not left to his own devices—no one had any doubt but that for their careful guarding, he would have immediately headed straight for the *Santo Cristo,* intent upon only one thing—freeing Maria.

There was not much conversation to be gotten from him; he was unnaturally silent, his face closed and shuttered.

He was obviously unwilling to reveal again the savage rage and painful anxiety that clawed its way through him. Only the hard shine of the emerald eyes gave any indication of the ugly and agonizing thoughts that he was experiencing, and even his friends walked warily around him, uneasily aware that at any time he might explode into rash action, driven mad by the powerful emotions that filled him.

That evening, a message arrived from Diego. It was blunt. If the buccaneers surrendered, he would give them clemency—if they did not, with the frigates that he had sent for from Caracas, and which would be arriving soon, he would sail to Maracaibo and would destroy the buccaneers utterly. Every man would be put to the sword.

A mirthless smile on his handsome face, Gabriel finished reading the message and tossed it back to Morgan. "Don't believe him," Gabriel drawled. "Delgato knows not the meaning of the word *clemency*—if you surrender, he will merely relieve you of your weapons and then slay you where you stand."

Morgan grinned wolfishly. "I never doubted it for a moment! I have called a meeting of the men to discuss this proposal with them—and I am certain of what their answer will be when they hear his terms."

The meeting was held in the center of the town, and as Morgan had predicted, the buccaneers were not interested in surrender—they had risked their lives to gain the booty that filled their ships and many had already had a taste of the "clemency" of the Spanish—they had no desire to taste it again. They would fight! And *damn* the odds!

Morgan's message to Diego was equally blunt. With a great flourish he had written: "Sir, having read your summons and having learned that you are so near, we shall save you the trouble of sailing with your nimble fleet to meet us, we shall come to you with all speed. As for clemency, yours we are acquainted with and wish none of it."

The next week passed in a flurry of wild activity as Morgan and his men prepared for battle, the buccaneers working from dawn till dark, arming their ships. For Gabriel, the constant work was the only thing that saved him from going quite mad. The nights were nearly unbearable, his restless dreams filled with images of Maria suffering brutality and cruel violations at du Bois' hands. It did him little good to dwell on the fact that du Bois was assumed dead, nor did it help to know that Maria was in her brother's hands. He strongly believed that while she might love Diego, Diego did not feel the same for her. Diego would make her suffer for marrying a Lancaster and as for the child . . . In the humid darkness of his room, Gabriel swallowed painfully. If she still carried the child, if these past weeks had not caused her to lose the babe, then its very existence would be a constant, infuriating goad to Diego. Who knew what he might do to her in a rage?

Gabriel had thought that nothing could have been worse than what he had gone through when the *Raven* had sunk and Elizabeth had died and he and Caroline had been forced into captivity, but he had been wrong. There were times when fear and frustration ate so painfully at his very soul that he was certain he would run amuck. He was full of rage, helplessness and fear, and there was *nothing* that he could do to relieve it. Nothing, for the moment, that he could do that would free Maria. Nothing except plan and wait for the battle that would come. No dreams of revenge crossed his mind as the days passed; there was only one driving, agonizingly insistent thought—find Maria and bring her to safety.

While the buccaneers worked busily getting ready for battle, Diego and the Spanish fleet were not idle either. On the same day that he had sent Morgan his demands for surrender, the *Santo Cristo,* nearly all her ballast and water thrown overboard, had finally been able to cross the bar that divided the Gulf of Venezuela from the Bay of Tablazo and the Laguna de Maracaibo. The big galleon took up her new position just off the Isla Zapara in the middle of the channel; *Soledad* and *San Luis* were anchored at equal distances to the starboard. Beyond them, but within cannon range, stood the recaptured Fuerte de la Barra, the fort on the eastern edge of Isla San Carlos which the Spaniards had been able swiftly to put back into some semblance of efficiency. With the Spanish ships blocking their only way out and the reinforced Fuerte de la Barra adding land support, the buccaneers were trapped. Confidently, from on board the *Santo Cristo,* Diego waited with growing impatience for his prey. He had those swinish buccaneers now! And thinking of the glory that would be his, of the honor and accolades that would be awarded him when he returned to Santo Domingo with Harry Morgan's corpse hanging from his yardarms, Diego smiled with glee. As for Lancaster ... His smile turned ugly. Lancaster, he would dismember before Maria's eyes and then toss the pieces to the sharks!

In the time that had passed since her arrival, Diego had become somewhat reconciled to her pregnant state. It made things difficult, but the unborn child also gave him a superior weapon to use against her ... she would do exactly as he ordered from now on, *especially* if she wished no harm to come to the bastard she would soon bear. Once the child was born, his sister would be totally at his mercy, the life of her child depending upon her obedience to his every whim. Diego's eyes glistened. Never again would she defy him! Never again would she upset his careful plans!

Maria had found the time on board the *Santo Cristo* a conflicting interlude of restfulness and agitation. She no longer had to live in stark terror that at any moment du Bois and his cutthroat crew might come bursting through the door to rape and murder her nor did she have to fear that she would die alone in the filthy cramped cabin of du Bois' pinnace, her body indifferently thrown into the sea. She was clean, she was well fed and her brother's cabin on the *Santo Cristo* was both spacious and elegant. Within reason she had the run of the ship and the young lieutenant, Miguel Colon, whose mistress had so inadvertently provided Maria with clothing, frequently escorted her for brisk walks along the decks of the *Santo Cristo*. But her heart was heavy, her spirit distressed, Diego's strictures and attitude making it dreadfully clear that she would never be allowed to see Gabriel again; that her child would be held hostage for her continued docile behavior. She was sickened when she viewed the future, almost preferring to die than to live as Diego would order. The coming battle with the buccaneers filled her with both fright and hope—she had no way of knowing positively, but she was convinced that Gabriel would be among them and that she might indeed be forced to watch the final horror, Diego's killing of her husband. But she also clung to the faint hope that somehow Gabriel would find her and that together they would confound Diego. Relent-

lessly, she racked her brain for ways of escape, planning
and discarding dozens of wild schemes, bleakly aware that
until after the child was born there was nothing she could
do to free herself. But once she had regained her lithe
form, once the babe was born . . .

Maria had no way of knowing that Gabriel had learned
of her situation; nor did she have any way of knowing for
certain whether Gabriel still lived—he could have been
killed in any number of buccaneer engagements since that
day he had left her on the docks at Port Royal. Stubbornly, she told herself that he *was* alive, that somehow
they would find their way to each other. But it was not
easy to keep hope alive, and there were moments when
she was nearly swamped by a feeling of utter despair, her
only joy the movements of the growing babe within her.
But there was not much else to give her pleasure, the
preparations for the coming battle with the buccaneers
were a continual unwelcome reminder that soon she and
her unborn child would be in the very midst of a vicious
fight; that the cannons of Gabriel's own ship might very
well unknowingly cause her death and that of their child.
It was a chilling thought, the alternative being equally
chilling—that Gabriel might die beneath the death-deal-
ing guns of the *Santo Cristo.*

There were daily reports brought to Diego from the
many spies he had set to watch the buccaneers, and from
these reports he gleaned much useful information. The
buccaneers were swiftly arming a large Cuban merchant
ship they had captured earlier in the lagoon and were
converting it into a flagship for their ragtag fleet. Extra
cannon were being mounted on the Cuban vessel and
much work was being done to reinforce her hull. It was
also learned that one of the sloops was being primed as a
fire ship. That news made Diego instantly take measures
to counteract this grave threat.

A fire ship was one of the most dreaded weapons in
naval warfare; it was particularly effective against anchored ships like the *Santo Cristo* and the others, the
great wooden vessels having no defenses against it if it
was their misfortune to be struck by such a weapon. Filled
and packed with every manner of combustible, these fire
ships were driven into their quarry, where they would

burst into flames and engulf the other ship, completely destroying it. Diego lined the decks of his ships with barrels of water and demanded that long brooms be cut to ward off such a menace. This done, he was ready, smugly confident that *nothing* could go wrong, that when the battle ended, he would be overwhelmingly victorious.

On the morning of April fifteenth, Maria was suddenly awakened by the sound of much frantic movement and with clumsy limbs, her advancing pregnancy making her awkward, she dressed. Completing a hasty toilet, she made her way to the deck of the *Santo Cristo,* and looking toward the Laguna de Maracaibo, with a leap in her pulse, she saw that the buccaneer fleet was now in sight, anchored just out of range of the Spanish guns. It was apparent that they were waiting until the wind and tide were in their favor before beginning the attack, and with a dry mouth, Maria stared at them, color rushing into her face when she finally recognized the *Dark Angel* among the buccaneer ships. Joy and terror surged through her body, and for one awful moment she thought that she would burst into tears—whether they were happy ones or frightened ones, she didn't know. One hand resting comfortingly on her greatly rounded stomach, she murmured with a mixture of delight and fear, "Oh, *chico!* He is there with them . . . I know it! He will be coming to rescue us soon!"

Across the wide distance that separated the Spanish ships from Morgan's fleet, from his position on the forecastle deck of the *Dark Angel,* Gabriel suddenly spotted the small female figure as Maria stood near the railings of the *Santo Cristo.* He froze, every nerve in his big body painfully taut. Hungrily he stared at her, knowing it was Maria, knowing that she was so close and yet so agonizingly far away from him. He could not make out her features across the width of water that lay between them, but some of the icy unnamed terror that had been his eased. She was still alive! His fist clenched, his dark face dangerous with promise. Soon, he vowed grimly, she would be safe with him!

To Gabriel's raging frustration and Diego's equally furious disappointment, it was two days later before the conditions the buccaneers were waiting for occurred. Diego would have brought the battle to them earlier, but in the shallow waters, with its hidden shoals and sandbars, he dared not try to maneuver, and he was forced to wait, his impatience and excitement growing with every passing hour. Soon. Soon, the battle would begin. Soon, he would show these arrogant dogs the true power of Spain!

At nine o'clock in the morning of the seventeenth of April the buccaneer fleet set sail—straight for the *Armada de Barlovento,* the Cuban ship proudly flying the English Admiral's flag. On one side she was flanked by the *Lilly* and on the other, the *Dark Angel.*

On board the *Santo Cristo,* Diego's lip curled in contempt as he watched the ships approach. His eyes gleamed as he recognized the *Dark Angel.* At last! At last he would rid himself of the Lancasterian swine, as he should have done years ago.

None of the three vessels which led the buccaneer fleet in Diego's direction appeared to pose much of a threat. The *Santo Cristo* towered high above them, and with her nearly three hundred fighting men and her sixty cannon, she was more than a match for this puny force! Alone she could take care of the three lead ships, and let the *Soledad* and *San Luis* blow the remaining privateer ships from the water. His hand tightened on the hilt of his sword. They would make short work of these impudent buccaneers!

The moment the privateer fleet came into range, the cannons of the Spanish ships began a furious assault upon them, and in the much smaller ships, with their far fewer guns, as was to be expected, the privateers took a terrible beating. But the buccaneers were not deterred, inexorably they came on and on, obviously determined to close and board, using their pistols and cutlasses to even up the odds against them.

Below in the captain's cabin of the *Santo Cristo,* Maria listened to the thunderous roar of the cannons, her face white, her prayers and every thought with Gabriel. Ah, *Dios,* she prayed, keep him safe! Do not let harm befall him! Restlessly she paced the floor, desperate to know what was happening above her, frantic at being locked in the cabin by Diego.

Above on the deck of his ship, Diego watched with narrowed gaze as the three lead ships suddenly divided—the

Dark Angel sailed smoothly toward the stern of the *Santo Cristo,* impervious to the cannon fire that came her way, the *Lilly* steered for the bow; and with flags streaming and cannons blazing, Morgan's flagship, the Cuban merchantman, was held to course. A course aimed directly to hit the galleon full amidships.

The collision came with a grinding and splintering of wood as the buccaneer flagship crashed mightily into the *Santo Cristo.* The buccaneers immediately flung out their grappling hooks and irons, locking the two ships together in a deadly embrace. All eyes were on the Cuban ship, Spanish troops preparing to board the insolent attacker, and no one noticed the small canoe that was suddenly lowered from the *Dark Angel* or the tall man who leaped into the frail craft and began to paddle furiously across the short distance that separated him from the massive galleon. There was not a moment to lose, and Gabriel was well aware of it; the Spaniards were about to be the recipients of a very nasty surprise when they boarded what they assumed was Morgan's flagship.

Only twelve men were aboard the former Cuban merchantman as she had rammed the *Santo Cristo,* but her decks had been lined with logs that had been painted and adorned with clothing to look like sailors. The interior of the entire ship was crammed with tar, pitch and any other highly combustible matter that could be found in the Maracaibo area, and even her decks and spars had been covered with inflammable material. More logs packed with gunpowder and fitted with short fuses had been placed in the newly cut portholes further to enhance the illusion that this was indeed the most powerful ship in Morgan's fleet. Once the Cuban ship had been tightly lashed to the Santo Cristo, the fuses would be lit and those few buccaneers aboard her would then leap into the water and swim frantically away from the stunning explosion that would follow.

Knowing that he would have precious few moments, Gabriel stood up carefully in the canoe, and even as the Spaniards rushed to board the Cuban vessel, he threw up a grappling hook, smiling grimly when it caught on to one of the railings of the poop deck of the galleon. He was, as yet, undetected, but that state could not last, nor did he expect it to. All he needed was enough time to get on board, then he would fight his way to hell to find Maria. But he didn't need to; as he swiftly scaled the dangling rope up toward the top, one of the windows that lined the stern of the ship flew open, and the dearest sound in the world came to him—Maria's voice.

"Gabriel!" she cried wonderingly. "In here, *por favor!* Quickly!"

He needed no further urging, and his dark face suddenly ablaze with vitality, he lithely swung into the captain's cabin. A second later Maria was swept into a powerful embrace, Gabriel's mouth warm and demanding on hers. The battle receded, the cannon's roar faded, nothing mattered but that they were together, their arms tightly wrapped around the other, their mouths meeting hungrily.

But almost immediately Gabriel firmly put her from him and muttered, "We must get out of here! Ramming the *Santo Cristo* was only a ruse; any second she is going to explode and engulf the *Santo Cristo* with flame!"

Maria's pale face whitened even further, but with her lovely eyes full of trust and love, she said calmly, "Very well then, let us leave—I have not liked my quarters very much anyway!"

Gabriel shot her a grin. "As you wish, madam!" For just a second his eyes dropped to her swollen stomach. His voice husky, he got out, "The babe? All is well?"

Maria smiled mistily at him. "I believe so—we have been through much together, but our child has caused me little trouble."

He crushed her to him for one moment more and then turned away saying, "It will be difficult, but do you think that with my help you can slide down the rope to the canoe?"

"With your help, I can do anything," she answered stoutly, ignoring the faint quiver of apprehension that went through her. But then, her purpose steady, she came to stand beside Gabriel near the window that he had entered bare seconds ago.

Gabriel glanced out the window, and his face a picture of resignation and, incredibly, amusement, he said, "I'm afraid that we have company, sweetheart."

The words had hardly left his lips when Jasper le Clair,

knife between his teeth, effortlessly swung into the room from the same window. Blue eyes gleaming with audacious daring, he removed the blade and said coolly, *"Mon ami!* Dĭd you think to have this adventure all to yourself? Didn't we all agree that once her brother had gotten her from the burning galleon, as he was certain to do, that we would then wrest her from him? I should have known that you would do something rash!"

Dryly Gabriel replied, "Following me wasn't rash? Besides, *you* agreed to the plan, I did not! I did not want to risk anything happening to her when Morgan's ingenious fire ship explodes—as it should at any second!"

As if he had conjured it up, the *Santo Cristo* was suddenly shaken by a violent explosion, the screams of dying men piercing the air, the ominous crackle of fire following almost instantaneously after the initial blast. His face grim, Gabriel said, "Since you are here, my friend, make yourself useful and let us get Maria away from here *now!"*

Mere moments had passed since Gabriel had first reached the *Santo Cristo,* and the sounds of the barbarous battle that was taking place all around them intruded unpleasantly. The roaring of the cannons as they belched forth death and destruction; the angry shouts of men as they rallied to fight and the pitiful shrieks of others as they lay wounded and dying; the softer, but equally deadly sound of the musket fire filled the cabin, making Gabriel sickly aware of the danger that faced them. Without further ado, he reached out for the rope that could gain them freedom, but even as he did so, the twisted length went limp in his grip. *Their presence had been discovered from above!* An excited shout from the poop deck confirmed this appalling news, and Gabriel wasn't at all surprised when a volley of musket fire whizzed downward. A swift look toward the water saw his worst suspicions realized—the canoe had been riddled with shot and was sinking before his eyes.

One arm protectively around Maria, his drawn sword firmly held in the other hand, he glanced wryly at Jasper. "It seems that we shall have to fight our way to the deck. If we dare to leave the ship this way, they will shoot us as we leap into the water and I, for one, do not intend to remain here to burn to death!"

The locked door gave the two men no trouble; they battered it down in a matter of moments. Through the opening billowed thick black smoke, confirming that the *Santo Cristo* was indeed ablaze. Lowering their heads, they plunged into the smoky passageway and stumbled forward; the stern hatch proved to be impenetrable, but they met no human resistance until they reached the main hatch and started toward the upper deck. It was there that they ran afoul of the four soldiers who had been ordered by Diego to bring Maria to him. Jasper and Gabriel wasted little time in swiftly dispatching three of the men, their flashing swords and knives efficiently banishing their opposition, the remaining Spaniard flying up the steps to warn those on deck. Maria had been pushed backward, away from the short ugly clash, but the skirmish pointed out clearly her helpless state and in a determined voice, she said, "I should have a weapon. A knife."

Breathing heavily, knowing that they had lost all element of surprise, the two men exchanged glances, and then his face hard and set, Gabriel handed her a long-bladed dagger. That once, long ago, he and Caroline had stood thus did not occur to him at the moment; all his thoughts were simply on getting Maria to safety. Even the knowledge that somewhere above him Diego could be found did not detract him from his goal, and together the three of them raced up the stairs, ready to face whatever lay ahead.

Pandemonium and disbelief reigned on the main deck of the galleon; the tubs of water so carefully placed along the sides of the ship had been useless against Morgan's crafty attack, and the *Santo Cristo* was fast becoming a flaming hulk. Seconds before Gabriel and the others had reached the upper deck, the ship's sails had been huge sheets of fire, and as the flames had shot higher and higher, the red and yellow-tongued fire had greedily consumed everything in its awesome path. As half-burned ropes and stays had given way, a rain of fiery debris had crashed onto the decks below, killing and maiming the astonished soldiers and crew. Amidship, where the Cuban vessel had rammed the *Santo Cristo,* the blaze was at its worst, smoke and gigantic waves of angry red fire exploding upward. There was nothing that could stop the uncon-

trollably destructive force of the fire, and the Spaniards
were frenziedly abandoning their once-proud galleon,
leaping with frightened disregard into the water far below them. The trap sprung, the privateers had rapidly
withdrawn. On the quarterdeck, Diego watched in
stunned fury the violent devastation of his ship . . . and
dreams of glory. He was ruined!

As Gabriel, Maria and Jasper struggled forward onto
the deck, their senses assaulted by the eye-stinging,
throat-clogging black smoke, the soldier who had survived the desperate fight near the main hatch ran up to
Diego. Gesturing wildly, he pointed in their direction.
Even across the smoke-filled distance between them, Diego's reaction was plain to see. The lips curled in a bestial
snarl; the black eyes slitted with loathing and hatred as
he stared at the trio below him on the main deck.

In one sweeping motion, Diego tore his blade free, and
his teeth bared, with a shriek of insane fury, he vaulted
nimbly over the rail to the deck below. Some of the others
still aboard the ship suddenly became aware of the intruders, and with Diego screaming orders, several of the
soldiers purposefully closed on Gabriel and Jasper.

The enemy aligned in front of them, Maria was hastily
shoved in back of Gabriel as his sword met the lunge of
the first man. Outnumbered, the deck littered with flaming obstacles and hampered by the need to keep Maria
safe behind them, inexorably the two buccaneers were
driven backward toward the towering forecastle deck at
the bow of the galleon. Gabriel and Jasper fought fiercely,
their swords inflicting terrible damage upon the Spaniards who had answered Diego's call, but still the desperate trio was driven further and further backward, until
there was no place for them to go except up the steps that
led to the forecastle deck.

Clumsily Maria stumbled up the steps, her heart
pounding, the dagger Gabriel had given her clutched securely in her hand. Wildly she looked around. Only the
breakhead of the ship lay beyond; this bit of deck would
be their last stand, and despairingly she glanced down at
the water which seemed so far below her. Blackened
pieces of spars and planks and the body of a dead man
floated past her eyes, and she shuddered, knowing that if

they were to escape that they were going to have to jump from this great height.

The sound of metal striking metal jerked her around, and with a combination of horror and hope, she watched as Gabriel and Jasper valiantly repelled the soldiers who had driven them so relentlessly to this final place. For a moment, it looked as if the Spaniards would be vanquished, and then suddenly, Jasper gave a cry as his sword arm was pierced by a thrust from one of the soldiers. His sleeve stained crimson by the wound, Jasper staggered badly, trying bravely to fight, but it was obvious that he could not. Gabriel redoubled his efforts, for the first time since he had held Maria in his arms in the *Santo Cristo*'s cabin, a thrill of fear shooting through him. Were they all to die here?

Busy savagely fending off the determined assault of the Spaniards in front of him, Gabriel had momentarily lost track of Diego. But then as the Spaniards retreated slightly to assess the situation, now that one of the buccaneer dogs had been wounded, Gabriel spotted Diego at the base of the steps. It was apparent that Diego had been waiting for his men to tire them before he moved in for the kill, and the disabling of Jasper seemed to be the cue that he had been waiting for.

The *Santo Cristo* a flaming ruin behind him, Diego stared upward at Gabriel. The few men between them seemed to disappear as they stared at each other, all the hatred they felt for each other plain to see on their faces. His voice thick, Diego commanded, "Leave him! He is mine!"

The soldiers scrambled away until nothing but the short length of steps stood between those two mortal enemies. Slowly, an ugly smile on his mouth, Diego climbed the steps, his swords held ready, his black eyes locked almost fondly on Gabriel's face. Very nearly purring, he said, "I have longed for this moment, English swine! And this time nothing shall stop me from killing you!"

Unemotionally Gabriel studied Diego's approach, deliberately clearing his mind of everything but what he must do to annihilate this one man. He cast a swift glance at Jasper and Maria. Jasper's face was haggard, one-half of his shirt drenched in blood, and Gabriel knew that his friend was very badly wounded. Maria stood nearby, her pregnancy painfully apparent, her skirts stained with Jasper's blood as she tried to prop up his sagging body, her face white and strained. She looked at Gabriel, all the love she felt for him shining in the sapphire eyes. Softly she murmured, "I love you. No matter what happens—I love you!"

Gabriel sent her a twisted smile, his heart swelling with love for her. Huskily, he admitted, "And I, sweetheart, have never loved you quite as much as I do at this moment ... I only wish ..." He stopped, spinning swiftly away, the gold hoop earring swinging wildly through the strands of the thick black hair as he leaped to meet Diego's charge up the last few steps.

As his big body surged smoothly forward to counter Diego's attack, there was no thought of vengeance in his mind, no thought of the past atrocities that he had suffered at the hands of this man; his thoughts were of the precious love that had come to him out of the vicious destruction Diego had made of his life so long ago. And so, in the end, he fought Diego not for the past but for the future, for the future full of love that awaited him in the warm, welcoming arms of his Spanish rose.

In the relatively cramped space of the forecastle deck, Maria and Jasper standing helplessly by, Gabriel and Diego fought their final duel. The ringing sound of naked steel against naked steel sang in the air as their flashing, darting blades met, disengaged and met again, each man determined to kill the other. Behind them, the *Santo Cristo* continued to burn, her debris-scattered decks now almost entirely deserted. Even the soldiers who had obeyed Diego's orders were no longer present; they, like most of the crew that remained alive, had leaped into the water to escape the ravening flames.

Gabriel fought with a cold ferocity. He displayed none of the intricate, elegant passes with his blade that usually characterized his fighting; instead he concentrated savagely on one thing, killing Diego. Twice, as his bloodstained sword slipped beneath Diego's guard, he had been certain that victory was his, but each time Diego had deftly recovered and escaped the fatal thrust. The ugly battle was a silent one, neither man having any breath left for insults and jeers, both men's breathing heavy and labored as they danced and leaped about the deck, the wicked blades glinting in the light of the flames that were consuming the *Santo Cristo.*

For Maria, watching this violent struggle with painful intensity as Jasper leaned half-unconsciously on her slender shoulder, it was her every nightmare come true. Even Jasper's blood, which stained the deck, had been in her nightmares, and the frightful sight of seeing her husband and her brother trying to kill each other was terrifying. But there was no longer the divided loyalty in her heart that there had once been; her every thought, her every prayer was for Gabriel. Despite everything, she did not wish her brother dead, but she despised him and pitied him and cared only that she and Gabriel escape.

But fate would not spare her and in that final moment, it was Maria herself who would swing the outcome of the desperate struggle. Gabriel was tiring, he had already fought several men this day before his blade had crossed Diego's, and it was beginning to tell, his thrusts not as strong and certain, his movements slower, less lightning-swift. His reflexes dulled by the strenuous battle, Gabriel's foot suddenly slipped on the blood-slick deck, and he stumbled to his knee, his guard down.

Like a snake, Diego struck, and Gabriel awkwardly turned the thrust aside as he struggled to regain his footing, but he was at a grave disadvantage and could not continue in this fashion. Maria was away from her position by the railing in an instant, and guided by blind instinct, with all the strength in her body, she drove Gabriel's dagger into Diego's left shoulder. Howling with rage and pain, Diego swung about to face this new threat, but in one clean, swift lunge, Gabriel's blade sank deeply into his black heart.

Diego stiffened and then an expression of utter stupefaction on his face, he fell forward, dead on the decks.

Maria covered her face with shaking hands and turned away, unable to bear the sight of her brother's sprawled body on the deck of the *Santo Cristo.* Gabriel was at her side instantly, and he pulled her into his arms, folding her close. "It is over, sweetheart . . . and now I'm afraid that we must face even more danger." He lifted her chin with a finger, and staring worriedly into her face, he said softly, "Maria, we're going to have to jump. I will try to shield your body with mine—but it is going to be dangerous . . . for you and the babe."

Maria swallowed. "I know, but there is no other way."

There wasn't. Though most of the crew was gone from the galleon, it would be impossible for them to recross her flaming decks, and their only chance for escape was to leap from the towering forecastle section into the waters many feet below them.

Jasper was still fairly cognizant of his surroundings, and as they prepared to jump, his voice slightly slurred, Jasper muttered gamely, "If I survive this, *mon ami,* remind me in the future *not* to intrude upon your adventures!"

Gabriel gave him an encouraging squeeze of the shoulder. "We will talk of this day when we are old men, my good friend. I promise you! Now *jump!*"

Maria's arms were locked around Gabriel's strong neck, and though he tried to protect her as much as possible from the impact, when they hit the water, she felt an agonizing jolt. Feeling as if her baby was being ripped from her womb, she hurtled down into the depths of the lagoon, hardly aware of Gabriel's arms holding her tightly to him. Of Jasper there was no sign. As the speed of their downward propulsion eased, with a powerful kick, Gabriel began swimming quickly toward the surface.

When their heads broke water, Maria's arms were still fiercely locked around Gabriel's neck, but the memory of that terrific jolt stayed with her. Was her babe hurt?

Jasper's voice nearby jerked her from her anxious thoughts. "A ship!" he cried weakly. "Yours! The *Dark Angel* come to rescue us!"

Moments later, Maria was gratefully aware of strong, eager hands reaching out for her and then of Gabriel kneeling beside her on the deck of the *Dark Angel;* Jasper, his breathing faint and shallow, lay next to her. One nightmare was over, but she feared that perhaps another was just beginning, that all was not well with her child.

Chapter Thirty-three

As Morgan's other vessels continued to harass the two remaining Spanish ships, the *Dark Angel* swiftly retreated to a safe distance from the fighting and dropped anchor. It was obvious that the buccaneers were winning the day, and with the captain's lady safe, the crew of the *Dark Angel* was jubilant. The only gloom on the horizon was Jasper's condition.

Gabriel had tenderly carried Maria down to the great room. Richard and the one-eyed Jenkins, supporting Jasper's sagging body between them, had followed, the ship's surgeon immediately behind them.

An hour later, Maria was sitting up in Gabriel's bed, drinking some broth that had been speedily concocted for her. She was wearing one of her husband's shirts, and except for the dark shadows under her eyes and the paleness of her skin, Gabriel decided with relief that she appeared to have suffered no lasting effects. His eyes full of concern though, he stood by the bed, and his hand gently brushing back the still slightly damp hair from her forehead, he asked for at least the tenth time, "Are you certain that you weren't injured when we hit the water?"

Keeping the unsettling notion that all was *not* well with her, Maria smiled wanly and murmured, half truthfully, half mendaciously, "I feel all right now. . . . Do not worry." Her smile faded and she asked anxiously, "And Jasper?"

Gabriel grinned. "The surgeon says that he has lost a lot of blood, but that the wound was not deep and that if he can be made to lie abed for a few days he will recover fully." His mouth curved wryly. "Keeping him in bed is going to be the problem."

Unpleasantly aware that other responsibilities called to him, but feeling that he could now safely leave her, Gabriel dropped a brief kiss on her mouth and said regretfully, "I must see how the battle goes—I will not be long."

While Gabriel had been involved with freeing his wife from the *Santo Cristo,* Morgan and the other privateers had certainly not been idle; in a remarkably short time, his battered little flotilla had completely destroyed the Armada de Barlovento. The *Santo Cristo*'s fate Gabriel was well aware of, but of the other two ships, the *Soledad* and *San Luis,* he did not learn their ignoble lot until he finally met Morgan aboard the *Lilly.*

He found an elated but frustrated Morgan angrily staring at the Fuerte de la Barra, the Spanish fort which still blocked their exit to freedom. Unless the fort could be destroyed, the buccaneers would remain trapped, and with Spanish reinforcements certain to be arriving soon, their situation was not good.

Morgan was both pleased and annoyed about Gabriel's bold rescue of Maria. "It is fortunate that you were successful," he growled, a twinkle in the dark eyes belying his unfriendly tone of voice. "Otherwise, I should have been compelled to bring you back from the dead to tell you exactly that I thought of your foolhardy daring . . . and Jasper as well!"

Gabriel smiled slightly, his features serene and relaxed as he lounged carelessly in a heavy oak chair, his feet propped up on a leather sea chest. Thoughtfully he commented, "That ruse with the Cuban ship was very clever, Harry. If the Spaniards hadn't been deceived by it . . ." He paused, then added somberly, "If they had guessed what you were about, we all might have failed."

Not one to be overly modest, Morgan preened and replied with forgivable smugness, "Yes, it *was* rather clever of me, wasn't it? But didn't I tell you that I am the greatest pirate who ever lived?"

Gabriel nodded, his green eyes alight with amusement. "Aye, so you did! And of course, you repeat that information so often that one is not likely to forget it!"

Not a bit disturbed, Morgan waved his hand languidly. "This is true, but it is only because of short memories!"

They grinned at each other, but then, his grin disappearing, Gabriel asked, "How bad is it, Harry? What happened to the other Spanish ships?"

Morgan grimaced. "We were magnificent today and the Spaniards fools—but we are still trapped! The *San Luis* tried to come to the aid of the *Santo Cristo*, but when the flames shot up, it was obvious that the *Santo Cristo* was lost; the *San Luis* sailed for the protection of the guns of the fort—hotly pursued by three of our ships, but once she came into the range of the fort's guns we had to draw back." He smiled and added, "When the tide fell, she beached herself on a sandbank!"

"And the *Soledad?*"

"Ah, now *that* is another tale. She is currently part of our fleet!" Morgan replied merrily. "Her captain gave orders to sail and though the cables were cut, apparently a rope stuck in one of the pulleys and she drifted out of control toward a mangrove swamp . . . out of the range of the cannon of the fort." Dryly he murmured, "Eagerly pursued by eight more of our ships and a fleet of canoes, even a simpleton could foresee the outcome. The Spaniards abandoned her and without a fight we seized her and made her ours!" His complacency vanishing, he said broodingly, "Only a fort full of armed, furious Spaniards who have survived today stand between us and freedom."

Leaving Morgan shortly, Gabriel went directly to the *Lucifer*. Entering Jasper's cabin and finding his friend comfortably ensconced in bed, his wound bandaged and his arm in a sling, Gabriel greeted him lightly. "I'm surprised," he said with a teasing glint in his eyes, "that this room is not filled with several of those pretty ladies from Maracaibo that you have been entertaining lately."

Jasper pulled a face, his color still very pale. "Today, seeing the lengths that a man in love will go simply to win a woman has made me decide that women are *very* dangerous creatures." He grinned crookedly and added ruefully, "And in my weakened condition, who knows what may happen—I could even fall in love!" He shuddered. "And to escape that horrible fate, I have ordered my first mate to keep them all away from me ... for a while."

Gabriel looked down at him and said quietly, "I want to thank you, Jasper. Without you, Maria and I would not have been able to overcome the forces against us. I will never forget what you did for us today."

Jasper moved uncomfortably and said roughly, "Oh, go away! I did nothing that you would not have done for me! Say no more of it or you will make me regret not leaving you to your fate!"

"How ungracious of you!" Gabriel retorted with amusement. "But then you always did save your charm for the ladies!"

Gabriel left the *Lucifer* heading for the one place he wanted most to be ... with Maria. Arriving at his ship, with quick eager steps he made his way to the great room, the great room which held everything dear to him.

Maria had been napping, the sensation that she had not escaped the plunge in the waters of the lagoon unscathed disturbing her rest. There was nothing that she could put her finger on, but something was wrong ... something with her baby. Gabriel's entrance woke her and eagerly she pushed aside her uneasy speculation, smiling warmly at her husband as he crossed the room to sit beside her on the bed.

The events of the past weeks were in both of their minds, but though they spoke softly of the things that lovers do, by tacit agreement, for the moment, they did not discuss du Bois, Diego or the burning of the *Santo Cristo*. They talked instead of the loneliness that had been theirs while apart, of their joy at being together again and of the future ... The future that was still so uncertain ...

On the following day, Morgan launched a savage assault on the fort, but to no avail; time and time again the buccaneers were beaten back without difficulty. The Spaniards had the better position, and they used their cannons and muskets to good avail, the buccaneers suffering considerable losses.

His face black with displeasure, Morgan had retreated. Continuing to mull over the problem, he ordered his ships back to Maracaibo to once again stock up with victuals for the journey to Port Royal. Finally, Morgan decided that he would offer peace to the grim defenders, as well as the release of all the prisoners the buccaneers had captured, if the Spanish would let the buccaneers sail free. The Spaniards, humilated and determined to crush these bold marauders once and for all, promptly rejected the offer. Not surprised, Morgan instantly set his mind on another course of action, a sly plan forming in his brain.

The plan was a simple one, its whole purpose to make the passage to the Gulf of Venezuela less dangerous by convincing the Spaniards to move some of their cannon. To the delight of the buccaneers, it worked. The fort's commander, Don Alonzo, stared hard the next day as canoe after canoe unloaded groups of pirates some distance away, and he grew worried. A land attack must be planned for tonight and a large one at that. Briskly Don Alonzo ordered some of his cannons moved to cover this new threat. The bait taken, tonight, under the cover of darkness, the privateer fleet would sail to freedom.

As night fell, with great stealth, the privateers made ready to sail and Gabriel wondered what the befuddled commander of the fort would think when he discovered that all those many trips the canoes had made back and forth all day had been with the *same* load of pirates! Pretending to disembark in the swamps a short distance from the fort, in reality, the buccaneers had concealed themselves by lying on their stomachs in the bottom of the canoes, and consequently only the paddlers had been visible to the Spaniards on the return journey to the privateer ships. The process was then repeated. And repeated. And repeated. It was, Gabriel thought amusedly, as he walked into the great room, an old trick, but in this case, oh so effective!

"What are you thinking about that makes you smile so much?" Maria suddenly asked beside him.

It was the first time that she had really been up, and dressed in some pieces of plundered finery, she looked quite fetching. Grinning hugely, Gabriel scooped her up into his arms and gently whirled her around the cabin. After kissing her soundly, he said teasingly, "Why, only of the pleasure you give me!" His mouth took on a sensual cast. "And of the pleasures we shall share again when the babe is born and I will be able to show you *precisely* how much I love you!"

A shadow crossed Maria's face at the mention of the babe. She had not felt truly well since the moment they had dived from the *Santo Cristo* and she had felt that powerful spasm of pain. But as there seemed to be no further indication of trouble, she had tried to tell herself that she was only being foolish. The low ache at the base of her spine today, however, had her deeply concerned, and she wished that Pilar were here. If only there were someone she could confide in . . . Determined not to add to Gabriel's worries at his time, she smiled slightly and asked, "When do we sail?"

"Soon!" he said happily and blissfully unaware that this was going to be one of the most momentous nights of his life, he left her and went above to wait for Morgan's signal.

The signal came, and in the darkness of the moonless night, the privateer ships slipped anchor and silently drifted with the tide toward the hazardous channel that led to freedom. Slowly the fleet approached within range of the guns of the fort. Would they succeed? And just as important, in this pitch-black veil of night, could their own navigators guide them through the treacherous waters?

Suddenly, the silence of the night was shattered by the roar of cannons, and with a frightened leap of her pulse, Maria knew that they had been discovered. She was alone in the great room, and her face contorted, as a strong, sharp spasm of pain tore through her. She barely had time to catch her breath, to guess the significance of that pain, when the fort's cannon boomed again, but the *Dark Angel*, along with the rest of the buccaneer fleet, continued to sail intrepidly, unwaveringly through the narrow channel that led to the Gulf of Venezuela.

The Spanish discovered Morgan's subterfuge too late, and the fleet had been able to pass the danger point with minor damage, but on board the *Dark Angel*, there was no sign of relief—the captain's lady was having her baby!

Racked by another powerful contraction, Maria had managed to call out and it had been Richard who had come to her aid. He had taken in the situation in a glance, and by the time Gabriel had come running from the upper decks, Richard already had Maria bundled into bed.

His face full of fear and anxiety, Gabriel stood by the bed, looking on helplessly as another pain gripped her. "Sweet Jesu!" he muttered. "Is there nothing we can do for her?"

The pain gone for a moment, Maria got out breathlessly, "It is not too bad . . . I think that the babe has just decided to arrive a little early."

The ship's surgeon had arrived, and when she twisted in agony as another pain struck her, Gabriel grabbed the man and snarled, "Do something! Do not let her suffer this way!"

The surgeon looked startled. "Me?" he gasped. "I am a surgeon, not a midwife! I know nothing of the birthing of babies!" At the murderous expression in Gabriel's eyes, he swiftly retreated from the room.

Unruffled, pragmatic Richard took control, saying calmly, "I will help her. A birthing is a birthing, and if you will leave us, your lady and I shall do splendidly all by ourselves."

The hours that then passed were some of the longest in Gabriel's life, and even the knowledge that the buccaneer fleet was now safe and entering the waters of the Gulf of Venezuela did nothing to relieve the tension and worry that was clearly etched on his handsome face. He yearned to be with Maria, but Richard had firmly banished him from the great room, stating bluntly, "You will only be in the way."

Some seven hours later, Maria, ably assisted by Richard, who said she did as expert a job as a fine Cleveland Bay mare, gave birth to her child—a small, but perfectly healthy boy. Red-faced and squalling lustily, Nathaniel Richard Jasper Lancaster was carefully placed in his mother's arms, and she gazed at his tiny, furious face with wonder. "Ah, *chico*," she murmured, "the adventures you and I have shared—it not surprising that you decided to arrive so early."

The news of the babe's safe delivery and the word that his mother was well spread through the fleet, causing the crews of the various ships to cheer boisterously; some even fired cannons. Surely, a great future buccaneer had just joined their ranks.

Gabriel, when finally allowed in the great room, could not tear himself away from Maria and his newborn son, and as the *Dark Angel* effortlessly glided through the shifting currents of the Gulf of Venezuela, he sat by his wife's side, staring bemusedly first at her and then at the small bundle in her arms.

Gabriel's features were gentle with love and awe as he stared at the tiny body. His son! Their child!

With shining eyes Maria watched the expression on his face, and then pushing herself up on one elbow, she asked proudly, "Isn't he beautiful?"

Gabriel glanced at her, noting the way the heavy black hair curled near her pale cheeks, the luminous quality of the dark blue eyes, the sweet curve of her rosy mouth. She showed obvious signs of being tired, the baby's unexpected birth nearly depleting her slender resources, but Gabriel thought that she had never looked lovelier. Huskily, he said, "Aye . . . but not unnaturally, I think that his mother is far more beautiful."

Maria flashed him a dazzling smile and Gabriel blinked at the sheer bewitching charm of it. With infinite tenderness, his warm hand cupped her cheek and he muttered, "I am so very happy about the babe, but if anything had happened to you . . ." He paused, the fear that had been his flickering for a second in the depths of the emerald eyes. Unable to help himself, he blurted out, "When I heard that you had been abducted by du Bois, I thought I would go mad, but tonight was in its own way far worse— then I could only imagine your distress, tonight I could *see* it!"

Smiling at him gently, she placed her hand against his mouth. "Hush! I know you have not mentioned his name before because you did not want to cause me pain, but let us speak of that time now and then put it away forever." Urgently, she said, "He scared and terrified me, but he kept his promise to my brother and did not molest me."

Anger at what she might have suffered surged through him, and thickly he got out, "If du Bois had harmed you, in *any* way, no matter where he would have tried to hide, I would have followed and found him, and with my bare hands I would have joyfully torn him apart, limb from limb."

Maria believed him, and resting her cheek against his broad chest, she said softly, "I know . . . I . . . the only thing I ever feared was that I might never see you again."

Gabriel pushed her a little away from him, and staring intently down into her face, he asked slowly, "And Diego? What of him?"

A flicker of pain crossed her lovely features, but gravely she answered, "He is part of the past too. I would not have wished him dead, but he gave us no choice. I am saddened that he had to die, but I would not undo what happened, terrible though it was, if it meant losing you or our child."

"You never will," Gabriel swore fiercely. "You are mine and I intend to make certain that you are always aware of how much I love you . . . *very* aware," he said raggedly as his mouth sought hers.

They kissed for a long time, all the pain and uncertainty, fear and misery that had been theirs in the past burned away forever by the power of the love they shared.

Two days later, just as dawn was breaking across the eastern horizon, the *Dark Angel*'s bow surged forward into the deeper, turquoise waters of the Caribbean, and Gabriel knew without a doubt that they were well and truly safe now, that all danger lay behind them.

He left his position on the deck and went in search of Maria. He found her in the great room, sitting near the windows at the stern, Nathaniel suckling hungrily at her breast. Hearing the door open, she turned around.

Gabriel smiled. Simply he said, "Come, come and let us watch the sunrise together . . . I think that it has much meaning for us this morn."

Together, Gabriel carrying Nathaniel securely in his arms, they made their way to the deck of the *Dark Angel*. Standing side by side at the bow of the ship, they stared at Morgan's triumphant fleet as it spread across the wide expanse of the Caribbean. The white sails billowed in the welcome breezes that propelled the fleet easily across the cream-crested waves, and Maria sighed with pleasure at the sight.

With Nathaniel held in the crook of one arm, Gabriel dropped the other arm around her waist and pulled her closer to him, saying quietly, "All the ships are full of riches, but I have the greatest treasure that I could ever want right here in my arms."

There was silence between them as they stood there together, Gabriel suddenly conscious that the long-carried, painful burden that had been with him since the day the *Raven* had been so ruthlessly destroyed had disappeared. He was, he realized with a start, free of the past. Once before he had set sail for Jamaica, full of dreams and full of hope; this time, he admitted slowly, he was also full of love. . . .

As if guessing what he must be thinking, Maria reached up to caress his cheek. Huskily she murmured, "It is all there before us, beloved, a wondrous future that we will fashion together."

And it *would* be wondrous, as wondrous, as glorious as the glowing, brilliant fingers of dawn which suddenly blazed across the *Dark Angel*, painting her gold as she sailed gracefully toward Port Royal, toward home, toward love. . . .